SHADOWBLOOD SOULS

BOOKS 1-3

EVA CHASE

Shadowblood Souls: Books 1-3

First Digital Edition, 2022-2023

Cover design: Moonchild Ljilja

ISBN: 978-1-998582-59-4

Shattered Vow

Before

Riva

When we said our goodbyes for the last time, the guys each held my gaze for a little longer than usual, as if they thought they could send some of their strength into me with their eyes.

The urge to hug all of them twined through my body, sharp as barbed wire when I resisted it. But I couldn't give in to the longing.

We never made a big production of parting ways at the end of the day, and we couldn't risk giving away that anything was unusual about this farewell. Not with the guardians watching: several in the gymnasium with us and others through the cameras mounted by the ceiling.

If we wanted to ensure that after tonight they could never separate us again, we had to be so careful. They had to believe that *we* believed we'd see each other in here tomorrow morning like always.

Who knew what they'd do to us if they realized what we were planning.

So far, the six of us had managed to act like everything was normal throughout today's training and socializing session. It helped that it'd been one of the easy days, basic testing rather than torment.

I'd raced Zian around the track twice as fast as any of the others could have run until our breaths came ragged.

Debated with Jacob about which of the knives would make the most effective long-distance projectile.

Plotted a hypothetical course across mapped terrain with Dominic's hesitant but thoughtful input.

Laughed at Andreas's banter while he decided to teach himself how to juggle, with only partial success.

Dropped onto the sofa next to Griffin during a break, when he put on the TV show only he knew was my secret favorite.

The other guys said the soap opera was corny with all the relationships that kept rearranging themselves after the characters' melodramatic outbursts, but Griffin pretended it was *his* favorite so that they'd heckle him instead of me. Because that was just how he was.

"You've got your tough-girl reputation to maintain, Riva," he'd told me once with one of his soft but brilliant smiles when I'd tried to say he didn't have to take the heat. "I'm allowed to be the sappy one."

But despite all our efforts, on the inside today's session didn't feel normal to me at all. The knowledge of what we were planning to do tonight weighed on my shoulders like a backpack full of bricks. Heavier bricks than any I'd actually carried before.

Our escape depended on me—on that toughness Griffin had talked about.

The weight became almost suffocating when I waved to the guys as the guardians escorted me and Griffin out first.

Andreas winked at me. "See you tomorrow, Tink." The silly nickname —born after we'd first watched *Peter Pan* as little kids and Drey had declared me as tiny as Tinkerbell—didn't do much to reassure me.

But then Zian mouthed the words that had become our mantra over the years as we'd prepared for this moment: *We are blood.*

With that phrase resonating through my body alongside my pulse, I walked out with my chin up.

Everything depended on me, but we were in it together. We were entwined by the strange powers that were ours alone and the eerie substance that ran through our veins.

The guardians always took Griffin and me first because our rooms were on the highest floor of the underground complex. In hushed conversations, the six of us had determined that Andreas and Dominic were one level below, and Jacob and Zian the level below that.

Beneath them were the training rooms we were leaving now. We had no idea how much farther down the facility might reach beyond that.

Sometimes I pictured it as a vast pit in the earth sinking down, down, down, all the way to the molten core some people called Hell. The image seemed fitting.

Hell seemed like exactly the word for the throbbing strain that would ripple through my body on the days they prodded my unearthly strength with their strange machines. For the sickening sight of the prop animals —and sometimes people—they tortured in front of me to gauge my reactions.

For the things they did to the guys in their own solo sessions that left them with anguish etched on their faces.

They probably thought they'd been *kind* to us today instead of just not totally horrific.

Even for a simple trip back to our rooms, the guardians always made sure to outnumber us. Four of them strode along in a ring around Griffin and me, the harsh artificial light glancing off their weird metal helmets and vests.

I sucked a little air in through my mouth, tasting and smelling it at the same time. The four today gave off pheromones with a faint tang of nervousness, but nothing extreme.

They weren't anywhere near as worried about what we could do as they probably should have been.

They didn't know I could now run even faster than I had in my race with Zian today. Or that the guy walking alongside me could not only pick up on other people's emotions but throw his own at them.

We'd learned to hide new talents as they emerged as much as we could during their brutal evaluations. And as long as our jailers didn't discover those talents in their tests, they wouldn't be guarding against them.

We marched up the blank white stairwell into a blank white hall to the blank white doors of what might as well have been prison cells. The guardians opened our doors across the hall from each other with a blue keycard.

Griffin raised his hand to my cheek and gave one of the silvery strands that'd slipped free from my braid a gentle tug. When we were little, he'd told me the pale streaks of hair falling over the slate-gray underneath looked like moonlight streaming through the night.

He smiled at me, a soft glint lighting in his sky-blue eyes. "Sleep well, Moonbeam."

"You too, Emo Boy," I retorted, and treasured the peal of his laugh as the door shut between us.

On the small table across from my bed, I found my dinner waiting: roast chicken leg, mashed potatoes, boiled carrots. I shoveled it down my throat without processing the flavor. It wasn't like there was a whole lot to miss anyway.

To pass the time afterward, I tapped the controls on the panel over the table to turn on the music channel I liked best. Lush melodies and thumping beats swept through the room.

Normally I'd have swayed along with them, maybe even gotten to my feet and let my whole body move with the music the way I never did when the guys could see me. I probably looked ridiculous when I danced, but I didn't care if I was on my own. It felt good.

It was one of the few specks of goodness I *could* cling on to in this place when I was alone.

But tonight I was too wound up to sink into the music. And if the guardians were watching from their cameras, my tension would become obvious the more I moved.

I couldn't let anything raise their suspicions.

Instead, I flopped down on my bed to simply listen. My hand rose to the pendant that rested against my sternum.

Griffin had brought pewter necklaces back for all of us one of the first times he'd gone on a solo mission in the wider world, using the cash the guardians had given him. I couldn't imagine they'd intended it for that purpose, but for whatever reason, they'd let us keep the gifts.

Maybe that tiny act of generosity made them feel better about everything else they inflicted on us.

My fingers clicked apart the metal cat from the sculpted ball of yarn it was curled around and then snapped them back into place on their rolling joint.

Click. Snap. Click. Snap.

The rhythm settled my nerves just a little bit. I closed my eyes as if I were tired from today's workout, though I hadn't pushed myself anywhere close to my real limits.

One song bled into the next until the lights went out. In the darkness, I kept my eyes closed and pretended to sleep. But my thoughts only got louder.

What would it be like, out in the wider world without the guardians controlling our every movement, jabbing and zapping us if we resisted—or just because they felt like it?

I'd gotten a taste of freedom on my own missions, but those had always been alone. Alone, and knowing that if I disobeyed my orders, the guys I'd left behind here at the facility would pay for my defiance.

Once we were out there and free… could I let them all know how I felt about them? All the longings and hungers that were so much more secret than what TV shows I liked or how I danced?

Griffin knew, because Griffin could absorb emotions like I inhaled stress chemicals. We'd never talked about it openly, but sometimes when a flash of desire or a pang of affection hit me around the other guys, he'd catch my eye and give me a subtle nod, as if to tell me it was all right.

"We're blood, remember?" he'd assured me once, without ever saying exactly what he was talking about. "We're going to be here for each other in every way. It's *better* if no one's left out. The other guys will see it that way too."

Could he really be so sure about that? There were definitely times when I got into a friendly bickering match with Jacob and thought there was more than just passion for the debate flaring in his eyes. Or when I wrestled with Zian and his breath seemed to hitch at the exact same time mine did as our bodies collided.

When Dominic scooted just a little closer to me while we sat together in companionable silence. When Andreas's gaze lingered on my lips while he paid me a compliment I'd otherwise have taken as teasing.

But that didn't mean they'd be okay with me wanting *all* of them. If soap operas had taught me anything, it was how pissed off people could get when someone wanted to kiss more than one dude at the same time.

I shoved away the images my mind had conjured. We could figure out the rest once we had the space to do it, without guardians monitoring and dictating our every move.

After a while, the music shut off too. That meant it was really late. I willed myself not to tense up, to keep lying there in fake slumber.

The lock on my door beeped, and my pulse stuttered. As the door swung open, I sprang off the bed, claws springing from my fingertips instinctively with a rush of adrenaline.

The guardian in the dim hall outside stared at me with a befuddled expression. Just behind him, I made out Griffin's face, taut with strain.

It must have taken more energy than I could imagine for him to push so much emotion on the guardian that the man had felt compelled to unlock not just Griffin's room but mine as well.

Now, I took over.

Before Griffin's emotional control could slip, I sprang at the guardian.

One swipe of my hand knocked the helmet from the man's head. My other fist whipped at his temple at just the right angle and power to knock him out.

Our jailers had trained us well. The guardian slumped to the floor with a thud of his ass and a faint groan.

One down, who knew how many more to go.

I heaved the man into the room and tore up my sheet with swift jerks of my inhumanly strong arms. One strip, I wrapped around the man's mouth to gag him. With the others, I bound his wrists and ankles to the bedposts.

He wouldn't stay unconscious for long, and when he woke up, I didn't want him raising the alarm.

Griffin darted in after me and patted the man down. He grabbed the blue keycard and grimaced.

"He doesn't have any of the other cards," he said under his breath. Our friends needed green or red for the rooms on their respective floors.

I sucked in my breath with a hiss of frustration, but we'd known we might have that problem. Which was why we hadn't set the plan into motion until we'd been sure of where the main control room was.

"Come on," I said, and dashed out of my room.

No warning siren had gone off, which meant whoever was on security duty this late at night hadn't noticed the altercation yet. We'd never made any trouble for our jailers, not in years and years.

Now the complacency we'd encouraged was working in our favor.

I hustled down the hall, only holding myself back so Griffin could keep up. We ran up the stairs to the floor just below ground level.

The moment I peeked out into the next hall and saw it was empty, I hurtled straight to the door to the control room.

I threw myself at the door with my full unnatural speed, smacking it with the entire side of my body. It flew off its hinges into the room as if hit by an explosion.

I ricocheted off the door and lunged at the solitary woman who had just whirled around in front of the array of displays and buttons.

She didn't manage to get out more than a gasp. I punched her with the same force I'd used on the guardian downstairs, and she sagged across her chair like her bones had turned into beanbags.

Griffin caught up with me. We stared at the touchscreens together, my heart thumping fast with the sense of the seconds slipping away from us.

With a hitch of breath, he pointed. "There!"

One of the glass panes had an image on it that looked like a blueprint. I tapped at it and managed to flip through different floors.

Level 3. Dominic and Andreas had checked the numbers beside their doors and passed them on: 3-7 and 3-8.

I poked at the first, and a window popped up with various options. I jabbed again: *Unlock door.*

The screen requested fingerprint authorization. Swearing quietly, I hauled up the woman I'd toppled. Griffin leapt in to press her index finger against the circle on the screen.

The room flashed in the layout. *Lock disengaged.*

A jolt of exhilaration raced through my veins. We were really doing it.

I sped through the commands and the press of the woman's finger: one, two, three times more. All the rooms open.

Then I spun toward the doorway. We had to make sure the way was clear.

Well, *I* had to. Despite all our training, Griffin wasn't much of a fighter.

We charged up the last flight of stairs to the landing up top and slowed to slip out through the main door into the night. The cool, fresh air washed over us.

Griffin dragged in a deep breath and grinned. "No one nearby," he said, meaning no guardians whose emotions he would have picked up on.

Just in case, I scanned our surroundings, taking in the parking lot, the fields, the fence, and the forest beyond.

Everything was still. Peaceful, even, as ridiculous as that seemed.

Stars twinkled overhead. A piney scent laced the breeze. I wanted to gulp it down like lemonade after a long, sweaty workout.

Right now, the guys would be hurrying up the stairs to join us. Andreas had used his charm and his talent with memories to learn how to hotwire a car. Zian's X-ray vision had given us the code for the gate.

Everything was in place. Nothing could stop us now.

A grin crossed my face with a burst of pure joy. I caught Griffin's eyes, and the matching excitement shining from his face turned him so gorgeous the sight took my breath away.

This time, when a familiar impulse gripped me, I didn't will it away like I had every time before. I let the wave of elation propel me toward him, slipped my hand around the back of his neck, and pressed my lips to his.

An eager sound reverberated from Griffin's chest as he kissed me back.

I could have gotten lost in him right then, forgotten everything but the feel of his body against mine.

Nothing had ever tasted sweeter than the collision of our mouths. It was like the perfect swell of melody in a song, resonating through every particle of my body and leaving me tingling.

This was what we could be. This was what we could *have*, once we were only ourselves, not anyone's belongings.

With the rush of giddiness came a starker, needier sensation clawing up through my chest. More. I wanted so much more than this.

But I hadn't completely lost my grip on reality. We weren't safe yet.

I forced myself to pull back, my gaze flicking over the terrain around us again—

And a boom echoed through the night.

Griffin's body spasmed, a dark splotch blooming on his chest alongside a puff of black smoke. As a cry I couldn't contain burst from my lips, his bright eyes glazed. His knees buckled.

I leapt to catch him before he could hit the ground. His body felt so limp and weak that a scream bubbled up from my lungs.

More blood gushed over my hands with the beating of his heart, alongside the dark mist that escaped our veins when we bled. I didn't know how to stop it.

Where was Dom? Where was—

The roar of engines rattled my eardrums, and my head whipped up, tears blurring my vision. Vehicles tore across the landscape all around me, sniper guns poking from windows and roofs.

I sprang up, claws slicing through the air, muscles braced. I wasn't sure what I was going to do, but I'd fight to the death to defend whatever life might be left in the boy at my feet.

Another shot rang out. Pain tore through my shoulder, slamming me backward.

Then a sharp zap of electricity blasted me. My nerves crackled and hissed like live wires; my mind reeled.

Footsteps thundered all around me. I lashed out with every ounce of strength I had left. Tears streamed down my cheeks, and the metallic flavor of my own blood seeped into my mouth from where I'd bitten my lip.

My fists and feet struck one form and then another—but another zap shocked me, shattering my control over my limbs. As I slumped over, the world beyond me hazed.

A horrible shout penetrated my growing stupor. "The others are secured!"

Rough hands grasped my arms and legs.

"It was a mistake to include a female with the rest," someone muttered.

Another voice chuckled as they hefted me off the ground. "Well, we're eliminating that factor now—and I hear we got a good price for her."

I groped for any remaining shred of control over my body, but everything went black.

One

Riva

It's been four years, eight days, and I don't know how many hours since I last saw my guys.

One of my current jailers cracks open the door to my room just wide enough to toss a bottle of water my way. The din of the growing crowd in the arena down the hall rises and then ebbs when he shuts the door again.

The bottle lands with a sloshy thump by my feet. I reach for it, the heavy shackles dragging at my wrists, and pop the cap immediately.

My throat is parched. Normally my keepers leave me with a few bottles on hand, but I finished my last one this morning, and the pricks didn't even bother to deliver a beverage with my dinner.

But obviously they expect me to be properly hydrated for this week's cage fight. Wouldn't want the star of the show giving a sub-optimal performance.

The lukewarm liquid slides down my throat, not half as refreshing as I'd like it to be. When I've finished chugging, I toss the empty bottle back toward the closed door with a grimace.

I roll my shoulders and glance toward the workout area of my room, but I usually give my body a break the day of a match. I only did a light round of stretches and cardio on the mat this morning.

I need to preserve my energy—both to win the fight and to make sure I win it *my* way.

In the past several months, the boss who runs this place has been arranging increasingly volatile opponents. If I'm going to meet whatever unpredictable moves they'll throw into the mix, I have to be fresh and sharp.

My gaze veers to the TV mounted on the concrete wall, the only entertainment I'm given in my new prison. I don't get to pick the content. From breakfast time until lights out, it broadcasts a steady stream of different shows that I assume my keepers chose.

All I get to decide is how much I tune in.

I don't want to watch the gaggle of friends on the screen right now laughing and clinking glasses, even with the sound diluted by the voices filtering through the wall from the arena. The image makes my stomach twist with the thought of how much I've lost.

I close my eyes, and for a moment, Zian is here with me. His dark brown eyes glint fiercely as he cuffs me lightly in the ear. *You're going to take these assholes down, even if you're a shrimp.*

I haven't managed it yet, I say to my imagined version of him.

I picture Dominic standing nearby, watching us with his usual pensive gaze. *You've done everything you can,* he says in that careful way of his as if he's measured out every word. *They haven't given you many options.*

They haven't. Except for the fights, I'm restricted to this room and these cuffs. I've seen enough guards march me to and from the arena to know the boss keeps a large force.

I could tear through five, maybe ten of them, sure—but then what? I'd end up riddled with bullets, with no chance at all of getting back to my guys.

Or worse, these bastards might report back to the facility that the property they sold is failing to meet expectations, and the guys would end up bleeding on my behalf too.

One of them has already died because of my failures.

The memory of Griffin's crumpled, bloody body flashes through my mind, and all my muscles tense against the prickle of tears. I don't want my keepers seeing the slightest vulnerability in me.

But not even the imagined figures in my head know what to say about my horrible mistake.

What if the other guys *aren't* still alive? What if—

My chest constricts. Without further thought, I flick out a claw and scratch it across the inside of my arm, just below the armpit, where dozens of matching scars crisscross my pale skin.

I've done this test before, so many times, but I need the visible confirmation.

A tiny trickle of blood spills out—and so does a wisp of black smoke. As I stare at it, my left hand drops to my upper thigh, where a tattoo marks my skin beneath my sweatpants.

The guys all had the same image etched in black in the same spot: a moon with a droplet dangling from its upper tip. The guardians pointed them out to us during our swimming lessons.

That tattoo shows that you all belong to the facility. You do your best for us, and we look after you.

Yeah, right. That worked out so well for us.

But the six of us are connected in other ways too.

I will even more memories of the guys to the front of my mind. Drey's broad grin. Jake's incisive gaze. Dom's steady voice. Zee's feral scent.

The tendril of smoke seeping from my arm trembles and then unfurls toward the wall in a thin but steady stream. One tiny piece of me relaxes.

We discovered this trick while messing around during one of our outdoor training sessions. The strangeness inside us seeks out its match if given a nudge.

We are blood.

As long as the smoke I bleed moves toward a target when prompted, I know the guys are still out there. Still someplace where I can find them.

If I ever get out of this shithole.

Pulsing bass draws my attention back to the TV. On the screen, characters bob and spin to the music at a house party.

I gaze at them for a few moments, but the sound doesn't stir even a fragment of the urge to join their dance. There's only one reason I move my body these days: to survive.

As the song fades out, the deadbolt rasps over again. Three guards walk in with guns and tasers at their hips. The empty water bottle crunches under a boot-clad foot.

I stand up, an ache of tension forming in my gut. The guards move briskly and silently to usher me out into the hall where more men are waiting, but when I inhale, whiffs of stress taint the air.

They're more anxious than usual—I might even catch a note of outright fear. But then, when the squad of guards came to escort me to last week's fight, I was keyed up and on edge because I'd realized yet another year had passed with me stuck in this place.

Another year apart from the guys who are my blood—the guys I love. Another year of failure.

That night, one of the guards pressed closer to me than I liked, and with my temper frayed, I elbowed him with more oomph than I intended. From the crack of bone when he slammed into the wall, I assume I broke his arm.

So I guess I can't blame them for feeling extra cautious tonight. I'll just blame them for everything else they put me through.

"Nice night, isn't it?" I say, glancing at the men around me for any hint of a reaction. Any clue that could help me, no matter how small. "Sounds like a good crowd out there. I bet the boss is *so* happy."

"Keep quiet, freak," one of them snaps.

The others ignore me, not even meeting my gaze. Their expressions look stern, impervious, but the prickle of fear in the air intensifies.

I *could* kill at least five of them before the others took me down, and they all know that. None of them wants to find out if they'd be among the unlucky ones.

My attention moves on to rove across the hall, but I'm as familiar with the details of this corridor as I am with my room. That air vent is too small for me to fit. That steel door leads only to a windowless storage room.

If there was an easy escape route, I'd have found it years ago.

The furor of the crowd gets louder as we approach the arena. My pulse skitters, just for a second.

It does sound like a big one, and plenty worked up already, more so than usual. Just who am I going up against tonight?

In the back of my head, Jacob gives me a cool smile. The chiseled planes of his face look so much like Griffin's it's painful, but his voice is more forceful than his twin's ever was.

No matter what they throw at you, you've got this.

I summon the cool composure I first developed during rounds of sparring at the facility. For the next half hour, nothing matters except the fight.

The guards in front shove open the door to the arena. A blast of unmuffled sound smacks into me alongside a riot of scents.

More than a hundred people—mostly men, but a woman here and there too—are poised on the chairs all around the fighting ring. They've been talking, both in friendly conversation and in argument, and the moment they spot me, their excitement rises.

A few whoops of encouragement reach my ears, but plenty of scoffing and guffaws come too.

"Look at that little thing. How's she going to beat anyone?"

"He'll crush her like a twig."

"They've got to be kidding with this. Where's the real fighter?"

Those are the newbies in the audience—the ones who've never watched my previous matches. The ones who know hush them ineffectively, but they'll find out how wrong they are soon enough.

My five-foot-one, one-hundred-and-five-pound frame is what makes me such a big draw and earns my keepers so much money at the betting table. No one ever seems to get tired to the spectacle of me taking down an opponent twice my size.

I let the voices wash through me, unaffected by them or by the stink of sweat, stale beer, and adrenaline that permeates the arena. My focus is narrowing down to the raised platform ahead of me. I stare straight ahead as we walk to the ring.

Just as we reach the steps, an icy wave of dizziness washes over me. I have to lock my knees for a second so they don't wobble.

I grit my teeth in annoyance. Get a grip, Riva.

I can't let anything these people do get to me. I can't do anything but *win.*

A guard unlocks the door on one side of the metal cage that surrounds the ring and shoves me inside. Normally I'd keep my balance without a hitch, but tonight I stumble just a bit.

Another flicker of cold shoots through my nerves, fracturing my concentration. What is wrong with me?

A hulking man with scars zigzagging across his bare chest and arms postures at the other side of the cage, clad only in horrifyingly neon green training shorts. He spins the machete he's selected from the weapons he was offered and laughs like he doubts he'll even need to use it.

Only my opponents get the benefit of a weapon. It's to make the fight a little fairer for them, though they rarely see it that way at first.

I flex my fingers and turn toward the guards to have my cuffs unlocked through the bars. As they fall to the floor with a clank, I tuck my cat-and-yarn pendant under the neckline of my tight tank top.

It's a risk keeping it on at all, but I don't dare leave it back in my room. It's a miracle my keepers have let me hold on to this one thing from my past life to begin with.

I'm not giving them the chance to take it away too.

I turn back toward my opponent, and the referee blows his whistle for the match to begin. That's the only way he'll intervene until it's time to declare the winner.

The boss likes it best when the fight is to the death, ending with a throat slashed or a skull cracked against the bars. But while my keepers can force me to fight, they can't dictate how.

If I have any other choice, if I can simply knock the other fighter out to end the match, I'll do it, even if it's harder.

Across some two hundred opponents, all but eighteen have left this ring alive.

The hulking man with the machete takes a step—to the side, rather than right at me. He might be confident, but he isn't stupid.

We circle each other at opposite ends of the ring, studying each other's movements. He's big, but I know from experience that the bulk will slow him down, requiring broader motions while I can be swift and precise.

At least, normally I can be. A little of the dizziness lingers in the back of my head. My feet push through the air like they're wading through shallow water.

A twang of alarm goes off inside me that's beyond simple frustration. Something *really* isn't right. Across two hundred fights, I've never felt like this before.

I flick my claws free from my fingertips, willing my feral side to the surface. My ears tickle where I know the shells have turned pointed and lightly furred. Inhuman strength thrums through my limbs.

But it's not quite enough.

The man lunges at me. I should have picked up on the shift in his intentions in the wafts of pheromones he's giving off, but my senses have dulled.

I fling myself to the side on legs that now seem to be pushing through mud rather than water. Too slow.

The blade of the machete stabs close enough to split the skin of my shoulder. Blood streams down my arm while a puff of smoke gusts up.

Recognizing his advantage, my attacker charges again, snatching at my braid with one hand while he slashes with the other. I manage to duck both his grasping fingers and the swing of the knife and kick him in the gut hard enough to slam him backward on his ass.

With a startled grunt, he skids halfway across the ring.

More dizziness clouds my mind, and I hook my clawed fingers around the bars of the cage for balance. My gaze veers beyond the enclosure and catches on the most prominent of my keepers: the corpulent, balding boss with the heap of gold chains around his neck, sitting in his raised section of the stands at the far end of the arena.

He must be able to tell I'm faltering. He should look horrified—panicked at the thought of all the money he's going to lose if I fall.

Instead, a hint of a smirk curves his lips. He takes a casual puff of his cigar, lounging deeper into his seat.

As I whirl back toward my opponent, a sense of certainty clutches me.

He knows something's wrong, and he *wants* me to fall.

Abruptly, I remember the last-minute water bottle after the stretch of deprivation. He needed to be sure I'd drink it.

What was in the bottle besides water?

My jaw clenches with a flare of anger. After four years, he's decided I've outlived my usefulness. Because of the incident with the guard last week, or was it always going to end now?

I'll bet he's wagered all his money against me for this fight. Probably with extra for seeing me pummeled all the way into oblivion.

The hulk comes at me again, a little more cautiously than before but still menacing. He heaves himself to the side and snatches at my wrist to yank me toward him.

I duck again and roll across the floor. My breath starts to burn in my lungs.

What will happen to me even if I manage to win? Will the boss order the guards to kill me like a dog that needs to be put down?

He'll be pissed off that I didn't bend to his whims—and he won't trust me to stay in line now that I've realized he's willing to sabotage me like this. The ungrateful fuckhead.

My attacker hurtles into me and bashes me against the bars for a second before I squirm free. As I spring away under his arm, I rake my claws across his side. My legs sway under me, but his are steady as ever as he barrels toward me again.

I may as well already be dead. I'm never getting back to my guys like this—there's no fucking way.

Gritting my teeth against the rising anguish, I throw myself into the man's charge, low to the ground. His knees buckle under him, but he slashes the machete across my hip as I tumble away. Pain spikes down my thigh.

I've failed them again. That bloated asshole in his prime seat screwed me over. And all the pricks in the audience are watching my downfall and cheering it on.

Their voices ring in my ears. Feet stomp on the concrete floor.

My opponent rams his fist into the side of my skull.

More fury sears up inside me, sharper and hotter than my misery. The boss is up there grinning like he isn't killing five people instead of only one right now. My guys are waiting for me, and he's fucking *smirking*.

I swore I'd get them out of our prison, and all these bastards just roar in encouragement as my attacker catches my arm.

His hand tightens to yank me right into the poised machete, and all my pent-up emotion explodes from my chest.

Rage sears up my throat and bursts from my mouth in an ear-splitting shriek. It rattles my bones and reverberates through every particle of my being.

The scream goes on and on, drowning out the cheers and the stomping, ringing through my brain. A twisting, ripping agony wraps around me, lacing my mouth with the metallic flavor of blood, and—

Two

Riva

I blink, my eyelashes sticking together briefly before pulling apart, and find myself staring down at the floor of the fighting ring. I'm hunched over, my hands braced beneath me, fresh score marks streaking from my claws through the scuffed beige surface.

The most horrible smell I've ever encountered clogs my nose. Like raw meat tossed into a putrid public restroom.

My stomach lurches, sending a spurt of acid up my throat. I sputter and raise my head, and then I just stare, frozen in place.

The scene around me is just as deathly still.

The scene around me is *death*.

None of the horrors the guardians subjected me to prepared me for this.

Bodies lie sprawled all across the stands around the arena, but they look nothing like bodies should. My gaze jars at the twisted shapes formed by the limbs and torsos, splattered with blood where the skin has cracked.

It's like a giant stomped all over the crowd—and then stirred them a little more for good measure.

My eyes jerk to the nearest body—the corpse of my former opponent, stretched out on the floor just a few feet from where I'm crouched.

His mouth gapes in a vast, broken maw as if someone grasped his chin with one hand and his cheek with the other and slammed them in opposite directions, taking his jaw right off its hinges. Uprooted teeth dapple the puddle of blood beneath his head. His lifeless eyes bulge so violently they've almost popped from their sockets.

His limbs lie akimbo, snapped and bent in a half a dozen places to form far more joints than any arm or leg is meant to have. Jagged ends of bone gleam where the flesh has totally split.

His torso is a crater, the ribs collapsed inward. A dark stain marks his neon-green training shorts, seeping into a yellow-brown puddle beneath his ass that suggests he both pissed and shit himself.

As I take the wreckage in, more bile shoots up my throat. I lurch forward in a full-out vomit.

My half-digested dinner of spaghetti and meatballs—because the boss always wants me primed on carbs before a fight—splatters the floor. I jerk my hands back, my stomach still roiling, and push myself to my feet to study the wider arena again.

As my attention trails over the carnage beyond the cage, where dozens of bodies lie wrenched and deformed like the one next to me, I become distantly aware that my legs are holding me perfectly steady. My gut is churning, and my chest has constricted with horror, but the dizzy unsteadiness brought on by whatever the boss drugged me with has vanished.

The boss. My gaze shoots to his high seat, and I suck in a ragged breath that floods my lungs with more of the awful stink.

He's strewn buckled backwards over one of the chair arms, his spine bent so sharply his head could touch the backs of his knees. His eyeballs dangle from their sockets, his jaw torn right off and resting on the seat next to them. The one arm I can see is rippled as if it was wrung out like a wet towel.

What the hell—what the hell *happened* here?

The last few moments before I blacked out rush through my mind. My desperation and fury, the boss's smirk. My attacker's hand clamped around my arm, and the scream reverberating up my throat like a bolt of lightning.

Like some kind of power.

My arms stiffen at my sides. I pull them up to wrap them tightly around my chest.

I couldn't have done this… could I? I've never had any kind of vocal power before—I've never damaged a body through anything other than physical combat.

But I'm the only one left standing, with all but one of the corpses lying far beyond my physical reach while I'm trapped within the cage. And that scream…

The memory of it sends a shiver up my spine, one that feels like anticipation almost as much as revulsion. I shudder and hug myself tighter.

Only a monster could have done something like this. A much more terrifying and inhuman monster than I've ever been.

Than I'd ever want to be.

The bouncy melody of a pop song erupts from the stands and shatters my shellshocked daze. Flinching, I jerk into a defensive stance—and realize it's a ringtone.

Someone's phone survived the carnage.

There are so many people here. So many mangled corpses. It won't be long before someone on the outside realizes there's a problem and comes looking.

But for now, I'm all alone.

My heart leaps high enough to overtake my horror. This is my chance. No one is standing in my way.

I can get out of here—I can go back for my guys like I've wanted to for so long.

I have to move quickly. As soon as any of the boss's people find this bloodbath and realize I'm missing, they might warn the guardians that I'm on the loose. I'll lose any element of surprise.

And I'm going to need every possible advantage if I'm going to break the boys out of the facility on my own.

My jaw clenches, my focus narrowing with the same cool detachment I bring to a fight, shutting out every consideration other than the job I have to get done.

First, I have to find a way out of this cage.

The guard who escorted me to the door lies at the edge of the ring where he'd stood waiting. Glancing away from the horror etched on his distorted face, I stretch my arm through the bars toward his hip.

I barely manage to hook my fingers inside his jeans pocket and snag the key ring. Breathing shallowly through my mouth, I push the key for the cage into the lock and twist it.

The door pops open. I'm free.

My limbs tense with the impulse to hurtle through the massacre to the exit, but I spot another object near the guard's fractured thigh: a pistol.

I prefer to work with my claws, but I can't deny that weapons would be an asset. Especially when I have no idea just how tightly secure the facility will be after our previous near escape.

The guys might not even be in that building anymore but moved to some place with additional protections.

I grab the gun and push myself onward through the deathly wreckage, scanning waists and hips and the items scattered in between, avoiding faces as well as I can.

There's another pistol, and a switchblade, and a thin knife that looks perfect for throwing, wedged beneath someone's contorted pelvis. My lips press flat as I yank it out.

It's all just meat now. Nothing worse than a butcher shop.

If I tell myself that enough times, maybe all of me will believe it.

I consider a fallen phone, but electronic devices are easily tracked. I do snatch up the least bloody wallets I spot—because I'm going to need money sooner rather than later—as well as a couple of lighters, a few pieces of jewelry that look pawnable when the cash runs out, and a voluminous purse with only a few scarlet flecks on the leather to shove my haul in.

Don't think about who this necklace or that bracelet once belonged to. Don't think about whether they were as immoral as the people who ran the cage matches or just someone who happened to get caught up with the wrong crowd at the worst possible time.

Don't think about how much they must have suffered, and who inflicted that suffering on them.

Jacob. Zian. Andreas. Dominic. All that matters is them. I'm finally coming for them.

By the time I've reached the exit, the one the audience arrives through that stands just beyond the boss's chair, I've added three more guns and another blade to my collection. One firearm for each of us, if the ammo lasts that long.

I don't know how many bullets they have in them, but I'm not lingering here to check.

My gaze flicks over to the boss's chair. To the thick gold chains looped around his purpling neck.

I bet they're worth plenty, but all of me recoils from the idea of taking anything of that man's with me.

I shove past the door into a wide but short hall that leads to a flight of stairs. Three more disfigured corpses sprawl on the floor here.

I don't want to think about the implications of that fact either. Or of the fact that the injuries I took in the fight aren't so much as stinging anymore.

With that sudden memory, I glance down at myself. The cut on my shoulder has sealed up, leaving only a ruddy line. The same with the one on my hip, visible through the slit carved in my sweatpants.

I've always healed quickly—we all did. The guardians remarked on it more than once. But not *that* fast. How—?

That doesn't matter either. I don't have to think about it. All that matters is there's no one standing in my way when I race out into the night.

I find myself under a single dim security lamp at the edge of a parking lot packed with cars I don't know how to hotwire or drive. All the things the guardians taught us, and they never bothered with that particular skill, the pricks.

I sling the strap of the purse over my shoulder cross-body and tighten it until the bag rests firmly against my back. After scanning the area for movement and seeing none, I extend my claws and sever my skin just below the scratch I made earlier tonight.

Blood trickles down, and smoke wafts up. Up and, as I hold my memories of the guys firmly in my head, to my right.

Now I know where I'm going.

I set off at a swift lope, my braid swaying against my back. The concrete building that holds the arena stands between several decrepit industrial buildings on what appears to be the outskirts of a town—or maybe even a city. I mark the position of the nearest highway when headlights cruise by and keep a healthy distance from the few cars passing by this late.

The shabby warehouses give way to scruffy fields and then stretches of farmland with weathered wooden fences and the occasional darkened house standing at the end of a long drive. I keep the same pace whether I'm jogging through rows of corn or along the edges of pastures.

After several houses, I come across a bike leaning against a post just down the drive. I yank it up and hop on.

Pumping the pedals, I can move so much faster, but I need some kind of firm path beneath the wheels. Thankfully the cars come even fewer between as the night creeps on.

I stick to desolate lanes when I can and sprint along the highway when I can't. Every now and then, I slow enough to squeeze more blood and smoke from my cut to confirm I'm still heading in the right direction.

It still feels too slow. I don't know how many hours of darkness I have left.

When I duck down in the ditch as a transport truck rumbles toward me, I decide to make a gamble. I drop the bike and dash over the shoulder at the last second to leap at the back of the truck.

Hooking my legs around the metal bar beneath the doors, I grasp one of the metal supports it's attached to. The truck keeps roaring forward with no sign that my intrusion has been noticed.

I prod a steady stream of smoke from my arm. It wavers through the ruddy glow from the lights on the back of the truck, pushing forward despite the rush of the wind.

We've sped past the fringes of another city, a couple of small towns, and a long stretch of forest before the dark wisp abruptly veers to my left instead of ahead.

With a hitch of my pulse, I spring from the truck. I roll over the grassy shoulder and stop with a smack of my side against a tree trunk.

It's only seconds before I'm on my feet and hurrying onward again.

Hustling through the underbrush, I stumble on an overgrown dirt lane… where the tufts of weeds have been recently pressed flat by tire treads. My senses go on high alert.

I run onward, gulping down air both for oxygen to fuel my muscles and for any trace of pheromone-emitting humans nearby. The lane weaves through the woods, across a stretch of tall grass, and into a denser sprawl of forest.

I don't encounter anyone. But then, the guardians would mostly be concerned about their wards getting *out*, not about anyone coming *in*.

When I spot a fence up ahead around a bend in the lane, I slow, still sticking to the shadows at the edge of the road. Slinking closer, I ease farther into the shelter of the trees.

Then I come to a stop several feet from where the forest thins. The certainty rings through every inch of my body that this is the place.

I don't think it's the same facility where the guardians held us before, but that's not really surprising. Their security had been partly breached.

It's a similar setup, though: a clearing the size of a few football fields surrounded by forest, with a lone concrete structure not far from the gate, looking no larger than a bungalow. There's no way to tell just looking at it how deep and wide the building extends underground.

No cars are in sight. The guardians must have added some kind of underground parking garage to keep them out of unwanted hands.

The fence is taller, about twice my height, with barbed wire coiled all the way around its top. Cables that run between the metal posts just above the barbed wire give me pause.

Then it clicks.

The fence is electrified as well as barbed. The guardians want to tear into anyone who tries to breach it in every possible way.

I wet my lips. I don't have much time. Dawn is creeping closer with every thump of my heart.

It doesn't appear that anyone has sounded the alarm about my escape so far, or else if they have, the guardians aren't worried I'll already have made it here. I only spot a few armed sentries ambling across the field around the building.

Even if my nerves are screaming for me to race straight to my guys, I have to be smart about this. I'm not screwing up what's probably my last chance.

I prowl around the edges of the field until I've fully charted it. One pine stands close enough to the fence and tall enough that I plan to return to it later.

Before I can do that, I need as many of the guardians as possible diverted by other concerns.

I slink back around until I'm on the side of the facility opposite my pine. Digging through my stolen purse, I produce one of the lighters.

With a flick of the dial, I confirm the flame still works. Then I grasp a fallen branch covered in curling, dead leaves, set it against a crumbling log, and send it up in flames.

Three

Jacob

I wake up too early, as always.

The room is pitch black. A faint burn still hums through my muscles from a workout that wasn't quite exhausting enough to knock me out all the way until morning.

They never are. I always find myself here in the dark, the firm mattress beneath me and the faint whir of the air filtration system overhead.

One more day I've made it to. Another day more than my brother got. Twenty-four more hours of useless existence under my belt.

The thoughts float through my head like shards of ice on a thawing river, freezing cold all the way through. I'm a void as endless as the total darkness of my cell.

Griffin would have told me to go easier on myself, to not let the past get to me. But Griffin is gone, and my awareness of the facts of my existence doesn't stir up my emotions anyway. It's simply the way it is.

Someone around here needs to see things clearly.

I close my eyes and focus on the rhythm of my breaths. Inhale. Exhale. Over and over. As repetitive as our days here are.

In an hour or two, the overhead light will blink on. A tray of breakfast will slide through the compartment on the door.

I will eat, and then I'll be tested, and then I'll eat again, and then I'll train. Then back to the cell for dinner. Then the lights go out.

Going through the motions, watching, waiting. Collecting all the little details that might someday add up to enough to make a difference.

I'm just thinking that when my chance arrives out of nowhere with the blare of a warning siren radiating through the walls.

I jerk upright on the bed, my heart thudding only a little harder than normal but my entire body gone rigid.

The alarm wails on and on through the darkness. Something's gone wrong.

The guardians have been disturbed, their plans shaken in some unexpected way.

It's an opening—it's exactly what we've needed.

At least, it will be if I can make use of it. This time, the first step in the tentative plan we've stitched together in fragments of conversation over the past few years depends on me, not my brother.

It should have been me all along. If it'd been me, maybe I'd have been the one who—

My mind snaps around the errant thought like a steel trap, shutting it away. I shove to my feet and step toward the door.

There, I tip my forehead against the cool metal surface, listening to the sounds from the hall with all my might. I don't have Zian's keen hearing or his ability to see through solid surfaces, but the people outside are making enough noise that I catch faint markers of their presence through the blare of the siren.

In the first moment I home in on the sounds, heavy footsteps are thundering down the hall by my door. By the time I register them, they've passed too quickly for me to reach out and catch hold.

I grit my teeth and strain my ears even more.

Is the situation bad enough that more of the facility's staff will come running, or has the opportunity already slipped through my fingers? This is the first time since we gathered all the pieces we needed for our plan that we've had our jailers at a potential disadvantage.

Who knows when it'll happen again.

As I listen, I press my fingers against the door as well, flexing my sense of my power from within my skull through my chest and arms. I need to be ready. And pulling this gambit off is going to take all my strength—all the strength the guardians have left me with.

Since we arrived at the new facility, we've all found our talents, even the ones we'd kept hidden, have been weighed down. Restrained. Something they're putting in the food or the air must be dulling us, taking the edge off the weapons inside us.

The guardians thought they could prevent us from staging another rebellion. But they haven't blanked us out completely. No doubt they'd have to send us into a total stupor for that, and they want us alert enough to jump through their hoops and carry out their orders.

It's taken longer to pull a scheme together than it would have otherwise, but we've made the most of the diminished skills we still have.

Nothing else reaches my ears except the continuing screech of the alarm. The emptiness expands inside me again, tugging at me to give up, to lie down on the bed, to return to the void.

But I owe my brother. I owe it to him to make every last person who hurt him pay.

What else have I held on this long for?

So I stay there, the metal a firm pressure against my forehead and fingertips, energy twining through my veins.

And then I hear it: a muffled holler and the thudding of more footsteps.

The slightest smile curves my lips. I push my hands harder against the door, let the sounds form a picture of the man running down the hall, and hurl all my concentrated will at the figure outside.

My nerves lurch as my talent slams home. I can *feel* him now, caught in my power like a fly stuck in a spider's web.

He flails against it, one foot skidding on the tiled floor, his head thrashing from side to side. But all I need is one finger.

At my full strength, this would be easy. As it is, sweat beads on my forehead and trickles down the back of my neck with the effort of yanking him over to my door.

My jaw clamps so tight my teeth ache. Deeper twinges run through my shoulders and down my spine.

The guardian bangs against the other side of the door. My forehead furrows as I focus on keeping his body there while I drag his hand toward the keypad of the lock.

The mechanisms inside it have some kind of safeguard I haven't been able to override with my telekinetic ability, at least at my current dulled state. No more keycards—they were too easily stolen. So we had to steal the codes instead.

I've seen the outside of my door a thousand times. I fix the image of the keypad in my mind and jab the guardian's index finger at the sequence of six numbers Zian was able to watch them tap in through the wall of his own cell down the hall.

They kept us farther apart this time, but not quite far enough.

4-8-9-1-3-4. The lock beeps, and the sequence of multiple deadbolts rasps over.

My muscles tremble with the effort it's taking to maintain my hold. I yank the man to the side, heave open my door to the full blare of the alarm and flashing red lights, and lunge at him.

It takes all of a single heartbeat to slap my hands against the guardian's chin and the back of his skull beneath his stupid metal helmet. One more beat to wrench his head to the side hard enough to snap his neck.

For all the training we've done, all the tests of our strength and speed, all the practice with weapons and targets, I've never actually killed someone before. Animals, yes, when the guardians forced me, but never a human being.

For a second, staring down at him in the pulsing crimson light, I brace myself for a surge of emotion—any emotion.

The man crumples on the floor with a clank of his helmet, and I feel nothing but a muted sense of satisfaction. The job is done. He got what he deserved.

I don't think Griffin would approve of that reaction either, but I'm the one here, so we're doing things my way.

I'm not really done, though. I step away from the guardian and race down the hall to the room with Zian's number.

Seeing his own code was easy, but he didn't have any way of entering it. I poke the buttons with the other sequence of numerals he gave me.

He's waiting, no doubt as revved up by the alarm as I was. The second the lock disengages, I jerk myself to the side, which is a good thing, because the next instant Zee's brawny frame is barreling past it.

He skids to a halt on the tiles outside, looming over me as his chest heaves with panted breaths. Normally he's only a few inches taller than my six foot even, but his partial shift has given him more on top of that, his muscles bulging wider.

Tufts of fur ripple across his neck and shoulders, the same black as the short-cropped hair on his head but scruffier. Tips of fangs protrude over his lower lip.

He whirls around with a growl, scanning the hall. Tension flexes through his limbs. But when he whips his gaze back to me, a tremor runs through his body.

He contracts just slightly into the still intimidating but more human guy I grew up with, the fur and fangs vanishing.

"The others," he rasps, his dark brown eyes alight with wild intensity.

As I nod, I'm already moving. We dash together to the nearest stairwell, Zian charging a little ahead but reining in the full speed I know he's capable of.

We hurtle up the stairs to the next floor, where Andreas's cell is. He scooped a guardian's memory of tapping in the keycode right out of the prick's head.

Whatever guardians were stationed on this floor, they've already charged off to deal with the emergency. I punch in the code and throw open the door.

Andreas lopes out, his usual easygoing energy keyed up enough that he bobs on his feet when he comes to a stop in front of me. His dark gray eyes catch mine with a flicker of a ruddy glow totally separate from the flashing lights.

"Better get Dominic," he says, offering a tighter version of his usual grin.

At the same moment, a guardian strides out of a room just a few doors down. His head jerks toward us, and a shout bursts from his throat loud enough to compete with the siren.

His hand flies to his com unit, but Zee moves faster. The massive guy all but soars across the tiles and bodychecks the guardian into the wall with the full force of his beastly strength.

The man sags to the floor with a dent in his helmet that turns the side of his head concave. Blood trickles out from beneath the metal to pool on the floor.

Zian stiffens, his teeth bared, his hands quivering at his sides. I freeze up, recognizing his struggle and not having a clue what the answer is, but Andreas is already loping to join him.

The leaner guy hooks his arm around Zian's burly one and nudges him toward the stairs. "Nice one, wolf-man. Can't get out of here without denting a few cans."

A halting chuckle that's half snarl erupts from Zee's chest, and he hurries with us to the next floor.

We had to rely on Andreas's skill to get Dominic's code too. It was a hell of a lot trickier than retrieving his own, since Drey has to see the person whose memories he's rifling through, and he can't pick and choose what he sees other than narrowing it down by other people present.

It was only a few months ago after over a year of trying that he finally caught enough small fragments to give us all the numbers.

We're just one level below the main one now, and a heavy thump reverberates through the ceiling. The flashing lights jitter—and a matching quaver of sensation echoes through my nerves.

I pause in the hall, scanning our surroundings while Andreas does the honors with Dominic's door. I can't identify the feeling that just came over me, but it's holding on, prickling into my skin. It isn't simple apprehension.

Dom darts out, his ever-present trench coat pulled tight around his slender frame and half of his dark auburn waves falling out of his sleep-rumpled ponytail to frame his tan face. As we set off toward the stairwell once more, my fingers curl toward my palms.

"There'll be more guardians upstairs, almost definitely," I say, pitching my voice to carry over the piercing wail. "We're going to have to mow through all of them."

Zian raises his fists, all traces of his momentary uncertainty vanished. "Not a problem."

Another odd flash tickles through my nerves. I frown. "And…"

Andreas glances back at me from where he's leaping up the stairs just ahead. "And what?"

"I don't know," I admit. "But just be ready. I think there's something else. Something… new."

Four

Riva

Another burst of flames licks up from a branch I've torched. I drop it on the heap of twigs I hastily pawed together and dash away.

Shouts ring out from within the compound. Guardians are charging over to the fence and through the gate to investigate the several fires I've already set, which are crackling and pluming smoke up toward the starry sky. The wavering orange light glints off the bars of the fence.

The fires might be enough on their own, but I want to bring as many of the staff as possible out of the facility. I don't know how long it'll take for me to get the guys out; I don't know what new security measures are in place.

The fewer bodies with guns standing between me and my goal, the easier it'll be.

I pull one of the pistols from my stolen purse and aim it at the treetops. I haven't gotten to practice my gunmanship in years, so the kick when I pull the trigger propels me backward with a jolt of surprise.

My aim is still true. The bullet smacks into a thin branch and cracks it at its base. It plummets to the ground, the crash of its landing punctuating the boom of the shot that split the air.

I don't want to waste bullets, but it'll work in my favor if the guardians think there's a whole army of hostiles out here. Darting in a semi-circle around the area where I lit the fires, I shoot five more times in quick succession, from spots farther apart than any one normal person could have traveled in that time.

Then the chamber clicks with a hollow sound. Empty.

I shove the pistol back in the purse in case we need it later once we can get more ammo, push the strap so the purse is pressed against my back again, and dash all the way around the compound to the pine I picked out earlier.

The gate stands open, but guardians are barging out through it—and I know without seeing it that at least a couple of them will hang back to stand guard. Trying to enter that way would send me straight into their midst.

But while they're all busy with the chaos I've created by the east end of the compound, no one's keeping watch over the southwest corner.

The tree comes into view up ahead. I sprint straight to it, flicking my claws from my fingertips, and leap at the trunk.

My arms wrap around it several feet above the ground, my fingers curling and claws digging in for a better hold. I brace my knees against the bark and scramble upward until I reach the branches. Then I start pushing off them to propel myself up faster.

As I near the top, the narrowing trunk sways with my weight. I swivel around it, take a split-second to confirm my distance from the fence, and then fling myself out into the air.

My braid whips out behind me. My back arches and legs splay to position myself in the perfect landing position.

I soar right over the barbed wire and electric cables and land with a soft thump in the grass far behind the aboveground structure.

A swift roll diffuses most of the impact of the landing. An instant later, I'm on my feet again and racing toward the building.

When I near the concrete wall, I slow to a prowl. Sticking close to the building, I slink along it and peer around the corner toward the lone entrance and the gate beyond it.

As I expected, two guardians have stationed themselves on either side of the gate, which is now closed while various other armored figures rush around beyond the fence near the growing blaze. As I hoped, even the two by the gate have their attention fixed on the forest rather than on the building behind them.

They think the threat is still out there. Suckers.

The door to the building stands half open, another guardian in the typical helmet and vest poised there as if waiting to see if her help will be needed too. I'm going to have to go through her—and fast enough to cut her off before she can sound a warning.

Her and anyone else who might be in the hall behind her.

My muscles coil. My jaw clenches. I don't have time to simply knock her out and truss her up for safekeeping like I did during our first escape.

She isn't a person. She's an obstacle between me and the men I need to set free.

She's one of the people who've treated *us* like objects to be tested and tormented for as long as any of us can remember. Why should I see her as more than an object herself?

I wait until her head turns away from me, tracking the continuing shouts from that end of the compound. Then I lunge.

I slam into her at an angle to send both of us tumbling into the hall, the door thudding shut in our wake. One clawed hand clamps over the start of a scream shooting from her mouth; the other slashes through her throat, hard enough to sever the artery.

Blood spurts up. Her body goes limp.

No one races to her rescue. I grasp at the first door within reach and shove the corpse into what looks like an equipment closet, swiveling her as I go so that her pants wipe away the worst of the blood on the floor.

Nothing to signal an intrusion to any other guardians who run by.

Now I'm alone in the hall. An alarm is shrieking, warning lights flashing red down the edge of the ceiling.

I can't let the clamor shake my focus. The control room has to be around here somewhere, most likely on this floor. They'd still keep it as far from the holding cells and the training rooms as possible, wouldn't they?

I lope down the short hallway, setting my feet as quietly as I can. One door opens to a meeting room with a boardroom-style table and chairs.

The next one gives me my jackpot.

Rows of monitors loom over consoles set up all around the square space. Warning messages blink on several of the screens.

To my surprise, the room is empty. Did I really freak out the guardians so much that they didn't leave anyone behind to monitor the facility from inside?

I grab one of the chairs and wedge it under the doorknob to hold off anyone else who might try to enter. My gaze darts over the controls.

There—the outer systems. It'll be good to have the gate fixed open when we make a run for it and the electricity in the fence turned off in case we have to take a more roundabout route.

The gate should wait until I have the guys with me, to give the guardians outside as little warning as possible. But I tap at the screen to turn off the flow of electricity through the cables.

That command doesn't require verification. Is that because someone with security access was using the controls recently enough that the system isn't asking for it again—or will the holding cells be a special case?

I'll have to try and see. I was counting on there being someone working in here for me to use.

But if I need a fingerprint for verification, I can always drag that woman out of the storage closet—or her hand, anyway. Hopefully she's got clearance.

I hustle around the spread of consoles—and jar to a stop.

There's the display showing the holding cells. It looks just like the one from four years ago. Except… four of those cells are already lit up and blinking, yellow against the blue lines of the layout.

Lock disengaged.

And beneath the numbers for each of the cells, there's a five-letter label in all caps. JACOB. ZIAN-. ANDRE. DOMIN.

My guys. They're already out.

How—is *that* why the control room staff left? Did the guardians realize I was behind the chaos outside and run off to drag the guys someplace more secure?

Where are they now?

I scan the displays for any that might give me a clue of where to go. My eyes snag on one in the corner with what looks like a blueprint lit up with little glowing dots. A few of them are moving—

The doorknob rattles. Before I can do more than spin toward it, something rams into the door with enough force to send the chair flying and pop the hinges.

The door crashes to the floor. A big, brawny figure barges in and stalls in his tracks, staring at me.

It takes me a second to recognize him with the four years that've transformed him from a buff teen who still had a touch of softness to his features into a hardened, musclebound man. But that peachy brown skin, those angled cheekbones, and the dark brown eyes glued to me now—they're all my Zian, so familiar and even more stunning than I remembered.

He takes my breath away. My heart thumps faster.

My voice comes out in a hoarse whisper. "Zee?"

Zian looks startled and confused but also almost… upset? Nothing in his face reflects the surge of relief that I felt the moment I realized I'd already found one of the guys I came for.

Before I can figure out what to make of that or say anything else, two more familiar, gorgeous men burst into the room behind him.

"What's the hold-up?" one of them is demanding, and my heart leaps at Andreas's familiar jaunty tone, even if there's a terse note in it right now.

He jerks to a stop too, his tight curls swinging at his temples. The other man beside him goes completely rigid, as if the sharp angles of his face and his pale blond hair were carved out of marble.

Jacob. It's the first time I've seen him since Griffin died, and the echo of his twin shines through his face so vividly that I can't help flinching with that past pain. His gaze sears into mine, he raises his fists—

And then Andreas is pushing ahead of both of the others, his expression a little wild but his voice insistent. "Zee, grab her and bring her. Jake, come on, we need the gate."

Jacob nods with a sharp snap of his chin, tearing his attention away from me. He and Andreas leap to the controls, and Zian springs at me.

My thoughts are too muddled with a mix of joy and bewilderment for me to dodge him.

Why would I need to dodge him? We're blood.

He snatches me right off my feet as if I weigh nothing at all and tosses me partway over his broad shoulder, his bulging arm wrapping tight around my waist. The heat of his body radiates all across my skin, his musky smell filling my nose and sending a tingling through my veins alongside the hum of adrenaline.

I want to hug him, to sob in relief that I've found them, that this is happening, but at the same time nothing about their reactions makes sense.

Why did they look at me like that? Why haven't any of them said a word to me?

But I don't know what they've been through on their end getting this far into the escape. And we do need to get out of here as quickly as possible.

I bend against Zian's massive frame, making myself as easy a burden as possible.

"I have—" I start to say, but my offer of weapons is cut off by Andreas's crow of victory.

"We're out of here!"

All three of them dash from the room without another word. The last of my four, the one I'd just started to worry about, gapes at us from where he's been waiting in the hall.

"What—?" Dominic says, and Jacob interrupts him with a swipe of his hand through the air. He points toward the door.

Nothing else is spoken. The four men barrel out into the night with me in tow.

I'd insist on being put down, but I can't say for sure that I can run faster than Zian, especially when I haven't trained at long distances in the last four years. My guys seem to have a definite plan already, and making a fuss could throw the whole thing off.

But as we hurtle across the field and through the gate, Jacob hurling both of the guardians there into trees with a shove of his invisible power, my stomach knots.

Yells careen through the night. The guys charge off the road into the shelter of the forest.

Zian's arm stays tight around me, his grip almost hard enough to bruise. His scent has flooded my lungs, but it can't wash away my uneasiness.

Bobbing with his strides, I stare down at the expanse of his back in the navy tee he's wearing and try again. "Zee?"

He doesn't answer. Doesn't give the slightest indication he's even heard me.

I don't understand.

I didn't know what to expect from our reunion, but it wasn't this. And all my instincts are quivering with the growing certainty that there's something I'm missing.

Five

Riva

Twigs and dead leaves crackle under the guys' thumping feet. I can't see much except the darkened ground flying by below.

When I try to lift my head, I jostle even more awkwardly against Zian's shoulder, but I catch a glimpse of flashlights streaking through the trees behind us. The guardians are giving chase, shouting to each other as they follow us.

The guys have taken a smart approach by diving into the forest. We've all trained for moving swiftly over uneven terrain, them probably much more recently than me. The guardians can't outpace us with vehicles amid the trees, and the trunks shelter us from bullets unless our pursuers manage to get closer.

But where are we going from here?

I was so focused on getting the guys *out* of the facility, with frantic adrenaline driving me from the arena all the way here, that I haven't taken much time to consider what we'd do after I accomplished my initial goal. All I know is I want to get us away from our captors, someplace they'll never find us again.

Which means we're going to need to put more distance between them and us than we can accomplish on foot.

Zian hurtles steadily onward, his breaths brisk but even with the rise and fall of his chest against my thighs. He'll be pacing himself, though—restraining his strength so he doesn't outrun the other three guys.

I can only make out fragments of their forms in the darkness, but at least one of the others is panting now.

I bite my lip against the urge to demand to know what they're planning next. The quieter we are, the more chance the guardians will lose track of us during the limited night we have left.

There's muttered communication between two of the others, and Zian veers with them to the right without adding any comment of his own. He leaps straight over a log like its nothing more than a twig.

I concentrate on balancing my weight against him for as long as I can bear to shut off my thoughts. But eventually, I can't help raising my head for another glance behind us.

What I see makes my pulse stutter. The faintest of glows is hazing the sky beyond the treetops, making the branches stand out in silhouette against what's now not black but a dark blue.

Dawn has arrived, and it's only going to get brighter.

Beneath the treetops, the forest is still dark as night. The guys must notice the emerging dawn, though, because they all push forward a little faster.

I can't hear any sound from our pursuers now, but glints of their flashlights still show in the distance. They've quieted down to focus on the chase.

If we dare to stop, they'll be on top of us in a matter of minutes.

All at once, we burst from the trees into a clear stretch of field. A sharply cool wind whips over me, licking across my back.

As the guys swerve farther to the right, my heart thumps faster with the sense of increased exposure. But in a few seconds, I understand why they've emerged from the cover of the woods.

We're dashing along the edge of a low cliff now—a cliff that looms over a four-lane highway. A couple of cars zoom by, but the road is mostly empty at this early hour. Headlights sear across the darkened landscape.

One of the guys sucks a breath through his teeth with a hiss. Another lets out a wordless sound of encouragement.

They're all ahead of Zian now, so I can't see them, but all at once, he starts running even faster. Then, with a heave of his chest, he launches us into open air.

A startled gasp breaks from my lips. He adjusts me against him as we plummet, cradling me closer to his chest. When we hit the ground with a smack, my body is tossed into his, cushioned by his brawn.

The impact is still hard enough to knock the breath from my lungs. His grasp loosens, and I squirm out of his arms to take in our surroundings.

We've landed on the flat bed of a moving truck, one that's roaring along the highway at what's got to be seventy miles an hour. The other guys have leapt on around us, Andreas swaying a little as he rights himself.

Dominic lifts the tarp that's covering the cargo of logs, which only covers one half of the truck bed, and motions for us to take cover under it. I scramble over, knowing we don't want the guardians seeing where we've gone if they make it to the cliff before the truck has zoomed out of view.

The moment we're inside our makeshift tent, I turn to face the guys. My gaze locks with Jacob's.

His handsome face hardens, a cold glint forming in his eyes. Without any warning, he throws himself at me.

The movement is so sudden and unexpected from a long-lost friend that my reflexes scatter and my muscles don't do much more than twitch before he's slamming me to the ground. My arms shoot up instinctively then, but his hand is already clamped around my throat and pressing in hard, cutting off my airway with a shock of pain.

Jacob glares down at me, his gaze pure ice now—icy hatred. Frigid enough that I shiver even as I squirm to shove him off.

Under normal circumstances, I could overpower him easily. But I'm tired from a night on the run, and he's got to weigh nearly twice as much as I do.

My wrists and ankles jar against the invisible hold of his telekinetic power. My thoughts are still too scrambled for me to come up with a coherent strategy to get him off me.

What the hell is going on? Why would Jake want to *hurt* me?

"So we got our freedom and you too," he says in a flat voice. "It's our lucky day. And now I get to—"

"Jake!" Andreas snaps, his tone sharp enough that Jacob's head jerks around, it's so unusual from the normally easy-going guy. "Get off her. We *need* her. She'll know things."

What is he talking about? I squirm more urgently against Jacob's hold, an ache digging into my lungs and my vision starting to waver.

But even with the choke hold he's got on me, the press of his muscle-hardened body against mine stirs a trace of old longings laced with horror.

I've wanted him this close to me—but not like this. Nothing like this.

"Drey is right." I recognize that quiet, even voice as Dominic's, though he's out of view.

Jacob swears, spittle hitting my cheeks. Then he shoves away from me as quickly as he sprang at me, as if he can't stand to be touching me for a second longer.

His striking features have always looked chiseled, but right now they might as well have been carved out of marble. He jerks a hand toward Zian.

"Stay by her. Watch that she doesn't make a run for it."

I stare at him and then at each of the other guys as Zian moves to stand sentinel over me, holding up the highest point of our makeshift tent. A strange energy crackles through the air between us, suffocating even now that my airway is open.

I'm surrounded by the guys I've spent more than four years dreaming of saving, all of us tucked into this cramped space little more than an arm's reach away. The awareness of their presence sends a giddy shiver over my skin even as I grapple with my confusion.

When I try to speak, my throat throbs. I swallow and cough and swallow again, and then manage to say hoarsely, "Why would I want to run? I—I came for *you*. Of course I figured we'd stick together. That's how it was always supposed to—"

Jacob steps toward me as if he's considering strangling me after all. "Shut *up*."

How can he be the same guy who once grinned so fiercely at me as we planned our winning tactics for a game of capture the flag? Who'd watch me spar with eyes alight with appreciation and call me "Wildcat" when he applauded a win?

Have the guardians done something I can't even comprehend to the boys who were once mine?

My bewilderment brings heat to the back of my eyes, but I clench my jaw against it. Breaking down in tears isn't going to help anything.

I need to stay calm and focused, and we'll get through this.

We have to get through it.

The guys have simply been watching my reactions. Andreas rakes his fingers back through his tight curls. His copper-brown skin has grayed, and I don't think it's just because of the dimness beneath the tarp.

"We know, Riva," he says. "Did you think they wouldn't tell us? That we'd just assume you were dead or something?"

I honestly had no idea what the guys would know about my whereabouts, but no matter what they believed, I expected them to be just as happy to see me as I was to get back to them.

I peer up at him, meeting the dark gray eyes that always used to shine with amusement or friendly warmth. "I don't know what you mean. The guardians took me away after— I guess they figured we were less likely to attempt another escape if we were apart."

It was a mistake to include a female.

Jacob lets out a scoff so ragged it's almost a snarl.

Dominic eases closer, hunched beneath the tarp even though he's the shortest of the guys, the plastic a few inches above his head. His dark hair hangs loose from its usual ponytail, but his pale greenish-hazel gaze is as pensive as it always was.

"There's no point in lying," he says in the same softly measured voice as before, bobbing a little with the vibration of the truck. "We heard about the deal—and everything."

My hands ball at my sides, but I will my frustration down. "It sounds like the *guardians* were lying. What deal? What 'everything'? I just broke you out of that torture building—"

Jacob snorts and can't seem to restrain his caustic remarks any longer. "*You*? When we found you, you were manning the control room, probably trying to figure out how to put the building in lockdown so we'd never make it out."

"Why would I be— I went in there to let you out, because I had no idea you'd already managed it."

"You had the door barricaded," Zian puts in, his words coming out in a low growl. "It seemed like you were trying to save yourself."

"Yeah, from the guardians." I gesture vaguely. "I'd already taken down one just getting into the building. I didn't know how many more were still inside who'd interfere."

Andreas cocks his head. "I don't remember seeing any bodies lying around when we left."

"I shoved her into a storage room so the body wouldn't tip off anyone else!"

"So there's also no proving it now—very convenient," Jacob sneers.

Why are they finding this so hard to understand?

I just barely keep my voice steady, my throat getting ever tighter with an ache that digs way deeper than any of the pain Jacob inflicted with his physical attack. "Why do you think the guardians went rushing out of the facility in the first place? How do you think you got your opening to break out of your cells? Why the hell would I have been doing *anything* other than trying to help you?"

Have you all gone fucking insane*?* I restrain myself from adding.

What did the guardians do to them? How have they warped the guys I loved so horribly that they don't even *know* me, not properly, anymore?

Jacob glowers at me, his expression so stark with loathing it cuts me right to the core. "I don't know what enemies those assholes have made who might have decided to mess with them. I *do* know that you bargained with the pricks for better treatment, gave up my brother as a fucking blood sacrifice, and then waltzed off to enjoy your cushy new privileges someplace you never had to see us again."

I'm shaking my head before I'm even consciously aware of the movement. Is that what they really think?

"I'd never have done that. How can you even believe— They caught us. Right outside the facility while we were waiting for you. We'd done everything according to plan, but they must have known and been prepared…"

"Why don't you tell us what exactly *you* claim happened that night?" Andreas says, still unusually terse.

I drag in a breath. Are we going to get somewhere now?

"Griffin used his ability to make one of the guardians want to open his door and then mine, just like we discussed. I knocked the guy out, but he didn't have keycards for the other floors. So we went up to the control room and opened all of your cells."

Zian nods slowly. "They opened."

Jacob flicks his glare toward the other guy before aiming it back at me. "And then?"

"Then we headed out to make sure the front yard was clear. We thought it was at first. Griffin couldn't sense anyone nearby, and I didn't see or hear anyone. It must have been a sniper who shot him."

A lump of grief blocks off my voice for a second before I recover it. "And then a bunch of guardians all rushed in, and they shot me too, and zapped me with tasers so I couldn't move…"

One of my hands lifts to my shoulder instinctively, but I know before I say anything more that they won't find my scar convincing—not if they're doubting everything else I said.

The guardians patched me up well before delivering me to the boss of the arena as merchandise. The remnant of the bullet wound looks more like it was a shallow stab mark, not a shot.

"That's all that happened?" Dominic asks.

My mind flits momentarily to the kiss—that giddy, glorious, *stupid* act that might have cost us everything. Every nerve in my body balks against admitting that one factor in my carelessness.

It doesn't make a difference… other than making me look pathetic.

"That's all," I say. "Obviously I wasn't alert enough—you have no idea how much I wish I'd picked up on the threat in time—"

Jacob folds his arms over his chest. "And where did you supposedly go that's kept you away for four years?"

I grit my teeth at the "supposedly" and force them to relax. "The guardians sold me to some crime boss who ran underground cage matches. I became his star fighter. It was either fight or they'd kill me, and if I was dead I wouldn't have been able to come back for you. He kept me under tight security. I never left my room there except for the weekly fights."

A ragged laugh sputters out of Jacob. "Such a fantastic sob story—and how perfect that you did it all for *our* benefit. How long did it take you to come up with that script? What a load of absolute bullshit."

I stiffen against a flinch. "It's not bullshit. It's what happened."

There's a stretch of stony silence between the guys. I can't tell if any of them are even really considering that I might be telling the truth.

Whatever story the guardians beat into their brains, they must have framed it awfully well. But still.

These were my guys. We were all each other had—we were in it together until the end.

We are blood.

They should know I'd never have turned on them.

Zian glances at Andreas, the tarp warbling against his hands as the truck sways around a curve in the highway. "Can you check her memories? That'd give us a quick answer about what really happened after."

Andreas grimaces. "Not particularly quick. There isn't much science to it, remember. I don't have much to narrow it down."

He lifts his chin toward me. "Do you have the name of anyone who was at this cage-fighting place—this crime boss and his goons who made you fight?"

I wince inwardly. "No. They barely talked to me, and I didn't get much chance to overhear anything."

Jacob shifts his weight with a shudder of the truck bed. "Isn't that convenient too?"

"Not really," I retort. "Since I'd *like* to be able to prove to you that I'm not some kind of murdering traitor."

Andreas's mouth has remained twisted. He clasps his lean hands together in front of him. "I'll try. Maybe I'll find something."

He doesn't ask my permission, just fixes his gaze on me.

The Andreas I knew would never have invaded my head without making sure I was okay with the intrusion. But when I look up, the ruddy glow of his power is already flickering in his eyes, as if the process of delving inside my head requires some part of him to burn.

I can't feel him inside my skull, but my skin itches with the knowledge that he's shuffling through fragments of images and conversations. But if it means he stumbles on the truth about that night, then it's worth it.

We hold there in silence through a few more jostles of the truck and the brightening of the daylight seeping through the tarp. Sweat beads on Andreas's forehead. His eyes jitter, and he yanks his attention away from me with a swipe of his sleeve across his hairline.

"I didn't come across anything definitive," he says to the other guys, his voice gone rough. "I got one glimpse of a cage fight, but no way to tell how often they were or whether she volunteered for it."

"Then we stick with what we know." Jacob scowls down at me. "And what we know is this bitch is a manipulative schemer who'd stab us in the back too the second she gets the chance. So why the hell don't you let me finish what I started?"

"Jake," Zian says, and then doesn't seem to know how to continue.

Andreas speaks up again, sounding weary but firm. "It's a sorry state of the world when *I'm* the voice of reason around here, but like I said before, we need her. If she's been working with the guardians right there in the facility, she must know things about their plans and how they'll operate."

Dominic inclines his head slowly. "She could know what steps they'll take trying to track us down, so we can evade them better."

"Exactly. And who knows what she's seen or heard that could help us with the next phase?"

"What next phase?" I demand. "And I don't know anything about what the guardians are doing, because I haven't even been in the facility or seen any of them for four years until last night."

The guys all ignore me. "Then we hold on to her until we figure out what we can get out of her," Zian suggests.

I want to believe there's a tiny bit of hesitance in his voice, but at this point I'm not convinced that's more than wishful thinking.

Jacob's lips curl as if the idea of keeping me around disgusts him, but he sighs. "Fine. But she is going to get what's coming to her one way or another."

He swivels on his heel and stalks to the edge of the tarp. Lifting it, he gazes out over the brightening landscape beyond the truck.

"Traffic's starting to pick up," he says. "And the guardians will probably be able to guess we ended up on a vehicle going one way or the other along this highway. We should get off while we can without being noticed and continue the conversation far away from here."

Six

Zian

Less than a minute after we've leapt off the truck, Jacob looks over at Riva where we're tramping through a sparse stretch of forest and holds out his hand. "Your bag. Let's see what you're carrying."

Riva's hand tightens around the strap for a second before she tugs it up over her head and hands it over. "It's just things I thought might help with the escape. Some of which I actually used. You can see one of the guns is empty."

It's an odd bag for her to be carrying to a fight, some kind of leather purse with a decorative fringe along the side. But she speaks with the same firm tone she's answered all our questions with so far.

"Weapons," Jacob mutters, and shoots me a look. He already told me to stick close to her, without needing to point out that I'm the only one in our group who can match Riva in strength and speed.

If she takes off on us, it's going to be up to me to catch her. The idea makes my stomach flip over, but it's already balled tight.

Where has she really been all this time? What was she doing when I stumbled on her in the control room?

She isn't *acting* like a person horrified that her closest friends think she betrayed them. Barely any emotion has flickered across her face, and most of what I have seen I recognize as anger.

If even part of her story is true—if she's been through hell for the past four years and came for us expecting a joyful reunion—wouldn't more of that show?

My mind darts back to the first moment when I saw her in the control room. I was so shocked the memory is blurry. Did her face light up right then, seeing me—more like she was happy than concerned that I'd broken in?

But even if it did, she could already have been putting on an act, realizing she was caught.

"Fuckload of guns and knives, wallets, jewelry…" Jacob fixes his gaze on Riva. "Did you just come back from a day trip robbing a bank?"

She glowers at him. "I had a chance to grab some stuff that seemed like it might be useful when I got away from the cage match place."

"Right, right." He paws deeper and lifts out a crystalline bottle of perfume. "And you figured smelling nice would help with our escape?" He tosses that back in and pulls out a ticket stub. "And going to concerts too. Busy woman."

Riva's jaw twitches, but her voice stays only terse. "I didn't bother to empty the purse when I grabbed it. I was in kind of a hurry, which shouldn't be a surprise. That stuff isn't mine."

"Uh huh. Looks more to me like you'd just come back from one of their stupid missions, with the benefit of a little R&R time." Jacob slings the purse strap over his own shoulder. "Zee, check her over and make sure she's not carrying more than what's in the bag."

Riva's shoulders tense, but she doesn't shy away from me when I step closer. Her fitted tank top and sweatpants don't leave much room for hiding weaponry. I can see with my regular vision that she doesn't have a pistol shoved in her waistband or a sheathed knife at her hip.

But because he asked, and because any tiny miscalculation could screw us all over, I stare a little harder, letting the tingling of my talent form in the back of my eyes.

I skim my gaze over her hips and back, jerking it away quickly from the curve of her small but sculpted ass with a flush of heat through my skin that I hope the other guys can't see. Then I move up beside her so I can give her front a quick scan, darting over her breasts with similar speed.

More heat trickles up the back of my neck and singes my cheeks. As I yank my focus back into regular sight, for a moment I simply watch her marching along next to me.

She looks so much like the Riva I knew. The same delicate features. The same odd hair, dark gray beneath and silver on top, pulled back in a typical if loosening braid.

The same deceptively slim frame that you'd think would snap in a swift breeze, when actually you're lucky if she doesn't snap *you* in half.

Still just as pretty—maybe even more so with the sharpening of her face with adulthood and the slight filling out of her modest curves. Still leaving me with the same urge to scoop her up and shield her by tucking her close against my much broader body.

I used to imagine holding her in other ways too, but my mind freezes up against those memories.

I thought I knew her. I believed the affection for me that I saw shining in her eyes, her determined commitment to all of us.

How could the girl I knew back then have turned on all of us—on *Griffin*, of all people—like that?

What kind of a woman is she now?

My temper stirs and simmers, but I hold back a full-out flare of rage. Wolfing out isn't going to help any of us.

And how can I feel angry and still have to hold my fingers back from brushing over her hair, her bare shoulder, as if I can reconnect with her that literally?

As if someone like me has any business touching *anyone* that way.

I wrench my mind away from those images—and a different thought hits me like a smack of frigid water.

"The trackers!"

The others all jerk to a halt, Riva last.

Jacob spits out a curse and jabs his finger at her. "Aren't you so glad your distraction made us forget?"

Riva blinks at him. "Forget *what*? What are you talking about?"

"We don't have time to argue about it," Andreas breaks in. "We have to get them out *now*."

Dominic clears his throat with an uncomfortable expression. "Riva might have one too."

She almost definitely does.

I step in front of her. "Open your mouth."

It'll be easier that way.

She knits her brow. "What—"

"The guardians put tracking devices in our teeth," I blurt out. I should have remembered it sooner—I'm the one who found them in the first place. "We figured it out after—after some things happened. Unless we pull the right tooth out, it'll be a homing beacon straight to us."

Something wavers in Riva's expression. Horror at the thought of yanking a tooth right out of her jaw or at losing some level of protection she thought she had thanks to the guardians she sold us out to?

It doesn't matter as long as we get this done.

Her lips part, and she opens wide. One of her front teeth is chipped, and another farther back looks like it's missing a chunk.

I don't think about that, only delve my gaze inside each of them searching for that bundle of metal.

There. "First molar on the top left, same as the rest of us," I announce, and hesitate. "I'm the one who needs to—"

"She's got the strength to do it too," Jacob snaps. "Let her deal with her own mouth. You can do mine first."

He steps forward, his stance rigid, and drops his jaw as far as it'll go. I tear my gaze away from Riva, revulsion coiling in my gut as I prepare to get down to work.

We talked about this part of the plan, and I pictured the process to try to prepare myself, but none of that could have matched the awfulness of actually having to reach into my friend's mouth, grip a tooth, and rip it out of his gums root and all.

As I pinch my thumb and forefinger around the right one, even more nausea fills in my stomach. "Sorry," I can't help rasping.

Then I wrench the molar out with a heave of my arm, as fast as I can manage.

Jacob is the most impervious of us all, but even he gives a ragged groan as blood spurts over his lips along with a puff of dark mist. Dominic is at his side in an instant, placing his palm against Jake's jaw by the wound. Dom's mouth presses flat, and Jacob's shoulders sag with released tension.

The sprig of wildflowers Dominic plucked up withers and disintegrates in his hand.

I want to apologize to him too, but none of this can be helped. All we can do is get it over with as quickly as possible.

"Break the tooth," Andreas reminds me in an urgent tone.

I set Jacob's molar on a flat stone and stomp my foot on it with my full inhuman strength. It shatters with a crackling of circuitry.

If the guardians were tracing us using that, the signal just went dead. But there are four more devices beaming out their radio waves.

Andreas is waiting when I raise my head. My stomach keeps churning as I perform the second extraction. He buckles over with a gagging sound, and then Dominic is there by his side.

A leafy twig crinkles away into dust from Dominic's hand. Then he faces me. "My turn."

I hate doing this one the most. Dom has been through all the same training as us, and I know his slender frame has plenty of muscle packed on it, but he's the smallest of us four. The least overt in how he's feeling.

I never know how he's really doing behind his quiet demeanor, but we all know he's got at least a few things haunting him.

Clenching my jaw, I tear out his tooth even faster than the others. As his hand shoots right into his mouth to heal the wound, I crush yet another tracker under my heel.

When I step back, Riva lets out a faint strangled sound. Shuddering, she grips the side of her face and drops the tooth she must have just dragged from her own jaw onto the stone. It smashes under the slam of her foot.

Blood dribbles over her chin, and her shoulders quiver. My gaze leaps to Dominic, but Jacob pushes between him and Riva.

"She waits," he says in a steely tone. "If she can deal out pain, she can endure a little. Take care of yourself, Zee, and Dom'll make sure you're okay first."

Riva's head droops. She doesn't protest, but something twists in my chest.

I hate what she did and everything that came after, but the viciousness of Jacob's rage is unsettling even me. And I'm normally the brute around here.

To get it over with as quickly as possible, I brace myself and catch hold of my molar. My muscles balk in the first instant against damaging my own body, but I push through the resistance and haul the tooth out.

Pain screams through my face. I sputter with it, and Dominic is by my side, palm against my cheek.

Soothing warmth blooms through my gums. When he pulls back, a dull ache remains, but the gaping hole is sealed.

We agreed beforehand that he'd only put in as much energy as it took to remove the possibility of infection.

He moves to Riva next, and Jacob doesn't argue. She holds perfectly still as Dominic works his healing power on her. Then she wipes the bloody spittle from her mouth with the back of her hand and stares at all of us with her bright brown eyes smoldering like coals.

I have to look away.

Andreas kicks dirt and fallen leaves over the crumbled remains of our teeth and the devices they contained. "We're going to want to hitch another ride as soon as we can, to get more distance between here and the last place they could have located us, yeah?"

Jacob nods. "We were heading toward another highway, weren't we?"

"It's at least a few more miles, but that's the idea."

"Then let's get going."

By the time the sun is well up in the sky, we're holed up in the back of a freight truck we spotted at a truck-stop diner.

Andreas grabs some apples out of one of the produce crates and tosses us each one—even Riva, after a momentary pause.

"Thank you," she says quietly.

I dig into mine, both savoring the tart flesh and wishing it was even half enough to settle the grumbling of my empty belly. I could really go for about five steaks and a side of bacon right now.

Jacob shifts where he's been sitting with his back against the wall near the door. "When we hop off of this ride, we're going to need to get more strategic. Focus on our goal."

My heart thumps a little faster. "Ursula."

We haven't been able to talk in much detail about any part of our plans while we were in the facility. We only sketched out the basics.

Now, the possibilities for our next steps seem to spill out endlessly in front of us.

"That one guardian suggested she might go 'back to Pennsylvania,'" Andreas points out, hunkering down against the crate. "It would make sense to start the search there."

I frown. "*How* are we going to search? All we've got is a first name and a few vague details. There won't be an official employee registry for the facility or anything like that."

Drey chuckles. "No, definitely not."

"What about a university?" Dominic says, pitching his soft voice just a little louder than usual to be heard over the rumble of the engine.

"We're the right age—we'd fit in pretty well. We'd have lots of other people around to blend in with. And there'd be libraries and computer rooms and all that, right?"

Other than one mission I've run, my experience with the American college system is restricted to TV show and movie portrayals. But his suggestion at least sounds reasonable.

"Who's Ursula?" Riva pipes up abruptly. "Shouldn't we just find someplace to settle in where no one at all can notice us?"

Jacob snorts. "Not if we want answers, but then, you'd probably rather we didn't get more of those."

I hesitate, not sure how much we even want to tell her, but Andreas shrugs. "We picked up enough info from the guardians to find out about someone important who worked at the facility in the past but then left—or got shut out. If we're going to figure out what exactly they did to us and what we can do about that, she seems like our best bet unless we figure we can take on the entire facility at once."

I can't help letting out a snort of my own at that suggestion, but a bittersweet pang shoots through my chest at the same time.

Is this actually going to work? Is it really possible we could learn something that could *fix* all the things that are wrong inside us?

Riva's forehead furrows. "Isn't chasing after anyone associated with the facility only going to make us more likely to get caught? What does it even *matter*?"

Jacob shoots her a cold look. "It matters to us. And if you were one of us, it'd matter to you too. But you're not going anywhere."

"I don't *want* to leave. I was just saying… Fine. Whatever the rest of you think you need to do, we'll do. I *am* one of you, and I'll be right there with you."

Jacob eyes her for a long moment. Then he glances at the rest of us. A hint of a smile touches his lips, one that chills more than warms me.

"We can't have Zian playing guard dog with her twenty-four seven," he says. "So we're going to need some other way of ensuring she stays true to her word. And I just thought of the perfect solution."

Seven

Riva

The second the words *perfect solution* leave Jacob's mouth, I can tell that I'm not going to like his proposal. Even so, I'm not prepared for his next move.

He extends his muscular arm, almost impressive enough to rival Zian's brawn, and squeezes his fingers into a fist. And a row of purple spikes shoot from his skin from the side of his wrist to just before his elbow.

My pulse stutters, my body tensing with the instinctive sense that whatever those are, they're a threat. They look like the spines on some exotic reptile.

Jacob never showed anything like that in the time I knew him before.

He stares at me with his ice-hard eyes as if daring me to comment.

Andreas clears his throat. "Jake, man, I'm not sure—"

"It's simple," Jacob interrupts. "I give her a mild dose of the poison. Then she'll have to stick with us so Dom can heal the damage regularly enough to keep her alive."

His lips curve into a tight smile, his gaze boring into mine. "I developed some new abilities while you were enjoying the high life. If I don't jab you much, it'll take a while before the toxin builds up enough to be fatal. But there isn't any regular cure—the guardians tested *that* very thoroughly. You take off on us, you're dead."

Zian's dark eyebrows have drawn together. I think he might protest this torturous suggestion, but instead he glances at Dominic. "But if Dom has to keep healing her…"

Jacob looks over his shoulder at Dominic, his face softening just slightly for the first time since we've reunited. Because he still cares about the other guys, just not about me.

"Only if you're okay with it," he says. "It shouldn't take *too* much, just once or twice a day, to keep her functioning. And hopefully we won't need her for too many days."

Like the boy I remember, Dominic takes a moment to think. I don't totally get why they're especially worried about him—will it really take that much energy to offset the effects of the poison?

He didn't seem all that fazed by healing our gums after we extracted our treacherous teeth. My tongue flicks over the new gap at the back of my mouth automatically, the tissue there still tender.

Dominic's stance looks a bit stiff, but before too long, he answers in his low, measured voice. "It's all right. I can do it."

Nausea unfurls up through my chest as I remember Jacob's phrasing. *Keep her functioning.*

"I might not *die*, but your poison is going to mess with my body, isn't it?" I say to him. "If the guardians catch up with us, I won't be able to help you fight them off very well if I'm physically sick."

Jacob turns to face me again, nothing but disdain in his expression now. How can he look so gorgeous and so cold at the same time?

"That's asking us to believe you'd be fighting against the guardians instead of with them."

I can't suppress the edge that creeps into my voice. "Yes, that *is* what you should believe, because that's what's fucking true."

At least the layer of frustration helps tamp down the anguish that's roiling through me underneath. Every quiver of that fraught emotion rippling through my chest makes me feel as weak as if I've already been poisoned.

It doesn't matter what the guys think right now. I have to prove to them that I'm the same Riva I always was, that I'll put all my strength toward defending them and keeping us together.

I can't do that if I'm falling apart.

"And yet somehow I'm still not seeing it," Jacob snarks back, and rolls his shoulders. "Of course, I still see just offing you as a viable solution too, if you're so upset about this option."

My mouth tightens into a flat line. None of the other guys speak up against his very explicit threat.

Memories flood the back of my mind: my dizziness last night, the shakiness of my muscles. He's asking to do the same thing to me that the boss did—the way the boss tried to murder me.

He wants to put me in a different kind of cage, with my own body trapping me.

A prickle creeps into my lungs—a tiny oscillation like something sharp-edged starting to vibrate within my ribcage.

Like a vicious, angry sound that wants to break free?

I stiffen up, clamping down on the impression and taking a deep breath to clear my lungs. That—that wasn't me. I won't let it be me.

There's no need to get angry about it anyway. Jacob is asking rather than ordering, at least.

He's telling me how this will go and waiting for my response. If I accept, if I show I'm willing to trust that they won't take it too far, that'll be one step toward convincing them that they can trust me too, won't it?

I'm not really sure what else I *can* do at this point.

I scoot across the floor of the cargo hold toward him. "Fine. Just remember that if I stumble when we need to move quickly or defend ourselves, it's not because I want to."

Jacob lets out a derisive sound. He grasps my hand, and in spite of everything, a tingle shoots straight through my nerves at the contact. My breath catches.

How can he not feel that we're all meant to be together, me included? That we really are blood in all the ways that matter?

We're connected in ways no other people on this planet are.

He'll have to realize it. I just need to keep trying.

Andreas steps closer, wobbling with the movement of the truck. "Are you sure you can control the dosing well enough right now? With our talents dulled…"

Jacob cuts a sharp glance toward the other guy. "You don't need to bring that up in front of her."

Andreas simply shrugs. "It's not going to matter by the end of the day anyway." He catches my eyes. "After you left, the guardians started drugging us somehow or other so we couldn't use our powers at full strength. Protective measures." His mouth twists into something halfway between a grimace and a smirk.

"It's already wearing off," Jacob says. "I know what I'm doing."

He tugs my arm straight in front of him and twists his arm so he can bring the purple spines protruding from it to my flesh. He lets just two of them rest against the skin and then presses them harder.

A stinging sensation like the needles the guardians sometimes injected us with shoots through my forearm and radiates into my hand and shoulder. Unlike with the needles, the sensation lingers, prickling in my veins even after Jacob has pulled his spines away.

That's the only effect of the toxin that I can feel so far. If that's all it is, I won't do too badly.

But that's probably too much to hope for.

Jacob is still holding out my arm as if he's forgotten that he no longer needs it. Because his attention has homed in on the front of my shirt.

I glance down at myself, wondering if I've gotten something on the tank top, just as his hand shoots out. He yanks on the chain around my neck to pull the cat-and-yarn charm out from its safe spot beneath the fabric.

A jolt of panic shoots through me with the thought that he's going to rip it right off my neck. My body reacts on instinct, my hand smacking away his before he can get a real hold on the necklace, my feet shoving me out of reach.

My back jars against the side of the cargo hold. Jacob takes a step toward me, chilling fury blazing in his eyes.

"They let you keep it. That was my brother's, and they let you— And you want us to believe you didn't win yourself special treatment?"

"I—" My fingers close around the charm protectively. My gaze darts from him to each of the other guys, and for the first time it sinks in that none of them are wearing their old necklaces. "What happened to yours?"

Zian's lips have pulled back with a growl. "The guardians took them from us as part of our punishment for trying to run."

They took even that from the guys—from Jacob? The one thing of his twin's he should have been able to hold on to?

My heart aches, but I don't know what to say. "I have no idea why they let me keep it. It wasn't part of any deal."

Jacob looms over me, his eyes narrowing. I brace myself for some kind of attack, but he just shakes his head with a derisive curl of his lips.

"Whatever. If you get totally out of it with the poison, say something, and Dom will balance you out. Until then, keep your mouth shut unless you're finally going to cough up some inside info about the guardians."

I frown at him. "I've told you already, I don't know any more about them than you do."

"Then you're basically useless, aren't you?" he retorts, and shifts his attention to the other guys as if I don't even exist.

My introduction to the state of Pennsylvania is a dingy clothing outlet store standing between two other big, boxy outlet stores just off the highway we've been driving down. Between the guys' talents, they were able to commandeer a seven-seater SUV in a mundane shade of tan from, as Andreas described it, "the kind of people who aren't going to be reporting their car stolen."

He's behind the wheel now as he pulls into the parking lot outside the store, a little more confident after his stint in the driver's seat earlier today. Have they managed to practice their driving skills since I've been gone, maybe as a little detour on missions?

I want to ask but I have the uncomfortable suspicion that any questions about their activities will come across as digging for info for my supposed guardian allies.

"Okay," Jacob says as Andreas parks at the far end of the mostly empty lot. "The three of us will go in and grab a few sets of low-profile clothes for all of us. Dom, you stay here with Riva."

I raise my chin from where I'm tucked away in the back seat. "Why can't I pick out my own clothes? I'm the one who brought the money you're using."

Jacob twists to shoot a glare at me. "You shouldn't look strange with that hair on a university campus, but out here in the boonies? We're trying to avoid getting noticed—at least, the four of us are."

I make a face at him, but he does have a point. My gaze slides to Dominic in the middle row, to the left of my seat.

I don't need to ask why the quietest of the guys is being left behind with me. Now that I've seen him by full daylight, I've realized that his posture isn't perpetually hunched after all.

He's got a small but noticeable lumpy area on his upper back, covered by the thin trench coat I haven't seen him take off once. Did the guardians perform experiments on him that left him disfigured?

Another question I already know will only make them more pissed off with me. But it makes sense that they wouldn't want bystanders noticing.

The other guys push open the car doors, letting a rush of cool fresh air waft over us. It's early fall, the leaves on some of the trees we've raced by already sharpening to reds and oranges with the crisp weather.

Then the doors thump shut again, and Dominic and I are alone.

I squirm in my seat, my nerves twitching with restless exhaustion and overall discomfort. I ended up dozing off for a little while on the truck and again here in the backseat after we found the car, but not nearly enough to make up for the fact that I've been on the run all night and the better part of the day after.

And Jacob's poison is gnawing away at me, setting off little aches in my joints and flashes of queasiness in my gut.

His strategy is so stupid. If we're attacked—if I need my strength—

I close my eyes for a moment, gathering my focus. Freaking out won't get me anywhere.

And the last thing I want is to provoke that sharp prickle in my chest again.

When I feel steady, I focus on Dominic, the sliver of his profile I can see from my current angle.

He's pulled his shoulder-length waves back into his usual ponytail, the auburn strands dark against his light brown skin. In the past four years, the line of his jaw has broadened a little, but other than that and the bulges on his back, he looks the same as the unassumingly handsome guy I knew then.

Dom was always the most thoughtful of the six of us: taking his time to consider every angle, stating his opinions carefully and waiting for our feedback. He wouldn't have jumped to conclusions or gotten caught up in righteous rage.

All the others had their silly nicknames for me, but he always called me exactly who I was.

I pull my legs up on the seat in front of me, hugging my knees. "You know this is ridiculous, right?"

His head turns a little, but he's looking toward the store rather than at me. "Getting new clothes? You've got blood on yours."

I wrinkle my nose at the stains not totally invisible in the black fabric and try again. "No. Treating me like I'm allied with the guardians. *You* realize I'd never screw the rest of you over, don't you?"

There's a moment of silence before he speaks again. "I don't think we should talk about this."

"I just need to know that someone here hasn't gone totally crazy. We're *blood*. I—"

Dominic swivels to meet my gaze then, the abruptness of the gesture cutting me off. His hazel eyes aren't as cold as Jacob's, but I don't see any friendliness in them either.

"You have no idea about anything," he says, quiet but terse. "You don't even know what I'm already giving up just keeping you around. So don't tell me I'm not doing enough."

I blink at him—at the back of his head, which is all I have a moment later. "What do you mean? What are you giving up?"

Before he can answer, if he even would have, the other guys are hopping back into the SUV.

Jacob tosses a plastic bag at me. "Get changed."

By the next morning when we arrive at the college campus the guys picked out, all of us look suitably student-ish, at least in attire. I've pulled on a black tee, a pair of dark gray cargo pants with a wonderfully excessive number of pockets, and a navy hoodie that I'm using to cover my silvery hair.

The guys have picked out a range of clothes from Zian's super casual sports tank and sweats to Jacob's dressier fitted button-up and slacks. Only Dominic has left on what he was already wearing.

I suspect he's not going to take off that trench coat in front of me any time soon. Maybe he never takes it off in front of *anyone*.

But from what I know from my limited and admittedly mostly fictional experience with college life, he'll still fit in well enough as some kind of alternative punk type.

We cruise down a street lined with narrow three-story townhouses attached in sets of two. Zian went ahead of the rest of us earlier and used his penetrating sight to find one building no one's occupied.

Since it's a couple of weeks into the typical semester now, we're hoping no one with more claim is going to try to move in while we're squatting there.

Jacob parks the SUV out front, and we clamber out. Zian hangs back by the door so he can walk over to the townhouse behind me, as if I need that much of an escort.

Uneasiness jitters through my body as I scan our surroundings.

Students are ambling around or hanging out on their front landings all up and down the street.

I haven't been surrounded by this many people since my last cage match. I haven't been surrounded by this many *normal* people—who expect me to be normal too—in more than four years.

It doesn't help that the twinges of nausea I felt yesterday have expanded overnight into a ball of queasiness that fills my stomach. I only managed to swallow a few bites of the fast-food breakfast we nabbed at a drive-through—and then regretted even that for the rest of the drive.

Sweat trickles down the back of my neck, adding to the clammy sensation creeping over my skin. I have to tense the muscles in my legs to make sure I'm keeping my steps steady.

But I will not complain. I won't give Jacob one more opportunity to accuse me of trying to weasel out of his security measures.

By design, Jacob reaches the door first. He lifts a fake key toward the knob, but we all know he's going to use his powers to actually open the lock.

A couple of girls are hanging out on the landing across from ours. One of the girls, a statuesque redhead with freckles scattered across her high cheekbones, glances across the lane at us and smiles. "Hey! New neighbors?"

"Yep," Andreas says in a carefully warm voice—friendly but not too encouraging. "We turned up a little late, but what can you do?"

"These places are great. So much better than the regular dorms. I'm Brooke, by the way. Let me know if you need any help figuring stuff out."

"Will do."

Jacob offers a brisk nod. Our neighbor's gaze travels over the bunch of us, locking with mine just for a second before moving on. Her brow furrows.

Do we look strange after all? Maybe she thinks it's odd for a girl to be living with four guys? Or are we giving off a vibe that says we don't actually belong here?

Before I can worry much about that, Zian is nudging me to follow the others inside.

The townhouses come pre-furnished with basic birch furniture and a sofa covered in a denim-like fabric. We find ourselves in a living room that's merged with a small dining room, an open-concept kitchen off to the side.

"There should be four bedrooms," Andreas says. "Two on the second floor and two on the third. I can take the sofa."

I'm getting my own space, then? Lucky me.

I take a step toward the stairs, wanting to find whatever bed will be mine and crash onto it. But I'm not concentrating enough, and weakness flares in my calves.

I stumble, knocking my hip against a side table when I catch myself. As I push myself upright again, my legs tremble under me. The ball of nausea swells into a boulder.

I might need the bathroom before I get to that bed.

The guys have gone silent, watching me. Jacob flicks his hand toward Dominic.

"I think she needs your first dose of healing. Don't patch her up *too* well."

Dominic nods and walks over to me. I try to catch his gaze, to search his eyes for any hint of understanding or a clue about what he suggested earlier, but he only looks at my forearm where he's resting his hand.

A soft warmth flows through my body, melting the nausea and the clamminess. My muscles relax, able to hold me up without extra focus.

A pinch of queasiness remains in my stomach, and I still don't feel quite like myself, but it's a lot better. Well enough for a flicker of heat to stir beneath my skin at Dominic's continued touch—and a pang of loss to hit me when he drops his hand.

"Thank you," I say to Dominic as he steps away.

He simply tips his head, still not meeting my eyes.

"Upstairs," Jacob orders with a snap of his fingers, and I find myself tramping with him up two flights to the highest bedrooms. He glances into both and points to the one he's decided should be mine.

"You'll stay in here unless we need you," he tells me. He hovers his hand over the inner doorknob, and the button that should allow me to lock and unlock it twists and crackles.

He's going to trap me inside with his powers. I swallow thickly. "You really don't need to—"

"Just a little extra protection for the rest of us," Jacob says coolly. "I'm sure you get it."

He stalks out, shutting the door behind him. There's a rasp, and I know he's engaged the lock.

Of course, I'm more than strong enough to break a regular dorm room lock if I need to. That wouldn't do much to prove my trustworthiness to the guys, though.

I glance around the bedroom. At least it's nicer than my last two jail cells.

A double-sized bed with a forest-green bedspread fills a third of the space, next to glossy birch bookshelves and a desk. The shag rug looks soft enough that I'd like to dig my toes into it.

And I have a window—the greatest of luxuries.

I walk closer to it and take in the view: the building across the lane. A figure turns by the window directly across from mine with a flash of red hair.

It's Brooke. She must have gone inside after we did—her bedroom matches mine.

I should yank myself back, but right then she glances out and notices me. A smile crosses her lips, and she raises her hand in greeting.

I don't know what to do other than wave back with an answering smile I hope isn't too tight. Then I back away.

Everything is okay. I'm okay. The guys are okay.

We got away from the facility like we always wanted. The rest we can figure out as we go.

I just have to stay strong.

Eight

Riva

I wake up to a brisk knocking on my bedroom door and roll over, rubbing my bleary eyes.

Evening has descended beyond the window, the world now painted in shades of blue and gray. My head feels muggy despite the sleep, but I'm not sure how much of that is natural fatigue and how much it's the toxin coursing through my veins.

The knocking comes again.

"What?" I say in a thick voice.

It's Zian who answers, a little gruffly. "Dinner. Come down."

The guys are letting me eat with them instead of merely bringing up a plate? I *have* stepped up in prisoner status.

I set that bitterly wry thought aside and pull myself out of bed. There's a clacking sound as Zian disengages the lock.

Whatever Jacob did to it, he's left it so the other guys can turn it from the outside too.

When I push the door open, Zian is waiting for me, all six-foot-five of him looming over my much smaller frame. When I slip onto the small landing, there's only a few feet of space between us.

I used to take comfort in his impressive size, but that was when I knew he'd only use it to protect me.

Not so much now, even if the sight of his massive body still sends a tingle through me that I can't explain. His expression looks strained, the normally warm peachy undertones to his brown skin dulled.

Because he isn't happy about how the others are treating me or because he isn't happy they're keeping me around at all?

Not the kind of question you can ask and expect a useful answer. I stretch my arms and glance toward the door between the two bedrooms with a twinge in my bladder.

"I need to use the bathroom."

Zian nods awkwardly and steps to the top of the stairs. "Just be fast."

The bathroom smells like artificial lemon from whatever the staff used when they cleaned it after the last occupants. I use the toilet and then splash water on my face, peering at myself in the mirror.

I'm not looking so great myself, my pale skin even ashier than usual other than the dark smudges forming beneath my eyes. I pat some water on the wisps of hair that are coming loose from my braid.

My hand rises to the lump of my cat-and-yarn pendant that's back under my shirt. I run my fingers over it, and a lump fills my throat.

None of this is going the way I pictured. None of this feels good.

But maybe I deserve it, even if not for the reasons the guys think.

I let them down. I was in the lead, clearing the way, and I got caught up in a silly impulse rather than keeping all my attention on making sure we were safe.

Griffin *died* because of me. I've never forgiven myself for that, so why should they?

Which means it doesn't matter what they think or say. All that matters is that I have to stick to the mission now—and do whatever it takes to keep these four men safe, because even after the hell they've been putting me through, I can't stand the thought of losing another of them.

With a renewed sense of resolve, I leave the bathroom and march stoically down the stairs ahead of Zian.

I don't like how sluggish my limbs feel, but at least the nausea hasn't expanded too much yet. When a whiff of greasy cheese and tomato sauce reaches my nose, my stomach gurgles with hunger rather than queasiness. By the time I reach the dining room, my mouth is watering.

The other three guys are already sitting around the table with a couple of pizza boxes popped open in between them. There are only four chairs, but they've pulled over one of the armchairs from the living room, which

Andreas has sprawled in with one lanky leg over the arm and his plate balanced on his belly.

He looks perfectly at home with that jaunty pose in his casual Henley and jeans—and as delicious as the damned pizza.

Not that it seems like he'd appreciate my thoughts on the matter at the moment. I tear my gaze away.

Jacob catches my eyes and jerks his hand toward the chair across from him. "Eat. No hunger strikes."

"I wouldn't want to starve," I inform him calmly, and pull off a slice of pepperoni and peppers.

Zian lets out a discontented rumble, looking over the offerings. "No meat lovers?"

Andreas arches his eyebrows teasingly at the bigger guy. "Take what you get, Zee. When was the last time you had the chance to eat *any* kind of pizza? It's not like we don't all know you'd rather be chowing down half a cow anyway."

Zian scowls at him without any real hostility. His love of every sort of meat—and knack for inhaling vast quantities of it—has been legendary among us since we were kids.

A trace of a smile touches my lips. At least a few things haven't changed.

I haven't eaten fresh pizza since one of my last missions years ago. Occasionally, my meals in the arena building included a slice or two, but always cold and a little stale, like they were leftovers from someone else's dinner a couple of nights before.

The first bite of this slice fills my mouth with the perfect blend of tart tomato, salty cheese, and spicy pepperoni. I can't restrain an eager hum of satisfaction.

Four gazes snap to my face. My skin heats five degrees in an instant.

For just that moment, the connection I always believed in between us thrums to life—but not quite the way I'm used to.

Then Jacob tears his attention away with a sneer and taps a few glossy brochures stacked on the table next to him. "I got a campus map, and I think I've worked out the best computer lab to do our research under the radar. We can get started tonight."

I take another bite, but this one slides down my throat with much less pleasure than the first. I still don't understand why we're risking staying here.

As if to punctuate my worry, exuberant voices filter in through the townhouse's front window as students meander by on the sidewalk outside. When I perk my ears, I catch the faint thump of bass reverberating through the wall between our side and the townhouse attached.

We're surrounded here—surrounded by people whose intentions and allegiances we don't know.

"Shouldn't we keep moving?" I say, tensing instinctively for Jacob's response. "Or totally lay low for at least a little while, until the guardians' initial search for us is waning?"

He aims his gaze at me again, but it's only chilly now. "And where do *you* suggest we go?"

I shrug, attempting a casual air. "There've got to be lots of places we could disappear to. Someplace in the wilderness where there'd be no one around to notice us. That's what we always talked about—"

"Before," he breaks in, his voice sharpening. "Things are different now."

"We need to find this person," Dominic puts in. "And the longer we wait, the colder the trail will get."

Zian grunts. "She might hear that we got out and decide to disappear herself."

"But what can anyone tell us that matters anyway?" I asked. "We are what we are. We should put everything about the facility and the guardians behind us and make our own—"

"*You* don't get to decide what we 'should' do." Jacob's voice is pure ice now. "No surprise that you wouldn't want us hassling anyone associated with the facility, though."

I grimace. "That's not what I'm saying. I don't see how it's going to help anything. And the more people see us, the more we're risking getting caught, no matter how much we try to blend in."

Andreas scoots a little higher in his armchair. "We need answers. Don't you trust us that we wouldn't be digging for them without a very good reason?"

When he puts it like that, I don't know how to argue. My teeth set on edge for a second before I will myself to relax.

"Who *is* this Ursula woman anyway? She worked in the facility? Why would she be able to tell you more than any other guardian?"

Jacob narrows his eyes at me. "Maybe you could tell us a little about that."

I frown back at him. "I've never heard her name before in my life."

Jacob considers me and then glances at Andreas. "You could confirm that, couldn't you? Search her memories for anything related to Ursula."

Andreas sits all the way up with a twist of his mouth. "Since I only have a very vague sense of who Ursula is, it might not get us anywhere, but I can try."

I go rigid in my chair, but don't protest when he fixes his gaze on me. What he sees should only prove my innocence in this one small way.

The shimmer of ruddy light comes into his eyes. He holds his stare for a full minute, not even blinking, the lines of his stunning face softening as he's absorbed by the search.

Then he drops his gaze. "As far as I can tell, Riva's never met anyone named Ursula. If she met her without knowing her name, I'm not sure I have a clear enough grasp to pinpoint that."

He drags in a breath and meets my eyes properly, something like an apology in his tone. "We think Ursula was someone high up in the facility, maybe even at the top at some point. Zian overheard a couple of the guardians who work in the testing area arguing about a change in policies—one of them saying she wouldn't have approved and the other pointing out that she wasn't in charge anymore."

"You don't need to tell her all that," Jacob snaps.

"Why not?" Andreas asks. "Even if she somehow went back to the guardians and told them, they already know a hell of a lot more about it than we do. We wouldn't be revealing anything new."

Zian looks uncertain. "The less she knows about what we're doing, the better, don't you think?"

"How else is she going to pitch in with the investigation?"

Jacob snorts. "You think we're letting her get involved with our mission? Did you get hit on the head on the way out of the facility?"

Andreas glowers at him. "What else are we going to do? Leave her locked up in her room here with someone always needing to play babysitter? If she says she wants to help us, we might as well give her a chance to prove it."

My spirits rise with a rush of hope, so swift it's giddying. Andreas believes me—enough to give me a chance, anyway.

I still don't think we're really safe sticking around here, but I'd rather be with the guys helping us get what they think they need than holed up in the bedroom twiddling my thumbs.

"I'll do whatever I can," I say quickly. "I'll be a little rusty on the computers, but I can handle the basics."

Jacob scowls at me and turns his attention back on Andreas. "If she wanted to be helpful, she'd own up to the truth about what she's been doing the last four years."

Andreas cocks his head. "Does that really matter as much as what she does *now*?"

Dominic clears his throat, and the others glance at him, recognizing that he's got something to say. He isn't the type to interrupt.

He glances at me and then the others. "The more she's around the other people on campus, there is more chance she could get across some kind of signal. If that's what she'd want to do."

"It's not," I mutter.

Andreas waves off Dominic's concern. "Isn't that already covered by the whole poison precaution? If she screws us over and loses your help, she's signed her own death sentence. Nothing to worry about."

Dominic hesitates. "I suppose we can cover more ground if she comes with us. All four of us can be working at the same time."

Jacob can't argue away the logic they've presented. He doesn't look happy about it, though.

He turns to Zian. "Are you okay with her running around on the loose?"

"No," Zian says, and my heart lurches. "Not when we can't be sure what she'll do."

"It won't really be on the loose," Andreas says in an exasperated tone. "We wouldn't let her go off on her own. One of us would always be with her."

Zian nods slowly. "Okay, that doesn't sound so bad."

"There you go." Andreas smiles at me—is that the first time *any* of the guys have aimed a friendly expression at me since I made it back to them?

I can't tell how much it's the novelty or relief or the way the smile turns his face twice as gorgeous, but a flutter of warmth fills my chest.

"It'll look better to the other students if we're all coming and going—like we really are attending classes," Andreas adds.

Dominic rubs his mouth, his expression turning even more pensive. "We should probably sit in on some lectures here and there too, just to keep up appearances so no one starts to wonder."

Jacob sighs and studies me again with his hardened eyes.

"You tell me what you need me to do to help out, and I'll do it," I say. "If this Ursula woman is so important, I'll dig up everything I can."

"Fine," he bites out, and grabs another slice of pizza with a hostile gesture as if it's offended him too. "But we're not letting you get anywhere near the computers. You can be on cover-story duty."

Nine

Riva

Before we arrive at the room for Introduction to Sociology, my nerves are jumping at the thought of crashing a class where we don't belong. Just how badly are we going to stick out?

Then I step through the doorway and jolt to a halt before the annoyed murmurs of the students behind me propel me onward.

The lecture hall is massive, practically a coliseum. There must be a thousand people packed into the folding chairs in the graduated rows that end maybe fifty feet above the level of the central stage.

Zian and I are both minor blips in the huge crowd—which would reassure me more if we weren't also surrounded by a swarm of unknowns.

I keep my hood up, even though I can spot girls with stranger hair colors than mine in a brief glance around the hall. All my senses are on the alert.

I'm no longer worried that we'll stick out in this crowd, but my instincts are screaming at me that there's no way I can keep track of every potential threat.

Zian drops into a seat at the top next to an aisle—easy to escape from as need be. In my apprehension, I approve of his choice.

As I sink into the padded seat next to him, he yanks up the little wooden desk surface that's attached to the chair and sets his notebook on it. I've got one of those too, and a couple of pens—all part of keeping up our front.

If anyone *does* wonder about the new arrivals in the townhouse residences, we want to give every appearance of being totally normal students. Definitely no freaks on the run from sadistic experimenters here.

The twitching of my skin gradually ebbs as the relaxed murmurs of the other students flow around me. How are the other guys faring in the computer lab?

My mind slips back to the memory of them leaving the townhouse, Jacob and Andreas looking like normal if breathtakingly handsome students but Dominic a little awkward in the padded parka he swapped his usual trench coat for. It obscured the lumps on his back completely, but he must be hot in it even keeping the front wide open.

But I doubt he wants to be trapped in the townhouse any more than I do.

My hand slips my pendant out from under my shirt. I click the pieces apart and snap them back together, willing myself even calmer, even more focused.

If a threat happens to come from anywhere in this horde, I'll be ready for it.

After the third *click-snap*, Zian glances over at me. My hand freezes, and then I stuff the pendant back out of sight, remembering Jacob's vicious response when he first saw it.

Maybe it's better not to remind the men of what I'm still holding onto from the guy we lost.

The professor walks onto the stage below, looking more like a doll than a person from way up here. He swipes his graying hair to the side of his forehead, takes his spot behind the podium, and activates his microphone with a brief fizzle of static.

"Good afternoon, everyone," he says in a drawling sort of voice. "Let's get started."

I didn't expect to pay all that much attention to the content of the lecture. My pen moves over the page, but I'm making notes about the kinds of clothes the other students are wearing, doodling their poses in their chairs.

I don't need to study Sociology. I need How To Appear To Be A Regular Human Being 101.

The short missions we went on under the guardians' instructions never lasted more than a day. We were never prepared to fully integrate.

Or at least I wasn't.

A fresh prickle of annoyance tingles through me. Why are we trying to blend in at all? It would be so much easier if we just vanished to someplace we could live off the land and avoided making the slightest ripple in anyone else's life.

Other people do that. And then I wouldn't have to be stressing about whether I'm making my ripples in just the right shape.

The professor's voice drones on with a flicker of bullet points changing on the projection screen. I study Zian from the edge of my vision, deliberating the best strategy to get through to him.

"Listening to an old dude talk for hours on end isn't what I pictured freedom looking like," I mutter under my breath in a dry tone.

Zian's eyebrow twitches, but he keeps his gaze on whatever he's jotting down in his notebook.

Still keeping my voice low so only he can hear with his keen ears, I tap my pen against my scrawled-on paper. "I wonder if we couldn't just grab a few computers and set up our own workstation someplace out of the way."

"We don't just need computers," he replies brusquely. "Once we figure out who she is, we need to find *her*. We can't just hide."

And what kind of a mess are we going to end up in if the guys insist on confronting this woman who at least used to work with the exact same people we're running from?

I scowl at my paper, but this isn't exactly an ideal setting for getting into an extended debate. And Zian isn't really the debating type—or he never was before, anyway.

There's so much I still don't know about the guys I used to be so in sync with.

But I have him to myself for just the next two hours. There's got to be some way I can start to convince him that their crazy plan is too dangerous.

As I stew over the problem, the professor's voice filters through my thoughts. "That brings us to the concept of tribalism. Now, obviously forming bonds with our fellow human beings is an important factor in our survival as a species. But our tendency to create 'packs' of sorts can also have major negative consequences."

I cock my head, intrigued despite myself—because my guys and I are basically our own little pack, aren't we? Does this bigwig think there's something wrong with that?

He rambles on for a little while about how human brains aren't capable of comprehending huge populations as a cohesive unit and the good that can come from collaborating with like-minded peers before getting to the points I'm more interested in.

"Once we connect with people we consider our tribe, though, there's frequently an impulse to view anyone *outside* that tribe with suspicion. At its worst, we see certain groups completely dehumanizing other people, thinking of them as if they aren't even the same species—and treating them as if they don't deserve the same kindness and respect. Slavery, genocide, and other atrocities can stem from that skewed perspective."

My fingers tighten around my pen. Unwanted images trickle up from the back of my mind of the guardians' demanding voices and harsh grasps. Always pushing us to perform for them and then shutting us in a cage when they didn't have a current use for us.

Because we were different from them. Strange. Freaks.

But they *made* us that way.

Anger stirs in my gut with a pinching sensation that brings me back to other memories. The fighting ring. The boss's smirk.

All those twisted bodies.

I close my eyes for a second and swallow down the uncomfortable emotions that've started to rise up. Then I forge my voice into an arch but light-hearted tone. "Sounds awfully familiar, doesn't it? Maybe the guardians should have taken this class."

Zian doesn't answer me, but the corners of his lips curve upward with a hint of amusement.

The tiny victory gives me a surge of exhilaration, washing away the last traces of my uneasiness. I press my advantage.

"But then, maybe *they* weren't really human. With that metal getup, they could have been secret robots for all we know."

Zian shakes his head at the absurd suggestion, but his smile grows.

"They definitely treated us like they didn't have any concept of humanity," I go on. "Like we were circus animals for their entertainment."

I pause and reach toward his arm to try to solidify the connection we do share, whether the guys have been willing to admit it or not. "And I don't know if they'll ever let us go, not—"

My fingertips graze Zian's smooth skin just above his wrist. In the very first instant, a jolt of warmth flows up my arm, catching hold of my heart and tugging me closer.

The very next instant, Zian is wrenching away from me, jerking around in his seat with a flash of bared teeth. A whiff of pheromones gusts off him that's stress and also something like… fear?

"*Don't touch me*," he snarls, low but so fierce several heads around us swivel our way.

I plaster a mild expression on my face and lean back over my notebook, pretending nothing's wrong for the benefit of our audience. Underneath, my insides are a shaky jumble.

Does he really hate me that much? What would he be *afraid* of?

I don't understand any of this.

It isn't fucking fair.

But nothing in our lives has ever been fair, has it?

From beneath my pained bewilderment, a surge of unnervingly volatile frustration rises up. It sends a prickling vibration through my lungs that chills me to the bone.

No. I don't want to feel that way. I don't want to feel *anything* that could lead me back to the horror show in the arena.

So I blank my mind and go through the motions of attentively scrawling out notes until the projection screen goes dark and the students stand up from their seats.

Oh. It's over.

I shake myself out of the sort-of trance I'd fallen into and get to my feet alongside the others. As we tramp out of the lecture hall, Zian doesn't speak to me, doesn't even look at me.

What would he do if I veered off in a different direction like I was going to explore the campus on my own instead of heading back to the townhouse like a good little girl?

After hearing the hatred ringing through his voice over a much smaller transgression, I'm not sure I'd want to find out.

I'm supposed to be showing I'm still a full, loyal member of our "tribe." That I'm willing to play along because it matters so much to me to re-earn the guys' trust. It'd be stupid to jeopardize that out of some momentary pique anyway.

Zian walks a little ahead of me all the way back to the townhouse, but I can tell from the tension in his muscles that he's tracking every move I make. As he strides up the three steps to the front door, a voice calls out to us.

"Hey, neighbors!"

It's the tall, redheaded girl from next door: Brooke. She's sitting at the patio table set up in the lane between our townhouse and hers, a textbook open in front of her, but at the sight of us, she gets up, flashing a bright smile.

As she ambles over, I freeze in place and then propel myself on up to the door, taking the steps at a pace I hope looks casual. I push my mouth into my best distantly friendly smile. "Hi."

Brooke comes to a stop beside our steps and sets her hands on her hips. "I realized I never got your names."

Her gaze flicks to Zian but quickly comes back to me, as if it was mine she was most interested in.

My smile starts to feel stiff, but I hold it up anyway. One of the names I memorized to toss out easily, similar to my own but common enough not to make me stand out, tumbles automatically from my mouth. "Rita. Sorry."

She laughs, but her attention still lingers on me. "It's okay. You were busy moving in yesterday."

"I'm Zack," Zian says gruffly, giving his own alias.

"Nice to meet you both. Are you getting settled in all right?"

"Yep!" I say in an attempt at sounding cheerful. "Just had our first class."

Brooke grins. "Looks like the prof didn't go too hard on you. What's your major?"

"Sociology." It's the only answer that makes sense, although I don't know what other classes we might end up sitting in on.

Then it occurs to me that I should probably return the question, since that's how small talk works. I'm so out of practice after getting nothing but grunts from my keepers at the fighting arena for four years. "How about you?"

"Double-major in History and Economics. You probably have some overlap! It's pretty amazing looking at society as a whole and all the crazy things we get up to, huh?"

"Yeah," I say, and wince inwardly with the suspicion that my agreement came out sounding weak. "It is," I add with a little more oomph.

She'd probably have enjoyed that sociology lecture. Suddenly I find myself wondering what it'd have been like to be sitting next to her, sharing observations about the professor's remarks.

Not that I *could* have shared with her even half of the things I'd have thought about.

Brooke tips her head to the side. "You know, Rita, a bunch of us are having a bit of a girl's night at my place tonight if you want to stop by and get to know some more people on campus. It'll be fun, nothing too crazy."

My brain stalls for a second. I've never been in a position before where I had people giving me personal invitations—people I expected to see again after I talked to them now.

I don't want to give any of the students here more chance to realize there's something off about me. But will it look suspicious if I say no?

My mouth opens and closes as I grope for my answer—and then the door to our townhouse whips open.

Jacob stands on the threshold, his bright blue eyes searing into me. "Let's get going," he says to both me and Zian in a sharp voice. "We've got work to do. You're holding us up."

I restrain a flinch at his tone, but he's given me the perfect exit. "Thanks, but sorry," I say to Brooke. "I've got a bunch of catching up to get through, but maybe another time."

I catch a glimpse of her brow knitting before I follow Zian inside.

The second the door thumps shut behind me, Jacob snatches my arm, his fingers digging in. "Don't even fucking try it," he snaps.

I stare at him. "What are you talking about? You asked me to come in, so I did."

He jerks his hand toward the front steps. "That whole weirdo routine with the girl next door. I guess you're trying to make her suspicious to sabotage our plans?"

I sputter a guffaw. "Are you fucking kidding me? I was trying *not* to make her suspicious. College students talk to each other."

At least, they have in all the shows I've seen. Brooke seemed to think it's normal.

Jacob scowls. "Not the talking. The awkward answers, the pointed hesitations."

I grimace right back at him. "I'm doing my best. Forgive me for not having socialized with anyone in four years. It wasn't by choice."

"If you go on about that sob story with the—"

"People!" Andreas breaks into our conversation with a brisk voice and a clap of his hands. When Jacob shuts up, he smiles and slings his arm around my shoulders.

It's the first gesture of physical comradery the guys have offered me since I broke them out of the facility. The first time *anyone* has touched me in an affectionate way since Griffin, right before…

I tense up instinctively, even as the rush of heat through my body sends my thoughts into disarray. I almost miss the rest of Andreas's comment.

"I'm glad you two enjoyed your class, but you haven't even heard the good news yet."

He lets go of me, just a brief, casual embrace, and I don't have time to miss it anyway. My stomach is sinking.

Somehow I don't think I'm necessarily going to agree about the "good" part of his news.

But Zian perks up. "What's up?"

Dominic steps into view from the living room, his parka exchanged for his lighter trench coat. "We found out who Ursula is."

Jacob nods, still scowling. "Ursula Engel. But we don't know for sure. She just seems to be the most likely person."

"There was a picture," Andreas puts in. "Not the best quality and from twenty-five years ago, but she matched the impression of her I got from the few memories of her I nabbed from the guardians."

"And she's a biochemist who did a bunch of work in this state up until around the time the facility must have been founded," Jacob continues. "Some of it for private security companies—the kinds of people who'd know how to set up a facility like that. But we couldn't find anything more specific than that."

"So, now what?" I ask, resisting the urge to hug myself.

Andreas aims his warm smile at me. "While those two were busy putting those pieces together, I tracked down someone who can help us find out all the details that aren't public on the internet." He pauses. "But of course, that help comes at a price…"

Ten

Riva

I stare through the moonlight at the waterfall tumbling fifty feet down the narrow cliff in front of me. "Oh, hell, no."

Jacob folds his arms over his chest, fixing me with a hard look. "Backing down already?"

I sigh. "No." Just extremely displeased with where my life has taken me.

Thankfully, Andreas insisted on coming along for the drive out into the wilderness too, and he balances out Jacob's harshness a little. He steps closer and gives the tip of my braid a gentle tug.

"I know you don't love the water, Tink, but you've got this. You'll be in and out in no time."

The warm confidence in his voice along with the old nickname—and the fact that he's showing any faith in me at all after the way the past few days have gone—steadies my nerves.

I don't actually mind water in general. Showers are fine. I can enjoy a quick dip in a warm swimming pool.

But immersing myself in the stuff sets my nerves on edge… possibly because of the same part of me that produces the claws from my fingertips and the pointed tufts of fur on my ears when I really give myself over to my animalistic side.

There's a reason Jacob used to call me "Wildcat."

And the faint spray lacing the air has already told me that this water is going to be cold. My skin is recoiling from it as if it thinks it can peel right off my body and avoid the whole production.

I square my shoulders and flex my fingers, feeling my strength. There's no running away from this expedition. It's the one thing Andreas's hacker wanted in return for his help—because there isn't much a hacker that good can't get on his own.

Right before we drove out here, Jacob let Dominic heal me. I can only feel the slightest prickles of the poison still coursing through my veins. But now he's watching me with a hint of a sneer.

I think he *wants* me to refuse so he'll have even more reason to question my loyalty.

No fucking way.

I point my index finger at him with a claw already extended. "I'm doing this even though I don't even think we should be bothering with this Ursula woman, because I know she's important to you and the other guys. And the four of you are important to me. That's the *only* reason I'm doing it. So keep that in mind instead of whatever snarky thoughts you'd usually be thinking while I'm getting myself chilled to the bone going up there."

Jacob blinks with a twitch of his eyelids as if he's trying to hide that he's startled. Then his mouth presses into a flat line.

Before he can let out yet another of those snarky thoughts, I stalk away from him toward the cliff.

Standing on the rocky bank several feet from where the water hits the shallow pond beneath, I study my target. It's a pretty ridiculous setup all around.

Some rich asshole our new hacker associate has a problem with built an off-the-grid cottage at the very top of this tall, slim plateau. I hate to think how much energy the prick is wasting pumping water the fifty feet up to the top only to have it spill back down again all around the house.

Apparently the only regular way in and out of the residence is by helicopter—if you can call that "regular." But he's never met a gal with superhuman strength and steely claws before.

The lights are off in the cottage. The hacker was able to tell us that his nemesis had a business trip keeping him away all night.

I don't need to see where I'm going, though. It's a simple matter of climbing straight up—and not falling.

Easy peasy.

I tug on the water shoes that are one piece of special equipment we bought for this endeavor and wade through the waist-deep pond in my leggings and long-sleeved tee, both black to blend into the night. The liquid chill bites into my legs.

The faster I pull this off, the sooner I can get out of it.

As I push right under the waterfall, I can't restrain a cringe at the tumbling water pummeling my hair. But there's a small gap between the flow of the falls and the rocky wall of the cliff, at least this far down.

I press myself into that water-free gap, swipe strands of drenched hair back from my face, reach up to hook my clawed fingers into the highest crevices I can reach, and haul myself upward.

The first half of the climb isn't so bad, as horrible pastimes go. My shoulders start to ache with the strain of hauling my weight upward, but I'm catching on enough nooks and crannies with my toes in their flexible footwear that I can propel myself up quickly and not rely on my arms for everything.

But the gap between the cliff and the waterfall narrows. First, it's just little streams hitting the back of my head here and there. Then, a continuous current gushes over my hair and down the back of my shirt.

I can't even shiver with the cold, or I might lose my grasp on the slick stone.

Gritting my teeth, I heave myself upward as quickly as I can without getting careless. Stretch a little farther. Reach a little higher.

Silently cuss out Jacob for deciding *I* should do this when Zian probably could have made the climb just as easily. More easily, really, since he's got no poison at all nibbling away at his muscles.

I'm one hundred percent sure Jacob's choice wasn't only because I might have an easier time sneaking into the actual building with my smaller frame.

Eventually, he's going to have to see that I'm completely on their side. There won't be any way he can deny it with that logical brain of his.

The worst section is the last ten or so feet right beneath the plateau. I have to grip the rocky ridges so tightly my fingers throb, digging my claws right into the limestone. My head stays bowed to the full deluge of water rushing over me.

Just a little farther. Just keep moving…

With my next reach, my hand finds no more stone surface above me. I grope forward and touch the flat plane where the waterfall originates.

With a gasp of relief in my throat, I throw myself through the roaring current, clambering all the way to a wooden deck that juts from the building ahead of me.

I haul myself out of the water and lie there on the buffed boards for a couple of minutes, catching my breath and letting my muscles recover. And also shedding the buckets of water that soaked into my hair and clothes. Then I stand up and wring even more moisture out of my shirt and leggings.

I slip off my water shoes and leave them on the deck. The "cottage" looms over me, a two-story structure that appears to be almost entirely glossy windows, framed here and there by dark wood.

How much money would you need in your accounts to feel comfortable throwing however many tens of millions it took to build and maintain this place?

But that's not my business. I'm just here to grab what I came for and go.

I slip around the house, searching for the entrance. The owner values his privacy—the only security cameras I spot are set up around the helipad at the far end of the deck area.

An alarm system wouldn't do him any good when he's disconnected this estate from the rest of society.

His mistake was assuming no one could possibly reach the place except by air.

The door isn't even locked. I stifle a laugh at the arrogance of that decision and ease inside.

Mr. Rich Dude also keeps the heat running even when he's not home. But I won't mock him too much for that, even in my head, because I appreciate the warmer air closing in around me and taking the edge off the clamminess of my damp clothes.

I take in the huge modern living room with its vaulted ceiling and leather furniture, every surface gleaming in the moonlight that seeps through the windows like it's all been recently polished—including the leather. A faintly smoky herbal scent lingers in the air, suggesting that the guy's been burning incense to set the mood.

Forget hackers and former facility bosses and all that. Why couldn't the five of us have a place like this away from the rest of the world?

Other than the fact that we don't have a billion dollars lying around, I mean. But I'd be happy with something several steps down on the fancy scale.

There's no way to argue with the guys about that right now, so I slink on through the expansive, airy rooms until I find the office.

At least, I assume it's the owner's office because there's a glass desk with two computer monitors and various other technological paraphernalia set up at one end. The rest of the space looks like a toy museum.

This is the only room I've encountered with no windows other than a couple of large skylights overhead. In the moonlight that seeps through the glass, dolls, action figures, and character statues stand poised along the built-in shelves that fill three of the four walls. Behind the desk, the one shelf-less wall holds several framed cards from what I assume must be specialized games, colorful art on the upper half and playing instructions on the lower.

This is where I need to be. But I'm looking for one item in particular…

I step closer to scan the shelves in the dim light. My gaze snags on a figure about eight inches tall, dressed in a purple suit with a black cape and gold detailing, still in its retail box.

Apparently this toy is super rare. Our hacker and Mr. Rich Dude used to be roommates once upon a time, and Rich Dude stole the collectable when he moved out.

And our hacker decided it was perfectly reasonable to send a bunch of strangers on a nearly impossible stealth mission to retrieve it.

I roll my eyes at the absurdity of the situation and pull out the watertight bags I kept under my shirt for the climb up. The action figure box slides into one well enough that I can seal the opening without a problem.

I tuck it inside the second bag for good measure, and then jam all that into a nylon backpack that's probably not at all waterproof. All it needs to do is make sure my cargo comes with me down the cliff.

Once I've slung the backpack over my shoulders, I tug the straps tight and secure the clip between them over my chest to make it extra secure. Then I hustle back to the front door, soaking up a little more warmth before I have to face the unpleasant scramble down.

I open the door—and halt in my tracks at the growl of an engine that's suddenly audible from overhead.

A helicopter is descending fast, the rhythmic whir of its blades already reaching my ears. Its lights cast thin but widening streaks across the landing platform just a few steps from where I'm frozen.

Fucking rich pricks and their way-too-insulated walls. Fucking hacker who was way too confident about the rich prick's schedule.

Every second I hesitate is another second closer to getting caught. I don't think I want to find out how Mr. Rich Dude would handle an intruder.

Hugging the outer walls, I dash around the house until I'm on the opposite side from the helicopter. I plunge into the rushing water beneath the deck and rush with it to the edge of the cliff.

Eleven

Riva

The current catches me and hurries me toward the waterfall—a little too fast. A twinge of Jacob's poison rattles my muscles at just the wrong moment, and my foot stumbles.

I careen forward, arms wheeling, and nearly tumble right down to the pond in a fatal swan dive.

My heart lurches. I try to throw myself backwards, teeter in the rushing water, and feel my shoes lose their grip.

As they slip right over the edge, I whip around and snatch out with my hands.

My arms smack into the water elbows first. One scrapes across a jagged piece of stone with a flare of pain through my forearm.

I gasp, and my other hand manages to snag on a knob of rock. My shoulder jars, the flow of the waterfall still battering me, but my body jolts to a stop.

Pain is splintering through both of my arms now, but I can't afford to hang out here in the middle of the deluge. The helicopter might already have landed.

I gulp air and ease down the cliff as fast as I can manage. Brace my feet, slide my hands down to the next holds, then clutch them for dear life as my feet skid farther below. Press my face close to the rough, slimy rock so I can suck in little puffs of breath.

I will the throbbing in my arms and shoulders as far back as I can. Clench my jaw until it's aching too.

Gravity is working with me rather than against me now, but a little too enthusiastically. It takes all my strength not to tumble with the falls into the shallow pool below.

By the time I'm close enough that I dare to jump the last several feet, tears burn in the backs of my eyes. Thankfully, the spray of the waterfall disguises any that have crept out.

I slog back to the bank on wobbly legs. The guys are gone—retreated to the car when they saw the helicopter coming, I assume. I'm too exhausted to even worry that they've abandoned me.

Regardless of how they feel about *me*, they really wanted the plastic superhero I'm carrying on my back.

The stretch of wilderness before I reach the overgrown track where we parked the car is totally black. I make my way more by sound and feel than sight. Finally, I catch the glint of moonlight off the windshield beyond the trees up ahead.

The moment I emerge, the engine rumbles to life. It must be Andreas behind the wheel, because Jacob leans out the passenger-side window to snap at me. "Let's go!"

As if I've been dawdling.

I stomp over to the passenger door, passing through the glow of the running lights. When I open the door to hop into the SUV's middle seat, Andreas has twisted in his spot up front.

"Are you bleeding?" he asks, his forehead furrowed with concern.

I glance down at my injured arm. The rock split the fabric, and blood streaks across the sliver of bare skin around the scrape, trickling down to the back of my hand. Somehow it hurts worse now that I can see how bad it looks.

"Just a little," I say nonchalantly.

Andreas lets out a rough noise and reaches for the key, but Jacob snatches his wrist before he can.

"I know how to bandage a cut too. We need to get out of here *now*."

Oh, joy. As Andreas reverses down the bumpy track, Jacob squeezes between the front seats to join me behind, bringing a first aid kit one of the guys had the foresight to stash in the glove compartment.

"I can do it," I inform him, not super keen on the idea of the guy who sent me cliff-climbing in the first place handling my damaged flesh.

"It's easier if it's someone else," he says curtly. Like he's annoyed that I'm inconveniencing him even while he's insisting on being inconvenienced.

I sigh and roll up my sleeve, biting my lip against a wince as the wet fabric rubs over the scrape. Jacob grasps my hand with the bare minimum of care and dabs the moisture from my arm with a folded piece of gauze.

Then he pauses. "You did get it, didn't you?"

I wrinkle my nose at him. "I know better than to come back without your prize. It's in the backpack, exactly as planned."

He lets out a huff as if even that fact doesn't please him and dabs antiseptic gel on my arm. As the stinging radiates through the muscle, he wraps some fresh gauze around my forearm.

Annoyingly, even while he's been such a jerk, other parts of my body have woken up with little tingles at his closeness. Someone should really give me a good shake.

And I shouldn't want it to be him.

"There, all patched up," Jacob says briskly, and pushes to the other side of the seat to get as much possible distance from me. You'd think I'm the one who goes around poisoning people with a touch.

"You okay, Riva?" Andreas asks.

Is he worried about the cut still or what fresh hell his friend might have wreaked on me?

I decide to assume the former. "It was pretty shallow. More an irritation than a real danger. Better I lost some skin than my whole skull going over the falls."

Jacob frowns, but just this once, his bad mood isn't directed at me. "That computer punk shouldn't have said the guy would be gone all night if he wasn't sure."

"Maybe plans changed at the last minute," Andreas says. "But you can lay into him when we get to the meetup if you want. Just don't wreck his doll." He pauses and then speaks again in an eager tone so familiar in my memory that it brings a fresh burn of tears to my eyes. "Did I ever tell you guys about the man I saw on the subway who used to work at a toy shop?"

"Probably," Jacob mutters, but he can't totally disguise the note of curiosity in his voice.

The guardians never let us hold on to much in the way of physical possessions, but Andreas built up a collection of a different type. Every time he'd go off on a mission, he'd delve into the memories of any person he saw who caught his interest and come back with the most interesting stories he was able to dig up.

He falls into that yarn-spinning cadence now as he turns the SUV off the track onto a proper road. "It seemed like he hadn't ever really wanted to run a store—especially one full of toys. He'd inherited it from an uncle, and when he first found out, he was outright pissed off. But then…"

As Andreas unravels his tale, I curl up against my window and let my eyes drift closed. It feels almost like old times, if I let myself focus on nothing but his voice.

By the time he's switched on the radio instead, I'm drifting off to sleep, exhausted enough that even my damp clothes can't keep me awake. It's a long drive back to the city. When I wake up with the cutting of the engine, the fabric is pretty much dry.

The hacker is waiting in the back room of a foreclosed arcade. When the three of us come in, his head jerks up with an eager flash of his pale eyes.

Zian and Dominic, who've been waiting with him and sort of standing guard, straighten up with pinched expressions like they've had a little too much caffeine to stay awake this long.

"You—" Jacob starts to vent, but I don't have the patience to listen to him harangue the guy. The expedition is finished now. We all survived.

I wave him quiet. "Let's just get this over with."

I unzip the backpack, meeting the hacker's gaze. "We got what you wanted."

When I pull out the action figure, still encased in its translucent watertight bags, the guy's face lights up as if I've brought him the elixir of life. He reaches for it automatically, but Andreas steps in.

"You know we got it. Now you need to dig up the information we need. Then we pay."

"Yes, of course." The hacker grins at me. "You have no idea how much this means to me. They only ever made a hundred with that specific detailing, and most of those have ended up in the trash over the years. That one—my dad helped me buy it, just a couple of months before cancer finally got him."

Oh. Maybe it's a little more than just a silly toy after all.

I offer an awkward smile and tuck the box under my arm. "We'll take good care of it until it's time to hand it over."

He chuckles, and his smile turns slyer. "I bet you will, if you had the skills to get it in the first place. I'd have liked to see you in action."

I don't know how to respond to that. His tone sounds oddly flirty, not that I'd be a good judge of that.

He can't really think I've come back from his death-defying mission looking for a hookup, right?

"There wasn't much to see," I reply. "It was very dark."

"Hmm." The hacker sidles close enough that he can trace his fingers over my forearm—the unwounded one. "But so many fun things can happen in the dark, especially with a girl as—"

"Get away from her," Zian snarls, shoving between us so abruptly that I stumble backward. Before I can even catch my balance, another hand grabs me by the elbow and yanks me farther away from the overly optimistic hacker.

I glance around and find Jacob gripping me, his eyes searing cold as he glares at the other guy with just as much hostility as Zian is giving off. "She isn't on the menu."

"Whoa, whoa," the hacker says, holding up his hands and backing up a few paces. "No offense meant. Just like to take my shots when they present themselves. I didn't realize you were together like that."

"She's with us," Zian says with a growl, and even though I know he doesn't mean like that, that he might mean simply as a prisoner, something low in my belly wobbles giddily at the sight of his protective stance.

"Sure, no problem. Here, initial gesture of good-will—I have the fake IDs you wanted too."

He hands Andreas the counterfeit driver's licenses with our photos and birthdates that make us all drinking age—which we might actually be, not that we plan on drowning ourselves in alcohol. We never celebrated birthdays in the facility, and the best we can figure is we're around twenty or twenty-one.

The hacker takes another step back and gives us a flippant salute. "I'll get on with your search… and maybe with fielding a phone call from one very pissed off trust-fund kid too."

A smile touches his face as he says those words, but it tightens almost as soon as it's formed. A shadow passes over his expression. He tramps out the door without another word.

I watch him go, a strange pang echoing through me. His happiness about getting his toy back didn't last very long, even if the figure had a special meaning to him.

How much did his former friendship mean to him? Getting this one thing back might not be enough to heal all the wounds dealt when it was stolen.

I look around at the guys I've reunited with and somehow found myself so much farther apart from at the same time, and suddenly all I want to do is burrow under the covers on my bed and imagine we could start this whole situation over from the beginning. And that it'd turn out better this time.

Twelve

Andreas

Riva doesn't act all that different even when she thinks she's alone. At least, I assume she believes she's alone.

It was more than a year after she disappeared that I stumbled onto one of the new extremes of my talent—in front of a couple of the guardians, just my luck. I was in the middle of a testing session, trawling for memories in the mind of some random woman they'd pulled in from who knows where and pretending I couldn't find half of what they asked for, when I started thinking about how nice it would be if I could just erase *myself* from all their minds.

Technically, I could have. Or, it'd have been possible if my talents hadn't been blunted by the drugs they kept us on. I could right now if I really wanted to—simply wipe all memory of my existence from every mind in the world but my own.

It wouldn't be the first time I've essentially erased someone.

But my skill with memory doesn't come with that many gradients. I could destroy one set of memories at a time, person by person, or I could sear away all impressions in a massive wave.

I'd be screwed if even my friends couldn't remember me. And it wouldn't have gotten me very far with the guardians anyway, since they'd still see me right in front of them and know something was up. The digital records of me wouldn't disappear.

All those thoughts passed through my head in a meandering sort of way, with the wish to vanish getting increasingly strong—and then I glanced down at my hand and realized I could see right through it to the chair arm I was resting it on.

Invisibility should have been a super useful skill, but all the accidental discovery accomplished was giving the guardians even more to prod and question me about. The few times they tapered off the drugs enough that I could pull off a full disappearing act, they had me in an ultra-secure exam room I couldn't escape from anyway.

Most of the time, when I tested myself in the semi-privacy of my regular room, the best I could manage was to hide a limb or two. Not enough to factor into our plans in any significant way.

But the drugs wore off completely a few days ago, and I feel like I'm breathing unclouded air for the first time in years. When Jacob suggested I follow him and Riva up to her room invisibly and keep an eye on her for a couple hours, it was a piece of cake to come along.

I slipped into the room after her while he held the door open and propped my transparent body in the corner away from anywhere she might walk, since she could still bump into me. And since then, I've been watching.

But really, there hasn't been much to see.

She sits on her bed for a little while with the same serious expression that's been alternating with annoyance on her face since we found her, pulling out her necklace and clicking it around. Then she hunkers down on the floor and runs through a series of exercises—pushups and crunches before getting back up for some squats and lunges.

It's impossible not to appreciate the strength that flows through her deceptively delicate-looking frame. As her face flushes with the exertion, tingles of heat course through my own body.

I'm not any kind of peeping Tom, though. When she moves to swap her now-sweaty tank top for a clean one, I turn toward the wall until I'm sure she's done.

It's not my fault images of what her slender curves might look like play out in my mind anyway. Riva was the only girl I ever really wanted, even after I had a chance to meet others—if briefly—on my missions into the wider world.

No matter what else has happened since, some feelings don't just vanish, even if you'd like them to. As I'm pretty sure Jacob could attest to if he was willing to own up to it.

When the rustling of fabric fades, I let myself look again. Riva walks over to the window and pushes it open a few inches so a waft of cool autumn breeze can seep in.

Good. I think we'll both benefit from that.

There's a digital clock on the dresser. I've been in here a little more than an hour. I flex my muscles, checking for any sign of flagging energy, but there's no indication that maintaining my invisibility is wearing me down.

At least not that way. I've gone as long as several hours in the facility's exam room, with none of the aches that creep in if I've been poking around in people's memories for too long. But the sensation always rises up after a while that I'm permanently fading—that if I wish my body out of view for too long, I'll never be able to bring it back.

It's probably just paranoia, but I don't plan on pushing myself to the limit just to test that assumption.

Riva sits back down on the bed and flips idly through a magazine she grabbed on our foray into the campus convenience store. It doesn't appear to be doing much to captivate her.

Jacob is going to be disappointed that I can't report back some vast conspiracy that she's been conducting behind her closed door.

Boredom itches at me. I could slip into her memories again, but so many of them I'm already familiar with because I was there too—and I'm not totally sure how well I'll hold my invisibility if I divert my concentration that much.

I fish in my pocket for the smooth shoelace I picked up a pair of along with our new clothes and twist it between my fingers. One knot, another knot, another knot, until I can't tie any more and I need to pick them all apart again.

The shoelace isn't as good for my fidgety habit as the length of woven cord I kept in my room at the facility, not quite slick enough to unravel quickly, but it keeps the restless itch at bay.

Soft strains of music start to filter through the open window. Someone in one of the townhouses nearby is blaring an upbeat pop song, like they're trying to pep up the neighborhood.

And Riva begins to sway.

At first, I can't say it's a definite motion and not just my imagination as I tune into the beat. But the gentle rocking of her torso becomes a little more pronounced, so it's obvious she's absorbing the music.

I can't tell whether *she* realizes she's moving with it. Her gaze is still focused on the glossy magazine pages.

Then her head tips a little to one side and the other, forming a more complex rhythm separate from her shoulders. Her chin bobs a little with the beat.

All at once, her eyes leap to the window. She stiffens abruptly, as if she's worried some horrible backlash is about to descend on her.

She gets up and shuts the window. When she flops on the bed again, she holds herself perfectly, rigidly still.

My gut twists. I remember now—catching glimpses of her here and there when we'd have a TV show or a movie on with a prominent soundtrack, or when the guardians pumped music into the training room while we exercised. Little moments when she'd slip into the melody with a few graceful motions.

Her momentary lapse with the music is the only thing I've seen during this stint of spying that's at all different from how she's been behaving around the rest of us. The only time she hasn't seemed totally self-aware and controlled.

I'm still turning that fact over in my mind when the lock rasps in the door and Zian calls in to Riva that it's dinner time. He pulls the door wide, as planned, and I hustle out ahead of her.

By the time she makes it down to the first floor, I'm helping dish out the pasta the others managed to cook, every part of me as opaque as it's meant to be.

I glance over my shoulder at her with a grin to cover a twinge of guilt. "How hungry are you, Tink?"

It's like an unexpected gift, the way her expression softens just slightly when I use her old nickname, taking her from pretty to ethereal. My heart skips a beat.

I have to be careful I don't start expecting that gift—or enjoying it too much. It's when you assume you know how things are going to go that everything turns upside down.

"Just a little," she says, sinking into the chair that's become hers. "But it smells good."

She offers me a quick smile in return, because she's assuming *I* cooked it rather than spending the last two hours studying her in secret.

"I think Dominic deserves most of the credit for that," I admit, and bump the other guy lightly with my elbow as he grabs his plate. I get a small smile out of him too, so that's a double victory for the meal.

The fact that *I* can still smile as much as I do shows the difference in how the past few years have hit us. It's hardly been a laugh riot for me, and I've felt Griffin's absence every single day, but I know nothing I've been through compares to the worst of what the other guys have faced.

If I can distract them a little from the burdens they're carrying, at least I'm helping in some small way.

Zian needs it too. He digs into his pasta enthusiastically enough, but when Riva leans past him to grab the salt, her arm almost brushing his knuckles, I catch the slight tensing of his shoulders. The tick in his jaw before he starts chewing again.

The flicker of uneasiness in his eyes.

No, I'm definitely not the only one feeling the draw of Riva's presence—but I can't even begin to imagine all the turmoil it'll have stirred up in him, after… everything.

"I told Dom to fry an extra package of ground beef for the sauce just for you, Zee!" I call over to him from my armchair perch.

He rolls his eyes at me, but his expression softens with resigned amusement. The teeniest of tiny victories.

Maybe if I keep trying, I'll eventually stumble on a larger one.

We're just finishing eating when there's a knock on the door. All five of us stiffen, our heads jerking toward the front of the townhouse.

When no armed guardians follow up the knock by bashing the door right off its hinges or smashing through the windows, I chuckle and get up, setting my mostly empty plate on the table. It isn't as if an enemy would knock first anyway.

I open the door to find the girl from the next building over—Brooke, that's her name—waiting on the front steps. She offers me a sunny smile, but her gaze flicks past me toward the room beyond as if she's searching for something.

"Is Rita here?" she asks. "A bunch of us are going out—I thought she might like to come with."

There's no way in hell Jacob is going to okay Riva going off for a romp with a bunch of strangers.

"She's deep in a study session," I say. "Hates to be interrupted."

Brooke's eyes narrow—only for a moment but enough to set me immediately on guard.

"You boys keep her on a pretty tight leash, huh?" she says in a casual tone that I suspect isn't casual at all.

Apprehension prickles over me. If she gets convinced that something unpleasant is going on, she could raise a fuss with the campus authorities, draw attention to us that we don't want.

I prop myself against the door frame, offering my best charming grin. "Nah, she just takes the school stuff very seriously. I keep telling her she should lighten up. Where are you off to? Maybe I can persuade her to take the evening off."

I'm convincing enough that confusion flashes across Brooke's face before she catches her reaction and gives a friendly laugh. "Oh, we're heading to our favorite club downtown. It's kind of a Friday night ritual."

"And what's so special about this particular club?" I ask with a playful arch of my eyebrows.

"Just that we love the DJ who's up on Fridays. And there are four-dollar drinks until ten."

"Well, now *I'm* tempted, anyway." I shoot her another grin, and a hint of pink colors her freckled cheeks.

I've spent enough time in the wider world to determine that if I hit the right notes, very few women are totally impervious to my friendly facade. But that doesn't stop a greasy sensation from creeping over my skin, knowing I'm using it to distract her from her concern for Riva.

Riva doesn't need her concern. I'm looking after her.

This college girl has no idea what any of us have been through, what we even *are*. She'd only make things worse.

But her mention of the DJ brings my mind back to seeing Riva sway with the distant music upstairs. Encouraging her to let loose a little doesn't sound like such a bad idea.

She should have the chance to really breathe too.

"Let me know the name of the place, and I'll see what I can do," I tell Brooke. "If I can work a little magic, we'll see you there."

After she tells me and leaves, I shut the door and walk back to the dining area where the other four are waiting with wary expressions.

"At least she went away," Zian says.

"For now," I say, clapping my hands together. "I wasn't lying. I think we should all go dancing."

I notice Riva goes even more rigid in her chair.

So does Jacob. "Are you fucking kidding me?"

I give him a pointed look. "I think we *all* could benefit from a chance to blow off some steam. Let down our guards a bit and show how we can fit in."

His mouth twists, but he doesn't argue further.

"That doesn't sound like my kind of thing," Riva starts to say, her fingers curling tightly around her fork.

But Zian has perked up, getting into the spirit of the thing. "No, it is a good idea. We don't have much else to do while we're waiting on that hacker guy anyway."

I aim a softer but still bright smile at Riva. "Come on, Tink. We've got our freedom. Don't you want to live a little?"

"Your new best friend isn't going to let up until she convinces you to hang out with her somewhere," Jacob adds in a mutter.

Riva hesitates and then lets out a halting laugh. "Fine. Let's hit the club—but only for an hour or two."

Thirteen

Riva

I tug at the sides of my hoodie as we walk up to the dance club's entrance. It's the only piece of clothing I'm currently wearing that I actually feel comfortable in.

I swear Jacob must have been cackling evilly to himself when he grabbed this sparkly halter top and jeans so tight they're practically painted on. But I couldn't even argue that my comfy tank tops and sweats make appropriate clubwear.

How the hell did I let the guys talk me into this? Oh, yeah, because it's the first time they've asked me to do *anything* that actual friends would do.

Even if it's hard to imagine from Jacob's current sour expression that I've made any progress at all with him.

The pulsing bass emanating from the club makes me uncomfortable too, in a different way. The beat is already resonating through to my bones, tugging at my limbs.

But I've never danced in front of anyone before. Now I'm going to be surrounded by both strangers and three of the four guys I was most nervous of showing my few secrets to.

I can't be glad that it's only three out of four, because Dominic is the one I'd worry least about judging me for my physical grace. But he wasn't going to get away with a parka or even a trench coat in a dance club, and the other guys accepted him begging off without argument.

They know why he keeps himself so covered up—I'm sure of it. One more way I've found myself outside of the circle of trust that was once so solid between all of us.

Well, I don't have to let myself really tear up the dance floor. For all anyone here knows, the most I'd ever want to do under the flashing club lights is bob a little with the rhythm.

The bouncer waves us in, and warm air rushes over us with a tang of alcohol. It's still pretty early in the night, but a lot of people must agree with Brooke's assessment of the DJ or have a craving for cheap drinks, because figures are swaying and laughing all across the long but narrow room.

The space is painted all dark purple except for splotches of white that give off an unearthly sheen under periodic sweeps of black lights. The bar counter that stretches along the side wall gleams glossy white too, making the drinks set on its surface glow like some alien tonic when the black lights wash over them.

A tremor runs up my legs, prickling through my flesh with the toxin that's nibbling away at my insides. Ignoring it, I hold my head high and walk farther in as I scan the space for Brooke's bright red hair.

It was her idea that I come, so I'd better make sure she knows I did. Maybe now that I've accepted one invite, she won't feel the need to keep extending more.

Our neighbor spots me first—she emerges from the crowd at my right and taps my arm, grinning widely.

"You made it!" she hollers over the thumping music. "It's good to see you here."

"I'm not much of a dancer," I say in a pre-emptive apology.

She makes a dismissive gesture and motions me over to the bar. "Get a couple drinks in you, and you won't worry about that. They make the best cosmos here."

The idea of gulping down the fermented liquid I can taste in the air sets all my nerves on edge. The guardians had us try alcohol a few times, just to ensure we'd be prepared for it if we encountered a situation where we needed to drink—or decided to give it a try out of curiosity's sake—on one of our outside missions. But I never enjoyed the impression of my senses going fuzzy.

I'll feel better if I can stay fully alert.

"Not right now," I tell Brooke hastily, buying myself a little time before I have to get into any questions of why I wouldn't drink at all, and fumble for an easy excuse. "I already had something before we left. Don't want to go too fast."

I think that's the sort of excuse I've heard people offer in made-up stories, and it appears to work well enough in real life.

"Oh, for sure," Brooke says without any sign of concern, and grabs me by the wrist to drag me over to where her friends are dancing.

The other girls all offer tentative smiles and then go back to shimmying with the music. Thankfully, this isn't the kind of place where anyone would expect a proper getting-to-know-you conversation.

Maybe Andreas was actually brilliant suggesting that we take Brooke up on her invite. Not only are we putting on a better show of being regular college students, I'm getting in some normal socializing without actually needing to be all that social.

And soon we'll be moving on from the campus and we won't need to pretend anymore. I hope.

I shuffle from side to side and wiggle my arms with the beat, feeling incredibly dorky but at least in control. One of Brooke's friends catches another's hand and spins her around. Another throws back a shot and weaves away from us to order another.

Brooke giggles with them and bops along with the music, doing nothing more elaborate than I am but somehow looking like she fits in here perfectly. I guess most people around us aren't pulling off fancy moves anyway.

My gaze travels over the crowd—and snags on Jacob about ten feet away. He's turned with his profile to me, but there's no mistaking the breathtakingly chiseled planes of his face, turned even more ethereal when the black lights hit his blond hair and pale skin.

I'm not the only one who notices that either.

A couple of women in club gear skimpier than mine, strapless corset tops and pleated skirts, are fawning over him. As I watch, one trails her hand down his arm from shoulder to elbow. Another leans close to murmur something in his ear, a sly smile curving her darkly stained lips.

My fingers flex automatically, my claws itching at the tips. I squeeze my hands into balls and yank my gaze away.

Going feral cat in the middle of a dance club will not help our cover one bit. And who am I to get possessive over Jacob?

He's made it one hundred percent clear that he has warmer feelings for a piece of used gum stuck to his shoe than for me.

But the next place my gaze lands is on Zian, standing a couple inches taller than even the biggest of the other guys around, and the ring of girls clustered around him, twirling their hair with their fingers and peering at him coyly through their eyelashes.

My stomach lurches, and I rip my eyes away again—only to find myself watching Andreas aiming a flirty smirk at a dark-haired woman in a skintight dress as they move with the beat together.

Is *that* why he wanted to come—why the other guys agreed? So they could find a pretty girl or two for a quick hookup?

It shouldn't bother me. We were never together that way, no matter how much I craved an even deeper connection before. But a now-unsettlingly familiar vibration resonates through my chest, scraping against my insides.

The guys are all rubbing it in my face: how much they prefer the company even of strangers over mine.

I close my eyes for a moment, willing the thrum of anger down. The bitterness keeps creeping up my throat.

At a gentle nudge of my shoulder, I glance up and find Brooke studying me. "Are you okay, Rita?"

"Yeah—yeah, I'm good," I mumble, and focus abruptly on the fresh drink in her friend's hand.

Maybe having my senses a little muddled would be helpful for getting through tonight. Just one cocktail shouldn't affect me very much.

It'll simply dull the sharp edges of that awful feeling inside me.

"I think I'm ready for a cosmo now," I add, not entirely sure what a cosmo even is. If Brooke likes them, they're probably okay.

She grins and comes with me over to the bar, where she orders one for herself too. The pink concoction arrives in a wide-mouthed, narrow-stemmed glass that I raise cautiously to my lips, half afraid I'm going to snap the stem by accident.

The cool liquid slides down my throat, both tart and citrusy sweet, with a sour tang potent enough to make me shudder. I only take a few small swallows, and then I follow Brooke back into the crowd.

I go back to my bobbing and swaying, taking sips in between to drain the glass. By the time I set it on the tray of a passing staff person handing out shots, there's nothing left in my chest but a soft fizzing sensation.

There, that's better. Now I might as well enjoy myself.

It feels perfectly natural to meld into the bass, to let the melody flow through my limbs and direct my muscles. A sense of elation washes over me.

I swivel and dip, sidling one way and twisting another, and the music holds me in its grasp like the perfect partner. It always tells me exactly where to go to match it.

As one song fades into another, Brooke gives a little cheer. "You've got some moves!"

One of her friends shoots me a thumbs up, and I grin hazily at her.

Was I worried about this before? Everything's good.

I'm getting hot, though, sweat trickling down my back under my hoodie. Everyone else is wearing short sleeves or none at all. Even having it unzipped isn't giving me enough air.

I tug the hoodie right off. It slips from my fingers and gets tugged away under nearby dancing feet, but I find I don't really care.

My hands soar toward the ceiling, and I undulate beneath them. I can really move without the extra fabric holding me back. Now I'm soaring.

When I notice Brooke again, her gaze is fixed on my arms. I glance at one as the black light sweeps over the dance floor. The scars that mark my flesh, just a little paler than the rest of my skin, flare with a momentary glow.

Brooke is frowning now. "What happened to you?"

I consider my arms, still swaying the rest of my body with the rhythm of the song. I don't have *that* many scars, do I? A few here and a few there. The cluster of tiny ones under my right arm are too small to show at all in this atmosphere.

"I got into lots of fights," I say, pleased that I can tell her this, and it's true, and it doesn't really reveal anything.

Brooke's frown doesn't go away. "Fights about what?"

I shrug. "Who would win. Don't worry. It was always me!"

I whirl around and laugh at the exhilaration of the movement. Brooke scoots over so we're facing each other again.

"Are you in any kind of trouble, Rita?" she asks with that serious expression.

I don't want her to look like that. Brooke is nice—Brooke should be happy. It was her idea for me to come here, and I'm having such a good time.

"No trouble," I assure her with a broad grin. "I left all the trouble behind."

"If there's anything—"

Fingers close around my elbow from behind. I turn to see Andreas standing over me, his usual warm smile looking a tad tense.

Is he getting serious too? What is up with people tonight? I thought we all came here to have some fun.

"Hey," he says, and directs his smile at Brooke for just a second before returning his attention to me. "You lost your hoodie."

"It was too hot," I inform him.

A little furrow forms in his forehead. "Well, I think you're going to want it later. Let's have a look and see if we can rescue it."

I pump my fist in the air. "It's a mission!"

Andreas tugs me away from Brooke and her friends, but instead of prowling through the mass of dancers searching for my wayward hoodie, he pulls me right over to the far wall where the whoops and chatter of the other dancers don't drown out our voices quite so much.

"How much have you had to drink?" he asks me, looking me up and down.

I do a little shimmy, wondering if I can get him to point the same flirty grin at me that he did for the other woman. "Just one. It was good!"

Andreas's expression only gets more serious, which is absolutely the wrong direction. "Maybe we should head home."

"What?" I protest. "No. We just got here, like, five seconds ago. I'm having fun."

He quirks an eyebrow at me, which at least brings back a bit of his normal easygoing vibe. "Are you really?"

I plant my hands on my hips. "Yes. Tons. I haven't been able to dance since—even when I was alone in my new room, there were the shackles, and I didn't like thinking about the boss watching—but now I don't care! I didn't realize it could be this much fun to dance *with* other people."

I don't know how to describe Andreas's expression anymore. He looks kind of like he isn't any more sure what he's doing with his face than I am.

With a surge of boldness, I tap him right on his toned chest. "Why don't *you* dance with me?"

"I'm not sure that's a good idea," he says dryly.

I grimace at him. "Why not? We could have fun together. We used to."

A sudden melancholy sweeps over me, dragging my spirits down into the toilet. I glance at my arm again, at the scars Brooke noticed and the smaller ones near my armpit.

"I always needed to be sure, you know," I say, running my fingers over the lines carved by my claws. "Bring out a little puff of the smoky stuff to make sure it still pointed toward the rest of you. That you were still out there somewhere."

Andreas's throat bobs with a thick swallow, and I'm abruptly captivated by that motion, my previous thoughts flitting away. I step closer to him and touch his neck.

"Riva," he says roughly.

"I really am so glad I found you," I tell him, and tip my head so it rests on his shoulder.

Some distant part of me expects him to shove me away, but the rest of me doesn't care. And that isn't what happens anyway.

Andreas's arms come up to wrap around me. He hugs me to his lean frame so tight that tears I can't explain spring into my eyes.

He smells just like he should, like sunshine and warm amber. I want to sink right into him.

Then he's detached himself after all—not shoving but pulling himself away, backing up a step as my head comes up to look at him. He opens his mouth and closes it again, and his gaze veers to someone beyond my shoulder.

I pivot and wobble on my feet with a wave of dizziness. Jacob's come up behind me—he catches my arm to steady me, his face set in that stupid scowl I'd like to punch right off it.

I yank my arm away. "I don't want to dance with *you*. You've been so mean to me over things I never even did."

Jacob blinks at me, startled enough for his stern expression to break, and glances at Andreas. "What the hell happened to her?"

Andreas's mouth twists. "She says she had a drink. Just one, and with that girl from the residences hovering over her I don't think anyone could have slipped something in it, but the alcohol could be interacting oddly with the poison."

"That's right!" I say triumphantly, as if Andreas has given me a trump card. I jab my index finger at Jacob, who is continuing to be way too gorgeous even when he's annoying. "You poisoned me too. Definitely no dancing."

My legs quiver under me again, even though I haven't moved them this time. I list to the side before catching my balance against the wall. "The floor's getting tippy."

Jacob swears under his breath. "We don't want her collapsing in here, for fuck's sake."

"Nope," I agree. "Then everyone would know just how big a jerk you are."

He glowers at me, which really isn't helping his case.

I glance away from him and notice Zian making his way over. One of the corset-top girls is trotting along behind him, pawing at his arm. And just like that, I'm sad again.

"He doesn't want me touching him, but these girls he doesn't even know…"

Andreas grips my shoulder. "It's okay, Riva. But we'd better head home. You've gotten kind of… sick."

I do feel that way now—all topsy turvy, like my stomach is flipping in somersaults.

I pivot, and Brooke is there, her big kind eyes even wider than usual with worry. "Is everything all right?"

My good mood returns in a flash. I snatch at her hand.

"Yes! Let's dance some more. It's definitely not time to go home yet." A whoop careens up my throat, loud enough that several nearby dancers glance our way. "Let's paaar-ty!"

Andreas keeps his grasp on my shoulder, the spoilsport. "We think she's been roofied," he says to Brooke. "She… doesn't normally act like this, even when she goes out."

Brooke's eyebrows draw together. "I can't believe someone—we've never had any problems here before. I can help get her back to the campus. It was my idea."

"It's fine," Jacob says, coolly and smoothly. "We all came together. No need for you to interrupt your night."

"I want to do *something*."

"You could keep an eye out for her hoodie," Andreas suggests. "We still haven't figured out where that got to."

Brooke doesn't look convinced, but I'm dizzy again, my thoughts too muddled to come up with an argument in my favor.

Zian reaches Jacob's side, his fawning fan gone off someplace else finally, and studies me with a flex of his arms. "Is something wrong?"

"She's out of it," Jacob says. "We need to get her home so she can sleep it off."

"Not sleepy," I mumble in an ineffective protest.

In the face of all their concern, Brooke eases back. "All right. If I find her hoodie, I'll drop it off in your mailbox."

"Thank you," Andreas says, flashing a smile, and then they're ushering me out of the club.

I grumble my displeasure as they stuff me into the back seat again, but relaxing into the pliant leather comes as an unexpected relief. My head lolls to the side when the car takes a corner, and my stomach churns.

I bring my hands up to cover my face. "I want to go to bed," I say, my voice muffled against my palms.

"That's what we're working on," Andreas says. He's stayed in the back with me, rubbing my shoulder reassuringly.

At the townhouse, I stagger up to my bedroom between Jacob and Andreas and crash onto my bed. Dominic is there, still in his trench coat costume, his face tight.

Is he angry with me? I don't know what I did wrong. There's so much I don't understand.

A little moan slips out of me, and he rests his hand tentatively on my belly. "You'll feel better soon, Riva."

Everyone else is gone. The room is dark. The tingling energy flows out from his hand and melts away my nausea and the shakiness in my limbs, but my mind still feels like it's floating someplace far above us.

He's mad at me, but he's here helping me anyway. That's what Dominic is like.

I want him even closer. I want him—

He stands up, and all at once I can't bear for him to simply walk away. The words tumble out.

"I missed you, you know. All of you. But especially…"

Dominic stops near the door. He watches me, a shadowy figure in the darkened space.

"Especially what?" he asks in a low voice.

I grope for the words to capture the memories trickling through my head. "When you weren't there, I'd sometimes still imagine the four of you. And *you*, you always had the right thing to say, like you'd thought it all out and gotten to the best answer like you always did."

I pause, and one more swell of grief rolls over me. "I wish I knew the right thing to say to you to fix whatever I broke."

Dominic is quiet for long enough that I almost forget he's in the room. Exhaustion drags my eyelids down.

Then his voice reaches my ears, steady but a little gruff. "Don't worry about it. It was already broken a long time before anything you did."

The comment makes me frown. The door clicks shut behind him, and I sink down into a hazy sleep.

Fourteen

Dominic

The marigolds give off a pungent scent, as bright and bold as their orange petals. I pour the last of the liquid from the small watering can over the raised garden bed and then sit down on the back step next to it.

Something that's balled tight and hard in my chest relaxes just a little as I take in the vibrant colors and the life the flowers exude. I don't know whether past student residents planted them or if the garden is something the campus staff normally maintain, but I'll take the little fragment of peace I get out of looking after them.

The only plants I ever got to handle in the facility were the ones the guardians expected me to kill. And then when that wasn't enough—

I shut those memories out of my mind and lean against the steps as well as I can without provoking a jab of discomfort at my back.

There are a lot of things going on in the house behind me that I can't really take care of, but then, it's been clear for a while that my talents are a lot more superficial than any of us would like to think. The damage we're dealing with has roots that run far deeper than our physical bodies.

And Riva…

Before my mind can stray very far in that direction, the sound of ragged panting has my head jerking up. As I get to my feet, Jacob jogs into view from the alley that runs behind the townhouses.

Well, kind of jogging. He's limping as much as he's running, his face gone waxy sallow.

I catch my lips before they can pull into a full grimace. The worst damage might be way down deep, but Jake does like pushing it as close to the surface as he can get.

"I'm okay, I'm okay," he mutters in a rasp as he makes it to the back steps, as if he doesn't look like he's just risen from the grave. He staggers on his way up the stairs, and I catch his arm.

He shoots me a glare that's plenty sharp despite how badly he's exhausted himself. "I'm *fine*."

Sure, he is. Just like he was fine all the days he collapsed at the side of the track in the training room, hair and clothes drenched with sweat, chest stuttering with strained breaths.

Back there, the guardians hauled him off and forced hydration into him—and whatever else he needed. Here, it's only me.

But he didn't think about that before he drove his body past every conceivable limit again, did he?

The moment the flash of resentment passes through me, shame burns it up. I know why he punishes himself like this—and what he's running away from while he does.

As if any part of it is his fault. The only person here who could possibly have saved Griffin is me.

And I didn't. I didn't even get close enough to try.

So I hook Jacob's arm around my neck, ignoring the pinch at the back of my shoulders, and support him on his stumbling feet into the living room. The other guys are somewhere else in the house, which is probably for the best.

Jacob has set himself up as de facto leader of our troop. It wouldn't be good for morale if they saw him half-dead.

Jacob grunts with annoyance, but he lets me lower him onto the sofa. "I just need some water," he grumbles.

I pour him a glass and sit next to him as he gulps it. He hasn't actually burned out *all* of his strength like he has in the past, but from the way he's set his legs, that one calf is still bothering him.

"You sprained something," I say.

He waves me off with an uncomfortably weak gesture. "It's not a big deal."

It will be if the guardians track us down here. If he's torn the muscle, it could take weeks to fully heal.

If we leave it to mend itself naturally.

There isn't a question in my mind about whether I'll do this—I can, and Jake needs me, so that's all there is to it. But there's nothing alive in the room around us.

I think about the marigolds outside. Picture snapping a couple of their stalks, and wince inwardly.

No, I can do this one all by myself.

As I bend over to set my hand against Jacob's lower leg, he sets down his glass. "Dom, you *really* don't need to—"

"I do," I interrupt in as firm a voice as I'd ever use with him. "If you don't want me needing to heal you, then don't go breaking your body."

I'm ashamed all over again at the trace of resentment that creeps into my tone, but Jake simply lets out a resigned sigh, accepting the criticism. And then, as I will a little of the energy inside me through his pantleg into his flesh, he says in a low voice, "I'm sorry."

I find a real smile somewhere inside myself. Even with the frustrations bubbling under the surface, I *am* glad I can help him this way.

"Don't worry about it. Like you said, no big deal."

Through the pressure of my hand, I sense the muscle and the fibers of tissue that've frayed. Closing my eyes, I will them to bind back together, to smooth out and strengthen.

My power flows out of me in a stream of warmth—and tugs at my gut at the same time. A prickling sensation ripples through my own limbs, little nips of discomfort here and there, spread out over my entire frame.

No big deal.

"Okay," Jacob says after several seconds. "It's good enough now. You don't need to do more."

The concern that leaks into his voice makes my gut twist in a different way.

Does he have any idea how much I worry about *him*? Every time he wears himself to the bone like this, he's risking toppling over some edge he can't come back from.

And I'm not totally sure he isn't looking forward to the day when that happens.

But I don't know what to say to him. Riva claimed last night that I always had the right advice, but she hasn't been with us to see the wreckage she left us in.

I can't tell whether any of the comments that flit through my mind would make Jacob feel better or worse, so I keep my mouth shut.

He's just slumping into the sofa in a more relaxed pose when Andreas comes thundering down the stairs with Zian at his heels.

"Our hacker came through," Andreas announces, waving his phone. "He's got something big on Ursula Engel. We can meet up with him tonight to hand off his collectable for all the details."

Jacob sits up a little straighter, still wan but mildly re-energized by the prospect of making progress with our search. He flicks his damp hair away from his eyes. "All right. Now we're getting somewhere."

Zian frowns. "Will Riva be okay to come after last night? I guess one of us could stay back here with her…"

Jacob shakes his head, his lips curling into a sneer. "If he doesn't see all of us, he'll wonder what's up—and he particularly noticed her."

I'm not sure whether the edge that's crept into his voice is directed more at the woman upstairs or the hacker.

"I couldn't sense any lingering effects from the alcohol that wouldn't have cleared up by now," I put in.

"And if she wanted to be at the top of her game, she shouldn't have been hitting the booze to begin with."

I stiffen at Jacob's tone. I might be pissed off about the past, but even I can see he's not being fair—how could Riva have known that a single drink would interact badly with the poison he insisted on infecting her with?

But I can't see how pointing that out will do any good. Or how wondering aloud whether the information this hacker dug up is really going to help us will either.

Maybe this opportunity won't get us where we need to go, but we have to put ourselves out there if we want to make any progress at all. If we're not even going to try to find answers, what's the point of even continuing the lives the guardians inflicted on us?

I push myself to my feet. "I'll make sure she's in decent shape before we head out. What time do we need to leave?"

It only takes a few seconds after we've gotten out of the car before I'm wishing I just stayed home. The night air has cooled enough that my parka isn't totally uncomfortable while unzipped, but it's still a heavy weight I'd rather not be lugging around.

I veer closer to the closed buildings along the shabby commercial strip near the industrial district where the hacker asked to meet us. Having the thicker shadows draping over me settles my nerves a little.

If no one can see me, then no one can speculate. No one can even notice the things I wish weren't strange about me.

Not that there's anyone much around here to notice regardless. Voices travel down the street from a few women wobbling out of a bar behind us, but they're the only people out and about nearby.

Zian scans the road and the darkened buildings along it warily. "We couldn't have parked right by the meetup place?"

Andreas runs his hand over his head, scattering his tight curls. "He gave specific instructions about parking at least two blocks away. I think he's a little paranoid."

Riva lets out a short huff of amusement that draws my attention to her. She's walking surrounded by us as usual, behind Andreas and Jacob and ahead of me and Zian—as if at this point we really have any reason to suspect that she's going to bolt on us.

It doesn't take much for her to catch my gaze. Honestly, when she's nearby, it takes a conscious effort *not* to be tracking every movement she makes.

Even her slightest gesture seems to reverberate through the air into my skin as if she's touched me.

Sometimes the sensation brings out the impulse to touch her in return, to pull her as close to me as I possibly can. But whenever that happens, other images dart through my mind: of how her expression would change if she saw all of me now, or of that scene from four years ago while Griffin lay dying…

My heart hardens up and my ribs seem to lock tight around it.

She said last night that she wishes she could fix what was broken, but some things aren't fixable. No, she isn't to blame for plenty of our problems, but for her to talk like that when *she's* the one who smashed our tight-knit group to pieces—the memory makes my hands clench.

How can I feel that way but not be able to shake the certainty tugging at me that she belongs with our broken shards?

I'm lost in those thoughts rather than paying attention to the world around us, so the man who lurches out of the shadows next to another bar we're passing takes me by surprise.

From the sour smell wafting from the alley and his jerk of his jeans, he was just pissing on the ground. That's all I have time to register before he's letting out a whistle and making a grab at Riva's ass.

Rage flares through my body. Even though there are three guys around me who are all more skilled at fighting than I am—not to mention Riva herself—my fist is flying before I've realized what I'm doing.

I punch the guy right in the face, catching his cheek and the side of his nose. An ache radiates through my knuckles, and his head snaps to the side with a pained *woof* of air escaping his mouth.

Zian has leapt to join me a second later, but the jerk is shuffling off, swearing under his breath and cradling his bruising face.

I lower my hand, staring at it for a second as if it could tell me where that split-second reaction came from. A faint hum of fury is still humming through my gut.

Riva has turned to peer at me. When I hesitantly meet her bright brown eyes, she offers me a slanted smile. "I could have walloped him myself and saved your hand. But thank you for defending my honor."

Jacob snorts at the second comment, and I feel twice as awkward about my reaction.

"Yeah," I mutter, ducking my head.

But I remember how Jake reacted when the hacker guy started putting the moves on Riva. I wouldn't be surprised if he'd have punched this jackass if he'd seen him first.

She belongs with us. She left us behind, but now she's back, and she is *ours.*

Even if I don't like thinking that way, the understanding is here, simmering away in the back of my skull.

No one speaks again the rest of the short walk to the out-of-business restaurant where we're meeting the hacker. The back door is unlocked, as promised.

We step into a room quite smaller than the one before, empty other than a couple of bare shelves and the smell of stale bread. Zian stays poised near the exit, and Jacob immediately moves to the inner door to check it as an escape route.

As he rattles the doorknob, it jerks in his grasp. He backs up a step so the hacker can step into the room with us.

The beady-eyed man looks us all over, his arms crossed over his chest. His attention narrows in on the bag Zian has slung over his shoulder.

"Where's my payment?" he asks.

Zian pulls out the action figure in its box but keeps it close.

Andreas cocks his head. "Where's our information?"

The hacker turns to him. "Your target was difficult to trace. Someone's done a lot of covering of her tracks. She must be important. But they weren't quite good enough to completely throw me off."

"So, what do you have, then?" Jacob says sharply.

The hacker shrugs as if our impatience means nothing to him. "I was able to confirm that she worked in a very hush-hush branch of a specific security company starting about thirty years ago, for several years after that. I have the address for the office where she was located. I can't tell you what happened to her after that, but the people there might have more answers for you."

After that, she probably moved on to the facility. It's the right timeframe.

My heart beats faster. Jacob motions for Zian to come closer, and the bigger guy does, carrying the action figure.

The hacker pulls a folded piece of paper from his pocket. "Full directions and coordinates," he says. "I didn't slack off on you."

"I should hope not," Jacob grumbles.

Andreas holds out his hand. As the hacker extends the paper to him with one arm, he reaches the other toward the box. The exchange happens perfectly simultaneously.

The hacker shoots us all a broad grin. "A pleasure doing business with you." Then he vanishes into the front of the derelict restaurant again.

While Andreas unfolds the paper, my breath catches in my throat.

"All right," he says. "Let's see where we're heading tomorrow."

FIFTEEN

Riva

With every passing minute of the drive, watching the terrain that reminds me of the forests around the facility, my skin creeps more. It's like we're going backward, heading closer to the people we should be running away from.

The information Andreas got from the hacker didn't show any reason to believe the company that owns this property is associated with the guardians or the facility we broke out of. Ursula Engel was only employed there until twenty-four years ago, definitely at least a couple of years before we could have been conceived.

But that doesn't mean there is no connection, or that the guardians are unaware of their former colleague's past work and that we might seek her out. We have no idea how much they know or don't.

Just this once, I wish Jacob was right that I was privy to a whole bunch of their inside info.

Andreas is driving while Jacob consults the GPS on the phone they've been sharing. In a particularly dense section of forest, he holds up his hand. "We're almost there. A couple of miles northeast of here."

Zian leans forward from the middle seat. "We should go through the brush, right? We don't know how closely they're monitoring the area."

Jacob nods. "Let's find a good spot to pull over, and we'll cover the rest of the distance on foot. Stay alert for any sign of guards."

He glances back at me pointedly, although in the middle of the woods, Zian's ears are going to pick up anyone patrolling faster than my enhanced senses. Especially since as far as we know, anyone patrolling around this building has no reason to be stressed out just yet.

I can't help thinking it's an understated jab about my becoming the opposite to alert the other night in the club. It's all a blur in my mind, nothing horrendously shameful sticking out, but he's made it clear that I both embarrassed myself and nearly jeopardized our mission.

Willing back a blush at the memory, I tip my head in acknowledgment. I'm here—he should know I'm going to help any way I can.

Even if I don't really think we should be sticking our necks out like this at all.

About a minute later, the shoulder widens enough that Andreas can pull the SUV all the way off the road. We ease out of the car, shutting the doors as softly as we can, and set off through the forest with Jacob and his phone map in the lead.

All of us know how to move quietly across any kind of terrain when we're not running for our lives. The faint rustling of our clothes and rasps of our footfalls blend into the wild sounds of the forest.

The fresh pine scent carrying on the lightly cool breeze puts me a little more at ease. We're not under the guardians' thumbs anymore; we're walking free.

I just hope that we're not currently walking straight back into our cages.

As we come up on the coordinates, Jacob slows even more, and the rest of us follow suit. We slink between the trees until we come within view of a cleared area up ahead.

It isn't like the facility, not really. There's no fence at all, let alone one beefed up with electricity and barbed wire. The structure standing in the middle of the grassy clearing is plain brown brick with a slanted roof, looking more like a bungalow than a place of industry. It's maybe twice the size of a typical single-story house, although for all we know there's more underneath.

A man in a gray uniform stands near the edge of the clearing toward the front of the structure, a few paces from where a narrow driveway leads into a small parking lot that holds two vehicles: a sedan and a jeep. He has his hands slung in his pockets in a casual pose, although I bet he knows how to use the gun holstered at his hip just fine.

No metal helmet or armor. Nothing on him that reminds me of how the guardians dressed. I relax a little more.

These people could still be dangerous, but at least they're not the exact same kind of people we fled from.

At Jacob's gesture, we prowl farther around the clearing until we determine that there's only one other guard on duty, strolling back and forth behind the building. From his bored expression, I don't think he's anticipating any significant trouble either.

Somehow I can't find it in me to feel particularly sorry for him. This company may not be affiliated with our facility, but if they employed someone who ended up helping run that facility, I doubt they're the most wonderful folks in the universe either.

We pull back deeper into the woods to confer.

"Since we have time and they're stationed where they can't see each other, I can knock the guards out one after the other," Jacob murmurs. "Then we tie them up and gag them so they can't get in our way once they come to."

He glances at Zian, who's got a bag with the lengths of cord we brought along as well as other equipment the guys felt was necessary. Andreas has already stolen one of the cords, twisting it around his hands with a knot tied in the middle.

We return to the edge of the clearing, standing in the shadows out of view. I'm not totally sure what Jacob means about knocking the guards out, figuring he's going to hurl a rock at their heads with his telekinesis or something, until his face goes rigid with concentration.

The guard's mouth clamps shut. As his lips twitch with a muffled grunt of surprise, his eyes widen.

His hands jerk to his throat. He gropes at his neck, the suppressed sounds he's making turning thinner, his cheeks turning bluish… like he's being strangled.

I can't see any marks against his throat, but understanding jolts through me. Jacob is using his talent in a much more subtle way. He's either compressing the man's airway right inside his body or willing the air not to move in and out of his lungs.

Both will have the same effect.

The guard tries to run for help, but his legs wobble. He sways and staggers toward the windowless back of the building.

My pulse lurches with sudden recognition. He's trying to throw himself against the wall so he can make a loud enough sound to alert the other guard—or whoever's inside—that way.

The threat of being discovered propels me into action without another thought. I hurl myself forward, racing across the short span of grass and yanking the man away from the building just as his legs give completely.

Zian catches the guard with me as the man slumps down unconscious, not that I need the help supporting a single ordinary person's weight. We lay him down on the grass carefully, and Zian fixes the cords in place. Then we carry the man into the shelter of the trees.

Jacob watches us return, his expression unreadable. His gaze lingers on me for a second. He dips his head, just for an instant, and stalks on around the clearing toward the other guard.

Well, I guess that's better than him spitting venom at me as if I sabotaged him rather than saving his ass.

With the other guard, Jacob nudges him toward the edge of the forest while he cuts off the guy's air, so we have no repeat of the last potential disaster. We leave that man hidden among the trees and walk over to the building's front door.

Zian peers at it with a momentary distant expression. "There's no one right on the other side," he says quietly.

"Be ready just in case." Jacob twists his hand by the door handle, and the lock disengages.

We brace ourselves. We discussed during the long drive out here that we wanted to question the people working here, which means we need them alive. But I know all of us are prepared to kill if it comes down to us or them.

An image of twisted bodies and splatters of blood flashes through my mind, and my stomach clenches.

Jacob eases the door open. The hall beyond with its light gray walls is empty, as Zian said, no one rushing out to confront us. A faint clicking sound carries from farther within, like someone tapping on a computer mouse.

We creep inside: Jacob and Zian in the lead, me in the middle, Andreas and Dominic behind me. The guys never leave *me* unobserved even when we've got much bigger fish to fry.

Zian stares at each of the doors we pass before giving an all-clear motion. The first rooms we peek into aren't even locked. They open to what look like studio apartments with a twin bed, a love seat facing a TV, and a kitchenette with a tiny table, all close to identical except for a few personal belongings and decorations scattered around.

"The employees must live here at least part of the time," Dominic says under his breath.

The work rooms appear to be at the windowless back of the building. We pass a storage room full of boxes of test tubes and latex gloves and reach the doorway the clicks are emanating from.

Zian scans the wall and holds up his hand with two fingers raised. "Scientists," he murmurs, so low the word is barely more than a breath.

Probably not also fighters, then.

Jacob glances at all of us as if to check that we're ready. He hovers his hand over the door handle, but it must be unlocked too, because I don't hear any sound before he's shoving it open.

We barge into a lab room with sleek black countertops set up with microscopes and other scientific equipment I don't recognize. Two figures in lab coats and protective goggles freeze at their workstations—and then an instant later, both whip their hands toward their pockets.

The gesture sets off an alarm inside me before I even see the shape of pistols emerging. Zian springs at the man who's a little farther away, and I leap right over the protruding counter to pounce on the woman who's closer.

She hits the floor with a soft grunt and a wince when I smack the pistol away. Andreas is already there, snatching the weapon up as well as the one Zian freed from his scientist. He hands one gun to Dominic and then peers down at our captives.

The woman beneath me is giving off whiffs of fear. "Who the hell are you—what are you doing here?"

She sounds young. I jerk up her goggles to properly see her face beneath her short brown hair and find myself staring at a woman who couldn't be more than a few years older than most of the college students we've been hiding among.

Andreas grimaces. "She isn't going to know much about anyone who worked here two decades ago." He stalks closer to the man Zian has pinned and shakes his head. "Neither of them would have been around at the right time."

"Check them anyway," Jacob says.

"Check us for what?" the guy demands. "We're just following orders here—we don't—"

Zian clamps his hand over his captive's mouth. When the woman starts to sputter, I do the same to her. Zian and I exchange a look, a hint of exasperation crossing his face, and a weird but welcome sense of comradery stirs in my chest.

This is how it's meant to be—all of us working together toward the same goals.

Andreas kneels down next to the woman. His eyes flare with a ruddy sheen, and I know he's searching her memories for any interactions with Ursula Engel.

His grimace makes it clear that he got nothing, as expected. He moves on to the man, studies him for a few beats, and then straightens up.

"They never met her."

Jacob's eyes narrow. "Is it just the two of you working here?"

The woman nods beneath my grasp, and the man does the same a moment later.

Dominic frowns. "There was a family photo in one of the apartments —everyone in it Asian. Neither of these two would fit, and the guards wouldn't either."

Trust him to have paid that much attention to the details. We all pause, listening for any sign of another presence in the building.

Our captives stay silent, but mine's stress spiked at Dominic's comment. It's possible that whoever that photo belonged to isn't here at the moment, but I'm willing to bet they are.

"We should search the other rooms," I say.

Jacob scowls at me, but it's the obvious next step. He motions to Zian.

"Let's get them tied up and gagged, and then we can move on. Make sure they don't have any other weapons—or phones—on them. We can always question them more later if nothing else pans out."

I suppose we could at least find out what they're working on here—although whether it'll have much to do with what Ursula Engel would have been working on nearly two and a half decades ago, there's no way to know.

Once the scientists are bound, we venture on down the hallway. There are just a few more doors.

The first leads to a records room with shelves stuffed with textbooks, binders, and storage boxes. The next is merely a washroom.

Zian gazes through the doorway and shakes his head with a frown. The door swings open to reveal another lab room with a single counter and then two desks with computer equipment, and no one in view.

I step inside, my nerves prickling uneasily. The woman I caught was worried about us finding *something*. What are we missing?

A faint tang in the air interrupts my thoughts. It's a trace of nervous adrenaline—fresh, tainting the air.

Someone *was* in here, recently, and now they're not.

Or at least they're not anywhere we can see.

The guys have started to pull back, but I wave at them to catch their attention. They watch me as I slink farther into the room, Jacob with unrestrained skepticism, the others curiously.

I make a circuit of the room, taking several breaths, and stop where the scent is strongest. Where a tiny, renewed whiff reaches my nose.

I point at the wall behind the desk and turn to mouth the words to the guys: "There's someone in there."

Zian hustles over. His eyes widen as his penetrating vision must confirm my suspicions. He beckons Jacob over and points to where I suppose the opening mechanism for the safe room must be.

The people who run this place weren't prepared for anyone like us. Jacob focuses on the wall, flicks his fingers, and a hidden panel detaches itself from the edge it sat flush against, whirring open.

Zian didn't just see the woman who's hunched in a corner of the narrow room on the other side. The second the panel glides open, he lunges at her and snatches the rifle she was lifting out of her hands.

As he snaps it over his knee, she flinches and cowers back against the wall.

She must be the one who stays in the room with the photo Dominic saw. She looks Chinese or maybe Vietnamese, her smooth skin beige in contrast with Zian's peachy brown but her rounded features reminding me of his.

Her black hair is streaked with gray, and tiny lines have formed at the corners of her eyes and mouth. *She's* definitely old enough to have known Engel, if she's been working here that long.

Zian grasps her wrists to hold her in place. There's no need to gag her when there's no one left for her to call out to.

"We're not here to hurt you," he tells her gruffly. "We've just got some questions."

"I don't bargain with terrorists," she snaps.

Andreas laughs. "It's a good thing that's not what we are, then. We're looking to tone down the terror, not increase it."

He ambles over and crouches down next to Zian. "I don't suppose you ever worked alongside a woman named Ursula Engel?"

The flicker of surprise the woman can't suppress sends a surge of triumph through me. We're going to get some real answers after all.

Andreas doesn't ask anything else out loud. He stares into the woman's eyes, already rummaging through all her memories of the woman in question.

Our captive flinches and twists away as well as she can, but Andreas doesn't need the eye contact. Zian keeps his hand clamped around her wrists. "You're not going anywhere."

Andreas starts to speak, his voice distant as if he's in a trance. Which I guess he sort of is, still riffling through her mind.

"It seems like they worked together a little more than two years. Dr. Gao here mentioned it when Engel was getting ready to leave. From the discussions they had, they were working on 'compounds' and 'chemical enhancements' for improving the focus of soldiers in the field—strength and sensory acuity and things like that."

Dr. Gao squirms in Zian's hold but doesn't get anywhere. She hisses through her teeth in panicked frustration. "What are you *doing*? How can you—"

Zian shuts her up with his other hand. Andreas keeps watching her, delving through her skull with his gaze.

"She saw a paper Ursula tried to hide—a deed to some land. Someplace out in Kansas. She bought property out there, not long before she quit, and she was being cagey about it, which caught Dr. Gao's attention. I think I can make out the coordinates if I focus—someone get me a piece of paper!"

Dominic dashes off and returns with a notepad and a pen. Andreas moves the nib over the paper without breaking his gaze, pausing a few times with a furrowing of his forehead.

He's silent for another few minutes. A sheen of sweat has broken out on his brow. I bite my lip, hoping he isn't pushing himself too hard.

"Engel left behind some bits and pieces in her office," he says finally. "Nothing anyone figured was important, but they stuffed it all in a box that they put in the records room just in case they wanted to go through it later if something came up. It might still be there. That's the only other useful thing I'm seeing."

"That's great," Jacob says, his voice unusually soft. "You got plenty, Drey."

He must be able to tell the strain Andreas has put himself through. A tremor runs through the leaner guy's legs as he stands up.

But he isn't done yet. He focuses on the scientist again and gives her a thin smile. "Don't worry. You won't remember any of this—or any of us —after we're gone."

Zian starts tying her up. Andreas waits there to complete his work and sear away the newest of her memories—all of those we feature in.

When Jacob prods me toward the door, I tear my gaze away. He, Dominic, and I hurry back to the records room.

Dominic spots the right box first. A peeling, yellowed label on the side has ENGEL written in small caps. He pulls it off the shelf and sets it in the middle of the floor so the three of us can sit around it.

A sour smell rises up out of the box the moment Dominic lifts the lid. I wrinkle my nose and start digging out the various bits of paper and other odds and ends alongside the others.

It quickly becomes clear why Engel wasn't worried about leaving any of this stuff behind. The highlights include a post-it note that simply says, *More coffee!!* and an empty chip bag. I don't understand why they didn't just throw this stuff in the garbage.

But down near the bottom of the mess, I unearth a magazine clipping. Unlike the rest of the contents, it hasn't been affected by age quite as much, because it's encased in a sealed plastic sleeve. The photo that fills the clipping is still glossy, the colors sharp.

I stare at it, tightening my grasp as a wave of emotion sweeps through me.

It's a snowy forest scene, but not like this place or the facility. There's a log cabin nestled between the trees, amber light glowing through its windows in welcome.

I can almost taste what it would be like to step through the doorway into the warmth and peace, so far away from the rest of the world.

Jacob knits his brow. "Is that another property she bought?"

Dominic leans closer to examine it. "I don't think so. Look at bits of text where it was cut out—I'm pretty sure that was from a magazine, not a real estate listing."

I finger the plastic covering. "It was something that mattered to her, though. She wouldn't have sealed it so carefully otherwise."

"Yeah." Dominic nods slowly. "And look, there are tack marks on the corners of the plastic. She had it hanging up somewhere—so she could see it regularly, I'd guess. Maybe it's someplace she *wanted* to have or go to?"

I swallow thickly. Is it possible that Ursula Engel dreamed about the same kind of escape and peaceful isolation that I do?

How absurd is that?

I want to tuck the picture into my pocket, but I'd have to fold it to fit, and that seems wrong. Zian and Andreas join us a minute later, and I slide the clipping into Zian's now mostly empty bag.

We've pawed through the rest of the box's contents, and nothing else has jumped out. We all stand up, clustered in the records room.

"All right," Jacob says. "We got everything these people can offer that might be useful. Andreas will wipe all memory of us from their minds, and I'll untie one of them before we go so they can all get free. No point in killing them. They don't seem to have had anything to do with the facility anyway."

Zian cracks his knuckles. "And then what?"

Andreas is looking at the phone. "I guess we head out to Kansas? It'll take a couple days, but if we leave right now—"

I blink at him. "You want us to head straight to this other spot from here?"

Jacob scowls at me. "Why not? Do you have a better idea?"

"I just…" Every inch of my body balks at the idea of charging off on a quest into some new unknown when we've only just survived this venture.

Do we really have to race straight into sticking our necks out all over again?

With each step we take, we're getting closer to Ursula Engel's connections to the facility. Closer to the enemy. Why can't they see how dangerous that is?

I drag in a breath and speak before Jacob can sneer at me again. "We pushed ourselves pretty hard here. Wouldn't it be smarter to go back to the townhouse and take a day or two to go over everything we've learned and rest up? We're tracing what this woman did more than twenty years ago—it's not like a couple of days is going to make a lot of difference to that."

Andreas rubs his head. I suspect from the flattening of his lips that he's fighting off a headache.

"She does have a point," he says. "I'm not sure I can even drive right now."

Jacob raises his eyebrows. "So you're going to trust *her* judgment?"

Andreas shrugs. "She did help us here a lot. She stepped up every time we could have expected her to, even when she didn't need to."

He smiles at me, and I smile back through a rush of warmth. Maybe a couple more days will be enough to convince them to see this situation completely my way.

Jacob scoffs. "We don't know if the guardians might catch on and start covering their tracks—or Engel's. Every minute could count."

A spark of inspiration hits me. "But shouldn't we scour the townhouse to make sure we're not leaving anything that could be used against us? It'd be careless to leave it without making sure we've totally covered *our* tracks. We didn't expect to be abandoning it when we left this morning."

Dominic's mouth twists. "That's a good point."

Zian rubs his hand over his thick black hair, his forehead furrowing. "Should we come up with some kind of story too, to explain why we're leaving all of a sudden? So that our neighbors don't ask too many questions?"

Jacob glares at him as if annoyed that even the guy whose main focus is brawn is coming up with solid reasons to go along with my suggestion. But now it's four against one, and while he's pissed off at me, he isn't so spiteful he's going to screw his own mission over just to stick it to me.

"Fine," he bites out. "We'll go back for *one* night and tie up loose ends. But we don't want to waste any more time than that. We could be risking the entire mission."

Andreas hesitates, and for a second I think he might change his mind. The others would probably follow.

He glances at me, and I let my smile slant wryly as if to say, *There he goes, being a grumpy jerk again.*

Drey's expression relaxes. "Until tomorrow," he says.

I can't deny that there's a flutter of hope in my chest that maybe Ursula Engel's tracks *will* be covered before we can follow them any further.

If there's no trail to follow, then the guys will have to stop chasing her down this reckless path.

SIXTEEN

Riva

By the time we make it back to the townhouse, night has draped itself over the sky, blotting out all the light except a speckling of stars and the artificial glow in the windows along the street.

Jacob parks out front in the usual spot. As the guys open the doors, laughter drifts out through the living room window of the townhouse next door, which they've left partly open to enjoy the warm early autumn air.

I scoot along the back seat and clamber out, discovering when I set down my feet that the poison in my system has been gnawing its way deeper again. A prickling jolt races up the legs I haven't used in a few hours, and I lurch to the side.

My hand slams against the side of the car to catch my balance. I take a breath and steady my body before starting forward again.

The prickles pinch at my muscles all the way up to my hips and dig into my gut. I don't like asking him, because there's something about the process he obviously doesn't like, but I think I'm going to need to get Dominic to work his healing skill on me again sometime tonight.

I roll my shoulders and walk a little stiffly to the front steps, uncomfortably aware of how Zian has hung back near me and the other guys are waiting for me rather than going on in. Not because they're concerned about my well-being, but because they still see me as a potential threat to be monitored.

Well, Andreas is actually concerned. He catches my gaze and offers a sympathetic grimace.

I've just gripped the railing next to the stairs when the door on the other side of the lane opens, letting the buoyant voices spill out louder. Brooke emerges. She trots down the steps with a little wave and strides right over to us.

"Hey!" she says, taking all five of us in with a glance, and then focuses on me. "I'm glad I caught you, Rita. I was really hoping I could talk with you for a sec."

I push my lips into a smile as I pray to whatever higher powers might or might not exist that I can improv my way through the unexpected conversation. "Sure. What's up?"

That's what college-student-type people say to their friends, right?

With a flick of her gaze toward the guys poised around me, she purses her lips and tilts her head toward the lane. "Just the two of us, away from the street? It's kind of… private. Girl stuff."

She shoots another, more pointed look at the guys.

Jacob frowns, but he knows how weird it'd look if my supposed roommates start dictating whether I can even talk to another person without their presence.

Andreas speaks up for all of them, with a casual motion of his hand toward the back of the buildings. "Go have your girl talk."

The guys troop inside as if it's no big deal, but my nerves creep as I follow Brooke down the lane to the small patios that border the alley behind the townhouses. I have no doubt at all that Zian is following my movements through the wall. Most likely Jacob will keep watch surreptitiously from one of the back windows as well.

As if I'm going to be plotting their downfall with a history student who's probably never encountered anything more dangerous than an A minus.

Brooke stops by the patios and leans against the wooden fence that borders her townhouse's. It's even darker back here beyond the reach of the streetlamps, just a couple of dim security lights illuminating the alley.

She pushes her hair back behind her ears and studies me. "I get that you might not be ready to talk about this yet. It might be hard to even think about it. But I want you to know that if you decide you need help, you can reach out to me, and I'll do whatever I can."

I stare at her, too bewildered to gather my words for a moment. She *can't* be referring to any of the things I'd actually need help with, so what the hell is she talking about?

"I don't know what you mean," I manage after an awkwardly long silence.

Brooke's mouth tightens. "Look, I've been there before. This guy I dated for a year in high school—I know what it looks like. How it feels. You might not want to believe it, but the way they're treating you isn't okay."

She's talking about my guys—what exactly has she noticed? A chill tickles through me.

"I'm not dating any of them. And nothing's wrong."

Brooke drops her voice. "It is, though. They don't ever seem to let you out of their sight. They didn't even want you to come talk to me—I could tell. They expect you to do whatever they say, I bet."

"It's not like that," I say quickly. "We're just—we're all new here. We rely on each other."

She knits her brow. "And what happens when you don't go along with what they expect? Sometimes it looks like you're trying not to limp, and those scars on your arms… I don't want to get you in trouble with them, but you've got to realize that's not normal. That's not how anyone who cares about you should act."

As she's spoken, my stomach's gotten so twisted up it probably looks like a pretzel now. *She* cares, clearly. Way more than someone who's only had a few brief occasions to get to know me really should.

But she's obviously more compassionate than the average person—and sharper-eyed. I don't know how to explain the things she's observed in any way that could make sense given what she'd be willing to believe.

I have to try anyway. I don't want her stressing out over my situation when she doesn't need to—and it's better for us if she thinks everything's fine over here.

I tug my hoodie closer around me. "I told you—I've gotten into fights. And not with those guys. I go to martial arts classes. Sometimes things get kind of rough in the sparring."

That seems like a reasonable explanation, but Brooke's expression stays skeptical. "Like I said, I understand if you don't want to talk about it. As long as you remember I'm here if you change your mind."

I wet my lips and stiffen against a wave of dizziness. Shit.

I wish I'd gotten Dominic to heal me up during the drive. She's really going to freak out if I start swaying around like I did at the club.

"I swear," I say, "I can see how it might look bad, but it's really—"

My deflection is cut off by the bang of the back door slamming open and a flurry of bodies springing out of the shadows from all around us.

I yelp and instinctively dive for cover behind our patio's planter. All four of my guys are barging out of the house—and at least a dozen black-clothed figures have burst from the darkness down the alley and between the other buildings.

In the first couple of seconds as my pulse stutters and my mind scrambles to make sense of the scene, I register the black helmets that cover all but the intruders' eyes and a slat around their jaws. Just like the helmets the guardians wore in the facility, only painted for stealth.

Our jailers have found us.

A startled gasp bursts from Brooke's lips, and one of the armored figures lunges straight at her.

Panic flashes through me. I leap back over the planter, hurling myself between my unexpected friend and her attacker with my claws flicking from my fingers—

But my weakened muscles react too sluggishly. I lash out a foot shy of the incoming guardian, who barrels straight into Brooke before she can emit a full-out scream and stabs a curved blade into her neck.

Her voice cuts out with a gurgle. Blood gushes down her fuzzy sweater and splatters the ground I've just fallen to.

A cry of protest tears up my throat.

No. No. She didn't do anything—she was just standing there—she barely had anything to do with us.

The guardian shoves Brooke's body away, and it topples over like a puppet cut off its strings. Every nerve in my body clamors to snatch her up, to drag her away from these menaces as if there's any way to keep her safe now, but her attacker is already spinning toward me.

I spring backward, falling into a defensive crouch. My heartbeat thunders behind my ears, but not loud enough to drown out the smacks and grunts careening from the patio.

The man whips up an odd-looking gun. I hurl myself to the side just in time to avoid a dart that clatters off the brick wall behind me.

They're trying to tranquilize us. Of course.

The bastards don't want *us* dead, only back under their control.

I can't let the brute I'm facing off with get another shot at me—I have no idea how badly the drugs in those darts will react with the toxin already in my veins. I roll to the side, leap off the wall, and ricochet straight toward him.

As I crash into him, an electric crackle sounds from where he's tried to pull some kind of taser-like device from his pocket. But it's his own thigh that spasms with the electric jolt, and then I'm gouging out his throat like he did to Brooke, the closest thing I can get to poetic payback.

Fury sears through my chest. He won't hurt anyone else who didn't deserve it now.

My gaze passes over her slumped, bloody form, and anguish floods me in turn.

Fucking damn it. If I'd just made it to him faster…

Another figure sprints toward me. I jerk around to defend myself, but before I need to, an invisible force wrenches him off his feet. It smashes his helmet against the corner of the neighboring townhouse, the metal denting right into the man's skull.

Jacob is standing by the planters, his face rigid with concentration, his hands slashing through the air as he directs his talent. He flings another guardian against an electrical post hard enough that the crack of a spine echoes through the air. Then he yanks another that's gotten too close right toward him—impaling him on the purple spines now jutting from his forearms.

The victim of his full dose of poison twitches like a fish flopping on a dock, spittle spewing from her lips before she collapses.

A massive form charges forward, so familiar and alien at the same time that my mind jars as it tries to process what I'm seeing.

It's Zian, and yet it's not—not any version of him I've ever seen before. Coarse, dark fur has sprouted from his peachy golden skin all across his shoulders and down his arms to where his own vicious claws protrude from his fingertips. His face is partly human but partly beastly, a stunted, wrinkled snout protruding where his nose and mouth used to be, huge fangs protruding over his wolfish jowls.

He slams straight into two attackers one after the other, bashing one's head around so far the neck snaps, driving his claws into the other's gut and ripping out a heap of intestines.

I catch a glimpse of Dominic farther away by the other end of the patio, silhouetted against the dim glow of the distant alley light. He's pulled off his trench coat, and *something* long and sinewy is lashing out from his upper back toward the incoming attackers.

One of those snake-like tendrils stretches out and yanks a man toward him, close enough for him to wrench off the guy's helmet and pummel him unconscious.

Andreas appears beside me out of thin air, panting. His voice comes out in a rasp. "Are you okay, Riva?"

Because I've been frozen in shock for the last several seconds. I heave myself out of my daze, toward the fray, making my actions an answer to his question.

The guys are fighting off a bunch of the guardians, but even more are converging on us. They knew this was going to be a tough fight.

Even as I throw myself at the nearest figure with my claws extended, I see another beyond her aiming a tranquilizer gun at Jacob.

"Jake!" I shout, tackling my target to the ground. The next second, Andreas is blinking into view behind the shooter and plunging a knife into the side of her neck.

He vanishes again an instant later like he was never there. I don't know how to wrap my head around that, but there isn't time to.

More footsteps are thumping toward us. More triggers are clicking with launched darts.

They aren't going to be happy until they have us caged and ready for their tests and torture all over again.

The fury that sparked when I watched Brooke fall blazes through my body. The pressure of it reverberates through my chest and sears the base of my throat.

Something is swelling inside me, something that wants to burst free through my mouth. Something that wants to rend every asshole around me limb from limb and make them *pay*.

A chilling certainty grips me: I could demolish them all, wrench them apart until they're made of nothing but pain—and then death. I could make them all fall.

They'd deserve it.

The vibration heightens to a caustic thrum resonating all through my body, condensing in my lungs. Fuck them. Fuck them all.

My lips part, but in the same instant, my gaze catches on Jacob. A fresh flare of anger rushes through me with the memories of all the shit he's hurled at me, followed by an icy splash of fear.

The scene from the arena rushes through my mind. All that carnage, all that savage destruction.

Like some creature way more monstrous than Zian looks right now rampaged through. Do I want to find out if I'll become that brutal beast?

I clamp my jaw shut. I can't—I don't know what I'd even do. I don't know how much I can control it.

There are so many things and so many people that've infuriated me in the past several days. So much emotion churning inside me, more than I can grasp hold of.

I don't know that my frustration wouldn't get away from me and ruin the people I want to save too.

I suck in a breath, forcing down the rage resonating inside me, and dizziness whirls through my head. I push myself forward regardless.

Slash. Shred. Smash. Stop every one of the pricks who're gunning for us until there's no one left—in my usual way.

The safe way that doesn't make my nerves wobble and my throat ache with a disturbingly potent hunger.

Bodies hurtle through the air. Flesh rips. Bones crack. My guys are a blur of motion around me.

The urge prickles up from my lungs again and again, and I shove it down harder each time.

And then there's no one left in front of me.

I sway to a stop, my legs trembling, my gut knotted with queasiness and exhaustion. The alley and the patios are painted with blood and draped with bodies.

Far off, a siren is wailing.

"Come on!" Dominic hisses, yanking his trench coat back over his slim form before I get a closer look at the shapes protruding from his back. He pushes Jacob toward the lane, spurring the other guy into motion.

I stagger after them, and Zian catches me up like he did at the facility. His face has morphed back to normal now other than a hint of fangs curling over his lower lips; the fur has vanished. As he heaves me over his shoulder, I spot Andreas wavering in and out of sight, each time a few steps closer to the sidewalk.

Without another word to each other, we dive into the SUV. Zian looks at Jacob and then jumps into the driver's seat. He starts the ignition with a roar of the engine.

We tear off into the cover of the night.

Seventeen

Riva

The guys mentioned before they were getting Zian and Dominic up to speed on the basics of driving so the responsibility didn't all fall on Jacob's and Andreas's shoulders. Zian must have caught on quickly, because he steers the SUV out of the campus without running us into any lampposts or trash bins, although a few times it's a near miss.

The vehicle sways with another sharp turn, and the engine roars as he presses on the gas again. I bump against Andreas's shoulder where he's thrown himself into the back seat with me and realize that shoulder doesn't look totally… right.

I blink, doing my best to focus through the muddle in my head, and my stomach lurches. He's technically visible now, but I can make out the seams in the seat and the edge of the window through his translucent body.

His hands have clenched on his lap. When a shudder runs through his lanky frame, my gaze shoots to his face.

His eyes are wide, gleaming with fear.

"Drey?" I say, my throat tightening with the same emotion.

His voice comes out in a strained rasp. "I'm trying. I can't quite…"

His body wavers, becoming closer to opaque and then more translucent again.

I don't know how to help him—I don't even understand what exactly is happening—but I can't just sit here and watch him struggle. My hands shoot out to grasp one of his, squeezing it tight between my fingers as if I can hold him fully in this world.

"You're here," I say, more babbling than with any clear strategy. "You're here with me. I can see you. You're going to stay right here with us."

Andreas stares down at my hands clamped around his. His breath evens out a little.

I give him another squeeze. "Don't you dare go anywhere. This is where you belong."

A shaky laugh spills out of him, and then he inhales deeply. With a couple more heaves of his chest, he's fully solid again.

His gaze lifts to meet mine, so fraught I don't know what to say but can't tear my eyes away either. "Thanks," he says roughly.

I swallow and force myself to loosen my grip on his hand, my fingers sliding away from his. "What was that? Are you okay?"

"Seems like it, now." He sags back against the seat with a humorless chuckle. "Every new talent has to come with its fun side effects, huh?"

His body was acting up like that because he was turning himself invisible earlier? I haven't seen him do that before—but then, I guess I wouldn't necessarily know about all his abilities.

He couldn't do that back when I was in the facility with him, though. How often has he practiced using the skill? It sounds like he didn't realize it could mess him up that badly.

Zian's panicked voice draws my attention to the rest of the vehicle. "Uh, where exactly am I going from here? What's the plan, Jake?"

It's Dominic who answers, from the middle seat where he's kneeling next to Jacob. "Get on a highway. The first one you find. We want to get away from this city fast. The rest we can figure out later."

He's clutching Jacob's shoulder. As I look at them, he gives the other guy a shake.

Jacob barely moves, sitting so rigid he might as well be a mannequin.

My pulse stutters. Something's gone wrong with him too.

I scramble past Andreas to the middle seat, falling back against the door when Zian swerves again. My head knocks into the edge of the window, and a hiss of pain escapes me with the spinning of my thoughts.

Andreas is grabbing my arm to steady me a second later. "Dom, you've got to heal her. The poison was getting to her even before the fight."

Dominic's gaze darts from me to Jacob—who remains totally motionless other than a brief blink of his staring eyes—and back again. He must decide my situation is more critical, because he reaches over the arm of the seat to press his hand against my sternum. "Try to stay still."

"Easier said than done," I mumble, but I let myself lean against the door, hoping the manufacturers didn't cut any corners with the lock mechanism on this thing.

Between that and Andreas's supportive grasp, I manage to only jostle a little while Dominic's warmly soothing power flows through me. My strength solidifies in my muscles; my stomach and my thoughts settle.

When I feel like I'm stable enough that I won't be causing more problems than I'm fixing, I pat Dominic's arm to indicate that he can stop. As he draws back, I hold on to the back of his seat and peer at Jacob.

From this angle, I can see that Jacob's fingers are flexing where his hands are braced rigidly against his thighs. A tendon tics in his jaw, every plane of his chiseled face pulled taut.

An uneasy shiver ripples through me. "Is *he* going to be all right?"

Andreas frowns. "He pushes himself too hard sometimes—just keeps going and going until he bottoms out."

Dominic's forehead furrows as he studies his seatmate. "He isn't normally quite like this. It's nothing physical—nothing I can tackle. It's like his mind is stuck in one place."

He touches Jacob's arm again, trying to jostle him out of it, but at the same moment, Jacob's hand outright clenches. And the front passenger seat starts to crumple over.

The steel frame inside the padding groans as the fabric frays. Zian flinches, the SUV jerking to the side before he recovers his grip on the wheel. "What the fuck?"

"Jake!" Dominic says, pitching his voice loud even though he's right next to the other guy's ear. "The fight's over. Snap out of it!"

His yank of Jacob's arm and the wave of his hand in front of Jacob's face don't interrupt whatever the other guy is caught up in. With a creaking sound, the headrest pops right off the seat back and smacks into the glove compartment hard enough to dent it.

What's Jacob going to aim his powers at next—the doors? The engine?

He could have shattered the windshield just now if the headrest had shot off sooner.

The urgency of the situation propels me forward. I scramble past Dominic and plant myself right in front of Jacob, sitting on his knees and gripping his face between my palms.

"Wake up, Jacob! We're getting away. You don't want to hurt—" Well, maybe he does want to hurt me, but not the others. "You're making it harder for Zian to drive. You're freaking out Dominic and Andreas. And me. Stop it!"

The twisting metal shifts from groaning to shrieking. Jake's eyes don't even flicker.

Wincing, I extend my claws from my fingers and take a quick swipe across his jaw.

Four thin lines of blood spring up in his pale skin, and Jacob's muscles jump. The metallic screeching halts. His eyes sharpen into focus—and fix right on me.

In that first second while I'm poised over him, our gazes locked and our faces just a couple of feet from each other, my emotions scramble like someone's taken a beater to them.

The last time I was this close to someone who looked like him, it ended with a kiss and then catastrophe. My body is caught between the conflicting urges to lean closer and wrench myself away.

But only for a second, because then Jacob moves—slamming his hand into my throat to heave me against the back of the driver's seat. He pins me there, his eyes flaring with icy rage. "You fucking traitor!"

Some distant part of my mind asks, *Haven't we already been through this?* I smack at his arm and squirm against his hold, not wanting to do any more physical damage than I already have.

Dominic and Andreas dive in, and between the two of them they dislodge Jacob's arm enough that I can flounder to the side and push myself away.

"She was helping you—helping us," Andreas is snapping. "For fuck's sake, dude, you almost wrecked the goddamned car."

"I—" Jacob's gaze shoots to the deformed passenger seat, and the harshness of his expression falters with a rush of bewilderment. He looks at his hands and then at me again.

"How do you think they found us?" he demands. "She must have alerted them somehow."

"What?" I burst out. "*You're* the ones who've been putting us out there, interrogating people and stealing stuff. I've spent this entire time trying to convince you to lay low!"

"She didn't exactly have much of a chance to send any messages either," Dominic reminds him in a steadier, quieter voice. "She hasn't been alone except in that one room, and Zian checked her carefully for any kind of devices."

At the mention of the fifth member of our group, my attention jerks to the driver's seat. Zian's fingers are clutched around the steering wheel, his knuckles pale with tension. Through the windshield, the wide stretch of shadowy road ahead suggests he found his way onto a highway, at least.

But just minutes ago in the fight, he wasn't himself any more than Jake or Drey were just now.

"Are you all right, Zian?" I ask quickly. "You didn't get hurt in the fight or—or anything?"

I don't know how else to ask about lingering effects of his transformation, but his grimace suggests he can guess what I'm getting at.

"The monster's back inside," he says with a trace of a growl. "Nothing to be afraid of right now."

Even though "monster" is exactly the word I'd normally have used to describe how he looked in his beastly state, my mind balks at accepting it —or the bitterness in his tone.

"You're not a monster," I say automatically.

All Zian responds with is a dismissive snort.

Jacob slumps in his seat, looking exhausted, but he still manages to aim one more glare my way along with a caustic mutter. "Still not convinced I shouldn't have killed you when we first caught you."

I wish those words didn't sting as much as they do.

Andreas scowls at him and tugs me back to our original seats. He tucks his arm around me, but I'm too twisted up inside to let myself relax into his offer of comfort.

Jacob isn't totally wrong to be angry. I might not have called the guardians down on us, but if we'd gone with his approach and headed straight to Kansas, we'd never have been back at the townhouse to begin with.

I was the one who argued that we should stick around the campus for another day or two. If I'd given in, we wouldn't have faced that attack.

And neither would Brooke. She'd still be alive, smiling and hanging out with her friends, studying for her double major and going out dancing…

The memory of her bloody body rises up in the back of my mind, and queasiness that has nothing to do with any poison bubbles in my stomach.

One more death of someone I should have protected that's now on my shoulders. One more stupid mistake.

There's a stretch of uncomfortable silence, and then Dominic speaks up, his voice low. "I suppose we should drive toward Kansas now, since we're already on the road."

Jacob lets out a huff. "As long as the traitor didn't tell the guardians all about that too."

I resist the impulse to kick the back of his seat. It's not that hard when I'm weighed down by guilt.

My other impulse is to argue against the plan, to point out all the reasons we'd be safer staying away from anything to do with Ursula Engel. But after the battle I was just part of, can I really say that's even true?

Somehow, the guardians tracked us down to that townhouse on a university campus where we hadn't gotten into trouble with anyone. We'd only been living there for a week.

Who's to say there's anywhere they couldn't trace us to?

Even that rich prick with his off-the-grid, waterfall-top cottage wasn't impervious to intruders, so how the hell could anyplace we hole up ever be totally safe?

But it's not just that. I think I understand now why getting answers is more important to the guys than staying out of danger.

I already knew they'd changed since I last saw them, but I hadn't realized how much. Their powers have expanded and shifted... and so have the consequences of those powers.

How much more are they struggling beyond what I've even seen so far? What have they done or think they might do that they want so desperately to find a solution to?

Because that's what this is all about, isn't it? Find Engel, get her to explain what she and the other experimenters did to make us what we are... and hope that somewhere in that explanation, there'll be a way to fix us too.

To make us something better. Less erratic. Less monstrous.

Is it possible she'd know how to turn off the thing inside me too? The brutality that wants to claw its way out and...

All those bodies around the arena. The sickening angles they were broken and contorted into. Like someone had taken *joy* in mutilating them...

I rub my eyes, willing down another wave of nausea.

It wasn't me. I didn't *want* to do that. I can't even say for sure I did.

But the knowledge pricks at the back of my mind: If I ever let that rage loose again, it will be my fault.

My guys have changed, and so have I, so maybe we're not so different from each other after all.

I don't want them seeing the thing inside me; I don't want it ever coming out. But it's possible I should have let them see more of *me* if I wanted them to trust me, instead of trying to prove myself with strength and stubbornness.

At the very least, I can admit that I've been wrong and that their quest matters to me too.

"I'm not a traitor, but I am sorry," I say into the silence that's fallen in the car, the words coming hesitantly. "I've been arguing with you all about going on this search for answers the whole time instead of just believing you that it was important."

"No kidding," Jacob grumbles.

I ignore his remark. "I can see—I can see why it *is* important. For you and for me. I'm not going to try to convince you against it anymore. I say we get to Ursula Engel and take back all the things people like her stole from us."

"There," Andreas says, his arm tightening around me. His light tone sounds a little forced. "Destination settled. Now, have I told you all about the woman I met who…"

As he spins his story to diffuse the tension hanging in the air, I close my eyes, and picture a future where this mess could all be just a memory too.

EIGHTEEN

Jacob

The new car is the best we could nab in the short timeframe we were working with, but I don't like it. The engine makes a periodic coughing sound, we need a whole minute to bring it up to full freeway speed, and one of the back doors nearly falls off its hinges every time we open it.

We also realize as soon as we set off in it that it's only got about an eighth of a tank of gas, but at least that's something we can fix.

I stand in the early morning darkness next to the pickup truck I found parked by a farmhouse, about a mile down the road from where we parked. At the tug of my mental energy, a steady current of gasoline flows past the open fuel cap into the large jug I'm filling for the third time.

My nose wrinkles at the cloying chemical smell. I breathe shallowly through my mouth until the jug is full, replace both its cap and the one on the truck, and set off toward our sort-of camp, lugging the sloshing weight.

Part of the reason we stopped was to crash for the night and catch up on our rest. I've only slept a couple of hours, but that's okay. Keeping busy stops me from thinking about anything but the task at hand.

We're not doing so badly. We destroyed the guardians who came after us. We ditched our former SUV in a lake where it vanished well beneath the surface, leaving no sign of us behind.

Now we're another fifty miles farther away, down a winding path of several obscure country roads the guardians have no way of tracing us down.

At least, they shouldn't.

The thought of how they found us at all is an uncomfortable niggling in the back of my skull. I scowl as I march through the grove of trees that shelters our camp from the road.

There's nothing down the overgrown lane but a small, rusty storage shed that's missing its door, but we didn't need much.

Zian is keeping watch at the moment, leaning against the shed next to the doorway. He gives me a nod when I emerge from the trees.

Andreas is dozing in the back seat of the car. Dominic sprawls in the tipped-back passenger seat, the collar of his trench coat pulled up so it'll shade his eyes when the sun peeks over the horizon.

I told Riva to take the shed. It's the only spot with just one exit for Zian to monitor.

I ease open the fuel cap on our new junker and propel the current batch of gas into the tank by sheer force of will.

We should almost be full up after this. I'm hoping we can cross a couple more state lines before we have to do anything as blatant as stopping at an actual gas station.

The process only takes a couple of minutes. I tuck the jug into the trunk in case we need it again and step away from the car.

A light breeze washes over me and rustles through the leaves of the poplar trees looming over us. I amble a short distance away, drinking in the fresh air and the silence of the night.

It got this dark in my cell in the facility, but that darkness was tight, controlled, suffocating. Standing here, I can feel the entire world stretching out around me with no walls holding me back.

There's only one path I want to take, but there's still a relief in the freedom. I close my eyes, absorbing the quiet and the openness and letting it carry all my thoughts away so I'm nothing but an empty vessel.

The scuff of footsteps breaks my reverie. I turn to see Riva emerging from the shed in the hint of a dawn glow that's just starting to touch the landscape.

As I watch, she nods to Zian with a quick smile. "Thanks for keeping watch," she murmurs, as if she doesn't know he was guarding *against* her as much as for her. "Are you going to be able to get some more sleep too?"

I don't like how his posture turns a bit awkward as if he's concerned about how she'll feel about his answer. She shouldn't matter to any of the others any more than she does to me.

She cut herself off from us the second she decided getting a few privileges was worth more than Griffin's life. But apparently the others are soft enough to be willing to forgive the past.

They never did see things as clearly as I did—and it wasn't *their* brother she sentenced to death.

I step closer before Zian has to answer and motion him toward the shed. "You should rest a little more. I can keep an eye on things."

On her.

A frown crosses Zian's face, maybe as he tries to calculate how much rest *I've* gotten, but he's never been the type to enter a debate voluntarily. He pushes himself off the shed wall and ducks inside.

Riva stalks toward me.

She stops a few feet away from me with a hesitant expression that irritates me even more. If she doesn't like how she knows I'm going to respond to her, maybe she should leave me the hell alone.

I fold my arms over my chest and keep my voice low so I don't disturb my sleeping friends. "Do you need something?"

Her shoulders come up for a second at my purposefully cold tone, but she appears to force them to relax a moment later. The movement of her body makes me annoyingly aware of the wiry grace with which she holds herself—and the rise and fall of her breasts behind the fabric of her hoodie.

Her presence stirs up all kinds of sensations in me, but most of them I choose to ignore. They don't matter either.

Her voice comes out soft but steady. "I just wanted to say that I understand why you're upset with me. I was right there, and I didn't—You have no idea how much I've beat myself up for not realizing something was wrong sooner—" She shakes her head. "I still think about Griffin every day."

My spine stiffens at her last comment, a sharper anger flaring inside me. "Keep his name out of your mouth. You don't deserve to even talk about him."

Riva's head droops for a second before she catches my gaze again. "I'm sorry. I hate what happened, and I know it must have been harder for you than anyone. I thought I should say that. Before, I was so focused on getting us away and keeping us all alive—I didn't show how much I cared."

And I'm supposed to believe she does now? This is obviously all part of the sob story she keeps trotting out to try to wear down our defenses and steal our trust.

But I never would have believed the girl I knew four years ago, the girl I—

I never would have believed that girl could have turned on us as viciously as we all know she did. I'd hurl a derisive laugh in her face if I wasn't still trying to stay quiet.

"Sure," I say instead. "You care so very much—about making sure *you* stay alive to get whatever the hell it is you're after now."

Riva's face twitches with a flash of emotion. It isn't right that she still looks as pretty as she always did—more so, even, with the last hints of childhood faded from her features, all striking, powerful woman now.

But not as powerful as she used to be. I've clipped her wings so she can't pull another sudden flight.

She wets her lips, and I don't let myself track the movement of her tongue, focusing on the burn of anger in my chest. Her voice comes out even quieter than before.

"Is there *anything* I can say or do that would make it easier for you to believe me?"

She's even worked a hint of desperation into her voice. I start to glower at her, and a flicker of inspiration shoots up inside me.

The other guys wouldn't let me destroy her, and maybe they were right, but I still intend to pay back all the pain she dealt out. And if she's going to offer herself up so willingly in her charade of innocence, why shouldn't I take her up on it?

There is a chance that I'm protecting all of us at the same time.

"Come here," I say with a jerk of my hand toward the trees.

Without questioning, Riva follows me into the grove. Leaves rustle under our feet. The faint beams of dawn light seeping through the branches catch on her silvery hair.

I don't want to do this where the other guys could see if they got up. They'd probably interrupt.

When the tree trunks block clear view of the shed and car, I stop and turn to fully face her. She stands stiff and ready, her chin raised.

Even that annoys me.

I let my gaze trail over her body with a detached expression. "It's possible you led the guardians to us without even knowing."

Riva knits her brow. "What do you mean?"

"There could be another tracker on you that we didn't find."

"But Zian scanned me—he would have—"

I shake my head. "Zian can only *see*. They could have implanted a device that would blend in with whatever it's up against. But I can test you with my power, make sure nothing moves that shouldn't or in ways it shouldn't."

It's unlikely she has any kind of tracker on her, really. It wouldn't have taken the guardians a week to find us on that campus if they'd had a signal pointing straight to us.

But it isn't impossible. It could have been something that needed specific circumstances to activate.

It could be something *she* needed to activate and couldn't right away. So even making the request is a test in itself.

Riva simply shrugs with no sign of concern. "Then you should definitely check. If there's anything like that in me, I want it out right away."

I fix her with a hard gaze so she knows I mean what I'm saying. "It's going to hurt. Your joints and veins aren't going to like me prodding them."

Her jaw clenches slightly as if she's bracing herself. "That's fine."

So fucking stoic. Part of me wants to *admire* her response the way I used to get a rush of elation watching her race through a brutal training course, throwing herself over every obstacle, and then circling back to help Dominic or Griffin if they needed it.

The rest of me wants to strangle that first part.

"Good," I say. "We'll start at the bottom."

I aim my attention at her feet, encased in the black sneakers we picked out for her. Reaching out with the force of my talent, I can trace the lines of bone and sinew, tendons and cartilage, all through those delicate appendages.

Then I start to twist them.

A little here and a little there. Nudging and tweaking every surface and strand of flesh. Watching for something that feels a little too hard or that shifts amid the rest in a way no part of the human body is supposed to.

Riva's breath gives a slight hitch. That's the only sign she reveals of her discomfort.

So far.

I work my way up, from her ankles to her calves to her knees. Her legs tremble, and I glance up at her face just for a second, taking in the flat line of her mouth with a jolt of satisfaction.

Griffin must have suffered so much—the agony when he realized she'd betrayed him, the blast of the gunshots ripping through him. She's still only gotten a small taste of payback, but it's a start.

"You could sit down if you want," I say.

She squares her shoulders. "No. I can handle it."

"If you insist."

I continue my upward journey, clamping down on the flush of heat that ripples through me around her groin. I can't ignore it, because if the guardians were going to trick us, that's exactly the sort of tactic they'd use, but I move over it quickly and efficiently, no lingering.

This won't be a very good test if it compromises *me* too.

Onward and upward; organs, ribs, arms. When I tug at her spine near the base of her skull, she sucks in a little gasp she couldn't quite suppress.

I restrain a smile.

But I reach the top of her head without any sign of a hidden piece masquerading as bone or tissue. Releasing my focus, I shake the tension out of my own body from the intense concentration of the last several minutes.

Riva's shoulders slump a little, but she isn't shy with her smile. "There's nothing? They couldn't have traced me?"

The brief satisfaction I got out of this ordeal vanishes in a snap. "Not like *that*," I retort, and my gaze homes in on the chain around her neck. "There is one more thing."

My hand shoots out faster than she could have been prepared for, but Riva's reflexes are sharper than mine even in a weakened state. She jerks backward, her own hand whipping up to cover the lump of the pendant under her shirt.

"What are you doing?" she asks with a flash of teeth.

This is what gets her upset? Not all the jabs of physical pain I just sent through her body—the thought of me so much as touching the necklace that my brother bought?

My teeth grit with the impulse to bare them in return—like Zian would, as if I've got an animal lurking inside me, mutating my body, too.

"They could have hidden a tracker in there," I snap. "Give it to me."

It's not as if she deserves that piece of him anyway, not when the rest of us had our last connection to Griffin stolen from us.

Riva pulls the cat pendant out but keeps her fingers closed around it. "You don't need to take it. You tested everything else without even touching me."

She's right, but that doesn't mean I have to like it. "It should be mine. He was my brother."

Something both fierce and haunted flares in her bright eyes. "It's the only thing I have left. We—we can look for the other ones—we'll get them back someday. But he gave this one to *me*."

Her voice turns ragged with the last few words, anguished enough that I find myself hesitating despite my best intentions. And that pisses me off more than anything.

"Fine." I glare at her hand, which she unfolds tentatively so I can at least see the little silver sculpture, and press my talent against every nook and joint to confirm it doesn't contain hidden circuitry.

I could break it so easily. One swift twist, and the cat and yarn would crack apart for good. But I'm not quite angry enough to do that.

It isn't just hers. It was Griffin's too.

When I sigh with the release of my attention, Riva tucks the pendant away. "Nothing there either?" she checks eagerly.

My teeth set on edge. I aim the full force of my glare straight into her eyes.

The other guys might be starting to forget who she's proven herself to be, but I *never* will, and I won't let her forget either.

"No," I say, flattening my voice so it's hard as steel. "But it doesn't make a difference. It doesn't matter even if you really are trying to help us now. There's nothing in this hellhole of a world that you can do to make up for what you've already done. You killed *all* of us that day, one way or another."

Riva flinches. "Jake—"

"Don't you *dare* talk to me like I'm still your friend." I take a step forward, looming on her tiny frame. "The only reason I've hung in here is so I can annihilate everyone who had a part in destroying my brother, and that is always going to include you."

My anger doesn't feel hot anymore. My veins might as well be full of ice.

I whip around before Riva can try to respond and stride back to the car, lifting my voice to wake the others.

"Let's go! The sun's coming up, and we have gas—we've got to get moving before those pricks find us again."

Nineteen

Riva

Given that the town we've stopped in is about the size of a postage stamp, it shouldn't surprise me that the local version of a supermarket is all of three aisles and a single dingy wall freezer. I peer through the smudged glass at the offerings, feeling strangely adrift.

I've shopped for food before, but only to grab a quick meal during a mission. The idea of building up a stash of groceries to last across multiple days, even weeks… and there are so many different options I've never tried…

I guess regular people have their whole lives to figure out what they like and don't, so they can casually stroll through a place like this and chuck stuff in their basket without even thinking about it.

Staying away from the frozen stuff seems like a good idea right now, considering we don't even have a fridge. I pull myself away from the tubs of ice cream and meander to the pre-prepared food section, where at least everything is already organized into a full meal instead of separate ingredients.

Jacob stalks by and pulls a loaf of bread off the shelf behind me. My skin tingles with his passing, the sensation sharpening into prickles that dig deeper inside.

My limbs have felt shakier ever since he checked me over for hidden devices. Little aches have formed in my joints and in the back of my skull, not quite the same as the pangs and twinges set off by his poison.

But I'm not going to act like a liability. I won't go begging Dominic to heal me up yet.

For however much longer Jacob keeps his stick up his ass when it comes to trusting me, I need to be more prepared. I need to adjust to this new normal of physical discomforts so they don't slow me down if we end up in another fight.

So I'm never again tempted to let out that shrieking, vicious thing inside me.

If I had, even if I managed to focus it completely on our attackers, what would the guys have thought of me after? Once I started to wonder that, I couldn't shake the question.

None of them are happy with their own talents. I don't think they'd appreciate an even more horrible one from the girl they already see as a traitor.

Please, let this Ursula Engel woman know something that will help us turn back to normal. Or at least closer to normal. I can live with retractable cat claws and a sensitivity to bodily chemicals.

I pick up some premade sandwiches that look vaguely appealing, a smile crossing my face when I catch sight of one stuffed almost to bursting with three different kinds of deli meat. I wave it in Zian's direction where he's just come around the aisle toward me. "This one's obviously for you."

His gaze latches onto it, and an answering smile springs to his lips for just a second before his mouth flattens again. He pushes on past me without a word.

My heart sinks. Okay, after last night's battle, maybe reminding him of his carnivorous tastes wasn't the best call.

Naturally, I turn around and catch Jacob glaring at me as if he thinks I was rubbing the subject in Zian's face on purpose.

I resist the urge to grimace back at him and meander farther down the aisle to the snacks and desserts.

Memories of past group meals flit through my head. A little of my good mood returns as I snatch up a box of chocolate fudge brownies and a bag of coconut macarons.

We meet up near the counter, and Jacob looks over my selections with a scowl but no complaints. I hope he remembers that I'm the one who provided the money so we can do this shopping at all.

Back at the car, we drop the bags in the trunk. Andreas hits the gas the second we're all inside, me crammed to one side next to Dominic and Jacob. It'd make more sense for me to take the middle seat given how much smaller I am than even slender Dom, but apparently Jacob can't stand the thought of so much as brushing up against me.

About a half hour outside the little town, Andreas veers down a scruffy lane and parks on the shoulder. We pile out to eat picnic-style in a secluded overgrown field. Zian does take the particularly meaty sandwich, I notice with a flicker of triumph.

I grab the two desserts and carry them over to our circle too, with a gesture toward Dominic. "Since you've got the real sweet tooth, I figured you should get to pick which we have today and which we save."

Dominic glances up at me, startled in a way that's mostly gratifying.

The other guys haven't bothered with desserts when we were eating at the townhouse, probably because Jacob was in charge of the shopping and focused on practicalities. But I haven't forgotten how Dom's face used to light up when the guardians would include cookies or chocolates with our shared lunches.

Now, he hesitates and seems to draw into himself a little more, like he can merge with the parka he's switched back to wearing despite the warming weather as we veer south.

"Thanks," he says without meeting my eyes again, as if it costs him something to accept.

I set my offerings down in the grass in the middle of our circle and sit down to take a bite of my ham and cheese sandwich, but my stomach has condensed into a solid lump.

Maybe I was too distant with them before, too cool and stubborn. Too focused on my own sense of practicalities and not considering the turmoil they're obviously dealing with.

But I'm trying every way I can think of to show them that the friendship we shared hasn't died, and nothing I do seems to be going right.

It shouldn't be this hard. We're blood; we have each other's backs. We always did.

How the hell did Brooke manage to hit it off with all those friends just by hanging out and talking with them?

My frustration awakens a shiver of that caustic vibration in my chest. I close my eyes and then stand up to walk back to the car.

Maybe they need me to give them a little space—and maybe I could use some too.

I slide into the back seat, leaving the door open so the mildly warm air can flow through, and peel off my hoodie since I'm starting to sweat in it. I'm about halfway through my sandwich when Andreas ambles over, a couple of macaroons in his hand.

"Mind if I join you?"

The tightness inside me eases. I have made progress with *one* of my guys.

"Of course not," I say, offering him a smile I don't need to force at all.

He drops into the seat by the open door and holds out one of the macaroons. "I thought you might like one too. We can't let Dom eat *all* of them. It'd be unhealthy or something. We're saving him from himself."

I laugh and take the lumpy cookie. My first bite dissolves on my tongue with a mix of sticky sugar and creamy coconut, and just for a moment, everything feels like it could be okay after all.

Andreas considers me as I alternate between the cookie and the rest of my sandwich, his own dessert polished off in a matter of seconds.

"Are you nervous about what's up ahead?" he asks when I'm licking the last crumbs of coconut off my fingers.

Is that why he thinks I went off to eat on my own?

I swallow thickly, the sweetness that lingered on my tongue turning sour. I'm not sure I want to have this conversation.

But if I can't talk to even him, then what am I doing here?

"A little," I say. "But I know we can handle a lot. We'll figure out what we have to do when we get there."

"You just seem kind of tense."

I look down at my hands and then at him. Andreas gazes back at me with his usual warm, open expression.

Just the sight of that handsome face with his dark eyes so focused on me makes my pulse flutter, but *that's* not what my issue is really about either.

I wet my lips and make myself say it. "Everything's all messed up. Between the five of us, I mean. Between you guys and me."

Andreas's smile falters with concern. "Riva, it's not—it's complicated. And you can't let Jake get you down. He's got his own stuff that he's working through."

I duck my head again. "It's not just Jacob, and you know that. And I could tell things were wrong when I first got you guys out, I saw that you didn't trust me, I just— I didn't know it would last this long." The last words catch at the back of my mouth, but I push them out. "I miss you."

I missed them so much, for all those years, and now they feel farther away than ever. But saying that much only feels pathetic.

Andreas reaches over to grasp my hand. "I'm here. The others will come around."

I clutch his fingers and speak past the lump in my throat. "I just thought you all knew *me*, that you would know I'd never have done anything I thought would hurt Griffin on purpose. It was a stupid mistake."

I stop there with a flush of shame and embarrassment. I hadn't meant to say that part.

Andreas studies me. "What mistake?"

Every particle in my body recoils from the idea of telling him about the silly, careless kiss. "Not paying enough attention to what was going on around us," I say vaguely. "Not catching on that we were in trouble soon enough to prevent it."

Andreas frowns as if he can tell I meant more than that, but I *really* don't want to continue the conversation in that direction.

I grope for a change of subject, lifting my gaze to fully meet his eyes again. "That thing last night where you were… fading—has that happened before?"

It's Andreas's turn to hesitate. His gaze drops to our linked hands.

"Not like that. Sometimes using the power makes me feel a little strange, but it hasn't had an obvious physical effect before. But then, in the past I've never gone back and forth between the two states so many times that close together either."

"I guess that could do it."

He manages a crooked smile. "Hopefully I won't have to pull any more stunts like that again."

Picturing him fading away sends a jolt of fear through my chest. I can't imagine how *he* feels about the possibility.

I squeeze his hand tight, seeking out his gaze. "If you need to use that tactic again, I'll do whatever I can to keep you with us afterward. I always will."

My voice gets a bit rough with those words. Andreas blinks at me, emotion shimmering in his eyes, and then he's scooting closer to me so he can wrap me up in his arms.

His warm, summery scent fills my nose. As my head tips against his shoulder, sudden tears prick at the backs of my eyes.

It's like our embrace in the club—except my memory of that earlier moment is blurred by the alcohol, and I initiated it. This hug is all him.

He pulls me even closer, tucking my head right under his chin, one hand stroking over my braided hair and the other resting against my side. His thumb sweeps up and down over the thin fabric of my tank top.

With each movement of his fingers, a starker heat sparks beneath my skin. It flows over my limbs and through my veins, as potent as Jacob's poison but exhilarating instead of draining.

I draw in a breath, and even more of Andreas's scent floods my lungs. A hot, heady pressure forms low in my belly.

I think the hug was only meant to be friendly, but my body clearly has other ideas. With these guys, it always has, but the flare of attraction has never swept through me quite as strongly as now.

I haven't been quite this close to any of the guys, not like this, since I found them again. And we're nothing like kids anymore.

It isn't just me, either. A new tang reaches my nose alongside the delicious smell of Andreas's skin: a waft of pheromones that's not stress but desire.

Of their own accord, my fingers curl into Drey's shirt where they were resting against his chest.

Andreas's hand dips a little lower to where my top has ridden up from my cargo pants. His thumb hooks under the fabric and glides over my waist skin to skin.

My breath catches. That simple motion lights flames across my torso.

I want him to tease his touch higher—lower—everywhere. I want everything.

If I tipped my head just a little back, I could brush my lips against his neck, flick my tongue across his throat. Taste his scent as well as breathe it in.

The rush of need blots out the rest of my thoughts for only a second before a chilling wave crashes over me.

What's wrong with me? I can't let myself get wrapped up in this crazed impulse that's sending all my thoughts spinning.

The last time I got distracted like that, it ruined everything.

The image of Griffin's slackening face and sagging body flashes through my mind, and I jerk out of Andreas's arms. My hand fumbles for the door handle behind me.

Andreas stares at me as if he's just woken up from a daze. "Tink?"

Somehow the old nickname makes the guilt punch even deeper. I shove open the door and scramble out into the sunlight.

"We should—we should probably get on the road again," I say, as if that makes any sense when I'm getting *out* of the car while I'm saying it.

But the other guys are already heading over to us. I should be thanking the stars above that Jacob didn't see Andreas and I before I broke our embrace.

Instead, my gaze snags on Drey's uncertain expression, and a twinge of regret shoots through me.

He's the only one who's been here for me, and I just pushed him away.

Twenty

Riva

As far as I can tell, Kansas is basically one really big grassy field. With some extra grass on the side.

The lonely road we're cruising along winds through those stretches of grass, up and down and around low hills, and past the occasional more cultivated stretch of fading corn or other crops I can't identify. We haven't seen a building up close in over an hour.

Jacob is driving now, with Dominic studying the specifications Andreas wrote down from Dr. Gao's memory of Ursula Engel's land purchase. His head dips and rises as he shifts his attention between the notepaper and the GPS map on the guys' joint phone.

"We should be just about there, from what I can tell. But I don't know what the property will look like."

He glances over his shoulder at Andreas, who's sitting in the middle now, squished between me and Zian. "You didn't see any mention of the usage of the property or buildings on it?"

Drey shakes his head, the slight motion sending a ripple of heat through my body that only amplifies my regrets about how I responded to his touch yesterday.

"It was definitely listed as a land purchase, not a house sale or something like that," he says. "But that was more than twenty years ago. Who knows what she did with it?"

Zian gazes out the window with a frown. "At least if there are guardians around, we should be able to spot them way in advance."

He's right, but there doesn't appear to be anyone at all around. I haven't even spotted a tractor in the last thirty miles.

Something makes Dominic lean forward in his seat. "There's a fence up ahead. That could be the boundary of the property."

My expectations have clearly become skewed by life in the facility, because when he says "fence," I immediately anticipate a ten-foot-tall monstrosity topped with spikes of barbed wire. What actually appears on the other side of the shallow ditch is a weathered wooden fence that'd only come up to my chest.

Here and there, boards are sagging or have fallen right off it. I crane my neck to get a better look past the guys. "I don't think anyone's been maintaining this place for a while."

"Or they just want it to look that way," Jacob mutters.

"We have no idea if it was ever connected to the facility," Andreas points out. "Who knows how many projects Engel might have had going on?"

Jacob lets out a brusque huff. "We go forward assuming they're here. That's a hell of a lot safer than assuming they're not."

For once, I agree with him.

Dominic points at the windshield. "There's a gate up there, so probably some kind of driveway. Should we head up that way in the car or on foot?"

Jacob slows the car as we come up on the gate. We all peer at the landscape around it.

There *is* a dirt lane, so overgrown with tufts of grass that it's barely visible amid the larger field around it. No recent tire marks have crushed the blades or dug into the soil. The padlock securing the gate is blotchy with rust.

Beyond the gate, the field stretches out perfectly flat as far as my eyes can see. There's no sign of any people, not a single building. Not even a freaking bush.

"Maybe she never actually used the property?" Zian ventures. "Or she tore down whatever she built here before she left?"

Dominic rubs his mouth thoughtfully. "If it's the latter, we should still check it out. There could be remains that'll give us an idea of what she was doing here."

Jacob scans our entire surroundings and makes the final call. "We'll drive up. It'll look stranger for there to be a car stalled here on the side of the road. Let me get the gate."

Not bothering to turn off the engine, he tenses his shoulders and makes a brisk motion with his hand.

The padlock clicks open. It floats through the air to hang on one of the fence boards.

With another shove of his power, Jacob pushes the gate wide. Its hinges let out an ear-splitting creak that has us all wincing.

He drives us through with a brief pause to heave the gate shut again. The flattened grass from our tires would give our arrival away, but only if someone looks closely.

The car creeps onward slowly as both Jacob and Dominic crane their necks to trace the faint path of the overgrown lane through the field. The bumps in the road jostle us, and my stomach starts to churn.

The effects of the poison have been sinking deeper into me throughout our drive here, but I've mostly been able to tune them out. I grit my teeth and focus on the terrain outside.

When Jacob hits the brakes, we've traveled far enough that I can't see the road or the gate anymore when I check the rear windshield. "I think the lane ended here," he says.

Dominic tips his head in agreement, and we all get out to scope out the area. The grass is noticeably thicker beyond the front bumper, supporting Jacob's theory.

But there's still nothing useful around us. Just grass, grass, and more grass.

We spread out through it, our eyes fixed to the ground for clues. The tall blades rustle against my calves. I walk slowly so that I don't miss anything—and so that the tremors shooting through the muscles in my legs don't have the chance to trip me up.

Every now and then, Dominic bends down and yanks a slightly taller plant out of the ground by the roots. Without comment, I watch him tuck the weeds and wildflowers into the pockets of his parka.

Someday he'll tell me what's going on with him. Pushing the guys to open up hasn't gotten me anywhere.

I don't want him to have to do anything for me that he isn't happy about.

We've been scouring the area for at least ten minutes when Zian gives a little shout. He's staring at the ground just in front of his feet, but when we all hustle over, I can't see anything there at all.

I mean, other than grass.

He motions toward the ground. "I've been trying looking *through* the soil as far as I can. A couple of feet down right here, there's more than just dirt. I think it's cement."

My heart skips a beat. "There's an underground building. Like the facility."

Andreas glances across the field again. "Except it's either a hell of a lot bigger or they didn't bother with the aboveground part."

Jacob's brow furrows. "Whoever was using it must have had some way to get in."

You'd think so, but another half hour of searching, with Zian guiding us as he traces the outline of the building through the earth, turns up nothing remotely resembling an entrance. Or any other sign that anyone at all has come out this way in the last couple of decades.

It's Dominic who calls out to us next. While we rush to join him, he kneels down in the grass.

He's crouched by a small metal grate, a circle no wider than his shoulders. "Any underground structure would need ventilation."

Jacob claps his hands together. "That's our way in."

Andreas cocks his head skeptically. "I don't think we're going to fit. How big is the vent under it?"

"Only one way to find out."

Jacob untwists the bolts holding the grate in place, and Zian heaves it up with a rasp of degrading metal. He leans down to poke his head inside, but *his* broad shoulders won't even make it through the opening.

"It looks even tighter in there," he announces with a faint echo.

Jacob's attention fixes on me. The other guys' gazes follow him.

My skin tightens up, but it's the obvious answer. I'm by far the smallest of us.

"Sure," I say before Jacob even needs to volunteer me. I'm part of the team; I won't shy away from doing my bit. "You want me to just crawl in there and…"

"Look for a way into the building, and then find a better way to get *us* in," Jacob says in a tone like I'm dim for not realizing that right off the bat.

Maybe it should have been obvious. My brain has started to feel kind of wobbly too, like little bursts of static electricity are crackling through my thoughts.

"Right." I peek down into the dark passage. "Anyone have a light?"

When Jacob hesitates, I let myself glower at him. "I know you don't want me armed, but what do you think I'm going to do with a flashlight that I couldn't with my fists? There obviously aren't any windows down there. I'm not finding any entrances if I can't even *see*."

He grumbles something under his breath and jogs back to the car. When he returns, he passes a keychain-sized LED light to me. "Get on with it."

"Happy to." I give him a mocking salute and bend down to squirm into the vent.

I have to go head-first, because there's no room to turn around once I'm inside. My gut twists and shudders as I squeeze into the space that's tight even for me.

The smell of aged metal clogs my nose, like long-dried blood. I swallow down the acid that creeps up my throat, switch on the light, and army-crawl forward.

The vent stretches out into hazy darkness ahead of me, all smooth metal with no markings to tell me anything about where I am. The tremors from my legs quickly migrate to my arms and shoulders, nibbling away at my muscles while I propel myself along.

Just keep moving. I can do this. I'm stronger than Jacob's stupid poison.

My back starts to ache too. The narrow space presses in on me, and my breaths become increasingly shallow.

Is there even enough air down here now?

A wave of dizziness sweeps over me. I pause, bracing my head against one hand.

I can't stop now. What am I going to do—just die here in this underground tunnel like a sniveling kid?

The guys wouldn't even know what happened to me.

Somehow, that last thought is the most terrifying of all. They'd probably assume I've abandoned them purposefully.

Fuck that.

I shove myself onward, my teeth clenching so tight my jaw throbs, which at least distracts me from the expanding aches and queasiness everywhere else in my body. The tunnel veers to the right, and I contort myself to follow it, the corner jabbing my belly.

A new addition to my collection of bruises. Hurray!

A couple of body-lengths after the bend, the vent slopes sharply downward. I hesitate at the top of the incline, clutching the tiny flashlight.

But where is there to go other than forward?

Elbow by elbow, I haul myself forward and down. When my thighs slide over the edge of the slope, gravity yanks me forward with more force than I can brace against.

I skid the rest of the way down at a freefall, bumps in the metal scraping against my stomach while my shoulders and hips bang against the metal sides. I try to shove my arms forward to shield my head, but the surface drags at them in the opposite direction.

The next thing I know, the top of my skull is slamming into a wall.

The impact radiates through my mind. My ears ring, and more bile creeps up my throat.

I hold still until the splintering pain eases off enough that I don't feel like my head's going to fall right off my neck when I move it. No sound reaches my ears.

If my thump was heard by someone down below, there's no sign of it.

Cautiously, I peer around me. I've come to a stop at the bottom of the incline, where the vent branches out in two directions like the head of a T.

Left or right? In the glow of the flashlight, both directions look almost the same. But I think I spot a slight ridge on the floor of the passage to the left, like there might be an opening there.

I heave myself around the corner and drag my body over to it.

There *is* an opening, a square a little smaller than the grate on the surface, with slats to let the air flow through. The space beneath it is pitch black.

I hold perfectly still and listen for several minutes. There's nothing but silence down below. Not the faintest flicker of light either.

As far as I can tell, if anyone is still using this place, they're nowhere nearby.

Tensed to jerk it away at the first sign of trouble, I aim the flashlight downward so I have some idea what I'd be dropping into. The glow catches on a tiled floor, a cupboard off to the side, and the edge of what I think is a desk.

Okay. Time to get out of this torture chamber.

I flick out my claws and dig at the edge of the grate. To my relief, a few sharp tugs are enough to dislodge it. I drag it out and push it down the passage across from me.

The real problem is compressing myself enough to fit through the hole. I hunch my shoulders together and wriggle, dropping an inch at a time until they pop through—and my hips catch me in mid-fall. Dangling upside down, my head whirls.

Just a little farther. I tug at my body with little hitches that send my gut roiling again and finally plummet to the floor.

I manage to roll in mid-air to land on my hands and knees, if not my feet. The thud when I hit the floor makes my whole body stiffen in alarm.

No footsteps come thundering over to investigate. And when I lift my hands, I find my fingers are smeared with grainy dust.

It's been a long time since anyone came into this specific room.

Grimacing, I wield my flashlight and stagger out through the doorway. My entire body is throbbing now, and I think my stomach may have permanently flipped upside down, but I haven't completed my mission yet.

My sneakers leave a trail through the dust coating the floor, down the hall and to the doorways of a couple more rooms that hold nothing but bare furniture and walls. Then I push open a door and find myself gaping at a smaller replica of a very familiar control room.

The screens mounted on the wall are thicker and outdated, the consoles beneath them similarly old-fashioned-looking, like something out of an old sci-fi movie trying to imagine the future within the current style. I run my light over the rows of buttons and switches.

There. A small cluster of controls off to one side has the label BACKUP GENERATOR overtop. I punch the ACTIVATE button with my thumb.

Thankfully, that particular control doesn't require any special identification. A whirring sound emanates through the room, and the overhead lights flicker on.

Hallelujah. It's a fucking miracle.

I scan the rest of the controls faster in the clearer illumination—as fast as I can through the pulsing headache that's emerged in the back of my skull. Where the hell is the FRONT DOOR control?

Finally I spot a lever and a couple of buttons that say ENTRY. I jab at them and yank the lever.

Something I did works, because a low mechanical groan reverberates from the hall outside.

I stumble to the doorway and stare with bleary eyes as the ceiling at what appeared to be a dead end in the hall unfolds. While part yawns upward, steps unfurl down to the floor.

A sliver of sky emerges above, expanding into a huge square at the top of the new staircase that appears to go up at least a couple of floors in height. No wonder Zian couldn't spot this entrance from up there.

I clutch onto the doorframe for balance, thinking I should yell just in case the guys somehow missed the giant trap door opening in the middle of the field, afraid that something much more solid than words might come out of my mouth if I dare to open it. The headache bangs on my skull like a toddler with a xylophone.

It's only a minute before the guys' voices become audible. They ease down the stairs, Jacob and Zian in the lead, walking a little faster once they've spotted me waiting.

"Wow," Andreas says, peering around him as they reach the hallway, and shoots me a grin. "Nice work."

I attempt to smile in response and promptly vomit all over the floor.

Twenty-One

Riva

I'm lucky that Zian can move as fast as he does, because he catches me right before I crumple into the puddle of grossness I just spat up. There's a flurry of motion around me: Zee tugging me off to the side and resting me against the wall, Andreas rushing over with frantic questions about how I'm feeling, Dominic coming to stand over me with one hand deep in his pocket.

And Jacob, of course, walking up behind Dom and sneering down at me like *I'm* the one who poisoned me. "This isn't really the time for dramatics."

I'd give him the middle finger, but my limbs appear to have transformed into lead, too heavy to lift. Andreas pats my cheek firmly, and I blink at him.

His face doubles before my eyes, and I sputter a choked giggle.

He glances up at Dominic. "When was the last time you healed her?"

I can't focus on Dom's face—my head won't lift either—but his voice comes out tight. "Yesterday afternoon. It has been a while—but she didn't say anything. She seemed fine."

"Maybe if she couldn't tell you hate doing it, she wouldn't pretend she's fine until she's literally falling over."

"I haven't been refusing. I can't help it if I'm not jumping for joy—I'm doing as much as I can."

"Well, if you wiped the poison completely from her system this time, we could all stop worrying about it."

Jacob cuts in. "And then we'd have to worry about her taking off on us instead."

"You can't really think—"

"Guys!" Zian breaks into the conversation in an urgent tone. "Look at her. I think Dom had better heal her *somehow* right now."

My chin has come to rest against my chest. A weird shudder is running through my body. I'm sinking and drifting away at the same time —and then a hand rests against my sternum just below my face.

The warmth that flows from Dominic's touch brings me back to earth and my body back into focus. My heart thumps steadily; my breath flows in and out.

There's a floor beneath me. A wall against my back. I'm still here. I haven't gone anywhere.

Dominic rasps something to the other guys about getting him "more," which doesn't totally make sense to me, but my mind is still too hazy to follow what's going on. Footsteps stomp one way and another.

A second rush of warmth washes over me, and my vision clears. Yes, I'm sitting on the floor, in the hall under the wavering lights powered by the backup generator. A sour smell laces the air—oh, right, because I puked.

I make a face and manage to push myself upright and away from the puddle in the same motion. Dominic straightens up too, brushing what looks like more dust off his hand against his parka.

He doesn't meet my gaze. Andreas said he *hates* doing this—hates having to heal me.

I tried. I tried so fucking hard not to need him, but it didn't work.

Andreas touches my arm tentatively. "Are you doing okay now?"

My face flushes with shame. I *was* doing just fine until… until I wasn't.

"Yeah," I say roughly. "Sorry. It caught up with me too fast. I'm fine."

My gaze flicks back to Dom. "Thank you."

He gives a slight nod in acknowledgment. I can't read his expression to tell whether he's pissed off or just tired.

Jacob strides past us. "Let's see what the hell we've stumbled on here."

As the rest of us follow him down the hall, I tuck the no-longer-necessary flashlight into my pocket. "There's a control room that looks a lot like the one in the facility—both of the facilities I've seen."

Andreas's mouth is still slanted at a worried angle, but he perks up with curiosity. "Are there stairs going farther down?"

"I haven't seen any, but I wasn't specifically looking for them. I wanted to let you all in first." I kick at the dust on the floor, sending a few fluffy bunnies floating into the air. "I don't think we have to be on guard for anyone still working here, though."

Zian snorts. "Not unless they float and are really bad at cleaning."

We pass the room where I dropped out of the ceiling and continue to where it branches out much like the ventilation system did. Down the passage to the left, we come across several rooms with thick control panels that send a shiver of recognition through me.

They look like the locks we had on our cell doors.

The rooms aren't locked, though. The doors stand slightly ajar. Peeking into one, I find myself staring at a low table, a plain dresser, and a crib.

Everything's covered in the same thick layer of dust we've encountered in the rest of the underground building. The furniture is as barren as in every other room—nothing hanging on the walls, no trinkets on the desk or dresser, no blanket in the crib.

There are marks of life, though. A shallow dent in a wall as if a toy were flung at it with greater than expected strength. Notches in the finish on the crib's slats as if the wood was tested with budding teeth… or claws.

I tear my eyes away and move to tug open the dresser drawers. Those are empty too, just a faint plasticky scent drifting up from them.

"They stripped the place down but must have decided it'd be easier just leaving the larger pieces behind," Jacob says from the doorway. As he takes in the room, his face remains a rigid mask, betraying no emotion.

Six of the locked rooms have the same layout. Exactly six. A queasy sensation unfurls in my gut that I don't think Dominic could heal.

A couple more doors down, we arrive at an office that's more compact than the larger meeting-style rooms near the entrance. The furniture is nicer, though: an old oak desk that actually smells like wood rather than plastic or metal, a heavy leather rolling chair, a couple of tall bookcases that match the desk.

The bookcases have a little motif carved into the upper section of the frame, like a forested skyline rippling with the points of evergreen trees. It reminds me of the preserved clipping of the cabin in the woods that we found in Ursula Engel's things at her former workplace.

A sense of certainty settles over me. "This was *her* office. Engel's."

Andreas runs his fingers through the dust on the desk. "She owned the property, and this is the nicest workroom we've seen so far. She must have run this place."

"It sounded like she was pretty important to the facility, right? Or at least she used to be? She made a lot of the decisions?"

"Something like that," Zian says in a low voice, shifting his weight from one foot to the other. "It was hard to tell from the snippets I heard. You don't think…"

"This is where we started," Dominic fills in when the larger guy doesn't go on. "This was the first facility, from when we were too young to remember. We must have moved when we were still really small."

An uneasy silence settles over us all. What are the chances that his explanation *isn't* accurate? The guardians up and moved once before, after our escape attempt. There's no reason they couldn't have other times in the past.

Once upon a time, a woman named Ursula Engel bought this property, had this structure built, and held the nicest office. This was *her* project.

And she raised six very unusual babies within these walls. Why? Where did we come from?

What did she want from us?

"Did she leave anything at all behind that's useful?" Jacob asks, pushing into the room. "Zee, check for any compartments in the walls."

Jacob starts testing the bookshelves for moveable panels. I peek behind the bookcases and then crouch down to peer beneath and behind the desk before checking inside the drawers.

In one of the lower drawers, my groping fingers catch on a small paper wedged right at the back. It tears a little as I tug it free, but when I smooth it out on my lap, it's still perfectly readable if faded.

My pulse stutters.

"What's that?" Jacob demands, turning toward me, but my throat has constricted too much for me to immediately answer.

It's only the size of a post-it note, but I recognize the handwriting from the box of Ursula's things, a distinctive mix of curly and spiky. And that handwriting has formed my name at the top of the note.

Riva

54 days – 9.5lb – 20.7"

First smile today. Like she was so pleased to see me. Lots of cooing. Lovely to hear.

My fingers tighten around the scrap. Am I imagining the affection in those words?

It sounds like… like she actually cared about me. About how I responded to her.

About whether I was happy enough to smile and coo.

Who was this woman, really? And if she raised us from when we were infants, if we mattered to her… why can't I remember her?

Twenty-Two

Zian

Andreas sighs and frowns down at the console he'd been prodding. "I still can't even get the screens to turn on. Any luck over there?"

On the other side of the room, I shake my head and glower at the buttons in front of me as if I can intimidate them into functioning. "The power's on from the generator. The door opened. There's got to be some way to get the rest of the system going."

My gaze slides down from the waist-height controls area across the smooth base of the console that stands it on the floor, where most of the electronic workings must be hidden. "Maybe there's something inside that needs to be fiddled with. I'll check if I can make out the problem."

As I plant myself on the floor so I don't have to crane my neck, Dominic peeks into the room.

"Still nothing," Andreas tells him before he has to ask, and lets out a rough breath. "Man. How long do you figure they kept us in this building before we moved to the first one we remember?"

"It couldn't have been many years," Dominic points out in his typical contemplative way. "If we were here when we were much older than three, we'd definitely remember the move."

"I wonder *why* they moved us," I murmur, as much to myself as to the other guys. It's hard to pay attention to their conversation while I focus in on the console wall in front of me.

With a faint fizzing sensation in my eye sockets, I direct my vision through the thin plastic surface to the nest of cables and circuit boards I find behind it. Sliding my gaze across those features feels like dragging my eyes through mud rather than air.

My eyeballs are already kind of tired from scanning so much of the ground overhead. Hopefully I can figure this problem out fast.

My attention homes in on a cluster of cables off to one side. The coating around the wires has melted together into a lump.

The connection there must be broken. Maybe if I cut out the melted part and twist the wires back together, that will get the juice flowing through the system properly.

It can't be that hard, right? Just match up the wires by the color of their coatings. A toddler could handle that.

"I think I might see how to fix it," I say, glancing up for a second, and realize I'm alone in the room. The other guys must have gone off to investigate more of the building.

They probably either told me they were leaving and I was too zoned out to hear, or they didn't want to interrupt my concentration. No big deal. I'll patch things up and call them back in once I've saved the day.

Or the computer system, or whatever.

I can't see any proper way to open up the base of the console, but I can take care of that easily enough. With a few well-placed smacks of the side of my hand, I create a rectangle of cracks in the plastic and then snap out the chunk I've outlined.

The fused ball of wiring is right in front of me. Scissors would be nice, but my hands will work just fine for that too.

It doesn't even take that much of my strength to snap the cables at either end of the mess. I chuck the melted ball into the far corner of the room and get to work peeling back the coating so I can twist the wire ends together.

A couple of sparks shoot from one of the wires and zap my fingers.

"Shit," I sputter, smacking them against my thigh to stop the stinging.

"Are you okay?"

My head jerks around. Riva's standing in the doorway, the color back in her cheeks—a welcome sight after she got so sickly pale for a minute when we first trooped in here.

I don't welcome an audience now, though, especially when the first part of the show was me looking like an idiot.

"I'm good," I mutter. "It'd take more than a little wire to hurt me."

Riva walks over and crouches a few feet away from where I'm sitting to consider the severed cables. "I could probably hook them up faster." She waggles her slim fingers. "One of the few benefits of being tiny."

She's poised that close to me, her coolly sweet scent wafting into my nose. All at once, a whole lot of me wants to tell her that even if it would still make total sense for me to call her "Shrimp" like I always used to, she's absolutely perfect exactly the way she is.

The perfect size for tucking into my arms and carrying to safety. The perfect size for shielding if danger descends on us.

But I'm not supposed to be worrying about *her* safety. We still don't know for sure that she isn't going to put the rest of us in danger.

The guys are the ones who stuck with me. She's the one who left.

My irrational impulses need to remember that.

"It means there's less of you to spread out a zap, so you might get totally fried," I retort. "I'm managing."

She doesn't argue, just watches as I attach a couple more wires. "You figure getting those connected will be enough to get the full console running?"

"Not sure yet, but it seemed worth a try."

Riva hums in apparent agreement. "It'd be pretty amazing to get into the records they'll have stored in that thing. If they didn't wipe the hard drive before they left."

Somehow I hadn't even considered that possibility, I was so intent on simply getting the damn thing up and running. I scowl more at myself than her and push onward, grasping the next cable.

I've come this far, and there are only a couple of wires left. We have to at least check.

Who knows how many answers could be hiding behind those blank screens?

The last cable gives me another zap as I connect it, hard enough that I shake my hand and let out a few more curses. So I'm already irritable when I stand up and poke at the controls on the console.

Nothing happens. The screens stay dark, taunting me for my useless work.

I glare at them, a growl slipping from my lips. The skin along my neck and shoulders prickles with fur itching to spring free.

This whole thing is garbage. I might as well smash the console all for the good it'll do us.

Riva's even voice breaks through my rush of frustration. "Technology never works the way you want it to when you want it to, does it?" She wrinkles her nose at the controls. "I think artificial intelligence already exists, and it thinks it's fun to mock us."

Hearing her echo my annoyance takes the wind out of my own anger. I swipe my hand across my mouth. "Yeah."

Bashing it up would only be satisfying for a few moments while I'm letting out the rage. After, I'd feel rotten about it.

It'd make me even more like the monster the guardians turned me into.

Did this Engel woman intend for my weird powers to emerge so blatantly and physically once I got older? Did she have any idea how I'd turn out?

What was the point of any of this?

I hunker back down on the floor, gritting my teeth against the turmoil inside me. I know I'm more than a monster.

I *have* to be more than that.

"There could be something else I missed," I say, peering at the other cables and the panels of circuits.

A couple of the panels look scorched to my untrained eyes, the green surface marred with black and grey smudges like miniature storm clouds. Is that normal wear and tear or a sign that *they've* been fried beyond functioning.

I scoot over to gaze through the unbroken side of the console to get a different example for comparison. The circuit boards on that side look pretty similar, which isn't helpful.

Which part of the console do we know for sure is working? Whatever connects to the backup generator and the controls for the entrance to the facility.

I move even farther to crouch by the area beneath the spot labeled for the backup generator. There is some circuitry there too, and a cluster of cables that aren't at all melted.

I stare hard at the circuit boards through the shell enclosing them, but it's too hard to make out the details when it's all so dark. Grimacing, I crack open that part of the console as well and let the light spill in.

There. Glancing back and forth between that panel and the other ones I've exposed, I can see that the scorched-looking marks aren't necessarily normal after all. The circuits for the backup generator don't appear to have them. And the details of the little bits and pieces look… sharper somehow, like the other panels have melted a tiny bit too.

Did the people who worked here fry the rest on purpose to make the system inoperable? Why would they have bothered if there was nothing to see if we got in anyway?

It seems too strange that *everything* would be significantly damaged except for a couple of key controls that have stayed pristine. They must have been worried there was some kind of data still retrievable inside this thing.

But I don't think I can unmelt circuits. I sure as hell don't know how to unscorch them.

I frown at the messed-up panels. "If we could find enough functional circuit boards, ones that look the same, maybe we could swap the panels out…"

"We can't take anything that's working with the generator," Riva reminds me. "Nothing will work if it shuts off."

Right, of course. I eye the area of the console near the entrance controls, but I don't think it's wise to fiddle with those either.

What if the door closes and then we can't get the circuits hooked up properly to re-open it? Riva can scramble out through the vents, but the rest of us would be stuck.

I suck in a breath, grappling with a fresh surge of frustration.

Okay, so I don't have the materials here. Think it through, Zee. You have a brain in the middle of all those muscles somewhere, right?

I'm not just the freak that sprouts fangs and fur and hurtles into a fight. I'm *not*.

I could take the messed-up boards… and bring them to some kind of electronics store. See if they could make a functional copy of them.

A smile darts across my lips. That's an actual plan. It'd mean having to leave and come back, but totally worth it if we can get access to the computer systems afterward.

We could find out exactly what the guardians did to us when we were just babies. How it all began.

And if we can see how the freakishness started… that might also tell us how we can end it.

High on hope, I reach for the nearest panel without giving myself a chance to second-guess my idea. My fingers grasp around it, feeling for the connection points where it can snap free—

And another electric jolt, twice as potent as the last one that shocked me, crackles up both my arms simultaneously.

The bolt of electricity sears through my nerves and stabs pain all the way to the roots of my teeth. My body rears back defensively.

In all of a second, fur ripples across my back, fangs gnash in my extending muzzle, and I slam my fist into the circuit board.

It sputters and sizzles, and I roar at it. Only as I catch a shaky breath do I come back to myself, staring at the bashed panel that's now way more of a mess than when I found it.

The metal bits have fractured. Most of the green board is cracked into little shards. A few of them patter to the floor as I watch.

There's no way any tech expert is piecing *that* disaster back together.

My face snaps back into human shape. I stare at the damage I did, panting, my fingers opening and closing at my sides.

Fucking hell. Of all the times to lose my grip on my temper…

But that grip is tenuous even at the best of times. I shouldn't have even tried.

"It's okay," Riva says softly. "Even if we could fix it, they must have wiped all the data too. There might be people like that hacker guy who could dig something out if they got the power on, but none of us know how. And we can't lug this whole console to a computer expert to ask for help."

I know that's all true. And when I glance over at her, braced for her expression, I don't see the slightest hint of horror in it.

She just saw me partly transform—right in front of her under the beaming lights, not at a distance in the dark like during the fight at the college—and she didn't cringe away. She's looking at me like I'm the exact same person I always was.

Fuck, how much do I wish I was that person.

My body starts to lean toward her as if drawn by a magnetic pull. She always understood better than the others, with all that savage strength in her own tiny frame—

My gaze drops to my hand lifting as if to touch her arm, and an image blazes up through my memory. This hand, clawed and bloodied. A scream ringing in my ears. Blood, so much fucking blood, on me and around me…

I jerk myself away, shoving to my feet in the same motion. "You don't know anything!"

Riva blinks at me, her body tensing exactly the way I expected it to before. "Zian? I was just trying—"

My voice tumbles out with a growl woven through it. "Don't *try* anything. Just get out of my way. You have no idea what I'm dealing with. All *you* ever do is grow pretty little claws and pointed ears."

"I—"

I don't want to hear a single thing she has to say. "You have no fucking clue how bad—You don't know anything. So just stay the fuck away from me."

Because I hurt people, and even after everything, I don't want to hurt you.

I don't say that last part out loud. It sticks in the bottom of my throat, but maybe it wouldn't make any difference anyway.

Riva's expression twitches. Then she scrambles up and darts out of the room, giving me the space I demanded.

And leaving me feeling like even more of a monster than I did before.

It's better this way, I tell myself as I slump back to the floor. We're safer this way.

Both of us.

Twenty-Three

Riva

It's on my fifth pass through the halls that my gaze slides along the wall outside the crib rooms at just the right angle, and I notice the tiniest of seams in the otherwise smooth surface.

I stop and back up a couple of steps to confirm what it took my mind a second or two to process. There *is* a nearly indecipherable line of shadow down the wall, like the edge of a partition.

"Guys!" I call out, moving toward it and pressing my hand against the surface right by the seam. "I found something else."

My prodding doesn't shift the partition at all. Jacob and Andreas come jogging over first—Jacob frowning, naturally.

"You found the wall?" he asks with an edge of sarcasm.

I roll my eyes. "I think there's a hidden doorway here like there was in the lab where Engel used to work. If you look at the right angle from the right spot, you can *just* see the edge."

Andreas has already stepped closer, cocking his head. He lets out an awed chuckle.

"There it is. Zian must have missed that."

"Too busy trying to play engineer," Jacob mutters, but there's a note of fondness alongside the exasperation that I've never heard when he mutters about me. "He was mostly looking in the actual rooms, not the halls."

He lifts his voice so it'll carry farther. "Zee, get your ass over here. We need those X-ray eyes of yours."

His call brings not just Zian but Dominic, who wanders over from the rooms he was searching.

As Jacob motions to the area of the wall, I step farther to the side, giving Zian as much space as I can. His tirade from earlier rings in my ears.

You don't know anything. Stay the fuck away from me.

Even the memory brings a burn into the back of my eyes. I inhale slowly and deeply in an effort to even out my emotions.

Zee has always had a volatile temper, one he has trouble keeping on a leash. He probably didn't mean all of what he said as harshly as it sounded.

But he's never spoken to me like that before, not even in the past week while Jacob's been laying into me. Is he *more* upset with me now than he was before?

How the hell did that happen? How am I still screwing this up?

I don't have the answers to those questions, so I do my best to focus on the conversation about the wall.

Zian must have spotted the internal mechanism to open the partition, because he's motioning to a specific spot farther over from the seam, around chest height. Jacob positions himself there and rests his hands against the wall to help guide his talent through.

He closes his eyes. The chiseled planes of his face tighten with concentration, turning him even more starkly gorgeous than usual.

We all wait, breaths held. There's a stretch of silence, and then a mechanical rasp within the wall.

The seam widens, pulling back to reveal not an opening but an actual door: solid, natural wood unlike the painted steel ones that fill the rest of this place. It even has a bronze doorknob.

We stare at the thing for a second as if afraid it's going to launch some kind of killer door attack. Then Andreas shakes his head with a self-deprecating guffaw and reaches for the knob.

It turns in his grasp, this part of the entrance unlocked. As he pushes it inward, lights flicker on automatically with the movement.

We slink into the hidden room one by one. Andreas lets out a low whistle. The rest of us just gape.

Like every other room we've entered in the old facility, a layer of pale dust coats every surface, dulling the colors with a grayish sheen. But even so, it's immediately obvious that this space isn't at all like the others.

As with the door, the walls are paneled with natural wood, slightly curved as if to mimic the undulations of stacked logs. Vividly grained boards show when I swipe my foot over the dusty floor too.

The room's been stripped down, leaving only the largest furnishings—the items I guess it'd have been most difficult to quickly and discreetly remove—but even those are totally different from anything else we've seen in the place.

A suede sofa, so plump my limbs twinge with the urge to sink down into it and discover how comfy it'd be, stands along one wall. It faces a stone-lined fireplace that's empty other than streaks of black that confirm it was used at some time. Or maybe those were painted on for aesthetic effect.

Built-in bookcases line the wall to one side of the sofa. Next to us, near the door, stands a wooden chest large enough that Zian could have curled up inside and the lid would still have shut.

A strange sense of recognition quivers through my mind. I sink down in front of the chest, getting a whiff of its dry but sweet cedar scent, and brace my hands against the lid to lift it.

There's an image in the back of my head, a sense of what I *should* see when I push it open. I can't quite get a firm grasp on the impression, but when I shove upward and reveal only an empty hollow inside, inexplicable disappointment sweeps through me.

No. There was, before—

"We've been in here," I say slowly, testing out the words to make sure I agree with them before I continue. "There used to be—I feel like this chest should have something in it."

"That's what chests are usually for," Jacob snarks. "Holding things." But his tone is milder than usual, a hint of uncertainty and confusion touching his face as he scans the room.

"That's not what I mean. Something specific."

I shut the lid and stand up, gesturing for the guys to come over. Only Dominic responds.

He gazes down at the chest with an oddly dreamy expression and kneels down in front of it like I did. As he pushes the lid up with a squeak of its hinges, his eyes flicker.

"Yeah," he says, almost a whisper. "I can almost see—I think there were toys in here."

The second he says the word, the impressions floating in my mind sharpen. "Yes! A stuffed blue bear. And a wooden helicopter with a metal propeller that spun."

Dom runs his hands over the rim of the chest, his gaze going even more distant. "A set of puzzle blocks you could fit together into different shapes."

The other guys have gathered around us. "You remember all that?" Andreas asks.

I bite my lip. "It's not like remembering. I don't have a clear image of it. Just kind of a hazy sense of what's missing."

I turn and walk deeper into the room. Other tingles of recognition and dissonance ripple through me.

The sensations guide me to the dusty floor near the fireplace. I sit down and rest my hands on either side of me, opening myself to the fragments of memory tickling at the edges of my awareness.

"I think there used to be a fur rug here. I can almost *feel* it, coarse but soft—running my fingers into it…"

Zian crouches down next to me and runs his hands tentatively over the space. "Yeah," he murmurs.

Jacob crosses his arms over his chest. "The guardians would bring us in here, then? Run some of their tests in this room?"

"Maybe." That doesn't sound quite right.

I scoot backward and lean against the sofa, still trying to sort through the jumble of hazy impressions. "I don't get the sense that we did anything I didn't like in here. It was somewhere just to relax. I looked forward to those times."

Dominic nods. "It was just us. Us and… her, I think. Like it was a special thing when she'd bring us in here to play."

Andreas's eyes light up. "Yeah. I can almost catch that feeling. Holy shit."

Looking around the space, I realize that while it's furnished very differently from most of the facility, there is one room it resembles a little. "She had wooden and leather furniture like this in her personal office. And she had that picture of the cabin in the woods at her old office. Maybe this is what makes her feel at home."

"And she wanted to share that with us," Dominic says softly.

I ignore Jacob's light scoff. Dom is right. She brought us in here, her little charges, and watched us simply play and soak up the warmer atmosphere.

It's hard for me to wrap my head around that kind of motherliness compared to all the interactions with the guardians I recall so much more clearly.

Where did Engel go afterward? Why did she step back from our lives and let them transform into all cool detachment and rigid schedules?

I frown at the room around me. "Do you think she *wanted* to leave the facility, or did the others force her out?"

"From the things I heard, it didn't sound like her time with them ended well there," Zian offers.

Andreas nods. "Yeah, there was a lot of tension in the few memories I caught."

And part of the path to those answers could be right here in front of us.

I glance back at the guys. "If these are the sort of surroundings she liked most, where she felt most at home, then if she left the guardians and went off someplace even the hacker couldn't track her down… maybe she got herself a cabin in the woods just like that picture."

Andreas hums to himself. "I wouldn't be surprised."

Jacob's mouth twists. "There are a lot of woods with a lot of cabins in them all over the world," he says. "Even if you're right, that information doesn't get us very far."

Dominic gets up and treads lightly in a circuit around the room. "It's a start, something to narrow things down."

"Maybe we could find another, *better* hacker—" Zian begins, and halts with a stiffening of his stance. His head jerks to the side, tipping one ear toward the ceiling. "I think I hear a car. Coming close."

We all tense up. Jacob moves first, waving us toward the door. "Come on. We'd better see what we're dealing with."

Twenty-Four

Riva

The five of us hustle together through the halls of the old facility to the massive staircase that leads to the outside world. By the time we've reached it, I can hear the car too—or cars, more like it. At least two different growls of engines hitch as they travel along the uneven lane.

It would probably make the most sense for me to sneak up and take a peek, since I'm the smallest, but Jacob must figure I might actually flag our pursuers down or something. He marches up ahead of everyone else, slowing cautiously as he reaches ground level.

After a moment, he returns to us. "Only two vehicles: a van and a normal-sized car. They're definitely heading this way—they just came past the gate."

Zian's forehead furrows. "Only two? Even with the van, those can't hold anywhere near as many guardians as they sent after us back at the college."

I swipe my hand across my mouth, my body still braced for battle. "They might not realize it's us. We have no idea if they figured out we went to Engel's old workplace."

"That's true," Dominic says. "They found us on the campus, not there. There's a decent possibility they have no idea what trail we're on."

Jacob glances toward the control room, his expression dark and pensive. "It'd make sense for the organization to have some kind of alert connected to the opening of the door, even after all this time. I should have thought of that. We should have moved faster."

"They're here now." Zian grimaces. "And I guess we'd better not let any of them leave to tell everyone else what we were doing."

Jacob cracks his knuckles. "Absolutely. Even if Drey could wipe us from their memories, these people must be affiliated with the current facility. Whoever questions them about what they encountered here will know what the gaps mean."

Andreas raises his head, looking haunted for a moment before his eyes narrow. "We need to keep at least a couple of them alive for a little while—so I can search their memories about Engel. We need to know more."

"Right. We can try to question them about what went on in this place too." Jacob glances around at the rest of us. "Target the oldest ones for that, as well as you can tell. They're the ones most likely to have worked with her and to know about the facility's history. Everyone else, we take out as quickly as we can."

"We should stay down here," I say, letting my back rest against the wall. "Out there in the open, it'll be too easy for them to get shots at us."

"Of course. Spread out and get ready to pick them off."

Jacob shoots a final look at Zian, who responds by moving with me when I back up to the entrance to one of the offices. He's still playing babysitter, even after everything.

I bite back a caustic remark and prepare myself, extending my claws from my fingers. We fended off the last bunch of guardians, even though there were more of them then and they took us by surprise. There's nothing to worry about here.

Other than the fact that they've gotten so close to us twice in just a few days.

The rest of the guys duck into other doorways where they can watch the hall without being seen. Zian's lips pull back from his teeth in a silent snarl, but he stays in completely human form.

From the way he's talked, I suspect he prefers to remain that way when he can keep control over himself. I can't blame him, not when I'm keeping my own most destructive inclinations locked up.

The way he looked when I got a clear glimpse of his transformation in the control room—his face twisted into a distorted fusion of animal and man. Not an actual wolf so much as the kind of wolf-man you might see in a horror movie, a deformity more than an enhancement.

But he was still Zian, no matter how much fur leapt from his skin or how his face contorted.

I hope he knows that too.

Low voices carry from outside, too quiet for me to make out the words. If they say anything that Zian picks up with his keener ears and finds concerning, he gives no indication.

Footsteps travel down the steps with a faint rasp. They know *someone's* down here, and they're trying to catch those intruders unawares.

That's another sign that they don't know who they're dealing with. The guardians are aware of Zian's sharp hearing—I think they'd expect him to have already noticed their arrival if they knew he was here.

They aren't prepared for his supernaturally penetrating sight either. He taps my shoulder and flashes seven fingers at me. That's how many people he can see have entered the building so far.

The footsteps tread lightly toward us. My muscles tighten in anticipation.

The muzzle of a gun comes into view beyond the edge of the doorframe.

Zian and I spring out simultaneously. We leap at the closest of the figures, him instinctively letting me take the closer one with my shorter reach.

I slam the rifle against my thigh to bend it beyond use and haul the man who was holding it into the office room. He crashes to the floor with a clang of his helmet and vest.

They might not have realized who was in this place, but they pulled on their usual guardian gear regardless.

The man swings a fist at me and pulls a knife from a sheath at his waist. I kick the weapon away with a snap of breaking bone and yank up his helmet to get a look at his face.

He's young, not much older than my guys—not a good choice for Andreas's memory interrogation. I hesitate for just a second, but then the man rams his knee toward my belly while groping toward a holstered pistol at his hip, and I slash out with my claws.

His head lolls as blood gurgles from his throat. I shove myself away.

Bangs and thumps are echoing through the building all around me. Zian has already bashed his first target against the wall and left the woman in a crumpled heap. He has a man pinned under his immense frame now, one who looks closer to middle-aged.

"Did you know Ursula Engel?" he growls at the guy while restraining his struggling limbs.

"Let Andreas figure that out," I tell him, and dash back to the doorway.

Three more bodies litter the hallway outside, two with the bashed in helmets I know were Jacob's doing and another with a couple of bullet wounds to the chest that could have been dealt by any of the guys. In the room across from ours, Jacob has another man glued to the wall with his telekinetic force, the strands of gray in his hair suggesting he's the oldest of those we've seen so far.

"Get what you need," Jake snaps at Andreas.

Andreas stands rigidly next to him, staring at the guy with the ruddy gleam shimmering in his eyes. "I'm trying. He's—he's doing something that's muddling things whenever I try to focus in."

The man manages a sickly smile of triumph that makes my blood run cold.

What new techniques have the guardians figured out that are messing up Drey's talent?

Before I can worry much about that, more footsteps pound down the steps as a few guardians who initially hung back charge in to defend their companions. Too late.

I dart back out at the same time as Dominic emerges from the control room, a gun in his hand. With his brisk motion to the right, we understand each other.

I hurtle at the two figures on the left, my feet pushing off the ground so swiftly the soles of my shoes barely brush the floor. Dominic fires off several shots in quick succession at the two on the right.

As his targets crumple, I slam into a woman who's just aiming her rifle, too sluggish to match my unearthly speed. Even as I snap her neck, I'm already spinning my torso around to kick the man behind her in the face.

His helmet dents inward, puncturing his skull with a fleshy cracking sound like Jacob's preferred tactic. I land on the floor surrounded by the four limp bodies.

The scene brings back a flicker of the arena. My stomach lurches, and I yank my attention away, toward the entrance.

I'm okay now. We're all okay. We dealt with them all without needing any extra brutality… didn't we?

No other voices or footfalls carry from outside. I sprint up the steps to peek out into the cooling air of what's now evening.

Nothing stirs around the van or the car that've parked a short distance from our vehicle.

I race back down to the hall. "That's all of them!"

But we don't know how many reinforcements could be on the way. Will the last of this bunch have called for backup before they descended?

They might not have been able to say *who* they were fighting, but they'd have realized the situation was bad.

When I reach the room where Jacob and Andreas were working on the one man, I find Zian has dragged his captive over there too, restraining him in the corner several feet from the first.

Andreas is frowning, sweat beading on his forehead as his eyes flare and dim.

"Fucking hell," he snaps, and glares at the man pinned to the wall. "If you don't let me in, we'll just have to kill you."

He glances at the other guy too, who I guess he also tried. "That goes for both of you."

The man Zian is holding sputters a little bloody spittle over his lips. "You're going to do that anyway. I'm not giving you a thing."

Dominic has come in beside me. We exchange a glance, neither of us knowing how to help.

"I can make the killing a whole lot more painful," Jacob warns, and twists his hand to the side. The man he's pressed against the wall lets out a grunt of agony, his features spasming.

Andreas elbows Jake. "That doesn't help," he says under his breath. "If their brain is fried with pain, I can't get much out of it then either."

Jacob scowls but eases up on the pressure.

I hug myself, uneasiness wobbling through my chest. If we can't get any answers from them, then where do we go from here?

Jacob was right that there are millions of places Engel could have set up her cabin, if she even did that.

The hovering man's gaze catches on me for a moment, and I catch the slightest softening in his defiant expression. It's there and then gone, but for a second I thought I saw a hint of… concern?

My first response is a jolt of anger. Who the hell is he to feel sorry for me?

Then understanding clicks in my head.

The hostile words Zian threw at me less than an hour ago. All Jacob's sneering comments about my "sob story." The reason I was so popular in the arena for all those years.

I don't look like a threat. I'm a short, skinny girl you'd think you could snap in two. My only outwardly unnerving feature is my claws, and I've retracted those back into my fingertips.

I hate it when people see me as someone weak and fragile… but maybe that's what we need right now. Maybe I can use the illusion of vulnerability to distract this guy from whatever technique he's using to close off his mind.

Stir up sympathy to rattle his emotions and his concentration in a totally different way from pain.

Even though it's my idea, my body balks for a few seconds before I can propel it forward. My skin prickles with discomfort as I place myself within clear view of both of our captives. Might as well see if the gambit will work on both of them.

"What the hell are you doing?" Jacob snaps at me, giving me the perfect opening.

I hunch my shoulders and let my voice come out quavering. "I'm just trying to help. Please don't yell at me."

Jacob's expression contorts with so much surprise I'd laugh if I wasn't aiming to give off the complete opposite impression. I turn back toward the captives, brushing my hands past my eyes as if swiping away tears.

I've got tears in me somewhere, the burn of grief and frustration I've felt more times than I can count since I reunited with my guys. Since all the way back to watching Griffin collapse in front of me and knowing I'd failed us all.

Blinking hard, I open up a channel inside me to bring those feelings to the surface rather than stuffing them as far down as they'll go like usual. Heat builds behind my eyes.

I don't want to risk faking it. If this is going to work, the deluge of vulnerability needs to come as fast and effective as possible.

So I open my mouth and let all my weakest thoughts tumble out, gazing vaguely at the floor, pretending I'm speaking to my guys rather than putting on a performance for our hostages.

"I always just want to help, but you never believe me. You've made me weak and sick and then you get mad at me because I can't do enough. I'm *trying*. I'm trying so hard to make things right, to be what you want, but that's never enough either."

A lump I don't have to force rises in my throat. A couple of very real tears slip down my cheeks. I take a ragged breath, leaning into the display of patheticness and ignoring the screaming of my dignity.

The guys are silent around me, but I don't dare look at them or our captives. I can't tell whether they're shocked or skeptical or if they've figured out what I'm trying to accomplish here.

I squeeze my eyes shut for a second, and more tears trickle out. "You want me dead too. I've spent the last four years thinking about nothing but getting back to you and getting you free, and all you seem to think about when you see me is how much pain you want to put me through. How horrible it is that I'm around. How much of a burden I am. I don't know what else you want from me."

My voice breaks on the last word of its own accord. I can't stop myself from sniffling, but maybe that's a good thing.

I hug myself tighter, hoping I look as frail as I feel right now with all my emotions stretched to fraying.

"You can all hate me as much as you want, but you know what? You can't hate me more than *I* already do. The mistakes I've made, the disasters I couldn't control… But I have never wanted to hurt any of you—not Griffin, not the rest of you—and every second of my life when I had the choice, I did whatever I could to protect you. If you can't ever believe that, then… I don't know."

My legs tremble beneath me, and I let them give. I slump down on the floor as if I'm totally defeated—and in that moment, I kind of am.

What if even this doesn't work? What if I've just made a fool of myself and still gotten us nowhere?

I can already hear the caustic insults that Jacob is probably forming in his head right now. A sob I can't contain hitches out of me.

I drop my head into my hands. I want to curl up in a ball so they can't see me, so I have some kind of shell against the world again, but that would defeat the point of this demonstration.

Just hold on. Just stay here in this awful stew of emotions for as long as I can…

"I've got it," Andreas says in a low rasp. "I got everything."

As I raise my head, a strange ache spreading through my chest, Jacob sucks a breath through his teeth—and two spines crack simultaneously, our captives' heads going slack.

Twenty-Five

Andreas

"We shouldn't stay in this junk heap of a car any longer than we have to," Jacob announces as he marches us out of the underground building. "We don't know if these guardians radioed details about it back to wherever they came from."

He glances over at me. "Where exactly are we going?"

"I'm figuring that out," I say without looking up from the phone I've taken control over. It'd be a hell of a lot easier to do this search on a computer with a big screen and proper keyboard, but I'm making do with my thumbs because I don't have a choice.

The conversation I plucked out of the one guardian's memories replays through my head. I've been concentrating on nothing but that since I recognized it was our best shot at finding Engel.

She's going all the way up to Glen Lily?

And a stretch farther north, it sounds like.

Must be fucking cold up there.

It was obviously a place, not a person named Glen. I squint through the reflected sunlight at the search results that pop up on the screen.

"Sometime when she was packing up to leave the facility—at least, I think that was what was happening—that one guy we caught was monitoring things from outside her office with another guardian. They made a few comments to each other about where she was going." I frown. "The main thing popping up is someplace in Kentucky—I can't tell whether it's an actual town or just, like, a landfill site or a road name."

Zian perks up. "Kentucky isn't too far from Kansas."

"Yeah, but… it doesn't really make sense with the other things they said. They were talking about her going 'all the way up' there. Kentucky isn't 'up' from any of the facilities we know about."

"Keep digging and see if you can find anything else," Jake orders.

As we reach the car, the other guys yank open the doors. I lower the phone for a moment to glance at Riva.

She hasn't said anything since her breakdown in front of the guardians—however much it was actually breaking down and not a sort of performance. But her silence now makes me even more certain that even if she released all that emotion on purpose, there was nothing fake about the anguish in her voice.

The tears that streaked down her cheeks have already dried, but there's still a hint of redness along the rims of her eyes. Her gaze has gone distant as if she's pulled back inside to collect herself.

To rebuild the dam that kept the torrent of grief and despair shut away before.

If the outburst hadn't really taken anything out of her, if it'd only been an act, it wouldn't still be affecting her now. And I didn't really think it was an act even in the moment.

I had to focus on our targets, on watching for their mental defenses against my talent to weaken, but the pain in her voice matched the brief comments she made to me in the car yesterday.

I move to get into the back with her, wanting her to know I'm still with her even if she pushed away from me before. I don't know what's going through her head, but it's a hell of a lot more than we've acknowledged.

Before I reach the door, Jacob gives me a sharp look and motions me to the front passenger seat as he gets in behind the wheel. My jaw clenches, but we don't have time to argue about this.

If I'm going to end up navigating, it does make more sense for me to be up front. He might not even be trying to separate me from Riva.

Given how he's treated her since the first moment we crossed paths with her, though, I'm pretty sure that's at least an equal part of his motivation.

The second all the doors are closed, Jacob hits the gas. I dive back into my search results.

I dig deeper and try a few different added words, and then sigh. "Nothing looks quite right."

"Are we sure that going after Engel is still our best option?" Zian asks from the back seat in an impatient tone. "I mean, we could just stick around here and more guardians will show up… If we're prepared for them, we could pick off a few to question."

Jacob shakes his head. "Those are grunt workers—expendable people. No one who's in charge with a real understanding of the big picture would be running into a fight. Anyone else who has an in-depth understanding of what they did to us will be behind all the facility's security."

"And it seems like Engel's the one who painted the big picture to begin with," I say as I continue skimming the internet. "She'd know more than anyone."

"Do you think they'll take her into protection after they realize we broke into that place?" Dominic asks.

We all sit in momentary silence as his question sinks in.

Jacob grimaces. "It's possible. But they shouldn't have any idea how we ended up at the old facility or why. Engel wasn't around us enough when we were older for us to have any memories of her—there's no reason for them to assume we were focused on her."

I nod. "As far as they know, we shouldn't even be aware she exists. And they don't seem to *want* her around the facility anymore. The guardians I just checked had no memories of her that seemed at all recent. Nothing where they talked to her about us escaping, for sure."

It's Riva's voice that pipes up next, low but clear. "That's why she's the best option. We were her project first, and the others shut her out somehow. The guardians are willing to die to keep their secrets. We could interrogate dozens of them and not get anywhere. But Engel… she might even think we deserve to know. Maybe that's why they kicked her out."

"Right," Jacob says, sounding a little annoyed to be supporting her point even as he agrees with her. "So, we track her down and see where that gets us. And if it turns out the guardians have brought her back under their wing to shield her, then we're in the exact same scenario we'd face if we never go looking for her."

Zian sinks deeper into his seat. "So… where exactly are we going, then?"

"I'm still working on that." I jab at the screen, flick through another list of results and another. "I guess it's possible I misunder—oh, wait!"

Jake glances over. "What have you got?"

"There's a town called Glenlily in British Columbia—Canada. That's definitely up north." With excitement bubbling up inside me, I flick through to the photos that come with the search and smile. "Jackpot. That looks like snowy cottage country to me, don't you agree, Tink?"

I hold the phone so Riva can see it from the back seat.

She sucks in a breath. "That's exactly the right kind of place."

Dominic lets out a hitch of a chuckle. "British Columbia's quite a hike from here."

"Maybe we should check Kentucky first, just in case?" Zian suggests.

I balk at the suggestion. "That's in the opposite direction. We'd lose days. The longer we wait, the more chance there is that the guardians will catch on."

Twisting in my seat, I catch Riva's gaze. She nods, understanding the question I'm asking without needing words.

I turn to Jacob. "I say we go straight to BC. It's our best shot by far."

Jake hesitates for a second and then waves his hand toward me. "Let's do it. Give me our route and see where we can look for a new ride along the way."

With a few beats of my thumb, I bring up the map for our location. I meant to focus on the roads streaking across the state around us, but as I study the landscape, another detail catches my eye.

I zoom in and trace the markings crisscrossing the map. "What if we didn't get a new car right away?"

Jake's gaze flicks toward me as he propels our current vehicle down the bumpy country road that brought us here. "The guardians could already be on the lookout for this one. We don't want—"

I hold up my hand. "That's not what I meant. They'll be looking for us in cars in general. We've got a long way to go—it wouldn't be a bad thing if we could get some rest while traveling too. There are a bunch of freight train lines through Kansas. We could hitch a ride like we did with the truck before."

Dom speaks up from the back. "Would we be able to catch one that goes all the way up to Canada?"

I tilt my head, studying the screen. "I don't know what the typical routes are, but there's a network with tracks that go northwest all the way up to the border. It looks like… we could pass through Nebraska, then

Wyoming, and then Montana, and cross into BC there. We'd have to check the GPS periodically, and I suspect we'd need to switch trains at least a couple of places, but they could get us most of the way there."

Jacob's expression turns pensive. "That method could be faster or slower depending on how consistently the trains are running. But we can always hop off once we've gotten some distance from this place and grab a car somewhere there's less heat on us."

I nod. "Yeah, exactly. The more we mix things up, the harder it'll be for the guardians to predict what we're doing or where we're going."

"All right. Figure out the best place for us to catch a ride nearby—and where we could ditch the car easily too."

I shoot Jake a tight smile in return. "Already on it."

The light in the train car gradually fades with the sinking of the sun. We eat the rest of our stash of food, making plans to pick up more wherever we get off this first train, and sway with the jostling of the car on the tracks.

Every half hour, I check the phone to confirm our progress on the line this freight train is traveling along. When I curl up on a musty canvas sheet next to the stacks of wooden crates to try to get a little rest, Jacob takes over.

I'm not sure he's been sleeping at all. He always pushes himself to his limit, even when he doesn't have to, but how the hell any of us could convince him to take a break, I don't know.

I wake up to a soft creaking and the sight of Jake and Zian peering at the phone with the electronic glow splashed across their faces. Dominic is lying against a different stack of crates, the hood of his parka pulled up to cushion his head, but when I move to join the others, he stirs and sits up.

All I can make out of Riva is her sneakered feet poking out from the thicker shadows where she's tucked herself in an alcove between more of the boxes.

"Don't leave it on too much," I say in a hushed voice, sinking down next to Jacob. "We don't know when we'll be able to recharge the battery."

"We got that extra battery pack," he mutters.

"Yeah, and eventually that needs to be recharged too."

He sighs, but he turns off the phone. "We're coming up on an interchange. Based on how fast this thing has been moving, I'd say we'll get there in twenty minutes or so. Then we'll have to see whether it keeps going the way we want, stops to unload, or veers off in the wrong direction."

We might have to get off, he means. I nod and glance toward Riva. "Should we wake her up?"

"No point until we know for sure, right?" Zian says before Jacob can answer.

Jacob grimaces. "If she is even sleeping and not pretending so she can listen in."

Listen in to what? What secret plans are we making that he thinks she'd want to spy on?

I fight down the urge to shake the guy. I know I don't understand how it's been for him in the past four years, but at some point, he needs to open his eyes and see that he's imagining a monster that isn't here.

Dominic moves closer to Riva with quiet steps and rests his hand gently on her calf. "She's definitely asleep," he murmurs a moment later. "Pretty deeply too. I don't know how much rest she's gotten in the last few days."

If she can't hear us, then Jake can't object to me bringing up the specific issue that's been niggling at me more and more during those few days. I turn to him, making my voice as firm as I can manage.

"I think it's time we got rid of the poison."

Jacob snorts. "So, you've totally fallen for her fragile victim act, huh?"

I glower at him. "She *hasn't* been acting like a victim, and the only times she's gotten fragile are when the toxin has worn her down. She's *killed* for us in at least two different fights with the guardians, even if you don't believe she hurt any of them when we first escaped. Whatever happened in the past, she's obviously on our side now."

"For how long?" Jacob demands, his voice harsh even as he keeps it low to avoid waking her. "You saw her back there, getting all weepy and whiny. Either that was a fantastic show of acting, which means we can't trust anything still, or she thinks she shouldn't have to prove herself after everything she did before."

"Is that what you got out of the things she said?" I shake my head. "We've been beating her down this entire time, and she's been taking it. Do you really think she's *enjoyed* it? If she cares at all about us, which she clearly does, then of course the way we've treated her would be hard for her. But she didn't say a word about it until she realized even that could help us."

"And when she was drunk."

"That wasn't her fault either," Dominic says. "The alcohol mixed with the poison really messed things up."

She's shown a little of the pain inside her only to me, too, but I'm not going to mention our conversation in the car. I encouraged her to see me as the one person among us she could open up to, and I'm not bringing up what she said then when all it'll get me is more snarky remarks from Jake.

"She's doing what she needs to do to survive," Zian says abruptly. "If something happens to us, she knows the poison would kill her. We can't be sure if she cares for any reason other than that."

Okay, now I want to shake him too. Why does he have to bring out his bull-headed stubbornness now?

"There's too much on the line," Jacob says before I can keep arguing. "If she tips off the guardians somehow at this point, we'll lose all the progress we've made, and we might never be able to find Engel again. We'll have nothing."

He meets my gaze steadily. "Once we've found out everything we can from the scientist, then we can talk about fully healing her."

Jake is always way too good at making his perspective sound like the most reasonable one. My jaw clenches, but I don't actually have a counterargument that I can imagine him accepting.

And Dom, the only one of us who could override Jacob's decision on the matter if he wanted to, has gone back to his typical silence.

I feel the need to try one more time anyway. "Even if back then she got caught up in some promise the guardians made or—"

Jacob doesn't even let me get to my point. He jerks forward, even the little warmth he'd shown me a moment ago vanishing behind the ice of his eyes.

"*If*? We *know* what she did. Don't try to wave it away now. Griffin deserves a hell of a lot better than that."

My mouth clamps shut. There's nothing I can say when the guy who's no longer with us is invoked. Even if inside, there's a question that's started tugging at me and won't go away.

Do we really know even that much?

The train car jostles with a metallic squeal, and Riva flinches where she was sleeping. She shoves herself upright looking both panicked and bleary-eyed, strands of her rumpled hair that've come free from her braid floating around her face.

"We must be at the interchange," Jacob says, ignoring her and pulling out the phone. "Let's see where our ride is going to take us from here."

As he studies the screen and the car shudders again, Riva slinks closer. She sits cross-legged a few feet from any of us, clearly not feeling comfortable outright joining our circle. In the thin light, the weariness etched on her pretty face makes my gut tighten up.

I want to pull her into my arms and hug her tight like I did before, but I'm not sure how much she'd welcome the gesture. It wouldn't actually do her much good anyway.

Instead, I motion to Dominic. "You should heal Riva up in case we need to make a run for it."

Dom moves to her side despite his tight expression, because that's an explanation they'll all accept—not to cure her completely, but to make sure she doesn't become a liability. Because apparently that's what we're now reducing this girl to.

The girl who was once just as vital to our group as Griffin was.

A memory rises up in my head of some afternoon not that long before our escape attempt, when Riva and Griffin were standing near each other in the training room, and he leaned over to say something by her ear. She laughed with that secretive little smile that made her whole face shine…

Only he could ever make her light up quite like that.

I also remember the jab of jealousy that ran through me even as I basked in the sight. I could make her laugh, sure, but not quite like that. There was always something a little more with him.

The one thing I've never understood, no matter what we've seen, was how she could have given up that light. Not just given it up—destroyed it and the guy who sparked it.

But what if she didn't? What if we've been completely wrong all this time?

If anyone's going to figure it out, it's got to be me—both because she *has* started opening up to me, and because none of the other guys are willing to even consider the possibility.

And if I'm going to figure it out, then for all our sakes, I'd better do it soon.

The train jolts and rattles, and Jacob looks up from the phone. "It's taking the southwest route. This one isn't good anymore." He gets to his feet. "Everybody ready to jump?"

Twenty-Six

Riva

Stones rattle under my feet along the side of the train tracks. The occasional kicked pebble patters off into the brush where it's too dark for me to follow its path.

Enough moonlight streams down over the tracks as they cut through the sparse woodland for me to make out the two guys ahead of me, though they aren't much more than silhouettes. Jacob marches forward with purposeful strides like he could keep going all night—and maybe he could. Dominic looks like he's drooping a little, though.

It's hard to judge how Andreas and Zian are doing from the crunch of their footsteps behind me, but they don't sound particularly energetic. No one's spoken in ages.

My muscles could keep going for hours longer, but my eyes are starting to get heavy. I only managed to get an hour or two of sleep on the train.

I suppress a yawn and peer through the scattered trees alongside the tracks. We're following the route that should take us closer to our intended destination, but since we set out, no trains have come rushing by. We haven't spotted any ideal place to steal a vehicle of our own either, although I'm not totally sure what criteria Jacob is going by to make that decision.

After several more minutes of trudging, the tree line peters out at our left. Fields sprawl out for miles, leading to low hills faintly outlined against the night sky.

Dominic's head turns to gaze out over the same landscape. I sense his pause before he speaks.

"There's a house down there. No lights, and the garage roof looks damaged. I don't see any vehicles in the driveway. Maybe we should scope it out and if it's abandoned, use it to crash for the rest of the night?"

Jacob lets out a disgruntled sound, but he seems to consider the possibility before he answers. "That might not be the worst idea. We're not making a lot of progress like this, and who knows when the next train will be by."

"We might be able to scrounge up something useful in the house," Zian adds.

Andreas comes up beside me, stretching his arms. "I could use a longer rest on a floor that's not shaking me around."

No one asks my opinion, but I'm perfectly happy to tramp with the others down through the weedy grass and across the field toward the house. Imagine if the place still has *beds*.

Such luxury.

As we get closer, I make out a sign on a post out front. By the time we reach it, I can read the thicker letters even in the darkness.

"The place is for sale," Zian says in a low voice, frowning at it.

Dominic motions to the smears of dirt on the sign and the crumbling edges. "That's been here for a long time. Doesn't look like anyone's been trying to show off the property lately."

Jacob squints at the garage roof, half of which appears to have caved in. "Could be once the roof went, they gave up, or at least couldn't be bothered to get it fixed right away."

We poke around the edges of the property, confirming there are no vehicles squeezed into the still-roofed side of the garage or parked elsewhere out of view. No one else stirs in or around the house.

Zian scans the walls with the tensed expression that comes over him when he's peering through things. "I don't see anyone inside. It's pretty empty—like they left some basic furniture for buyers to see but that's it."

Jacob walks up to the front door. "All right. Might as well make use of what we've been given."

I can't tell whether the door is already unlocked or if he uses his talent. Either way, we're walking into the front hall moments later.

The place is still and silent other than the creak of the floorboards under our shoes.

Like Zian suggested, the furnishings are totally spartan. The living room holds only a futon sofa and a plain coffee table.

There's a dining room with only the table and four chairs, nothing along the walls. All the kitchen appliances are on hand, but the fridge and the cupboards are bare.

"I guess room *and* board would have been a little much to ask for," Andreas says dryly, and then tries the tap. The faucet sputters and then expels a stream of water into the sink.

His eyebrows shoot up, and a smile crosses his face. "I, for one, could go for a shower before I get back to snoozing."

My skin itches with the grime I'm abruptly aware of coating it. "Me too."

Jacob gives me a pointed look. "You can have your turn last." Then he glances at Andreas. "Go ahead, but don't take too long. We have no idea how much hot water we might get, if any."

Andreas nods and jogs upstairs. He's already ducking into the bathroom when the rest of us follow.

There are only two other rooms up there, a larger bedroom and a smaller one, both with double mattresses on blocky wooden frames and no other furniture. Jacob considers them and then heads back downstairs.

I figure he'll tell me I need to sleep on the floor while he and the other guys share the beds, and at this point I don't even care. I rub my hand over my mouth to suppress another yawn and wait for my chance at the shower.

The guys are at least considerate enough to heed Jacob's instructions and keep their time short, although that's probably more for each other's benefit than for me. I don't think Jacob considered that by having me go last, I can take as long as I want, since there's no one left to delay or stiff on the hot water.

I strip off all my clothes except my necklace, with a faint twinge of uneasiness like Jacob might try to steal it if I remove it from my neck even for a second. Then I start the shower running.

The tub area doesn't come with any toiletries, but there's a pump bottle of liquid hand soap on the sink that's damp from earlier usage. I bring it right into the tub with me.

Luke-warm water pelts me, but it's better than the nothing-at-all I've had for days before. I rub the pearly white soap all over my skin.

My fingers graze the moon-and-droplet tattoo on my thigh. I glance at it, blinking through the spray, abruptly choking up.

One more sign that I belong with the guys I came here with. One more fact they've somehow decided doesn't matter.

I yank my gaze away and finish scrubbing myself down.

My hair's been tied in the same braid since the last time I showered, which was enough days ago that I've lost track. I pull off the elastic, but the strands catch on each other, refusing to fully unwind. So I work the soap into my scalp as well as I can and rinse it off, figuring that's good enough.

As I'm shutting off the water, the door squeaks open, and there's a soft thump on the floor. "We found some clothes in a box in the basement," Andreas says. "And a washer-dryer set. Figured you might like the chance to wear something clean too, even if it's a bit big. I'll grab your old clothes to take them down, if that's okay?"

"Thanks," I call out, feeling weirdly exposed even with the opaque curtain between us.

When he's gone, I ease out to find he's left me with a simple cotton dress that's only a little loose around the waist but falls to my calves when I think it was meant to be knee-length. And it's not exactly my usual style. But I'll take it if it means I can have my hoodie, tank top, and cargo pants back clean in a few hours.

He took *all* my clothes, including my panties and sports bra. Which I'll be glad to have clean too, but I feel oddly exposed even with the dress draped over me like a curtain.

Girding myself, I pull on my sneakers and head out.

Jacob is waiting by the top of the stairs dressed in a tee that's stretched on his muscular physique and a pair of gym shorts, both obviously borrowed like my dress.

"I'm escorting you to your room so the rest of us can get our sleep," he says.

I blink at him. "My room?"

He gives me a chilly smile and gestures for me to follow him.

We walk downstairs and through the kitchen to another, dingier flight of steps that leads to the basement. A damp, mildewy smell tickles my nose as we descend into the depths, but the guys have risked turning on the light down there where there are no windows, so at least it's not pitch black.

On one side, there's a laundry room where the washing machine is rumbling away. On the other side is what I guess is meant to pass for a guestroom to potential buyers, with a steel-framed twin bed and a tiny side table that holds the lamp responsible for the room's light.

It doesn't seem like such a bad deal until Jacob starts back toward the stairs with a caustic remark tossed over his shoulder. "The basement is the only part of the house we can lock from outside the room. You can stay down here until we come for you."

Oh. I'm not being given the gift of privacy but the punishment of a prison. I really shouldn't have expected better, should I?

I sink down onto the edge of the bed and wait for the sound of the door thudding shut at the top of the stairs. Instead, there's a murmured conversation I can't decipher until the end.

"Fine," Jacob mutters. "But you should get some rest too."

It's Andreas's voice that answers. "I will. I need to wind down a bit first anyway."

His lanky form appears, ambling down the steps. He's swapped clothes too, though the new tee hangs more loosely on his leaner frame and he found a pair of jeans that seem to fit him pretty well.

I peer at him. "Adding to the laundry?"

Andreas stops near the foot of the bed and offers me a smile that looks oddly hesitant. "No, I just thought… you might appreciate a little company, without Jake hovering around like a thundercloud. Unless you wanted to go right to sleep?"

My pulse skips a beat, both startled and happy. "No, I'm kind of wound up still too."

And I'll soak up every bit of friendship my guys are willing to offer while I can get it.

There's nothing to sit on down here other than the bed. I debate for a second and then scoot all the way over to the head where the limp pillow is lying. Then I pat the blanket a few feet away in offering.

As Andreas lowers himself onto the edge of the bed at the opposite end from me, giving me plenty of space, my mouth dries up. I haven't really talked to him—to any of the guys—since I let myself break down in front of them in the old facility.

Stalling, I reach back to try to work at the knots in my hair again. Drey watches me for a moment, taking in my wince as I yank on a few strands harder than I meant to.

"It's tangled up pretty bad, huh?"

"That's what happens when it's left braided for days on end." I let out a sigh and dig my fingers between two twisted locks. "It'll be even worse if I sleep on it like this." Maybe I'll have to cut the whole rat's nest off.

A twinge runs over my neck at the thought of leaving it bare, as if my hair is really any protection.

Andreas sets his hands on the mattress and then ventures, "Do you want help? At least I'll be able to see what I'm doing."

My body seems to sway toward him and recoil simultaneously, wanting him close but afraid of wanting too much. I wet my lips, and the trace of disappointment that crosses his gorgeous face at my hesitation defeats my doubts.

"Sure. I'm obviously not getting very far on my own."

I twist on the mattress so that my back is partly to him, and he eases close enough to reach my hair. His knee comes to rest against the small of my back through the thin fabric of the borrowed dress.

Suddenly I'm twice as aware of the fact that I have nothing at all on under that thin layer.

But Andreas simply lifts the tangled locks and starts loosening one knot carefully. Of course, his hands brush my bare neck with his movements.

Each brief contact sends a flash of heat over my skin. It's pooling in my face—and lower down, where at least he won't be able to see it.

Then his next words douse me in cold. "Do you think about Griffin a lot?"

"I—" My voice catches in my throat. I have to swallow before I can continue, wishing I could see his expression now. "Of course. Every day."

"I don't think *he* would like the way Jake is trying to 'avenge' him."

The comment relaxes some of the tension inside me. Drey isn't leading up to an accusation.

A pang of guilt radiates through my chest anyway. "I guess that's hard to know."

While the agony of the bullet tore through him, in the moment when he must have realized he was dying, did some part of Griffin curse me for making such a stupid move? Would he agree with his twin that it was all my fault?

Andreas wiggles a few strands free and lets them drift down across my shoulder. I have to hold myself back from leaning into his gentle touch.

"Do you remember that time with the cookies when we were really little?" he asks.

"The cookies…" I repeat, combing back through my recollections.

Andreas hums to himself, his knuckles gliding across my neck. "We were sitting around the table in the training room having lunch, and right after Griffin asked to use the bathroom, the guardians on duty brought out a plate of chocolate cookies. It was the first time they'd given us any dessert in weeks. We each downed ours like we were sugar-deficient, and Griffin still hadn't gotten back—"

The moment flickers up from the depths of my mind, provoking a twitch of my lips. "And Dominic took his."

Andreas chuckles. "Right. Dom snuck that last one and inhaled it, and then Jake noticed Griffin's was gone and demanded to know who'd stolen his brother's cookie. He was kind of a self-righteous dick even back then, wasn't he?"

I'm outright smiling now. "I think I'd better plead the fifth, or next time he'll have me sleeping in the garage."

Andreas's hands falter for just a moment before they resume their work on my hair. "Zian got all flustered and guilty-looking even though he hadn't done anything, because he was *usually* the one who'd eat the most, so he figured he'd get blamed. But Jake pointed out the extra crumbs by Dom's spot and started glaring at him."

"I thought Dom was going to faint, he looked so agonized." The image swims up through my mind of the much younger version of the man I know now.

"No kidding. So Griffin finally gets back and Jake wastes no time calling Dom out, Dom sits there all horrified with his eyes starting to well up with tears, but just before he can babble a gazillion apologies, Griffin just smiles at him. And says if Dom took it, he must have wanted it a lot, so it's okay."

My throat constricts. "Yeah. That was just… how he was." Griffin would have been able to sense how awful Dominic felt about his petty crime without the other guy needing to say anything.

Andreas shakes his head in bemusement. "Funny how that guy was more mature at five or six than the rest of us are even now."

I arched an eyebrow on the side he'd be able to see. "Speak for yourself." But an unexpected sense of peace has settled over me, as momentary as it might be.

I haven't let myself think about Griffin *that* far back in a long time. Mostly I've just beaten myself up with images from our last night together.

Twisting my head as far as I dare without disrupting the detangling session, I peek at Andreas's face. "You've always been our memory-keeper as well as the memory-reader, haven't you? Keeping track of all our history."

He smiles at me. "I like my collection of stories."

Yes, all the stories he's compiled from the people he saw on missions whose minds he dipped into. The remark sparks another jolt of curiosity. "Did the guardians still have you all go on missions after—after we tried to escape?"

"Yeah," Andreas says, casually enough that my anxiety around asking fades away. "Not as often as before, and they'd still have us on a low dose of whatever drug they kept us doped on so we couldn't do anything too crazy. And the same old threat hanging over us that if we acted out, the others would pay for it."

His smile twists. "After they saw how we reacted to losing Griffin, they must have been even more sure of how effective that warning would be."

Losing Griffin, he says. Not losing both of us.

Because they didn't think of *me* as being lost—because they assumed I'd left them behind on purpose, for reasons I still don't totally understand.

But I don't want to bring that up again now, not when it's gotten me nowhere before and we're having this moment where things feel almost okay.

I gaze across the room toward the washing machine. "Any good stories I missed?"

Andreas clicks his tongue against his teeth. "Let's see. What would the best ones have been…?"

He lowers what must have been an entire section of the braid, now knot-free, and moves to a matted area closer to the middle. His fingers graze my spine.

"There was this woman I noticed in a park in Seattle one time," he says. "She looked like a very bookish, cautious type—hair in a tight bun, cardigan buttoned all the way up, plaid skirt down to her ankles. Sitting there with a book on her lap and a notebook she was writing in propped against it. I figured she had to be a super-committed student studying for exams."

I inhale slowly, resisting the urge to sink back and take in even more of his warmly musky scent. "But I'm guessing that's not what you found in her head."

"Nope. I got all kinds of memories of going out scuba-diving. Cruising around in this boat with fancy radar-checking maps. Swimming way down to find ruins of sunken ships, showing off artifacts she'd found online." He laughs. "An underwater Indiana Jones. I bet she was actually taking notes on what her next dive site could be."

"I bet she'd have lots of interesting stories too."

"Looking for my replacement already?" Drey gives my hair a playful tug. "I've got a whole library in this head. You don't need anyone else."

"Fine," I say, wishing it could be like this with him—with all of the guys—always. "Tell me another one then."

He's silent for a moment, thinking and unwinding my hair. Then he starts to speak in a softer voice than before.

"The last mission I did, I saw an elderly couple in a coffee shop. I noticed them because the woman was gazing around all dreamily while the man looked just… beaten. Sad and weary. I couldn't help wondering how they'd ended up like that—why he'd stayed."

My stomach clenches in anticipation of an awful explanation. "What was it?"

"Well, I searched his head for memories about her. And there were tons of them, going back decades to when they must have been only in their twenties. And in most of the memories, they were so happy, having a blast, building their life together… But then the ones from recently, when they looked a lot older, she was forgetting things, getting cranky, often not even recognizing him…"

An ache squeezes my heart. "She had Alzheimer's."

"Or something like that," Andreas agrees. "But it was hard to say it was a sad story, you know? Because they'd had so many years together before things got bad. And even the way they were right then—while I was watching, there was a moment when she turned to him and said his name and just beamed at him, and all his sadness disappeared. He looked like he figured he was the luckiest guy alive."

The ache expands into something brighter and bittersweet. The words just tumble out. "Griffin would have loved that story."

"Yeah, I bet he would have."

Andreas rests his hand against the back of my shoulder, not quite an embrace but like an offering of one. When I hold still, he moves it to finish teasing apart the last tangled bits of my hair, and I wince inwardly against the pang of my regret.

"He was the heart of our group," Drey goes on. "I mean, it was obvious even when he was there, but it got *really* fucking obvious when he was gone. I've tried to fill that gap, because the other guys sure as hell don't know how to, but I'm not sure I've done all that great a job."

His voice has gone raw. The sound cracks something inside me.

I reach back and grasp his forearm. His hands go still.

"You've been here for me," I say. "You have no idea how much that matters to me."

Andreas swallows audibly. He tips his head forward so I can feel his breath tickle over my hair. My whole body wakes up to tingling alertness and a starker craving I can't pretend away.

But how can I even be thinking about him like that when—

As if he's followed my train of thought, Andreas's voice comes out halting but gentle.

"Tink, there's something you haven't told us about what happened when you and Griffin were getting out of the facility, isn't there?"

Twenty-Seven

Riva

The instant Andreas's question hits me, I choke up. "I—"

No other sound will emerge.

There are things I haven't told them about our failed escape attempt, yes—and reasons I haven't, too.

Andreas combs his fingers through my unknotted hair before trailing them down my arm from shoulder to elbow. His other hand shifts to grip mine where I reached for him.

"Maybe if you explain it to me, I can make the other guys understand. *I* know you wouldn't have hurt any of us on purpose."

Tears well up behind my eyes. For a second, I can't even breathe. I grapple with the impulse to wrench myself away from him—because I'm not really sure I deserve the compassion he's offering.

But he just admitted his own worries to me. He told me stories when I asked.

How can I shut him out when he's the only one who's even tried to let *me* in?

I want someone to know. My mind balks against the admission, but at the same time I have the sense of relief just beyond my fingertips.

I start slowly, my body braced to jerk myself back if the territory starts to feel too treacherous. "It all happened the way I already told you. Until

—we got outside, and we were waiting for the rest of you, and it *seemed* like no one was anywhere nearby. And I just—it was so stupid, doing it right then—but I'd wanted to for so long, and it felt so good being so close to getting free—"

My voice fades out. Andreas waits, a patience to his silence that doesn't feel like pressure.

"I kissed him," I whisper, and suddenly I'm blinking back tears that have overflowed. "I kissed Griffin instead of keeping watch or checking the surroundings, and the second we stopped kissing, they shot him, just like that, he was just *gone*, and I— I couldn't even stay with him or say anything to him while he died because they tackled me and dragged me away."

A sob cuts off anything else I would have said. My head droops.

Both of Andreas's arms come around me. He hugs me close like he did in the car before, but an incredulous note colors his tone when he speaks. "Is *that* the big mistake you've been feeling so guilty about?"

"I screwed up," I mumble between hitches of breath as I fight to regain control over my emotions. "What kind of idiot goes for a kiss when we were in the middle of the most dangerous mission we could possibly attempt—when everyone's lives were on the line— I wanted all of us out there more than anything, and I gambled it all away for a few seconds of… of *that*."

"You said you'd wanted to for a long time," Andreas says hoarsely.

"Yeah." My voice drops even lower. "I loved him. So fucking much. But it didn't do him any good in the end, did it?"

I pause, and then raise my head to meet Andreas's gaze.

He looks strangely stricken in that first moment despite his reassuring words, but he appears to yank his reaction under control. "Of course you did. And it makes sense. You thought you were safe. If you cared about him that much—"

All at once, it feels incredibly important to make one thing crystal clear. Griffin took my secret to his grave, but maybe it never should have been a secret to begin with.

Maybe if my guys had known all along how much my world revolved around them, they never could have believed I'd have betrayed them.

"I loved all of you," I interrupt, with enough force that Andreas's mouth snaps shut. I rub my hand over my face, wiping away the dampness on my cheeks. "I wanted to kiss all of you. I wanted to have what that old man you saw had with his wife—with all of you, for just as many decades or even more. But nothing could happen while we were in the facility anyway, and I had no idea how you'd all react. Griffin knew, because he always knew how everyone was feeling, but I couldn't figure out what to say to the rest of you."

Andreas's eyes have widened. Whatever discomfort he was struggling with before, I can't see any trace of it now.

He raises his hand to the side of my face and strokes his thumb over my cheekbone. A little of his usual good humor dances like a spark in his eyes.

"I can't help noticing you're using the past tense," he says. "I guess we haven't been so loveable lately, huh?"

His tone isn't exactly playful. There's too much pain mixed into it too.

I tip my head into his touch, still holding his gaze. "Things have gotten pretty messed up. But I still think we all belong together. We just have to make it back to where we were before—or maybe it's that we need to figure out something new that works with who we are now. But we're blood. That'll always be true. I've loved you basically my whole life, Drey. A couple of weeks isn't going to erase that."

The relief I tasted before floods me, sweeping through my nerves and washing away the weight I've been carrying as if now I could float right into the air.

This is freedom. This is escape. Part of the answer was inside me all along.

Andreas's jaw works, a less familiar emotion shimmering in his eyes. Then he slides his fingers down to my chin and draws my mouth to his.

I'm not prepared for the maelstrom that hits me with the meeting of our lips. Heat flares between us, and my fingers clutch at the front of his borrowed shirt like I'm holding on to him for dear life.

All the hunger that's simmered up inside me every time we've touched fills my body. It propels me closer, pressing my mouth harder against his with an urgency that burns right down the center of me.

But that heat isn't enough to sear away the icy jolt of panic that hits me at the same time. Even as I cling on to Andreas, my spine stiffens.

I want to fall right into him, and I want to wrench myself away before some horrific catastrophe crashes down on us.

Andreas tips his head to break the kiss with his forehead resting against mine. He caresses my jaw like he did my cheek moments ago, over and over in a gentle motion as my pulse races with the spike of frantic adrenaline.

"It's okay," he says softly. "See? Nothing horrible is happening. You can't ruin anything with a kiss. It wasn't your fault then, and you aren't screwing things up now either. I promise."

My breath hitches with a strange mix of anguish and affection. He understands, and… he's right. There's no blast of gunshots or thunder of footsteps barging into the house.

Nothing about this moment feels like a mistake.

My fingers tighten in his shirt, and I'm yanking him back to me before I have a chance to hesitate in doubt. And if any doubts *had* been rising up about whether he only kissed me to prove a point, the rough sound that escapes him and urgency with which his mouth claims mine erase them in an instant.

Once we've started again, we can't seem to stop. Our lips collide over and over, every kiss even more addictive than the last. I'm inhaling him, downing him like the sweetest of cocktails, and I can't get enough.

A heady energy flows through my limbs, as if the smoky stuff that trails out of us when we bleed is reaching from my veins to pull him even closer. As if it's seeping out of our skin and melding us together, breath to breath and blood to blood, in a way no normal human beings could experience.

Andreas's fingers delve into the strands of my hair he so recently untangled. His other hand slides down the side of my body, marking a scorching trail all the way to my hip.

Then he lifts me right onto his lap, grasping the skirt of the dress as it pools around my thighs so I can straddle him. He sucks my lower lip between his teeth with the slightest prick of pain that sparks into something so much more delicious.

He could eat me whole, and I wouldn't mind one bit. I want to be lost in him, completely intermeshed.

"Riva," he murmurs between kisses. "Wanted you for so long. *Loved* you for so long. You're ours—and mine. All mine."

I let out a whimper of agreement that he drinks straight from my mouth. His hand glides up beneath my dress to cup my bare breast.

The swipe of his thumb over my nipple has me gasping and rocking in his lap. Andreas groans, his other hand dropping to push me closer against him—against the bulge that meets my pussy through our clothes.

The press of him against me sets off a jolt of pleasure so intense it sweeps through my mind. I'm barely thinking any more, barely aware of anything except the roar of unfulfilled need. The tendrils of smoke in my blood writhe as they reach out toward him.

I didn't know that it could feel like this—that I could ache for someone so badly I'm almost sobbing with the sensation. The desperate impulse to sate my hunger has me pushing even closer against him.

"Riva," Andreas mutters again, followed by a series of muffled swear words as he tips us over on the bed. His mouth brands my neck, my shoulder, and my collarbone before he yanks my dress up high enough to close his lips over the peak of my breast.

I cry out, my pussy outright throbbing now. My fingers rake down his chest and up under his shirt, claiming the lean planes of muscle as he devours me.

"Drey, please," I gasp out.

"Fuck," he rasps again with a blissful wash of breath over my nipple, and shoves his hand down between us. At the first stroke of his thumb over my clit, I jerk against his touch.

Bliss sings through my core and amplifies the siren call within me that's wailing for more.

It isn't enough—we could be even closer—every particle of my body is quivering with need and wrenching at me—

I don't know exactly what I'm doing, but I've seen enough poised Hollywood versions of this moment to understand the gist of what's required. My hand gropes at the fly at the loose waist of his jeans, and I manage to pop the button.

We're meant for this. We belong together. For the longest time, I've known that down to my bones, and the anticipation of finally uniting in the most concrete possible way resonates through my soul.

Andreas strokes me more forcefully, the wetness seeping from me turning his fingers slick, his breath coming ragged. As he squirms out of his jeans and boxers with my fumbling assistance, my hand grazes the rigid shaft between his legs.

So hard and so hot, because of me.

At that point, I'm not sure there's anything that could have interrupted our passionate collision. Andreas braces himself over me with just a second's tensing of his arms, his chest heaving, his lips parting as if he means to say something but can't quite find the words.

I wrap my hand around his cock and lift my hips to meet him, and all that escapes him is another groan as he plunges into me.

Being filled is a different kind of burn, giddying and searing and sending a fresh ache of need radiating through my body. I cry out, and Andreas bows his head over me, touching my face even as he drives into me again.

"Don't want to hurt you," he says with the same edge of desperation that's gripping me.

I sway to meet him, clutching at his back, his shoulder. "It's not—it's good. Don't stop."

If we even could.

A strange ringing fills my ears, as if I'm in my head but also not. Like I'm inside Drey as much as he's inside me, breathing with him, moving with him, coasting on the bliss that's swelling wider and faster.

We're disintegrating and recombining as if we're two beings made entirely of the dark haze in our veins, merging into one. One motion, one rhythm, one ripple of pleasure echoing on and on through both of us.

My claws spring from my fingers. The flavor of desire courses into my nose and mouth until my lungs are drenched in it.

Andreas's eyes shimmer red. He lowers his head right next to mine, shaking and thrusting and mumbling words by my ear like a frantic prayer.

"Mine. Love you. Always. Need you. Riva. Stay."

As if there's anywhere I could go. As if there's any part of me that isn't fused with him, caught up in the power resonating through us in tandem.

I dig my hand into his hair, managing to curl my fingers away from his scalp. He inhales with a hiss and bucks into me faster.

And I shatter apart.

I'm a whirlwind, careening in every direction, the final surge of bliss reverberating through me like the blaze of a firework. Andreas lets out a choked sound, and I feel him explode with me, both of us spiraling up and out—

And then back down, together, entangled on the bed, still half-dressed and damp with sweat.

Andreas kisses me long and lingering, looping his arm around my back to hug me to him. Then he nestles his head next to mine while he holds me against him as if he never plans to let me go.

A shaky laugh spills out of him. "That was—that was really something."

"Yes." And somehow something in me wants even more. My nerves quiver like there's still a fire smoldering on deep inside.

Andreas eases back and frowns, touching my collarbone with a tentative finger. "Did you have a bruise here before? I didn't mean to get rough like that."

I glance down, unable to see what he's pointing to, but my gaze catches on his chest. I reach up and brush my finger over the top of his sternum. "You got one too."

There's an imprint on his coppery skin, fingerprint-sized and round, but it doesn't exactly look like a bruise. Or maybe it does, but one formed by the smoky part of our blood rather than the red stuff. Like a dab of shadow risen to the surface of his flesh.

The sense of our beings twining and merging comes back to me with a heady shiver. I glance up at him.

"We got so close we left a mark on each other."

He studies the spot for a few beats longer before lifting his gaze to meet my eyes. A fond smile crosses his lips, the corners of his eyes crinkling with so much affection I automatically smile back.

"I hope that's what it is," he says. "I prefer that to the symbol they marked us with."

I skim my fingers down his side to the tattoo on his thigh that matches mine. His gaze follows their trail and halts on my torso.

He touches a raised ridge of scar that slices across my ribs. Another, shallower but wider, near my belly button. Another, just a thin white line cutting down toward my hip.

His voice comes out taut. "These look pretty new. You got them… from the cage fights?"

I nod, feeling abruptly, weirdly shy. "It was hard to get through them totally unscathed. I did a pretty good job."

"I'm not criticizing you." His jaw tightens, his lean muscles flexing against mine. "When we're finished with this mission, we're going to track those assholes down and obliterate them from existence in every possible way."

My stomach gives a little lurch. He has no idea how thoroughly they've already been obliterated. But that's the last thing I want to talk about—even think about—right now.

Instead, I pull him into another kiss. Our lips move together more tenderly than before, but a fresh waft of desire flares between my legs.

Andreas eases back just an inch with a shaky laugh. "It's amazing, being with you. I feel like… like every part of me is more *alive*."

My smile stretches wider, my momentary uneasiness fading away. "Yeah."

We sit up together, Andreas's arms wrapped around me, and he kisses my forehead, but a trace of tension returns to his stance.

"I want to just stay here with you," he says, "but I've got to— Jacob and the others have to pull their heads out of their asses and see what idiots they're being. You haven't deserved any of this. The bullshit has to end *now.*"

Twenty-Eight

Riva

The second Andreas leaves the basement, his borrowed jeans hastily pulled back on and his tight curls still rumpled, the room feels achingly empty.

Sitting on the bed, I rub my arms, but that only rekindles the memory of his hands running over me, his body moving against mine, reminding me of what I'm now missing. I've become a live wire, my nerves risen up through my skin so that every sensation is twice as sharp.

My claws are still out; I can't quite will them to retract. The scent of our shared desire still laces the air, thickly enough that I taste it with every breath.

My blood thrums on through my veins, pulsing with an exhilarated energy I don't know where to aim.

I touch the spot on my collarbone where Andreas said I was marked. A fresh tingle ripples through my body.

I can sense him—vaguely, but with enough of his flavor that I know it's him. He's standing still, high enough above me that he must be on the second floor.

That's all I can tell, but the knowledge sends a new thrill through me. If we're separated again, I don't need to cut myself open to track him now.

Did it happen simply because we had sex, or was there something more to the heightened emotions of that collision that bound us together more tightly than before?

Can he sense me too?

A smile touches my lips, and the washing machine rumbles to a stop with a harsh beep.

Apparently I'm on laundry duty since I'm the one stuck down here. I spring off the bed and go over to move the damp clothes to the dryer.

It's a small load, so it shouldn't take long. I can't wait to get back into my regular clothes. This dress makes me feel like a dwarf.

Someday, maybe I'll have a proper wardrobe, multiple outfits to pick between… that I don't have to leave behind after just a few days because brutal guardians launch an attack. Not that I have high fashion aspirations, but a little variety would be nice.

As I set the dryer running, a whiff of a different sort of emotion reaches my nose. The tang of stress hormones unfurls through the air.

Those aren't coming from me, and there's no one else in the room. Frowning, I turn my head and prowl through the space, trying to follow the trail.

I end up underneath a vent for the furnace, which isn't currently running. Another waft of tension prickles into my lungs from above.

The vents will run all through the house. In my overly sensitized state, a trace seeping down from the higher floors must feel like a lot.

But how upset must the guys be for even a trace to trickle all the way down here?

I push up on my toes toward the vent and realize I can make out voices too. Way too faint and muffled for me to distinguish any words, but they're obviously raised, curt and hostile.

Is Andreas arguing with the other guys—about me? I guess it would be an argument if he's trying to convince them to stop being such jerks.

I shift my weight, uneasiness coiling around my gut. I don't want him fighting my battles for me, all alone.

If he's arguing on my behalf, I should at least be there to back him up.

I don't really expect to get anywhere, but my restless feet carry me up the basement steps, my nerves outright buzzing now. My fingers clutch the knob—and it turns smoothly.

I freeze for a second before understanding hits me. Drey didn't bother to lock the basement when he left.

He didn't see any reason he needed to.

A pang of joy thrums through me alongside my apprehension. I *can* go up there and stand with him, then.

Before I can think any farther ahead than that, my body is already rushing forward. My bare feet pad across the worn floorboards to the main staircase and up it, moving swiftly but silently with the stealth that comes automatically to me.

The voices come into sharper clarity as I hurry upward. Andreas is speaking, so terse his tone alone makes my heart ache.

Then I register what he's saying.

"…the whole reason I started 'getting cozy' with her was so she'd open up about things she wouldn't have told us otherwise. I held up my end of the deal. Now you've got to listen."

What?

My legs lock at the top of the stairs. I stare through the doorway into the shadowy bedroom ahead of me where Andreas stands by the bed.

All three of the other guys are poised around him, but he's facing Jacob, whose gaze slides from Andreas to me. A glitter even chillier than usual lights in his fierce eyes.

"Yes," he says, giving Drey a smile so sharp it could flay skin. "That was the deal. And now she knows it too."

Andreas turns, his gaze snagging on mine. His mouth opens, but no sound comes out.

My feet propel me forward, one step and another, through the doorway. Then I can't bear to get any closer to him.

My own voice catches in my throat before I force out the question. "You were acting friendly just to trick me into telling you things?"

Andreas's expression goes sickly. "It wasn't like that, not exactly. And it isn't like that now."

"It was exactly like that," Jacob interjects, focusing on me again. "We had a little conversation right after we arrived at the college, while you were locked up in your room. I wanted to keep you out of our investigations, but Andreas insisted that we should get you involved so we could see if you'd give something away in the moment. He promised he'd convince you to trust him so you wouldn't be as guarded."

Pain lances right down the middle of me. My fingers flex at my sides, the tips aching around my claws.

"You argued in front of me about whether I should come along," I say, my voice not much more than a rasp.

Jacob brings out his vicious smile again. "Yes, we did. We had to sell the idea in a way you'd believe. And it gave Drey his first chance to play your champion."

They staged the whole conversation. They *all* knew.

My gaze jerks to Zian and to Dominic, and their tensed expressions confirm it. There isn't a hint of surprise from either of them, only trepidation about how I'm going to react.

"Riva, I swear that has nothing to do with tonight or—or—" Andreas stumbles and then recovers. "I believe you. I realized we were wrong. I—"

"He's very good at it, isn't he?" Jacob interrupts. "Got you to let your hair down and everything." He glances at Andreas. "You can stop now. I can't see how you'll get anything more out of her than you already have."

"Will you shut the fuck up, Jake?" Andreas snaps, but my mind is already spinning back through our interlude in the basement.

He brought up Griffin. Told a story about guilty secrets. He prodded me about there being something I hadn't told them about the night Griffin died.

That whole thing—the affection he offered, the supposed confessions he made—it was all to lull me into thinking I could open up.

Did he come up here and tell them just how very much I opened up to him? Jacob is talking as if he knows everything.

"Why would you— How could you—?" I don't know how to voice the question that's choking me. There's a wail lodged in the base of my throat, expanding with a dull throbbing.

I loved you. All I ever did was love you, and you all…

Jacob narrows his eyes at me. "You actually think you deserve better?"

His sneering tone sparks a spurt of anger that sears up through my chest. It rattles through my ribs and grips hold of the vibration building at the back of my mouth.

My hand shoots up to close around my pendant. My thumb clicks the cat and yarn apart and together, apart and together, but the rhythm does nothing to settle the anguished fury that's thrumming through my nerves, rising to a roar.

I could hurt them just as much as they've hurt me. I could tear them a-fucking-part.

I glance at Dominic and Zian again, my voice hoarse. "Are both of you okay with all of this? Really?"

Zian's mouth opens and closes and opens again. "We needed to know —we needed to be sure…" he says weakly.

Dominic's face has hardened with tension. "We've had to look out for ourselves."

Themselves. The four of them together and me on the outside, where they've shoved me as hard as they can.

My teeth grit. The prickling vibration jabs its way up my throat.

No. I close my eyes, willing down the vicious urge that's shaking me from the inside out. But I'm too raw, too churned up already. I can't get a grip on it.

And Jacob's voice follows me into the darkness behind my eyelids. "You don't have to play *our* friend anymore now. You're not getting anywhere with that. So let's see who you really are already."

My lungs ache to scream right back at him, to show him what he's daring me to do. To make him wish he never mocked and berated my misery.

No, no, *no*.

My thumb wrenches at my pendant again—and the joint cracks. The two pieces fall apart in my hand, the ball of yarn tumbling against my palm, the cat still dangling from the chain around my neck.

I broke it—Griffin's necklace.

Like I broke him. Like I could break *all* of them if I just let myself—

"Riva," Andreas is saying, and I get the impression he's been talking longer than I've been hearing. "He's being a fucking idiot. Listen to me. I—"

He takes a step toward me, and my body recoils. A sliver of a shriek hitches from my throat.

I clap my hand over my mouth, but I see him wince. I taste the pain that one brief smack of the power in me provoked.

The thing squirming and thrumming inside me craves more. It's clawing its way up from my chest, on the verge of exploding.

I am going to destroy everything, and part of me is going to revel in it.

Jacob steps toward me too, his eyes glinting like ice. "That's right. Tell us how you really feel."

I yank my gaze from him to Andreas, who's frozen in his tracks. He's looking at me as if he can see the storm of emotion raging inside me—or maybe it's so close to the surface now it's written all over my face.

I back up, and the door slams shut behind me with a heave of Jacob's talent. He stalks closer with that cruel smirk I want to scratch off his face.

Break him, twist him, make him suffer. And the rest of them just standing by, watching him hurt me. Lashing out in their own ways.

Show them all what real pain is.

No.

The protest barely stems the surge of rage inside me. My vision starts to haze.

I have to get away.

My hand shoots out, snapping the chain with the movement. The necklace slips from my fingers and clinks onto the floor.

"Stay away from me," I gasp out. "I don't want to hurt you."

But I also do, I do.

And the only escape from the pressure howling through my body is to throw myself toward the window that's between me and Jacob.

My shoulder slams into the pane first. I'm hurtling fast enough to shatter the glass and careen out into the open air.

Shards slice across my arms and calves, but I barely notice those tiny pains. For a few seconds, I'm in freefall, hurtling through the air.

My body rotates on instinct, and I hit the ground with a puff of exhaled breath and a jolt through my limbs.

Voices are already carrying from the building behind me, my name ringing out through the jumble of shouts. Panic races through me ahead of a renewed roar of anger.

They're going to come after me.

They won't let me go.

My legs propel me forward. I sprint across the grass as fast as my feet can fly, veering away from the lane and the road.

Farther down, near the train tracks, scattered saplings offer a tiny bit of cover. I race toward them automatically, my pulse thundering in my ears, my lungs shuddering with the power that wants so badly to burst out.

I'm a monster. Only a monster would want to put the men she's loved through the agony I can sense I'm capable of.

Only a monster would *enjoy* the idea.

My name pierces the air again. Someone's hollering at me to stop.

No, I can't. I can't.

They've poisoned me and beaten me down with words and lies. Maybe they're monsters too, and not because of the powers inside them.

Maybe I'd be right to destroy them.

Shut up!

I just have to get away, far away, and then…

And then what's left? My whole life has been them, us.

We are blood.

If we aren't, if I'm nothing to them, if everything I thought we had has been washed away, how can I be anything other than a monster?

My legs pump; my feet pound against the uneven ground. A different sound emerges from up ahead: the rumble of an engine.

The train's lights flash between the trees. It's whipping toward me, just seconds away.

Tears blur my sight, and still the hunger inside me to deal out a deluge of pain screams on and on. It won't let me go either.

Not while I'm still alive.

I don't think. My body swerves of its own accord, closer to the tracks. To the one simple solution that could kill both the monster and my own agony.

It's gravel rattling under my feet now. The train roars toward me with a blare of its horn.

I fling myself onward to meet it, and one final cry penetrates the anguished haze in my head.

"Wildcat, *no!*"

Jacob's voice. Jacob's old nickname for me, that he hasn't used once since I found him again.

It hits me like a plea echoing up from the past, yanking me back to where I always thought I was meant to be.

What the hell am I doing?

I wrench myself to the side, but it's a little too late.

The full force of the speeding train catches the side of my body. It whips me around, knocking my arm out of its socket, shattering my ribs.

Pain blazes through every particle of my being as I crash into the grass beyond the shoulder. Then my mind fizzles out.

Twenty-Nine

Dominic

Riva looks so fragile with her small frame silhouetted by the train's headlights. I was worried before, but the image sends a bolt of pure terror through me.

She wouldn't really— She doesn't mean to—

Even as my mind makes its silent protests, I push my legs forward even faster, or at least I try to. My balance wavers on the uneven ground.

The others have all pulled ahead of me, but they're still not close enough. My arm shoots out as if I can grab her across that distance and wrench her to safety.

Jacob's voice rings through the night, raw and frantic. "Wildcat, *no!*"

At his shout, Riva appears to swing in the opposite direction. But before even a wisp of hope can rise up inside me, the side of the onrushing locomotive slams into her.

She spins into the air with a spurt of liquid blood and smoke that shocks a cry from my throat. The mutilated form that falls to the ground near a cluster of saplings barely looks human, let alone like our Riva.

"Dom!" Jacob yells in the same panicked tone as before.

It comes down to me. I don't know how we're going to fix any of the mess we found ourselves in that sent her running to begin with, but I'm the only one who can ensure she's even alive for us to try.

If there's enough left of her to save. If I can make it to her in time.

A surge of my own panic pushes my limbs beyond what I thought I was capable of. The train roars on past us, but I'm barely aware of the cars rattling along the tracks.

There's only that small, shadowed form lying motionless by the trees.

Zian gets to her first. He falls to his knees and reaches his hands out to her, clenching his fingers before he actually touches her like he's afraid he'll somehow make it worse.

He leans backward, his face contorting with his wolfish features, and tips his head toward the sky. An anguished groan reverberates through the air.

My open coat flaps against my sides. I yank at it as well as I can without slowing down, heaving it from my shoulders and letting it whip off me.

I'm going to need to bring every bit of my ability to this moment, every piece of me that can contribute. No hiding, no holding back.

Andreas stumbles to a stop by Zian. With one glance at Riva's body, his eyes widen and a mumbled curse falls from his lips.

Jacob is already there, dropping down and bringing his hands to her face with a sudden gentleness I had no idea he still had in him.

His fingers slide down to her neck. "She's still got a pulse. Not much of one but—*Dom*. She needs you."

"Coming," I gasp out, hurtling the last several paces to where she's lying.

Even in the dim moonlight, partly draped in the spindly shadows of the saplings, it's a horrifying scene. She looks like a jointed doll who's been smashed on the floor by a malicious kid.

Her one arm is drenched with blood, arching away from her body at an angle that makes me wonder how much it's even still attached to her shoulder. On the same side, her torso is crumpled in, more blood drenching the pale dress and the grass beneath her. Her motionless face looks pure white except for the speckling of blood across her lips.

Streams of dark smoky stuff gush up into the air, twining with the shadows.

I collapse to the ground next to Riva, already flinging one of my extra appendages around the nearest sapling. As the suckers dig in tight to the smooth bark of the trunk, I wrap the other around her waist and set my hand on her throat.

Jake pulls back to give me room, his whole body trembling.

"Do *something*," he says, but his voice is so hoarse I know he doesn't mean it as a criticism.

Just this once, I'm the strong one, and the rest of them can only watch helplessly.

He was right about her pulse. It stutters, faint and fading against my palm.

I focus on that, close my eyes, and haul all the energy I can from the tree I'm gripping.

The sapling is full of life—vibrant, green, growing. So much fucking potential that I can see the massive tree it'd have eventually grown into in the back of my mind.

I drag all of that out of it, quivering across my back, and pour it into Riva.

I don't know all the parts of her that might be shattered or crushed, but it doesn't matter. My power senses what to align and seal.

My own heart thuds on at a sickly frantic rhythm as I pull more life, and more, and more out of the sapling.

The tree bows, its branches sagging, its bark blackening. Beneath my touch, Riva's flesh fuses back together.

Bones snap into place and meld their broken edges. Blood vessels reattach themselves.

I will more of the vital fluid to form in her arteries and veins. The flavor of raw meat forms in the back of my mouth and my stomach roils, but I ignore both sensations.

I'm inflicting death as much as I'm giving life, but only the second part matters.

Only Riva matters.

Flashes of memory dart by behind my closed eyelids. The moments when we'd figure out the answer to a problem in the same moment, and she'd shoot a softly sly smile my way to match my own.

All the times when I'd be lost in a tangle of emotions after a session where the guardians pushed me to use my talents in ways I'd never have wanted to, and she'd come over to work patiently alongside me until I'd decided what I wanted to share.

The day when she begged one of them to put a wildflower from the outdoor training field into a pot for me so I could keep it in my room, because I'd commented on how it was going to get trampled before too long.

The time Andreas challenged me to run her all the way around the track piggyback style, and we collapsed at the end in a fit of laughter, the most ridiculous but also the most free I'd felt in ages.

And then there's the moment when I healed her after the club night, when she talked about how much she wanted to fix things. The way she's hesitated to ask for my help even when she was on the verge of collapsing, because she could tell I don't like what my power costs me.

How could we not have realized sooner that the guardians were the ones who'd deceived us? How could *I* not have realized sooner?

I was so concerned about my monstrousness, about the deformities sprouting from my back, but it wasn't my physical strangeness she ran away from. No, it was my attitude, cold and silent while Jacob laid into her, shying away from her gestures of friendship.

I can't even hate what I am right now, even if it was the guardians' awful tests that grew most of this part of me, because my strangeness is what's saving her.

The sapling dwindles completely, crumbling into deadened dust. The blood seeping from Riva's body has slowed, but I can still feel it trickling out of her as both smoke and viscous liquid.

Shifting my position, I extend my appendage to the next nearest tree. Another surge of life energy, another being I'm consigning to death.

The woman beneath my hand is breathing now, in little spurts of air. Her pulse remains sluggish, but it beats stronger against my fingers even if it's slow.

She's coming back to us, bit by bit. Please let her make it all the way.

As the worst of her injuries bind back together, I become aware of the toll the healing has taken on me, even when I'm only acting as a conduit. Pain throbs at the base of my skull; my mouth tastes like ash as well as blood.

A tremor runs through my bones, and a hand rests on my back to steady me. "You're doing good," Andreas says raggedly. "You're really doing it, Dom."

The scuff of footsteps tells me Jacob is pacing. I don't need Griffin's talent for reading emotions to sense the tension rolling off of the guy.

Zian lets out another pained grunt. "Is there anything else you need? Anything we can do?"

I open my eyes and peer down at Riva, inhaling deeply as I do. The headache splinters right through my brain, and I'm not sure I can propel any more energy into her until I've rested at least a little.

"Does anyone… have any water?" I croak. Both she and I could probably use it.

Jake stops and makes a brusque gesture toward Zian. "You can get back to the house fastest. There are a few bottles in the bag that had the food."

Zee dashes off without hesitation, and Jake stoops over Riva, staring down at her face. From his hard expression, I'd think he's as coolly emotionless as usual if it weren't for the anxious flexing of his hands.

His gaze jerks up to meet mine. "Why hasn't she woken up? Did you fix everything inside?"

Drey frowns, his hand adding more reassuring pressure to my shoulder. "He's obviously been doing everything he can, as well as he can."

I cough and manage to speak a little clearer. I don't want to tell him that I can't say for sure whether she *will* wake up.

"I think I healed all the most important parts. She seems to be stable." Another thought jabs at me, too insistent for me to ignore. "I'm going to heal the poison out of her too."

Jacob's features twitch with what might be a suppressed flinch. "Of course," he snaps. "Heal everything. Just get on with it."

I try to swallow past the dryness of my throat. "I'll—I'll keep going, I just need a moment—"

"It's fine, Dom. That was amazing." Andreas gives my shoulder another squeeze, but when he looks down at Riva, there's no mistaking the anguish that contorts his face.

"She ran right at that train," he says in a low voice.

Jacob swipes his hand over his jaw. "She was running away from us. She wanted to get away from us *that* badly…"

His voice trails off with a rasp.

"I don't think it was only that." Andreas hesitates. "Just for a second, while you were riling her up, I felt— *We* all had new talents emerge in the past few years. We haven't seen anything like that from her. Yet."

My attention drops to the unconscious woman we've surrounded. I study the body I've been melding back together.

Does she have her own unnerving abilities that she's keeping to herself, as much as I've done the same?

I didn't sense anything physically unusual about her while I healed her, but I'm not sure if I would have.

"It doesn't matter," Jacob snarls, shoving himself to his feet. "We fucked up. I fucked up, so much—"

His voice cuts off with a strangled sound—and the tearing of roots from soil. One of the other saplings rips right out of the ground, yanked by his power, and whirls across the field.

Drey tenses. "Dom might need—"

I don't hear the rest of his sentence, because right then Riva's eyelids flutter. Flutter and open, the bright brown irises shining up at me.

Thirty

Riva

Everything hurts.

I'm not even exaggerating. I mean, there's my chest and my ribs and my stomach and my head. My shoulder and my hip and my knee, all consumed by a deep ache that rises and ebbs with my breath.

But even my ears prickle. My big toes throb. My fucking pinky finger twinges with pins and needles.

What the hell— Where am I?

I blink and find myself staring up at Dominic, his shadowed, handsome face etched with worry and strain. Stars speckle the night sky beyond him.

I'm lying on my back. Grass tickles the backs of my bare arms. The air is cooling damp patches all across my torso and legs.

Dominic lifts his hand from where it was resting at the base of my throat. Something else shifts across my belly; something thin and sinewy… like the things I can see sprouting over Dom's shoulders.

The shapes of them are vague in the moonlight, but I make out the curves of rows of suckers along the undersides of the things. I blink again, but the view doesn't change.

He has two *tentacles* growing out of his upper back.

The words slip from my lips before I have a chance to think about them, more a creak than a voice. "When did you become an octopus?"

Dominic's expression shutters. I can feel him closing himself off from me, and the memories from what happened right before this moment rush back to me with a jolt.

The farmhouse. Andreas, in the basement. And afterward—everything they said—all the things I hadn't realized—

I close my eyes, sinking back into the physical pain that's somehow more comforting than the swell of anguish that wants to swallow my whole mind. And Dom answers my question.

"About three and a half years now. We've all been evolving."

His voice is tight but even, no hostility in it. More pieces click together in my head.

This is what he's been hiding under his ever-present coats—what I saw him flinging at the guardians when they attacked us at the campus townhouse. What he never wanted me to see.

"Why…?" I rasp, and can't quite form the question.

Dominic's hand comes to rest on my sternum. "I'm healing you. You—you got bashed up pretty bad. I'm patching you up as quickly as I can, but it's a work in progress."

When I open my eyes again, his are shut. A rush of warmth flows through me, some at my chest where his fingers are pressed, but mostly from the tentacle lying across my abdomen.

The sensation radiates through my flesh. If the healing energy he conjured before was a stream, this is a river, coursing through every crack and gash that needs to be knit together.

The other tentacle, the one not wrapped around my belly, veers off toward… a nearby sapling. The tip curls around the thin trunk.

Its branches are sagging, the whole tree bowing toward the ground as its bark darkens as if overtaken by rot.

Dominic must notice my gaze. "The energy has to come from somewhere. It all balances out one way or another."

Oh. The flowers and weeds I saw him picking before—he was using them for healing energy.

As I bring my attention back to him, the arc of the tentacles I can see arcing over his shoulders *expands*. Just a little, maybe half an inch, but unmistakable. Like they're pulling farther out of his skin.

"They're growing," I mumble.

Dom lets out a ragged chuckle. "They do that. When I use my power."

Understanding hits me like a smack across the face. Oh, shit. "That's why you didn't want to— You don't have to. You don't—"

His other hand closes around mine—gently so that he doesn't provoke fresh pains in the delicate joints there. "It's fine, Riva. You need this. I'm *glad* I can do it." His voice dips. "I'm glad you're still with us."

I need this… because of the train. That final memory roars up to the surface, and I wince instinctively as if I'm feeling the impact all over again.

Footsteps stomp closer. "Is she okay? Don't do anything that could hurt her."

"I know," Dominic says, almost a growl, as my gaze flicks from him to the other man now standing within my limited view.

Jacob stares down at me, his expression tense, his normally cold eyes blazing as if they've been lit with blue flames. His hands are clenched at his sides, the tendons standing out in his arms.

I jerk my gaze away with a lurch of my heart that sends a new ache through my chest. I don't want… to see him, speak to him, deal with any more of his bullshit.

Jacob lets out a grunt of frustration, and then there's a groaning sound, like a weakening branch pushed by the wind. Somewhere beyond my field of vision, Andreas swears with a rustle of footsteps over the grass.

"You can't keep doing that. Calm the fuck down."

"How am I supposed to calm down when she—"

Another set of footsteps thumps toward us from farther away, bringing Zian's breathless voice with them. "I brought three water bottles—totally full." He stops with a hitch. "Is she awake?"

I'm not sure I want to see or speak to Zian either. I close my eyes again, descending into the painful darkness of my body.

"Give one to Dom," Andreas is saying. "He's wearing himself ragged. Maybe Riva should have some too."

Dominic speaks in an uncertain tone. "I don't know if her stomach and… everything that connects to it are fully recovered. She was hit pretty hard all the way down her side."

Jacob pipes up next, with an edge that rankles me. "Then get on with healing the rest of it."

"He's doing his best," Andreas snaps. "Why don't you find something more useful to do than tearing up trees?"

At a whisper of fabric and a shift in the air, I know Andreas has knelt at my other side, across from Dominic. I *definitely* don't want to look at him—don't want to think about the vulnerability and passion I offered him when his only goal was to unravel me.

I can't do this anymore. I don't wish I'd embraced the train head on, beyond repair, but that one fact hasn't changed.

If I stay with my guys any longer, either they'll tear me apart or I'll do the same to them. Maybe both.

They don't want me. What's the point in sticking around anyway?

Dominic's hand against my sternum goes abruptly limp. The current of warmth fades away, but I realize I'm not half as achy as I was when I first woke up. I don't feel all that much worse than I have on average over the past several days, with Jacob's literal venom eating away at me.

As if he's sensed that thought, Dom brushes his fingers over my forehead, swiping stray strands of hair away from my eyes. "I drew all the poison out of you too. You won't have to deal with that anymore."

As he's probably happy about, since it means he won't have to deal with it either. Although if he's going to be mad at anyone about however much staving off the toxin's effects have expanded the tentacles he's so intent on concealing, he really needs to take that up with Jacob, not me.

Part of me wants to sink right into the earth and never return, but I'm aware that's not a viable strategy.

I force myself to open my eyes. Focusing on the shadowy landscape beyond my feet rather than any of the men around me, I flex my muscles and ease into a sitting position.

Halfway up, I sway. Dominic's hand shoots out to steady me, with a tremor that runs through it as he catches my weight.

How much did the healing process take out of him?

I lean my hands into the grass so I can hold my own balance, tensing and relaxing each section of my limbs to get a sense of how much they can endure.

I might be able to walk right now. I think running is probably out of the question. Definitely no scaling cliffsides or squeezing through ventilation shafts.

Thankfully I should never have to do either of those things again, since they weren't my idea in the first place.

There's a moment of silence, as if the men are waiting to see if I'm going to say something. Andreas clears his throat.

"Riva, I'm sorry," he says, his voice hoarse despite his efforts. "So sorry. I only wanted to make sure we could trust you—and I'd seen that we could. Tonight wasn't about trying to trick you. I really did want to just talk with you. The rest… The rest I wasn't expecting at all."

A noise comes out of me that's something like a snort. At the same time, ridiculous tears burn at the edges of my eyes.

I am not going to fucking cry over this manipulative lying asshat.

Andreas goes on, still strained but not showing any offense at my response. "I went upstairs to tell the guys that they'd been wrong—*we'd* been wrong—and that you'd been telling the truth about everything. I would have told you the whole truth once I knew they'd come around."

Easy for him to claim that now.

My hand lifts instinctively to my neck, but there's nothing for my fingers to close around. With a jab of anguish, I remember that I broke the necklace. Dropped it.

It's probably lying on the floor back there in the farmhouse. Not that it matters when it's cracked apart—

Another form crouches right in front of me, hand outstretched. I'm about to recoil from Jacob when my gaze catches on the glint of sliver resting on his fingers.

"This is yours, Wildcat," he says, his eyes piercing into mine. "I twisted the broken bit back together. It should hold until we can get it properly soldered."

I don't want to take anything from him—but it doesn't really count when the thing was already mine anyway, does it?

My hand darts out to snatch the pendant from his hand. I tug the chain around my neck to attach it in its proper place, feeling abruptly like I'm a wild animal they're all trying to coax into tameness.

I'm not the one who's been going around savaging and shunning people for no reason at all.

"Okay," I say stiffly, my voice still a little weak. "I'm healed enough that I can get by. You can all go back to your quest now."

Zian steps into view and stalls at the edge of my vision. "What are you saying?"

Do I really have to spell it out?

"You don't need me. You don't want my help. I'm finally getting the message loud and clear. You can stop jerking me around, and I'll go find something else to do with the rest of my life and you can go on with yours."

"Riva."

Andreas touches my shoulder, but I jerk away from him. I glare at him before casting my gaze around me at all four of the guys.

The tears well up again anyway. I cracked something open down in the basement with Andreas, and apparently all Dominic's work didn't stitch that part of me shut again.

My emotions bubble up to the surface faster than I can catch them. "I thought we were blood, and we'd be there for each other like we always used to be. That you'd see how much you all still meant to me and know I hadn't changed. But that was obviously stupid of me, so I'm accepting reality."

I move to get up, but Jacob catches me first. He looms over me, his knees coming to rest against mine, his hands framing my face and holding it so I have to look at him.

Unless I close my eyes.

But even though I refuse his gaze, he speaks anyway, his voice taut and emphatic. "It wasn't stupid. I have been the biggest fucking asshole and an idiot on top of that. I don't know what I'd have done if we'd lost you too, if I'd pushed you all the way to— Please don't go."

It was his voice that brought me back before I went too far; his nickname, his plea. The memory makes my skin tighten.

Even after everything, his touch and his closeness send a heated tingle over my skin. I don't *want* that. No fucking way.

I squirm backward so fast Jacob releases his hold, but I bump into Dominic. With a strangled sound, I finally push myself to my feet.

My legs wobble but hold me. The torn dress clings to my body with drying blood—*my* blood, from injuries now sealed.

"I don't know why it suddenly matters to any of you," I spit out, blinking hard against the tears I refuse to acknowledge. "You couldn't have known or liked me very much even before if you believed I turned on all of you that easily."

Zian's mouth twists. "You don't understand."

"No," I shoot back. "I don't. But I don't need to."

Andreas steps toward me again but doesn't try to touch me this time. "I can show you."

My gaze darts to him of its own accord. There's so much fraught emotion in his eyes that my throat closes up at the sight.

"I can project the memory into your mind," he goes on. "My memory of what happened that night for the four of us who never made it out of the facility. It doesn't justify anything, but it might explain a little."

My body balks, but curiosity gnaws at the back of my mind. What could possibly have happened that would make a difference?

Maybe it won't. Maybe I'll feel just as done with them as I do now.

Either way, at least I'll know.

I glance around to check if any of the other guys is going to object to his offer, but they stay quiet, braced and waiting. I turn back to Andreas.

"Fine. But make it quick."

He hesitates. "You might want to sit down."

As much as I hate to admit it, he has a point, given how shaky my muscles still are. I lower myself onto a patch of grass that isn't soaked with my blood, and Andreas kneels a few feet away from me.

He focuses on me with the ruddy sheen coming over his eyes, and the moonlit fields around me disappear.

I'm dashing out through my cell's doorway, catching Dominic's eye as he bursts from his room farther down the hall.

"They did it," I say with a grin stretching my face, but it's Andreas's voice. Because this is Andreas's memory—I'm seeing everything that went down through his eyes.

We race into the stairwell, flinging ourselves upward to reach the others as quickly as possible, and a troop of guardians barrel into view.

As if they were ready the whole time. As if they knew we'd be coming.

I hear a grunt from below, and then a tranquilizer dart has already struck me in the neck. Another guardian leaps forward with a taser that spews electricity through my body. I stumble on the steps—

A momentary blackness. Then I'm sitting in one of the smaller training rooms with Dominic, Zian, and Jacob arranged around me. All of our hands are cuffed behind our backs.

A few guardians stand around the room with weapons braced at their sides. Another paces back and forth in front of us.

"What you tried to do tonight was highly irresponsible, ungrateful, and totally misguided. Did you really think there was some wonderful life waiting for you in the world out there, without our help?"

Andreas's jaw tightens at the suggestion that we *need* the guardians, that they're helping us rather than holding us down. We all keep quiet.

The guardian goes on. "At least one of you had the foresight to realize she was better off making her own arrangements with us than spending the rest of her existence on the run."

Andreas's head jerks up unbidden. I stare at the guardian through his eyes, the others doing the same.

There are no thoughts or emotions in the memory, only what I can interpret from the sensory details, but I think they all must have noticed that neither I—as Riva—nor Griffin were in the room. They must have been wondering what happened to us.

The guardian swipes a tablet off a desk at the side of the room and stalks back toward us. "We're all built to look out for ourselves. You're lucky we take as good care of you here as we do. Remember this the next time you have the urge to start scheming."

He spins the tablet toward us with a video playing on the screen. Surveillance footage, dark and a little grainy because of that darkness.

It's a view of the empty front yard outside the facility, lit only by the hazy glow of a few security lamps. A moment later, two figures dash into view.

Me—the actual me—and Griffin. I'm distantly aware of my real heart thumping faster in horrified anticipation of what I know is going to come.

I didn't realize—I don't really want to watch him die all over again.

But I can't close my eyes, because they're Andreas's eyes, and he took in every second of this.

The figures on the screen scan the area. The one that's a younger me pauses and then steps toward Griffin, pulling him into a kiss.

Andreas flinches.

Just as the real me lets Griffin go, the shot comes, blasting into his body. His frame jerks, his legs crumpling.

But that's not even the most horrifying thing.

The me on the screen doesn't scream out and struggle against an onslaught of attackers the way I know I did. She looks calmly down at Griffin's body and then raises her head to nod to someone outside the footage.

A small squad of guardians appears. One of them pats my shoulder in a way that looks almost friendly.

They march me over to a truck and let me hop inside. I smile at them from the window before the truck drives away.

I fucking *smile*.

Back where Andreas is, Jacob thrashes against his handcuffs, pushing himself toward the guardian. "Where is he? Where's my brother? What did you do to him?"

The guardian flicks off the tablet and gives Jacob a nonchalant look.

"I'm afraid your brother didn't survive. An important reminder of the potential consequences when you step out of line."

"You fucking bastard!" Jacob snarls—and the memory falls away.

I'm sitting in my own body again, surrounded by cool fresh air and rustling grass. I gulp in a breath, my eyes burning all over again.

"It wasn't true," I burst out. "That isn't how it happened. I never—they attacked me too. I tried to fight them—I tried to get to Griffin—"

"I know," Andreas says softly. "I believe you. They must have doctored the video to splice in footage they faked."

I stare at him. "But you did believe it. You believed it this whole time."

Dominic speaks up, quiet and a little ragged. "When they showed us the footage, we were already in shock. And then seeing that Griffin had died… It messed with our heads, made it hard to know what to believe. And you never did come back."

I thump my hand against the ground. "I did. I did as soon as I fucking could."

"You did," Jacob agrees. "And we made a total mess of that too. Me more than anyone." His jaw works as he lowers his gaze.

And maybe that does make sense, considering he was the one the most messed up. It was his brother who died—his twin.

But just looking at him makes something in me cringe away with the memory of all the harsh words and vicious commands he's hurled at me since I broke them out.

I don't know what to do with any of this. I don't know where to go. Here I am in nothing but a ragged, bloody dress that doesn't even fit right, not even sure what state I'm in, no money, no food…

With a monster lurking inside me, just waiting until someone makes me angry enough.

I swipe my hand across my mouth and look at the guys again. "What do we do now? The way you're picturing it, anyway."

They hesitate, exchanging glances. Jacob speaks first.

"We keep going after Engel. Find out what we can about what we are and how to fix what they've done to us—and how we can destroy the assholes who did it to us. They're the ones who need to pay. For Griffin. For everything."

Zian hunches his shoulders in apparent discomfort. "I just want to get rid of this shitty 'talent.'"

"We are close," Andreas says. "We could reach her in just another couple of days. And after we see what answers we can get… then we could decide where we go from there."

I draw my knees up to my chest and hug them, my mind whirling with everything that's happened, everything I've learned.

I want answers too. I want to meet the woman who was pushed out of the facility she built—who recorded my first smile like it gave her joy.

It'll be a hell of a lot easier getting to her if we're all working together. A hell of a lot easier to make sure the guardians don't recapture us if we have each other's backs.

Do I trust the guys to actually have *my* back now? I guess in a way they always did. Even when they thought I was a traitor, they stepped in every time I faced the slightest threat.

The only people they didn't protect me from was themselves.

I know what I'd prefer, and I know what makes sense, and they aren't the same thing. But if I have to choose…

I've survived more than a week of them treating me like the enemy. I can make it through a couple more days of their company while they're *not* being assholes, right?

As long as they aren't acting like jerks and pissing me off, they shouldn't incite the twisted power inside me.

And the poison is gone. If I change my mind, I can leave whenever I want.

I sway to my feet again and square my shoulders. "All right. Then let's stick to the plan."

THIRTY-ONE

Riva

The chilly autumn breeze winding between the trees north of Glenlily licks under my braid and makes me wish I had a proper jacket instead of just this hoodie. We didn't want to risk going into anywhere as public as a store, and the old clothes we found in the farmhouse didn't include any outerwear.

At least I'm back in my comfortable shirt and cargo pants instead of that overlarge dress.

I tug the zipper right up to my chin and tramp on, aware of the guys around me at the edges of my vision. We've spread out through the hilly terrain both so that we can select paths where we'll make the least noise picking our way through the brush and so we have a wider view between us over our surroundings.

We skirted the tiny town called Glenlily about an hour ago, already having left behind the pick-up truck we commandeered after crossing the border into Canada by train. If the guardians suspect we might come this way, they'll definitely be watching the roads.

We have no idea how much farther their surveillance might reach. There might not be any of them up here at all if they haven't considered that we'd be interested in their former boss—or whatever exactly Ursula Engel was to them.

But we need to keep watch not just for possible attackers but for Engel's property itself. Andreas has only gathered that it was somewhere north of Glenlily. He has no idea exactly how far.

I'm hoping "north" was at least relatively accurate. It'd be awfully easy to walk right by a secluded home in this dense forest.

There was a single gravel road stretching north from the town for the first mile or so, which we were initially following along. But it petered out into what was more of a private lane, and then an overgrown path I'm not totally sure most vehicles could even navigate.

Zian is keeping it within range of his penetrating sight, though, since we have to assume Engel has *some* way to bring supplies up here. Somehow I doubt she's living off the land right through the Canadian winter.

Can you subsist on maple syrup and pine needles?

A stone dislodges under my foot, but I catch my balance before I even fully stumble. Two pairs of eyes immediately shoot to me—Dominic's at my left and Jacob's at my right.

But this time, neither gaze holds any hint of hostility. Dom veers a little closer with a lifting of his eyebrows that I know is a question, asking if I'm okay.

I give him a quick nod. My insides still twinge at random moments, like there are a few tiny cracks that weren't perfectly fused, but I spent most of yesterday resting in one train car or another.

Right now, I feel *better* than I have for most of the past couple of weeks.

And that's mainly because I no longer have any poison trickling through me, wearing me down bit by bit.

I ignore Jacob's gaze, even though I can feel it lingering on me as we weave onward between the trees. Something about the night when the train nearly ended me spun him around from accusing to ashamed, but I haven't totally recovered from the emotional whiplash of the switch yet.

How can I be sure he won't change his mind all over again with some other move I make?

I inhale deeply, filling my lungs with the cool piney air, and freeze at the sound of a twig snapping.

Crack, crack, crack, three times in quick succession. That's the signal Zian said he'd give if he spotted anything.

Without a word, the rest of us slink through the forest to join him.

He's pulled a little ahead of the rest of us, standing now at the crest of a low, mossy cliff.

He waits until we've all gathered around him and points down the steep slope. All I can make out are more trees, but Zian must be looking right through them.

"The path branches in two directions just up there," he says under his breath, barely louder than the rustle of the wind through the leaves overhead. "There's a small hut right at the junction, and I think someone's inside it."

Andreas peers in that direction as if he thinks he might see through solid objects too if he tries hard enough. "You figure it's a guard house?"

Zian nods. "Or something like that. I guess it could be a park ranger thing, but… if the glimpse I got is what I think it is, the guy inside is wearing a metal helmet."

A guardian. My pulse hiccups, and my muscles tense instinctively.

Jacob's mouth sets in a grim line. "We go down there and question him, but we have to be careful about it. There might be others around, and he's probably got a way to alert them if there's trouble."

Dom looks at him. "If there's no one else nearby when we get close enough to check, you could yank him right out with your powers before he even sees us."

Andreas shakes his head. "Not at first. Remember the guardians that caught us in the old facility? This one might be able to block me from getting a good look at his memories… if he knows he needs to be blocking me."

Jacob offers him a hesitant smile, as if he isn't sure how Andreas will take his interjection even if it's in agreement. "Yeah, Drey should take a peek first and find out as much as he can that way before we get into a physical altercation."

I assume we've settled it, but Dom's gaze slides to me. "What do you think, Riva?"

It's the first time any of them have asked my opinion while they're working out their strategy on this mission. For most of the past couple of weeks, they've been ignoring my opinion even when I insisted on giving it.

I hesitate, feeling the pressure of their combined attention on me. I don't really have anything to add. My skills aren't going to be especially helpful in an interrogation.

At least, not the typical ones.

"It all sounds good," I say. "But if he catches on, I guess I can bring out my sob story again to distract him from blocking Andreas."

Jacob's jaw ticks at the words "sob story"—his dismissive phrase, flung more than once in my face.

Andreas shoots me a smile even more uncertain than the one Jacob gave him. "I'll do my best to make sure you don't have to."

I shrug as if it's no big deal, but I'd really prefer to avoid baring my soul for some stranger all over again if I get a choice in the matter.

If I have to, though… I just want to find this woman and finish the mission. Then we'll know what we actually have—and whether there's been a point to any of this.

We ease down the hill, setting our feet even more carefully than before. By the time we've reached the base of the cliff, I can make out a few slivers of a structure through the trees. The hut is built out of wood to blend into the forest, but the logs have darkened with the beating of the weather over the years.

Andreas takes the lead, since it's his talent's range that matters for this first part of the plan. He walks slowly and softly through the brush, his gaze fixed straight ahead.

When he stops, we all do as well, a few steps behind him.

For several minutes, we all just wait there, making no more noise than breathing. Andreas stays still and silent too, but I can see the effort he's making in the stiffening of his stance.

His shoulders come down abruptly with a faintly ragged exhalation. He treads back toward us.

"He definitely works with Engel," he whispers, "but he's been interacting with her for a long time. I can't tell which of the memories I've seen are the most recent, and none of them showed how to get to the house from here—or even for sure that the house I saw *is* all that close to here."

"Could you tell how many other guardians there might be around?" Zian asks, scanning the forest with a worried expression.

Andreas grimaces. "He definitely had memories of talking with her while there were one or two others with him, so I don't think we should count on him being here alone."

I hug myself. "Did you see anything about him hearing that we might show up?"

"No, but I can only narrow what I see by direct interactions. He's never seen us in person. If someone talked to him about us or showed him pictures, I wouldn't necessarily find that."

Dominic frowns. "We could simply sneak past him and try one of the paths, and if that doesn't get us anywhere—"

His suggestion is cut off by a sudden blare of electronic noise that makes us all startle. As it resonates through the woods, Jacob slaps his hand to his pocket.

"The phone. What the fuck? I had it on silent."

Andreas motions at him wildly. "It's got to be some kind of emergency alert. Shut it off!"

But it's too late. Even as Jacob jabs at the screen, the door to the hut thumps open.

"Jake!" Zian growls, low and urgent, and I know he isn't hassling him about the phone now.

Jacob spins toward the guardian who's marching toward our side of the forest with gun raised and whips out his hands.

The rifle hurtles away in one direction. The man crashes to the ground in the other, letting out a startled grunt.

We rush through the trees to the weedy path where the guardian fell. He glares up at us from beneath the brim of his helmet, his hands wriggling where Jacob's power has pinned them away from his sides.

From the twitching of his lips where they're pressed tightly together, I suspect Jacob is holding his mouth shut too. Only muffled sounds of consternation seep out.

"Check him for other weapons or anything he could communicate with," Jacob orders, with just a hint of strain in his voice.

We all dash in. Andreas hauls off the man's helmet. Zian jerks open his metal vest and pats down his shirt while Dominic checks his hip pockets.

I yank off one boot and then the other, peering inside them for knives and then tossing them away into the forest. Wouldn't want to make it any easier for this asshole to run.

The guys retrieve a walkie talkie and a pistol. Zian hands the second of those to Dominic, who needs the offensive boost the most.

As he clutches the walkie in his broad hand, Jacob glowers down at our captive. "You're going to answer our questions, or you're going to die very slowly and painfully. I think that should be an easy choice."

It wasn't for the guardians we interrogated before, though. This man doesn't look like he's going to be much more talkative. His eyes narrow, dark with anger even though I can smell his fear at the threat.

"Where would we find Ursula Engel's house?" Jacob asks.

He must have loosened his grip on the man's mouth to give him the option of speaking, but when the guardian's lips part, it's with a hasty inhalation that sets all my nerves on edge.

Only a fragment of a shout of warning slips from his mouth before Jacob has slammed his mouth shut again. The man lets out a frustrated whine and squirms as well as he can against the ground.

"Wrong answer," Jacob snaps, and swivels his fingers. The man's thumb twists with a crack of breaking bone.

A fresh whiff of stress pheromones tickle my nose—and an idea sparks in my mind. Maybe there is a way my usual talents could help get us some answers.

"Wait," I say, holding out my hand.

I expect Jacob to argue, but he goes silent, watching me. I walk up to the man and step over him so I have a foot planted on either side of his chest.

Setting my hands on my hips, I stare down at him, getting to be the taller person in a confrontation just this once.

This man doesn't know what powers I might have. Even the guardians who were in charge of our captivity must realize by now that we've shown skills we kept hidden from them before.

So let him imagine I'm reading his mind.

I pin him with my gaze for a few thumps of my heart and then point to the left path. "We go this way."

Nothing shifts in the air. I furrow my brow as if I'm picking up something new and then let out a little chuckle. "Oh, no, you're not tricking us that easily. It's this way."

When I point to the righthand path, the spike of stress I expected wafts into my nose. A grin crosses my lips with a flicker of exhilaration.

I have him.

"Definitely that way," I say with increased confidence, and eyeball the path to the right for a moment before peering at our captive again. "Now let's see how much company we can expect to tangle with along the way, and exactly how to get the jump on them."

Another spurt of nervous pheromones. There *are* other guardians down that way, and now he's worried for their safety.

With his own animalistically heightened senses, Zian catches on to my tactic first. He steps closer to the man, looming into his view with his brawny arms flexing.

"He's trying so hard to yell. There must be someone pretty close."

"Yep," I say when I get a whiff of confirmation. "But we just need to take care of that one and then one… no, two…" There's another surge of anxiety. "Two more. Three altogether, and we're home free."

Zian cracks his knuckles and grins at me, the admiration in his eyes warming me despite my intent to stay totally detached from these guys. "That shouldn't be too much trouble."

"I wouldn't think so. Especially since they've only got guns like this dude, and maybe a couple of tranqs."

Another flare of stress confirms my guess. He wouldn't be worried if I was underestimating his colleagues, if they had some other trick up their sleeves.

I study him for several seconds longer. "Too bad for the guardians that the ones back home didn't think there was much chance we were headed up here. They couldn't be bothered to send a whole army."

The man grimaces at me, unable to express his futile anger in any other way. My statement must at least be close to the truth, because it's pissed him off and frightened him all over again.

I shove myself away from him and glance at Jacob. "I think that's all we need to know."

Jacob gazes steadily back at me and inclines his head, a gesture of trust that sends an unexpected ache lancing through my heart. He believes me, just like that.

He turns his attention on the guardian and, without a word, snaps the man's neck.

Zian moves automatically to haul the body into the woods out of sight. Andreas catches my eyes and lets out a soft whistle.

"That was pretty badass, Tink. We'll have to remember that trick."

I look away, my nerves jumping at the compliment and the affection in his tone. "Let's hope we don't have to. Come on. We've got three more of these assholes to deal with."

And then, if I'm right, we'll come face to face with the woman who started it all.

Thirty-Two

Riva

The house reminds me so much of the magazine clipping from decades ago that I have to stop and stare for a moment to make sure I'm not hallucinating.

The trees surrounding it aren't draped with snow, but their needle-laden boughs swoop around the log walls in a woodsy embrace. Those walls rise two stories above the low slope where the house is perched, to a sharply peaked roof that makes me picture a vaulted ceiling beneath.

Large windows gleam darkly glossy, reflecting the forest around them. The afternoon light is too bright to allow any glimpse of what's inside.

To my eyes, anyway. Zian peers at the place and then glances at us.

"I'm going to sneak a little closer to get a better look inside. Make sure she doesn't have other guardians in there with her."

Jacob nods. "Just be careful."

As Zian treads lightly between the trees to approach the house, Andreas rubs his mouth, his expression unusually pensive. "All of the guardians we tackled on the way here—in their memories of talking to her, it seemed more like they were her jailers than her protectors. She always sounded like she was irritated that they were insisting on staking out the house."

There were three more guards stationed along the path through the woods, just as I'd thought I'd determined from the one we questioned. None of them revealed anything more useful than the first, though—other than what Andreas just said.

I think back to the other things we've learned about Ursula Engel. "They pushed her out of something she set up… They're probably worried she's going to reveal secrets they don't want getting out."

To us? Or to the general public?

What *would* ordinary people think if they found out that people like me and the men around me exist?

An image of Brooke's crumpled body flashes through my mind. That wasn't our fault—but we've dealt out plenty of violence ourselves.

Somehow I don't think we'd get a cheerful reception from the average human being. Every monster movie I've ever seen, the strange creatures, the mutants, and the freaks are greeted with screams and gunfire, not open arms.

But the woman inside that house knows what we are and cared for us almost like a parent. She had some part in *making* us, I have to assume, whether directly or just instructing others.

And maybe we're about to find out how and why.

Andreas motions toward me, his fingers skimming the air a few inches from my arm without quite touching me. "Riva, can I talk to you for a second?"

He's beckoning me away from Jacob and Dominic. As the other guys give him a curious look, my legs balk instinctively.

Andreas swallows audibly, a trace of queasiness crossing his face. "Please," he adds. "I'll give you plenty of space. I really just want to talk."

It was talking that ruined everything to begin with, but the rawness of his voice tugs at my heart against my will.

If I don't like what he has to say, it's not as if I can't march right back to the others without finishing hearing him out.

"Fine."

He leads me back through the brush in the opposite direction from the house until the others are just fragments of color between the trees. Then he stops, keeping a good five feet of distance between us as promised, and turns to face me.

Andreas has always been the most fun-loving one of us, the quickest to toss out a joke or latch on to an opportunity for amusement. But there isn't the slightest trace of humor in his expression now.

His gray eyes are shadowed, his lips pressed in a tight line. His normally rich brown skin looks tarnished even in the bright daylight, as if the base color has been leeched out of it.

In spite of everything, seeing him like this makes me want to grab him in a hug. My arms itch with the urge, but I hold them rigidly at my sides.

"I'm sorry," he says abruptly in a low voice. "I know I said that before, and I know it's not enough—I just don't know what else to do, and we're about to walk into that house, and I don't know what's going to happen."

He stops to drag in a shaky breath, and I just stand there silent, my stomach twisting itself into knots. How can I ache so much with both the agony this man inflicted on me and the pain I can hear twined all through his voice?

Andreas holds my gaze with a glint of determination lighting in his eyes. His hand twitches as if he wants to reach for me but held himself back.

I can taste his nervousness. He thinks that what I do here, what I say, could hurt him.

"I shouldn't have believed the guardians' story or that stupid video," he goes on. "I should have realized you were telling the truth from the first moment you came back to us."

My jaw clenches. "Yes, you should have."

His head droops slightly, but he doesn't break eye contact. "I was wrong and an idiot, and I'm going to do whatever it takes to make up for that, however long it takes. But I need you to know—that night in the farmhouse, I'd been trying to convince Jake that we could trust you beforehand. I *knew* you were on our side. I wanted to understand everything you'd been through, and I was hoping if I had more of the story I could make him see what I already had."

"You still…" I grope for the words through the constricting of my chest. "You nudged me in the direction you wanted. You manipulated the conversation. You told me those stories, talked like you thought *you* were failing the other guys—"

"That was all true," Andreas breaks in with a rough laugh. "Hell, I have been failing. They all fell to pieces, and I'm the only one who wasn't really shattered, and I still couldn't figure out a way to put them back together, not properly. And now I've failed you too."

"*I* can't fix that."

"I know." He drops his gaze for just a second before catching mine again. "But I meant everything I said that night. Every single thing. I love you, and I've loved you for as long as I had any idea what the word even meant. It's a fucking *honor* to be connected to you however I am."

His hand rises to his chest, to the spot where I know his skin is marked beneath his shirt. "I fucked it up, I broke the most precious thing I've ever been given, and no matter what happens, no matter what those assholes come at us with next, I'm going to be fighting to my last breath to make it right again. I just hope my last breath doesn't come in the next hour or two."

His words have sent wave after wave of churning emotion through me. The last sentence jars me out of the haze. "You think it's that dangerous, going in there?"

Andreas grimaces. "I don't know. But this is big, and we don't have anything close to the full picture… I can't shake the feeling that we might be walking into something we can't come out of, one way or another. And I didn't want to take the chance of that being true without telling you how much you mean to me."

He touches his chest again, over his heart this time. "We are blood."

My fingers curl toward my palm of their own accord, wanting to rise to the same spot on my own chest.

"We are blood," I murmur. "I don't—I don't know how the rest will go. But I want to find out exactly what that means. And then… whatever else we do, whatever else happens, it'll begin there."

"Yeah."

Andreas searches my face for a moment, but if he was hoping for more absolution from me, I can't give it to him. Dominic did an amazing job mending the torn-up pieces of my body, but my feelings are still jagged shards scraping against each other from the base of my throat all the way down to my gut.

Drey doesn't push for the answers he wants this time. He simply dips his head and turns slowly to give me time to recognize that he's returning to the others, so we can walk together.

I keep the same definite distance the whole way back, but maybe some of those broken pieces inside me don't scrape quite as sharply as they did before.

We reach Jacob and Dom just as Zian does from the other direction.

"I couldn't see anyone else inside," he says quietly. "Engel is there—or at least a woman who looks like how Drey described her. Sitting in the living room with a mug and a book. The rest of the place is empty."

We all exchange a glance. I raise my chin and speak before Jacob can give the final command.

"What are we waiting for, then? Let's see what she has to say."

Thirty-Three

Riva

Jacob uses his power to unlatch the basement window and nudge it up bit by bit with the softest of rasps. Zian's keen sight spotted an alarm system mounted near the doors on the house, but Engel hasn't protected the windows as well.

One after another, we slip into the dark space. The tang of pine sap hangs in the air, no doubt from the stacks of logs that fill most of the unfurnished room.

The chill follows us in from outside. As soon as Zian has squeezed through, the last of us, Jacob eases the pane shut again.

Who knows if Engel is sensitive enough to notice a strange draft? But then, she's going to know we're here soon enough.

We prowl between the stacks of logs to the narrow staircase that leads to the ground level. There's no door at the top of the stairs, only a rectangle of light that a current of warmth wafts through.

Andreas goes first based on prior agreement. We don't know if he'll be able to get a look at Engel and read her memories surreptitiously, but if he can get the chance to, we want him to take it.

She might be at odds with the facility we escaped, but we have no way of knowing how she'll welcome us.

Zian described the basic layout of the house to us from his

observations, and what we emerge into matches what I pictured from his words. The main floor is an open-concept space with the basement doorway at the far end of the expansive kitchen. Dark wooden cabinets and black appliances gleam around us.

A matching kitchen island, several feet across, sections off the kitchen from the dining and living rooms beyond—and hides us from the rest of the building while we stay crouched. We creep across the smooth tiles toward it.

When he reaches the island ahead of the rest of us, Andreas peeks around the side. He cranes his neck for a few seconds and then glances back at us with a frown and a shake of his head.

He can't see Engel to get a lock on her mind from here. We're going to have to rely on our other skills—and her potential willingness to talk.

Jacob makes a gesture of caution, reminding me of the instructions he gave before we entered. *We approach slowly, staying alert, watching in case she has a weapon. I'll be ready to disarm her if I need to.*

We shouldn't go in too strong, Dominic put in back then. *She might not be a real enemy. We have to give her the chance to let this be a peaceful conversation.*

Jacob made a face but nodded. That's what we're all hoping for—no more fighting, just answers.

Is it crazy for us to even hope?

I can't see Engel either, but the whisper of a turned page reaches my ears. The clink of her mug set down on a side table.

The sounds give me an impression of her in my mind's eye, off to the left side of the room where the ceiling looms highest. The second floor only fills half of the space, over the kitchen and dining room. Dark beams crisscross the far wall of the living room around towering windows, stretching so high I can see them even crouched behind the island.

This isn't how accepted guests are supposed to enter, but we can't risk slipping back out and simply knocking on the door, not knowing how she'll react. Instead, we rise cautiously to our feet.

The woman who's only been a name to me before now flinches in her armchair beneath the tall windows. Her book falls from her hand to thump on the floor.

My eyes skim over her, absorbing my first real view of the woman I've wondered about so much.

Her hair, a mix of fawn-brown and gray, curls lightly where it's tucked behind her ears. Her oval-paned, wire-rimmed glasses slide down her nose with a flinch, revealing pale eyes with crinkles of age at the corners. A cozy sweater and faded jeans clothe her softly rounded frame.

I can't help thinking she looks almost motherly, even in her startled state. Like the moms I've seen on TV screens, sending their grown kids off to college or comforting them through breakups.

It isn't hard at all to imagine her offering a warm hug or reassuring words —I mean, if she wasn't staring at us like we've nearly given her a heart attack.

Andreas has raised his hands in a gesture of surrender. "I'm sorry for sneaking up on you like this. We were hoping to speak with you—we don't mean any harm."

As long as she doesn't try to harm us, he means.

The rest of us stay perfectly still, watching. Engel nudges her glasses up her nose to study us through them. Then her hand swipes downward in an odd motion I don't totally understand.

It looks almost like she's reaching for her mug, but instead her fingers dip between the arm of the chair and the side table. Just a brief skim before she's folding her hands in her lap.

Jacob tensed beside me for a second, but once both her hands are in view and empty, he relaxes again, just a smidge.

"Do you know who we are?" he asks, managing to sound more curious than hostile, although I don't think he's capable of completely erasing the demanding note from his voice.

A hint of a smile curves the woman's lips, enough to send hope flitting through my chest.

"My shadowblood children, all grown up," she says in a crisp but gentle voice. "I haven't seen pictures in years, but you haven't changed that much since the last time."

That voice. The faintest of recollections, not even really a memory it's so vague, wisps through my head like the hazy impressions I got in the playroom at the old facility.

I've heard that voice lilting in a lullaby before—I'm sure of it.

Now that I can see the living room properly, it occurs to me that it looks an awful lot like that playroom. Log walls, suede seating, a fireplace where flames are crackling away over pine logs.

An image so familiar yet distant it sends a pang of homesickness through my chest.

If we ever had a real home, it was something like this.

As I take that in, Engel's brow knits. "It's only the five of you?"

She doesn't know about Griffin. The realization jabs me in the gut like he's dying all over again.

I swallow thickly, but Dominic speaks before I can. "He's gone. Four years ago—we tried to get out, but it didn't work."

"Ah." Engel appears to hold her emotions close, but a flicker of sadness crosses her face. "I heard about the attempt but not the entire outcome. My condolences."

She leans forward slowly, and it occurs to me that she must feel just as wary of us as we are of her. She doesn't know how much we know or what we think of her.

Picking up her mug, she gets to her feet. "I can be a proper host, even if the visit was unexpected. Before we get into the talking, how would you like some hot chocolate?"

A whisper of a memory passes through my head of buying a cup once while on an outside mission. I remember the sting of burning my tongue better than the actual flavor.

But the fact that she's offering at all sends a quiver of elation through my chest. "That would be nice," I say automatically.

Jacob casts a wary glance around at the rest of us, and I know what he's thinking. As friendly as she's being, we need to watch her—and probably we shouldn't actually consume anything she gives us even if it looks safe.

Still, I can't help relishing the idea of simply holding a mug radiating heat and breathing in the sweet steam rising off it.

As Engel approaches the kitchen, the five of us move like one being, both giving her space and keeping our own out of our honed sense of self-protection. We cluster to the right of the island as she passes by on the left and then gather around its far side, leaving it between her and us like a barricade.

I get the sense that she wouldn't mind us sinking onto the cozy seats in the living room, but none of us is ready to relax anywhere near that much.

Engel moves through the kitchen with soothing ease, pulling out a pot and setting it on the stove, grabbing a measuring cup and a box of cocoa powder from the cupboards. As she gets a carton of milk out of the fridge, she shoots a soft smile our way.

"It's impressive that you found your way here. But then you were always quick studies, the bunch of you."

I can't keep quiet any longer. "You had something to do with— You started the first facility. You were there from when we were born."

She picks up on the question I'm asking before I've figured out exactly how to ask it. "I arranged for you to be born."

"We're not just people," Zian says abruptly. "We have…" He raises his hand, extending his wolfish claws as he does. "We can do things no one else can."

"Yes. You are very special, my shadowbloods."

Something about Engel's tone itches at me, but my mind latches onto that last word—one she used before. "What does 'shadowblood' mean? What *are* we?"

"That's why we're here," Jacob adds, setting his hands on the edge of the island. "We want to understand what was going on at the facility, how we turned out like this."

Dominic speaks up, his voice quiet but steady. "And why."

"I see." Engel pours the milk from the measuring cup into the pot. "I suppose we have time to get into that story."

We all lean a little closer in anticipation. A crimson sheen glimmers in Andreas's eyes. He's searching her memories even as he listens alongside us.

Engel's lips purse, her expression momentarily tightening as she adds more milk to the pot. Then she turns to face us while she unscrews the lid on the cocoa powder.

"You know that you don't bleed exactly the way a regular human does."

I touch my arm where I scratched open my skin so many times. "There's smoky stuff that comes out too."

She inclines her head. "Like shadows. That's why I've always thought of you as 'shadowbloods' in my mind."

As she spoons some of the dark brown powder into the pot, my pulse skips a beat. "Our tattoos." A moon for night—for shadows? And a droplet… of blood?

"Yes, that was the inspiration for the design, although it wasn't my idea to imprint it on you." Her mouth tightens again. "But as for what and why… Many years ago, when I was younger than you, I found out that there are creatures that enter this world that are pure shadow. They don't bleed red at all, only that dark haze."

"Creatures?" Zian prods.

Engel swirls a whisk in the pot with a faint clinking as it taps the sides. "All the things from fairytales and folklore, all the monsters and myths we'd have liked to believe were only made up. They sneak into our world and blend in among us as well as they can, using us, preying on us..." She sucks in a sharp breath. "And barely anyone knows."

Uneasiness prickles over my skin. Monsters and myths... with powers like ours?

"But some people do know," Jacob says. "*You* know."

"Yes. And those who know push back as well as we can. My sister and I joined a group of those aware, under the name the Company of Light. Light to combat the shadows. We thought it was very clever."

Engel's expression darkens. "After some time, it became clear to me that we couldn't do enough. Even if everyone in the world knew, it might not be enough to protect humanity when the fiends we were up against had so much strength and were so difficult to destroy."

"So you made us," Andreas says with a distant quality to his voice. My head jerks toward him, but his gaze is distant too, still with the reddish glow over his irises.

He must be talking about something he's seen in her memories.

He inhales sharply and goes on. "You thought *we* could fight them if you made us strong enough."

If it bothers Engel that Andreas has picked that information up from her mind, she doesn't show her discomfort. "Some members of the Company had been capturing the shadow creatures and running tests on them, experimenting with the essence they're constructed of, toward a goal I suspected was untenable. But I saw the possibility for taking some of what made the fiends such formidable foes and enhancing humans with it."

Jacob's mouth twists. "So, we have some of that monstrousness—that essence—mixed up in us?"

"Yes. I wanted to create humans who could match our enemies while standing alongside us." A trace of wryness colors Engel's tone. "Unfortunately that required starting from scratch at infancy, but this war has always been a long game."

A lot of things suddenly make so much more sense than they did before. "That's why we've had all that training," I burst out. "Keeping us physically strong, making sure we could fight, practicing our powers." I'm not sure what the missions were for—maybe the little tasks they sent us on worked against these shadow creatures in some way we didn't realize?

Did the guardians justify the more torturous parts of the training thinking they were preparing us to face something even worse?

Andreas frowns. "But why did the other guardians make you leave? It was your project—you set everything up… You haven't seen us since we were around ten, it looks like?"

"And we haven't seen you at all since… since as long as we can remember," Dominic adds.

Engel whisks the heating chocolate mixture some more, trickles of steam starting to rise from the pot. "Yes. Over time and with changing circumstances, I came to have different ideas about how the project should proceed than most of my colleagues did. About what our specific goals should be, about how you should be treated."

A slight edge creeps into her voice. She wasn't happy about how they treated us.

"But if you were the one who started everything, couldn't you decide for the others?" Zian says.

Engel sighs. "I didn't have all the power—I'd needed to seek funding and guidance. I was overridden, limited in my involvement and then pushed out completely, other than when they feel the need to consult me."

The bitterness in her tone sends another quiver of uneasiness through me, but I can't explain why. It sounds as if they treated her badly—why shouldn't she be upset?

The question tumbles out of my mouth. "What did you want to happen to us?"

Did she see how cruelly the others were treating us and want to set us free? Is that why she's seemed so calm about us showing up like this?

Her smile returns, appearing to confirm my guess. "I'll be able to show you. Now that you're here, I can see my intentions through."

"Is there a way to take *out* the shadow parts of us?" Dominic asks abruptly. "If we don't—if we'd rather not—"

The shoulder area of his parka shivers where his tentacles must have twitched underneath.

"I'm afraid not," Engel says, "or I'd happily do that for you. But the shadow essence is entwined with your genetic code. It would be like attempting to carve the musical talent out of a violin prodigy or the coordination out of a natural athlete."

Dominic's face falls, and Zian's expression tenses too. My gut clenches.

If there's no way to remove the thing that's been growing inside me, trying to take me over…

Jacob crosses his arms over his chest. "What do we do now? How do you see things going from here? The guardians will probably figure out we came up this way soon, and—"

Engel pauses in her stirring and cuts off his concerned statement with a dismissive wave of her hand. "You don't need to worry about *them*. When they mentioned you were roaming around, I told them I doubted you'd have any interest in me, that they shouldn't waste their resources up here. The nearest reinforcements are hours away. I knew they'd only want to recapture you."

Her comments should be reassuring, but my apprehension rises more. She hasn't actually answered the question, has she? Despite the fact that both Jacob and I have asked.

As she clicks off the burner on the stove, I take a step toward her, scanning her posture, trying to figure out what my subconscious is picking up on. "What do *you* want?"

"Give me a little more time to gather my thoughts, and we can get into that."

Engel gives me another smile, but the scent that catches in my nose at the same time makes me freeze in my tracks.

She *sounds* calm, and she's acting as if she's glad we're here, but she's giving off an unmistakable tang of stress. If she isn't worried about the guardians crashing in on us, and she isn't worried about us hurting her, then what could be wrong?

I drag in a deeper breath, and recognition sets off a spike of alarm through my nerves.

It isn't the same kind of stress I tasted from the guardians we've interrogated, sharply metallic with fear. It's closer to the pungent anticipation I breathed in so many times in the fighting arena, from opponents both worried about my reputation—and determined to crush me.

Like she sees us as enemy combatants, ones she stands a real chance against.

But she isn't fighting us—she *wouldn't* stand a chance if she tried—

Full understanding clicks in my head. She's stalling. Because she's waiting for something else.

Before my thoughts have quite caught up with me, I'm spinning around. I dart across the living room to the chair where she was sitting when we first came in.

My fingers dip between the chair arm and the table where hers did in that brief, odd gesture I couldn't make sense of and then forgot—and catch on the edge of a button hidden beneath the lip of the table.

Engel's posture stiffens. I whirl around toward the guys.

"There's a control here—it's got to activate some kind of alarm system. She's signaled for someone to come."

All of the guys immediately jerk into defensive stances. Jacob's gaze turns searingly cold.

"Who did you—"

Before he can even finish spitting out the question, a swarm of dark-clothed figures swing into view from above and smash straight through the high windows in a shower of shattered glass.

Thirty-Four

Riva

As I fling myself away from the windows, glass shards slice at my hoodie, one scraping across my jaw. Heavy feet thud onto the ground inside Engel's house with enough force that the floorboards tremble.

With the ear-splitting booming of the first shots, a broad hand snags around my arm and yanks me farther away from the intruders with supernatural strength. Zian and I tumble toward the kitchen island, propelled by his backward lunge.

He was standing ten feet away when the attackers burst in. He leapt *toward* them rather than away just to pull me to safety.

A bullet whizzes across my upper arm, clipping me and searing through my skin. As I bite back a yelp of pain, Zian grunts, flinching where he's still gripping me. My heart stutters with panic.

"Here!" Jacob's voice rings out, taut and furious. Scraping, creaking sounds surround me, mingling with the thunderous rattle of the gunfire.

I roll onto my feet and spin around, flicking my gaze over the chaos that now surrounds us.

The other guys dove down by the island too. Jacob's turned this spot in the middle of the house into a sort of triangular fort, with the sofa and the overturned dining room table yanked close by his powers to form the other two sides.

The reason we haven't leapt *behind* the island is obvious from the cacophony of sound battering my ears. Some of the shots are blaring from the kitchen. Others from the front of the house, opposite the living room.

Our attackers entered from all sides—front, back, and up from the basement. We're surrounded.

And those are actual bullets, not any kind of tranquilizer. Blood is soaking through my hoodie from the shallow gouge in my arm, and Zian—

Zian's right shoulder has completely sagged, a splotch of red blooming fast around a bullet wound right where his shoulder meets his chest. I can't tell whether the bullet is still lodged inside or tore straight through, but if it'd been even a few inches farther to the right…

He almost died, pulling me to safety.

The figures shooting at us almost *killed* him.

Something Engel said echoes up from the back of my mind with chilling clarity. The disdain in her voice when she talked about the guardians. *I knew they'd only want to recapture you.*

In the moment, I'd thought she'd meant as opposed to letting us keep our freedom. The sickly certainty coiling in my stomach tells me it was just the opposite.

She didn't want us to even survive.

The prickling vibration resonates through my chest. I clench my jaw against it and force myself to focus on the battle.

The initial barrage of gunfire has dwindled for just an instant. One benefit to being surrounded is that our attackers can't pelt us with bullets wildly without significant risk of hitting their colleagues.

Of course, the benefit only lasts as long as they can't get close enough to shoot us like fish in a barrel.

My claws jolt from my fingers, my nerves buzzing with combat alertness. But there isn't much I can do to fend off the pricks without charging out there on a suicide mission… or letting lose the stirring power inside me that has a mind of its own. A vile, vicious mind I don't want anything to do with.

Near me, Jacob's face has gone tight with concentration, his hands jerking as he throws his telekinetic force through the room around us. Bones crack and pained groans reverberate through the air.

Andreas grimaces. "I can't project memories to distract them from down here where I can't see them. But if I—"

He cuts himself off and vanishes into thin air in the next moment.

All at once, several of the sets of footsteps around us start stumbling. Shouts of confusion echo them.

Andreas has slipped out there among the enemy combatants unseen, muddling their minds.

There are too many of them, though. Bodies thump closer to our makeshift shelter, and Dominic bobs higher, his tan face turned greenish. Having shed his parka, he lets his tentacles whip free to smack away the gunmen attempting to get at us.

Another figure charges up to the overturned table. I spring at him before he can get in his shot and slice my claws right through his forearm.

Blood spurts and tendons sever, but the man still slams his other fist toward me.

Zian roars. The massive guy pummels my attacker in the face hard enough to bash in his skull and wrenches the rifle from his grasp in the same moment.

I spin toward my protector, my pulse stuttering at the thought of the wound he's already taken. More blood is leaking out through his shirt, but he shoves me out of the way while scanning the room beyond the table warily.

In his protective rage, his wolfish fur has sprouted from his skin all across his neck and arms. His jaw has extended with the beastly folds of flesh, widened nose, and protruding fangs.

But his dark brown eyes are still Zian's even as they flash with fury. Only a brief shudder through his massive frame reveals the pain he's in.

Even shot, he's right here with me, looking out for me like we always promised to do.

All of the guys are. We fend off the attackers in a weird sort of dance, Zian and I hurtling up to tackle anyone who gets too close, the other guys keeping most at a distance.

As I slash through the calf of a gunman who's jumped onto the island, Dominic heaves out his tentacles to bat away a second foe I hadn't seen launching herself at us. There's a clatter and a splash as the woman must stagger into the pot of hot chocolate.

When another enemy shoves the muzzle of his rifle through a gap between the table and the sofa, I shatter his jaw with a kick moments before Jacob hurls him away.

And all the while the yells and mutters of confusion tell me that Andreas is working his powers, keeping our attackers unsteady. One of the fighters manages to snatch my arm in mid-swipe, and Drey appears for just an instant behind him, jabbing a knife between his ribs.

Even if the bonds of friendship—and whatever more we could have had—have fractured between us, we're still a team. Right now, in the midst of the fray, not one particle in my body doubts that I could trust each of these men with my life.

And I'll be here for them too, whatever it takes. We are not letting these assholes take any of us down.

If the battle weren't so fraught, maybe I'd take comfort in the thought. But just as I start to think we might be able to withstand the onslaught, they throw a new tactic in to the mix.

One of our attackers hurls an object over our barricade. I yelp out a warning.

Jacob whirls in time to heave it away before it hits the floor—but as it soars away, it explodes in mid-air.

We all fling ourselves to the floor instinctively under the hail of shrapnel. Jacob's body spasms where he's fallen next to me.

I jerk myself onto my hands and knees to see him clapping his hand to his temple. Blood streams out from under his fingers. His eyes twitch as if he can't quite focus them.

"Dominic!" I cry out. I don't give a shit about what a jerk this guy has been to me when he's fading before my eyes.

Dominic stretches a tentacle to encircle Jacob's head, but his gaze darts around us with a panicked expression. There's nothing here for him to grab onto to suck in the life energy he must need to heal a serious wound.

If he took it out of himself, would *he* be the one crumpling?

Andreas must have seen and recognized the problem, because the next second he's flitting into view near the table and flipping one of our attackers right over it, headfirst. Dominic's other tentacle lashes around the intruder's neck, tight enough to strangle, but another of our enemies shoots at Andreas in his momentary visibility.

Andreas flickers translucent and throws himself to the side, not quite quickly enough. His torso lurches with the impact as the bullet catches him in the back.

He staggers toward us with a choked gasp, snapping back into completely solid form. Zian and I lunge together to haul him into our shelter.

He collapses there, wincing as he struggles to push himself more upright. "I can't—I need to—"

Blood is pooling beneath him. Jacob is still bleeding too, as quickly as Dom is trying to stabilize him. Footsteps close in around us again.

Panic chokes me. And the vibration within me that I've been suppressing thrums up through my lungs too forcefully for me to ignore.

I can stop them. I can shred them apart and make them wish they'd never tangled with us.

My claws dig into the floorboards with the wrenching longing to do just that.

I open my mouth, and my gaze snags on the faces around me. Dominic's, tight with urgency and strain. Jacob's, fighting the slackness that's creeping over his muscles. Andreas's, his eyes glazing with pain. Zian's, his anguish showing even across his wolfish jowls.

In that instant, I can feel that I'll be able to shield them from the vicious rage. I'm not angry with them, not right now. I can aim this brutal energy beyond the boundaries of our little barricade, away from those within.

But that's not the only problem.

The growing shriek at the base of my throat makes me feel sick even as the urge clamors through my nerves to set it free.

What will the guys think of me after they see it? Once they know what I'm capable of doing—what I'm willing to do?

What some part of me will revel in?

They only just started believing that I'm the girl they always knew, and I can shatter that illusion with a single scream. Make them think they were right to distrust and shun me before.

I *am* that girl. I never asked for this power. It isn't *me*.

The wrongness of this whole situation sweeps over my body, and it's a question rather than a scream that bursts from my throat, aimed at the woman I have to assume is still somewhere in this house with us and the soldiers she summoned.

"Why? Why are you doing this? You *made* us."

Is there anything that could change her mind, make her call off the slaughter?

Ursula Engel's voice carries from somewhere behind me, crisp as before and somehow steady in spite of the battle that's being raged around her.

"I'm sorry. I didn't plan for it to end up this way when I started. But I did make you, so it's my responsibility to unmake you when no one else is willing to take that step."

"But—"

Her tone is so cool and dispassionate it lances straight through me. "I've been arguing for this since you were toddlers, when the Company of Light was destroyed by a hybrid not that different from you. I demanded it again and again when I saw how quickly your abilities were evolving and expanding, when my colleagues started pushing for you to be sent beyond the protection of the facility. But no one would listen to my warnings, and they shut me out."

"You're insane," Dom shouts at her in a ragged voice. "We're not—"

Engel cuts him off. "You're monsters of the worst kind. Abominations growing out of control, without even the few weaknesses that make the other creatures vulnerable and not enough humanity to rein your impulses in. That's not what I meant to create. So I've gathered my own guardians to my purpose, and now I can end the catastrophe I set in motion."

She must give some signal, because the booted feet thump toward our shelter again. My stomach lurches, but I know then that this is the end.

I have no other choice. I can kill the girl I wanted to be, for myself and for the guys around me, or I can watch us all die.

It isn't even really a choice.

As my lips part, it occurs to me that Engel doesn't even know. She's so confident her soldiers will be enough.

She screwed herself over by going rogue. The regular guardians haven't been filling her in on all the details. She didn't know Griffin had died; she probably wasn't aware of some of the guys' newer powers.

And she clearly has no idea about the destruction I wreaked in a cage-fighting arena two weeks ago, whether I meant to or not.

Not a single person in this building is prepared… including me.

Andreas gasps a ragged breath, and our attackers throw something that hits the dining table with a smack. The wooden surface blasts apart in a shower of splinters.

And the last of the control I was holding onto snaps.

The shriek that's been swelling in my chest claws up my throat and sears from my mouth. It screeches out of me so loud my ears ring with it.

My vision hazes. My body sways where I'm braced against the floor, the power of the scream threatening to consume my entire consciousness as it careens through the room.

I dig my claws deeper into the boards beneath me, holding on, refusing to be as overwhelmed as I was last time when it took me by surprise, when I had some toxic drug dragging me down.

If this is me, then I have to own it. I have to be awake enough to make sure I only hurt the people who're trying to hurt us, not the men who are my blood.

Whether those men still want any kind of bond with me after this moment or not.

The piercing wail keeps pealing from my lungs and ricocheting through the room, and a sense of the figures around me ripples back into my body like some kind of echolocation. I've pinned them in place, six men still standing in the front area beyond the dining table, eight in the living room who'd been approaching the sofa, three in the kitchen behind me.

And Engel. I can feel her too: a slightly different, more familiar quiver that runs through the lancing energy I'm throwing at them.

She's tucked away at the top of the basement stairs where she must have been watching from, as paralyzed as the others.

"Riva?" I hear one of my men murmur, so distant through the scream that I can't even tell who it is.

I ignore him, plummeting deeper into the current of the scream as it radiates through every cell inside me. Hunger courses with the vicious energy, prickling all the way down to my gut.

My awareness of my captives sharpens with the heightening of the shriek. I can follow the thumping of their pulses, the trembling of their straining muscles.

All the nooks and crannies where the pieces of their bodies fit together. All the soft and tender spots filled with fragile nerve endings.

My attention homes in on the closest man. His feet.

I snap the balls up toward his shin so fast I turn the arches inside out.

The crack of the bones sets off his guttural cry, and the blaze of pain flows back into my lungs. But it doesn't hurt *me.*

No, it's like drinking the freshest lemonade on the hottest day, a balm to every place inside me that's been craving relief.

I need more. More.

They have to pay.

I close my eyes, lost in the ringing in my ears, the screech of my own voice, and the bodily reactions reverberating into me. Every sensitive spot on our attackers lights up in the picture painted by my new senses.

Crush his knee caps. Burst his balls. Crack every bone in his spine from the tailbone up—but careful not to sever the cord.

Let him feel every tremor and stab of agony I'm inflicting on him. I can only gulp it down if he tastes it too.

Pop his elbows inside out. Mash every finger from tip to knuckle. Break his ribs and shove the shards down into his kidneys.

The stream of anguish widens into a torrent. It floods me, shockingly exhilarating.

Somewhere way deep down in the back of my mind, there's a flash of horror, but not enough to distract me.

The current halts as the man blacks out, his mind short-circuiting. Nothing more to gain from him. I wrench his head around to end him completely, my awareness already leaping to the next.

One and then another and another. Faster with each iteration as I gain momentum.

Tendons rent, sinews torn, bones fractured. Organs punctured, joints unhinged.

The glorious flood of agony tingles over every inch of my skin. I'm vaguely conscious of the wound on my shoulder sealing up, the flesh smoothing out like it was never split.

The last lingering tears that even Dominic couldn't totally heal inside me meld together good as new.

I'm stronger—so strong. Stronger than I ever imagined I could be. Stronger than anyone else could have guessed.

More foes fall like dominos, and the surge of giddy elation propels me to my feet. My scream still resounds through the building.

With every thump of my pulse and heave of my lungs, I obliterate another life.

Until there's only one left, other than the four clustered around me.

One woman huddles at the far end of the kitchen, trembling with both rage and terror. Spittle flecks her lips as she tries to force out words.

I don't want to know what the experimenter who made us has to say about me now. If I'm a monster, then I learned it from her.

She made us, she raised us, and then she set us up to be slaughtered. How *dare* she expect any better in return.

My shriek hitches even higher. Bones burst into cutting shards from Engel's toes across her feet, through her ankles and knees up her legs.

They carve waves of pain out of her to feed the fire burning inside me. It's so fucking bright now.

I could take on the whole facility. I could raze an entire fucking town.

But her torment is most satisfying of all. The closest thing we ever had to a mother—the attempted murderer of her own children.

Her spine bows back. Her ribs split from her chest.

Every horrible thing she thought about us, every vicious plan she had for our demise will disintegrate with the agony ravaging her mind.

Then I wrench her heart in two, and she collapses into a puddle of blood and urine.

The scream whips around for a new target, and I suck it in with a gasp.

No. No fucking way. We're done now.

We did what we needed to do.

The hunger clamors for more, but I tense my entire body, hauling it back. I will not let this horror take me over, not completely.

The sound peters out. My jaw swings shut.

And I find myself standing, my muscles quivering with restrained power and the flavor of blood coating my mouth, in the middle of a tableau of carnage.

Contorted bodies lie sprawled all around our shelter. The sight of them sends a jab of shame and a splash of revulsion over me, but the high of the moment is still humming through my veins.

The guys are standing too, staring at the massacre: Jacob gripping the edge of the island, Zian's shoulders held at a lopsided angle but looking full human again, Andreas with his arm looped around Dominic's shoulder while one tentacle mends his wounded body. The guardian slumped at their feet lies still and lifeless, but nowhere near as grotesque as the deaths I wrought.

Their gazes slide from the deformed corpses to me, and the bottom of my stomach drops out.

I rescued us all. I seized our freedom.

And deep down inside, I loved every second of the butchery I carried out.

Now I get to find out whether I've lost everything after all.

The Girl We Knew

(A Jacob POV Bonus Scene)

What made Jacob realize he was wrong about Riva and decide to race to her rescue when she ran toward the train tracks? Find out in this alternative POV scene from his prespective…

It takes way too long for Andreas to come upstairs.

The other guys have already crashed on the bed in the second bedroom. I've staked myself out next to one of the two windows in the main bedroom, the open door giving me a view of the stairs.

Mostly I'm looking out over the lawn toward the road. With the moonlight gleaming down from the clear sky, the fields outside are cast in shades of gray.

If the guardians track us all the way out here somehow, they'll most likely come from that direction—from the road. And if they try to swoop in by helicopter or hitch a ride on a train like we did, I'll hear the engine well before they get here.

Finally, the stairs creak. I don't glance over until his form appears at the top of the stairs in at the edge of my vision.

I can barely make out Andreas's face in the darkness. He might as well be a specter haunting the house. But something about his stance as he comes to a stop in the doorway makes my muscles tense up with frustration.

He's done something he shouldn't have. I can sense it in everything from his curly hair gone askew to the determined gleam in his eyes to the way the jeans that aren't his hang on his hips.

My fingers curl toward my palms. I'm not surprised at all when the first words out of his mouth are, "We need to talk about Riva."

"I told you on the train," I say without even needing to think about it. "We'll revisit that subject *after* we've gotten whatever we can from Engel."

As he walks into the room, Drey shakes his head with a rustle of his curls. "No. All the venom—in every form—needs to stop now. It shouldn't have gone on for even this long."

I glower at him. I wasn't totally convinced his plan was going to get us anything useful instead of coming back to bite us in the ass, and obviously I should have listened to those doubts.

"It isn't up to you. You don't get to make the call."

He folds his arms over his chest, letting his voice rise a little. "You're not in charge here either. We're in this together—isn't that how it's supposed to go? You're not always right, Jake, and this one time you're incredibly wrong."

My teeth set on edge. "I guess you can make your case once everyone's awake. In the meantime—"

"We're awake." Zian appears in the doorway, rubbing sleep from his eyes, with a weary Dominic behind him. "What's going on?"

Of course his sharp hearing picked up on the tense conversation even while dozing. I glare at Andreas to drive home the fact that he's woken up our friends, who needed their sleep, but he can't even be bothered to look guilty about it.

"We've been wrong about Riva," Drey says, focusing on the other guys now. "I got the whole story out of her, and she hasn't lied at all. She didn't turn on us even a little bit."

Zee's forehead furrows. He trudges across the room and sinks down onto the edge of the bed, his head hanging for a moment as he appears to absorb the claim. "But we saw—"

"I know what we saw," Andreas snaps with a jerk of his hand through the air. "It's what made even *me* treat her like shit when we should have been welcoming her back. But they must have faked it—we should have realized that."

Dominic frowns where he's stalled just inside the doorway. "It looked awfully real."

I let my lips curl with a sneer. "Drey just *wants* to think it was fake so he can feel better about getting cozy with the traitor."

Andreas's eyes flash. "She's not a traitor. You think you're so smart, Jake. Do you really figure the people running the facility are skilled enough to genetically engineer us into whatever the hell we are, but they couldn't handle doctoring a minute of video footage?"

My hackles rise. "I figure there was no reason for them to bother."

"No reason? How about giving us someone to be angry at other than the guardians—who're the ones who actually killed Griffin? How about adding that little sliver of doubt about whether we can trust even each other to try to deflect another escape attempt? The second part didn't work, but the first sure as hell did."

I tense up despite my best intentions. Even the second part did at first. I remember way too well how for the first few months after I watched Griffin fall, even the three guys around me transformed into strangers to my eyes.

"You don't *know*," I retort. "You've bought into her victim routine and now you want an excuse to make that okay."

Andreas's jaw clenches. "Do you even listen to yourself? We *did* know Riva. She was one of us, right there with us through all the shit they put us through, and she has been since she came back too. Why the fuck we ever trusted what the guardians showed us over what we'd seen our whole lives—that's the crazy part."

"I planned out every part of that escape down to the minute. We didn't let a hint of it slip. How else could they have known to be waiting for us like that?"

"Oh, so that's what this is really about," Andreas says. "You can't admit that you might have slipped up somewhere, or that maybe you simply weren't quite as brilliant as you'd like to be."

I shove myself to my feet. "It's not about me at all. It's about Griffin, who's dead, because she—"

"She *loved* Griffin," Drey cuts in. "Which you wouldn't doubt at all if you ever bothered to listen to her instead of the angry story you've built up in your head."

My stomach balls into a scalding knot. "And I suppose she told you that she loves you too, huh?"

Andreas's determined expression doesn't falter even slightly. "She loves all of us. Or she did, anyway, but it seems like she could still love even you in spite of what an asshole you've been to her if you got your head on straight."

I hadn't thought there was anything left in me other than resolve and rage. But those words pierce open something way deep down inside me and set loose the tiniest flicker of hope.

My stance goes rigid, a renewed wave of fury rushing up through me. How can I want something even a little bit that Griffin had first, that he can never have now?

All that fury expels itself in Drey's direction. "What a stupid fucking fairytale. And you believe all this bullshit she's been spouting, huh?"

"Yes," Andreas says firmly, "I do. Because I've been watching her and listening to her for days, and everything adds up to it being true. In case you've forgotten, the whole reason I started 'getting cozy' with her was so she'd open up about things she wouldn't have told us otherwise. I held up my end of the deal. Now you've got to listen."

As the last words tumble from his mouth, a movement just outside the door catches my eyes. Riva has jerked to a stop where she's slipped up the stairs, her face gone rigid with apparent horror.

A sick sense of satisfaction fills me so completely I don't even mind that she's somehow gotten out of the basement.

"Yes," I say, yanking my gaze back to Andreas with a tight smile. "That was the deal. And now she knows it too."

Let's see how long she can keep up her innocent act in the face of this revelation.

Riva walks through the doorway, her eyes glued to Drey, and then halts. Her voice comes out scratchy. "You were acting friendly just to trick me into telling you things?"

For once in his life, Andreas seems to grope for his words. "It wasn't like that, not exactly. And it isn't like that now."

Oh, please. He needs to realize how much bullshit that is too.

"It was exactly like that." I turn my attention back to Riva, shaping every word to cut through whatever fantasy she thinks she's caught him up in. "We had a little conversation right after we arrived at the college, while you were locked up in your room. I wanted to keep you out of our investigations, but Andreas insisted that we should get you involved so we could see if you'd give something away in the moment. He promised he'd convince you to trust him so you wouldn't be as guarded."

Riva's mouth twists, her claws slicing through the air at her sides. Already prepared for a fight.

"You argued in front of me about whether I should come along," she says, as if that means anything.

I smile coolly at her. "Yes, we did. We had to sell the idea in a way you'd believe. And it gave Drey his first chance to play your champion."

Andreas, the fool, is still trying to pick up the pieces like there was ever anything worth fixing here. "Riva, I swear that has nothing to do with tonight or—or— I believe you. I realized we were wrong. I—"

I interrupt him before he can babble on any more. "He's very good, isn't he? Got you to let your hair down and everything." I cut my gaze to Drey. "You can stop now. I can't see how you'll get anything more out of her than you already have."

"Will you shut the fuck up, Jake?" Andreas snaps, but Riva is deathly silent. Taking it all in, understanding just how much she threw away four years ago.

She's never getting us back. None of us. I'm making sure of it, like I should have to begin with. For Griffin.

Her lips part. "Why would you— How could you—?"

She doesn't seem to know how to go on. Does she think those puppy-dog eyes are going to work even on Andreas now?

A twinge of uncertainty quivers through me, rankling my nerves. Enough with the charade.

I glare at her. "Do you actually think you deserve better?"

She reaches up to grasp the damned necklace that Griffin gave her, as if she has any right to hold on to a gift of his friendship. She glances at the other guys who've remained still and silent by the bed.

"Are both of you okay with all of this? Really?"

Zian looks sick, but he doesn't deny it. "We needed to know—we needed to be sure…"

"We've had to look out for ourselves," Dominic grits out.

Riva's jaw clenches. Her eyes close, but I'm not letting her check out of this conversation.

"You don't have to play *our* friend anymore now. You're not getting anywhere with that. So let's see who you really are already."

Riva winces, and her fingers tighten around the pendant so abruptly there's a metallic crack. Her eyes snap open; she stares down at her hand.

How can she look so anguished about it even now?

Andreas has been rambling again, trying to cajole her back—with insults aimed at me. "Riva, he's being a fucking idiot. Listen to me. I—"

He moves toward her, and she jerks away with a sharp yelp that shudders through my bones. Andreas flinches.

Her body tenses as if she's bracing to lunge. Her eyes darken, turning stormy with anger.

Good. We've almost shattered this stupid farce.

"That's right," I say. "Tell us how you really feel."

She backs up a step, as if she can escape the reckoning. Oh, no. With a flick of my fingers, I send the door banging shut.

As I walk closer to her, she aims a glare at me. Her mouth twitches with all the caustic words I'm sure she's itching to finally let out.

But then her hand wrenches away from her chest, the chain of her necklace breaking and flying from her grip, and all she lets out is two hastily gasped commands.

"Stay away from me. I don't want to hurt you."

Then she hurls herself at the closer window.

She twists her slim frame at just the right angle to crash straight through the glass. Her body tumbles out in a shower of shards.

I've stopped breathing.

"Riva!" Andreas yells, dashing past me to the window. There's a thump below, and then she's off, her silver hair streaming out behind her in the moonlight.

Moonbeam, Griffin always called her.

"Where's she going?" Zian demands, and Drey is ranting something at me about how I was laying into her, but my mind is stuck on the last moment before she dove through glass to get away from us.

I can't shake the impression that it was terror more than rage on her face. That those last frantic words weren't a threat but a plea.

I bend to pick up the broken pendant off the floor. Zian is already charging out of the bedroom.

Andreas catches me by the elbow. "Are you going to help us get her back or not?"

I chased her away. That wasn't what I was trying to do, was it?

My thoughts seem to have jumbled, the righteous fury that was fueling me now petered out and leaving me even emptier than usual, staring at the ashes. I move at Andreas's tug, rushing down the stairs after him with Dominic right behind us, but everything in my head is a whirl.

I wasn't necessarily wrong, was I? She's trying to get away from us.

Because I just beat her down like my words were a cudgel. What the hell does that even prove?

That she's a human being. That what I say and what we do matters to her beyond the practicalities.

Fuck, fuck, fuck.

She isn't as fast as she probably would be at her best, fatigue and my poison wearing at her muscles, but she's still fucking speedy. By the time we burst out the door and dash across the yard, she's already a tiny figure halfway back to the line of the train tracks. Too far for me to reach with my power.

Where is she even going?

I push my legs as fast as they'll go, but the truth is I'm exhausted too. In less than a minute, my lungs are burning.

Zian has pulled ahead of the rest of us, hollering at Riva to stop. Andreas calls out her name.

My gaze stays locked on her distant figure, like a mirage of the girl we used to know. The one who'd laugh while she raced circles around all of us except Zee on the track. Who'd blush and duck her head when any of us tossed her a compliment… especially me, maybe because I never gave them out too freely.

Who'd squeeze in between the bunch of us on that L-shaped sofa in front of the TV and make sure the rare, treasured bowl of popcorn got passed around so everyone got plenty, keeping an eye on Zian's grabby hands. Who'd go off to the side and simply sit with Dominic on the days when he got back from solo training looking like someone had punched him in the soul.

And with the adrenaline blaring through my system, for the first time it really sinks in that Andreas might be right.

The woman fleeing from us right now might be that exact same girl.

And I have let out all my hatred and frustration on her instead of the people who really deserve it. Starting with myself.

I grit my teeth and throw myself forward faster, just as the roar of an approaching train reaches my ears.

The lights blink into view through the trees up ahead… and Riva swerves toward the tracks. Like she's running to meet it.

Like she welcomes the collision.

Horror blots out every other thought in my head. That's my Riva, *our* Riva, and I'm the one who's flung her toward disaster.

I'm too far away. I don't know how to stop her. But the words careen up my throat with all the force I can put into my voice.

"Wildcat, *no!*"

* * *

I hope you enjoyed this bonus scene from *Shattered Vow*! To find out what's next for Riva and her monstrous men, pick up Monstrous Power, the second book in the Shadowblood Souls series.

Monstrous Power

One

Riva

The room smells like death.

That's probably because of the copious number of dead bodies sprawled all across it.

It's like a house party of corpses, three dozen or so limp forms gathered around the kitchen and open concept living and dining room of Ursula Engel's expansive but homey cottage in the woods. Some slump on the floorboards and tiles, others loll across leather and hardwood furniture.

Most of them died because of me.

It's pretty easy to tell which ones I took out—at least, the ones I killed with the shrieking power that's now settled down inside me rather than with my claws. Those corpses are definitely not enjoying this undead party.

While the unearthly scream tore out of me, I saw right inside our enemies. I knew exactly where to twist and what to snap to wring every drop of pain out of them before their bodies shut down completely.

Limbs lie askew at impossible angles. Faces have locked in contortions of anguish.

The meaty, metallic tang of blood laces the air, but also the nauseating odors of urine and shit. A lot of my victims lost control over their bladders and bowels in the grips of my brutal talent.

I close my eyes for a second, but removing the gristly view doesn't stop my stomach from churning. Partly because it's not just the scene that's making me queasy, but also the stares of the four other figures who are still standing with me.

My guys. My fellow shadowbloods, who have the same dark smoke winding through their veins that I do that gives them their own unnerving talents.

The four gorgeous, tormented, vicious men who spent most of the past two weeks punishing me for a betrayal I didn't even commit.

They believed I was a monster. I wasn't back then, back when we were separated four years ago.

But looking at the carnage around us with my shriek still ringing in our ears, it must be difficult for them to see me as anything else right now.

I swallow thickly, willing down my nausea and the protests that want to bubble out.

I didn't want *to do this. It was the only way to save us.*

But those claims aren't totally true. Some part of me *did* want to wreak all this havoc, to savage and maim with wild abandon.

Some part of me reveled in it, drew strength from it. It took all my self-control to shield the guys from the sadistic hunger inside me.

I want to say it isn't me but some other being inside me, but I know that's not true. There's no alien in my chest that can be carved out and burned away.

The hunger is woven into my body, mind, and soul. It's etched in my DNA.

And the woman who lived in this house wrote that code, even if she didn't realize at the time exactly what abilities would emerge and grow in us.

I glance behind me at the mangled body of our creator at the same time Jacob does. The chiseled planes of his stunning face harden even more with the clenching of his jaw.

"Engel said reinforcements were too far out to get here quickly, but we don't know how true that was," he says, breaking the shocked silence. "Let's grab anything that could be useful and get out of here."

Dominic follows his gaze too, his dark auburn hair falling across his tan forehead to shade his eyes. He sways a little and catches the edge of the blood-streaked kitchen island for balance.

He's just spent the past several minutes healing the worst of the other guys' wounds—with the slim, orange tentacles arcing from the top of his shoulder blades to the backs of his knees. He grabbed most of the life energy he needed from the assailant now lying dead by our feet, but the process must have taken a lot out of him as well.

His voice comes out in a low rasp. "She really hated us."

The accusations our creator threw at us echo from the back of my mind. *You're monsters of the worst kind. Abominations. A catastrophe I set in motion.*

Of course, the bloodbath we're surrounded by doesn't exactly stand as evidence in our favor. I'm not sure any bystander would accept "She started it!" as a reasonable excuse.

Andreas rakes his hand back through the tight coils of his hair, his mouth twisting into a grimace. "Yeah. Well, I can't say I liked *her* all that much either."

None of us laughs at the darkly wry remark, but the rough attempt at humor stirs us all into motion. We tramp over the shattered chunks of the dining table that formed one side of our makeshift fort and pick our way between the bodies.

The search feels unnervingly familiar. I scanned a similar scene just a couple of weeks ago, appropriating weapons and cash, in the arena where I'd been forced into cage fights.

I don't look at the guys, but every now and then I see one pause with a flick of his gaze from a distorted body to me. Each time, my gut knots tighter.

They're moving slowly through the mess. Zian is still favoring one brawny shoulder, though it looks like Dominic was able to stop the bleeding. His wolfish features have vanished, but his normally peachy-brown skin has lost some of its warmth.

Andreas leans a little to the left and bends his knees when he checks something on the floor rather than tilting his torso. A bloody hole marks his shirt where the bullet caught him minutes ago, the wound sealed now but no doubt still painful.

And Jacob's blond hair is dappled crimson from the shrapnel cut that's closed but still an angry pink on his pale forehead.

Dominic speaks up again, quiet as usual and with a wary note in his voice that pricks at me more than I like. "You're not injured, are you, Riva?"

I shake my head quickly. "I'm fine."

I'm actually better than fine. The influx of our enemies' pain has left me energized and rejuvenated.

As the guys have probably noticed.

I shove my uneasiness aside and grab a rifle from where it's lying next to a hand lumpy with shattered bones.

We each pick up every gun we can find that hasn't been broken by Zian's wolfman strength or Jacob's telekinetic powers. I hold on to those that still have at least a few bullets, tucking one pistol into the back of my sweats and setting the other weapons in a growing common pile near the front door.

There's no way of knowing who we might have to fight next… and I'd rather fight with gunfire if I have the option.

That thought brings me to the huge living room windows that stretch from waist-height to the vaulted ceiling, two stories high. Most of their glass now lies in scattered shards on the floor, crunching beneath my sneakers.

A significant number of our attackers crashed in through these windows. I lean over the ledge into the cool autumn air and peer between the trees for any sign of where they came from—and any colleagues who might be on their way.

I can't see anything suspicious, and the fresh breeze filling my lungs is a welcome relief. My braid slipping over my shoulder, I tip farther out into the forest air just for a second.

Glass crackles just a few feet away, and I jerk to the side instinctively. A burning sensation sears across my waist.

I flinch again, glancing down. A shard still lodged in the frame has sliced into my bare flesh where my hoodie and tank top rode up.

Biting my lip against the pain, I jerk my shirts down over the cut and the puff of smoky stuff that started to waft from it and spin around. The wound throbs against my pressing elbow.

Zian has come up by the windows, his massive body looming more than a foot taller than me even in totally human form. He studies me with his dark brown eyes, probably wondering why I flinched so badly.

Or wondering if I'm going to hurl my power at him in response.

Before he can outright ask anything, I let out a stilted giggle. "Just a little jumpy after… all this. I'm going to check the second floor."

I hustle over to the stairs and dart up them, gritting my teeth against the deepening ache in my side. I am *not* going to beg Dominic for help, not when he's already wiped out.

Not when I now know that every bit of healing talent he uses, the beastly appendages he's so ashamed of grow even longer.

Engel's bedroom is painfully tidy, not a drawer ajar, not a wrinkle in her duvet. I can't help wondering whether she'd be more pissed off about the fact that I killed her or the mess I've made of her home below.

In the ensuite bathroom, I tear a chunk of thick fabric off a towel and fold it into a pad to stem the bleeding. Then I tie that firmly in place with a strip of one of Engel's sheets.

Such lovely linens she's outfitted her home with. I'm sure the thread count made her proud.

They bind my wound well enough. With my baggy hoodie overtop, you can't tell there's anything unusual underneath.

I stand in front of the bathroom mirror for a moment, digging my hands into my pockets and pressing the hasty bandage against my side. The throbbing makes my jaw tick, but a strange sense of peace settles over me.

This is one small fragment of what I inflicted on all our attackers downstairs. A reminder of what I did—what I don't ever want to have to do again.

If having that reminder helps ensure that I keep my most vicious hungers under control, it's a good thing.

The stairs creak, and I pull myself out of the ensuite into Engel's bedroom where I can make myself useful again.

It isn't Andreas coming upstairs after me, I realize with a faint tingling on my clavicle. I can sense him moving around on the level below through the little dark blotch on my skin—the mark that formed after we merged our bodies in more ways than we recognized at the time.

The mark that also appeared at the top of his sternum, that maybe he now wishes he could scrub off along with any other association with me.

I yank open the bedside and dresser drawers and find an envelope with a wad of hundred dollar bills in one and a jewelry box tucked into another. Well, we need any extra cash we can get from pawning Engel's valuables more than she's inclined to wear them in her current state.

I stuff the envelope into the ebony jewelry box and carry it into the hall just as Jacob makes an eager noise from the room next door. He comes out with a laptop clutched in his hands.

"Who knows how much useful info she's got stashed on this," he says, aiming a sharp but seemingly genuine smile at me.

I don't know how to respond when the vast majority of the smiles Jacob has shot at me in the past couple of weeks were cold and cruel. But I'm saved from needing to when Dominic calls up from the first floor.

"I found Engel's cell phone—and her car keys."

Jacob's smile widens. "All right. We make a swift getaway and then ditch it as soon as possible."

As we hustle back down the stairs, Zian rubs his jaw. "Should we drive back to the car we took most of the way here?"

Andreas shakes his head. "We don't know who might have found it by now. I say we head straight to the nearest active trainline and hitch a few more rides."

"Perfect." Jacob tucks the laptop under his arm. "Let's get moving."

His motion toward the door encompasses me as well as the guys. We all stoop to grab a couple more guns from the pile on our way out.

None of the other men look at me. As we tramp around the log house to the 4x4 parked off to the side, uneasiness prickles over my limbs.

We all need to leave—me getting caught would be a danger to the guys. Are they going to kick me to the curb after that?

Don't I *want* to leave, after everything they put me through?

We are blood, we always said to each other. But they've broken the promise of those words so many times since I found my way back to them.

I only came this far with them to get answers... and while we got plenty of those from Engel, what she told us only spawned new questions. I need to know more, and whatever Engel kept on her devices could be the key.

So I guess I'm sticking with them for now, at least during this brief reprieve while we save our skins. But who knows what horrible thoughts about me are winding through the guys' heads as we clamber into the vehicle.

This could be the very last ride we share.

Two

Riva

The glow of the laptop screen turns Jacob's face an even eerier pale than usual in the darkness of the train car. He glares at it and lets out a string of colorful curses before shoving it away.

Andreas glances over at him from where he's sitting by the wall and raises his eyebrows. "You didn't really think the genius scientist would forget to put password protection on her devices, did you?"

Jacob scowls. "It didn't seem like she got a whole lot of visitors she'd need to worry about prying into her stuff. There was hope."

He leans back against the stack of crates behind him, swaying a little with a bump on the tracks, and folds his muscular arms over his chest. "You'll just have to scrounge up another hacker for us."

Andreas tugs at the length of rope he picked up in the train yard and has been winding into knots to pass the time. "I can do that, as soon as we figure out where we're landing."

The smell of sawdust itches at my nose. I draw my knees up to my chest where I'm sitting across from Andreas and risk a question.

"Do you figure we should stay in Canada for now or head back to the States?"

We decided before we hitched our ride that it was better not to try to cross the border right away, not when we're so close to where the guardians may already realize we've come over. But we haven't picked a final destination yet.

Dominic stirs where he's been slouched near the car door. During our short wait for the train, he drained some of the life from a towering pine tree to heal up the other guys' wounds a little better, but the effort seems to have exhausted him.

His voice comes out steady enough, if typically quiet. "The guardians never sent us on any missions outside of the country. They'd probably expect us to cross back to more familiar territory."

Zian lifts his head from where he's been sorting through our collection of firearms, consolidating ammo where he can. "As far as we know, all of the facilities were in the States, right? The guardians probably know their way around better down there too."

Jacob nods. "I think we should stay up north while we regroup, until we've decided on our next steps."

His cool blue gaze slides to me, as if he wants my approval of the plan. As if my opinion suddenly matters to him after weeks of sneering at any suggestion I made.

He admitted to being an asshole and an idiot, with something like an apology… after he tore into me so brutally I had to run straight at a speeding train to make sure I didn't unleash my shrieking power on him. That was only a couple of days ago.

I don't know what to believe. Especially now that they know just how brutal *I* can be.

I press my elbow against the wound on my side—starting to seal on its own with the heightened ability to recover that all our bodies have, but still sore when I prod it. The pain lances through my torso, grounding me.

As I open my mouth to make a brief comment of agreement, the train car lurches. My arm bumps my side harder than before, and what comes out instead is a strained squeak.

All four of the guys sitting around me stiffen. A whiff of nervous pheromones reaches me.

I snap my mouth shut, my stomach flipping over. But I knew we weren't going to avoid this subject forever.

There's a moment of silence other than the rattle of the train over the tracks. Then Andreas speaks up, with a weird mix of wariness and concern in his tone.

"What happened at Engel's house—you didn't tell us you'd developed new abilities too."

I drop my chin to my knees, staring at the scuffed floor rather than holding his gaze. "It'd only… come out once before. I didn't want to think it would happen again."

I close my eyes and add, "I didn't want to think I'd done it in the first place."

I hadn't wanted my guys to realize I had something so horrifying in me. So much for that.

There's a rustle as Dominic pulls his parka closer around him in the cooling evening air. "It didn't look like you just killed them," he ventures.

My throat constricts, but I don't see any point in lying about it.

They saw everything. We might as well get it all out now so they can be as revolted as they're going to be.

My voice comes out scratchy. "The power latches on to any place it can cause pain. Like it feeds off hurting people as much as possible before they die."

"With that scream." Jacob taps the floor. "Like a banshee."

"A what?" Zian says.

I can hear Jacob's baleful glower without even opening my eyes. "Don't you remember that big fat mythology book we all passed around when we were kids? The one Griffin loved."

His voice goes just a little rough with those last few words, mentioning his twin. My hand rises automatically to grip my cat-and-yarn necklace, the one Griffin gave me.

The only thing any of us has left of him.

I can't grip it too hard, though—can't snap the rotating pieces open and shut like I used to when I was feeling tense. I broke it during that last argument with Jacob, and he was only able to partly fix it on his own.

As I let myself take in the darkened train car again, Dominic tilts his head to the side. "Weren't banshees the ones that screamed to warn that death was coming? I don't think they did the actual killing."

Jacob shrugs. "It's not as if our powers fit into neat little boxes. I don't remember any monsters that grew poison spikes and moved things with their minds." He runs his fingers over one forearm where his deadly spines can emerge.

The guys lapse into another momentary silence. Then Andreas fixes me with his gaze, almost like he's going to peer inside my memories, though no ruddy light comes into his dark grey eyes.

"That night at the farmhouse," he says carefully. "When you ran toward the train… You said you didn't want to hurt us. You were trying to stop the new power from coming out?"

I have the urge to curl up inside myself, to recoil from the question. But he obviously already knows.

I got so close to the verge that night, a little sound burst out of me. I saw him flinch. He's putting the pieces together.

I make myself speak. "I was—after everything—"

The words clog in my throat. *After we had sex. After the shadows in our blood tied us together.*

The act felt so precious in the moments after—until I overheard Andreas admitting that he'd gotten close to me just to dig for information. To figure out how much of a traitor I was.

He's apologized too. He's claimed that he wasn't trying to use me when we melded together like one being. But I don't know how much to believe that either.

I swallow thickly and propel myself onward. "After what we did, my nerves were all keyed up, my emotions whirling—and then with the argument, it was even worse—I *didn't* want to hurt any of you, not like that, but I could tell I was losing control."

More silence. I hug my knees tighter.

This is the worst. Not just the pain I can wield and revel in, but that some part of me was ready to inflict it on them.

No matter how awful they've been, they didn't deserve that—that all-encompassing, soul-rending torture.

Zian clears his throat. "So you… you would have let that train kill you…"

He doesn't seem to know how to go on.

"I wasn't really thinking," I mumble. "It was the only way I could stop myself for sure."

That's how bad it was. That's how close I got to tormenting the guys who were my only family, who I swore to protect, in the most horrific way imaginable.

I brace myself for accusations or recriminations. So I'm not at all prepared when Zian pushes away from his pile of guns and hunches down by my feet.

"We hurt you so badly," he says raggedly, his face so low to the floor his forehead must brush the gritty surface. "With everything we said, the way we'd been treating you—and you still would rather have *died* than hurt us."

My mouth opens and closes, my voice dried up in shock.

Zian goes on in my silence. "I'm so sorry, Riva. I should have been better. I shouldn't have trusted anything the guardians said. You were always there for us, doing everything for us—I am never going to forget that again."

I stare at the massive man kowtowing his apology to me for several beats of my heart before I can even process what's happening.

He isn't horrified. My confession has made him *more* regretful?

"Zee," I say softly, and don't know how to go on. My heart is aching as much with the memory of times he snapped at me as with the anguish he's expressing now.

He hasn't so much as lifted his head, as if he's waiting for some kind of judgment. My hand reaches out of its own accord toward the short tufts of his silky black hair.

My fingertips graze the top of his head, and Zian jerks away from my touch. Just an inch, but enough of a rejection that I yank my hand back.

"Sorry," he mutters to the floor. "Sorry. I—"

"It's okay," I say before he can go on. I'd rather not hear him explain why he's so adverse to me touching him.

He regrets a lot of things, clearly, but that doesn't mean he wants to get cozy with me either.

Zian eases up a little, his dark eyes searching mine. They're stormy, but lit with enough hope to send the ache in my chest jabbing even deeper.

I fumble for a fuller answer. "We've been through a lot. All of us. I don't really know where we go from here. But I'm not asking for anything."

At this point, I know better than to ask for anything.

Zee pushes upright, looking as if he's not totally satisfied with that answer but uncertain about what he would want instead.

By the door, Dominic draws himself a little straighter, his expression tightening. "You used the power at Engel's house. Are you sure… Are you sure you can control it *now*?"

He obviously isn't. And that's fair—that's closer to the reaction I was expecting.

I set my chin on my knees again. "No. That's why I want to understand everything Engel told us. How she made us—what she made us out of. I was hoping I could get rid of it, but if I can't, then there's got to be a way to at least rein it in more."

Ursula Engel admitted that she'd created us by combining human DNA with the essence of what she called "monsters." Maybe something on her laptop or phone will help us understand exactly what that means.

"We've all had issues with our talents getting away from us," Andreas says, but his tone is still wary.

When the rest of them lose control, none of them risks putting the rest of us through indescribable torture.

"It was only that one moment," I can't help replying. "There were other times when I could have used it, when it wanted me to let it loose, and I kept it under wraps. I *decided* to use it in Engel's house, because it was either that or we died."

"And it was fucking amazing." Jacob pushes to his feet, his penetrating stare sliding over the other guys. In the faint light with that resolute stance, he looks like a warrior guardian angel, just missing the wings.

He jabs his forefinger toward me. After the past couple of weeks, I can't restrain a wince even though his frown obviously isn't directed my way.

"Riva gave the pricks everything they deserved," he says fiercely. "She threw all the pain they've put us through back at them, right where it belongs. And she didn't give us so much as a papercut in the process. So don't any of you dare act like she's anything but a goddamned superhero."

I blink at him, startled speechless for the second time in minutes. How the hell did the guy who's been going out of his way to bully me at every opportunity suddenly become my biggest supporter?

Is he really, or is his attitude going to turn on a dime with the next shift in the wind?

The corner of Zian's mouth kicks up with a hint of a smile. "It was pretty spectacular watching them all go down."

Andreas tips his head to me. "We'll find answers—for all of us."

Dominic's attention has been drawn away by something beyond the door. He leans toward it before glancing back at us.

"We're coming up on the first junction. We wanted to switch trains here, right?"

"Yes." Jacob snatches up the laptop he cast aside. "The more times we divert course, the harder it'll be for the guardians to track us."

Zian stuffs the guns into the sack we found and peers around us through the walls of the car with his X-ray sight. "I don't see anything strange nearby."

A squeal pierces the air as the train's brakes grip the tracks. Dominic peeks out through the door again and motions to us when the coast is clear.

We hop out into the thickening night and slink along the side of another, motionless train to get a look at our options for transport.

As Jacob pushes ahead in his typical mode as our self-declared leader, Andreas touches my arm—just a fleeting gesture to draw my attention. He slows purposefully, and I match his pace even as tension winds around my gut.

What does he want?

He ducks his head with a slant of his mouth that looks more embarrassed than anything else and then glances sideways at me. "I realized—we got so caught up in the moment that night—I didn't even think about protection. Do we need to worry that you could be—"

I catch on before he even finishes the question.

"No," I interrupt hastily, my cheeks flaring. "The guardians fitted me with some birth control thing before we started going on missions, and they'd updated it just a few months before we tried to escape. It should still be working."

Even if it wasn't, with the stress and physical strain of my captivity at the cage-fighting arena, I haven't had a period in years.

"And that was the first time I ever… did anything like that," I add awkwardly, not really wanting to put a name on the act out loud. "So no diseases or whatever to worry about." I pause. "At least from me."

It's hard to tell in the dim light from the security lamps up ahead, but I think Andreas's face flushes beneath his coppery brown skin. His gaze drops to the gravel-strewn ground.

"There was only once before for me, and it was—the guardians arranged it, a couple months after they took you away. I think they figured we needed some kind of outlet. I didn't *want* to. But they would have been careful about health and all that."

A rush of cold washes over me. My feet stumble for a second before I recover. "You—they *forced* you? All of you?"

My gaze flicks to the guys ahead of us, but Andreas is already shaking his head. "They tried, but it… didn't go so well. That's why it was only the once, and only me."

His voice has gotten strained, but I have to ask. "What happened?"

Andreas's jaw ticks. He raises his head, but I can't tell which of his friends he's looking at. "That's one story that is definitely not mine to tell.

You should just know, while you were dealing with all that crap where they took you… a lot of shit went down for us too."

I'd already realized that, but I'd had no idea the guardians had gone that far.

Jacob motions to us, and Andreas picks up the pace to catch up. I follow him, my stomach churning.

Just how badly did our former captors damage the boys I loved?

And was it too much for them to ever really be those guys again, even if they want to?

Three

Andreas

I grip the handle of the door between our motel room and the adjoining one, and catch Dominic's eyes where he's sitting cross-legged on the bed. He looks a little bizarre, slouched there in his parka that disguises the bulge of his extra appendages.

He doesn't like any of us seeing his tentacles more than we have to. As if hiding them will make them less real.

"All good?" I mouth at him.

He nods, our phone pressed to his ear and his other hand resting on the laptop's keyboard. Then his attention veers back to the computer.

"Okay," he says to the woman on the other end as he taps a few keys.

The hacker I managed to connect with—by searching the right kinds of online forums for the telltale signals I've learned—is theoretically going to walk Dominic through the process of cracking the laptop's password from a distance. We decided Dom was the best choice for that job since he's definitely got the rest of us beat when it comes to staying calm and focused.

I don't want to see what Jacob or Zian would do to the computer after a few frustrating failures.

Me, I'd probably get distracted wondering about the hacker's other exploits and wishing I could peek inside her memories from over the phone.

I slip into the other room and shut the door with a click. When I turn around, I find Jacob perched on the edge of one of the double beds.

He hasn't got anywhere to go, but he's poised like he's about to charge into battle. Typical.

The muffled sound of sloshing water filters through the bathroom door. Jake notices my glance.

"Zee wanted to take a *bath*," he mutters with a combination of derision and bafflement that's almost funny.

My mouth twitches into a smile. "This is the first time he's really had a chance in ages. Might as well."

Even when we commandeered the townhouse on the college campus right after our escape, all its tiny bathrooms had were shower stalls. And I have a hazy recollection from the swimming lessons the guardians insisted on when we were kids: Zian stopping to simply float on the surface of the water in the big glass tank they used.

It might feel pretty incredible having that huge body buoyed up. Taking all the weight off.

Of course, I don't know how much water he can actually fit in the motel tub around all those muscles of his.

I make a mental note, adding to the long, invisible list I've been keeping in my head: We'll find a place with a proper swimming pool.

Eventually. When the guardians are no longer at our heels.

If that day ever comes.

Jacob jerks his head toward the door to my and Dominic's room. "You're sure this computer guru is going to come through?"

I shrug. "She only gets the rest of the money if she does. I didn't get the impression it'd be that hard for her."

"How long are we going to be waiting while she holds Dom's hand?"

I resist the urge to grimace at him. He doesn't really mean to be insulting, even if he sounds like it.

I know from experience and observation that the vast majority of the bitterness that spills out of Jake is actually directed at himself.

"She said it depends on the exact firmware on the laptop. A simple one could take just a few minutes. A more secure setup, she figured two to three hours. Shouldn't be more than that."

Jacob lets out a huff. "Engel would have had plenty of fucking security."

No doubt. But I'm not sure taking a few hours to unwind is a bad thing—for any of us.

My gaze darts to the door at the other end of the space. The one that leads into Riva's room.

A soft tingle ripples through the spot at the top of my chest where our interlude in the farmhouse marked me. I can sense her on the other side of the door, still there.

She looked so surprised when Jacob pointed out the room that was hers, without messing with the locks or posting a guard outside. So fucking surprised it kills me.

The ache reverberates through my chest alongside the urge I've been fighting ever since that night at the farmhouse. Every particle in my body wants to go to her, to wrap her up in my arms, to tell her I've got her, I love her, it'll all be okay.

But it isn't okay. She thinks I betrayed her.

Because I *did* betray her… just not quite as badly as she believes.

Riva doesn't want me touching her. She barely wants to talk to me.

And maybe she isn't entirely wrong, because the other image that flashes through my mind when I think of her is from Engel's cottage.

Jaw stretched open impossibly wide. Every plane of her face gone taut. Her eyes hazed white.

And the little quivers that passed through her body with each pulse of her scream—eager, almost *giddy*. Like twisting and snapping those bodies while they cried out in agony was a thrill.

I swallow, ignoring the twinge of nausea that ripples through my stomach at the memory. She called on that power to save us—and however she felt about it in the moment, there was no mistaking the horror and revulsion in her expression when we prodded her about it after.

She didn't ask for her new talent any more than Zian asked for his feral rages or Dominic his growing tentacles.

I have to show her I understand that too.

I turn back to Jacob. "I'm going to take Riva to go pick up supplies at the mall. We need to replace what we lost at the townhouse now that we have a chance."

Jacob springs to his feet, his gaze immediately twice as intense. "I'll come with you."

I hold up my hand, not at all surprised by his declaration. "It's better if you stay here. Dom's occupied, and Zian obviously needs a break. Someone needs to be standing guard, right?"

Jacob's eyes narrow. "The mall is more exposure. If they find you there—"

I raise my eyebrows. "We're in the middle of nowhere, four train hops and a drive from the last place the guardians could locate us. And if they find us anyway, Riva can look after herself."

"But—"

"Jake," I say, and he stops at the firmness of my tone.

I hesitate, because this isn't the kind of thing we've normally talked about. It isn't the kind of thing we've normally been *able* to talk about with the guardians watching over us in the facility and charting every weakness.

But I suspect it'd be good if we were all a little more honest about how we feel.

"I screwed up with her," I say quietly. "In some ways worse than you did. I need to take my chances to make it up to her when I can get them."

Jacob's jaw tightens, but he lowers his eyes at the same time, looking vaguely abashed.

"Fine," he mutters. "Get more phones too. If we're going to be splitting up sometimes, we need to be able to reach each other."

I nod. "Totally agreed. Thank you."

His gaze flicks back to me, his pale blue eyes now stormy. "Just don't be gone too long."

I grab some of the money from our stash and knock on the door to Riva's room. My gut clenches in apprehension about her response before her voice calls out, clear but hesitant. "You can come in."

She can probably sense that it's me just like I'm aware of her presence beyond the door. I ease it open to see her setting down the TV remote next to her where she's poised in the middle of the bed.

I felt her there and she's been at the forefront of my mind for days, but seeing her directly sends an extra jolt of anguished affection through my heart.

She looks so small and delicate with her hoodie hugged tight around her and her shoulders warily hunched. Her skin shines nearly as pale as the silvery strands of her hair that twine with the darker gray underneath.

She flips her braid over her shoulder and studies me with her bright brown eyes. They gleam with feline alertness even when she's in fully human form.

Riva isn't weak or fragile, not really. I've seen so many times how much strength her tiny frame contains.

But somehow that knowledge makes it worse. She endured so much from us, took the accusations and the venom—both metaphorical and literal—and even when she finally cracked, her first instinct was to sacrifice herself to save us.

It's hard to imagine how we let ourselves question her devotion. I have to find a way to show just how devoted to her *I* can be.

I don't care how vicious her new abilities are or how well she can control them. It doesn't matter if she ends up hurting me by accident.

Anything she could deal out would be worth it just to stand by her side like I should have to begin with.

"I'm going to that mall we passed to pick up some changes of clothes for all of us and a few other things," I say. "Do you want to come along? I figured you might like getting to choose your own outfits this time."

Riva blinks, and that flash of startled emotion flits across her face again. The last time we bought new clothes, Jacob forced her to stay back in the car under guard.

And I let him get away with it.

She unfolds her limbs with her usual careful grace and pushes herself off the bed. "All right. I would like that."

We leave through her outer door, Riva stepping close enough to me that I catch a whiff of her sweetly metallic scent. My fingers itch to stroke over her hair or trail along her jaw, but I curl them into my palms.

She'd only flinch away.

She tucks herself into the passenger seat of the sedan we made off with —clunky but functional enough. I let her sit in silence as I start the engine and turn onto the country highway toward the suburban mall about ten minutes down the road, nestled between a couple of minor towns.

There isn't a whole lot else on the highway other than a diner that looks like it caters mostly to truckers and a building that's not much more than a shack with granite lawn ornaments poised for sale out front. Just after noon on a weekday, the mall's parking lot is pretty desolate too.

That suits our preferences just fine.

Riva tugs her hood up over her distinctive hair before we get out of the car. I run my hand over my tight coils and hope that they and my brown skin won't stand out too much in small-town Manitoba.

The guardians always sent us to decently big cities for our missions.

I've gotten more uneasy glances roaming across the more out-of-the-way parts of the continent in the past couple of weeks than in my whole life beforehand.

Before we reach the mall doors, I pass several bills to Riva. "Grab whatever you want, wherever you want."

Another flicker of surprise passes through her eyes. "You want me to go off on my own?"

As we push inside, I offer her a crooked smile. "As much as I'd like to offer my services as bodyguard, I know you can kick a hell of a lot more ass than I can."

We both know that's not what she meant, but she ducks her head in acknowledgment. As she takes in the sprawl of shops ahead of us, just a hint of a smile touches her lips.

I spot a clock mounted near the entrance and point to it. "We'll meet back here in an hour?"

"Sounds good."

Riva sets off at a more energetic pace, making a beeline for a store with sporty tank tops and sweats in the display window. I watch her go for a few seconds before propelling myself in my own direction.

I don't actually like leaving her to her own devices, but only because I won't immediately know if she's under threat.

There isn't a whole lot I'd be able to do that she couldn't. What I said to her about our relative self-defense skills was accurate, though.

And there's no denying how much the freedom meant to her.

I've tried apologizing for my epic screw-up with my words, and that hasn't been enough, understandably. So I'll just have to prove how much I trust her—how much she matters to me—with how I act as well.

It's not as if I've completely lost track of her anyway. As I move briskly through the men's section of the one department store grabbing the shirts and pants I know the other guys will want that aren't too pricy, as I pick up cheap but sturdy looking backpacks at a luggage shop and four more prepaid phones at an electronics kiosk, I'm constantly aware of Riva's position relative to me in the building.

But I can't sense anything other than where she is—no emotions, no other impressions. If she was in distress, I'd have no idea.

I work through my mental shopping list so quickly that I still have plenty of time left when I reach the end. I pause by a store directory and scan the other options.

What else could I offer Riva as a gift of sorts? A token of my affection?

I riffle through my large collection of captured stories—from other people's memories, from TV shows and movies and books. How do you pamper the woman you love?

I've never had the chance to before. I doubt Riva's ever been pampered enough to have any idea how she'd like it to happen.

Which only makes it more important that *someone* start doing it now.

She's already getting whatever clothes she likes. I can't imagine her wanting any jewelry other than the necklace from Griffin that I've never seen her take off except that one night when everything went to hell.

My gaze settles on a bath and body shop. If even Zian can appreciate a nice soak in the tub, why wouldn't Riva?

It seems like as good a place to start as any.

I pop into the shop, the mingling floral perfumes flooding my nose, and try to pick out something to Riva's tastes. I don't think she wants to smell like a rose garden—but then, what do I know?

In the end, I grab a selection of different options and stuff the bag into one of the backpacks so I can keep it sort of a surprise.

When I make it back to the front entrance with ten minutes to spare, Riva is already waiting there. The jeans she's wearing look the same as before, but they're tucked into a pair of lace-up leather boots totally ready for ass-kicking.

She waggles one foot at me with a slightly larger smile than I saw before. "I figured I should be prepared for more forest hikes. And snow. If we keep ahead of the guardians for much longer, we'll be dealing with winter weather too."

"Very wise," I say casually, like my heart hasn't skipped a beat taking in the rest of her. She's swapped her old navy hoodie for a deep maroon one that brings out the gold tones in her vibrant eyes.

A couple of plastic shopping bags dangle from her arms, so obviously she hasn't held back. Good.

A little of her previous uncertainty returns as we head across the parking lot. "Do you need the cash I didn't use back?"

I shake my head immediately. "We should all have at least a little money on us in case we get separated. Oh, and I got a phone for you. We'll have to program in each other's numbers once we're back at the motel."

She takes the package from me and holds it tightly for a second before slipping it into her bag. "We're really getting our act together this time."

"It should have been like this from the start." I open the trunk and toss my bags inside, then glance back toward the mall. "We should probably do a little grocery shopping too. Non-perishables. The money'll go a lot farther that way than with restaurants."

"Good point." Riva rubs her hands together as if she's already envisioning the meals to come.

The supermarket attached to the mall contrasts starkly with the rest of the space, a chill in the air and the overhead lights twice as harsh. I can't help noticing one of the clerks drifting along behind me while supposedly checking that the shelves are properly organized.

Does he think I'm going to rob the soup and sauces aisle?

I fill the basket I picked up hastily, including a box of cookies and a tray of tarts in recollection of Dominic's sweet tooth. I rejoin Riva in the fruits and vegetables section, where she's contemplating bags of lemons.

"Looking for something to stuff down Jacob's throat?" I ask wryly.

The corner of Riva's mouth quirks upward, and she shakes her head. "I was thinking that I kind of liked that drink I got… with Brooke… at the club. It was kind of citrusy and sour. But I'd rather have it without the alcohol."

Brooke—who lived in the townhouse next to the one we were squatting in on campus. Who died when the guardians ambushed us there.

I wince inwardly at the memory and motion to the lemons. "You should get them, then. Experiment. Why not?"

"Yeah. There's no one to tell us what to do now. Why not."

I wouldn't call her peppy, but by the time we return to the car for a second time, her stance has definitely gotten looser. So when we reach the motel and I'm sorting out her bags from mine, I only feel a little awkward getting out the bath and body stuff.

"I bought something else for you," I say, handing it over. "In case you want to just chill out for a bit while we can. There's regular salts and a bunch of different scented stuff…"

Riva peeks inside with a trace of confusion and lifts out one bottle full of pearly blue liquid. "Bubble bath?"

I grin and spread my hands. "Maybe you want to relive the childhood we never got."

When she gives me a pensive look, I let my hands fall back to my sides. "You've been through a lot, in general and recently… and a lot of it is because of us. You deserve a chance to relax."

I can't read her expression, but at least she doesn't appear to be pissed off. She glances into the bag again and cocks her head.

"Maybe I will."

She goes in through her door and I knock on Jacob and Zian's, not wanting to disturb Dominic if he's still deep in hacker-consultation mode.

Jake flings the door open as if he thinks I've come to warn him of the impending apocalypse. Zee only pauses briefly where he's pacing the room, his hair still damp from his own earlier bath.

"No emergency." I hold up the bags. "I've got clothes, phones, and food—and packs to stash them in so we can keep everything with us wherever we go."

Naturally, Jacob grabs the bags from me and immediately starts sorting the clothes into their respective backpacks, deciding without asking what belongs to who. But he knows us—it's not like I can say he's wrong.

"Is Dominic still on the call?" I ask Zian.

The big guy nods and resumes his pacing. He's only crossed the floor a few times before he pauses to contemplate the grocery bags. "What did you get to eat?"

I suppress a laugh. "Mostly stuff we don't have to worry about going bad anytime soon, like protein bars and dried fruit. But for tonight I did find some premade subs. Yours is meatball."

Despite his obvious tension, his eyes light up. I pick up that bag and stick the subs in the fridge before he gets any ideas about having that dinner just a couple of hours after the drive-through lunch we gulped down on the way here.

At his frown, I toss him an apple. "You do need a few nutrients other than protein."

He glowers at my teasing tone but takes a bite as he goes back to his pacing.

Jacob carries one fresh change of clothes into the bathroom and takes the world's fastest shower, probably worried we'll somehow descend into catastrophe if he leaves us alone for more than a few minutes. The hiss of the running water tugs my thoughts back to Riva in the other room.

Is she soaking in her bathtub right now? My mind conjures the image of her small but soft curves, the pert nipples I stroked my fingers over, the slim hips that rose to meet me…

Heat floods my body. Now *I* need a shower—a cold one.

Maybe one day she'll trust me enough to invite me into a bath with her.

That idea sets my mind down on another dangerous path. I borrow Jacob's tactic and start pacing to distract myself.

Jake stalks out of the bathroom with a flick of his gaze toward the door to Riva's room. I can tell from the momentary tensing of his expression that he wants to go check on her and is holding himself back.

He looks at me next, and the heat that filled me earlier fades away under his scrutiny.

I'm not totally sure if Zee and Dom realize just how close Riva and I got the other night, but Jacob has definitely guessed. Knowing that sends a weird pang of guilt through me.

As far as I know, I'm the only one of us who's experienced sex once, let alone twice. Even if the first time wasn't by choice, some part of me enjoyed it by the end.

It's pretty hard for a teenage boy to convince his body not to react to certain kinds of stimulation.

I sure as hell hope the other guys don't envy me that first time. The suffocating agony of fighting against your physical reactions with all your willpower and still losing… I wouldn't wish it on anyone.

They might envy me about Riva, though.

She turned to me out of the four of us because I was the one who was there for her. But the allegiance I offered her was partly under false pretenses.

I'm not sure I really deserved to get to know her that way first. She admitted she had feelings for all of us.

There's nothing I can do about it now, though.

I hold up another apple. "Hungry?"

Jacob is just tossing the gnawed core into the trash bin when Dominic shoves open the adjoining door, the laptop clutched in his hands. We all freeze.

"I'm in," he says breathlessly, his hazel eyes unusually wild. "And I found something—we had no idea—"

Riva nudges open the door opposite, obviously having heard him. She's rebraided her hair, but a few strands stick damply to the sides of her pretty face, and I can't repress a shiver of satisfaction that she used my gift.

"What?" she demands. "What have you got?"

Dominic motions us over and sits on the end of one of the beds where we can easily gather around him. The open folds of his parka pool around him.

He points to a file open on the screen. A tremor runs through his hand.

"There could be others," he says. "Other shadowbloods like us."

FOUR

Riva

In the first few moments after Dominic's declaration, all of us simply stare—at him, at the laptop screen. My head is spinning too fast for me to concentrate on the words.

"What do you mean?" I blurt out. "We never saw—the guardians never said—"

Dominic waves at the screen with a rustle of his parka. He must be sweltering in the thick coat even with it unzipped, but I've never seen him display his tentacles unless he absolutely has to.

"It's not obvious whether they actually *did* create more hybrids. But I found a file that refers to different processes that Engel used. There's an original one, labeled first gen and dated almost twenty-two years ago."

"Around the time we would have been conceived, however that happened," Andreas fills in, looking ill.

Dominic nods. "And then there are two others, one from about five years after that and then another after two more. Some of it is in shorthand notation I don't understand. But it seems like she's reminding herself of where she left certain things out."

My stomach has balled into a massive knot. "She didn't want to make more people like us. She didn't even want *us* to keep living. She said by the time we were toddlers, she'd already changed her mind."

Jacob frowns, leaning his weight onto his hand where it's resting on the comforter next to me. He isn't paying any attention to me, but I'm abruptly aware of how close he is.

How close they all are.

I scrambled onto the bed at Dominic's beckoning without thinking, just wanting to know what he's found. Now I'm perched on my knees with Jacob just a few inches at my right and Andreas equally close at my left.

And Dom is right in front of me. I could tip my head onto his shoulder if I wanted to.

An unwelcome tingle of warmth races over my skin. Suddenly I wish I never took Andreas's suggestion of a soak in the tub, as brief as I made it.

I figured the regular salts he got might be good for the wound on my side that's still raw. If it gets infected, I'll *have* to ask Dominic for help.

But now my skin is scrubbed clean under my crisply new clothes. The sensation is energizing in ways I'd rather not tap into.

No matter how badly these men hurt me, some part of my body—maybe even my soul—believes that I belong with them. As close to them as I can get.

Thankfully, it's my mind that gets to make those decisions.

I stay stiffly still where I can still see the screen but avoiding easing any closer to the guys.

Jacob makes a vague gesture at the computer. "She was the one who figured out how to make us, but she said there were other people who had control over the facility—who could boss her around. They wanted to keep us. Maybe they wanted to make more too."

Zian lets out a rough chuckle. "She could have given them instructions that were missing pieces so it wouldn't actually work. Pretended it was a fluke they produced us."

"Or the new process worked, but without the parts she thought made us too dangerous," Dominic says quietly.

I shudder. "There could be a bunch of shadowblood teenagers being put through all the same tests we were."

Or even younger kids. There's no saying the guardians wouldn't have used Engel's processes more than once after she handed them over.

"Is there anything else in there that would tell us for sure?" Jacob demands.

As Dominic starts clicking through more files, I scoot farther back on the bed. Could there have been other people like us, with wisps of smoke in their blood and monstrous powers, at the facility where we grew up?

There were an awful lot of doors on the same levels as our cells. For all we know, the guardians had separate training rooms elsewhere in the building.

And we know we lived in at least three different facilities over the course of our captivity. It's also possible they kept younger test subjects in a totally different place.

Or maybe Engel screwed her colleagues over and they never managed to create anyone else even sort of like us. She didn't seem bothered that it was just the five of us who showed up, other than wondering about Griffin's absence.

Dominic makes a discontented sound. "There are more documents with that weird system of notation I don't know how to read. I don't see anything definite about other 'shadowbloods,' but she doesn't seem to have any files even on us here. I'll keep digging."

"You got into her phone too?" Andreas asks.

"Yeah, but she must have deleted everything whenever she used it. No call history, no saved contacts, nothing."

I restrain a sigh and push myself right to the edge of the bed. My limbs itch to return to my own room where the guys' presence won't niggle at me, but I want to hear the second Dominic finds something.

It could be there's nothing useful on the laptop at all. That we're even more adrift than when I first broke them out of the facility, when they had the goal of finding Engel to see what she knew.

The TV remote is sitting on the bedside table. Aimlessly, I pick it up and start flicking through the channels.

Zian gets up and comes around to get a better view of the TV, but he sits carefully on the other bed, a few feet away. I know I don't have to worry about *him* getting up in my personal space.

He shoots me a cautious glance, but his voice comes out with a friendly warmth despite its gruffness. "Do you figure a massacre in that little cabin will make the news? Stuff like that can't happen very often near some tiny town."

I consider the question seriously, lingering on a news report about traffic conditions. "Engel's place was so isolated, it'd have been the guardians who found it. And they'd have covered it up."

"Like it never happened."

"Yeah." I cross my arms, tapping my elbow against the rebandaged wound that's hidden under my hoodie.

I wish I could erase what I did completely out of existence, as thoroughly as Andreas can wipe out memories.

I wish I could erase the ability right out of *me*.

I flip the channels a few more times and pause with a jolt of recognition. The faces on the screen, the slightly hazy lighting, and the dramatic swell of music are all so familiar they send me back more than four years to the TV breaks we got in the middle of training.

A woman with billowy hair and an elegant dress wags a manicured finger at a stern-looking man with slicked-back hair. "Don't you dare," she says, drawing the words out.

He squares his shoulders, glowering down at her dramatically. "You're the last person who should be threatening me, Carolina."

Andreas has lifted his head to see what I'm watching. A soft chuckle escapes him. "That's the crazy soap opera Griffin always wanted to watch."

Jacob's gaze jerks up too. At the flexing of his jaw, I feel like I have to explain—to make it clear I didn't mean to rub salt in a wound.

Even though my own heart aches with the memory of watching these storylines play out tucked next to his twin on the sofa.

Heat tickles across my cheeks as I make myself speak. "It was actually —I liked it. Griffin just knew, and he knew you guys would tease me about it if I said *I* wanted to watch the show."

From the tick of Jacob's eyelid, I can't tell whether my admission made things better or worse.

Andreas arches his eyebrows, but his tone stays mild. The same careful way he's been speaking to me ever since his last apology.

"I think you're allowed one or two interests that are a little girly, Tink. We would never have forgotten that you could take us down in two seconds flat in a sparring match."

Zian gives a huff. "The rest of you, maybe."

I squirm a little, still embarrassed. "Everything in this show was just so different from the facility. They were always going to fancy places and meeting fancy people. And when they got angry, they'd just stare and snap at each other instead of stabbing or shooting."

Not to mention that watching the characters' melodramatic relationship issues made me feel a little less ridiculous having a crush on all five of my best friends.

Before anyone can talk about the soap I secretly adored any more—before it can provoke any further painful memories—I shut the TV off and turn back toward Dominic. "Anything else on the laptop?"

He's brought one hand to his mouth, resting his knuckle against his lips as he scans the current batch of files. "I mean, there's a lot on here. Some of this is kind of interesting—she's got notes on different types of 'monsters.'"

We all perk up.

"Like, what kinds we were made out of?" Zian asks.

Dominic shakes his head. "Nothing connecting them specifically to us. Just observations and data, abilities and possible weaknesses."

Jacob grimaces. "Either to figure out what she wanted to fuse into us or how we were supposed to go take the things down."

Engel had said that she originally created us in the hopes that we'd be powerful enough to fight the creatures she called monsters. Then she decided we were even more dangerous than the original monsters were.

I draw my legs up to my chest. "We've got to figure out more about what we are and what we can do, somehow. If the full monsters can go around mingling with humans without most people noticing, *they* can obviously control their abilities just fine."

So there ought to be ways that we can too. Ways to make it easier to contain my urge to shriek when I get angry.

Ways to ensure Andreas doesn't fade away after he uses his ability to turn invisible. Ways to tame Zian's wolfish rage.

Maybe even a way to get Dominic's tentacles to shrink back into him instead of growing.

Dominic rubs his chin. "It doesn't seem like anyone at the facilities would know. Engel made us, and I don't think she ever shared the full process with anyone else."

"We'd have a hell of a time trying to go straight at the guardians on their home territory anyway," Andreas says.

Zian hesitates and then catches my gaze. "What about—the place they sent you to, after we tried to escape?"

I suppress a shudder at the thought of the cage-fighting arena where I was held—the weekly matches against armed men twice my size, the shackles that weighed down my arms in between, and the mix of fear and hatred that emanated off my keepers.

"They didn't know anything," I said. "I'm not sure they had any idea what I was other than, to them, a freak."

Jacob's eyes narrow. "We need to pay them back too. They're going to regret everything they put you—"

"They already regretted it," I break in, and jerk my gaze away. I don't want to watch their expressions while I admit this. "That's the first time my new power came out. I took out the boss and all his people who were around… and the whole audience."

My shoulders come up defensively, but I refuse to outright cringe. The memory of that much larger massacre still makes me queasy, but it got me free. It brought me back to my guys, even if our reunion hasn't exactly gone the way I hoped.

If it wasn't for the carnage I dealt with my scream, I'd still be in those shackles in the room where the boss kept me, all alone.

There's a moment of silence, like the other guys aren't sure what to say. Then Zian grunts. "Good."

Jacob's mouth curves into one of the hard little smiles that until recently were normally aimed at me. This one is on my behalf. "Yes. They got what they deserved."

I'm not sure the other two guys feel quite the same way, but Andreas at least changes the subject so we don't need to dwell on my past brutality.

"If we can't get more answers about our 'monstrous' talents from the people who put them into us," he says, "what if we asked the things that have their own talents?"

Zian knits his brow. "You want to talk to the *monsters*?"

Andreas holds up his hands. "I'm just saying, they're the only other direct source of information. We don't have to make friends or anything, just find one or two and question them."

As his suggestion sinks in, I find myself nodding. "And we don't know how monstrous those monsters actually are. Engel said they're horrible… but she thought *we* were horrible too."

The guardians are against the things they call monsters, and they want to enslave us. So we share at least one other thing with the creatures: a common enemy.

"We'd still need to be cautious," Dominic points out.

"Of course. Trust no one." Jacob rolls his shoulders as if he's warming up to launch into an interrogation right now. "Any idea from her notes where we'd be best off looking for these creatures?"

Dominic tilts his head to the side, studying the screen. "It sounds like most of the ones that mix with humans regularly like to do it where there are lots of people to blend in with. So a big city seems like it'd be our best bet."

Zian relaxes a little. "That'll mean more people for us to blend in with too. Should we stick to Canada still? What's the biggest city up here?"

"That would be Toronto. Bigger than most of the cities in the States too." Andreas glances around at us with a slow-stretching grin. "What do you say we head a little farther east to do some monster-hunting?"

FIVE

Riva

"This is part of downtown too?" I ask, peering through the windshield at the buildings we're cruising by. "How much of it is there?"

Andreas laughs from behind the wheel. "I told you it was a big city."

He brakes at a red light and glances over his shoulder toward the guys. They're crammed together in the backseat… because Zian insisted I should get to ride shotgun even though his bulky body needs the space way more than I do.

I'm not totally sure whether he was being considerate or ensuring there was no chance he'd end up squished next to me if Jacob demanded the front seat instead.

"One time I crossed paths with a guy who grew up in Toronto," Andreas says, falling into the slightly lilting cadence he takes on in storytelling mode. "He had a bunch of memories of this place. Worked somewhere downtown. Lots of hustle and bustle."

"I don't suppose he had any memories of monster encounters?" Jacob asks with a hint of impatience.

Andreas lets any implied criticism roll right off his back. "Nah. The most interesting thing I saw was he climbed that whole tower once."

He points toward one of the back windows where a slim building with a bulge partway up, like an olive speared on a toothpick only a whole lot bigger, juts up toward the clouded sky. It's got to be twice as tall as the highest skyscrapers nearby.

"Climbed the outside?" Zian says doubtfully.

Andreas chuckles. "The inside, going up the stairs. Seemed like they went on forever. Then he got to the top and puked."

"And that's your idea of a fun story?" Jacob mutters.

"It didn't seem like he minded so much. He laughed about it after, and then his friends caught up and they had a little celebration in this restaurant up there."

I frown at the pedestrians ambling by on the crowded sidewalks. Just like all the other sidewalks we've passed, none of them stand out as anything other than human.

Curiosity tickles up inside my head. "I wonder if you've ever looked inside a monster's memories. I wonder if you *could*."

Andreas cocks his head. "I don't know. I've never run into anyone whose memories I couldn't see. But hopefully the real monsters aren't blending in so well that I wouldn't notice pretty quick once I peeked inside."

"If they don't remember doing anything monstrous, then they're probably not all that bad," Dominic remarks in his quietly thoughtful way.

We all sit with that thought for a minute as the car creeps along through the traffic. Then Zian sets his hand on his belly.

"Since we haven't figured out where to go yet anyway… maybe we should grab some dinner?"

Jacob lets out a huff, but Andreas nods. "It'd give me some time to concentrate on the people around and see if I can stumble on any unusual memories that'd point us in the right direction."

"Fine," Jacob says. "But let's pick someplace low key where they don't expect us to be dressed up or anything."

He looks pulled together enough, wearing a combination of collared shirt and slacks that Andreas picked up for him at the mall. Andreas could probably blend in anywhere that's not high-level fine dining in his Henley and khakis.

The rest of us, though… I've got on my new favorite hoodie, the inside velvety soft against my arms, and a new pair of cargo pants with a couple of knives stashed in the pockets and a pistol in the back of the waist, just in case.

Zian's in his preferred athletic casual, sweats and tee under a track jacket, and Dominic—well, he's going to look a little strange keeping that parka on inside no matter where we go.

Every one of the men is still absolutely stunning, though. I jerk my gaze back to the windshield and instruct myself to stop noticing, as if that strategy is going to work this time after it's gone *so* well before.

"I think I see a good option." Andreas pulls the car into a tight parking spot and motions to a storefront farther down the street.

We all clamber out into the cool autumn air. I suck in a deep breath, both to clear my lungs and to see if I catch any unusual tastes that might lead us to our target—and Dominic twitches where he's stepped out next to me.

I only see it from the corner of my eye, and when I glance at him he looks perfectly calm, but I think that was a flinch. A faint tang of nervous adrenaline reaches my nose before the breeze washes it away.

I probably gulped a bunch of air like that right before I let out my killer shriek.

The thought weighs on me as I tramp alongside the guys to a restaurant with a faded sign proclaiming it the Daffodil Diner. The windows are a tad grimy and the leather seats I can see inside are sporting a few cracks, but it's not crowded and definitely not fancy.

I'll take it.

Jacob pushes inside first with his usual commanding air and scores us a booth in the corner next to the front windows. I'd imagine he wants to keep an eye on everyone passing by outside throughout the meal.

This may be a big city that we're blending into, but that doesn't mean the guardians couldn't track us down here.

Apprehension prickles over my skin. I hardly notice how Jacob has ushered the guys into the seats until he's motioning for me to sit down across from him.

He's arranged so that I get to sit on the end of the bench, where I'm not boxed in. The exact opposite of how he'd have handled this scenario a week ago with his fears that I'd take off on them.

I'm next to Zian, who's left me plenty of space beside his brawn—for both of our benefits, no doubt.

I accept one of the menus the waitress brings us, my gaze darting between it and the window.

If the guardians *did* somehow find us here, we'd see them coming, right? It looks like there's a back entrance over by the washrooms.

And if we really need to make a fast getaway, glass is always breakable.

When I finally convince myself to give the menu my full attention, my mouth starts watering. We haven't eaten anything except grocery store offerings and drive-through fast food in days.

The burgers look tasty, but I've had a ton of those already. And so many of the other options sound good.

Even if this place isn't five-star dining, it'll at least be different from the stuff I've spent most of my life subsiding on.

I lick my lips. Andreas catches the movement with apparent amusement.

"Already know what you want, Tink?"

"I want the whole menu," I mutter. "They have fish and chips *and* lasagna. How am I supposed to decide?"

One corner of his mouth ticks upward. "I was eyeing the lasagna. How about I get that and promise you a piece of it?"

My eyes flick to him. I evaluate his expression, but he looks totally relaxed about the offer—and maybe a little hopeful.

I don't want to feel like I owe him for the kindness. But I also really want both dinners.

I set down my menu. "It's a deal. We'll trade part."

Zian hums to himself. "Ribs or steak? They should have a combo."

Dominic casts his pensive gaze around the restaurant's interior. "At a place like this, I think ribs would be a better bet."

"Not like I'm that picky about my steaks," Zian replies.

I've generally been trying to look at Jacob as little as possible, but it's hard when he's sitting in front of me. When my gaze snags on him next, his eyes are just narrowing, his attention fixed on the window.

My head snaps around with a hitch of my pulse, just as a man on the sidewalk outside fumbles his cup of takeout coffee. The steaming liquid splashes all down his shirt, and he yelps loud enough for me to hear it through the glass.

As the guy hustles away, I glance back at Jacob. A small but satisfied smile has curled his lips.

He catches me watching him and draws himself up a little straighter. "That jerk was eyeing you like he figured he'd have *you* for dinner."

So it wasn't just clumsiness but a little telekinetic push that spilled the coffee.

I glower at Jacob. "Being looked at isn't going to hurt me. And if he tried to do more, I can handle some random dude just fine."

Jacob shrugs. "A more subtle approach is better for us than bringing out claws in public."

He has a point, but I fold my arms over my chest. "Or you could just not pick fights over imaginary insults."

Jacob pins me with the full force of his cool stare. Somehow it doesn't feel all that chilly at the moment, though.

"You can still be angry at me, and that's fine," he says, low and even but with a terse edge that suggests he isn't really all that happy about my feelings. "It's not going to stop me from protecting you."

Says the guy who spent most of the last few weeks torturing me every way he could. It's really not fair that the vehemence behind his words sends a flood of heat licking over my skin.

"We all are," Zian puts in, glancing toward the window as if he thinks there might be some new threat out there for him to take on next.

Before I have to figure out what to say to my self-declared bodyguards, the waitress swoops in to take our orders.

After she leaves, Jacob turns to Dominic, taking the pressure off me. "You kept looking through Engel's notes while we were driving. Did you find anything else that could help us ID the monsters?"

Dominic's mouth twists. "I'm not sure. Even in the parts that aren't using her special shorthand at all, I can tell there are a lot of gaps, things she didn't bother explaining because she already understood."

"There has to be something, or no one would ever realize they're around," Zian says.

"I mean, in the write-ups on different types, she mentioned 'common characteristics.' Things like a werewolf is likely to have pointed ears or fangs or claws. But obviously they don't go walking around like that all the time."

Andreas rubs his jaw. "Maybe they do show some outward signs, though. Otherwise, why mention it?"

Zian frowns. "None of us have anything noticeable." He pauses, with an expression like he's just swallowed his tongue. "I mean…"

"Other than me," Dominic says mildly, though he's looking at his napkin rather than at us.

"It'd be hard for anyone who did have obvious inhuman physical features to blend in," I point out. "So maybe they'd hang out places where it's usually darker, like nightclubs or bars or whatever."

Jacob lets out a short laugh. "Places where everyone's a little weird. Every city's got venues like that."

I try to think of any I saw, but… "It's hard to tell which ones are weirdest from the outside."

"Maybe we need to start popping into some places, then."

Zian's forehead furrows. "I don't know. The more we stick ourselves out there, doesn't it get more likely that *we'll* be noticed?"

I let the guys hash out their concerns a little longer while I peer out the window to where evening is falling. The streetlamps flicker on, casting their glow over the sidewalk.

Dozens more people walk by, but none of them are flashing fangs or swishing tails.

If it was easy to tell who the monsters are, wouldn't *everyone* know about them?

The waitress bustles over with our food fast enough that my stomach has only just started to pinch with hunger. The sight of the golden battered fish and thick but crisp fries raises my spirits.

I definitely made the right choice—both of them. Andreas's lasagna bulges with heaps of meaty tomato sauce and creamy cheese.

I half expect him to balk, but he immediately sets about cutting off a quarter of the slab. He drops it onto his saucer and slides it over to me.

"If you like it enough that you want more, let me know."

I glance down at my main plate and lift one of the three battered filets onto my own saucer to offer up. "It's a trade."

"You really don't have to—"

"It's a trade," I repeat firmly. "I do want to still be able to *walk* after this dinner."

A fleeting smile crosses Andreas's face. "Okay, fair."

I would grapple with the weird sense of friendship that I don't want, except right then Jacob stabs his fork down on my plate. The metal tines clang against the china.

I arch an eyebrow at him as he lifts the fry he speared off my plate. "Defending me from my dinner now?"

He swivels the fork in his fingers to show a black blob pierced by one tine. "A fly landed on it."

For a second, I can't speak. He must have used his power to hold the fly in place for him to have caught it like that.

I think.

Without missing a beat, Jacob pushes out of his seat, walks to the counter, and sets the utensil down on the formica surface.

"I need a new fork," he says, calm but insistent.

The waitress who's working behind the counter area slides one over to him without bothering to ask why. She probably figures he just dropped his on the floor.

My insides are starting to feel all jumbled up, so I dig into my now fly-free dinner to distract myself. The fish is perfectly tender and the sauce that came with it deliciously tart. When I pop a forkful of the lasagna into my mouth, I have to close my eyes in a silent swoon.

Tomorrow we'll be back to protein bars and grocery store sandwiches. I'd better savor all this while I can.

To no one's surprise, Dominic ordered breakfast for dinner to suit his sweet tooth. He's got a plate heaped with syrup-drenched blueberry pancakes and a couple of pieces of bacon on the side.

After five hasty bites, he's waving his fork at Andreas. "Put maple syrup on the grocery store list for next time. I think I could live on this stuff."

Then he turns to me, with a gentler motion of the utensil and a hint of hesitation. "Do you want some? It's way better than table syrup, and the pancakes are great too."

I open my mouth and close it again.

He hasn't gotten to have food like this any more often than I have. The guardians usually kept our meals very plain so that we'd appreciate any little treats they rewarded us with—and every now and then they'd let us go without as some kind of test.

He's probably *never* eaten fresh pancakes like this—and he's offering a portion to me.

Is he trying to make up for his reaction when we got out of the car?

Before I can answer, Zian's eyes widen. He tears another rib off the row he's been working through and holds it out in offering. "The ribs are really good too, if you want to try."

"Um," I say, starkly aware that they're not offering to share with each other. This generosity is all about me.

An easy way to prove a point? Am I supposed to forgive everything that happened before because of a bite of pancake and a BBQ rib?

My gaze darts to Jacob of its own accord—somehow he's the safe one since he's the only one who hasn't attempted to share. He meets my gaze and glances down at his plate, the same fish and chips I ordered.

"It seems a little redundant, or I'd join the club," he says, as if he thinks I was looking at him as a demand rather than an escape.

"It's okay," I say quickly. "Really. I've got lots of food already."

I should probably thank them, but somehow right now that feels too close to accepting apologies I don't think I'm ready to yet.

I'm saved from getting even more flustered by the return of the waitress. "How're you all doing?" she asks with a warm smile.

It occurs to me then that we have a perfect resource right here.

I push my own mouth into a smile. "Great! We were wondering though… Are there any good places you'd recommend around here if we wanted to go out for drinks or to, er, party a little after dinner? Somewhere really interesting, like a crowd you wouldn't normally find outside the city. We want to get the full experience."

I don't know if my attempt at explaining sounded odd to her, but either it sounded like a reasonable request or she just wants to make sure she gets a good tip. She taps her pen against her lips.

"Well… if you want something on the quirky side, more of an extreme atmosphere, there's a punk venue just a few blocks east from here. And a little farther than that, there's a bar that I think still does Goth nights. Those are the closest ones I can think of."

"Sounds perfect," I say brightly, whipping out my phone. "What are the names? I don't want to forget."

She dredges them from her memory, and I tap them into my notes app. As she walks away, Andreas lets out a soft whistle.

"Very smooth, Tink."

Jacob is grinning, which if you know him is simultaneously both breathtaking and terrifying. "We know what our next stop is. Finish up, and let's get back on the road."

Six

Jacob

It's possible that none of the people in this club are monsters.

It's also possible that all of them are.

The patrons swarming the place are doing a good job of imitating dangerous beasts, at least. The streaks of ruddy light that cut through the dimness keep catching on spikes that I mistake for spines or horns for an instant before the full picture becomes clear and I see they're only embellishments on a jacket, wrist cuff, or choker.

The smell of leather permeates the large, low-ceilinged room, mingling with the sour notes of various alcoholic spirits. The same material's texture covering so many of the figures gives brief impressions of animalistic hides.

And then there are the tattoos and piercings sinking right into the patrons' actual skin. Rings and gems and more spikes, flashing in the light. Dark imprints crawling across forearms and necks and even faces, sometimes with clear images but sometimes just abstract patterns.

I scan every one of them, my body tensed for the first sign of anything definitely inhuman. But every pair of eyes I glance into and every form I consider appears normal enough once I've studied it.

Those pairs of eyes are studying us in turn. Most with skepticism, mixed with either curiosity or hostility.

We don't really fit in. I didn't realize this place would require a uniform.

Andreas, Zian, and I look way too overtly normal in our varying styles of college-guy clothes, no piercings and no tattoos within view. Dominic just looks odd, wading through the crowd in his parka.

Imagine how this bunch of supposed toughs would react to what he's hiding under that coat.

Riva is the only one who looks like she could belong. She strides along in her combat boots, her hands tucked into the pockets of her dark hoodie, the silver layer of her hair reflecting the lights.

She's always moved with a certain assurance, the knowledge that she can tackle any physical challenge that comes her way. I remember watching her stride through the arena, her eyes flashing with determination to take on whatever crap the guardians were going to throw at us next.

That confidence has hardened in her over the years we were apart. If before she was fire, now she's got plenty of steel in her too.

But also a tender underbelly she protects so well, I almost convinced myself it wasn't there until the truth of it was smacking me in the face.

I stick close to her—as close as I can walk without provoking a flinch. There aren't a whole lot of women in here in general, and none as pretty as her. Most of the gazes that travel over her body are at least curious if not outright leering.

My hands stay balled at my sides. If we weren't on a reconnaissance mission where we need to not stick out any more than we already do, I'd jab all their fucking eyes out.

It doesn't help that Riva is swaying just a bit with the chaotic rhythm of the music blaring from the overhead speakers. Every motion makes her lithe, athletic grace more obvious.

I want to slide my hands down her sides and tug her tight against me. I want to bury my face in her hair and drink in the scent I never let myself appreciate before.

But she'd probably jab *my* eyes out if I even tried. I wouldn't even blame her.

I jerk my gaze away. My nerves jump with the restless energy winding through my limbs that I have no outlet for.

There's so much emotion churning inside me that I don't know what to do with. Regret and desire and shame and devotion.

I've been so empty of anything other than vengeful rage for so long that the deluge sets me off-balance. Like I'm a ship, and sudden swells of waves keep rocking me in directions I can't always predict.

I fucked up. I fucked up so utterly and completely.

I put the woman next to me—the woman I spent so much of my life loving—through total agony, both physical and emotional. I did it on purpose.

It's a fucking miracle she even accepts being in the same room with me.

I have no idea how to heal the damage I did, how to make her feel good in any way that could come close to making up for the awfulness I put her through.

All I can do is be right here to protect her from the slightest threat. Make room for her voice when she has something to say.

Bit by bit, I *will* make her believe that I treasure her. That I know she's my equal.

That she never deserved one particle of the shit I threw at her.

And if that's not enough for her to ever do more than tolerate my presence, well, it'll be my own damn fault, won't it?

The thought sends a harsher smack of anguish through my chest. My hands squeeze tighter.

I'll protect her from everyone out there and from *me*.

And from the power inside her she's still afraid of. We need to find one of these monsters and get them to cough up their secrets.

I haven't spotted a single clue around us so far. My jaw clenches with frustration, a looming sense of failure—and a jump of my nerves as my own power sparks.

One of the lights overhead crackles out with a spurt of shattering glass. A few of the patrons shout as the tiny shards drift down on them like vicious snow.

Shit. I didn't mean to do that.

Well, there's no way any of these dorks could connect the little mishap to me. Still, I grasp at the shifting energy inside me, grappling for a better hold on it.

We veer to the left, making a circuit of the space. The music isn't quite as ear-rattling near the bar.

The crimson lights help disguise Andreas's talent as he flicks his attention from one head to another. I can tell from the brief, starker flares of red over his dark irises that he's delving into the patrons' memories, searching for anything that might identify a target.

Zian is carrying out his own inspection, using his X-ray sight to peer beneath layers of clothing for any monstrous appendages they might be hiding like Dominic does. There's no outward sign of his talent other than the twitches of grimaces that cross his broad face.

All the flesh he glimpses must be human if not particularly enjoyable to look at, because he keeps stalking on without nudging me.

A guy who's about my height, his short hair dyed like green leopard spots, bumps his shoulder against mine—hard. My head jerks toward him.

"What the fuck are *you* idiots doing in here?" he demands over the rumble of bass guitar. "Get lost on the way to a kegger?"

I smile sharply at him, resisting the urge to bare my teeth like I'm as much a wolfman as Zian. "We're right where we wanted to be."

He opens his mouth again—and, oh what a tragedy, his mug of beer on the bar counter next to him suddenly topples over.

As he yelps and the bartender rushes to mop up the mess, the five of us merge deeper into the mass of bodies.

The others have been too focused on other things to notice the minor altercation. But when we get farther down the bar, a guy in a studded leather vest reaches out his hand and snaps his fingers at Riva like she's a dog.

"Why're you hanging out with these dipshits, beautiful?" he hollers. "Come over here and let a real man buy you a drink."

Riva rolls her eyes, but my shoulders have already stiffened with a jolt of fury—and jealousy, as if some stupid part of me thinks she'd actually take this imbecile up on his offer.

Three bottles whip off the shelves behind the bar. One of them whacks the jerk in the back of his skull.

Oops.

Somehow I can't summon any grief over that little slip-up.

But as the asshole whirls around to yell at the bewildered bartender, Riva's gaze snaps to me. So do my friends'.

Riva gives a brusque motion for us to move away from the bar. The second the crowd filling the room has closed around us, she spins on me.

"What the hell was that?"

"He was being a prick," I protest, and wince inwardly. I don't want to argue with her.

And I really shouldn't have let my power slip the reins again. What the hell *is* wrong with me?

I already know the answer to that.

She's glowering at me from just a foot away, and there's nothing wrong about *her* at all, only how badly I screwed things up.

"We're supposed to be keeping a low profile," she says, crossing her arms in front of her.

Andreas nods with an apologetic grimace. "We should keep any visible talents to a minimum, right? Don't want to scare off any monsters *or* risk the guardians catching wind somehow."

"Yeah, yeah, I know," I mutter.

How can I admit that I didn't even mean to brain that guy? I'm the one who's kept us all on track.

I can't go flying off the rails now. Not when Riva needs me too.

As much as she needs any of us. Her steps might bounce a bit with the rhythm, showing the fluid grace that compact body is capable of, but I can see the strength in every motion.

I remember how she brought all those soldiers to their knees with her voice alone.

She isn't a monster. She's a fucking marvel.

But we still need to find the actual monsters.

I catch Zian's gaze, and he shakes his head. Andreas is frowning, a crease forming in his brow as he stretches his abilities again and again.

Maybe Engel's fearsome creatures aren't into the punk scene. It's not doing much of anything for me.

I turn toward Dominic, who's looking even more hunched and awkward than usual in his parka. I'm about to suggest to him that we leave and check out some other place, because if he agrees then I'm probably being strategic rather than just giving up, but right then a bellowed voice socks my ears from behind me.

"What the fuck did you just say?"

I pause and glance over, my body going even more tense. Two beefy guys who could almost rival Zian in size are glaring at each other while several others who might be their friends look on with uneasy scowls.

"You heard me," the one guy growls through his thick red beard. "Twilight Zombduds totally sold out with that last album, and they should be dead to all of us."

The other guy jabs his thick finger at the bearded guy's face. "They paid their fucking dues, and that's my uncle's best friend's cousin you're talking about."

I don't really understand what the hell they're so worked up over, but the next thing I know, Beardie is swinging his fist. Suddenly the cluster of figures around them transforms into a seething mass of angry yells and bashing hands.

The atmosphere in the room goes from mildly ominous to war zone in an instant. I shove between Riva and one of the combatants who ricochets her way, taking an elbow to the ribs before I heave him out of range.

If they mark her with so much as a bruise…

My pulse thunders; my nerves sizzle like they've been tapped into an electric current. Two more lights shatter across the ceiling.

Didn't mean to do that either. Fucking hell.

I whip around toward the others, every cell in my body buzzing. I have to get us out of here—both to get Riva and my friends away from the fight, and to make sure *I* don't expose us.

The others are already pushing through the crowd toward the door, but the club patrons are jostling in every direction. Some are shoving toward the fight, either to join it or cheer them on.

My heart starts hammering twice as fast. I slam between them to push my way back to Riva's side.

Bodycheck one asshat to the side here. Punt a slowpoke out of the way there.

Clear a way to the door.

Ignore the bottles flying off the bar shelves and smashing every which way.

Ignore the groaning of the floor that might be some part of me prying at the boards.

Just get out. Just get away. There was nothing in this dump for us anyway.

We stumble out onto the sidewalk with a stream of other people who weren't interested in the fight. Some asshole grabs Riva's arm.

I lunge at him, but she gets there first, slamming her knuckles into his nose. He swears at her and staggers off, and I jar to a stop beside her with a growl.

The sign over the club windows screeches, one end starting to wrench forward.

Riva looks at me. I clamp down on my power with all the will I have in me, every muscle going rigid.

I'm going to defend her. I won't be one of the things that's threatening her—not ever again.

Get your head on straight, Jake.

The storm of emotions I still don't know how to master roils on inside me, but nothing else breaks. I feel as wiped out as if I've sprinted a mile just from tamping it down.

I'm way too out of practice at feeling things.

Andreas nudges us all on down the street. I breathe evenly through my nose, letting the chilly night air wash over me.

In that moment, I wish I was back in the forest. Nothing but trees around us and bare earth beneath my feet.

Then Riva freezes in her tracks a couple of steps ahead of me.

We all halt too. She points toward the other side of the street, farther down.

"That woman there," she murmurs. "The one with the green dress. I think she's what we're looking for."

Seven

Riva

I don't know how to explain it, which is too bad because the guys will probably think I'm insane. But the longer my gaze remains on the woman down the street, the surer I am that somehow she's one of the creatures Engel would have called a monster.

A quiver runs through my veins, small but tangible, like the faintest breeze rippling the shadows in my blood. Like I recognize her on a bodily level even if I don't with my eyes.

Then she's vanishing from view, slipping through a doorway on a storefront near the corner.

"I could just… feel it," I say to the guys, who are staring after her from where they're standing around me. "That there's something about her that's like us and not like regular people."

Zian nods slowly, his eyes wide. "After you pointed her out—I think I could sense it too."

He shoots me a hopeful smile, and my mouth returns it automatically. My heart skips a beat at the gleam of affection in his eyes even though the rest of me knows it doesn't mean what I want it to.

What I *used* to want it to.

The other guys still look puzzled. Maybe it makes sense that Zian and

I would have the keenest awareness of other beings that are kind of like us, since we're the ones with the most honed physical senses in general.

There's always been something a little more beastly about us than the others, at least in the most literal sense.

The feeling isn't even all that strange. A different sort of shiver passes through me like an icy finger down my spine.

I've had the same sensation of recognition before. I had no idea what it meant at the time, but during my missions, there were at least a couple of people who set off that tiny quiver through my blood.

And that skyscraper in San Francisco—the one I couldn't help stopping and staring at, what must have been almost ten years ago. Was that a place built by monsters, or for them?

The clap of Jacob's hands brings me back to the present. His gaze is fixed on the building the woman slipped into.

"Let's go see what she is and what she can tell us, then."

His gaze flicks to me, but not in challenge or accusation. It's happened often enough in the past few days that I know I'm not imagining that he's looking to me for *approval.*

My certainty doesn't make the act any less confusing. But really, what else are we going to do?

I suck in a breath and nod.

We cross the street and amble toward the building. I usually avoid paying much attention to Jacob at all, shying away from the uncomfortable memories his presence stirs up, but now I study him surreptitiously.

He got a little wilder in the punk venue than I've seen him… ever. Or at least since we were little kids.

He's always prided himself in being coolly incisive, staying in control and on top of every scenario we could encounter. He'd dive into any exercise requiring strategy with a fierce sort of focus, tugging us all along with his swift observations and decisions.

From what I've seen since we reunited, those habits have only amplified.

Except after that one attack from the guardians, when we were at the campus townhouse, that is. While we were driving away, it seemed like he'd gone into a sort of daze, lost in his head somewhere.

He practically destroyed the front passenger seat with his telekinesis before I shook him out of it.

He wasn't in a daze in the bar, though. Tonight he's appeared as alert and focused as ever.

But then, I haven't had much of a chance to really get to know all the nuances of who he or the other guys have become in the past four years. They've kept me at a hostile distance until just recently... and I can feel how much painful history they're still keeping bottled up inside.

We ease to a stop outside the building. The cursive letters on the sign up top declare it *The Royal Lounge*.

Most of the front windows are covered by a purple velvet curtain, only a sliver of the interior visible near the door. There, amber light washes over pale, glossy wood and delicately pebbled leather.

The few patrons I can see are dressed similarly to the woman I spotted: subdued but elegant evening wear.

Andreas's gaze has already slid over the five of us. "I don't think we want to stick out in there like we did in the punk club. Jake and I are probably fine. Zee, I got you the one polo shirt in case we all needed to dress up a bit."

Zian makes a face. "Let's go get it then."

We've been keeping our backpacks full of all our new clothes and other belongings in the trunk of the car. As long as we have them nearby at all times, we can hope that we won't lose everything again.

As Zian digs through his pack, I open up mine. "I got a sweater that'll look better than the hoodie."

My dark jeans might go over better than the cargo pants in a swanky setting, but I'm not going to strip down that much. Angling my body so the side of my waist with the bandage is hidden from the guys, I peel my hoodie off and pull the soft black sweater on over my tank top.

When I turn around, Zian is tugging the collar of the navy polo shirt. His mouth is slanted at an awkward angle, but I have to suppress a swoon.

The color compliments his dark hair and peachy brown skin perfectly. And I've never seen him in anything other than athletic gear before.

Zee cleans up nice.

He glances toward me, and I jerk my gaze away before he can realize the flush creeping across my cheeks has anything to do with him. Instead, I find myself facing Dominic, who's looking even more awkward in his parka.

He ducks his head, the short ponytail he's pulled his smooth auburn hair into sliding across his shoulder. "No one needs to say it. I realize there's no way I won't stick out like a sore thumb."

In a shirt or a coat thinner than the parka like the trench coat he used to wear, the lumps of his tentacles will be obvious on his upper back. He doesn't have any workable options.

A pang resonates through my chest. This isn't the first time we've left him behind.

All the childhood training sessions that required immense strength and endurance, Dominic and Griffin always faltered first. The echo of a flinch rises up from the memory of watching the guardians zap them with their electric prods if we slowed down too much to help them along.

Sometimes they didn't mind us working together, but other times the goal was for all of us to be pushed to our limits… whether we liked it or not.

Jacob hesitates. It's clear he doesn't want to say anything that would make Dominic feel worse about his limitations.

I can't help appreciating his obvious concern, as much as I want to be annoyed by everything about him.

"You can stake out the place from outside," he says after a moment. "Pretend you're waiting for someone to show up. Give us a warning if it looks like trouble's brewing."

We don't have any reason to think we'll face a sudden onslaught of danger from outside, but it's a reasonable compromise.

Dominic offers Jacob a tight smile. "It's a plan."

Trying to look casual, we walk back to the lounge. Dominic props himself against the wall next to the neighboring building, and the rest of us venture inside.

As we step into the warmly lit space, moody classical music wraps around us, full of swelling violin and a tinkling of piano. It smells a hell of a lot nicer than the punk venue, the alcohol tang still present but mingled with a mix of smoky florals. I suspect there's incense burning somewhere beyond view.

The long, narrow room in front of us holds a bar that's only smallish, a semi-circle with a glossy black counter about halfway through the space. In the front half of the room, several sleek leather sofas and armchairs squat in clusters around low mahogany tables. At the far end, patrons stand clustered around taller, smaller circular tables.

A couple of groups are relaxing with their drinks on the seats near us, but I don't see the woman in the green dress among them. Most of the activity appears to be happening at the back anyway.

We stroll over, Andreas stopping at the bar to order drinks for him and the other guys, I guess to keep up our front of being regular customers. He glances at me, but I shake my head.

I don't have Jacob's poison winding through my body anymore, but just remembering the dizzying effects of the one cocktail I drank while I did makes me queasy. I'd rather not even hold one.

A couple dozen people are gathered around the high tables in the back. Once we've approached, I see it expands to twice the width of the front, as if the lounge intrudes on the neighboring building.

The other patrons are chattering and laughing and sipping from their drinks demurely. Nothing about them looks at all monstrous.

The woman in the green dress isn't among them. Has she left already?

Or maybe there's a second floor or a basement level.

I'm about to suggest that to the guys when the faint quiver that drew my attention to her ripples through my veins again.

My gaze snaps to a slim man who looks to be in his late twenties, standing in the far corner by a table on his own. His fingers curl loosely around the stem of his wine glass.

He's watching the other patrons with a nonchalant expression, but I'm abruptly sure that he's actually sizing them up. As prey?

Zian nudges me with a brief tap of his elbow against my arm. He flicks his eyes toward another man, a little older, with a stout frame and a broad grin as he says something that gets his several companions laughing.

The moment I look at him, another quiver hits me. The sensation is more obvious now that I'm getting used to feeling for it.

Jacob motions for us to head to one of the few tables that's unoccupied, over by the wall where we can talk somewhat discreetly. He's only taken a few steps when one of the elegant women sashays up to him and lays her slender hand on his forearm.

"I haven't seen you here before," she purrs.

I've witnessed the kind of interest these guys get from women before—at the dance club where I had that one drink. It's not really surprising considering how stunningly handsome they are.

And I don't even *want* Jacob, any way at all.

But the second she touches him, a growl catches in my throat and my claws itch to spring from my fingertips.

Last time he got this kind of attention, he didn't seem to mind. Tonight, he pulls his arm smoothly but firmly away and steps to the side.

His pale blue eyes turn icy cold. "Not interested," he says in a voice that could slice through glass.

The woman winces, clearly startled by his forceful rejection, and Andreas steps in. He holds up his hands in a placating gesture, keeping his own tone mild. "Sorry. We're taken."

They are?

The woman's gaze darts to me, and my cheeks flare twice as hot as they did just checking Zian out.

Oh. Er.

I kind of want to shout that I'm not taking *any* of them, let alone all of them, but that would send all hope of keeping a low profile right out the window.

It's better if the guys stay focused on our current mission anyway, right? No matter what excuses they give to explain it.

I march on to the table we were heading for without commenting on the situation. By the time the guys have followed me a few moments later, I've willed my blush to retreat.

"No green dress," Andreas comments in a low voice for just us to hear.

"There are two more. I think," I say. "That guy by himself over in the corner and the chubby one with the big crowd around his table."

Zian nods. "That's what I'm sensing too. Can you look into their memories, Drey?"

Andreas turns the glass he hasn't actually drunk from between his hands, considering his potential targets. "I'm a little concerned that they'll notice if I use my power on them. We don't want to put them on the defensive right away."

"It's not their memories we need anyway," Jacob puts in. "We want to know their basic supernatural tactics. But once we have one of them ready for interrogation, you might as well take a peek then. It could be useful to know what they're up to in general."

I study the two men as subtly as I can manage. "How do we get them 'ready'? We wouldn't want to get aggressive up front when we're not sure what they're capable of."

Zian follows my gaze and frowns. "The loner seems like he'd be easier. We'd want to get him outside where no one else is going to interfere, right?"

Jacob hums thoughtfully and brings his drink to his lips, but I can tell he doesn't actually sip the amber liquid. "Let's do a bit of a test run. Zee, you're the most intimidating out of the four of us. Take a walk around the tables, going past both of them, and we'll see if there are any interesting reactions. Could be the loner is way more dangerous."

If Zian minds being put forward as bait, he doesn't show it. He picks up his own drink and immediately sets off to navigate the room.

He keeps a casual pace and doesn't linger anywhere for too long, but it's impossible for him to be completely unnoticeable. He's got to be the tallest and brawniest guy in the lounge, and gorgeous on top of that.

He brushes past the loner's table without looking at the guy. The slim man's gaze only rests on Zian for a moment before it returns to the other patrons. I don't catch any hint of supernatural talent.

The popular man glances over his shoulder before Zian has even reached him, as if sensing some kind of approaching threat. I think I glimpse a brief yellowish sheen passing over his eyes before he returns his attention to his fan club.

Jacob tenses at the same moment. He saw the reaction too.

As Zian circles back toward us, a woman who's been giggling with a few friends spins away from her table. The wobble of her legs suggests she's had a few too many of those martinis.

But I don't think her stumble is entirely accidental. She falls right into Zian, grabbing the front of his shirt and already aiming a sly smile up at him.

I yank my hands below the level of the table just in time to hide the instinctive spring of my claws before I can will them back into my fingertips. At the same moment, eyelashes fluttering, the woman parts her lips as if to make some coy remark.

But Zian shoves away from her.

His mouth clamps tight as if he's bitten back a yell. His eyes have gone wild and his muscles rigid, as if she attacked him rather than making a pass—albeit a forceful one.

"No," he says with a tremor in his voice that he masters a second later. His arms had come up as if to ward her off and now sink to his sides.

"Are you okay?" he adds gruffly, his stance still tensed.

The woman blinks at him, looking totally bewildered, and then sways back to her friends, who are all giving Zian the stink-eye. He hustles back to us with his head low.

My stomach has knotted. I've seen women fawn over Zian before, but not quite so aggressively.

It isn't just me he doesn't want touching him. The flash of emotion that contorted his face in that first instant—it looked like *panic*.

I'm obviously not the only one who noticed. Andreas has knit his brow.

"Zee," he starts when the other guy reaches us.

Zian shakes his head brusquely. "I'm fine. Who are we going for?"

Jacob waits for a beat as if checking to confirm Zian really is fine and then tilts his head toward the loner. "The guy in the corner didn't show any sign of powers or seem to notice anything unusual about you. I think your first instinct was right—we go for him."

Well, if we're all going to pretend nothing weird just happened, it's easiest to play along.

I raise my eyebrows. "So now we just have to convince the monster-dude to leave the lounge without looking like we're harassing him. So simple."

A small smile crosses Andreas's lips. "Maybe it's time I took a little risk and peeked inside his head, then."

His eyes flare briefly with a ruddy light. Then he motions to us. "I've got something I can use. Come on."

Jacob lets Andreas take the lead this once. We weave our way over to the loner's table as a group.

With all four of us in front of him, the slim man can't really look anywhere else. He cocks his head. "Can I do something for you?"

"We've got a message for you from Frond," Andreas says.

Whatever he saw in the possible-monster's head, it delivers. The man twitches straighter, his nonchalance fading away. "About what?"

Andreas jerks his thumb toward the lounge's back door. "I think it's better if we discussed it with fewer people around, yeah?"

The man nods slowly, casting another wary glance over us before moving from his table. We all tramp out of the lounge and into the wide, shadowy lane out back.

There, the slim man turns to us and crosses his arms over his chest. "All right, let's hear it."

The words have barely left his mouth before he's slammed back into the opposite wall by an invisible force. Jacob strides forward in the wake of his power and adds his hand to the man's throat.

Apparently he's decided there's no point in even pretending this could be a friendly conversation. To be fair, he might not be wrong about that.

As we all stalk closer, Jacob fixes the monster-man with his icy stare.

"We have some questions. It shouldn't take too long if you answer quickly."

The man sputters a choked guffaw. "Who do you think you are?" His eyes narrow, and all at once, his face goes sallow. "What the fuck *are* you?"

"None of your fucking business. Now, we can—"

Jacob isn't even finished saying the first part of his threat when the man simply… vanishes.

One second he's there, shoved up against the wall, and then next, Jacob is lurching forward with his hand smacking into the bricks. He whirls around with an angry grunt.

I spin on my feet, craning my neck to scan the alley, but I can't see the slightest hint of our target.

"What the hell?" Zian says, his muscles flexing.

Andreas wets his lips, his expression tense. "It looks like the real monsters have more tricks up their sleeves than we realized."

EIGHT

Riva

"You're not welcome in here anymore," the stately woman says from the front entrance of the lounge.

We stall on the threshold, where she cut us off. The back door had locked behind us, so we'd come around thinking maybe we could get something out of the portly man or even find the woman in the green dress after all.

Instead, our way is blocked.

Jacob lifts his chin. "Why not?"

The woman raises her own head at a haughty angle, a little taller even than Zian thanks to her heels and being up a step from the street. "We don't allow anyone to harass our patrons. Leave before I have to take further measures."

Oh, shit.

We retreat down the street, Dominic moving to join us. An uneasy vibe runs between all of us.

Andreas is frowning. "Someone must have looked out back while we were confronting the guy."

"In the split-second we had him before he disintegrated," Jacob mutters, and glances at Andreas. "He didn't just turn invisible—not like you do anyway."

Andreas nods. "I still have some kind of physical presence. It looked like he simply wasn't there anymore."

Zian makes a discontented sound. "How the hell are we supposed to get any answers out of them if they can disappear in a snap?"

Dominic has been watching and listening silently, and must be able to put enough of the pieces together to understand what happened. "Whatever skills one monster has, the others don't necessarily have too," he points out. "We don't share many abilities."

I pull myself straighter with a renewed sense of purpose. "That's right. We just have to find another one."

The slight movement pulls at the lingering wound on my side with a jab of pain. I think I broke the scab again when I leapt to search for the vanished monster-man in the alley.

That's fine. It's a reminder of how dangerous any of these creatures could be, considering I got the sadistic power inside me from their kind.

"Come on," I say to distract myself from the deepening ache. "The more ground we cover, the more likely we'll find someone tonight."

As we head back to the car, Jacob nudges Andreas. "Did you see anything interesting in the monster's memories?"

Andreas grimaces. "I only dipped in briefly, just long enough to pick up a name that seemed meaningful to him. I was trying to avoid freaking him out. Looks like we did anyway."

The guy did act particularly startled right before he vanished. What was that all about?

"He's probably not used to people who seem human recognizing what he is," I say.

We pile back into the car, me taking the front passenger seat again. I want a good view so I can notice anyone who gives me that weird quivery feeling right away.

Jacob takes the wheel this time, his hands squeezing tight around it. He's pissed off that the woman barred us from the lounge.

"Maybe when we do find another one, we should try a more diplomatic approach first," I suggest, a little tartly.

Jacob lets out a huff, but he doesn't argue. "Let's see *who* we find before we make any decisions."

We cruise along the streets through the thickening night, sticking to the commercial areas with shops and restaurants. It doesn't seem likely monsters would be hanging around in the middle of a residential street.

Do they own houses? Do they hide away in caves in ravines and forests?

We have no idea how these things even live. Engel said they were like the supernatural beasts from stories, but how much of those stories are true?

Plenty of pedestrians are still out on the streets, most of them in pairs or groups. I watch a girl who looks about my age rush up to a cluster of other women and throw her arms around each in turn.

I almost had a girl friend. Brooke, our neighbor on campus, tried to be there for me.

Maybe if we'd stayed there, eventually she and I could have become BFFs or besties or whatever the current word for it is. But because she was trying so hard to be there for me, she got caught in the crossfire when the guardians found us.

I can't make any friends other than the uncertain ones I have right now. It's too risky—for them far more than for me.

The thought sends a jab of loss through me that's sharper than the ache from my injury. I swallow thickly and keep skimming my gaze over the sidewalks outside.

We're passing the thicker shadows of a large, treed park when one of those quivers finally races through my veins again. I jerk forward in my seat, biting back a wince at the jolt of pain that sears through my side at the sudden movement.

"There," I say, pointing toward the far end of the park. "There's someone… Someone's sitting there next to that bench."

The figure is barely more than a lump of layered fabric topped by frizzy hair, but there's no denying the increasingly familiar sensation tingling through my blood. Jacob parks by the curb, and we walk over cautiously.

It's a middle-aged woman, hunched next to the bench with a grimy blanket pulled around her shoulders. Dirt smudges her plump face.

She looks like a homeless person. Is that a disguise she's putting on, or can a monster actually be down and out just like a regular human being can?

Or are my senses going haywire, and she *is* just a regular human being?

Zian prowls ahead of the rest of us, his muscles taut beneath the preppy clothes he's still wearing. He shoots us a look with a swift nod of confirmation.

He can sense it too. I'm not going crazy—well, any crazier than I might already be.

The woman stares up at him with a scowl, even less friendly than the guy we tried before. I aim a warning glance at Jacob and step past Zian to stand in front of her.

"Hey," I say in the warmest voice I can manage, and think that I should have volunteered Andreas for this role rather than me.

Too late now, I've already committed.

I force a smile. "We were hoping we could ask you a few questions. Because… we think you're kind of like us."

The woman's gaze flicks over the five of us. Her scowl deepens.

"I'm not an info booth," she says in a dry rattle of a voice.

I hold up my hands, tuning out the increased ache in my side at the motion. "I understand that. But we've been pretty out of the loop when it comes to… unusual stuff. Things those people wouldn't understand." I wave vaguely toward the pedestrians sauntering by on the other side of the road.

Andreas must be able to tell I'm floundering a bit, because he comes around beside me to join in with his smoother warmth. "We don't want to make any trouble for you. Just to get a little advice on using certain skills that we wouldn't want the average person noticing. You have some experience with that, I'm guessing?"

His smile looks a lot less stiff than I'm sure mine does. His eyes stay their normal dark gray, not attempting to scan her mind.

He doesn't want to freak her out either. We don't know what *she* might be capable of.

The woman studies us again, her tongue flicking over her lips, and a shudder ripples through her pudgy frame. She pushes abruptly to her feet.

"I'm not having anything to do with you."

"Wait!" Jacob snaps, lunging forward.

As the woman rushes backward, away from us, his hand snatches at her arm. An instant later, his fingers close around nothing but air.

The woman is gone, wisped away as abruptly and completely as the man in the alley.

Jacob glares down at his hand and then at the spot where the woman disappeared. "Seems like they can *all* give us the slip just like that. Fucking hell."

Dominic shifts his weight on his feet. "It's getting late, and we don't really know what we're dealing with. Maybe we should head back to the apartment, get some rest, and do some new planning tomorrow morning."

My throbbing waist thinks that's a great idea. All I want is to flop on a bed away from the guys and will my emotions back into order as well as my body.

"Dominic's right," I say.

His glance my way looks a bit startled, but Zian nods too, if with apparent reluctance. "We're not getting anything done like this."

Jacob sighs. "Fine. There's got to be a way to make these pricks stick around and talk."

Andreas cuffs him lightly on the shoulder. "We'll figure it out, Jake. We haven't come this far for nothing."

The Airbnb he was able to arrange for us is located in a dingy neighborhood on the outskirts of the city proper, which is probably why it was available on such short notice. But it's got three bedrooms with four beds between them and a pull-out sofa, so at least there's enough space for all of us.

One benefit to my guys' newfound sense of generosity is that they announced that I should take the main bedroom that comes with its own ensuite bathroom. The moment we've stepped into the boxy three-story house we're renting the top two floors of, I pull the pistol out of my waistband to leave it with the duffel of weapons and make a beeline for the stairs.

Even after sitting still for the drive, my side is still aching. As I reach the staircase, I adjust my backpack on my shoulders, careful not to let too much weight rest on that side.

I mustn't be as subtle about it as I intended, because Dominic speaks up from behind me. "Are you feeling okay, Riva?"

"Yeah," I say quickly. "Just tired and kind of disappointed. I'm going to go take a bath and chill out."

In theory, that should stop any of the guys from insisting on keeping me company. In actuality, Andreas follows me up the stairs to the door to my bedroom.

When I pause with my hand on the doorknob and raise my eyebrows at him, he holds up his phone. "I figured out how to download music onto the prepaids. I could show you if you want to have some tunes going with your bath."

There's something so hopeful in his dark eyes that my stomach twists with my refusal. "That's okay. I think silence might be good right now."

I just want to get away from all of them, to have some space where I don't have to keep my vulnerabilities walled off. Where I'm not constantly having to remind certain parts of me that these guys are as likely to hurt me as help me.

Andreas nods, his face only falling a little. "Maybe later."

"Yeah." I might actually like that, even if I don't feel like telling him so right now.

He pauses, his gaze searching mine, and his voice drops. "You know if there's anything you think of that I could do—that would make you happier or feel safer or *anything*—you only have to tell me, and I'll make it happen. Whatever it takes."

The tightness in my stomach climbs up my chest to squeeze my throat. When he looks at me like that, talks to me like that, I can't totally suppress the memory of the night when everything went so horribly wrong.

Of the part before everything went wrong, when he made me feel like I was someone worthy of being cherished rather than punished. When he told me he loved me in the same voice he used just now.

And then I found out he'd been *pretending* to support me from the start just to see if I'd betray some secret evil agenda.

The boy I knew before, the one who could always find the right wry remark to break a sour mood, the one who'd enrapture us with dramatic retellings of tales he'd read and movies we'd watched—or, once we started our missions, true stories pulled right from the minds of people he'd crossed paths with… He would never have been that callous and calculating with his charm.

I have to keep reminding myself that I don't entirely know who these men actually are anymore.

My teeth set on edge. "I don't know what it would take for me to totally trust you again. I don't know if I ever will. But me telling you to do something and having no idea if you're just going through the motions definitely isn't going to work."

Andreas winces. "Fair. But the offer still stands, whether it helps you trust me or not. I won't try to rush you."

He steps back, and I slip into the bedroom.

The moment the door closes behind me, my breath rushes out of me. I toss my backpack on the bed and peel off my sweater.

Lifting the hem of my tank top, I find that a little blood has seeped through my latest bandage. Thankfully I grabbed some gauze when the guys weren't looking at one of the stores we stopped at for supplies, so I can re-dress it.

After that bath.

The wafts of steam that rise from the running water settle my nerves. I let the sensation carry my mind away from everything but the scratched-up but deep tub.

I hadn't been sure I'd actually enjoy baths, considering anything more than a brief swim is about as much water as I can generally appreciate. But anytime I've been dunked before, it's been in water with at least a bit of a chill.

Turns out even the cat-girl can find an approximation of a hot tub relaxing, at least in small doses.

I still have some of the bath stuff Andreas bought for me, so I toss the plain kind of salts in as well. Then I sink into the hot water.

It encloses my limbs in warmth and licks around my neck. I slide down until the back of my head is completely submerged. Then I loosen my braid and let my hair flow out around my shoulders.

My hand moves to my cat-and-yarn necklace, nestled against my sternum, making sure it's still holding together. I haven't taken it off since Jacob gave it back to me.

Then my fingers drift lower to trail over the tattoo of the crescent moon on my outer thigh. The moon with the dark droplet dangling from its upper tip—the one all the guys have too.

Shadowbloods, Ursula Engel called us. Because we were made with essence from the things she saw as monsters woven into our DNA, and we can see it in the smoky stuff that wisps from our veins when we bleed.

Maybe it's fitting that the full monsters seem to somehow merge into the shadows when we try to confront them. Would it be easier to restrain them by daylight?

My mind lingers over that idea, contemplating scenarios. The heat of the water lulls me into a mild daze.

But when a thud and a shout carry through the walls from downstairs, I spring to my feet in an instant.

"Back off!" Zian growls, and there's a smash that could be from either my guys or some unknown intruder.

My heart thudding against my ribs, I snatch the towel and wrap it around me as I race through my bedroom. I burst into the hall, charge down the stairs to the living room—and jerk to a halt on the bottom step.

All four of my guys are poised there in defensive stances, staring at the new fifth figure in the room.

A figure that's eight feet tall with horns poking from its purple skin and menace glowing in its ruddy eyes.

NINE

Riva

The purple, horned man—I assume, because he looks more male than female with that square jaw and those bulging pecs—glowers at the five of us. He's standing just a few feet from the apartment's front entrance, but I know none of the guys would have opened the door for him.

He got inside without them needing to.

A shiver runs through my ears as they sharpen into furred points. My hand that's holding the towel closed around my torso clenches tighter. Claws prick through the nubby fabric and spring from my free hand.

Those are the only weapons I have. My knives are in my discarded cargo pants upstairs, and all our guns are piled in the duffel bag near the intruder's feet.

If a blade or a bullet could do anything against a creature like this anyway.

I slide one foot back, bracing in case I need to spring. All my attention remains on the intruder.

His horns, glowing eyes, and purple skin aren't his only inhuman features. All he's wearing is a black strip of fabric like a loincloth around his hips, and a short tail with a devilish tip protrudes from a gap in it.

The tail lashes back and forth like he's a pissed-off cat. And as I watch, his immense form rises several inches off the floor.

He's hovering in mid-air. A ripple of energy washes over me, jangling through my nerves.

I don't need to strain any of my senses to recognize this man as a monster.

"What do you want?" Jacob demands, his voice taut enough that I can tell he's nervous. One of the dining-room chairs floats next to him as if he's readying it to hurl at the intruder.

I'm guessing he was responsible for the smashing sound I heard, via the vase now lying in pieces on the floor a few feet from the purple beast.

The monster bares his teeth in what could maybe be considered a grin if it wasn't full of so many sharp, ominous fangs.

"I came here to ask *you* exactly that question," he says in a guttural rumble of a voice that shakes up my insides even more. "I heard you've been hassling beings who'd rather be left alone."

His gaze slides over us again, and his mouth curves into what is definitely a frown. He adjusts his pose in the air with a twitch of his muscles.

As if he's preparing *himself* in case he needs to go on the defensive. A strange wobbly sensation travels down the center of me.

Nervous pheromones lace the air, but I think most if not all of those are from my men. Maybe monsters don't give off the same kinds of chemicals humans do.

But I can see that this beastly man is definitely a little afraid… of us. What the hell?

Andreas's eyes have flared with their own reddish glow, but it fades as he focuses back on the present. "We didn't mean to bother anyone. We were just hoping to ask a few simple questions."

The creature lets out a derisive sound. "Your approach hasn't sounded all that peaceful to me. What *are* you? Where did you come from?"

Zian folds his brawny arms over his chest. The wolfish hair that's sprung from his neck and the tops of his shoulders ruffles with a flex of his muscles, but he's managed to keep the full wolfman face under wraps.

"How's that any of your business?" he asks with strained bravado. "We didn't go breaking into anyone's apartment like you just did."

"Unexpected situations call for unexpected measures," the monster retorts. "You want to ask some questions? Answer mine, and maybe I'll have a little advice for you."

There's a sneering note to those last words, but his stance remains wary. What exactly is he afraid that *we* might do?

The guys hesitate, but I don't see any point in drawing out this confrontation longer than we need to. It's not as if we need to worry about this beast reporting what we tell him back to the guardians—and anyway, I wouldn't be sharing anything they don't already know.

I lift my chin a little higher, tucking the ends of my towel under my armpit to free both hands. "We were being held captive by people who made us… kind of like you. We managed to get away from them, but there are a lot of things we don't understand about our powers."

Dominic speaks up in his usual softly even voice. "The people we ran from don't want to tell us anything. Mostly we'd like to get better control over our abilities."

"People," the purple giant says. "You mean humans?"

The five of us exchange a glance. "As far as we know," Andreas says.

The monster's lips curl with what looks like disgust. "And they *made* you? From…" He shakes his head as if he doesn't even want to consider the possibilities.

"We don't really get it either," Jacob says, sounding peeved. "We wouldn't have 'hassled' anyone if we did."

"But you're part human, part shadowkind," the beastly man clarifies. "The two mixed together?"

"Shadowkind?" I repeat, confused.

His gaze veers to me, and he flashes his fangs again. "That's what we call ourselves. Maybe your makers called us 'monsters.' Most humans use that word."

Gosh, I wonder why that would be.

But his words send a quiver of rightness through me at the same time. Shadowkind. Like the shadowy haze that seeps from our wounds.

I swallow thickly. "They called us shadowbloods."

The monster—shadowkind—whatever he is—makes a sound like a snort. "And what do you bleed? Red liquid or black smoke?"

"Both."

Somehow he manages to look even more upset about that fact than he already was. He draws back toward the door.

"I'm not interested in playing anyone's mentor. I just look out for my city to make sure no one's stirring up trouble."

"We'd stir up a lot less trouble if any of you would actually talk to us," Jacob mutters.

The beastly man glares at him. Then he pauses, a more pensive expression coming over his fearsome face.

"I have heard that there's a powerful shadowkind down south who caters to odd ones. He has a hotel—in the city called Miami. You could go down there."

I can't tell how much he's trying to help us and how much just hoping to get us out of his territory.

From the twist of Dominic's mouth, he's wondering the same thing. "How would we find the right hotel? Who is this guy?"

"I believe his name is Rollick. But I don't promise anything." The purple giant shoots us another glower. "Leave the shadowkind here alone and go ask your questions someplace else."

His gaze falls on the small duffel full of our confiscated guns. His lips draw back in a silent snarl.

"You brought mortal weapons. Is there *silver* in some of those?"

I have no idea why he'd object to silver—or whether we've got any fancy firearms. But the monster doesn't wait for an answer.

"You'll be a little less trouble without these."

He whips the bag off the ground into his arms. Then he blinks out of existence just like the two monsters we tried to interrogate earlier did, taking our entire stash of guns with him.

"Shit," I mumble.

The room's ceiling fixtures are shining brightly. So much for my hope that light might help us keep the monsters in one place.

When he doesn't reappear, the tension wound through me releases just a little. I pull my claws back into my fingertips and hug myself over the towel.

"Well," Andreas says wryly, "that was a fun little visit. I guess bullets won't do much against things like him anyway."

Then his gaze slides toward me—and jars to a halt. The other guys glance over too, and suddenly a different sort of scent wafts through the air alongside the heat that's sparked in their eyes.

I'm abruptly aware of my wet hair sending a trickle of water down my back… and of the fact that I really am wearing *just* a towel. My body is totally naked underneath.

The towel only falls halfway down my thighs, and the two ends have opened to show a triangle of flesh almost to my hip. Damp patches cling to the sides of my breasts.

I try to tug the fabric over more of me without flashing any extra skin in the meantime. "I didn't know what was going on—I didn't have time to get dressed."

Jacob is staring at me with his normally cool eyes searing, as if he's on the verge of marching across the room and peeling the towel right off me. I'm torn between the conflicting desires to recoil and to welcome that hunger.

Zian makes a rough noise and jerks his head to the side.

Dominic clears his throat, his tan cheeks gone ruddy, and tears his gaze away to look at the other guys again. "It seems like at least in this city, the monsters communicate with each other. Look out for each other."

Yes, thank God, let's focus on something other than my state of undress.

I nod. "I don't think it'd be a very good idea to try to approach any others around here. I don't know what abilities that guy had, but he felt like he had a *lot*."

"Yeah." Zian frowns at the spot where the purple shadowkind was floating, still keeping his eyes carefully averted from me. "Do you think we should believe what he said about that guy in Miami?"

Jacob seems to shake himself out of a trance. He grimaces. "He just wanted to get rid of us."

"He was pretty specific about it," Andreas puts in, and pauses. "I mean, maybe this Rollick monster—or shadowkind or whatever—is actually a dude who eats humans for breakfast and our new purple friend figured that was an easy way to eliminate us for good, but I'm pretty sure a Rollick with a hotel in Miami actually exists."

"Did you see anything in his memories about that?" I ask.

Andreas shakes his head. "There were some dark, murky moments that I couldn't make much sense of, and some where he just appeared to be watching people around the city. One time when he beat up a smaller, creepy-looking dude for reasons I don't know. Nothing very useful. I didn't have much time."

"That's okay," Jacob says. "We can look up hotels in Miami, see if we can figure out which place someone named Rollick owns before we head all the way down there."

Dominic exhales with apparent relief. "Yeah. Get all the information before we make a decision."

Jacob cuts his gaze back toward me, with another flare of heat that flushes my skin. "And you'd better go finish your bath, Wildcat."

He says it mildly enough. But maybe because of that show of self-control combined with his obvious hunger and his use of my old, fond nickname, an unwelcome ache forms between my thighs.

Yes, I had better.

I whirl toward the stairs. "I'll be out quick to hear what you've dug up."

Then I flee from the longing that tugs at me from each of my men—and the answering pang rising up inside me.

Ten

Riva

There's something inexplicably satisfying about twisting half a lemon around the notched peak of a juicer. Feeling the ridges dig into the pulpy flesh against the pressure of my fingers, watching the glass base fill with pale yellow juice.

It makes me feel like I'm actually accomplishing something, which isn't a sensation I've had much in the past couple of days.

Andreas watches from where he's nursing a mug of coffee at the apartment's small dining table. "Had a craving you couldn't resist?" he asks in a lightly teasing tone.

I make a face at him. "I had to take advantage of the equipment while I have it. No motel is going to have a juicer. And I've been carrying around that bag of lemons since The Middle of Nowhere, Manitoba."

Zian stirs at the other side of the table, where he's been gulping down breakfast sausages—another benefit of having a proper kitchen for once. "We don't know for sure that we're leaving today, do we?"

His gaze slides to Jacob, who's sitting on the sofa across from the kitchen with Engel's laptop propped open on his knees, now connected to the apartment's Wi-Fi. I turn toward the kettle that's just started to whistle.

We took shifts all night keeping watch in case the big purple dude decided to encourage us to leave town more forcefully. The guys tried to insist that I should sleep straight through until I pointed out that they weren't going to convince me that they trust me now by refusing to let me do my bit to protect us.

But I'm not sure how much Jacob slept at all, even when it wasn't his shift. He stayed up into the wee hours in the same pose he's in now.

When it was my turn on watch, he made a point of going into the bedroom he's sharing with Dominic, but I thought I heard keys clicking when I came back up to get more sleep.

As I pour the hot water into a measuring cup, he sighs. "I haven't been able to find *anything* about a person—or whatever he is—named Rollick in Miami. Or the whole state of Florida either."

"Maybe it's time for some fresh eyes," Andreas suggests mildly. "Dominic got pretty comfortable with that computer—he could—"

"I know what I've already tried," Jacob interrupts with an irritated edge. "And that's just about everything."

He shoves the laptop onto the coffee table and sinks back into the sofa cushions.

I dip a spoon into the bag of white sugar that came with the Airbnb and drop the grains into the hot water before consulting the recipe on my phone. It *says* that I should use two tablespoons, but I'm going for alcohol-level sour here.

I stir the one spoonful in and reach for the lemon juice. I can always add more sweetness later if I want.

"What else do we really need to know?" I say as I add the juice and fill most of the rest of the cup with cold water. "It'd be dangerous continuing to talk to shadowkind around here. The only other place we know for sure we should be able to find some is Miami."

Dominic has just stepped into the kitchen area to pour himself some coffee from the pot Andreas brewed. He glances over at me. "We have no idea how dangerous following that one monster's advice might be."

I shrug. "We don't know how dangerous *anyplace* might be. And… we're pretty dangerous too. I think these 'monsters' can tell. Why do you think they all ran away from us?"

I don't really like bringing up the threat we can pose, especially when I seem to be the biggest threat of all. But we can't just sit here playing house.

Zian makes a thoughtful sound. "Even the big guy yesterday seemed kind of nervous of us."

I pour my mixed liquids into a drinking glass I've already added several ice cubes to. They tinkle against the sides. Picking up the glass, I turn to face the guys.

Jacob studies me as I raise the glass to my lips. I'm not sure what he's looking for, so I focus on the first sip of lemonade washing over my tongue.

Oh, that's fucking good. So tart it wakes up my taste buds like a punch in the face.

Who needs coffee when you've got this? And I'm never drinking a cocktail again.

As I take a larger gulp, restraining a pleased shiver at the shock of sourness, Jacob rubs his mouth. "It is our only lead."

Andreas nods. "And there's a chance the guy was telling the truth. It's not like shadowbloods are crashing his city so often he'd have a system set up for screwing us over."

"I vote that we try Miami," Dominic says quietly. "Being careful, but we would be anyway."

Zian swallows another bite of sausage. "If you all think it's the best idea, then I'm in."

"All right." Jacob grabs the laptop and stands up. "We should get going right away then. The faster we get there, the less time there is for these shadow monsters to make their own plans if they want to screw with us after all. Everyone eat what you need to and pack up anything that isn't packed up, and we head out in an hour."

Andreas throws back the last of his coffee. "I call first dibs on the shower!"

As he and Jacob head upstairs, Zian digs into his ample breakfast with even more haste. Dominic takes a long gulp of his own coffee.

I drain the rest of my lemonade, reveling in every bite of the tang, and set the glass down by the sink. There's a grocery store danish left, cherry and cream cheese, but I'm not sure how much that appeals.

Without thinking, I stretch upward to tug open one of the higher cabinets—and pain lances from my side from my re-opened wound.

My fingers twitch. My mouth snaps shut against a gasp, my jaw clenching tight.

I slow the movement, relaxing my torso as I ease the cupboard door open. The pain quickly fades to a dull ache.

I'm okay. No big deal.

But nothing in the cupboard makes the sacrifice worthwhile. I scowl at the stacks of dishes for a moment and then grab the danish. "I'm going to get packed up."

Dominic sets down his mug and trails behind me up the stairs. I assume he's going to his own room to pack as well, but as I open my bedroom door, he catches me by the elbow.

The second I stop, my pulse jumping at the unexpected physical contact, he drops his hand. His hazel eyes search mine.

"When did you get hurt?"

My stance goes rigid, and I curse my carelessness downstairs. Of course Dominic would notice the signs of an injury.

"It's fine," I say. "I'm taking care of it. Nothing to worry about."

His mouth tightens. "It's not *fine*. We haven't gotten into a fight since Engel's house—that was days ago. If it's still bothering you—"

"I'll deal with it. It isn't your problem."

A shadow of anguish crosses his face, so blatant I can't miss it. He swallows audibly and then tips his head toward the room behind me.

"Can we talk—just the two of us?"

I could be a brat and point out that it's just the two of us right now, but we both know that the other guys could walk into the hall at any moment. With those sharp ears of his, Zian might even be able to pick up on this conversation from downstairs if he tried.

If Dominic had demanded rather than asking, I'd have said no regardless of that fact. But the agony in his expression has left my gut all twisted up.

I step into the room without speaking and prop myself against the wall a few feet inside, my arms crossing over my chest.

Dominic follows cautiously. He nudges the door shut behind him and stays poised in front of it, his posture awkwardly stiff.

"I'm sorry," he blurts out in a tone much rougher than his usual measured voice. "I can't remember if I've ever said it this clearly before—I should have. I'm sorry I made you feel like healing you was a problem."

I glance at the lumps vaguely visible under the shoulders of the new trench coat Andreas picked up for him—so that when he's only around us, he can cover up with something lighter than the parka. "It is a problem, though, isn't it? Every time you use your power, they grow."

"That doesn't fucking matter. Making sure you're okay matters a hell of a lot more."

He pauses and swipes his hand over his face. "I messed up before. A lot. I know that, and you have no idea how sorry I am for everything. I should never have let Jake do his trick with the poison in the first place—I should have figured out that the guardians lied. *You* never gave us any reason not to trust you."

My response bubbles from my throat with a sourness that's less pleasant than my lemonade. "You still don't trust me."

Dominic goes even more rigid than he was before. "What do you mean?"

I might as well spit it out now.

"You're scared of me because of what I did at Engel's house. I saw how you looked at me—and on the train, you were worried about me controlling that power. I've noticed you flinch like you think I'm suddenly going to scream at you."

Dominic closes his eyes for a second. His jaw works. When he looks at me again, his eyes have darkened so much they make my chest ache.

"That's not because of you either," he says, and taps the side of his head. "I know up here that you'd never hurt me. It was just that seeing you destroying all those people like that… it reminded me of the worst parts of *my* power. It isn't your fault. That's my damage to deal with."

I frown. "What do you mean? You only hurt things when you have to so that you have the energy to heal someone."

His head droops. "No. It seems like my extra limbs added another new dimension to my original powers. The guardians forced me to test it out plenty of times."

There's no mistaking the bitterness in his tone. My body tenses up with instinctive defensiveness.

In so many ways, they hurt my guys. Does it ever fucking end?

"What did they do?" I ask with a vibration of the caustic energy inside me that for once I don't even totally mind.

Dominic's voice drops even lower than before. "I can steal the life out of things even if there's nothing to heal. And it's the most incredible feeling…"

His expression contorts with revulsion—at himself, nothing to do with me.

"I've never done it except when they insisted, when they said they'd hurt one of the other guys if I didn't," he adds. "But once I got started—I don't know if I could have stopped before whatever plant or animal they wanted me to work on that time was dead."

"Dom." I don't know what else to say.

In the back of my head, I can see the quiet, pensive boy who'd always dash in to help if any of us showed the slightest injury. Who used to spend a bunch of the little free time we got poring over the medical books the guardians agreed to bring him.

He always hoped he could get even better at using his talent, help even more. Instead he got saddled with a matching curse.

And the guardians forced him to act out that curse over and over.

The ache has crept right up my throat, clogging it. I want to reach out to him, but part of me still balks.

Dominic lifts his gaze again to meet mine. "I told you before that the things that are broken, they broke before you came back. It's true. I think it's true for all of us. And it's our own fault for letting our damage get tangled up with what we believed about you. I won't get mixed up like that again. You've always been here for me, and *nothing* would make me happier than being here for you too. However you need me. Whatever it does to me."

Sudden tears prick at the back of my eyes. I blink, grappling with the growing surge of emotion inside me.

I believe him. He's standing here in an enclosed room with me just a few feet away, talking about things that he has every reason to think would make me angry, and I can't taste even a hint of fear in the air.

Really, he's always been the one I was the least angry with anyway. Jacob was horrible, and Andreas manipulated me. Zian snapped at me and berated me more than once.

All Dominic really did was not interfere—and fail to totally hide his discomfort. I completely understand his conflicted feelings about using his powers now.

But there is still one hitch.

"*I* don't like the idea of making things worse for you," I say, my voice strained.

A little of the tension gripping Dominic's face fades with the smallest of smiles. "It wouldn't be worse, in the balance of things. I swear to you, I'd rather know I did everything I could to make sure you're not in pain than keep these stupid things a tad shorter."

The lumps of the tentacles twitch under the thin coat.

I wet my lips, still torn. Not least of all because when he looks at me like that, every inch of my body tingles, and definitely not with pain.

But we don't know what we're going to face in Miami. It'll be better if I'm not working around an injury.

And it isn't as if I really need the constant reminder of how awful my new ability is. My memories have been vivid enough to cover that just fine.

I grasp the hem of my hoodie. "I guess you could take a look at it. There's nothing in the apartment you could draw energy from anyway."

As I lift the bottom of the hoodie and the tank top underneath away from the bandage on my waist, Dominic steps closer. He rests his fingers gently at the edge of the bandage, waking up my skin even more.

"Go ahead," I say, struggling to keep my voice steady.

He peels back the adhesive ever so gently and considers the mostly-scabbed-over cut. His mouth slants downward. "When did this happen?"

"Engel's house. After the fight. I had an unfortunate encounter with a shard of glass in the window frame."

"It's barely healed. You've been prodding it so it won't totally seal up on its own?"

I grimace. "I… I wanted the pain to remind me of the kinds of pain I'm trying *not* to inflict unless I absolutely have to."

Dominic looks up at me with so much compassion in his eyes that I forget how to breathe. He's less than a foot away now, and the familiar urge tugs at me to bring him even closer.

"I can heal it by myself," he says. "It'll only take a little out of me—the same amount of hurt spread out over my whole body. Easy to recover from."

"Dom…"

He ignores my conflicted protest. "Please, let me?"

It's the "please" that does me in. I incline my head, not trusting myself to speak.

Dominic rests his palm over the wound, just barely grazing the scab. It only takes a moment before the warmth of his healing energy flows into my waist.

The severed flesh knits together. The scab smooths over. The lingering ache melts away.

And more warmth washes through the whole rest of my body.

It's less than a minute, and then Dominic lowers his hand. He doesn't look any worse for wear.

He looks as pensively handsome as usual, his face just inches from mine.

He doesn't draw back. He lifts his other hand to touch my cheek, and our gazes lock together.

"Thank you," he says softly, as if I've done *him* a favor.

My pulse skitters. I want to lean into his touch—but the longing brings a jolt of panic.

The last time I let one of the guys get this close to me, my heart ended up torn in two.

Before I can clamp down on my nerves, my body is jerking away, taking a few steps back.

Dominic stays where he was, his fingers curling toward his palm. His face has shadowed again.

But this is for the best, isn't it?

I shouldn't be letting myself get distracted from the larger mission. I shouldn't be indulging in my teenage fantasies of some kind of epic romance anyway.

"Thank you," I say, because I definitely owe him that much. "We should get packed up before Jacob starts cracking the whip."

Dominic manages another little smile, although it's tighter than before. "Right. I'll see you downstairs."

After he's left, I don't actually have much to do. I wash up in the bathroom, not bothering with a shower after my soak in the tub last night, and stuff a few lingering odds and ends into my backpack.

When I tramp down to the lower floor, I find the guys gathered in the living room already, packs slung over their shoulders. I guess we're heading out a little early.

Jacob motions us toward the front door wordlessly. As we follow him, Zian's head snaps to the side as if he's tracking a sudden sound. He halts in his tracks.

"Wait," he mutters, and moves to the window.

He scans the street outside, holding perfectly still, his eyes narrowing. His broad shoulders tense.

He glances back at us, wide-eyed. "There are guardians out there, staked out around the building. They've found us."

Eleven

Riva

"Are you sure?" Jacob asks as he edges toward the window. As if Zian would make up an invasion of guardians.

Zian is staring at the street outside again. He nods.

"There's this clinking sound their stupid armor makes… It's not very loud so I almost didn't hear it, but I'd know that noise anywhere."

His muscles twitch with restrained power.

My own body has gone rigid with alarm. "How many are there?"

"I've only seen two." He tips his head toward the window. "There's one around the corner of a building across the street, and another ducked next to a car."

Dominic frowns. "I doubt they'd only send a squad of two to try to take us down. There are probably others too far out of view for even your X-ray vision to catch them."

Zian lets out a faint growl. "Yeah."

"At least you caught on so you could warn us," Andreas says in a typical attempt at optimism, though he looks as unnerved as the rest of us. He grips the strap of his backpack against his shoulder and jerks his chin toward the door. "We've got to get to the car."

Jacob lets out his breath in a huff. "Yeah. No good waiting here for them to finish ambushing us. If that fucker yesterday hadn't taken our guns…"

Zian draws back from the window. "We managed without shooting anyone before. Out in public, and in daylight too, they'll have to be careful how they attack us, right?"

A shiver runs down my back. "We have no idea how far they might be willing to go. But I hope so."

"Be ready," Jacob says. "They might simply try to tranq us like before, or they might have decided it's better to just take us out, no matter what Engel said. I'll use my powers to keep them as far away as possible."

Zian glances at me. "Riva and I can smash anyone who gets close."

"I'll muddle anyone I can see with projected memories," Andreas says. "It's worked before. We're not trapped this time. We can make it."

"As long as it's just them." My throat constricts. "Do you think the shadowkind monster last night tipped them off somehow? What if more of *them* are out there too?"

We all pause for a moment in uneasy consideration. Then Jacob shakes his head.

"The guardians won't negotiate with us, and they *know* us. I can't see them collaborating with the things they wanted us to kill."

"That doesn't mean it wasn't the shadowkind who gave us away somehow," Dominic says quietly. "Maybe we didn't get out of the city fast enough to make him happy."

Zian grimaces. "It doesn't matter. Let's just get going now, and then we'll all be happy."

He has a point. I roll my shoulders to loosen them and move with the others toward the door.

The house we're staying in has an outer staircase built against the side of the building to allow outside access to the second floor. Our car is parked by the garage around back.

So close and yet so far.

Jacob goes first, easing the door open and peeking outside. I'm immediately grateful for the solid concrete wall that runs along the landing and the stairs to waist height, even though it looked dreary to me when we first showed up.

"No sign of them yet," Jacob mutters. "Stay low, but move fast. Maybe we can get out of here before they're even fully in position."

He launches himself toward the stairs, his knees bent and shoulders hunched to keep him mostly below the level of the wall. It's more a scuttle than a run.

Zian motions for the rest of us to go ahead of him. He's planning on bringing up the rear, which isn't a bad strategy.

Once we get to the bottom of the stairs, we may need someone big and strong to cover the rest of us in our sprint to the car.

I slink forward behind Jacob, extending my claws from my fingertips. The tension of our escape brings the caustic vibration into my chest, but I suppress it with gritted teeth.

I can't let out a shriek like that without knowing where my targets are. I'm not sure I could even hone the power enough to make sure it only captured our enemies and not random bystanders as well.

The busy activity of the city makes it an ideal spot for us to hide away … but also difficult to avoid collateral damage.

Jacob has almost reached the middle landing when his feet appear to slip from under him. He stumbles and sprawls forward on his hands and knees.

"What the—?" He scrambles up, his head jerking around as if he's looking to see what he tripped over.

Before I can say anything, it hits me too: an invisible surface smacking against my ankles. I teeter and snatch at the railing for balance.

Not a surface, I register through the sudden thudding of my heart. An invisible *force*, like Jacob's telekinetic talent—

Footsteps thunder across the pavement below us. Jacob snarls and slashes out his hand.

The rest of us barrel down to catch up with him, to help him.

Something clatters on the ground; projectiles rattle against the side of the stairwell. A dart whizzes past my ear.

They're still not trying to kill us. But what the hell was that energy that tripped us?

I catch the flashes of sunlight glancing off helmets below—a fuckload more than just two of them. The guardians sway this way and that as Jacob shoves them back.

He dashes farther down the stairs with the rest of us at his heels. Andreas's eyes flash red, and a couple of shouts ring out with a familiar tremor of confusion.

Then a spurt of flame roars into being partway down the stairs.

We jerk to a halt, gaping. A glint of movement catches in the corner of my eye just in time for me to yank Dominic down.

Another dart streaks by, inches from his head.

Then dark vines ripple out of nowhere over the top of the wall. Swallowing a yelp, I aim a punch at one that looks ready to snatch at us.

My hand flies straight through it, my knuckles banging against the concrete.

I stare, and something clicks in my head. "It's an illusion. How—"

As my head spins, there's only one explanation I can think of. I bob up just for a second, my gaze searching.

Most of our talents require seeing our target, if not being directly within reach. Whoever's responsible is probably nearby.

There. By a bus shelter beyond the end of the driveway, a girl who doesn't look like she could be more than sixteen is poised with a guardian on either side of her.

When our eyes lock, her mouth drops open. Then I'm ducking low again to avoid a barrage of darts.

"There's a guy on the other side of the street," Zian mutters to me as he crouches at the back of our pack. "A *kid*, but he's doing something."

I swallow thickly, a difficult task now that my mouth has gone totally dry. "They really did make other shadowbloods."

There are kids out there, teens just like we once were, and somehow or other the guardians are forcing them to attack us.

What kinds of torture have *they* been through across their lifetimes?

Jacob swings his arm, and a few more bodies thump on the ground beyond the stairs. But he can't focus enough to do a ton of damage when he's dealing with a whole army of them at once.

The flames lick up toward the sky, but they haven't expanded beyond their patch. Andreas jabs his forefinger toward them.

"Just charge right through them and keep going until we get to the car," he says. "Same plan as before."

Jacob pushes the attackers back, Andreas confuses them, and Zian and I rip apart anyone who gets through them. And Dominic is here to patch up whatever wounds our attackers deal out along the way.

We all nod and dash forward.

The guardians have been keeping their voices down, but more mutters and footsteps carry from beyond the staircase. We hurtle onward.

I veer to the side so the fire only flicks across my limbs with a brief searing before I'm past it. Then we're out in the open.

Jacob swings around, darts flicking this way and that with the movements of his arms and head. They clatter against the side of the building or plummet to the ground rather than hitting us.

A few of the incoming guardians stumble, their hands flying out as if to grapple with something only they can see, but more are rushing toward us.

Zian barrels straight into one who's wielding a taser. He roars, his distorted wolfish muzzle protruding from his face, and wrenches his thick claws straight down the man's torso.

I duck under the swipe of a baton and plunge my own narrower claws into my attacker's gut. As I yank sideways to ensure this one won't come at us again, blood and bits of flesh splatter me.

I leap and tumble, slashing a throat here and kicking out hard enough to break a thigh bone there. I'm only vaguely aware of Zian fighting alongside me and the other three guys racing to the car.

The engine roars. The sedan zooms toward us and screeches to the side, the trunk ramming into another guardian who'd just lunged forward.

The back door whips open. Dominic beckons us from inside.

I punch the nearest attacker with a crunch of shattering jaw and fling myself into the seat.

Zian springs after me and fumbles to haul the door shut in his wake. Andreas is already slamming on the gas pedal.

As the car lurches around and races onto the road ahead, I crash into Zian's lap with the turn. He grasps my arm to help right me, and his posture goes abruptly taut.

"Riva!" he cries out, half protest, half groan.

When my head snaps up, his expression is frozen in an expression of horror, his face caught halfway between its fully human and wolfman forms. His wrinkled jowls draw back from uneven fangs; the whites of his eyes gleam with apparent panic.

A howl bursts from his lips, one so agonized that my heart nearly stops. At the same time, it raises the hairs on the back of my neck.

Any guardians out there trying to follow us won't miss that sound.

"Zee!" I hiss, trying to push myself away in case our closeness is the problem. But he keeps clutching my arm, his gaze raking down over me.

His whole massive frame shudders. "No, Riva, no, no."

All at once he jerks back from me, his shoulder slamming against the car door hard enough to dent it. "Dom, you have to help her—you have to—I didn't mean—"

The warbled words make no sense until I follow his gaze, looking down at myself. I'm drenched in blood and gore—does he think some of it is *mine*?

You'd think he'd be able to tell from my face that I'm not in the middle of death spasms, but he's gripped by some response beyond logic.

Dominic has reached over from my other side to clasp Zian's shoulder.

"Hey," he says in a gentle but nervous tone. "Zee, we got away from the guardians. Riva isn't hurt. Everything's all right."

But Zian's attention is fixed completely on me. His breath is coming in hoarse pants. He shakes his head frantically.

I've only seen him close to this panicked once—almost ten years ago, when the guardians took us out to some lake for swimming practice. I plunged in right to the silty bottom and glided around seeing how long I could hold my breath, and when I surfaced Zee was crashing through the water shouting my name.

But that time, he calmed down pretty quickly as soon as he saw my apologetic smile. I don't know what's wrenching so badly at him now.

With a stutter of my pulse at the memory of his reactions to my touch before, I move my free hand to curl my fingers around his, squeezing tight when he tries to jerk it away.

I'm not letting him this time. I don't understand his reactions, but my instincts propel me onward.

He needs to know I'm okay.

I hold his gaze and manage a smile. "I'm good, Zee. Nothing's wrong. Just the blood of our enemies—like it's meant to be, huh?"

I stroke my thumb over his palm. He blinks at me, his head twitching.

His posture starts to relax. I carefully pull at the wet fabric of my open hoodie and the tank top beneath so he can see there are no tears.

"I'm totally fine. Not hurt at all. Only the ones who deserved it are."

A long, shaky breath rushes out of Zian. His wolfish features fully contract, leaving him as the gorgeous man he normally is, if slightly sickly looking at the moment.

His fingers twist against mine—and squeeze back, just for a second.

He doesn't always hate my touch.

"You're all right?" he croaks, scanning my face.

"Absolutely, one hundred percent all right," I assure him. "Other than being annoyed that those assholes ruined my new favorite hoodie."

He lets out a startled guffaw and then pulls his hand from mine. This time I let him go.

His head droops. "I'm sorry. I just—I got so worried—"

"It's okay," Dominic says before I can figure out how to answer. "It could have happened to any of us."

Zian shoots him a look as if he's thinking that it really couldn't, but he sags deeper into his seat rather than arguing. I ease away from him onto the middle seat and tug off my backpack.

At least those made it with us through the fray.

"I *am* going to need to get changed soon," I announce to the car at large.

Zian isn't coated with gore. Benefits of being bigger than most of your opponents so they aren't bleeding all over you as they die.

The thought of the battle we just fled surges back into my mind, and my stomach lurches.

"Did you see them?" I add. "The teenagers who were there?"

Dominic knits his brow. "Teenagers?" He mustn't have heard Zian's comment.

"Around the building. I saw one with the guardians, watching from farther away, and Zian did too."

As Zian dips his head in acknowledgment, Andreas lets out a rough sound. "I did see a high-school age kid watching from a window on one of the other buildings with a weird expression. I thought he was just watching the fight as a startled bystander…"

"Something tripped me and Jacob," I say. "And there was the fire that started out of the blue, and the vines that were only an illusion. Things like what we can do."

Dominic sucks in a sharp breath. "That's right. You said something about shadowbloods—I was so focused on getting out of there."

"We all were," Jacob says. "And it doesn't matter anyway. We're heading to Miami now."

I scowl. "Of course it matters. We can't just— If they have other kids they're torturing like they did to us, we have to help them."

"Why? If you're right, then those kids just helped attack us."

"They might not have had a choice," Zian says, his voice still ragged. "Or they might have thought that we were the real problem. We know what kinds of tactics the guardians use."

If they could turn the guys I grew up with against me, it would be pretty easy to convince a bunch of strangers who have no idea who we are that we were a greater enemy.

"We don't have to figure it out yet," Andreas says. "It's not like we're in a position to stage a prison break right now anyway."

He pauses. "But I agree with Riva. When we *do* have the chance… we can't let them keep doing to other people what they did to us."

I manage a tight smile in gratitude, and then another unnerving thought hits me. "What if that's how they found us? What if the other shadowbloods can use their talents to track us down?"

An uneasy silence settles over the car. Jacob's voice breaks it, even grimmer than before.

"Then we'll just have to keep on moving so they never have the chance to catch up."

Twelve

Riva

It turns out that I didn't really need my new favorite hoodie anyway, because Miami in September is freaking hot.

We cruise along the main strip with the air conditioning blasting, but I can still feel the heat radiating through the windows of our new car alongside the bright late-afternoon sunlight. Jacob and Andreas nabbed this one not far outside Toronto, since it seems likely the guardians who survived the battle will have taken note of our previous vehicle.

The station wagon is clunky and a bit of an eyesore, but the back seat is more spacious than our most recent rides. I stretch out my legs where I'm perched next to the lefthand window.

Just this once, I managed to convince the guys that Zian should get a chance at riding shotgun. Both he and I need to be scanning the streets for possible monsters. Or shadowkind. Or whatever we're going to call them.

The sun isn't the only thing radiating through the windows. Thumping bass seems to reverberate out of buildings on every street and through the windows of open car windows on the road around us.

I kind of like it. It's like the city is one big dance party.

Which is a good thing, because we're doing a lot of cruising without any success so far.

There are a lot of hotels in Miami, and none of them come with signs announcing "Get your monsters here!" So we figure our best shot of finding the one we want is hitting up the local potential clientele.

Hopefully at least one of them will be a little more open to answering questions when that question is a simple, "Do you know where we can find a guy named Rollick?" But in the four hours since we crossed the city limits, Zian has spotted one woman who gave us the monster vibe, and she took off on us before we could even get the whole question out.

"We could go down to the beach," Zian suggests with an unmistakably hopeful note in his voice.

Jacob kicks the back of his seat. "We're not here to sunbathe. If the guardians have some way of getting the younger shadowbloods to track us, we can't stick around here any longer than we absolutely have to."

Zian lowers his head, abashed. "I know. But maybe monsters like the beach too."

He pauses. "It's supposed to be that in the ocean you can float no matter how heavy you are—because of all the salt. I never had the chance to try that."

Andreas lifts his right hand from the steering wheel to tap Zian's arm with his knuckles. "We'll get you some beach time in there somewhere."

At the obvious fondness in his voice and the fact that he wanted to reassure Zian at all, a twinge runs through my gut. That's Andreas for you, always keeping his friends' spirits up.

When he talks like that with Zian, he totally means it, no hidden agenda. Not like all those words of encouragement and reassurance he offered me in the first couple of weeks.

"After we've made some progress," Jacob grumbles.

I jerk my mind back to the present and frown at the high rises we're passing by. "We might have better luck after it gets darker. We only found the two monsters in Toronto when it was getting on into the evening."

"Shadowkind sticking to the shadows," Dominic murmurs from beside me. He's been looking even more pensive than usual since we left Toronto.

He's going to be uncomfortable even in his thinner trench coat anyplace without air conditioning. When we stopped to approach that one woman, he stayed in the car.

Maybe the creatures that call themselves shadowkind can teach him something to help with that problem too. Even if he can't get rid of the tentacles, it's possible there are other techniques for hiding or distracting attention from them that we simply haven't discovered.

We leave behind the commercial strip for a row of ritzy-looking condo buildings, stark white against the deepening blue of the sky. As Andreas flicks on the turn signal to head back downtown, my gaze slides over the front courtyards—and stalls on two kids playing on a tiled walkway.

There shouldn't be anything remarkable about them. It's a boy and a girl, both of them I'd estimate around seven years old.

At least, that's how old they *appear* to be. Because when my attention halts on them at the first niggling awareness, the now familiar tingle of recognition shivers through me.

It hits me twice, as I study each of them.

"Wait!" I call out.

Andreas takes the turn he already committed to but pulls over to the curb just a few car-lengths down the intersecting street. "What's up? Did you see something?"

He twists in his seat to meet my eyes as the other guys watch me too.

I motion over my shoulder toward the condo buildings. "I know it's going to sound ridiculous, but there were a couple of kids back there, hanging out in front of a building. They both gave off that shadowkind feeling."

Zian's forehead furrows. "Kids?"

Andreas cocks his head. "They might not actually be young. It could be some kind of illusion or other supernatural effect they're putting on."

Jacob tilts forward to get a full look at my face. "It was definitely them you got the vibe from?" he asks, with no sign of dismissiveness, only concern.

I nod. "I did a double-take after I got the first impression. It didn't make sense to me either."

"Let's see what the kiddies have to say for themselves, then." He glances at Zian. "Maybe you'd better hang back with Dominic, Zee. We don't want to look like we're ganging up on a couple of children."

Zian grunts but stays put while Jacob, Andreas, and I climb out of the car. At the corner, I tip my head toward the two kids who are giggling as they poke at something on the ground with sticks.

They still look exactly like real, human kids. But I can't ignore the jittering awareness that something isn't quite right about them.

Something a lot like what isn't quite right about me.

We walk over with a casual air that Andreas doesn't even need to remind Jacob to maintain. The kids don't glance our way until we veer off the sidewalk into the courtyard.

They pause, eyeing us, and the fat beetle they were prodding trundles away.

Andreas slings his hands in the pockets of his slacks and aims a warm smile at the two of them. "We're a little lost and were hoping you might be able to help. Any idea where we could find a man by the name of Rollick?"

"He owns a hotel around here, we heard," I put in.

The boy's face pales. He flings himself away from us so fast I don't have time to react, and then he's vanished by the hedge.

The girl scrambles up too, but there's a flicker of curiosity in her expression that stops her from outright fleeing.

"Please," I say, taking another step toward her. "We won't bother you any more than this."

Her gaze darts over me, and she hugs herself. "Beach Bliss," she spits out, and takes off in the same direction her partner went.

Jacob prowls after them with a huff of frustration, but Andreas already has his phone out. His thumb whips over the keypad, and a wider grin curves his lips.

"Beach Bliss Hotel and Nightclub," he says, raising his head. "It's just a twenty-minute drive from here."

On the outside, the Beach Bliss Hotel fits perfectly with the other hotels along the prominent beachfront strip where it's located. All white-washed walls and sleek modern styling, it stands a little taller than its nearest neighbors, though hardly a skyscraper at ten stories.

Its street-facing front glows with scarlet neon in the dwindling daylight. I can't help thinking that color choice seems a little ominous compared to the pinks and blues on either side.

Even from across the street, my ears catch the pulsing of rhythmic music from the nightclub section that fills one half of the first two floors. More vivid lights flash through the otherwise dark windows.

It might be early in the evening, but the party appears to be in full swing already.

In the short while we've been watching, we haven't seen anyone go in except for a few obvious travelers dragging wheeled suitcases. Either the club-goers are all hotel guests who've already checked in, or there's an outer entrance beyond our view, maybe on the beach side.

"So…" Zian says with a doubtful expression. "We just walk right into the place?"

Jacob draws his already rigid frame up a little straighter. "Walk in, look for anyone monster-y, ask them how we'd speak to Rollick. Simple enough."

He glances at Dominic, who's still in the car, eyeing the hotel through one of the open car windows.

"I'm coming too," Dominic says. "I shouldn't be too noticeable in the club lighting."

He gets out, the sleeves of his trench coat rolled past his elbows to allow him more relief from the heat. The air is just starting to cool as the sun sinks out of view.

We set off across the street and skirt the side of the hotel, picking up our pace when we spot a trickle of patrons heading into the building from a patio around back. Just in that first glimpse, the quiver of supernatural awareness wriggles through me.

I don't have time to figure out which of the figures triggered the sensation before they've stepped out of view. Thankfully, it looks like the club dress code is awfully loose—there's a woman going in with just a sarong over her bikini and sandaled feet, and a couple of men in khaki shorts and tees.

My tank top and cargos should blend in just fine.

It doesn't appear that security is particularly tight. No one is vetting people right at the door, although I do spot a couple of big dudes in professional-looking uniforms standing off to the sides just past the doors.

Because it's early, the dance floor is only about half full, and most of those people are simply talking in clusters and maybe bobbing a little with the rhythm rather than outright dancing. I have to suppress the spring that wants to come into my step at the emphatic melody winding around me.

We're not here to dance. We have a mission—one that's all our own.

My gaze skims over the drifting groups, and my feet stall beneath me. Zian jerks to a halt too.

Inside… this place doesn't look normal at all. The quivers hitting me are melding together into an electric shock.

At least a third of the people I glance at set off that reaction in me. It might be closer to half.

The whole club is packed with monsters.

Welp, we're definitely in the right place.

The other guys pause and look at Zian and me, taking in our reaction. I motion them all over to a quieter corner beyond the end of the marble-topped bar.

"There are tons of them," Zian says in a low mutter before I can speak. His muscles flex beneath the thin fabric of his tee. "I don't like this."

My fingers curl instinctively around my pendant, itching to pop and click the cat around the yarn like I used to. "Yeah. If we piss anyone off… we could be in big trouble."

Jacob inhales sharply and studies the room again, his mouth tightening. "We have to try."

"Why don't we ask someone on staff?" Dominic suggests. "The security guys or the bartenders? Even if they're not shadowkind, they've got to have some idea how to reach out to their boss."

Andreas snaps his fingers. "That's the ticket. Come on."

He strolls over to the not-yet-crowded bar and leans his elbows on the counter. The nearest of the two bartenders—a tall, slim guy with a cleft chin—comes right over, sending another quiver through me.

I don't know if all the staff are shadowkind, but that dude definitely is.

"Hey," Andreas says in his usual easygoing way. "We'll get a round of Sangrias—and we were hoping to have a word with the guy who owns this place. I think his name is Rollick?"

The bartender's eyes narrow. He looks us up and down, and I catch a tick in his expression that looks like surprise.

"He doesn't normally chat with random visitors," he says, calmly enough.

"Well, if there's a way to make an appointment or something, we'd appreciate any tips you can give us." Andreas offers a warm smile. "We were pointed this way by someone who thought he could give us a hand."

"And who was this someone, so I can pass on a name?"

"He didn't give us one," I pipe up, speaking just loud enough for the bartender to hear us but not any nearby fully human patrons. "It was a big purple dude with lots of horns who enjoyed floating, hanging out in the Toronto area, if that rings any bells."

The bartender's jaw works. I can't tell whether he looks more unnerved or irritated.

"Give me a minute, and then I'll get to those drinks."

As he walks off, Jacob grimaces. "Are you sure that was a good idea, Riva?"

I shrug. "I could tell he's one of them. And he could obviously tell there was something different about us."

"If giving him that info makes it more likely this Rollick guy would talk to us soon, it sounds good to me," Zian says.

Jacob still doesn't look happy. "Stay on guard. We don't know how friendly our welcome is going to be."

It can't be more than a minute before the bartender reappears from wherever he went off to and starts pouring our drinks. He slides them across the counter to us and accepts Andreas's cash without a word.

I curl my fingers around the sweating glass, wrinkling my nose at the sour-sweet smell. I wish I had more of my custom lemonade instead.

"Now what?" Zian asks.

Andreas considers the rest of the club. "I say we stick together and wait. I don't think it'd do us any good to badger anyone else at this point."

He sips his drink with an approving expression. I simply hold on to mine for appearances, having no interest in fizzing my thoughts with alcohol.

More people drift into the club. Quite a few of them aren't actually people, from what my heightened senses tell me.

One song bleeds into the next, and the colored lights sweep over the figures, more of whom are dancing now. The beat thrums through my muscles, but I'm too on edge to immerse myself in it even if I wanted to.

We move away from the bar as more customers come over. My skin starts creeping with uneasiness.

"What if—" I start to say, and just then a woman saunters up to us out of the growing crowd.

I immediately know she's shadowkind. Even if I didn't have any special sensitivity, she'd look unearthly with her statuesque height, her sharp cheekbones and jawline, and the feral grace to her movements.

"Rollick will see you now," she says, briskly and simply, and turns as if expecting us to follow.

There isn't a whole lot else we can do. With a wary glance at each other, we trail behind the woman past the bar and through the rest of the club to a door that blends into the dark gray walls.

She unlocks the door with a press of her hand and leads us up a flight of stairs and down a short hallway to another room. When she's opened that door, she ushers us in ahead of her.

We step into a large but sparsely furnished office. A thick crimson rug covers most of the floor, leading to an old-fashioned wooden desk with a leather chair behind it. A matching liquor cabinet stands nearby, and that's it.

Well, other than the man who's getting up from the leather chair as we file in.

Like the other creatures that call themselves shadowkind that I've met so far, this man's outward appearance is totally human. Extraordinarily handsome human, like one of my soap-opera hunks stepped right out of the screen with lighting effects and makeup intact, but not monstrous in any way.

Our escort shuts the door behind us, standing with her back to it as if to block us for making an escape.

The man ambles closer. The bright glow from the light fixture gleams off his tawny hair.

He smiles, but it's a measured smile, like he isn't sure how much warmth he wants to offer us yet. He's as tall and muscular as Jacob, which doesn't mean much against my or Zian's supernatural strength—but who knows how much power *he's* hiding.

When he stops, still about five feet away from us, a waft of that power tingles over my skin. He's giving off enough don't-fuck-with-me vibes to make the hairs on the back of my neck stand on end.

"So," he says in a silky drawl, "a purple dude in Toronto told you to come looking for me."

He's quoting my words back at me. I feel it's my job to respond. "He said that you… you might be able to do something for us. That you help out shadowkind who are 'odd.'"

The man who must be Rollick arches his eyebrows. "But you're not shadowkind, are you?"

"We're hybrids," Jacob says tersely. "We have powers."

Dominic clears his throat. "We were brought up by human experimenters who I'm sure knew a lot less about living with those powers than actual shadowkind would. We just want to get a better idea how to handle that side of our nature."

Andreas nods. "That's all we were looking for. A little guidance. Not trying to make trouble or get in anyone's way."

Rollick crosses his arms over his chest. "And these experimenters are the ones responsible for your hybrid state?"

"Yeah," Zian says, and hesitates. "I don't think— Have there been other hybrids before that you know of?"

Good question. The shadowkind guy didn't sound particularly surprised by the idea that we could exist at all.

"Not like that," Rollick replies in a bland tone that doesn't really answer anything. He studies us in silence for a long moment. "I don't run tutoring sessions."

He seems to be entertaining the idea of helping us, though. If the purple floater sent us here to be decimated, wouldn't the guy in front of us be getting on with that already?

"We just want to make sure that we're not disturbing regular people by accident," I say. "And to figure out if we can stop the people who made us from tracking us down. Things like that. Maybe you were born knowing it, but we have no idea what we're doing."

Rollick chuckles. "You obviously have a lot to learn, starting with the fact that shadowkind aren't born."

He rubs his jaw and then adds, "Well. It could certainly be interesting seeing what you've made of yourselves so far and where you could go with it. And I'd rather not have beings of any type running amok drawing attention to our existence."

"Does that mean you can give us a hand?" Zian ventures.

The unsettling man eyes us for yet another stretch of apparent contemplation. My skin starts to itch.

Then he swipes his hands together as if washing them of the dilemma. "Let's see what you can do, and I'll set you up in the hotel for a few days while I decide what I make of it."

My flare of hope is shaken by a jolt of nerves. A few days in one spot?

Andreas has clearly been struck by the same concern. "We appreciate the generosity, don't get me wrong, but I don't think it's a good idea for us to stay in any one place for very long. The people hunting us down managed to track us to Toronto in about a day."

"They might have just gotten lucky," Dominic adds. "We managed to stay in one location for about a week earlier on. But we can't know for sure."

Rollick hums to himself. "Someplace to stay while staying on the move. I might have an idea how you can accomplish that too. But it'd be dependent on you staying close enough to stop by and meet with me every day. Could you accept those terms?"

Jacob lifts his chin, his jaw set at a firm angle. "I think that depends on what your idea is."

The shadowkind man grins as if delighted by the answer. "They didn't experiment all the brains out of your heads, I see. It just so happens that I met an odd bunch several years ago who had a very useful method of transportation…"

THIRTEEN

Dominic

Zian runs his hands over the granite countertops and shakes his head, still not over his amazement. "This has got to be the nicest place I've ever stayed in, and it's a fucking *car*."

"Recreational vehicle!" Andreas calls cheerily from the driver's area up front. He's enjoying our new ride too.

I take in the RV from where I'm sitting on the convertible sofa that served as one of our beds last night. It is hard to believe that what looks like a luxury apartment is on wheels, although the faint rumble of the engine and the occasional sway as Andreas eases us through a turn give it away.

This sofa and the one across from me boast soft, dove-gray leather. The cabinets in the kitchen and overhead gleam with dark wood, and the kitchen area comes with a full-sized fridge and microwave along with a stove top and small oven.

Between the king-sized bed in the official bedroom at the back, the bunks across from the bathroom, the pull-out sofa, and the loft over the driver's seat, we even all get our own beds. The only possible comfort we could complain about missing is a bathtub, although we do have two separate bathrooms complete with glass shower stalls to make up for it—the one in the main space and the bedroom's ensuite.

And somehow the mysterious Rollick produced this amazing home-slash-vehicle for our use in a couple of hours.

I shift in my seat, my extra appendages flexing uneasily against my back. "Are we sure it was a good idea to take a gift *this* nice from a guy who openly admitted he's a demon?" Whatever exactly that word means in real-world rather than movie terms.

"I wouldn't exactly call it a 'gift,'" Jacob says from where he's poised in the seat next to Andreas's, watching the Miami suburb pass by beyond the windshield. "He made it clear that if he doesn't see us every day, he'll have it confiscated."

"Still, it's awfully generous."

Rollick didn't just hand over the extravagant vehicle but a credit card to keep it gassed and us fed as well. Which I appreciate, because it meant that we could keep cruising around the outskirts of Miami all night, taking shifts while the rest slept, but it is a lot.

"I wonder how all this works," Zian murmurs as he crouches down on the floor by the oven. I can tell from the tightening of his face that he's using his X-ray vision to study the inner mechanisms, but he hasn't completely zoned out of our conversation. "Rollick was pretty curious about us."

"Or nervous," Riva puts in as she emerges from the main bedroom, which we all agreed should be hers.

Out of all of us, she needs her privacy—and her distance from the rest of us—the most.

Her pale skin has a rosy glow from the shower she just took. She's already wound her hair back into her usual braid, and she's wearing a typical tank-and-cargos combo.

But I can't stop the brief flash of memory that sends me back to seeing her wrapped in nothing but a towel a few nights ago.

At the twitch of my dick, I yank both my thoughts and my gaze away. With the way she flinched away from me after I healed her, she couldn't have made it clearer that she doesn't want me *that* way.

And why would she? Who the hell would want to make out—or anything more—with a guy who's got two gruesome tentacles sprouting from his back?

Tentacles I admitted to her I've stolen lives with… and enjoyed it.

Jacob hums in response to Riva's suggestion. "He definitely wants to know more about what we can do with our powers. Or to make sure we aren't going to use them destroying his city."

Andreas chuckles. "If he was *that* worried, I don't think he'd have let us leave at all."

Riva's mouth twists at an uncomfortable angle. "I'm not sure he wanted to find out what might happen if he tried to stop us."

She leans against the wall next to the bathroom, her eyes downcast. A different memory rises up: of her yesterday evening, setting her mouth in a flat line while Rollick cajoled her into demonstrating her most potent power.

He brought in a little rat-like creature from someplace, a beast the size of his hand with a strange mohawk of fur down the middle of its back and eyes that shone eerie green.

Just give it a little jolt. Shadowkind are awfully resilient. You're not likely to kill it unless you really *try, and it'll heal quickly enough.*

I suspect the only reason she forced herself to go along with the request was her hope that Rollick would know how she could keep a tighter grip on that particular talent. Finally, she fixed her gaze on the creature, her body tensing, and seemed to work up to the brief shriek she pushed out.

It wasn't much more than a squeak, but the rat-thing squealed as one of its legs dislocated from its hip.

That's not the problem, she told Rollick after, when he commented that she'd restrained herself just fine. *The problem is when I'm upset. It gets so much harder to rein the… the hunger in.*

But Rollick hadn't looked as if her clarification was a deal-breaker. He gave us all a homework assignment for today that we're off to complete now before checking in with him later on.

Now we know that our talents—and Riva's in particular—*can* work on monsters as well as regular men, though.

What would it feel like to drag the life energy out of one of those unnerving creatures? Out of a demon like Rollick, who made the air quiver around him with all the power he contains?

I suppress a shudder and yank my attention back to the present. "We don't know much about the shadowkind. What they want. How they think. The guardians obviously have mixed up priorities, but that doesn't mean they're totally wrong to see what they call monsters as… well, monsters."

"And that's why we're going in with eyes wide open and ears pricked for any sign of trouble," Andreas says, and pauses. "We definitely should stay cautious around Rollick, generous or not. I managed to sneak a few peeks inside his memories, and… he's bashed some creatures up pretty badly at least once himself, for reasons I couldn't tell."

An uneasy shiver travels through my gut. "Then he doesn't have too many qualms about resorting to violence to get his way."

"We don't trust him," Jacob agrees. "But I'll point out that for all we know, the things in that memory deserved it."

"True." Andreas hauls on the wheel. "Here, this looks like a good spot."

We've ended up in an industrial zone on the edges of the city along the coast. Drey pulls into a vast shipping yard where a few pieces of steel machinery stand derelict.

The concrete storage building attached to this yard appears to be vacant. A grimy FOR LEASE sign hangs crookedly in one dim window.

The back of another long, low building stretches along the far side of the shipping yard, and a line of tall metal fencing creates a barrier to our left. A few narrower buildings stand across the street, with little visible activity, though I see a truck rumble toward them as Andreas parks.

Nice and secluded. No one nearby enough to see us flex our talents.

Andreas has brought the RV all the way over to the unused building, as far from any potential passersby as possible. We step out one by one into the warm fall air.

It only takes a matter of seconds for humidity to start building beneath my trench coat, even though Andreas picked up one about as light as they get. But I'm not risking flashing my monstrous extras around in plain view, no matter how isolated this spot is.

Jacob draws himself into a commanding stance. "All right. Everyone ready for this assignment?"

I think his gaze lingers a little longer on Riva than the rest of us. If she notices, she pretends not to.

Zian rubs the knuckles of one hand with the other. "We're just trying to bring out a little of our power and use it without going overboard, right?"

Andreas nods. "Yeah. Get a feel for it, seeing how gradually you can extend it bit by bit. It makes sense. If we get more comfortable with our abilities, they shouldn't get quite so overwhelming even when we're under attack."

He smiles easily at all of us, but I know he's worried about his own talents and how they affect him. I saw him struggle to make his body completely solid again after he blinked in and out of visibility too many times in a row not that long ago.

How can I resent the things growing out of my back when Drey has to face the possibility of literally *disappearing*?

Zian glances toward the RV. "I guess I'd better stay totally out of view if I'm going at all wolf-man."

He's trying to sound blasé about it, but his muscles tense as he strides around the vehicle so he's sheltered between it and the vacant building.

Jacob swipes his hands against each other. "We should spread out some so we're not feeling observed and self-conscious."

I don't know how self-conscious he ever feels about *his* powers, but I can appreciate what he's saying for Zian's benefit. "Good idea."

He strides off to the left toward one of the looming machines, which maybe he's planning on manipulating with his telekinetic powers. I'm not sure if he's planning on bringing out his poison spines today too.

"I'd better pick a spot pretty far out of the way too if I'm going to be dipping in and out of visibility," Andreas says with a crooked smile, and heads to the right where there's a shadowed alcove in the side of the building.

Riva lets out a huff, her arms crossed tightly over her chest. "I guess I need to look for something alive. Do bugs feel pain?"

A little shiver passes through her body, and she catches my eye just for a second. "I don't really want to torment even them."

I offer what I hope is a reassuring smile. "I guess it's worth it in the long run if it makes sure you don't torment anyone you *really* don't want to hurt later?"

"Yeah." She bites her lip and then wanders off across the grit-strewn yard, scanning the ground.

I have a similar task ahead of me. I need to see if I can just kind-of kill something… get the high of stealing its energy without sucking it dry.

The thought makes my stomach list queasily. I don't like tapping into that side of my powers at all.

But that's exactly the problem Rollick is trying to help us tackle. If we shy away from the parts of ourselves we're afraid of, how can we learn how to master them?

I might not trust him, but I don't think he's wrong in suggesting this strategy.

Whether bugs can feel pain or not, they can definitely die. And avoiding taking enough energy to kill them will definitely require particular finesse.

I meander forward, not in the exact same direction as Riva but keeping her within view from the corner of my eye.

As much as I hate the vicious aspect of my powers, I've at least had to face it dozens of times in the past under the guardians' orders. This is all totally new to her.

She might not want me getting physically close to her, but I'll guide her through any emotional trauma that might rise up as well as I can.

Assuming I can keep a handle on my own. Memories flicker up—the nervous squeal of a pig, the death groan of a golden retriever that's etched on my soul—and I flinch inwardly.

I didn't want to. I never would have if our jailers hadn't made the consequences of refusing their orders worse than the orders themselves.

But always, in the end, some part of me couldn't get enough.

We've crossed about half of the sprawling yard before I spot a fat beetle trundling along looking lost. My gut clenches tighter, but I know it's perfect for my purposes.

I pluck it up and tuck my hand under the flap of my coat so one of my suckers can rest against the hard-shelled body.

When I'm not already trying to heal, it takes a certain amount of concentrated effort to start siphoning energy. Especially when my initial impulse is to balk at the idea.

I drag in a slow breath and focus on the soft twitching of the bug's legs against my unwanted flesh. On the faint tickle of life I can sense inside its form.

Take just the smallest sip. Only the minutest of tastes.

Let it be stunned but not killed.

Let it recover.

I hone my attention even more and then give the slightest tug with my talent.

A jolt that's barely larger than a splinter shoots through my nerves—a split-second tingle that's so temptingly exhilarating I've grasped for more before I'm even conscious of it.

I catch myself an instant later with a mental slap. It's too late.

With a sinking heart, I bring my hand back around and peer down at the beetle. It lies stiff and still in the middle of my palm.

I don't need to wait to see if it'll snap out of a trance. I already know it's dead.

That fact becomes even more obvious when I move to set it down, and its desiccated body crumbles into dust.

Guilt tangles tight through my chest. I swallow thickly, forcing myself to step forward, to look for another target to try again.

But deep inside, all I really want to do is strangle myself with my own fucking tentacles.

Maybe this is pointless. I've never *needed* to use this part of my power outside of the guardians' experiments. Who knows if I ever—

Movement from the direction Riva went in interrupts my thoughts. My head jerks around in time to spot three burly, leather-vested men marching toward her where she's standing not far from the metal wall.

Riva has seen them too—I mean, they're difficult to miss. She braces herself defensively, frowning at them as they approach.

"What are you doing here?" one of them demands. "This isn't some playground."

"I'm just taking a walk," Riva replies. "What's your problem?"

I have no idea what it might be, but apparently the men have a pretty major one, because they all launch themselves at her without another word.

Under normal circumstances, I wouldn't intervene. Not even when I see one of them flash a knife.

Riva can handle herself in a fight. If I dashed in, chances are I'd only get in the way and make it harder for her to defend herself.

Her limbs slash around her petite body like a whirlwind—an absolutely gorgeous one. But as her fist catches one of the attackers in the nose and her knee rams another in the gut, two more men who look like they came in a matching set with the first three hurtle right over the fence a short distance behind her.

One of the newcomers is gripping a knife… and the other has a pistol clasped in his meaty hand.

Alarm blares through my nerves. I'm leaping forward before I've even fully processed my panic.

She's distracted by the first bunch—she doesn't know the new attackers are coming. And no amount of feral strength can stop a bullet to the skull.

Even my powers wouldn't be able to save her if that prick shoots her in a particularly vital spot.

I threw myself toward her believing I had the chance to save her before the threat even got to that point, but I'm no sprinter. I'm still ten feet away when the jerk with the gun raises it, his fingers curling around the trigger.

The other has swung toward me, brandishing his knife. Getting in my way.

But even without that obstacle, I wouldn't make it in time.

Not with my hands and legs.

Understanding hits me in a chilly smack. It's broad daylight—there are multiple witnesses—but I have no time for doubt.

I can protect her, so I will.

I don't hesitate, despite the pang of anguish that sears through me. With one swift yank, I fling off my coat and whip my tentacles at our assailants.

FOURTEEN

Riva

The man stabs his knife at my shoulder, and I just barely manage to duck—blocking his friend's punch at the same time. Some distant part of my mind is protesting, *What the hell is going on?* but my fighting instinct overrides any other consideration.

These three pricks don't look like guardians—no armor, no helmets. They don't seem to have any idea what they're dealing with.

But whatever their reasons, they're trying to hurt me. And they're going to regret that decision.

I have my own blades in my cargo pants pockets just in case, but it's easier working with just my body. I knock the knife from the one guy's hand with a punch so hard the bones in his wrist crack.

He stumbles to the side with a grunt of both shock and pain. The other guy lunges at me—and does a double-take when I flash my claws at him.

I take advantage of his surprise to kick him in the gut, sending him careening through the air to sprawl several feet away.

Only then do my ears pick up the scrape of other footsteps behind me. I whirl, clocking my third attacker in the face as I pivot on my feet.

He reels backward, and I find myself staring into the barrel of a gun—just as a long, sinewy tentacle smacks into the man pointing it at me.

The gunman's arms slam sideways. The shot goes wild, clanging into the metal fence.

Dominic rushes in, his trench coat shed, both tentacles whipping around us. Another attacker, this one clutching a knife, lies slumped on the ground in his wake.

I leap in and wrench the gun from the shooter's hand. He barely seems to notice me.

His broad face has gone sallow as he stares at Dominic. At the inhuman appendages protruding from Dominic's back.

"What the fuck!" he spits out. "What kind of freak—"

A sharper fury than when it was only me they were attacking roars up inside my chest. I ram my fist into his mouth before he can finish his question.

His jaw jerks right off its hinges. With a moan, he sinks to the ground, clutching it.

Dominic stares down at him, panting. He looks almost as sickly as the man staring at him does.

He's put so much effort into hiding his strangeness. This is exactly why.

He knew what reactions he'd get.

But he let these assholes see him, let them gape at him in horror like all of them are now, to save me.

Other, more welcome footsteps thud toward us. Jacob, Andreas, and Zian race across the lot, their faces taut with confusion and anger.

"Who the hell are these fuckheads?" Jacob growls, leaning mainly toward anger as usual.

I step farther away from the five men, all fallen to the ground with their various injuries and staring at all of us. Their aggression has given way to fear.

My mouth twists into a frown. "I don't know. I haven't seen any guardians around."

Zian marches up to the guy with the broken wrist, bristling with fury. "Who sent you at us? What do you want?"

The man flinches at the bellowed questions. "None of your fucking business," he grits out, but he still looks bewildered.

"I don't think they had any idea who we are," I murmur. Or what.

"You're—you're *monsters*," mumbles the guy I kicked in the gut, scrambling to his feet. His gaze is fixed on Dominic, his face gone waxy.

Andreas snorts in derision. "I'd say the monsters are the ones going around randomly attacking people."

He grips Dominic's shoulder, and the other guy stirs out of the agonized daze he seemed to have slipped into.

"Grab your coat," Andreas says, quiet and gentle. "I'll wipe you from their memories. They'll have no idea what they saw. It'll be like it never happened."

Dominic nods shakily and hurries to where he dropped his coat. My gaze follows him, my heart wrenching on his behalf.

It did happen. *I'm* not going to forget it.

I already knew he was willing to let the monstrous parts of himself grow to heal me. But revealing himself like this… doing that might have been even harder.

As Andreas turns toward my injured attackers, Jacob looms over the nearest one and slams the guy's back into the asphalt with a stomp of his shoe against his ribs.

"You'd better tell us what the hell you were trying to do here, or a whole lot more of you is going to end up broken. In ways you can't even imagine."

Whether because of Jacob's fierce expression, the venom in his tone, or the inhuman features he's already seen, the man lets out a whimper of surrender. "It was just a job. We got some cash and some pictures—we were supposed to get more if we offed the girl."

"Who gave you the job?"

"I don't know! It was just an envelope—left in our car a half hour ago telling us to come right away."

Andreas is studying him. "I think he's telling the truth."

"If he is, then it doesn't make a whole lot of sense," Jacob grumbles.

"It doesn't."

Andreas's eyes flare ruddy. After a minute, he shakes his head. "I'm not seeing anything that would connect these jerks to the guardians."

Jacob grimaces. "I guess you'd better wipe *all* of us from their memories then."

He turns to glower at the injured men. "You're going to walk us over to your car, give us the pictures and the cash, and then we'll let you drive off to the hospital like none of this ever happened. Or we can kill you right now and take all your stuff anyway. It's up to you."

"We'll give you what you want," rasps one of the other guys.

I rub my arms, my nerves still clanging with uneasiness. I don't like this at all.

"After that," I say, "I think we'd better have our next chat with Rollick sooner than we'd planned."

◡

If I had any doubts that the self-proclaimed demon took the threat of the guardians seriously, the fact that he's left behind the comforts of his hotel to meet with us elsewhere erased them. I don't know how much we can actually trust him to have *our* best interests at heart, but he seems awfully practical when it comes to his own security.

We drive into the immense underground parking garage he directed us to with our eyes peeled, but there's no sign of any danger within. After we've parked not far from the exit ramp and eased out into the cool, dim space, Rollick wavers into being near a concrete column several feet away without warning.

All of us flinch, our hands jerking up defensively.

Rollick chuckles, the corners of his eyes crinkling with well-worn smile lines. "I didn't mean to startle you. If you're going to be keeping much shadowkind company, you'd better get used to abrupt comings and goings."

Jacob studies him intently. "How do you do that? The shadowkind we tried to talk to before—some of them just vanished, as fast as you appeared right now."

Rollick raises his eyebrows. "There's a reason we got our name. The realm we came from is made mostly of shadow, and that's our natural home. We can meld into and out of the darkness of your world whenever we want."

Zian looks down at himself as if expecting to see his own body blending into shadow. "*We* can't do that."

"That doesn't surprise me. The only other hybrid I've ever met needed a lot of practice to tap into that particular skill, from what I hear."

Curiosity jolts through me. "You know another hybrid like us?"

"Not exactly like you," Rollick says with a twinkle of amusement in his eyes. "She came by her combined nature through more natural processes, no experimentations by nosy humans."

Andreas has perked up too. "Where is she? Maybe we could talk with—"

Rollick gives a dismissive wave of his hand. "I've already attempted to reach out to her and gotten no reply. She's kind of a flighty being, in more ways than one. But also prone to taking on projects of various sorts. No telling how long she might have dropped off the grid this particular time. But I did bring a few other associates for you to meet."

He makes another motion, and three more figures solidify into sight in a semi-circle facing us.

Like Rollick, they look human as far as I can tell, but they give off an obvious vibe of supernatural energy. My muscles tense.

Is this some kind of ambush?

But Rollick goes on talking without any hint of aggression. "I thought these three might be of some use if your 'guardians' come calling again. Cinder can manipulate electricity."

The wiry-thin woman at his left snaps her tan fingers, and sparks shoot up. More dance in her pale eyes.

Rollick indicates the stockier man with a head of thick, chocolate-brown curls next to her. "Slick has a knack for tracking down objects and coaxing them into his possession."

The man tips his head toward us with a blink of his heavy-lidded eyes.

"And I insisted on coming along because you all seem so interesting!" the woman at Rollick's right pipes up.

She grins at us with no sign of self-consciousness. Her hourglass figure in its silk dress gives her a sultry look that's offset by her dimpled cheeks and the youthful glow in her smooth face.

Rollick clears his throat. "Pearl was watching from the shadows during our first meeting. But she's selling herself short. As a succubus, she can persuade most mortals to do just about anything."

"Doesn't even have to be dirty," Pearl says with a bell-like laugh, and considers the men standing around me. "Although for the bunch of you, I certainly wouldn't mind taking a—"

A snarl of warning vibrates up my throat before I'm aware of my reaction. My claws have sprung from my fingertips, and the mark that formed after Andreas and I had sex burns.

Pearl holds up her hands. "Hey, now! I don't touch where there's already a claim."

She lowers her eyelashes and peeks at me through them. "I'd mention my offer extended to *you* too, but I have a feeling it'd be the rest of them growling then."

As it is, the guys around me have stiffened at her final remark. I will my claws back into my fingertips, my face flushing with embarrassment.

"It isn't— We're not—"

But some part of me is clamoring to tear her limb from limb if she suggests so much as touching any of them again.

Rollick claps his hands together. "Well, that's the introductions. How did your first training session go?"

Jacob's attention flicks back to the demon, his eyes narrowing. "How do you *think*?"

"Well, from the tone you're taking, I'm going to guess something unexpected was involved. You'll have to tell me what that was, since I have no idea."

Rollick's tone has stayed glib, but that could be an act.

"What Jake is getting at is that we were attacked," Andreas says. "Well, mostly Riva was. A bunch of men—humans—who looked like they were part of some gang said they'd been hired to try to kill her."

Zian bares his teeth. "We sent them running."

Dominic shifts on his feet. He hasn't said anything so far, just standing a little back from the rest of us with his head drooped lower than usual.

I glance at him with a twinge of concern, but his expression gives away nothing but a mild discomfort.

What happened during the attack—revealing himself, taking in the assholes' reactions—is obviously still weighing on him.

Rollick cocks his head. "These guardians of yours caught up with you already? That's awfully competent for mortals."

"No," I say. "That's why it's strange. The attack doesn't seem to have had any connection to the guardians at all."

Rollick pauses, and then a change comes over his body that I can't totally explain. He doesn't shift the way Zian does, his physical form altering, but somehow his presence feels *bigger*, more potent, in a way that sets all my nerves jittering.

He swivels toward Slick. "You were talking about testing them, provoking them. I *told* you to leave it be."

Any hint of good humor has left his voice. His tone is dark and cold enough to make me shiver.

Slick's eyes widen. "I wouldn't have—you know me, Rollick—"

"Yes, I do know you. And you know *me*. If you lie to me again, you won't be around to do it a third time."

The other shadowkind man draws his posture stiffly straight. "We don't know what they might be capable of beyond what they were willing to admit. We needed to see—"

Rollick's hand lashes out so quickly I barely see it. Thick black claws have protruded from his fingertips.

They slice through Slick's neck deep enough that a torrent of black smoke gushes up from his flesh.

Slick staggers and vanishes. Rollick turns back to us, his ominous energy simmering down, his claws gone. He looks perfectly calm, and so do the women on either side of him.

My body has gone even more rigid. "Did you *kill* him?"

Rollick shakes his head. "It'd take a lot more than that to kill a shadowkind. Which I could have done if I wasn't feeling mildly merciful."

He glances into the shadows behind him. "Slick knows he'll need to give a full accounting when he's done recovering from his just punishment."

My throat has constricted. This is the kind of creature we're dealing with. A demon ready to deal out a painful, even fatal punishment in an instant at being disobeyed.

The fact that he did it on our behalf doesn't set me particularly at ease.

I suspect my men feel similarly. They've all eased a little closer to me at the display.

Well, all except Jacob, who probably figures a truly "just" punishment would have been slaughtering the offender. He's stepped toward Cinder.

"Electricity," he says. "Can you use that to heat things up just like real currents—if we wanted to melt something, for example?"

The slim woman gives him a puzzled look. "What are you looking to melt? I don't do grilled cheese sandwiches."

Despite everything that's unnerving about this situation, the corner of my mouth twitches toward a smile. Then Jacob motions to me.

"Not cheese. We have—*Riva* has a necklace that's very important to her, and it broke, and none of us can fix it properly with our powers. But you might be able to work the metal so it's good as new again."

Oh. With a lurch of my heart, my hand flies to my cat-and-yarn pendant. "I—I don't know."

Jacob told me he'd find a way to see it fixed. Apparently he was so committed to the task that he's taking the first opportunity he's spotted to do so, no matter how bizarre.

Cinder considers me. "If it's your trinket, it's up to you. I could do it —it wouldn't be hard."

I hesitate and then force my hands to move to the clasp on the chain. Why shouldn't I let her if she's offering?

It's not as if she has any reason to damage the pendant.

"Very good," Rollick declares as I tentatively pass the necklace to Jacob, who hands it straight to Cinder. He turns toward Dominic. "Before we get down to larger business, I've given the matter of your tentacles some thought. Given your hybrid status, I'm not sure how this would go. But I don't think it'd be a horrible risk to attempt carving them right off you."

Dominic's body goes rigid as he stares at the demon. My pulse stutters.

He did say something about how uncomfortable they made him to Rollick during our demonstrations of our abilities yesterday. Maybe he indicated even more disgust with them than I realized.

Dom's voice comes out rough. "That's good to know, but I don't think —let's not go to that extreme an option first."

"I do have someone who's close to an expert to consult." Rollick drops the subject as if it didn't mean much to him anyway and sweeps his gaze over all of us. "Now let's hear a full accounting of what you all accomplished with your time when you weren't fending off random miscreants. And then I'll decide what I should send you off to do next."

FIFTEEN

Riva

As Andreas steers the RV out of the parking garage, I flop onto one of the narrow sofas. The cat-and-yarn pendant slides across my chest with the movement.

I curl my fingers around it. But even though Cinder said she'd fused the metal bit I snapped fully back together, I'm too nervous to test it by clicking it apart and back together on its joint in my old fidgety habit.

Jacob watches me in his intense way that's somehow amplified in the past week. "It should be fine now. Exactly the way it was before."

I don't know how to reply to that statement. The necklace is never going to be exactly the way it was before, because I will always have broken it once, no matter how well it's fixed.

Just one small object out of the many things I've broken when I lost my self-control, but the one that matters the most.

And I was losing control because of him. Because of the cruel words he was hurling at me.

"Do you think there's really any point to this?" I ask instead. "Talking with Rollick, doing his 'homework'?"

Zian glances around us. "He did hook us up with this nice ride. It's a lot better than driving around squished into cars and staying in dingy motels."

He does have a point there. I sigh and rub my hand over my face.

"What else would we be doing?" Andreas asks from the driver's area. "If we're going to escape the guardians or take them down—and rescue the other shadowbloods they've made—we need better control over our powers."

"I already have excellent control," Jacob mutters.

I can hear the roll of Andreas's eyes in his dry tone. "You have excellent control until you get so wrapped up in it that your brain short-circuits."

Jacob grunts, unable to argue against this point.

Zian looks down at his hands, flexing his thick fingers. "I feel like practicing with the smaller shifts helped me get a handle on it. But it's hard to tell when we're not in the middle of a battle anyway."

I glance at Dominic, who's sunk onto one of the benches by the dining table. He must have given our situation plenty of thought—that's what he does.

And I have no idea how today's experiment went for him. He hasn't said anything about it.

He still hasn't said much of anything, period. Not since he threw off his disguise to leap to my rescue.

My stomach twists.

When I was wounded and refused to say anything, he insisted on helping. Just now he rushed to my defense, regardless of the consequences.

I want him to know that I'm here for him just as much. That I believe he's on my side enough that I can be on his side too.

I push to my feet. In these small living quarters, there's no way to do this without being obvious about it, so the other guys will just have to deal with being excluded.

"Dom," I say gently. "Could I talk to you for a minute?"

His head jerks up. He blinks at me, looking a tad dazed.

Has he been considering Rollick's offer—wondering whether he should cut the monstrous part of himself right off, possible consequences be damned?

Jacob and Zian watch us too, puzzled and maybe even a little wary. I ignore them.

Something firms in Dominic's eyes. He gets up with a determined energy to his stance. "Of course."

I motion for him to follow me.

There's really nowhere we can go that's at all private—and has space for both of us to comfortably fit—except the main bedroom at the back of the RV that the guys have declared mine. As I step inside, seeing the bed right there, my pulse wobbles.

I don't want to sit on that while I'm in here with him. It reminds me too much of the things I've spent so much time longing to do with all of my guys—of the things I did with Andreas in memories that are now soured.

I glance around and hop up to perch on the ledge beneath the TV. My legs dangle against the drawers built into the wall there.

Dominic slides the door shut and stands a couple of feet away from me, looking me over. Concern darkens his eyes.

"Did you get hurt when those pricks attacked you? What do you need?"

Oh. That's why he came so easily—he thinks this is about me again.

It never even occurred to him that I'd notice *he* needs help.

I swallow thickly. "I'm fine, Dom. But you're obviously not."

His stance stiffens. "I'm totally okay. They didn't even touch me."

I hold his gaze. "Not with fists or blades. I know it couldn't have been fun hearing the way they talked about you."

Dominic's head droops. He shrugs. "It doesn't matter. It was nothing I didn't already know."

I make a rough sound. "It isn't true. There's nothing wrong with you—just because you look *different*, doesn't mean you're horrifying."

He lifts his eyes just enough to study my expression. "The tentacles bother you too, though, don't they?"

"Why would you say that?" I ask, frowning.

His lips curl into a grimace. "The other night—after I healed you…"

The memory clicks into place before he needs to finish, and guilt squeezes my gut. "I'm sorry I pulled away. It wasn't—"

"I understand," Dominic says quickly. "With how I am—*what* I am now—I'd never expect—"

"Dom!" I break in, and wait until he meets my eyes. "It had nothing to do with how you look. It had nothing to do with you at all."

My voice wobbles. It's my turn to lower my gaze.

"Everything got so messed up after I broke you all out, it's hard to know how to come back from that. I don't know if I even *want* to with the others. And even with you… I guess I'm just scared."

A moment of silence stretches between us. Then Dominic steps forward and wraps his hand around mine.

I'm starkly aware of his thigh just inches from my knee. Of his presence right in front of me, his pensive gaze searching my face and trailing heat over my skin in its wake.

"If you really— Whatever you need, Riva. However long it takes. Even if you never decide to try again at all. I'll be right here."

I look up again, my heart skipping a beat. "I matter that much to you?"

His fingers tighten around mine. "You always did; you always will. From the first moment I was old enough to think about you as more than just a friend, I've been in love with you."

He jerks his head toward the lump beneath his coat on his left shoulder. "You know what I thought when Rollick talked about seeing if we could take these things off? No. No fucking way. Even if it could be permanent. Even though I hate them. Because they saved your life, and maybe they will again someday, and nothing could be more important than that."

More love than I knew I was still capable of feeling swells in my chest. My lips part, but saying those three words doesn't seem half as good as showing them.

"Can I see them?" I ask quietly.

Dominic's gaze stutters, startled and maybe a little disturbed. "You want…"

"To see them. Properly. To see *you*, all of you, the way you are now."

I haven't really before. The only times he's brought out his tentacles, I was either too wrecked or too distracted by a fight to really take him in.

Dom hesitates and then reaches for his trench coat. He eases it off carefully and lays it on the end of the bed.

Then he stands there with his profile to me, tensed for my appraisal.

He's taken to wearing T-shirts with a broad necklines, this one with notches cut in the back as well to offer more room for the tentacles. They protrude on either side about an inch down his back, each halfway between his neck and the peaks of his shoulders.

I lean forward and trace my fingers across the bare skin above his shirt collar. There is no clear line that separates Dominic's flesh from the new appendages.

It's as if they're not poking out of his skin but a fully integrated part of it. After the first inch or so of his normal light brown skin tone, their mottled surface takes on an orange hue, but it's a gradual transition.

Two rows of small suckers dapple the undersides, from about half a foot down all the way to the tips. They're about twice as long as his arms now, though thin enough that he can coil them against his back.

They aren't frightening or horrifying. Like I said, they're just different.

They're a part of this boy—this man—who I loved and maybe still can.

I glide my fingertips right around the base of the closer tentacle. Dominic inhales with a hitch, and I jerk back my hand.

"I'm sorry. Does it hurt?"

A hint of red blooms in his cheeks. "No. The opposite."

A flush sweeps through me in turn, its heat pooling between my thighs. I can't resist extending my fingers again and stroking the base of the tentacle lightly.

Dominic closes his eyes. The whiff of pheromones drifting through the air gives proof to his statement.

My nerves quivering in anticipation, I slide my fingers farther along the tentacle.

Its flesh is softer than the skin of his back, almost satiny. And when I dip my thumb cautiously right into the cup of one sucker, I find that surface has the texture of velvet.

My pulse thrums through my veins. An impulse grips me, and I can't think of a single reason not to chase it.

What better way is there to show him how fully I embrace everything he's become?

I curl my fingers around the tentacle and guide it toward me. Then I dip my head down to press a kiss against one pair of suckers.

Dominic shivers, but the thickening of the desire lacing the air tells me it's not with discomfort.

"Riva," he murmurs in an unusually husky voice.

The suckers are pliant against my mouth, embracing it gently in return as if they're kissing me back. The crisp tang of Dom's scent wafts over me, and my pulse thumps even faster.

I part my lips and flick my tongue over the hollow of one sucker.

A strangled sound escapes Dominic, and then he's twisting toward me, grasping my shoulder. He buries his face in the crook of my neck, matching my kiss with the emphatic press of his lips against the sensitive skin there.

Heat sears across my chest. I wrench my head around at the same time Dom does.

Our mouths collide with a surge of heat and a longing that clamors through my veins. All I can do is emit an encouraging murmur and kiss him even harder.

Dominic loops his arm around my back and pushes closer, nudging my knees apart to give him access. While one hand holds me close, the other strokes down my side and along my thigh.

His breath wavers against my mouth. I tug him into another kiss, drinking it down.

I want him. I need him. The feral darkness winding through my blood propels me onward.

More. More. More.

Just like it demanded when I was with Andreas.

My muscles clench up despite the peal of hunger inside me.

Dominic freezes. When he starts to pull away, I grab his tee in my hands.

"No," I mumble, my mouth still just inches from his. "I—"

Words escape me. I tip my head forward, and he catches it against his shoulder, his arms coming around me again.

A tremor runs through his body. The same desire that's baying for release inside me must be reverberating through him as well.

But he holds himself still, waiting for me.

My voice spills out haltingly against his shirt. "The only other two times I've gotten close with anyone, things ended really badly. The first time with the boy I kissed dying. The second time with *me* almost dying, because of everything that happened after."

Dominic squeezes me close.

"I can't promise anything about what the guardians might have up their sleeves," he says roughly, "but I've got no secrets left. You know everything there is to know about me, Riva. Things I've never even told the other guys."

I let his words sink in. I believe them.

I'm scared. So fucking scared, more scared than I've been the entire time since that night with the train.

Am I going to let the fears own me, or am I going to take what I actually want? What every particle in my body knows I deserve?

Resolve twines with the longing in my heart. But one more thing holds me back—a concern that's not for me but for the man who's wrapped me in his embrace.

Andreas's words when he checked with me about the risks of our hookup rise in the back of my mind.

The guardians arranged it. I think they figured we needed some kind of outlet. It… didn't go so well.

I don't want to do this if it's going to stir up horrors from Dominic's past too.

"Dom," I venture. "Andreas told me that the guardians—that after I was gone, they brought a woman…"

That's all I need to say for him to know what I mean. I can feel his understanding in the tensing of his body against mine.

"It was sick. But I guess they figured that out too pretty quickly."

I nestle my head deeper into the crook of his neck, grappling with the clamoring of my desire. I didn't check with Andreas before— I didn't know it mattered. I need to be sure.

"You're not—Doing this isn't bringing up any bad memories?"

Dominic lets out a shaky sigh. "There isn't much to remember about that part. She took Andreas into another room, and then after…"

He stops, awkward around the thing Andreas didn't want to talk about either.

Something awful happened that day. But I'm not going to demand it from him if he isn't ready to talk about it.

"She never got to me," he goes on finally. "So I never had to… do anything. After that, they stuck to broadcasting porn onto the screens in our cells for a half hour a day to encourage us to get any hormones out of our system or something."

I wince. "That sounds incredibly horribly uncomfortable."

Dom manages a laugh that's only mildly strained, light enough to soothe my worries. "Better than their original plan. At least it might have given me some basic idea of what I'm doing."

He eases back just enough to meet my eyes. "Not that I'm assuming we're going to— I'd never want you to do anything you're unsure about."

I wet my lips, renewed longing flaring beneath my skin at the hunger in his gaze and the way it tracks the movement of my tongue. "Do *you* want to?"

He tips his forehead against mine. "Riva, right now I don't think there's anything I've wanted more in my entire life."

My heart hitches with exhilaration. Maybe, just maybe… we could both be okay.

Maybe it could be something as beautiful as making love is meant to be.

I tip my head and nudge myself upward, and he meets the kiss I'm offering. The hunger thrums through my veins again, melding our lips together with our kindling passion.

I grip him tighter, my fingers sliding into his soft hair. The elastic holding his short ponytail dislodges so the strands slide free across my knuckles, but he gives no sign of minding.

His mouth sears into mine. Our lips part, our tongues dancing against each other with a giddy thrill.

My hands drift down the front of Dominic's shirt to grasp the hem. Without speaking, he raises his arms—and adjusts his tentacles—so I can peel the fabric off him.

A starker heat washes over me at the sight of his slimly toned torso laid bare in front of me. Then one of Dominic's tentacles traces along my waist, and my skin turns outright scorching.

Would other girls run screaming in terror? Let the idiots flee.

This man has two extra limbs to caress me with. To love me with.

A lump rises in my throat. I haven't said it yet.

I raise my head and gaze straight into Dominic's smoldering eyes. "I love you."

Something like awe flickers across his expression, and then his mouth is crashing into mine again.

I press against him, the heat of his body coursing into mine. The caress of my hands over his bare chest brings a groan to his lips.

More, more, more.

He yanks up my tank top, our lips breaking apart for just long enough to toss it aside. As his fingers fumble with the clasp of my bra, both of his tentacles tease over my ribs and across my belly.

I shiver with need. It isn't even close to enough.

I thought the desperate wildness that came over me with Andreas had to do with it being my first time. But it seems it was because it was my first time with *him*, and the shadows inside me crave the new connection with Dom just as much.

Or maybe it'll always be this intense with any of the guys, no matter how many times we've already been together. All I know is the haze coursing through my veins alongside my blood is straining toward Dominic.

The hunger has become a keening echoing in the back of my ears. My fingers dig into Dominic's naked back, and I have to will my claws to stay in.

Some part of me wants to split him right open and mingle our essence in that way too.

The deepest ache pulses between my legs. As Dom cups my freed breasts, swiveling his palms against my nipples, I whimper, both at the sparks of sensation and the yearning for connection not yet fulfilled.

I want to savor this moment, but my body is crying out in agony to completely unite. I arch into his caresses—and cant my hips toward the bulge behind his jeans.

Dominic groans against my mouth. He kisses me with even more force, applying the same principle to my breasts with a sharp tweak of my nipples that leaves me gasping.

Before I can even think about it, my hands have leapt to his fly.

"I want…" he mumbles. "I need… Oh, God, Riva."

I nod my head in little jerks, my fingers yanking at the button. "Yes. Please."

Neither of us has much idea what we're doing. I've only collided with someone like this once before, lost in the passion of the moment, and he's never been with anyone for real.

But the shadows rippling through us know what they want. Every movement comes to me without needing to think. Like it's meant to be.

Shove Dominic's pants down his thighs. Pump his rigid shaft through his boxers. Inhale his moan into my lungs.

He hooks his fingers around the elastic waist of my cargo pants and yanks them down. They skip over the ledge I'm perched on and tumble off my legs.

His hand delves between my legs, somehow both satisfying some of my desperate hunger and sending my desire spiking even higher.

"You are perfect," he insists in a low voice as he wrenches my drenched panties off me. "Fucking perfect. Every part of you. Everything you can do."

I don't argue—I can't. I'm soaring too high on the heady sensations, tangled up too much in the writhing of my blood.

I grip his ass and tilt forward, and he plunges into me like he was always meant to be there.

Yes. Yes. This is what I needed most.

This is how we become complete.

We rock over the drawer unit, Dominic bucking deeper and deeper into me. His breath has gone ragged, but so has mine.

His tentacles trail up and down the sides of my body, drawing even more pleasure from my flesh. I kiss him wildly, lost in the same sense of merging I felt with Andreas.

Our essence is flowing together. Our breaths are mingling.

We move together as one being, bliss blazing through both of us in tandem.

My claws pop out. Dominic's tentacles shudder.

He sweeps them right over my breasts and grips my hips to pull me even tighter against him. His cock sinks so deep it hits a spot inside me that makes my thoughts spin, and then fragment, and then—

Ecstasy roars through my body, overwhelming every other sensation. The shadows in my blood dance.

The words tumble out of me like a plea. "Come. Come with me. Stay with me."

Dominic lets out a raw cry and slams into me one more time. His hips jerk as he follows me into release.

He sways in and out of me a few more times before coming to a stop. His head bows over mine, his body braced against me where I'm still balanced on the ledge.

The intensity of our joining thrums through me. I should have expected this too—this electric sensation like all my feelings have risen up to the surface of my flesh.

Just like it was with Andreas.

I lift my head, seeking out one more kiss. For comfort, for confirmation, for—something.

Dominic meets me halfway. His body trembles with the expended energy of our collision, but the kiss is so sweet I want to drown in it.

When we ease apart, my gaze drops to his chest. I touch the dark dab that's formed on his skin at the top of his sternum.

"I marked you too," I mumble in my surprise.

Dominic's thumb sweeps along my collarbone. "You had one on this side already, but now you have another to match."

He pauses. "Was that—was that because we—does it do anything?"

"I don't know how it works or why it happens," I admit. "But I—I always know where Andreas is, if I concentrate on it. It'll probably be the same with you now."

A smile crosses Dom's face, bright enough to melt any momentary insecurities about whether he'll mind being permanently branded.

"That's perfect too," he says in the softest voice I've ever heard from him. "Then I'll always be able to find you if you need me."

Unexpected tears spring up behind my eyes. I sling my arms around his shoulders and hug him to me.

Without warning, Dominic lifts me off the ledge. He spins us together and carries me onto the bed.

He lies down with me nestled against him and brushes a kiss to my forehead.

"You asked me to stay. I'm staying until you decide it's time to leave."

An ache radiates through my chest, but it's the most delightful kind of pain. Choked up, I tuck myself closer against him and let my eyes drift shut.

I have one of my guys, finally, properly. And the possessive hunger inside me will just have to accept that one might be *all* I end up taking.

Sixteen

Zian

My sharp hearing paved the way for both of our escape attempts. It warned me of the guardians' attack in Toronto.

So normally, it's one talent I totally appreciate. But right now, I wish I could carve my eardrums right out of my skull.

I brace my hands against the leather seat of the sofa, clenching my jaw with my effort to hold my claws in. I don't think shredding the upholstery in the fancy RV that isn't really ours would be a good move.

Another stuttered gasp reaches my ears. An extended rustle of fabric, like a piece of clothing pulled off.

My emotions churn inside me, burning away at my gut.

It shouldn't matter. I can't offer Riva what Dominic is obviously giving her.

I'm too fucking messed up.

I should be glad she's recovered enough from the shit we've all put her through to want *any* of us like that.

But somehow the faint sounds of their interlude are stirring up both searing jealousy… and a well of heat at the base of my groin.

I probably should not stand up anytime soon. My stupid dick that refuses to get the memo is at half-mast.

Part of me wants to duck into the bathroom and rub the growing tension right out of me, but just thinking of it makes me flush with shame.

How the hell would I ever look Riva in the eye again if I do *that*?

Instead, I train my attention on the built-in appliances across from me. With a nudge of my vision, I can see through the surfaces to the wiring beneath.

I can see the inner workings of things. Sometimes it comes with a curious itch about how those things actually work.

If I could maneuver their parts without wrecking them like I did with the computer system in the old facility we broke into. But an RV's oven shouldn't be anywhere near as delicate as computer circuitry, right?

Not that I can concentrate all that well right now regardless, no matter how I try.

A stuttered breath filters through the bedroom door, followed by a moan. And Jacob's gaze jerks up from where he's sprawled on the smaller sofa across from me.

The noise wasn't that loud, but clearly it's gotten loud enough that he picked up on it. He lowers his phone, his expression tensing.

A groan that makes even Andreas's head twitch carries through the RV, followed by a muttered voice I can barely make out myself.

Jacob's entire body goes rigid.

A mug whips out of the RV's sink and cracks against the ceiling.

Andreas glances over his shoulder, easing on the brake at a red light. "Perfect control, huh?"

"Fuck off," Jacob snaps. He sinks back down into the leather cushions with obvious effort, putting on a picture of being relaxed without remotely looking like he actually is.

Andreas switches on the radio, and a jangly tune flows through the RV, washing away the more provocative sounds from the back bedroom.

I wince inwardly. If I'd thought to ask him to do that earlier, maybe the two of them wouldn't even have had to notice.

"It's fine," Jacob mutters, more to himself than either of us. "It makes sense. I fucking poisoned her, and Dom healed her. Of course she'd forgive him first."

His hands flex and ball against his lap, but no more objects careen through the air. Looking at him, I get the impression that if he's angry with anyone right now, it's only himself.

"Maybe we should start our sleeping shifts," I suggest awkwardly. "Rollick wanted us to meet him pretty early tomorrow."

Andreas nods. "I'm good to keep cruising around for at least a couple more hours. I'll let you know when I need to switch."

If he's particularly bothered by what he'd heard, he isn't showing it. But then, I can't see much other than the back of his head.

And Drey has always been the best of us at putting on an easygoing attitude no matter what's going on inside him.

I clamber up into the loft over the driver's seat, where the radio will completely overwhelm any sounds from the other end of the RV, and pull the blanket over me. When I close my eyes, images of what Riva's face might have looked like as she made those sounds float by behind my eyelids.

It's a long time before I actually fall asleep.

The RV takes the turn onto the ramp into the underground parking garage with a slight lurch that has me clutching the steering wheel.

I can't say I like driving *any* vehicle, but the massive house-on-wheels is my least favorite so far. It reminds me of my own body when I'm in a shift: too bulky, too easy to accidentally smash something—or someone—into smithereens.

But I can't leave it to the other guys to do all the work.

When I can finally stop the RV in the same spot we parked yesterday and turn off the engine, my breath rushes out of me in a whoosh of relief.

I guess it'd be a little too much to ask the demon if he could supply us with a rotation of chauffeurs on top of everything else, huh?

Although, who knows? If these shadowkind creatures can merge into any patch of darkness, we could already have been carrying around unknown passengers who've been spying on us this entire time.

The thought sends an uneasy prickle over my skin. We don't really understand what we're dealing with when it comes to these monsters.

At least, *I* definitely don't.

Is Rollick helping us because he cares at all whether we survive? Or because he sees us as a potential hazard that he wants to contain?

Would he have already slit all our throats if he was sure he could get away with it unscathed by our powers?

Those are the kinds of questions I'd expect Jacob to have thought through the answers to. And Dominic.

Who still hasn't emerged from the bedroom where he spent the whole night with Riva.

I wouldn't say I'm the most sensitive guy ever when it comes to emotions, but I can *feel* Andreas and Jacob's awareness of that fact as we gather in the main room. The jolt of tension when the bedroom door opens seems to ripple through us all.

Riva strides out first, her chin high as if daring us to comment. But it's the hint of a soft smile lingering on her lips that tugs at my heart the most.

Dominic emerges at her heels, his arrival more subdued. He looks remarkably unrumpled, his auburn waves smoothed back into their usual short ponytail.

I think that's a different shirt from yesterday. Did he slip out sometime during the night to grab his backpack?

Did they *shower* together?

My fangs itch at my gums. But it's none of my business.

Jacob shifts on his feet and opens his mouth like he's going to say something.

Before he can get any words out, Rollick's languid voice reaches us through the door. "Are you all coming out, or did you see this as just a convenient parking spot?"

Jacob's mouth flattens. He hits the control to open the door, and we tramp out into the dank air of the dim underground lot.

Rollick is waiting there, seemingly alone. I know not to trust appearances on that score, though.

"There we are," he says in a satisfied tone. "Bright and early and ready for work. Such industrious students."

Jacob glowers at him. "You *asked* us to come here at this time."

"And I'm glad you showed up. Let's get started."

Rollick's gaze slides over each of us in turn. "After giving the matter more thought after hearing your accounts of your first training session, I've decided my misguided colleague wasn't totally wrong in principle. We need to work on how you react when you're *not* prepared."

Riva sets her hands on her hips. "So you're going to send us off to some other secluded part of town to get attacked?"

Rollick waves her sardonic suggestion off. "No, we can keep things much simpler. Those of you who have talents that come out reflexively in self-defense will take a stroll around this lot right here—separately—and my few associates who you currently can't see will emerge and test your ability to restrain yourselves."

He points at me, Jacob, and Riva. "That would be you three. Go take a hike."

Jacob balks. "What about Dominic and Andreas?"

The demon narrows his eyes at Jake. "I've brought in a friend who's particularly familiar with all things tentacle-y to take a look at Dominic's situation. And I'd like to personally conduct some minor experiments to see how Andreas's talent for disappearing might be related to our association with the shadows. Any more questions?"

His voice has stayed mild, but a slight edge underlies those last three words, more a warning than a legitimate offer. A prickling sensation courses through my limbs.

Experiments. Haven't we had enough of those?

Andreas doesn't look concerned, though. I guess it makes a difference when we have a choice.

When Jacob doesn't speak, Rollick motions us away. "Shoo. In different directions."

I don't like walking away from the others any more than I did yesterday, but I force myself to amble around the RV and then drift along the concrete wall at that side of the garage.

How good an experiment is this test, anyway? We *know* Rollick's buddies aren't going to actually hurt us.

My mind darts back to the thugs who surrounded Riva outside the shipping warehouse. Okay, maybe we don't actually know that.

The thought has just passed through my mind when a bulky form even bigger than I am bursts into view right in front of me. One bulging arm swings at me as if to pummel me in the face.

I give a startled bark and fall back a step, a surge of aggressive adrenaline rushing through my veins. Fur sprouts from my neck and shoulders, and my face juts forward into its fanged snout.

The big green-skinned dude who sort-of attacked me just drops his hand to his side and gives me a hard-edged grin. "The idea was *not* to react," he rumbles.

I make a face, which results in my wolfish lips drawing back in a snarl. With concentrated effort, I rein in my beastly side.

My jaw aches at the sharp contraction. I flex my shoulders, eyeing the figure in front of me, wondering if he'd call himself an ogre or a troll or something I've never even heard of.

"You seemed like you were going to hit me," I mutter, but I know that's a weak excuse. This guy's boss—or whatever Rollick is to him—just warned me minutes ago that I'd be tested this way.

The Grim Green Giant doesn't appear to be bothered by my excuse. He shrugs and motions me onward. "Try to do better next time."

The next shadowkind that leaps at me shouldn't scare me at all. It's the flirty woman who barely looks older than her teens that we met last time.

But she appears floating in mid-air with a swish of blond curls and her knee ramming toward my face, and my pulse jolts all over again. The next thing I know, I've wolfed out for a second time.

As she lands on the ground with a patter of her feet, I growl and contract my wolfish features. All this "test" is doing is pissing me off.

The girl—succubus?—whatever—cocks her head at me with a coy smile. "I'm honored that you think I'd need that much beast to take me down."

I scowl at her. "I couldn't help it."

She studies me with a vaguely curious air. "You don't like it, do you? Shifting like that?"

"What's there to like about it?"

"It makes you powerful." She laughs lightly. "Just FYI, from what I've seen in my experience, trying to *avoid* something your body actually wants to do means the urge will come roaring to the surface even faster when you can't help it."

She blinks out of sight again, leaving me frowning at the spot where she was standing.

Could that really be part of the problem? I'm fighting the wolf-man so much that it's become *harder* for me to control it?

What if I assumed that I *was* going to wolf out? What if I accepted at least a partial shift as inevitable, but as a tool I want to keep in my back pocket until it's totally necessary?

As I amble on through the parking garage, I reach inward to the parts of me that activate when I transform. I feel the shape of that monstrous face lurking behind my own.

Possibility coils through my muscles and under my skin. I'm ready. If I *really* need to, I'll go full beast on any threat.

My gut twists, still not totally happy with the idea. But when the slim electric woman, Cinder, leaps from the shadows at me with a shower of sparks, my flinch isn't half as bad as before.

My fangs spring free. A few tufts of hair burst from my flesh. But my face stays almost entirely human.

I could have, but this wasn't a situation that needed it.

I glance down at my hands as my claws sink back into my fingertips. I decided I could bring out the wolf-man… so I also got to decide when I *didn't.*

Cinder gives a brisk nod, not looking particularly pleased despite the sign of approval. "That wasn't bad. If I were one of those dim humans, I'd probably have assumed I imagined the little bit of a shift you showed."

As she slips away, Rollick's voice rings out through the parking garage. "Okay, I think our would-be banshee needs a little intensive attention. The rest of you, take a break."

I turn to see Riva stalking over to join him with a shadowkind man I haven't seen before walking next to her. From her peeved expression, she didn't ask for any special training.

My protective instinct tingles under my skin. I wander closer, wanting to keep her within reach of a short sprint.

The other guys drift to join me. Dominic peers at Riva over his shoulder.

"You can let her out of your sight for a few seconds," Jacob says in an icy tone. "You're not the only one who can take care of her."

Dominic yanks his gaze back to us. Something in me bristles at the tightening of his expression, like he's going to insist that actually he is.

But it fades just as quickly, and his mouth slants at an awkward angle.

"You know," he says haltingly, "last night—it wasn't something either of us planned."

Andreas offers him a smile that looks a little sad to me. "It's overwhelming. The first time, anyway. I don't know… Something about our blood."

Dominic holds his gaze, a mix of guilt and relief playing across his features. "Yeah." His attention slides back to Jacob, and his back draws up straighter. "I'm not going to apologize. We didn't do anything *wrong*."

Jake blinks at him. Then his stance droops, just slightly but noticeable on a guy who *never* backs down.

He flicks his eyes downward. "I know," he says tightly. "It's good that she trusts at least one of us."

A chilly shiver passes through me. What would have happened if she kept being wary of *all* of us? Would she have left?

I can't have her like that, but I still want to be with her in every way I can. As much as I can without fucking it up.

I might have said something to try to reassure Dominic that I'm not pissed off with him, but right then Riva raises her voice. My attention jerks to her.

She's hugging herself and glaring at Rollick. Five other shadowkind have gathered around her, close enough that my wolf-man self niggles at my nerves.

"I told you I don't want to," she says. "So leave it alone. Just because you're helping us doesn't make us your slaves."

Rollick looks vaguely amused, which only irritates me more. "I hardly think my suggestion was anything close to *slavery*. You asked for strategies to control your inner monster. We can't find ones that will work unless—"

"No," she interrupts firmly. "Forget it. What I've already tried was bad enough. There've got to be other ways."

"Look, if you'd just—"

I don't wait to hear the rest of his appeal before I'm marching over, anger coiling through my muscles. The other guys hurry with me, tension thrumming between us, all aimed at a source where we're much more comfortable directing it.

My voice comes out in a growl. "She said no. You have to—"

A screeching sound drowns out my voice—and a grid of lights overhead breaks off the ceiling and plummets straight at our heads.

Seventeen

Riva

At a thunderous groan from above, I fling myself to the side and duck at the same time, my arms whipping up to shield my head. Which is the right move, because an instant later, shards of glass careen through the air like shrapnel.

One sliver slices across my shoulder. As I grit my teeth, the pain shoots through my chest.

A hand clamps around my elbow and yanks me farther to the side. The jolt sends a fresh pang through my shoulder, sharp enough that I can't suppress a yelp.

A voice I recognize as Jacob's swears. There's a clanging sound nearby that could be another assault or his power lashing out—I can't tell which.

The parking garage has fragmented into wavering shapes. With the nearest set of lights shattered, shadows drape our section around the RV.

I glimpse Rollick and a few of his people tensed and staring off toward the garage entrance just before Jacob tugs me the rest of the way around the RV to relative shelter.

He's loosened his grip. As soon as he stops, he whirls around.

His gaze searches my body until he spots the cut. It's shallow, but blood is trickling down my arm.

Jacob's face goes rigid. One of the rearview mirrors snaps off its bracket like it was made of Styrofoam rather than steel.

Okay, that move was *definitely* him.

The other guys rush around to join us, their expressions panicked.

"Dom!" Jacob barks, low and terse. "Get over here. Riva's hurt."

Even after everything Dominic said to me last night, my body balks at the thought of him extending his powers. "I'm fine. It's shallow, nothing—"

But Dom is already next to me, his fingers curling around my upper arm just below the cut. The worry in his eyes and the whiff of fear he gives off stop me from protesting further.

As the warmth of his healing ability washes over my shoulder, Zian and Andreas close in tighter around us in defensive stances. They both shoot me concerned glances before peering across the dimmed parking garage.

"What the hell is going on?" Jacob mutters. "That wasn't any accident."

Zian's muscles flex. His frame grows a few inches in a partial shift with a spurt of fur along the back of his neck.

His voice comes out in a growl. "There's someone up near the entrance. A bunch of people."

A chill prickles through me. "Guardians?"

He pauses. "Yeah. It's got to be. I think I can see a few helmets."

"Fuck." Andreas glances toward the RV. "Let's get out of here. We can drive right through them if we have to."

The words are just leaving his mouth when an ominous warbling sound rises up from the RV's engine area. Like a rush of flames has just flared up inside it.

The image flickers from my memory of the fire started by one of the younger shadowbloods when the guardians ambushed us at the Airbnb.

I snatch hold of Dominic's sleeve and yank him with me. "Get away from it!"

All five of us hurtle forward, staying close to the concrete wall. The next second, the RV's hood blasts open with a burst of fire.

We're still close enough that the heat singes my skin. Zian lunges in front of me, wincing as a few bits of smoldering debris must hit him.

Our attackers must be a squad of guardians—they've managed to find us again. Did they track our presence to the garage after we left last night and lie in wait hoping we'd return?

Or have they developed some new way of finding us that takes them even less time than before?

Flames dance across the RV's inner workings. It's obviously we're not driving our house-on-wheels anywhere anytime soon.

But no footsteps come pounding across the concrete floor. I can make out several figures mostly poised by the far end of the garage now, lurking in the shadows on either side of the entrance, but they make no move to charge.

"Why aren't they coming at us?" I murmur.

The answer comes to us in the form of a shout echoing beneath the low ceiling. "Jacob, Andreas, Riva, Zian, Dominic. It's time you came home. You don't understand what you've gotten yourself into. Those monsters will eat your souls."

I flinch at the sound of my name, but as the man goes on, understanding sinks in. They've realized we were talking with shadowkind here.

"They're afraid of completely storming the place in case the 'monsters' fight them," Dominic says under his breath, coming to the same conclusion.

Why aren't the shadowkind *already* attacking the intruders after their aggressive arrival?

I look to where Rollick is standing and find him as tensed as we are. He doesn't look particularly afraid, but his mouth is set at an uncomfortable angle like he isn't at all pleased about the new arrivals either.

The few shadowkind who've kept their physical forms around him are watching his reactions. Cinder tips her head toward him and says something I can't hear.

They're all braced for a sudden movement, twice as on edge as he appears to be.

They haven't decided what to do. The guardians raised us hoping we'd be able to destroy shadowkind—they probably have other methods of striking out at our tentative allies too.

Even if those methods aren't particularly effective, why should the "monsters" we've turned to take the risk on our behalf? They could just vanish into the shadows and pretend this confrontation never happened.

My lips part… but I'm not totally sure I *want* to appeal of Rollick to help us get out of this standoff.

The guardians know a lot more about the shadowkind than we do. They've clashed with them who knows how many times.

They've seen enough horrors from the creatures they call monsters that they believed raising partly monstrous warriors to defend the human race was a reasonable measure.

And we've already seen horrors, haven't we? One of those shadowkind paid off a bunch of goons to try to murder me, just to test how we'd use our powers.

Rollick responded to that overstep by gouging his colleague's throat.

And just now, the demon was cajoling me into exercising my twisted powers. Insisting that I need to inflict more pain, refusing to try any tactic to simply keep that talent under wraps, no matter how much I hate it.

Was his insistence really for my benefit or for his, because some part of *him* enjoys seeing pain dealt out?

The guardian's voice rings out again. "Stop fighting and return to us, and we'll make sure you're safe. They can't touch you at the facilities. And anything they've already done that you might not even know, we'll fix it."

A creeping sensation tickles up my bare arms. I hug myself, shifting my weight from one foot to the other.

Is it possible? Could the shadowkind have inflicted powers on us that we haven't even noticed?

Of course they could have. They can slip in and out of shadows, move through the world totally invisibly. There could be thousands of them around us right now that we have no idea about.

Who knows how much else they're capable of doing without giving any sign at all?

Jacob's face has hardened even more than before. "I'm not going back to that fucking prison," he says under his breath. "*Those* monsters killed Griffin."

I swallow thickly. I don't want to go back to the facility—to one of the facilities, since it sounds like there are even more than we know about?—either.

"Can we get past them on our own?" I ask. "Without the RV? Zee, do you know how many we're dealing with?"

Zian squints through the dim light. "I think I've counted twelve inside. But we're too far away for me to look through the walls. There could be more ready to rush in if they have to."

To my surprise, it's Dominic who speaks up in favor of the

shadowkind. "If we're going to ask Rollick and his crew to help us, we'd better do it soon, or they might just leave."

I glance at him, taking in his taut but always handsome face in the wavering light from the flames still licking up from the front of the RV. "You think we should trust them?"

Andreas's mouth tightens. "We don't know what kind of deal we might be making if we ask for that kind of help. What it might turn out we owe them after."

"I don't see any way we're fighting our way out through who knows how many guardians and other shadowbloods too," Dom says. "Not on our own, not when they're ready for us, right between us and the only escape route. Maybe some of us would make it… but that's not good enough for me."

My stomach knots. I shake my head. "No. We stick together."

We are blood. The words we used to say to each other as kids and teens resonate through me.

I'm not ready to say them yet, not ready to call the guys who hurt me anything like family again, but I'm also not going to sacrifice them for my own escape.

My gaze slides back to the cluster of shadowkind, just as Cinder blinks out of view, along with one of the shadowkind men whose name I didn't get. My pulse hitches.

They're already starting to leave, deciding they have no dog in this fight. Why would they want to listen to the guardians talk to them like that?

They're our blood too. We're half shadow, half human like the guardians.

How can we know which side has our best interests more at heart?

What if neither of them does?

Zian stiffens, more fur sprouting along his shoulders as he does. "A few more guardians just came in. One of them was carrying something—it looked like a gun, but I've never seen one that big."

A shiver ripples through my body. Our time is running out.

As if to add emphasis to that suspicion, the man hollers at us one more time, sounding a little impatient. "You can't trust them. They'll use you and spit you out. Make the smart choice and end this now."

The slight edge in his voice raises my hackles. *Use us and spit us out*—isn't that exactly what the guardians have done all these years?

Why am I even considering believing a single thing they'd say?

The shadowkind might not have the exact standards of morality I'd prefer, but only one of them has actually tried to hurt us. The rest, as far as I can tell, have genuinely been trying to help, whether I've liked their advice or not.

Footsteps are starting to scrape across the concrete now.

I suck in a breath, my heart thumping, and turn to the guys. "I think we know who our real allies are, even if they're not perfect. We can't do this alone."

The guys all nod except Andreas, who hesitates. Then he tips his head too with a grimace.

The second I get his acceptance, I spin toward Rollick. He's waving off the massive green-skinned man, turning on his heel as if he's going to leave too.

Shit.

"Wait!" I burst out, darting over. "We—we can't fight them off alone. We still need your help."

Rollick halts and raises his eyebrows at me. "You want to throw in your lot with the monsters who'll steal your souls?"

I make a face at the wry note in his voice. "We're more like you than we are like them. Please. I don't know how we're going to get through this without you."

Rollick makes a gesture, and a few more shadowkind materialize around us. A quiver runs through my veins with the sense that there are definitely several more lurking unseen.

"What exactly do you want us to do?" he asks. "Our methods aren't necessarily pretty."

My guys have come up behind me. "Give those assholes everything they deserve," Jacob says in a caustic tone.

"But not the young ones," I jump in with a skip of my pulse. "The teenagers—they're like us. They're being forced. Just—just scare them off. The guardians knew what they were getting into. I don't care what you do to them."

Rollick nods. "Fine. Let's get this done before it turns into an even bigger mess."

"Do you want—" Andreas starts.

The shadowkind near us have already leapt into the shadows. I gulp a breath—and then the chaos starts.

There's a clang and a crunch of smashed bone. Shouts that sound more panicked than irritated bounce through the garage.

By the entrance way, the figures scatter, dark shapes rearing in their midst.

A clawed hand severs a helmet-clad head right off its neck. Electricity crackles through the air, and two bodies seize up in spasms.

The smell of burnt flesh reaches our noses. My stomach churns.

"Should we… go help them?" Zian says with an uncertain expression.

Dominic shakes his head. "I think we might just get in the way."

We thought we were skilled fighters, but we've got nothing on these, well, monsters who can leap in and out of shadows and wield their powers and supernatural strength with total confidence.

There's a boom, maybe from that gun Zian saw, and a large black mark appears on one of the cement columns. The shadowkind don't even slow down.

Gurgles and pained grunts fill the air. I spot a few figures fleeing out up the entrance ramp, away from the bodies now littering the floor.

That's what we called down on the guardians. That's what we asked for.

I'm as responsible for the carnage here as I was when my scream wrenched through our attackers before.

But I can't say I regret it. Not when the vision of Griffin crumpling flashes behind my eyes.

Not when I think of all the torment they put us through over the years and the stories the guys have told me about what happened after I was dragged away.

The guardians don't see us as anything but tools. They'd kill us too if they didn't want so badly to use us.

Two final figures scramble out into the streaks of sunlight. Several shadowkind emerge into view among the slumped corpses.

"Some army," one of them mutters disdainfully.

We hustle over to join them. My gaze skims over the fallen guardians—and jars on a smaller, skinnier form.

It's the girl I spotted during the ambush in Toronto.

Her dark hair fans out around her pale face, which is smeared with blood. Her chest has been gouged open, innards spilling across the ground and puffs of smoky essence drifting up.

Nausea rolls over me. I cringe away and jerk my attention toward Rollick. "You weren't supposed to kill the kids."

Rollick glances at the girl and shrugs. I can't read the emotion behind his dark blue eyes.

"In every battle, there'll be a few unexpected casualties. It's rarely a scenario that allows perfect precision. Would you rather that was *you* brought down by the mortals we just saved you from?"

A shiver runs through me. "No."

But I didn't exactly want this either.

Did we really make the right choice?

Rollick doesn't allow us any time to debate that question. He makes a sweeping motion toward the entrance.

"Mortals or not, they managed to find us here—and slip past my sentries, which I'll have to investigate. Clearly I underestimated this group. We need to get you out of Miami, now."

Eighteen

Riva

The ocean air gusts across the pier, filling my nose with the scents of seaweed and salt. And my mouth too, because my jaw is hanging slack as I take in the big white boat ahead of us.

Big is an understatement. *Boat* might be an understatement.

The vessel docked at the end of the pier is the seafaring version of a castle. The sleek white walls stretch across three floors above the deck to the gleaming metal bars of some kind of radio tower.

Several padded lounge chairs already sit in a couple of semi-circles across the open area of the deck, beckoning us to sprawl in them. Rectangular windows decorate the sides below deck, where that massive hull could hold an entire football field, as far as I can tell.

Andreas lets out a low whistle. "And I thought the RV was fancy."

Zian's eyes look ready to pop out of his head. "You couldn't fit that on a highway."

The Miami warmth still wraps around us, but the breeze licks a chill over my skin. I rub my arms. "I don't know about this. If we don't like how things are going, it's not like we'll be able to just leave."

The vast stretch of ocean around and beyond the ship makes my nerves itch. That is way more water than belongs in any place all at once —at least, any place I'm going to be.

Jacob shrugs. "That's the point, right? There won't be an easy way for anyone to get to *us* either."

His gaze slides to me, and his mouth slants in concern. "But if you think we shouldn't take the chance…"

I grimace. I didn't ask to be the deciding factor for the group, and I probably shouldn't be when my dislike of open water is more instinctive than logical. "I don't know. It just makes me nervous."

Dominic rests his hand on the small of my back—a simple gesture, but one that sends a much more pleasant tingle through my body.

I like that he feels comfortable offering little gestures of affection. I like that I no longer panic at the thought of receiving them—from him, at least.

"It makes sense to be wary," he says. "But if things get *really* bad, there have to be life rafts and things like that. It's hard to know where we'd be safe on land with how easily the guardians keep tracking us down."

"Yeah." I let out my breath in a huff. "Where did Rollick wander off to? Are we supposed to head on board or what?"

Andreas tips his head toward the other end of the pier. "Last I saw him, he was over by the harbor office. Maybe even monsters need to do paperwork."

Zian guffaws at the wry remark. I shift my weight from one foot to the other, restlessness winding through my body, and turn.

"I'll go see what's going on with him. If there's a problem, I want to know right away."

Dominic's touch falls away with my movement, and he reaches to grasp my hand instead. "I'll come with you. It's better if none of us go off on our own."

Jacob jerks to stiffer attention. "*I'm* coming."

Zian steps forward too, hastily opening his mouth. "I can make sure—"

I hold up my hands, stopping them in their tracks. "I don't need a whole entourage. I can look after *myself* just fine, remember?"

And if the shadowkind are up to something, it'll be a lot harder for me to slink over and find that out with my self-appointed bodyguards barging along after me.

Jacob grimaces, but I don't give him a chance to argue. Tugging on Dominic's hand, I set off toward the compact beige office building beyond the line of smaller boats.

Dom must sense my mood, because he keeps quiet as we approach the building. He's always been the type to walk softly, so he's really the perfect companion.

The fact that his closeness and our deepened connection make me a little giddy is just a bonus.

Rhythmic beats thrum through the walls of the office. Apparently no one in Miami is exempt from their dance music addiction.

The bass isn't loud enough to totally drown out Rollick's voice. I catch a few barely decipherable words and hustle closer as stealthily as I can.

We stop by the corner of the office building. Rollick is standing several feet beyond it near the edge of the main harbor area, gazing out over the rippling water as he talks into the phone at his ear.

"I'm hoping it won't be too long. But this is an unpredictable situation."

He means us. We're the situation.

I cross my arms over my chest, wishing I could hear the other end of the call.

Rollick pauses while his conversation partner must speak, his head bowing. A little of his typical cool confidence has fallen from his stance, as if what the other person says could alter his plans.

I always thought the demon was the man in charge around here. Does he have his own boss that he answers to?

Then he lets out a chuckle that's almost gentle, his voice dipping as well. "You know I'd rather not be away from you any longer than I can help, Quinn. I'll be sure to make it up to you *very* thoroughly the next time we're together."

My cheeks flush. Oh. I can tell by his tone that he isn't talking to a superior but to a lover.

"I'm sure it'll be fine," he goes on. "Some of my associates panic too easily. I won't keep Torrent away too long either. And you know you can call either of us any time. If you need us, we'll be there."

The unmistakable affection in his words calms my nerves. Rollick is capable of caring about *something*, clearly.

He isn't a sadistic beast, at least not all the way through, no matter what the guardians think of the shadowkind.

Dominic glances at me, and through unspoken agreement, we ease away from the office. We're halfway back to where the other guys are waiting when Rollick's brisk footsteps approach from behind.

"All right, all right," he says. "Everyone, on board. Let me give you a quick tour."

With less trepidation than before but still a healthy dollop of wariness, I follow him up the long, narrow boarding ramp with the others. He motions to the broad front deck with its lounge chairs first.

"Feel free to relax however you like when we're not working on those powers of yours. You have full access to the ship."

I guess there isn't much need for private spaces when he and his colleagues can slip into the shadows to talk in secret about anything they wouldn't want us to know.

Rollick leads us through a series of hallways with equally glossy floors and walls. There's a dining area that looks like an upscale restaurant, the smell of roasting meat already drifting from the kitchen beyond. A library room packed full of books and cozy armchairs.

Next we come to a lounge of cushioned seating facing a broad window that shows a view beneath the ocean water, one even I have to admit is breathtaking. And finally we peer into a huge space that could fit an entire apartment inside it that Rollick calls "the party room."

By the time we reach the section with the sleeping quarters, I'm so filled with awe I'm surprised it isn't floating me up to the ceiling like a helium balloon.

The RV was fancy, but it was still a cramped space with only the basics, as elegant as those were. This is like a full-out luxury vacation.

But the niggling voice at the back of my head reminds me that all this luxury might come at a price we haven't yet discovered.

"I'll be holding on to the main suite for myself, naturally," Rollick says. "But I don't think you'll find anything to complain about in your accommodations. And you'll all have your own rooms this time."

Each of the bedrooms he opens the doors to is as big as the entire interior of the RV. The cream-colored walls and leather finishings give off a soothing vibe.

The beds are big enough that I could sprawl at any angle and not come close to touching the edges. And they're each across from a larger TV than I've ever gotten to watch in my life.

I tread into the last room, which I decide on the spot will be mine, my feet sinking into the thick carpeting. What kind of channels can you access at sea?

No one has to know if I decide to hole up in here binging all the episodes of my soap opera that I've missed, right?

Rollick steps back with a satisfied smile. "Make yourselves

comfortable. We'll gather in the dining room in an hour to discuss strategy—and eat, of course."

The prospect of enjoying whatever his private chef is whipping up has my mouth watering despite my wariness. It wouldn't be *so* bad to enjoy the magical experience we've somehow landed in the middle of, would it?

Andreas gazes around the room with a breathless chuckle. "I've seen memories of cruise-ship vacations. Huge ocean liners with their own casinos and water slides and theaters. But none of them had cabins this nice."

"I'll take this over a casino any time," I declare, dropping my backpack on the bed to claim it.

The guys linger by the doorway. Jacob starts prowling through the room as if scanning it for threats.

I narrow my eyes at him. "You've got your own bedroom to hang out in."

He turns to me with a fierce flash of his eyes. "You're not sleeping in here alone."

I can't restrain a snort. "I'm not sleeping in here with *you*."

"I'll put a blanket down near the door. No one's getting past it without going through me."

Is he fucking kidding me?

My baleful look turns into a full-out glower. "The shadowkind can slip right around you without you even knowing they're there. And if *anyone's* going to keep me company overnight, it'll be Dominic."

My cheeks heat all over again with those last words, but the shy but brilliant smile that flickers across Dom's face makes the announcement worthwhile.

Jacob cuts his gaze toward Dominic, his jaw clenching. "No offense meant, but his skills are better for *after* a battle, not fighting one."

I plant my hands on my hips. "You're not—"

Before I can tell him off again, he raises his arms in surrender. "You don't want me right in here, I'll stay out. I can sleep in the hall outside the door."

My mouth twists with annoyance, but I don't know how I can stop him from doing that if he's going to insist. What does he even think he's going to accomplish?

"Sounds like it's settled," Andreas says, his tone dry but mild. "Maybe we should all take a few minutes to sort out our own space, though?"

Jacob grunts but marches out. The other guys follow, but Andreas hangs back for a moment at the doorway.

When I meet his gaze, he tips his head toward me, his expression softening. "How are you doing?"

I shrug. "Other than feeling a little smothered and wondering how far in over our heads we've gotten, I'm okay."

He wets his lips. "You know if you need anything—if there's anything you'd want me to do, for whatever reason—"

The pain I've worked so hard at suppressing springs up to clench around my gut.

"We're not there yet," I say quietly. "I don't know if we're ever going to be there. And I'm not going to forget that you're around without you reminding me. Just—just leave it, okay. We've got bigger things to worry about."

Andreas nods, but his face has tightened as if he's as knotted up inside as I am. "We do. But just for the record, none of this matters half as much to me as making sure you're happy."

He leaves before I can say anything else. I swallow thickly, so tangled up inside that for a second I can't breathe.

I don't bother unpacking my bag, because even at sea, it's always possible we'll need to make a hasty exit. I flop down on the bed and allow myself to revel in the fluffiness of the duvet for several minutes, but anxious thoughts keep gnawing at the edges of my mind.

This ship is amazing, but it's never going to be home. We can't stay on the run forever.

Are Rollick and his friends really going to carve out a path to a normal life for us? Or are we going to end up almost as trapped as we were in the facility, just with different types of captors, different sorts of tests?

I wish I had a better sense of the way forward.

To try to clear my head, I run through an exercise routine and take a quick shower. But when a speaker mounted in the corner of the room activates, I can't say I'm eager for the summons.

"All passengers please report to the dining room."

I'm both ready and not. I duck out into the hall at the same time as the guys step out from their various doorways.

Dominic looks up and down the hallway. "I don't remember which way the dining room is."

Zian takes a sniff of the air and strides forward without a hint of doubt. "I'm ready to dig in."

His nose leads us well. We emerge into the dining area I saw earlier and find a few of the tables pushed together to create one long one.

Serving dishes sit down the length of it, a couple heaped with spareribs that give off spicy and tangy-sweet scents. Others hold slices of baked ham, baby potatoes glistening with butter, and two different kinds of salad, one laced with mandarin slices and another with dried cranberries.

My mouth is already watering. There's no one else around yet—at least, no one I can see—so I grab a plate at random and add a little of everything to it.

Zian goes straight to the ribs, creating a little mountain on his plate that he tops with ham. He drops into a chair and pops the first bite into his mouth with gusto.

Obviously he isn't worried about trusting the food. But then, it *would* be a pretty bizarre scheme for Rollick to arrange a massive cruise just to poison us on the first night.

As we all take seats in a semi-circle at one end of the table, Rollick saunters over seemingly out of nowhere. "Eat as much as you like," he says. "Technically the rest of us don't *need* the food. Although I wouldn't associate with anyone who can't enjoy a good spare rib." He plucks one of the dry-rub morsels off its platter and carries it to his spot at the head of the table.

As if on cue, several more shadowkind waver into being by the other seats. Pearl plunks herself down next to me with a bounce of her golden curls and snatches a mandarin slice right out of the salad.

"Fruit is the best," she says in her cheery voice, and pops it into her mouth. "Don't you think so? They taste so good, and they carry the seeds to make more fruit! And I've heard mortals say they give you nutrions or something too."

My mouth twitches, but I'm afraid she'll be offended if I laugh. Offending a monster, even a not-very-monstrous-seeming one, feels like a bad idea.

"I think it's probably nutrients," I say. "Like vitamins and stuff."

"Oh! There are so many words. And that's just your language." She plucks up another slice. "Humans do like to make things complicated."

Okay, that's a fair assessment.

"That's what I like about you," the succubus goes on hastily as if concerned that she might have offended *me*. "It's so interesting on this side. Not that you're totally mortal. I guess we don't really know exactly how much you are one thing and the other. It's very exciting."

The other beings sitting around the table don't look all that excited. Some of them barely glance our way at all.

Others study us with apparent trepidation, as if they're as concerned about what we might do as we are about them.

What was it I heard Rollick saying on the phone—something about his associates panicking? They aren't *that* nervous about us, are they?

Why would they be?

My stomach momentarily tightens, but then I spot the dessert table over in the corner. Maybe a little sweetness will soothe my nerves.

I slip over to it, snatch up one of the smaller plates, and study the offerings. Slices of key lime pie and a cake that gives off a lemon-y scent, puffy meringues and plump cookies glinting with sugar crystals.

I scoop a piece of cake onto my plate and take one of the sugar cookies too. On my way back to my chair, I take a bite and restrain a moan at the perfect chewy, buttery dough.

Dropping back down between Pearl and Dominic, I turn to wave the cookie at Dom. "You have to try—"

As he glances up at me, my gaze slides to his plate, and I realize he's already grabbed two. Three, actually, counting the one there's only a chunk of left in his hand.

He must have gone straight to the dessert table before he even started filling up his dinner plate.

A laugh bubbles out of me, startled but genuinely happy. "I guess your sweet tooth is going to have a good time around here."

Dominic grins back. "No kidding."

As I alternate between the remains of my main dinner and my dessert, Rollick stirs at the head of the table. He folds his hands together on the tabletop and shoots a pointed look at an empty chair next to him.

A moment later, one final shadowkind being appears out of the shadows—a lean man with scruffy auburn hair, an oddly dented cheek… and two tentacles protruding from his waist, braced as if to help his balance.

Dominic brightens. "That's Torrent," he murmurs to me. "He talked with me this morning—he's going to look into reasons why my…" He waves toward his shoulders, where his tentacles are covered as usual by his trench coat. "…might act the way they do."

Why they keep growing when he uses his healing power, he means. It looks like that guy should have some idea how these things work.

Rollick clears his throat. "All right, folks. We can eat and talk. Try not to spew crumbs at anyone else, and it's all good."

He shifts his attention to our end of the table. "Our shadowblood guests of honor. You've been through a lot today, so I'll give you a break until tomorrow. But then I think our first priority should be determining exactly how you're able to trace each other's movements. Assuming your younger counterparts are using the same methods, once we've identified them, we may be able to find ways of deflecting the connection."

"May." Not "will."

No one here is really sure what to make of us, are they? Including ourselves.

But his mention of the younger shadowbloods brings back the memory of the bloodied girl this morning. My chest constricts.

We aren't the only ones who need help. Everything my guys and I went through at the guardians' hands, they're still experiencing it every moment they remain enslaved.

"And we'll just stay on this boat until we figure that out?" Andreas asks.

"I'm hopeful it won't be too extended a process." Rollick smiles with a hint of grimness. "But you should be safe here for as long as it takes."

He casts his gaze over his shadowkind companions after those last words, with a darkening of his eyes that looks like a warning. Is he worried that another of his associates might come up with their own ideas for how to deal with us?

My skin prickles. Luxury vacation or not, I don't want to be stuck in the middle of the ocean with this bunch any longer than absolutely necessary.

And the real answer might be something we were already hoping to accomplish for totally different reasons.

"What if there isn't any way to block the connection between shadowbloods?" I say. "Or they're using some method that we don't know about to even test?"

Rollick raises his eyebrows. "Then I suppose we'll figure that out as we proceed."

"Or we could solve the entire problem for good in one go."

His eyebrows lift higher. "What did you have in mind?"

I tap the table. "It's the other shadowbloods who are the biggest problem. The guardians only started finding us so quickly once they dragged the kids into the search. But they're prisoners just like we were. They don't deserve to be used like that. We should break them out of whatever facilities they're being kept in, and then the guardians *can't* use them anymore."

Zian nods eagerly. "Two birds with one stone. We have to help them."

Rollick pauses, and one of the other shadowkind, a tall gangly guy I hadn't noticed before, sits up straighter in his seat. The ropey muscles along his arms flex threateningly.

"We don't need more than five of the mutants running wild."

Rollick glares at him. "These are my guests you're talking about, Kudzu. They haven't caused us any trouble so far."

On the other side of the table, Cinder lets out a derisive sound. "We've come all the way out here because of them."

"Because we chose to." The demon's voice lowers ominously. "You're welcome to find yourself new employment whenever you like."

She tenses in her chair, ducking her head apologetically. But the tension still radiating through the air makes my skin creep.

"A jail-break!" Pearl pipes up, clapping her hands together. "I think that would be fun."

Kudzu snorts. "You think everything is fun. You're a newbie and a tourist."

She winces, looking hurt enough that my hackles rise on her behalf.

I raise my chin. "This is the most direct way to deal with the problem. And if you all were helping us, I'm sure we could pull off a 'jail-break' a lot faster than experimenting with interrupting a connection we don't even understand."

"I agree," Dominic says, quiet but firm.

Jacob leans his elbows onto the table. "It's just a bunch of mortals you'd have to tackle, right? What are you all so scared of?"

From the looks most of the shadowkind shoot us then, I get the impression it's not the guardians they're scared of.

Like the big purple dude back in Toronto, for some reason most of these beings are frightened of *us*.

Maybe even Rollick is behind his suave demeanor. He waves his hand through the air as if he can dismiss all the concerns raised on both sides just like that.

"It's an option I won't take off the table," he says. "But we don't know where these facilities even are. So why don't we start with what we have right in front of us?"

"Can you ask someone to start looking?" Andreas asks. "I wouldn't think it'd be too hard for shadowkind to figure out what locations fit—with the resources you've got, anyway."

"I'll see what I can do."

Even his noncommittal answer appears to be too much. Kudzu shoves away his plate. "You can't be serious."

Rollick studies him with a languid blink. "I believe in considering all the strategies available to us. It's worked in my favor before."

The gangly man mutters something under his breath that I can't make out. He vanishes into the shadows a moment later.

"This isn't like before," Cinder says to Rollick, her expression tense, and wisps away too.

And just like that, it looks like we've lost two supposed allies before we even got started.

Nineteen

Riva

When I flick out my claws and bring them to my arm, all four of my guys stiffen where they're standing around me.

"Riva!" Andreas protests, but I've already sliced open the skin beneath my shoulder in a shallow cut.

As a thin trickle of blood streaks down and a tiny whiff of dark smoke gusts up in the ocean breeze washing over the yacht's deck, Jacob lets out a sound like a growl. His hand jerks up as if he was going to catch my wrist but thought better of it.

"Never again," he says roughly. "You don't hurt yourself."

I look from him to Zian, who has tensed with anguish etched across his face, to Andreas's tight expression, to the horror in Dominic's eyes.

"It's no big deal." I motion to the tiny white scars that mottle my pale skin from elbow to armpit. "I did it at least once a week when they were holding me at the cage-fighting arena."

Zian's face contorts with even more distress. "Why would you—"

"So I knew you were still out there," I say with impatience I can't suppress. "That was before I knew you were all going to be asshats about seeing me again."

Standing beyond our little cluster, Rollick lets out a sudden sound that might have been a muffled snicker.

Jacob's stance has gone totally rigid. A faint creaking emanates from somewhere in the vicinity of the yacht's front cabin until Andreas gives him a punch to the arm.

Jacob shakes himself, his gaze searing into me in a way that sets all my nerves jangling—with both alarm and other emotions I'd rather not acknowledge.

"Heal her," he snaps at Dominic.

I scowl. "I can do this. I don't need—"

"You don't need to get hurt ever again," Jacob interrupts. "Not if we can help it. It's the least we can fucking do."

He turns to Rollick. "I'll handle the bleeding for the tests."

The demon shrugs. "It's up to you. I'd just like to get on with it, if you're done posturing for the woman who clearly isn't impressed by it."

A tiny smirk tugs at my lips. No, Rollick definitely isn't a completely bad guy.

Dominic has already rested his hand on my shoulder, but he searches my gaze before extending his power. Waiting for my permission rather than following Jacob's orders automatically.

I have made a lot of progress with my guys. With all of them, really, even if it's hard to know what could be enough from some of them.

"It's really fine," I tell him. "You know how quickly we heal on our own. It'll seal up in a matter of minutes."

The bleeding has already stopped. I'd have to prod it to get it going again, but I don't feel like provoking a longer argument.

Dom gives my shoulder a gentle squeeze. "If you're sure. I don't mind at all."

"*I* mind. The protecting each other doesn't just go one way, in case you've forgotten."

I reach up to squeeze his hand in return and then step away so it isn't a question anymore. We walk across the deck toward the bow while Jacob hangs back.

The test doesn't really work if we're standing right next to each other.

Rollick watches the proceedings with obvious curiosity. "The shadow part of your blood seeks out each other naturally?"

I shake my head. "It doesn't just happen. I had to concentrate on my memories of them."

Zian frowns. "How would the other shadowbloods be able to focus on us?"

"They could have watched recordings from our time in the facility," Andreas says. "There'd be years of footage."

I guess we have to assume that would be enough. Unless the guardians have found other connections we're unaware of.

Jacob pushes his rolled-up sleeve right over his elbow. The purple spines laced with his innate poison spring from his forearm.

He mustn't be affected by his own venom, because he twists his arm and scratches open the heel of his opposite hand without hesitation.

He dug in a little deeper than I did. A thicker spurt of smoky stuff streaks up toward the stark blue of the sky.

Jacob closes his eyes, his face turning into a mask of concentration.

After just a few seconds, the stream of haze curves. It wavers through the air across the deck toward the four of us.

Rollick hums to himself. When the trickle of smoke has nearly reached us, he gestures to what seems to be thin air on the other side of the deck.

A couple of shadowkind—Cinder and a slim man I saw at dinner yesterday materialize by a plastic storage box and shove it toward us before opening the lid. The guy cringes backward, and Cinder makes a face.

"Get yourselves some shields," Rollick tells us. "Let's see if the essence can still seek you out through that."

Essence. That's what he calls the smoky stuff. He told us earlier that it's *all* shadowkind bleed, no liquid at all.

The four of us march over to the container and find gleaming serving dishes inside. When I shoot Rollick a quizzical look, he offers a wry smile.

"Shadowkind can't handle silver and iron. Those were the easiest large pieces of silver we could obtain on short notice. Hybrids don't seem to have the same issues with the metals, but maybe it'll deflect the particularly shadowy parts of you."

Silver. Something twigs in my brain—the big purple shadowkind who confronted us in Toronto accused us of using silver, didn't he? With the guns?

Were Engel's murderous guardians shooting at us with silver bullets like we're werewolves out of a horror story?

Considering both those guardians and their guns are long gone, I guess it doesn't really matter.

I heft one of the serving platters, which stretches from my chin to my waist when I hold it in front of me, and position myself across from Jacob with the plate held firm.

The other guys join me. Jacob stares at us as if he finds the whole thing ridiculous but squeezes a little more blood from the puncture wound on his hand.

The smoke wavers up—and veers straight toward us within seconds of him closing his eyes again.

Rollick gives another pensive hum. "All right. That's not doing it. I figured it was wishful thinking. If it takes concentration to establish the connection, maybe concentration can ward it off too. All of you, focus on pushing back any essence that might be flowing your way."

I can't see how this is going to help us in the long run. We can't exactly wander through life constantly thinking about pushing monster-blood smoke away from us.

But to humor him, I close my own eyes. Draw up a mental picture of the waft of smoke drifting away from me. Narrow all my attention down to that image.

When Rollick coughs meaningfully, my eyes pop open. The first thing I see is the stream of dark haze that's yet again stretched out toward us.

I exhale with a grunt. "So much for psychic shielding."

The demon trains his gaze on me. "You mentioned something about there being other ways you were in tune with each other beyond your blood. What specifically did you mean by that?"

"I think we're all a little extra aware of each other when we're nearby," Jacob puts in, pressing his other hand over his cut to stop the bleeding. "I knew something was going on the night Riva came to break us out, even though I hadn't seen her yet. But I don't think that effect is strong enough that anyone could track us from a distance using it—if it's even a general strategy and not something specific to us because we grew up together."

He's never mentioned that to me before—that he sensed my presence in some way like that. But I'm too distracted by the actual thing I meant to give much thought to his assertion.

I resist the urge to hug myself against the awkwardness the subject stirs up inside me. Instead, I hook my fingers into the neckline of my tank top.

"It's more than that. There's—when one of the guys and I have, um, hooked up, we both had a mark appear on our chest. And since then, I've been able to sense where they are through it."

I ease down the fabric just enough to show the two small black splotches that mark my collarbone on either side of my sternum. Zian's head jerks around, and Jacob stares from the other side of the deck.

Looks like Andreas and Dominic never mentioned that little side effect to their friends.

Pearl pops out of the shadows next to me so abruptly my nerves flinch. It's only by sheer force of will that I don't jump ten feet in the air.

She waggles her finger at my chest. "You got shadow imprints from having sex? That's so cool!"

Cool is not the word I would have used. But maybe to a succubus, airing your bedroom activities in public is a lot less embarrassing.

"I… guess." I glance at Rollick. "Shadow imprints? Is that a normal thing?"

The demon ambles closer, his head tipped at a contemplative angle. "I've heard of some shadowkind who plant physical marks on beings over whom they're staking a claim, but generally those are mortals, and it's done purposefully. It sounds like you didn't mean to create them?"

I shake my head. "No, it just happened."

"Very interesting. There's so much we don't know about how hybrids might function."

He motions for me to pick up the silver platter again. "Hold it so it's totally covering the mark." Then he snaps his fingers at Andreas. "Go somewhere else on the yacht, wait five minutes, and then come back."

Cinder, who's still watching from near the railing, lets out a discontented sound.

Rollick ignores her. As Andreas lopes off, his attention stays focused on me.

"Can you follow his path without seeing him, even with the silver over the mark?"

I pause, letting my own attention center on the splotch that binds me to Andreas. A faint tickling sensation spreads through my flesh.

I try to map my sense of him onto what I remember of the ship's interior layout. "I can definitely tell what direction he's in and how far away he is. If I needed to get to him, I could find him no problem. He's stopped… I think that would be the library?"

A few more shadowkind pop into being around the edges of the deck. The gangly muscular guy who complained yesterday—Kudzu—crosses his arms over his triangular chest.

"None of this is working. They're not *like* us."

Rollick turns to him. "We've only tried a few strategies so far."

The other man grunts. "We're risking everything over—"

He cuts himself off with a jerk of his head, but the frustration in his voice digs into my bones. What's his problem with us?

Rollick looks as if he may have restrained an eye roll. As I set the platter aside, he strides toward his shadowkind companions, gesturing for them to gather with him near the front cabin.

"If you're so concerned about using our time effectively, you can use that thick head of yours to generate some other possibilities."

Kudzu lets out a huff, but he follows, along with Cinder and a couple of the others. The tentacled man—Torrent—appears out of the shadows to join their cluster.

Pearl leans closer to me, giving off a whiff of a smoky rose scent. She raises her finger as if to touch one of the marks on my chest, but I step back instinctively, releasing my shirt so the neckline springs back up to cover them with a jostle of my pendant.

The shadowkind girl claps her hand to her mouth with an abashed expression. "Sorry! I just—I've never seen something like that before."

"Me neither," I say dryly, eyeing the woman.

She's awfully nosy. Is that a succubus thing or just a Pearl thing?

Her smile springs back into place, and she waves to the slim guy who helped bring the silver platters over. "Billy, come meet them!"

The guy walks over to us tentatively, his pale eyes gone wide beneath his chaotic brown waves. As he gets close, I realize that two of those waves aren't hair at all.

He has spiraling horns protruding on either side of his head, closer to beige than brown and poking too high to be disguised by his locks.

"Billy's like me," Pearl announces, slinging her arm around his narrow shoulders. "Well, he's a faun, not any kind of cubi. But he hasn't been in the mortal world much. So many fun things to learn."

The horned guy's gaze roves over all of us, including Andreas and Jacob as they cross the deck to rejoin our group. His voice comes out breathless. "Have you ever gone in a plane before? This is my first time even on a boat. They say you can swim in the water, but I don't know..."

He tugs at a lock of his hair, glancing toward the ocean with a nervous expression. A pang reverberates through my chest.

I know what it's like to feel like a newbie in the world, even if not quite the same way as this guy.

"We haven't actually gotten to experience a whole lot so far ourselves," I say. "Most of our lives, we were locked up in one building."

Pearl tsks her tongue. "That's so unfair of them. You have all this amazing world to run around in and they shut you up in one tiny little part of it."

Is that why she's so overeager too—because she hasn't spent much time around people? Or mortals, as the shadowkind seem to call us?

That could explain the lack of manners and personal boundaries.

Dominic must be thinking along similar lines. "Where do you go when you're not here? I take it shadowkind don't start out in our world?"

Pearl laughs. "Oh, no. We come into being in the shadow realm. We can only get here through rifts. I *need* to make the trip, because I've got to feed, but I only became, like, a year ago."

Zian's brow knits. "You're only a year old?"

She motions to her curvaceous body as if putting herself on display. "We come the way we're always going to be. No growing up. We weren't there, and then we are."

"Like magic," Andreas says dryly.

Pearl claps her hands. "Yes. Just like that."

Billy ducks his head awkwardly, his face turning ruddy beneath his light brown complexion that's a lot like Dominic's. "I've been alive for longer than that. But I can't mingle with mortals when they'll notice these." He motions to his horns.

Jacob cocks his head. "Can't you just think them away like Rollick does with his claws?"

"Oh, no," Pearl says. "We can't leave our shadowkind selves behind completely. Everyone's got one thing that sticks."

She pushes up one fluttery sleeve of her dress to reveal a band of glittering gold that winds across the normal creamy skin. "It goes right across my chest to my other arm. But I can cover it up, or people think it's a strange tattoo."

"Some of us can hide our sticky features better than others," Billy says.

"Yeah." Pearl squints at all of us. "But you five don't seem to have any at all." She glances at Dominic. "Well, except for you, but you said those only grew in later. That's got to be a hybrid thing."

Footsteps rap across the polished wooden boards toward us.

"Keeping our guests entertained?" Rollick saunters over to our end of the deck with an amused expression.

Pearl grins at him. "Someone should with those grumps around."

The mention of the "grumps" brings back the knot in my stomach. I hesitate and then force out the question. "Why are some of them bothered by us? It seems like they're upset that you're helping us at all."

Rollick pauses before he answers, which makes all my nerves twinge with apprehension. He's trying to decide how to tell us something we won't want to hear.

"Our community, such as it is, has some… mixed feelings about hybrids," he says.

Zian glances down at his brawny frame. "They don't like that we're part human?"

"Not exactly." Rollick appears to weigh his words again before continuing. "None of us have much experience with beings like you. Honestly, before you showed up, I was only aware of three other hybrids in the entire length of my multi-millennia existence, and two of those were almost immediately snuffed out by our de facto rulers."

My body tenses. "They were *killed*?"

Rollick spreads his hands. "I'm sure it's difficult for you to understand from the inside. But to us, on the outside… You're the ultimate wild cards. You've already seen some of that. You have powers that can rival our own—in some cases, overwhelm most regular shadowkind—and none of the weaknesses that can keep us in check."

"We can't jump into the shadows like you," Jacob points out. "We can *die*."

I can tell from the edge in his voice that he's thinking of Griffin.

"Well, you may be able to do the former with some training. And we can die too, just with a fair bit of difficulty." Rollick offers us a crooked smile.

"So, they're… jealous of us?" I ask, still trying to wrap my head around where the resentment is coming from.

Rollick chuckles. "Maybe a little. But it's more that you're a threat. Past hybrids have proven difficult to control, as you yourselves are finding with your abilities. We don't know how destructive you might become—toward us, or toward mortals, which will draw attention to the rest of us."

Pearl nods, her voice dropping to an awed whisper. "They say the last hybrid nearly burned up the whole planet."

My jaw goes slack. "What?"

As my gaze slides to the grim figures watching at the other side of the deck, my spirits sink.

No wonder they're so hostile. No wonder we've seen signs of fear from even the powerful shadowkind.

We're an unknown quantity, and one that could screw them up and screw them over in ways they can't even prepare for.

We're lucky Rollick is sticking his neck out even this much.

My next question tumbles out, propelled by a sudden chill. "What do the others want you to do with us? Do they think you should kill *us* too?"

Rollick snorts. "Don't worry about that. *I* can see that you're not on the verge of burning up the whole world or anything so catastrophic." He gives me a meaningful look. "At least, as long as you give those powers more practice to make sure you have a grip on them."

As I squirm internally at his insinuation, he rubs his hands together. "In any case, Torrent has set off through the waters to head back to land. He'll make some inquiries along with other associates of mine to see if we can't track down these facilities your guardians are running."

Zian perks up. "We're going to go rescue the other shadowbloods?"

"We're going to see if that's a feasible course of action."

I should feel victorious. That was my idea, and Rollick is actually pursuing it.

But I can't shake the uneasy weight the conversation has placed on my shoulders.

He didn't say that the other shadowkind *don't* want us dead, only that we shouldn't worry they'll succeed in making it happen.

Is he the only thing standing between us and a total slaughter?

If the humans who made us think we're too dangerous to exist, and the shadowkind they've fought against feel the same way… where can we possibly belong?

Monsters exist, sure. And it turns out my guys and I are the only thing the monsters are scared of.

TWENTY

Andreas

Rollick motions to the glasses in front of us. "All right, drink up!"

Across the small, glossy table from me, Riva studies the amber liquid. Her mouth slants at an uncertain angle.

I can't help remembering the only other time she's drunk anything alcoholic since we got out of the facility: that night at the dance club when a single cocktail went haywire with the poison Jacob had inflicted on her.

That was the night she pointed out her scars to me and told me how often she'd taken comfort in knowing we were still out there. When she asked me to dance and looked so downcast when I refused.

When she pulled me into a hug I couldn't resist, and I got to experience the full, unrestrained bliss of her embrace.

I should have known for sure then. Hell, I should have known from the start that she was telling the truth.

But instead I treated her like an enemy, schemed against her, and now here we are. Even if we didn't have a table standing between us, there'd be an invisible wall dividing us that I can't climb over.

I curl my fingers around my own glass. "It's weak stuff, right?"

Rollick chuckles. "It wouldn't be a very effective solution to have you stumbling around drunk. I just want to see if having a little interference with your normal mental state might disrupt the connection."

I raise the glass to my lips and gulp it down. The mix of sweet and sour flavors coat my tongue and send a pang through my gut.

Riva hesitates a few moments longer and then downs her own drink.

Only a faint tingle in the back of my skull suggests that I've got anything like a buzz. I could definitely handle operating on this incredibly mild level of tipsy for a while if it meant the guardians couldn't track us.

"You know the drill," Rollick says. "Riva, you leave this time. Andreas, you see if you can find her."

Riva rises from her seat and slips out of the room without a word—or a glance at me. My throat constricts.

But I can already tell that the alcohol hasn't dulled the bond between us even slightly. Her presence nibbles at my awareness from the spot on my sternum.

She's turned left down the hall. She's heading through a doorway into another room—I think that far down, it'd be the observation lounge.

I can sense her existence from under my skin, but I can't touch her. Not anymore.

"It isn't working," I say without even bothering to get up. "I can feel her just as well as ever."

Rollick rubs his chin. "I still think these marks and the connection between them could be the key. They're something that's specific to you shadowbloods."

He gets up. "Well, let's go collect her. Maybe I'll think of another tactic to try along the way."

The chef bustles out of the kitchen just then and sets a platter on the buffet table along the dining room wall. He seems to emerge every hour or two during the day with snacks, just in case anyone's hungry.

Pearl and Billy, who've been hanging on our every move through Rollick's tests, bound over to collect some of the delicate pastries on offer. I can't summon any enthusiasm in myself, but I catch myself as I turn toward the door and go back to pluck a few to set on a plate.

Riva isn't much of a dessert person, but I know she likes sour flavors, so she might appreciate this lemon tart. Or the mini-Danish topped with what looks like a blob of cranberry.

Rollick waits for me without remark.

"The observation room," I tell him as I walk to rejoin him, our little fan club hustling along behind me.

When we reach the observation room with its tall windows that offer a view both above and below the ocean surface, Riva is lounging on one of the cushioned benches. In my first glimpse of her gazing at the watery landscape, she looks almost relaxed.

Almost *happy*.

It's a crime how seldom I've gotten to see her like that in the past few weeks. A crime that she hasn't been able to *be* like that very often in those weeks.

And the way her expression tightens when she sees me walk into the room, her momentary joy falling away, is an outright atrocity. One I committed.

The gift I've brought seems pathetic now, but I walk over to her anyway. "The chef brought out some pastries. I figured these were the ones you'd like the most."

Riva takes the plate from me and sets it on the bench's armrest. She considers it for a moment.

"I'm not really hungry," she says in a slightly apologetic tone that I can't say I deserve.

I give an awkward laugh. "It's okay. I didn't want you to go without in case you were."

I haven't even gotten a flicker of a smile out of her. Nothing like the soft curving of her lips when Pearl and Billy come rushing down the aisle between the benches.

Billy presses his hands to the window and gapes at the fish flitting by. "There are so many mortal creatures even down here."

He did say he'd never been on a boat before. I guess he hadn't made it down to this room yet.

Pearl turns toward Riva with a pop of her succubus hips that I suppose a guy might find appealing if his entire heart wasn't tangled up with a different woman. "You like it in here, huh?"

Riva runs her fingers over the leather cushions. Her eyes widen as she glances around the room, awe brightening her face in a way that makes my pulse skip a beat.

"I like the whole ship. It's incredible… I feel like I've stepped into a movie or a TV show."

"Much better than underground prison cells, I'm sure," Rollick says with a grin. "Well, you can enjoy it at your leisure for a little while. I haven't come up with any brilliant new brainstorms quite yet."

Riva hesitates, and I can feel her—partly in her body language, but maybe I pick up a fragment of her emotions through our connection too —weighing her options. Deciding whether she'd rather stay here and watch the ocean life when I'm in the same room or go someplace where I'm not around.

An uncomfortable heat prickles up my neck. I open my mouth to say I'm heading back to my room, but before I can get any words out, she's already sprung to her feet.

"Speaking of TV, I haven't gotten to do any real channel surfing for most of my life, so I think I'll keep catching up on that."

She shoots another smile at the shadowkind around us, not quite aiming it at me, and slips away.

I watch her vanish through the doorway, my stomach clenching. When I tear my gaze away, Rollick is watching *me*.

"It can be rather difficult to win over a woman who sees you as a villain," he says in a mildly wry tone. "But it's not impossible. I know from personal experience."

Somehow I don't think the supernaturally handsome demon in front of me has faced quite the same challenges that I have with whatever love life he carries out, but I'll take the sympathy at face value anyway.

I exhale roughly. "It's my own fault. I just don't know how to make it up to her."

I don't know if I even can.

Rollick ambles toward the doorway. "I can't say it's a swift process or an easy one. You might have to reveal things about yourself that you're used to hiding. But if it's worth it, it's worth it."

As he heads off to who-knows-where, Pearl sashays over to me. "Maybe I can help! This boat has *everything*. There's got to be something around that would impress her."

I don't think impressing Riva is the key, but who knows? Maybe the succubus's cheerful commentary will jostle loose some brilliant brainstorm of my own.

Relationships are her specialty, after all. Well, a certain type, at least.

"All right," I say. "Let's see if I've missed anything."

We amble through the halls, making a circuit of the ship's many common rooms. Pearl natters on about Riva's eating habits—"I heard her ask if we have any extra lemons!"—and her disinterest in the library —"I don't blame her; words are a lot more boring than being someplace."

There's a spa area I hadn't stumbled on before, but I can't see Riva letting me pamper her in any way that involves putting my hands on her body.

We step into the party room where someone has lowered a mirror ball from the ceiling, and Pearl sets her hands on her hips. "Too bad she isn't much of a party girl."

The comment sets off an automatic twinge of defiance in me. "Actually, she really likes music and dancing," I say. "But that could come with some bad memories too…"

I pause, gazing at the expansive room in front of me. An image floats up in the back of my mind of Riva's face rapt with awe like it was in the observation lounge—but years ago, tucked next of Griffin on the training-room sofa.

I feel like I've stepped into a movie or a TV show, she said today. And days ago, in the hotel room, she admitted to how much she loved that frothy soap opera Griffin would always arrange to put on for her.

The guys on that show were always screwing up and begging forgiveness. Maybe I can learn something from them.

The idea hits me in a bolt of inspiration, sizzling through my mind and knocking every other thought out of my head.

That could be perfect. It would be hard to pull off, and maybe it wouldn't do the trick, but I know her. I know—

Something inside me balks. Is that really the right direction?

If I pick something that personal, that specific to her—will she wonder if I've peeked inside her head with my talent? Invaded her privacy?

I swallow thickly, wavering between exhilaration and doubt.

Rollick said I might have to reveal things rather than hide them.

Riva knows I observe people all the time, that I remember all kinds of things about them. And doting on her in all the generic ways I can think of hasn't gotten me anywhere.

I have to try, don't I? I can't really fuck up any worse than I already have.

A little trepidation lingers, because I know it's not just her I'm going to have to win over but the other guys as well. First, though, I need to make sure my idea is possible to begin with.

"I think I've got something," I say to Pearl. "Do you have any idea where Rollick is?"

Her eyes flash with excitement. "I can find him!"

The next second, she's leapt into the shadows.

Billy, who's trailed behind us simply taking in the conversation, peers around the party room. "You're going to try to make Riva happy?"

"Yeah. I mean, it's a little more complicated than that, but… basically."

He offers me a small but genuine smile. "I don't know much about mortal parties, but I do know music. If you need any help. It comes with the whole faun thing." He motions to his horns.

An unexpected flicker of friendly warmth passes through me. I don't totally trust the shadowkind, but I'll take them over the guardians any day.

"Thanks," I say. "Let me think about this—if I can even get this idea off the ground."

Pearl hasn't returned yet, so I venture down the hall, not sure where I should head now. But I've only made it past a few doorways before the succubus blinks back into sight—with the demon right beside her.

Rollick arches his eyebrows. "Apparently there's some incredibly urgent matter you need to speak to me about."

I wince inwardly. "Sorry. It's not that urgent. But, since you're here now… Would you let me use the party room for something tomorrow night? And I'd need some supplies. I don't know how easy that'll be while we're at sea."

"I was already planning on docking tomorrow morning, just briefly, for other reasons. Give me a list, and there's very little I can't obtain. And I have no plans for any parties, so the room is up for grabs."

My heart leaps with more hope than I've felt in ages. "Great. Thank you. I'll get on with making that list."

"This is about Riva?" he asks.

I hesitate. "Is that a problem?"

The demon aims a crooked grin at me. "Not at all. I happen to think it's better for all of us if your little banshee-of-sorts found herself some more peace. See what you can do about that all you like."

He vanishes, leaving me with an uneasy knot in my gut. Why does he think it's better for *everyone*?

But then, he does seem to enjoy making vaguely ominous comments for his own amusement.

I hurry toward the residential quarters, my nerves twanging with both eagerness and uncertainty. The sound of voices from the games room draws me up short.

The other three guys are gathered around the pool table there, Jacob motioning from the cue ball to one of the others.

"You're supposed to hit it *into* that ball."

Zian frowns. "That seems like a pretty stupid way of doing things."

"Jake's right—those are the usual rules," Dominic says from where he's standing off to the side, studying the rack of cues. "But nothing says we couldn't make up our own."

They all fall silent when I stride into the room. Jacob's expression tightens.

"Training is all done for the day?" he asks.

"For now." I barrel onward before I can think better of the proposal I'm about to make—and how they might feel about it. "I need your help—I want us to do something for Riva. Something… big."

Twenty-One

Riva

I know before they even knock that Andreas and Dominic have come up to my bedroom door together. Their arrival sends two tiny pulses of awareness through the marks along my clavicle.

A strange mix of joy and apprehension tangles inside me as I reach for the door handle. I'm about to see one guy who makes my spirits lift and one who sets off painful pangs of memory.

And I'm tied to them both. Forever, probably.

I ease the door open and peer outside. A faint vibration runs through the floor under my feet—the yacht is cruising again after stopping at a harbor for a couple of hours this morning.

Both of the guys look at me with matching expressions of hopeful anticipation. Andreas is holding a large bundle wrapped in white tissue paper.

Dominic beams at me. "We've set something up for you. Really, Drey did, but we're all helping. We thought we might as well enjoy everything we've got on the ship while we're here."

"And we haven't really taken a moment to celebrate our freedom properly," Andreas adds, more hesitantly. "It's because of you we had the chance to escape the facility when we did. I don't know that we'd ever have made it all the way without your help. We definitely wouldn't have made it out of Engel's house alive. So, you're the guest of honor."

I open my mouth and close it again, my words startled out of me. Before I can figure out what to say, Andreas holds the bundle out to me.

"I wasn't sure what you'd like best, so I picked out a few options. I hope you'll change into one of them, but it's totally up to you. Dom will bring you to the party. You can ignore the rest of us the whole time if you'd prefer that, but I hope you'll come."

I accept the bundle, finding it soft and yielding like cloth. My nerves jitter with a mix of uncertainty and curiosity. "What exactly did you set up?"

A smile touches Andreas's lips for the first time with a hint of mischief that makes my heart ache. I've missed his playful side—missed being able to take it at face value.

"You'll see," he says mysteriously, and slips away down the hall.

Dominic holds my gaze, reaching out to give my forearm a gentle squeeze. "I think you should come. And I wouldn't say that unless I was sure."

My mouth twists. "I don't think a party is going to make up for everything."

"I know. That's not how Andreas sees it." Dom pauses. "He did speak up for you before that night, you know. In the train, while you were napping. He tried to convince Jacob and the rest of us that you were on our side and we should stop treating you like an enemy. None of us totally listened. That's on us. On me. *I* could have agreed with him and argued for you too, and maybe—"

So much anguish has crept into his voice that I can't bear to let him keep going. I step closer, leaning into him, and his arm rises to encircle me automatically.

"*You* didn't lie to me or manipulate me," I murmur against his chest. "I'm not happy about how things were back then, but you never pretended to feel anything you didn't. It's different."

Dominic swallows audibly and brushes a kiss to the top of my head. "I know. I'm just saying, when you and he—when you were with him that night—I don't think he was lying at all by that point either."

I'm sure Dom wants to believe that. Andreas is his friend—the four of them had only each other for the years after Griffin died and I was gone.

But the sharp words that greeted me when I followed him after we slept together ring through my memory, still painfully vivid. *The whole reason I started getting cozy with her was so she'd open up…*

He was saying that even after. Talking about the deal he had with Jacob.

It didn't sound like it was totally over.

"Just come," Dominic says gently. "I think it'll make things a little more right. It isn't about forgiving him—he's not going to make any demands, I promise."

I let out a soft huff and straighten up. "All right. But only because *you* asked me to."

Dom's smile soothes my uneasiness. "Thank you. Now I've got to go get changed too."

As he vanishes into his own room, I carry the bundle over to the bed, more puzzled than ever. I tear open the tissue paper and paw apart the three clumps of folded fabric inside.

They're dresses. Fancy evening gowns, leagues beyond anything I've ever worn before.

I hold them up one by one, staring at them. Then I drape them against myself as I consider my reflection in the wardrobe's full-length mirror.

Sleek black silk, so glossy I can almost see my reflection in *it*, tumbles down my frame from spaghetti straps.

Dark green lace flows into a princess skirt like an explosion of forest leaves.

A mesh neckline meets a pale blue bodice with a rippling waterfall of chiffon beneath.

They're all beautiful. They're all completely separate from anything I ever imagined my life could contain.

I linger over them, running my fingertips over the smooth fabric. I still don't know what Andreas is up to, but I told Dominic I'd give it a shot.

And I can't deny that excitement shivers through me at the thought of putting on one of those gowns. Seeing myself transformed into the kind of person who *would* belong in a life like that, if only in appearance.

Finally, I settle on the pale blue dress. It's the lightest and the most flexible to move in.

And when I tug at the folds, I discover pockets hidden in the chiffon skirt. I know where my knives are going.

Just because I'm getting dressed up doesn't mean I'm throwing caution to the wind. We've been attacked when we least expected it before.

Anyway, maybe I'm going to end up wanting to stab Andreas. Might as well be prepared.

I shimmy into the dress, which falls all the way to my ankles. To my relief, the solid part of the bodice covers my cleavage, only my shoulders and collarbone revealed through the mesh.

My two shadow marks show through the transparent fabric, one on either side.

The silver chain of my cat-and-yarn pendant dangles between them. The necklace doesn't exactly fit the elegance of the dress, but I can't imagine taking it off any more than I could erase those marks.

I'm just turning toward the door when Pearl materializes out of thin air right in front of it. A yelp of surprise bursts from my lips.

Pearl cringes with embarrassment. "Sorry, sorry, I forgot, I should have started outside and knocked. I can try again and—"

"No," I interrupt. "It's okay. You're here now. What's going on?"

"I'm helping!" She flashes a smile and holds out a pair of gray ballet-style dress shoes. "You picked a good dress. It makes your eyes look more gold."

Considering she goes around wearing cocktail dresses as casual wear, her approval feels reassuring. "I'm glad you like it."

"I can do something fancy with your hair too. If you want."

My gaze veers back to the mirror. My usual braid, slightly rumpled at the moment, doesn't really fit the elegant clothes.

"Are you a hairdresser now too?" I ask with a little wryness.

Pearl laughs. "I'm good at beauty stuff. Seems to be part of the succubus skillset. I can make it pretty but not too fussy. You'd like that, right?"

I exhale slowly. "Yeah, that sounds about my speed."

Pearl really must have some kind of cosmetician magic, because in the space of a few minutes, she's unwound my hair and fixed it into a swooping coil across my head with a few waves drifting down on one side. Not how I've ever pictured it, but looking at my reflection, I could almost believe I *am* someone else.

Pearl rubs her hands together in excitement. "I'll go tell the guys you're ready."

She vanishes again without bothering with the door.

I wiggle my toes into the shoes, which have enough give to fit my feet comfortably. No heels, which is probably for the best.

The next arrival does knock. I square my shoulders and answer the door.

Dominic is waiting on the other side again, but he couldn't look more different either. He's wearing a fancy suit with a collared shirt underneath, a bulge on the back showing where it covers his tentacles. His auburn hair is smoothed back in the neatest of ponytails, and his eyes are gleaming.

He looks absolutely dashing. I think I might be drooling.

It takes me a moment to shake myself out of the initial daze and realize he's awestruck too. A hint of a flush colors his light brown skin.

"You're even more gorgeous than usual," he says.

There's so much admiration in his voice, my nerves quiver with it.

He holds out his arm, and I take his elbow, pretending to be the people we look like now. As he leads me down the hall, I glance at the other bedroom doors, but they're all closed.

Dominic rests his hand over mine. "Everyone else is already there."

I open my mouth to ask where, but right then the first strains of music reach my ears. Not the thumping of club music that surrounded us in Miami, but lilting notes that suggest a more elegant sort of dance to fit our new getup.

Dominic directs me through the doorway of what Rollick called the party room. Which I guess makes sense, because Andreas called this a party.

But it's nothing like I'd have expected.

The room has transformed. Jewel-like lights twinkle across the ceiling. Swaths of gauze in reds, purples, and pinks cover the walls.

In one corner, a mahogany table holds several champagne glasses and a selection of bottles. Another farther into the room offers trays of delicate hors d'oeuvres.

And in the middle of it all, under the shifting light that reflects off the central mirror ball, my other three guys are waiting.

Zian stands awkwardly in his suit like he isn't quite sure how to wear it, but holy hell, does his brawny form fill it out well. Jacob looks coolly handsome as ever in his own.

And then there's Andreas. Dressed to the nines and with his normally loose coils slicked close to his head, he's outright devastating.

All three of them tense up at my first steps into the room.

Zian's eyes widen.

Jacob's expression goes totally rigid, his hands balling at his sides.

Andreas gazes at me so avidly I feel the tingle of his attention through our marks. His throat bobs as he swallows.

I can't stop myself from folding my arms across my chest, self-conscious. "I—I don't get it. You just wanted us to dress up?"

Andreas motions to the room around us. "I wanted to make it like something out of your favorite TV show. They were always going to fancy soirees and things. I thought you should get to have something like that in real life—as close as I can give you."

That's why this scene feels so familiar—it's like a moment out of the soap opera.

A nervous giggle bubbles at the base of my throat. "What do we do now?"

Andreas shrugs. "Eat. Drink. Dance. Whatever you want. Rollick said we can have the room for the whole evening."

"Back to tests and practice tomorrow," Zian puts in with a faint grimace.

My insides have gone all wobbly. I'm off-balance but thrilled at the same time.

For just this moment, we don't have to be fugitives or monsters or anything other than people at a party. Like we don't have any problems bigger than who's been making eyes at whom.

I turn toward Dominic with a smile. "Let's dance, then."

I don't actually know how to dance with a partner to this refined music, but it turns out that's okay. Dom sets one hand on my waist and takes one of mine with the other, I rest my fingers on his shoulder, and we drift around the room under the lights, stepping in time with the melody in slow circles.

My grip on his hand tightens as one song fades into the next. "I can dance with just you the whole time, right?"

Dominic leans in to give me a quick peck on the lips. "Whatever you want."

I steal glances at the other guys as we continue our swaying path around the room. They're doing a good job of at least acting like they don't mind being here.

Jacob has poured himself a glass of one of the champagnes, though I can't tell if he's actually drinking it. Zian plucks up the meatiest appetizers from the spread.

And Andreas leans against the wall in a casual pose, watching all of us like I used to watch the TV.

Like he isn't totally part of this scene he arranged.

After the first couple of songs, Billy materializes in the corner. He raises a pan flute to his lips and adds an accompaniment to the music that lifts my feet faster.

My mouth twitches with amusement. I tug at Dominic, and he takes that as his cue to spin me in front of him.

My skirt fans out. My heart lifts.

There's plenty of magic in this moment without the work of any supernatural powers at all.

The faun gives the next few songs a spirited extra melody. Then Pearl appears and draws him over to fill out more of the dance floor.

They beam at the décor and the rest of us as if this is a gift to them too—a little piece of mortal life they're getting to try out. My own smile widens.

It's been a while since lunch. When my stomach grumbles, I ease back from Dominic and wander over to the snacks table.

Zian glances up at me. His gaze skims over my body in the dress, and a whiff of attraction rolls off him potent enough to make my cheeks blaze.

He takes a step back as if realizing his appreciation is obvious—and potentially intimidating. I come to a careful stop and pick up a morsel that looks tasty, letting him have his space.

"Are you planning on doing any dancing?" I ask him before popping it into my mouth.

Zian's jaw works. "I—I don't think that's a good idea."

My stomach tightens, even though I should have expected his answer. "It doesn't have to mean anything."

He glances at the floor and then back at me, oddly tentative. His voice comes out gruff.

"It would, though. And I don't know— I like watching you with Dom. It's good seeing you happy. You should keep dancing with him."

It's the weirdest rebuff I've ever heard. I don't think even my soap opera heroines would have known how to answer him.

So it might almost be a good thing that Jacob approaches just then, with a wary air that's offset by his usual aura of authority.

"If you're looking to mix things up," he starts, and then hesitates as if he's not sure how to finish that sentence. He sucks in a breath. "I'd be happy to dance. We wouldn't have to get too close if you still feel uncomfortable. You call all the shots."

The way he's looking at me sets every inch of my skin tingling, but I don't want to explore the feeling. I don't want to let it cloud my memories of how he treated me before even a little.

"I'd rather not," I say awkwardly. "But, um, thank you."

Jacob dips his head in acknowledgment with a flicker of regret I can't help noticing. "It's a lovely dress," he says, the compliment coming out stiffly. "But it doesn't hold a candle to the woman in it."

My pulse flutters despite my reservations.

How do I respond to that either? I'm not going to tell him he looks stunningly gorgeous as always.

Dominic saves me, tucking his arm around my waist and tugging me back onto the dance floor. I bow my head by his chin, my voice dropping.

"I don't know how to do this. I don't know—"

"It's okay," he murmurs. "No one is expecting anything. It might be hard to believe it after everything, but we really all just want you to enjoy yourself."

Enjoyment isn't something I really got to expect from most of my life. But for another song or two, sticking close to Dominic and following the rise and fall of the melody, maybe I do manage it.

Then Dominic lifts his head and draws me into the center of the room. I realize that Pearl and Billy have disappeared.

Maybe to give us our privacy. Because as Dom eases away, Andreas walks over to meet me.

"I don't really want to dance with you either," I blurt out, and bite my tongue at my bluntness. As true as that might be, I'm also not out to hurt him.

Andreas's expression twitches with what might have been a restrained wince. But his mouth forms a crooked smile.

"That's not what I came over for. I didn't just set this up so you could have a soap-opera party. I figured you deserve a soap-opera showdown too."

Twenty-Two

Riva

I blink at Andreas, totally confused. A soap-opera showdown?

"What are you talking about?"

Andreas gazes steadily back at me, his dark gray eyes stealing my breath. "The characters were always confronting each other and letting out their grievances. A lot of times in places like this."

The corner of his mouth ticks a little higher. "I'm sure there are tons of things you could say to me that you've held back because… because that's who you are. But you can let them out. You can tell me just how pissed off you are with me. Yell at me. Slap me. Knee me in the balls. I deserve all of it. Lay in to me. It's the best moment I could give you to say your piece."

I know exactly the kind of moments he's talking about. I've seen them play out on the TV screen so many times.

Back then, I never dreamed that I'd be in a position where I'd have a similar tirade I could aim at one of my guys.

My gaze flits to the other three men standing around the edges of the room. They're all following our conversation but without any sign of considering intervening.

Andreas clears his throat. "They should hear this too. I'm not going to hide how badly I screwed up."

He sinks down onto his knees in front of me, so that I'm looking down at him rather than the reverse. My throat constricts.

There is so much pain and anger still churning inside me. The sense of betrayal aches like a wound that's never properly healed.

Maybe I do need this.

"You lied to me," I say in a rasp, trying out the accusation.

Andreas nods. "I did, and I shouldn't have."

He doesn't let his gaze waver from mine. Tears prickle behind my eyes.

My voice rises. "You pretended that you cared about me. You made me believe that I could trust you. And the whole time you were waiting for me to give away some awful secret for you to report back to the other guys."

My hands clench. I don't want to hit him, not even in anger.

I have none of the same qualms about shouting. It feels good hurling the complaints at him—a release without the nauseating horror I'm capable of at full rage.

The flesh-rending kind of shriek doesn't prod at me at all. The monster inside me knows this anger isn't about dealing out hurt but holding my own up as a banner.

"You came to me and acted so sweet. You let me open up to you completely—we shared something I'd never shared with *anyone*—and the whole time—it never would have happened—I never would have let you even *kiss* me if I'd had any idea why you'd been nice to me!"

"It's the shittiest thing I've ever done to anyone," Andreas says, his voice as strained as his agonized face. "I'm not going to make any excuses. I was so fucking wrong, and I wish I could go back and pummel some sense into me."

But as the words come out, I realize that I want more. I don't want him to justify what he did, but I need some kind of explanation.

"Why?" I say, abruptly choking up. "Why would you do that to me, after everything we'd been through before, after— How could you treat me like that?"

Andreas tenses. "Riva, I don't even want to try to say it makes sense—"

"But it did," I break in. "When it was happening, you thought you were right. Make me understand."

The last sentence reverberates through the air with the firmness of a command.

A shadow crosses Andreas's face, but he keeps gazing up at me. "I—I don't know if you'll understand. But I can tell you everything along the way."

I set my hands on my hips, the smooth fabric crinkling under my fingers. Resolve steadies me. "Fine. Do that. You're always telling stories about things from the past—make this one of them."

Andreas stares at me for a moment. Then he inhales slowly.

"You already saw how it started. The video the guardians showed us, making it seem like you knew Griffin would be killed, like you'd made a deal with them."

"The one they faked."

"We didn't know that. We should have, but we were freaked out and we'd just watched Griffin *die* and you never came back… They were always reminding us how you'd turned on us, rubbing salt into the wound, and with everything else they put us through, there wasn't a whole lot of time to step back and really think."

Andreas tears his eyes away from me for a second before dragging them back. "There were times when I wondered if it could really be true. But I thought if they'd made it up somehow, then you had to be dead too. Maybe some part of me would rather think you'd betrayed us but were still living out there somewhere than that you were gone forever."

The raw note in his voice makes my eyes burn hotter. "And then I did come back. I came back to save you."

"I don't know how to explain it," Andreas says, more ragged by the second. "I'd spent four years believing you were a traitor. You seemed distant. I could tell there was something you weren't telling us, even after you started opening up. I only made the deal with Jacob because the alternative was not even trying to find out what was true—and it was something I could do. A way I could make sure the other guys were safe. I've been trying so hard for so long to keep everyone from falling apart…"

He trails off.

I resist the urge to grit my teeth. "You let me fall apart."

"I didn't mean to. I didn't— the more time I spent with you, the more I was convinced that you were telling the truth, that you'd come to break us out and you wanted to protect us. But I couldn't get the other guys to believe it. And there was still that thing you were keeping quiet about… I had no idea it was only that you'd kissed Griffin."

I remember with a queasy lurch of my gut how nervous I was when I finally admitted that to him.

But he'd already known all along from the video. That much of the recording was real.

"I did tell you," I said. "When I thought I could trust you."

"And I was so relieved it wasn't anything else. That you were exactly the woman you'd always been. I thought everything was going to be okay."

A shudder runs through my body. "You thought it was okay to fuck me."

Andreas can't suppress his wince at my harsh phrasing. His head droops.

"You were still the woman I'd always loved, and you loved me too, and when I was wrapped up in the moment, it felt like that was all that mattered. And after I came out of the daze, all that seemed to matter next was making sure the other guys knew we'd been wrong so I could fix everything else. I didn't know you'd follow me—that you'd hear…"

"Were you ever going to tell me if I hadn't?" I have to ask.

"Yes," Andreas says hoarsely. "I'd already realized I was going to have to while I was walking upstairs to talk to the guys. But it was more important to deal with them first. I guess I don't have any proof that I definitely would have in the end."

He raises his head again and meets my eyes. "No matter what I do to make up for it, I know there's no way to simply fix how I screwed things up. But I will keep trying. For the rest of our lives, if that's what it takes. I'll go to my grave trying and not regret anything but the fact that I fucked up so horribly in the first place. I've loved you my whole life so far, and I'll love you for the rest of it, even if you spend the rest of yours hating me."

The truth of those words rings through his voice—and resonates through the mark on my chest. He means it, every bit of that statement.

And I don't hate him. Even at my angriest and most hurt, I've never hated him.

I'm not sure I'm even angry at him anymore after his confession. I can follow the road he went down without all that much difficulty.

The guardians screwed all of us over. They messed with our heads and battered our spirits.

They broke us in so many ways and put together the pieces badly.

How many mistakes have I made?

All he wanted to know was the truth. So he could be sure, for the guys he'd do anything to protect.

I *can* understand that.

But even as my shoulders start to relax, a thread of tension remains wound around my stomach. That echo of his voice wavers through my mind again.

The whole reason I started getting cozy with her was so she'd open up…

I have to know the whole truth too.

"Okay," I said quietly. "I want one more thing."

"Name it."

"I want you to show me your memory of everything that happened from when you left me in the farmhouse to when I caught you talking with Jacob."

A flicker of surprise races through Andreas's expression. Before he can speak, Jacob lets out a rough sound from where he's standing near the snack table.

My attention jerks to the other guy. "What?" A prickle of renewed irritation climbs my spine. "Are you worried it'll make *you* look even worse?"

Jacob swipes his hand across his mouth. His face hardens, but he answers evenly enough.

"I know it will. But that's my fault."

At least he can admit that much.

I tug my gaze back to Andreas. He nods. "Whenever you're ready."

Last time, when he showed me what they experienced after our first escape attempt, he suggested I sit down first. I lower myself to the floor and brace my hands on either side of me.

"Go ahead."

Drey's eyes shine crimson, and all at once I'm back in the basement.

I'm back, but not as myself. My silver-steaked hair, the stuff that made Griffin call me Moonbeam, unfurls across a blanket beneath my new view.

It's Andreas's eyes I'm looking through this time. Andreas's arms wrapped around a much slimmer, smaller body than his own.

Andreas's body tensing in the moment before he tells me he needs to go talk to Jacob.

I think I know why he started the memory here. Because while I can't read his emotions in the memory, I can feel the way he resisted releasing his hold on me.

He didn't want to let me go. He didn't want to leave me.

But he pushes himself swiftly up the stairs with an air of

determination that radiates through his body. He walks straight to the room where Jacob is sitting on the floor by the window and stops on the threshold.

"We need to talk about Riva."

The Jacob of weeks ago answers Drey with the same coolly dispassionate tone he used so often back then. "I told you on the train. We'll revisit that subject *after* we've gotten whatever we can from Engel."

As I watch from within, Andreas marches right into the room with a shake of his head. "No. All the venom—in every form—needs to stop now. It shouldn't have gone on for even this long."

Jacob's icy gaze turns into a glower. I can see why he didn't love the idea of me revisiting this conversation.

"It isn't up to you," he snaps. "You don't get to make the call."

Andreas crosses his arms in front of him. "You're not in charge here either. We're in this together—isn't that how it's supposed to go? You're not always right, Jake, and this one time you're incredibly wrong."

"I guess you can make your case once everyone's awake. In the meantime—"

Before Jacob can finish his dismissal, Zian and Dominic appear in the doorway.

Zian swipes at his bleary eyes. "We're awake. What's going on?"

Andreas turns to them with a sense of urgency winding through his limbs. "We've been wrong about Riva. I got the whole story out of her, and she hasn't lied at all. She didn't turn on us even a little bit."

I can't deny how emphatically he says the words, how strongly he clearly feels about making that statement. It's etched into the memory.

He was sure. He wanted to make things right.

Zian knits his brow and goes to sit on the edge of the bed. "But we saw—"

Andreas's tone turns terse with frustration. "I know what we saw. It's what made even *me* treat her like shit when we should have been welcoming her back. But they must have faked it—we should have realized that."

Dominic frowns from the doorway. "It looked awfully real."

Jacob's sneering voice would make me flinch if I were in my own body. "Drey just *wants* to think it was fake so he can feel better about getting cozy with the traitor."

Fresh tension tremors through Andreas's body.

"She's not a traitor," he retorts. "You think you're so smart, Jake. Do you really figure the people running the facility are skilled enough to genetically engineer us into whatever the hell we are, but they couldn't handle doctoring a minute of video footage?"

"I figure there was no reason for them to bother."

"No reason? How about giving us someone to be angry at other than the guardians—who're the ones who actually killed Griffin? How about adding that little sliver of doubt about whether we can trust even each other to try to deflect another escape attempt? The second part didn't work, but the first sure as hell did."

The part of me I'm still aware of within Andreas's mind starts to ache with the vehemence in his voice. I missed all this—I had no idea how hard he fought for me.

"You don't *know*," Jacob shoots back. "You've bought into her victim routine and now you want an excuse to make that okay."

Andreas clenches his jaw. "Do you even listen to yourself? We *did* know Riva. She was one of us, right there with us through all the shit they put us through, and she has been since she came back too. Why the fuck we ever trusted what the guardians showed us over what we'd seen our whole lives—that's the crazy part."

"I planned out every part of that escape down to the minute. We didn't let a hint of it slip. How else could they have known to be waiting for us like that?"

"Oh, so that's what this is really about. You can't admit that you might have slipped up somewhere, or that maybe you simply weren't quite as brilliant as you'd like to be."

Jacob pushes to his feet. "It's not about me at all. It's about Griffin, who's dead, because she—"

"She *loved* Griffin," Andreas interrupts. "Which you wouldn't doubt at all if you ever bothered to listen to her instead of the angry story you've built up in your head."

Jacob's face flushes with fury. "And I suppose she told you that she loves you too, huh?"

Andreas's voice doesn't waver in its confidence for an instant. "She loves all of us. Or she did, anyway, but it seems like she could still love even you in spite of what an asshole you've been to her if you got your head on straight."

Oh, Drey. I want to cry and I want to hug him, and a million other clashing desires.

Jacob practically sputters. "What a stupid fucking fairytale. And you believe all this bullshit she's been spouting, huh?"

"Yes," Andreas says firmly, "I do. Because I've been watching her and listening to her for days, and everything adds up to it being true. In case you've forgotten, the whole reason I started 'getting cozy' with her was so she'd open up about things she wouldn't have told us otherwise. I held up my end of the deal. Now you've got to listen."

The words don't strike the same chill in me hearing them now. He was using them as a club to smack Jacob into accepting his argument, nothing more.

The last painful shards that were still digging into me melt away.

I'm not happy about what Andreas did or the choices he made when we first reunited. But he wasn't scheming against me up until the end.

He really had realized his mistake, and he was fighting tooth and claw to correct the whole group's course the best way he knew how.

In the memory, Andreas's gaze has jerked toward the doorway where that past me has appeared, sickly pale and braced defensively. Then, with a hitch of my senses, I'm falling back into my own head, faced with Drey's worried eyes here in the present.

For the first few seconds, I can only stare back at him. My innards feel so jumbled up it's a wonder I'm still breathing.

Then I reach out my hand and touch his cheek.

Andreas closes his eyes at the tentative caress. A glint of a tear seeps out from beneath one lid.

"You've got it, Tink," he murmurs. "You've got all of me."

The armor I've built up must have cracked, because the declaration sinks right into me. And I believe him.

I stroke my thumb across his cheekbone. Then I stand up on wobbly legs, not entirely sure what happens next, but knowing this is my story now.

My soap opera. My melodrama.

I might still be hurting, but I can feel more than that. I want to *be* more than that.

I tug Andreas up by the collar of his dress shirt. He peers at me, uncertain.

The lilting music is still winding around us. So I say, "Dance with me."

Twenty-Three

Riva

Dancing with Andreas is the strangest feeling. Like a war is being waged inside me.

The mark he gave me tickles eagerly. My nerves clamor to push closer against him.

My muscles tense in resistance, not ready to let go of the wariness I've held on to for so long.

He's tense too, holding himself a careful distance away from me, never stepping any nearer. One of his hands rests on my waist so lightly I can barely feel the pressure.

The warmth of it blooms across my skin anyway.

His fingers twine loosely with mine, leaving the way open for me to pull away if I need to. As we turn in a slow circle with the elegant tune, he gazes down at me.

No red sheen colors his eyes now. I think he's watching for the slightest sign that I've changed my mind, that he's overstayed his welcome.

The silence between us starts to weigh on me.

"I liked all of the dresses," I tell him. "It was hard to pick. This one just felt the most right for how I'm feeling at the moment."

A hint of a smile touches his lips. "I'm glad. It was hard to know—I don't think I've ever seen you in any dress. Or with your hair up like that. Was that Pearl's idea?"

I laugh awkwardly. "I just let her do whatever she wanted."

"She did a good job. You look stunning. I could hardly breathe when you first walked in." He pauses, and his voice dips. "I can hardly breathe now."

I squeeze his hand instinctively and hear him swallow. "I don't know… I don't know if I totally forgive you yet. There are pieces of me that still hurt. They might for a long time."

"That's okay," Andreas says quickly. "I wasn't pushing for anything. I just—doing this was the only thing I could think of that came close to showing you how much you mean to me."

A lump rises in my throat. "I like the party a lot too."

His lips curve into a clearer smile. "Good. That's what matters the most."

Behind the anguish and the fear that I'll pull away after all, I can see the boy he used to be in his face. The Drey who'd always have a wry remark to break through a tense moment and a story to tell to lift us out of darker thoughts.

He had four years to marinate in the lies about me. To watch his friends struggling with their new talents and their grief, unable to help them.

Would I really have held on to my faith in my guys if the guardians had told me a similar story before they'd shipped me off? If they'd claimed that Griffin and I had been caught because one of the others had turned on us?

I don't really know. I'd like to say I would have, but I wouldn't have thought I could slaughter an entire arena of strangers either.

The truth is, I want to forgive Andreas. I want to sink into the sense that we belong together, that we'll stand by each other, and leave the pain behind.

It might not be the smoothest road, but I can start that journey now. I don't have to completely forgive him for the past to trust his devotion to me in the present.

With our next rotation, I ease half a step closer. Andreas's head dips with a shaky exhalation, his breath tickling over my forehead.

My gaze drifts away from him for just a moment—and snags on Jacob still poised by the snacks table.

Poised is absolutely the word for it. Every muscle in his body looks coiled with tension, ready to spring—whether to tear me and Andreas apart or to climb the walls in frustration, it's hard to tell from his taut expression.

And in that moment, taking in the chiseled planes of his face, I remember more of the conversation when I discovered Andreas's betrayal.

With every word after I made it to their room, Jacob jabbed the knife in deeper and twisted it. He *knew* everything I only just saw in Andreas's memory—he knew how adamantly Drey had fought for me and believed in me.

And even then, he did everything possible to convince me that the other guy was only playing at caring about me.

He's very good at it, isn't he? Got you to let your hair down and everything.

Then to Andreas, in front of me: *You can stop now. I can't see how you'll get anything more out of her than you already have.*

My feet stall in mid-turn. Andreas freezes, but the anger gripping my body now has nothing to do with him.

I spin toward Jacob. "*You* lied to me. You knew Drey was sure I hadn't done anything wrong, that he wasn't trying to mess with me anymore, but you talked like he was still using me."

How much of the pain tangled with my memories of Andreas are because of what he actually did, and how much is the wrenching sense of betrayal provoked by Jacob's jabs?

Whatever color Jacob's face contained drains from it. Somehow his stance goes even more rigid.

I half expect him to deny my accusation, but he squares his shoulders as if accepting a blow.

"I'm sorry," he says in a voice as tight as his expression. "I thought—I was pissed off—it was a shitty thing to do. You can come at me too if you want to. I deserve it a hell of a lot more than Drey did."

My fingers curl toward my palms, but from beneath the anger comes a twang of resistance.

I could yell at Jacob for the rest of the day and still not be finished letting out all my grievances. For just a little while with Andreas, I was starting to feel almost okay.

I don't want to ruin this moment that wasn't Jacob's anyway, by delving into all that pain too.

"I don't even want to *think* about you," I reply in a voice so flat and cold it could rival him at his worst, and turn back to Andreas.

Bobbing up on my toes, I sling my arms around Drey's neck and tug his mouth down to meet mine.

Am I aware that this move is guaranteed to twist the knife *I* just stabbed into Jacob? Hell yes, I am.

But the longing to get close to the man my body already claimed has been coursing through my veins for days, even if my broken heart has overridden the hunger. And the second our mouths collide, my desire is the only thing that matters.

Andreas lets out a soft, choked sound and hugs me to him tightly. Our lips meld together with a familiar electric thrill.

Every cell in me sings out with joy.

I've missed this man, I've craved him, and now he's back where he's meant to be.

The wave of emotion isn't as intense as the first time we collided. An ache to resolidify our connection completely forms between my legs, but I'm not going to hump the guy right here on the dance floor.

No matter what happened after the first time, his touch still makes me feel giddily alive in ways nothing else can.

But not no *one* else.

A nervous chill flickers through my nerves, and I draw back just far enough to seek out a different pair of watching eyes. I find Dominic where he's drifted over to the far wall.

I brace myself for anger or disappointment in his expression, but the moment I catch his gaze, he smiles. A broad, open smile, as if nothing could make him happier than seeing me reestablish my bond with his friend.

Unexpected tears flood my eyes. I clasp Andreas's fingers with one hand and hold the other out to Dominic to beckon him over.

Andreas stands with a relaxed posture as Dom comes to join us. I grip Drey's hand and tease my fingers down Dominic's lean chest.

"This is my party, right? I want to dance with both of you."

Dominic lets out a soft chuckle and sets a hand on my hip.

Andreas grins down at me, his eyes gleaming with affection. "What you want, you get, Tink."

Club music would work better for this kind of collaboration, but we can make it work.

I close my eyes and tune into the subtle rhythm beneath the melody. Sway my body from side to side with the dips and swells.

As I revolve between them, the guys follow my lead, turning with me.

Dom trails both his hands up my sides to my ribs and then down to my thighs. He leans in to press a kiss to my shoulder from behind.

Andreas shimmies a little one way and then the other, always staying in front of me. His thumb strokes over my knuckles while his other hand slips around the back of my neck.

I'm caught between the two of them, but I don't feel remotely trapped. They're the fuel to my fire, and feeding on both of them makes it burn even brighter.

I don't give a shit that the other two guys are watching. They picked their own paths away from me.

And if the shadowkind are peering at us from the shadows—let them stare if they want to.

I tip my head back against Dominic's chest and feel the faint hitch of his breath. His groin brushes my ass with a hardness that sends my hunger spiking higher.

There are some things I don't want an audience for. Things I want to share with just the two men who've marked me—and who've welcomed my mark in turn.

I caress the line of Dom's jaw and then reach to grasp the few coils that have swung free at the sides of Andreas's face. "I love the party you made for me, but I think I'd like to move on to a different kind of celebration."

Drey's voice comes out in a low rasp. "What did you have in mind?"

I draw his face closer to mine and speak so only he and Dominic can hear me. "Take me to my bedroom."

"Fuck," Dom mutters, and buries his face in the crook of my neck. The nip of his teeth against the sensitive skin there brings a gasp to my lips.

Andreas's gaze sears into mine as if he's searching for any fragment of doubt there. When he doesn't find it, he pulls me by the hand toward the doorway.

"I think the other guys will figure out the party's over."

A momentary twinge passes through me at the thought of Zian—but he didn't even want to *dance* with me. He doesn't owe me anything, but surely I don't owe him anything either?

And Jacob can go suck rocks.

I'm barely aware of the walk back to my room. My feet might as well be gliding over the carpet, and every inch of skin is thrumming with anticipation.

With the eagerness to immerse myself in the men I've branded as my own.

We duck into my bedroom, and I slip off my shoes instinctively at the edge of the bed. Then doubt coils around me.

What am I doing? I was already out of my depth hooking up with just one guy.

Andreas hesitates with a trace of his own uncertainty, but Dominic turns me toward him and seeks out a kiss. My body melts against his.

I know him. I know how we work together, with no past pain tarnishing what we've made together.

I push at the lapels of his jacket, pulling my lips from his just long enough to demand, "Off."

Dom's smile is a little shy as he shrugs off the jacket. He's cut openings in his dress shirt from the top of his shoulders to halfway down his back so his tentacles can slip easily through.

I reach behind him to tease my fingertips over the satiny skin. Dominic hums low in his throat and claims another kiss.

As we inhale each other's breath, Andreas eases closer. He dapples kisses along the curve of my shoulders and the back of my neck.

Every graze of his lips sets off sparks through my chest.

When he tugs off his own jacket, I lift my hand to run my fingers along the collar of his shirt. He groans, leaning into my touch.

"I missed you so much," he mumbles against my hair. "Dreamed about you every night. Ranted at myself for being stupid enough to lose you after you went through so much to find us."

"I missed you too," I admit in a small voice, and he hugs me against him from behind, nuzzling the corner of my jaw.

The air turns thick with the scent of anticipation and lust. But this moment is about so much more than simple bodily cravings.

I grip Dominic's collar and gaze into his bright hazel eyes. "I love you."

Dom cups my face in a gesture that couldn't make me feel more cherished. "I don't even know how to say how much I love you."

Andreas's arms tighten around me. I let my head tip back against him. "I love you too."

He sucks in a breath and bows his head beside mine. "Then I'm the luckiest man who ever existed on this planet. I'm going to spend every second I can making sure I'm proving how much I mean it."

Dominic's fingers find the zipper beneath my armpit and ease it down. The heat of the men's bodies on either side of me ward off any chill as he peels my dress off to pool at my feet.

I still feel abruptly overly naked, but there's an easy way to balance the scales. I grasp at the buttons on his shirt, flicking them open as quickly as I can.

When Dom takes over, tugging the shirt right off, I run my hands over his chest and tip forward to lap my tongue over one pebbled nipple. He lets out a rough sound and jerks my mouth back up to his, firm but not brutal about it.

His tentacles curl around his body to stroke over mine. The suckers press against my skin all along my torso in a multitude of kisses.

"That's hardly fair," Andreas mutters in a teasing tone. "How are my two hands supposed to compete?"

Dominic grins at him, so at ease with the reference to his strange appendages it makes my heart flutter. "You'll just have to make particularly good use of what you have. You could start by undoing her bra."

Drey hums and hooks his fingers around the band. As the pressure falls away with the drooping of the cups, I turn toward him.

Facing him again, more undressed than I ever was the one time we got intimate before, a momentary awkwardness settles over me. I don't know where to set my hands or aim my eyes.

Maybe sensing my shift in mood, Dominic's touch gentles. One tentacle wraps around my waist in a tender embrace while his hands slide around to cup my breasts as if to shield them.

Andreas gazes down at me, the rich brown of his skin even more vibrant than usual but a shadow of anguish still lurking in his eyes.

He glides his fingers along my jaw to my chin like he did the first time he kissed me, but he simply holds them there, his face still inches from mine. His tongue flicks out to wet his lips.

"Tell me what you want from me," he says, his voice raw. "I'm honored to be invited in at all, Riva. It only goes as far as you say. You have to know how much I want you."

I do, because the same need burns inside me. We merged our souls together but never had the chance for the wonder of it to sink in before it was spoiled.

I want to do this right.

The words tumble out. "Kiss me."

Andreas doesn't need to be asked twice. He bends down to capture my lips.

The same thrill tingles through me as did on the dance floor.

My hands slip under the hem of his shirt of their own accord to fan across his taut abs and toned chest. Drey groans and fumbles with the top buttons of his shirt before yanking it over his head.

Then he's diving in for another kiss, not waiting to be asked this time. He consumes my mouth while Dominic swivels his palms in deft circles against my stiffening nipples.

A whimper climbs up my throat. The ache between my thighs expands, torturously demanding.

All I'm wearing now are my panties, and I can tell they're drenched.

The next time Andreas releases my lips, Dom twirls me back toward him. He sweeps my small frame off my feet, his tentacles helping brace me against his body, and lays me down in the middle of the massive bed.

"I've been wondering…" he murmurs, planting a trail of kisses down my sternum. "I want to try… But I don't really know what I'm doing. You'll have to show me what feels good."

I sag back into the duvet, ready to welcome whatever he has in mind. "Go ahead."

His kisses chart a path all the way to the hem of my panties. He teases his tongue across the base of my belly as he guides that scrap of fabric off me, and my nerves jump with anticipation.

Then he lowers his mouth right over my pussy.

I knew this was a thing people did, but I had no conception of how glorious it would feel. A surge of bliss races up from my core.

My head arcs back against the pillow with a moan.

Dominic doesn't hesitate. His tongue flicks over every sensitive spot down below, and his lips massage every place it isn't touching.

I can't stop myself from bucking to meet his mouth. Pulses of pleasure rock me in endless succession.

With the gasps and cries slipping from my lips, I hope he can tell he's doing fucking fantastic.

Andreas lets out a ragged breath and sinks down on the bed next to me. He nips my earlobe and nibbles my jaw, but his gaze comes back to focus on Dominic's face between my legs.

As Drey fondles one of my breasts, rolling the nipple between his thumb and forefinger, the fresh jolt of pleasure makes me buck harder. Dom raises his head just a little, his tongue swiping over my clit.

"How does she taste?" Andreas asks in a tone so hungry I shudder eagerly at the sound.

Dominic's eyes gleam. "Sweeter than a sugar cookie."

He dives back in for more.

As I writhe with their combined attentions, Dom's tentacles stroke up and down my legs. Then one delves right between my thighs.

Dominic lifts his gaze again, swirling his tongue over that most provocative place while he gauges my reaction. The tip of the tentacle glides through the slickness of my opening.

Holy fuck. I tremble with the pleasure both immediate and promised.

"Don't stop," I mumble.

He slides his lithe appendage right into me. It fills me with a slim, flexible pressure not at all like his cock but thrilling in its own way.

As the tentacle pushes deeper, shifting forward with swift pulses, I moan. Dominic smiles against my clit and sucks down hard.

At the chorus of sounds spilling from my throat, Andreas swears under his breath and drops lower to lap the peak of my breast right into his mouth. I tangle one hand in his tight coils and the other in Dom's silky auburn strands falling loose from his ponytail.

The shadowy smoke in my blood doesn't wrench at me as urgently as it did my first times with each of these men. Instead, it quivers through my veins in a heady sort of dance, urging me on with a sense of reveling.

This is where we're supposed to be. How we're meant to be.

United like one being.

All at once, the fleshy tendril inside me twists. It curls around, increasing the feeling of fullness as its end spirals into a thicker ball.

I gasp, my grip on Dominic's hair tightening. He suckles me more eagerly—and thrusts that bulging tip into me like the thickest of shafts.

I'm already so aroused the burn that comes is nothing but ecstatic. I sway with the pulsing, welcoming his tentacle even deeper.

Pleasure swells through my torso, intoxicating and exhilarating. Then Dom scrapes the tips of his teeth across my clit, and I shatter.

I come so hard I sob with the impact, clutching on to both him and Andreas. A tidal wave of delight sweeps through me.

My body clenches and then goes slack. My vision spins.

"That's how we treat our woman right," Andreas murmurs as I sag into the duvet.

The words set off a pang of resolve that resonates through me. I don't want this interlude to be only about me.

We belong to each other; it goes both ways. I wouldn't have anything else.

As Dominic straightens into a kneeling position, I convince my muscles to move, twisting me up and around. Without giving him a chance to protest, I nudge him down on the bed, the pendant I'm still wearing swinging from my neck.

"Riva?" he asks, breathless.

I yank at his suit pants so hard the button pops. "I want to taste you too."

He inhales as if to form a protest that I don't need to, but I've already freed his erection from his boxers. When I wrap my lips over the head of his shaft, any words he might have said dissolve into a groan.

"Oh, fuck," he manages to mutter as I work my mouth farther down his rigid cock. "So fucking good, Riva. Never—felt anything like—*God*."

Hearing him unravel only heightens my enthusiasm. I have no more experience with this act than he had going down on me, but the awareness of his enjoyment floods my senses.

I stroke my fingers over the moon-and-blood-drop tattoo on his hip that matches mine.

We're bound together by blood and history, and my body knows exactly how to make his quake.

My tongue winds around his hot, straining flesh. I drink down his musky flavor.

Dominic's hips rock to meet me with obvious restraint. He touches my temple, his fingers trembling with the force of the bliss I'm conjuring in him.

Despite the force of the orgasm I've already enjoyed, a throbbing sensation forms in my sex at its emptiness. An ache for the same driving rhythm that's now focused on my mouth.

And I can have that, can't I?

I release Dom's cock for just long enough to glance toward Andreas, who's sat back on his heels to watch us with heated envy.

"Drey. I need you—inside me."

His eyes widen. Then he's scrambling to meet me, jerking at the fly of his pants at the same time.

"Fuck, yes."

He strokes his fingers over my opening first, but I don't think I could be any wetter. I suck Dominic's cock down at the same moment as Andreas's presses into me from behind.

Pleasure spikes through every nerve. I moan around Dominic's shaft, and he shivers at the sensation.

The shadows inside me flare. If they were dancing before, it's an all-out rave raging through my veins now.

The marks on my collarbone sing out. We're joined; we're together.

We're blood, and we found our way back to each other against all the odds.

Andreas's fingers curl around my hips. He rocks into me at an increasingly urgent pace that I match with the suction of my lips.

Dominic sways with me. His eyes have gone hazy with pleasure.

His tentacles still wind around my shoulders and arms. One makes its way between us to pluck at my breasts, and I can't hold back another moan.

Dom grunts. "Can't stop—Riva, I'm going to—"

I want it all. I down him as far as I can and savor the spurt of his release at the back of my throat.

As I suck him dry, his tentacles ramp up their attentions. My nipples tingle with the squeeze of the suckers.

Andreas bows over my back to kiss my shoulder blade. He tucks his hand around my waist and fingers my clit in time with his frantic strokes.

That's all it takes. I crackle apart again, bright and hot as a firecracker exploding.

My pussy clamps around Drey's cock, and he groans as he follows me.

Andreas loops his arm around my waist as he rocks to a stop. He presses more kisses down my spine.

Then he pauses with a shaking inhalation and tips his damp forehead against my flushed skin.

"I love you. Always."

Emotion swells at the base of my throat. I twist around, tugging him with me so I can nestle between both men on the bed.

"Never leave me again," I murmur, and I think they both know I don't mean just physically.

"Not a chance," Dominic swears. He captures my mouth in a quick but emphatic kiss, heedless of his flavor lingering on my lips.

Andreas hugs me close. "It'd take a goddamn apocalypse to tear me away from you."

But as I sink into the mellowness of the afterglow, a niggling chill seeps in.

I'm not entirely sure that an apocalypse is off the table.

Twenty-Four

Riva

Rollick leans against the railing around the yacht's upper deck, the cool breeze ruffling his tawny hair. "What exactly is your objection?"

I lower my gaze to the little crab he's set in a bowl on the small table between us. It clicks its claws and scrabbles at the sides too steep for it to clamber over.

It looks more like an alien creature than a thinking, feeling being. I wouldn't be able to make out agony in the stalks of its eyes or catch a gasp of its pain.

But that doesn't mean it wouldn't feel plenty. It's still *alive.*

It has just as much a right to live that life peacefully as I do, doesn't it?

I meet the demon's gaze again. "That's not who I want to be. I don't want to use my power—I wish I didn't even have it."

Rollick lets out a short sigh. "You know you don't have much choice. There is no operation that's going to cleave the talent—or the urge to use it—out of your body. Your options are master it or be mastered by it when you're unprepared."

I grimace. "But how is mastering it better than the alternative if it means I'm willingly torturing animals to get to that point? At least… at least when I've used it before, I had a good reason to. It was life or death."

"And you could be sparing this crustacean some pain now only to inflict much worse on some other innocent being later."

He's right. I know he's right. But—

I lift my chin. "I haven't had the urge lately, even when I've been upset. The last time I released the power, I managed to only work it on the people attacking us. Maybe… maybe I've got enough control already."

Rollick cocks his head. "You might be satisfied making that gamble, but I'd rather ensure more certainty than 'maybe.' As would my associates. If you want my help, this is a necessary condition."

I study the crab again. Nausea unfurls through my stomach.

A tremor of a deadly shriek tingles through my chest, but it wants to smack into Rollick, not the little beast in front of me. Show him what he's asking me to inflict.

But I don't. It isn't even difficult for me to resist the twinge of fury.

I hate the sadistic presence lodged inside me. Jacob and Zian can hone their brutal skills with inanimate objects that can't feel anything. Dominic can at least practice with plants.

And Andreas doesn't do anything that would physically hurt someone in the first place.

It's only me whose power *demands* agony to operate. Why did I end up like this?

But if Rollick decides we're not meeting him halfway, it won't be just me but all of my men who'll be kicked to the curb. I grit my teeth and prod at the viciousness inside me.

What kind of nerves does a crab have? What will I need to crack and sever?

The monster inside me will know. As soon as my scream ripples over its body…

I part my lips, but my throat constricts. The only sound I propel out is a choked grunt.

Frowning, I inhale deeply and try again.

The cruel shriek stays locked in my chest. The thin squeak I force out does nothing at all.

"I'm trying," I say, bracing myself for Rollick's anger.

He only studies me in his usual implacable way that always makes me feel like he's seeing way more than I'd prefer.

"But you don't want to try, and you don't have the proper motivation. You're working against your purpose."

With another sigh, he straightens up. "As much as I'd like to get on with this, I don't think enraging you is a great way to begin a regimen of self-control. I have some things to take care of on land this afternoon. See if you can't meditate on the issue and come to accept the act as necessary so you'll get out of your own way."

He doesn't say what'll happen if I *can't* manage to get out of my way, but his prior comment about necessary conditions is warning enough.

I swallow thickly and follow him down the steps to the main deck. The harbor of a city I can't recognize from the skyline is coming into view up ahead across the dark water, glossy high rises interspersed with older-looking structures in pale pastels.

"Where are we?" I ask. "And how long are we going to be here?"

"Havana. And how long depends on how quickly I can conclude my business. But I'd imagine you're decently safe with a good chunk of ocean as well as national borders between you and our foes."

Havana, Cuba. I've never left the United States before other than our brief foray into Canada.

But his reply relaxes me. I'm not sure how the guardians could figure out we've come here even if the younger shadowbloods are tracking us from back in the US.

They'd need to get in their own boats to narrow down our location across the ocean. Rollick's people would see them coming from miles away.

I think I'm starting to warm up to sea travel.

"Stay on the yacht," Rollick tells me as we reach the lower deck. "You should all do some meditating on deflecting your fellow shadowbloods too. You've got all those shadows in you—they ought to be able to work with you a little if you can focus them enough."

I nod. "We can do that. I'll get the guys together."

I'll even work with Jacob if it means we come up with better protection against the guardians.

But after the yacht docks, I linger for a few minutes by the railing, watching the activity in the harbor and the cars cruising by on the streets beyond. Whiffs of brine and gasoline reach my nose.

A strange pang forms in my chest, like I'm homesick for a place I've never been before.

Even though I have no marked connection to him, I recognize the solid footsteps that tread across the deck toward me as Zian's. He comes to a stop by the railing a couple of feet away from me and hesitates.

"Everything okay, Shrimp?"

He says the old, teasing nickname like he's testing it out. The sound of it in his gruff voice brings a sudden shock of heat to the back of my eyes.

"You mean, other than the fact that we're being hunted across the continent by slave-drivers who want to use us as weapons?" I say, matching the vibe he's offering.

Zian lets out a huff. "Yeah, I guess it's a silly question. You just looked kind of… sad. In a different way from usual." He glances down awkwardly and moves as if to walk away. "I didn't mean to—"

"No, it's fine." I turn my attention back to the city. "I was just thinking that maybe we could get away from the guardians if we just settled down in some distant country. They can't be all over the world, right?"

"It would be pretty crazy if they were. Drey says all the memories he saw from them, it seemed like they weren't talking with people far away."

"Yeah." I swipe my hand across my mouth. "But then I realized that they'd find us eventually anyway. Given enough time, they could probably track us down anywhere on the planet. Maybe we'd buy ourselves a week or a month, but would that really be worth it if we'd just have to pick up and run again?"

Zian stands in silence for a moment, contemplating the question. "No. Not really."

"And there's the other shadowbloods too. I don't want to just abandon those kids."

Not to the same horrors we went through. Not if we can spare them some of that torment.

Zian's muscles bulge as if he's already imagining an assault on a facility. "We won't. We'll get them out. You managed to get us four free, so with all five of us together, we've got to be able to pull off a whole lot of prison breaks."

In spite of the uncertainty lingering between us, the determination in his words makes me smile. "Let's hope so."

Maybe because of that momentary sense of understanding, I find myself glancing over at him. "Zee… Is something bothering you—about me?"

His gaze jerks from the scene ahead of us to me, startled. "What?"

My fingers tighten around the railing. "You obviously don't have to want to dance with me or whatever. But sometimes it seems like you're still upset with me or concerned about what I might do, or *something*. You apologized for distrusting me—it seemed like you weren't scared about my power—but if you still have doubts about anything that happened—"

Zian shakes his head so forcefully I stop speaking. "No. No, Riva, I —" He extends his hand toward me and then catches it before it's quite reached me.

We both gaze down at that truncated gesture for a moment before he lifts his head again, his mouth tight.

"It's not you," he says. "I swear it's not you. You have been so… incredible. Fuck, I'm grateful you're even talking to me after… after everything."

"Then…?"

He swallows audibly. "It's me. I don't know what *I* might do—I don't trust myself."

That doesn't make any sense. If he doesn't hold any animosity toward me, then why would he need to worry about doing something that could hurt me?

I drag in a breath, struggling for the words to ask him, and just then the other three guys come hustling out onto the deck.

As Zian and I spin toward them, several shadowkind, including Cinder and Kudzu, emerge as if ushering our friends out. None of the guys look happy, Jacob scowling darkly enough that it's a wonder the sun hasn't blinked out.

My pulse stutters. I push toward them, Zian stalking over at my side. "What's going on?"

Kudzu turns to us with his ropey arms folded over his chest. "It's time for you to go."

I blink at him. "What?"

"The five of you mutants. Get the fuck off our ship. Stay the hell away from Miami."

"But—Rollick said to—"

Cinder slashes her hand through the air with a crackle of electricity. "Rollick's got millennia under his belt. Staying alive even longer either doesn't mean that much to him or he's too curious to do the right thing. So we're deciding now. We're done with you."

She's serious. They all are.

My gaze travels over the faces of Rollick's colleagues, and every single one of them stares back at me with hardened eyes and determined expressions.

They waited until he was out of reach, and now they're staging a mutiny… against us.

"This is ridiculous," Jacob snaps. "It's not your call to make."

"I'm the one in charge while Rollick is away," Cinder says. "So yes, it is."

She snaps her fingers, and sparks shoot into the air.

As if summoned by the display, Pearl and Billy burst into being on the deck next to us. Pearl's normally coiffed locks swing in frantic disarray.

"What are you doing?" she demands, facing the other shadowkind. "You can't just—"

"As if you newbies get any say," Kudzu sneers at them.

Billy squares his narrow shoulders and steps toward him. The faun is a full head shorter than the smallest of our antagonists, but he doesn't let that stop him from glaring at them on our behalf.

"I might not have spent much time mortal-side, but I know that Rollick wouldn't like this. If you have a problem with what he thinks is right, why don't you—"

Kudzu slams a fist into the smaller man's face, hard enough to send Billy's slender form flying across the deck. Billy crashes to the floor with a groan and smoky essence pouring from beneath the hand clamped across his nose.

"Hey!" Zian growls.

He steps between Billy and the other shadowkind while Pearl dashes to her friend. Cinder sends up another threatening spurt of sparks, and a chilling rush of air sears over us from one of the other beings.

My heart thumps so loud it reverberates through my entire body. In a detached sort of way, it occurs to me that us leaving isn't want these shadowkind really want.

They want us dead. They want to know for sure we'll never cause any problems for them.

But they're still wary of us. They're not totally sure what we'll do if they attack us the way Kudzu just lashed out at Billy.

They're settling for running us off to preserve themselves. If we make it a fight, I don't know how long they'll stick to caution.

I don't know if any of us would survive that fight, outnumbered and against monsters who have a hell of a lot more experience wielding their powers than we do.

Dominic has rushed over to join Pearl and Billy, his tentacles shifting beneath his trench coat. "Is he okay?"

"He'll heal," Pearl murmurs. "But it'll hurt."

Billy's gaze seeks out mine from across the deck. I can see anguish in his eyes that isn't just because of his broken nose.

"I'm sorry," he mumbles. "I—" He shoves himself to his feet, glowering at the other shadowkind again. "We're not letting you do this."

My gut wrenches. The shadowkind who'd befriended us are willing to fight too, and their companions clearly aren't afraid to pull out all the stops to shut *them* down.

"No!" I call out before anyone can throw any more punches—or sparks, or whatever. "We'll go. Just let us grab our bags, and then we'll leave."

The guys' heads jerk toward me. I aim a determined look at all of them, willing them to follow my lead.

Jacob's eyes flash, but his shoulders come down through what looks like sheer force of will.

"What she said," he bites out, turning back to the shadowkind.

"Fine," Kudzu snarls. "You have five minutes to get your things and get the fuck out of here. But we'll be taking your phones first."

So we can't get in touch with Rollick. My stomach balls tighter.

He holds out his hand, and I can't see any option but to pull the device out of my pocket and toss it at him.

The guys follow suit, their expressions grim.

"All right, get on with it," Cinder says. "And that five minutes is one each. We're not giving you a chance to conspire together."

She motions to Zian, the closest to her. He glances at me as if for guidance.

At my sharp nod, he takes off into the ship.

Apparently he's worried about the shadowkind changing their mind partway through, because he hurries back onto the deck carrying not one but five backpacks—all of ours. He tosses them to each of us, shooting the shadowkind a challenging glower.

"We're going to tell Rollick what you did," Pearl declares, her face flushed with anger.

Cinder narrows her eyes at the shorter woman. "The two of you will keep your stupid mouths shut, or we'll smash you right out of existence. Maybe you've forgotten, but you can die in this realm."

"It's all right," I say quickly. "We're going."

I catch the guys' gazes and set off toward the boarding ramp. With obvious trepidation, they follow me one by one.

My heart feels heavier with each step over the frothing waters toward the pier. What if *this* gamble is the wrong one?

But the price of forcing the issue feels way too large for me to want to place my bets there.

I grip the straps of my backpack as we tramp through the harbor. At the city-side end, we merge into a bustle of other bodies, but apprehension keeps prickling through my nerves.

Most of the faces around us are tan or darker, framed by hair in shades of brown and black. Dominic and Andreas blend in just fine, and Zian might not draw attention from anyone who doesn't look closely at the shape of his features, but Jacob's pale coloring stands out starkly in the crowd.

And me—my moonbeam braid must shine like a beacon of abnormality.

My fingers itch to pull one of my hoodies from my pack, but sweat is beading on my skin even in just my tank top. I'll be a liability if I get heatstroke too.

We might draw a few odd looks, but the locals will simply assume we're tourists, right? They must be pretty used to those.

Voices flow around us, but the ones I make out are all speaking Spanish, which I know maybe three words of. I weave through the crowded streets beyond the harbor and finally find a narrow side-street to duck into that's little more than an alley between two tall stone buildings.

It's dim and quiet, which is what mattered the most to me.

The moment we've all gathered in the side-street, Jacob turns to me. "What are we doing?"

The question is brusque enough that my hackles rise. "Making sure we don't get murdered by bigger monsters than us."

His mouth twitches with a wince. "I wasn't criticizing. I just wondered what your plan is now."

Oh. I'm still not used to this new accommodating attitude he's taken toward me, and the memories stirred up last night have brought the early days of our reunion back into uncomfortable clarity.

I exhale roughly and peer at the busier street beyond us where men and women are ambling by, caught up in animated conversation. "That shouldn't be only up to me. But I figured we'd get our bearings and stake out the harbor someplace where we'll spot Rollick when he gets back."

Andreas's downcast expression brightens a little. "We can intercept him and tell him exactly what happened."

"Right." I might not want to put us or Pearl and Billy in the other shadowkinds' crosshairs, but the demon can look after himself.

Dominic's expression has stayed pensive. "We might not see him at all. He could go to the ship through the shadows."

"We should at least be able to tell when they're preparing to disembark," I point out. "They'll have to bring in the ramp. If that happens, we can rush over and make a fuss."

Jacob nods slowly. "Sounds like our best bet. We just have to pick a good vantage point so we can watch the yacht without those pricks noticing we're hanging around."

Zian cracks his knuckles, his lips drawing back from his teeth. "I wanted to pummel them into the deck. We might have been able to take them."

A queasy chill wraps around my gut. "We don't know that. And they'd have *wanted* the excuse to kill us. You heard what Rollick told us about how the shadowkind see hybrids."

A gloomy silence descends over us all.

Dominic adjusts his pack against the bulges on his shoulders. "Maybe we shouldn't go back right away. It wouldn't make sense for Rollick to dock for a five-minute errand. We can give the other shadowkind a little time to believe that we've left for good and go back to whatever they're usually doing all day."

Zian frowns. "What do we do until then?"

Andreas glances toward the street. "I've heard good things about Cuban street food. Who's up for dinner?"

"Will they take American cash?" Jacob asks doubtfully.

A flicker of a smile crosses Andreas's face. "Dom and I got Spanish lessons in the facility. I guess they were counting on sending us places like this to do battle with shadowkind while blending in with the locals. I don't have a ton of practice, but I'm sure I can manage to get some money converted. We'd just need to find a bank."

I ease toward the wider street and peer down it at the signs on the buildings. Even my limited grasp of the language doesn't prevent me from guessing what *Banco* must mean.

"I think there's one by the corner," I say, pulling back.

Dominic glances at the rest of us. "Maybe you three had better stay here where you won't be too noticeable. Drey and I can handle dinner."

My body tenses at the thought of watching them walk away, but I'll always know exactly where they are. And Dom has a point.

"Be fast," I say.

Dominic steps over to me and raises his hand to the side of my head to tug me close. He kisses my forehead and then manages a reassuring smile that soothes my anxious spirits just a little.

"I wouldn't stay away from you for long, Sugar," he murmurs. "We'll be right back."

The new nickname sparks a welcome warmth in my chest, followed by a flicker of heat across my cheeks when I realize where it's come from.

Sweeter than a sugar cookie.

Dom shoots me another smile that's somehow both shy and sly and steps away from me with obvious reluctance.

"I'll look after her," Jacob says in his commanding way.

I don't bother to hold back my snort.

As Dominic and Andreas slip out into the busier street, I lean against the smooth stone wall behind me. The faint pulse of my marks traces their journey away from us.

Jacob shifts his weight on his feet. "Riva."

He waits until I look at him. It's the first time he's spoken directly to me since I told him off in the party room last night.

My jaw tightens automatically. "What?"

He holds my gaze unwaveringly. "I know you hate how I treated you before. I hate that guy too. If I could kill him, wipe him right out of existence, so you never had to think about him again, I would. But if I did that, then I wouldn't be here to stand between you and the assholes who are still around. That's why I'm here. It isn't enough, but I'm giving it everything I can."

My throat closes up. I yank my eyes away, my hand rising to grip my pendant.

"You *are* that guy," I say. "Realizing you were an asshole doesn't turn you into a whole new person."

Jacob scowls. "No. I guess it doesn't. But if I can find a way to turn myself into one, I will."

He says the words so vehemently that I can't help believing him.

The trouble is, I don't think that way exists.

Zian clears his throat, cutting through some of the building tension. "The guys didn't even ask what we wanted for dinner. I hope they get something good."

A laugh tumbles out of me despite the ache around my heart. "I'm sure they know what you like by now."

As we wait, restless anxiety ripples through my limbs. The ache in my chest expands to encompass more than just my feelings about Jacob.

Is it my fault the shadowkind are afraid of us? I'm the one with the most brutal talent.

I'm the one who's refused to attempt the steps Rollick's asked me to take toward controlling it.

Why wouldn't they see me as a threat?

When we get back on board, when Rollick can sort this out, I'll do the practice he's asking for. I'll deal out a little pain to make sure I don't slip up when it really matters.

It's the least I can do when the shadowkind are risking so much just having us around.

The uneasiness tangled inside me doesn't loosen until Dominic and Andreas appear at the mouth of the side-street several minutes later, carrying several items wrapped in foil paper.

Andreas starts handing his cargo around, the heat of the contents seeping through the paper into my hands. "I caught a few happy memories from people who've stopped by this food stall a gazillion times, so I think it was the best of the bunch around here. If you—"

With a sharp hissing sound, a streak of silver sears through the air and plunges into his shoulder.

Twenty-Five

Riva

Andreas stumbles, a splotch of red blooming on his shirt sleeve. Even as the foil-wrapped food falls from my hands and I leap to him, more bolts hiss through the air.

Another strikes him across his temple, digging a gouge through his dark skin. Then there's a clattering sound like a shower of hail.

I fling my arms around Andreas to pull him closer to both the nearest wall and the ground. Dominic is already racing over to us, his face tensed.

As I press my hand to the wound on Drey's shoulder, as little as I can do for him with *my* touch, my head jerks around to seek out the source of the shots.

Jacob is crouched on the ground between the rest of us and the depths of the alley, his hands raised defensively. Several more gleaming bullets whip toward us and crash into the forcefield of telekinetic power he's pushing them back with.

Those aren't tranquilizer darts. Someone's trying to *kill* us.

A clammy sensation squeezes around my gut.

"I can't see who's attacking us," Zian says in a rough voice, his head swiveling as he scans the narrow street. "It looks like they're shooting from someplace above. There!"

There's a flicker of movement by a window. An arm jerking out, flinging something down toward us.

Alarm blares through my nerves. "Get out of here! Onto the street—where there's more people."

We hurtle out of the alley like one being, desperate for the shelter the crowded throughway can provide. Whoever's attacking us, they won't risk shooting innocent bystanders, right?

A *boom* reverberates from behind us, jolting the ground beneath my feet. I sling Andreas's arm over my shoulders, holding him awkwardly with my lesser height even though my muscles are up to the challenge.

He curls his fingers into my shirt but runs alongside me, only swaying a little. But the sight of the blood streaking down the side of his face makes my stomach churn.

Dominic dashes next to us, gripping Drey's hand. "I need something—" he gasps out. "The wounds are too deep—I have to get the energy from somewhere."

Oh, hell, I didn't even think of that.

The people on the sidewalk jerk away as we plunge into their midst, murmurs and exclamations rising up in our wake. I don't need to understand the language to recognize that they're disturbed.

Who wouldn't be?

I spot a sapling growing from a pot on the far side of the street. That's got to be enough, right?

I jab my hand toward it, and Dominic veers in that direction. Zian and Jacob thump along behind us.

"We've got to get farther away," Jacob rasps out. "Whoever they are, we don't want them following—"

He doesn't even have time to finish his warning. Hollers ring out, bouncing off the bright pastel storefronts.

Dominic lunges forward and smacks his free hand against the tree. I let Andreas slump against the pot and spin around.

A squad of figures in military-style uniforms are barging into the street from the same direction we came from, a few of them right out of our side-street. Whatever they're shouting to the pedestrians clogging the wider throughway, the crowd is parting.

People are hurrying off in either direction. Cars grind to a halt, some of them backing up to navigate nearby cross-streets.

The soldiers raise their guns and point them straight at us.

"Shit," Jacob hisses through his teeth. He catches my arm and pushes

Andreas forward, herding us toward another street just a few buildings down.

Then his hand lashes out behind him. Two of the figures running toward us topple like action figures kicked by a toddler.

The other soldiers are barking orders at each other. They dodge their fallen companions and start shooting again.

More of the bullets ping against Jacob's hurled power, but one whizzes right past my ear. I swallow a yelp and throw myself faster toward the corner, yanking Andreas with me.

The wound on his arm has to be killing him, but that's better than him being *literally* killed.

As we dart around the bend, I fling a quick glance over my shoulder at the uniformed combatants pursuing us.

They all look like locals. I don't see a single metal helmet either.

They aren't guardians. So who the hell are they, and why the fuck are they trying to kill us?

"What's going on?" I manage to say as we barrel past the bystanders on the less crowded street we've turned onto. "We haven't even done anything!"

Dominic drags in a breath, his forehead already shining with sweat—probably because he's managed to seal Andreas's injuries enough to slow though not stop the bleeding.

"They're saying something to each other about monsters. About the ones they were warned about."

The clammy sensation from before turns into blades of ice lancing through my gut. "They were tipped off."

Like the gangsters who came at me back in Miami—except a dozen times deadlier.

At least one of the shadowkind in Rollick's crew took a page out of his disgraced colleague's book.

Ursula Engel did tell us there were other organizations dedicated to ridding the world of shadowkind. One of our supposed allies must have found a local group and pointed them straight at us.

They found a way to arrange our deaths without having to risk their own hides even slightly.

Jacob lets out a string of curses through his gritted teeth. My own fury, sharpened by a sting of betrayal, surges up through my chest.

We never did a thing to the shadowkind. All we asked for was whatever help they'd freely give.

We turned to them instead of turning *on* them like our creator wanted, and they repaid us by trying to destroy us just like she did.

My power reverberates through me with the prickling of a scream at the base of my throat. But everywhere I look, I can't help seeing the startled civilians darting away from us as more yells echo from down the street.

Whether this group of monster hunters are actually part of the military or they've stolen uniforms to make it look like they are, they've found a winning strategy for clearing their way. My talent isn't as easy to aim as a gun, though.

Even as it claws at my lungs, begging me to pay our attackers back for the pain they've already caused the man beside me, I gird myself. I'm not going to tear through all these unknowing people on a rampage.

I don't even know if doing it would save us. Who can tell where more of these assholes might be coming from?

All at once, I'm wishing I had tormented a few crabs and the other creatures Rollick would have set in front of me. Maybe then I could have chosen who I ripped into.

We shove toward the opposite sidewalk where there are still enough confused bystanders around to offer us some cover and hurtle onward into a broad courtyard that opens up in front of us.

But our attackers have obviously been warned that we wouldn't go down easily. Another half a dozen of them come charging into view from the far end of the courtyard.

I whirl around, but the figures behind us are marching into view, closing in.

The two groups are trapping us between them. How much longer will Jacob be able to hold off even one set of bullets?

Andreas touches his still-bleeding forehead. "If I could mess with their minds—I can't concentrate."

"It's not your fault," I say urgently.

Zian waves his arm, his voice low and urgent. "Guys! Over here!"

We dash forward to an alley he's spotted at one of the unguarded corners of the square. The thunder of more gunshots blares behind us.

A body slams into me from behind. We spin, my claws springing out, and then I see it's only Jacob, wrenching me to the side.

Wrenching me to the side… while blood bubbles from the bullet he just took to his ribs.

He took it for me. Shielded me with his body when his power couldn't offer enough protection.

"Jake," I mumble, still scrambling forward.

His pale blue eyes dart wildly from side to side. "Just go. *Go*."

"Dom!" I call out instinctively as we throw ourselves into the dingy alley.

But our healer is already a few steps ahead, still helping Andreas along —and he's got nothing in this gritty laneway to draw energy from except himself.

If Dominic falters, then we might all be dead.

Jacob hustles along behind me, but his breaths sound labored, his steps uneven. Steadier footsteps and another barrage of shouts carry from the road beyond.

The lane swerves, giving us a momentary reprieve. We push ourselves faster, swing around another bend—

And find ourselves staring at a six-foot-tall wooden fence that blocks the entire passage ahead.

Zian lets out a snarl and hurtles toward it like a battering ram. He hits the fence shoulder-first.

The boards crack but hold in place.

As he backs up to try again, the rest of us hurry over around him. Jacob lists to the side, clamping his hand against the bullet wound on his torso.

And at the same moment, the first of our pursuers springs around the bend.

Bullets boom out. Jacob grunts and casts out his power, but not quite fast enough.

Even as I leap toward the wall, a metal bolt catches me in the back. It sears into my chest with a blazing pain.

My lips part. A croak tumbles out of them.

I can't get my breath. My lung is collapsing.

"Riva!" Jacob cries out, and sputters a sound that's as much groan as growl.

Then something else groans, with a grating earthen quality. The sound resonates all around us, behind us, stretching through the alley.

Zian rams his shoulder into the fence again, and three of the boards shatter completely. I stagger toward him and trip over a stone.

I spin to catch my fall against the stone building beside me—and gape as the far end of that building comes crumbling down over the man who shot me like a landslide.

It's Jacob. He's lifted his blood-drenched hand alongside the other, the muscles flexing through his arms as he hauls the entire three-story structures on either side of the alley off their foundations.

Chunks of stone roar down into the narrow lane. In a matter of seconds, the alley is blocked off as high as the second-floor windows still standing on the opposite side.

I get a glimpse of the wreckage, and then Zian's arm is whipping around me. He scoops me up against his brawny frame and hauls Jacob off the ground too.

"I've got them!" he shouts to Dominic, and heaves us through the remains of the fence.

Zian is supernaturally strong, but even I wouldn't have thought he could carry both me and Jacob at a sprint. Either I didn't give him enough credit, or I should be incredibly grateful for the effects of adrenaline.

I can't focus well enough to really think about it. The pain of my failing lung radiates through my body and my mind, and the next span of time fades into nothing but ragged gasps for breath and the caustic throbbing.

I'm vaguely aware of a cool breeze lapping over my face. My ass hits the ground, and a tendril it takes me a moment to recognize as one of Dominic's tentacles wraps around my torso.

"Bring him over here!" he shouts out.

Warmth washes through my chest. The pain jabs deeper—and then starts to melt away.

My wheezing smooths out. Air flows into both lungs with a renewed pang of pain, but also the relief of oxygen.

I open my eyes. We're sprawled under a short stretch of trees.

The one right over me is starting to sag, its leaves shriveling.

There's a creaking sound, and a crash. I jolt upright to see a car rocking where it's tipped on its side.

"Jake!" Zian snaps, grasping the other guy's shoulder.

Jacob has sat up too, his face so wan you'd think all the blood from it had drained into the splotch soaking his shirt. No fresh blood streams from his side now, but his face is frozen in a mask of tension, his eyes both dazed and fiercely frantic.

"They shot her!" he rasps out. "They fucking shot her."

Another car flips off its tires.

Andreas swears and waves his hand in front of Jacob's face. "We got away. We're all okay now. But we won't stay that way if you make it obvious where we've ended up."

"Fucking—asshole—pricks—I'll kill—every one—of them."

The words grate out in anguished hitches. A telephone pole snaps off its base like a twig.

I've seen Jacob like this before—not this bad, but the same basic state. After the guardians ambushed us on the university campus.

Ignoring the splinters of pain lingering in my lungs, I shove myself toward him. I can take the same tactic that brought him back to reality then.

Straddling his sprawled legs, I smack my palms against the sides of his face and yank it toward me. "We're out. You stopped them. It's done."

Jacob's pupils jitter in his eyes. His hands snatch at the air.

"Riva—they shot her—the fucking bastards—they tried to *kill* her—"

This time, one of the trees crashes over. My gut twists into a ball.

It's me he's so agonized about. Me he's still fighting for in whatever battle he's gotten trapped in inside his mind.

I shake him. "I'm right here. Dom healed me. I'm okay."

His twitching eyes don't see me. His body shudders in my grasp.

Dominic at least partly healed Jacob's physical wound like he did mine, but I have no idea how much other kinds of damage our escape has taken out on him.

I had no idea he even *could* tear down an entire building—let alone two of them—with his talent. And that was after he'd already deflected dozens of bullets.

"Jake!" I yell, as loud as I dare, and slap his cheek with a prick of claws. "I'm here. Listen to me."

The blow has no discernable effect. Jacob lets out another anguished groan, and something thuds and shatters down the street.

"Riva!" he calls out like I'm not there at all.

The shadows inside me tug me toward him, and I'm so worried that I let them.

I lean in with one last-ditch effort of convincing him I'm with him and slam my mouth into his.

Jacob's breath stutters against my lips. His hands fly up, fingers curling around my neck, tangling in my hair.

But not to choke me or torment me like he might have weeks ago. He holds me in a desperate embrace as another shudder passes through him.

His mouth drops from mine as his head bows.

"Riva," he murmurs in what's little more than a breath.

My insides feel as if they've been entirely rearranged all over again. "I—I'm okay. I'm here."

I push myself farther back so I can see his face. Jacob stares at me, still dazed but back with us.

I will down the flush burning my cheeks and scramble right off him. "We need to get out of here before they catch up with us. Can you walk?"

His mouth opens and closes. Instead of answering with words, he sways to his feet.

My own chest is aching, but I hold myself as steady as I can and glance around at the others. "Where do we go?"

A tremor runs through Dominic's body where he's leaning against the tree he sucked most of the life out of. He's burned out most of his energy too.

His gaze slides along the landscape beyond the trees. Following it, I realize we've come down to the coast again, though not the same stretch as the harbor where the yacht was.

In the near distance, a range of smaller boats bob in the water along narrower docks, stretching as far as I can see.

"We could find a boat no one's using," Dominic says hoarsely. "One we can figure out how to start if we need to. It'd be easier getting away on the water."

Zian hesitates. "Should we see if we can find Rollick?"

Andreas's mouth twists. "We don't know for sure that he *wasn't* in on that attack. And even if he wasn't, we're obviously not safe anywhere near his ship until he's dealt with the others."

I might have protested if I didn't feel so weak myself. We're in no condition to fight with several shadowkind along with any other unwitting human accomplices they rope into their campaign against us.

"We rest and then we regroup," I say.

Dominic's gaze slides to the wreckage around us. "We should definitely put some distance between us and this spot."

Jacob winces and trudges forward on wobbly feet. Zian falls back to steady him with a hand against his back.

Dom and Andreas fall in on either side of me. I reach to grasp Dominic's hand, as concerned about his well-being as he clearly is about mine.

We walk until I think I'm going to collapse. Zian picks out one of the larger private boats nearby and peers through the walls to confirm it's empty.

After we scramble on board, Jacob extends a little jolt of pressure to start the ignition. Andreas steers the craft away from its harbor, in search of a hiding spot where it won't be noticed in the descending darkness of evening.

The rest of us tramp down into the cabin area. There's only one level, but it has two cramped bedrooms and a set of freestanding bunks behind the stairs.

I don't bother to ask, just flop right down on the double bed in the first of the bedrooms. Before I can relax, Jacob sinks down next to me.

"I'm not leaving you alone," he says in a raw voice. "I'm not letting them get one more chance to come at you."

I could point out that I don't have to be alone even if he isn't in the room. Or that he can stand between me and any attackers just fine from anywhere else on the boat.

But I don't have the energy to fight with him. Not after all the fighting we've already done.

Not after seeing how desperate he was to defend me even after he'd already saved me.

"Fine," I mutter, and squirm under the blankets so there are at least two layers of fabric as a barrier between me and his side of the bed.

Then I close my eyes and sink into oblivion.

Twenty-Six

Jacob

I wake up with a pounding ache in my head and a flutter of unfamiliar emotion in my chest. My pulse hitches in the second it takes me to orient myself.

I'm sprawled on a bed that's rocking gently with the water that buoys this boat up. And Riva is lying next to me in the darkness, her fiercely sweet scent wrapped all around me.

My heart keeps thumping at its heightened rate. I lift myself gingerly into a sitting position and peer at her in the dim light that seeps through the bedroom's small, curtained window.

Her petite body swathed in the covers I'm poised on top of, huddled with her back to me right at the far edge of the mattress.

As far as she could get from me without falling off the bed.

The ache in my head has retreated, but a new one winds around the base of my throat. I only vaguely remember insisting that I would stay in here with her.

Did she let me because she understood or because she was too worn out to argue about it?

I close my eyes. *You are such a fucking prick, Jake.*

The thrum of my blood through my veins pushes me toward her.

Clamors at me to hug her close and prove to her how much she means to me.

But hugging her wouldn't accomplish that. She'd flinch away the second I touched her.

The only time she's willingly embraced me was when she felt she had to or I'd screw us all over.

My hands ball at my sides, my fingernails digging into my skin with pinpricks of pain.

My memories of the attack and our escape are hazy and disjointed, as much blaring anger and horror as any concrete imagery. But I remember the press of her lips against mine, the shock of elation and longing cutting through the savage emotions that were gripping me.

Elation and longing immediately tainted by my realization of how wildly my powers had been flailing around.

I saved us and then I practically called our attackers right back down on us. Nice work.

The thought sends a different sort of thrum through my body. The assholes who tried to gun us down are still out there.

They shot Riva. They almost killed her.

They *wanted* to.

My teeth set on edge, a surge of rage welling up inside me—the one emotion in me that's comfortingly familiar.

I can't change what's already happened. I can't undo all the shit I put this woman through.

I can't make different decisions years ago. I can't bring Griffin back to life.

But I sure as hell can make sure that anyone who's tried to hurt Riva never gets a second chance.

This kind of rage, the slow-burning kind like a forge smoldering inside my soul, wafts a cuttingly frigid sort of fire. My thoughts harden with cold efficiency.

Every movement, every consideration narrows down to the goal in front of me. Every thud of my pulse propels me forward.

I slide off the bed, pick my pack off the floor where I dropped it, and stalk out of the bedroom without a sound.

As I tug the door shut behind me with a soft click, a form stirs on one of the bunks beneath the cabin stairs. Andreas gets up and squints through the dimness at me.

Yes, that's perfect. He's the one I need.

"Zian's standing watch," he whispers, tipping his head toward the deck above. "He just took over from me."

"Where's Dom?"

Drey motions to the other bedroom. "Out like a light. I think he needs all the sleep he can get after patching the rest of us up."

I nod. "Can you stay awake a little longer?"

My friend studies me with a trace of hesitation that makes my gut twist. Though we've been there for each other through so much, his pause brings back all the ways I let *him* down too.

But all he says is, "What did you have in mind?"

I motion in the direction I think is toward land. "Those fake soldiers are out there. Probably still looking for us after I bashed up their city. I think we should find them first."

"And then?"

A tight smile grips my mouth. "And then we make sure they never get anywhere near Riva again."

Andreas swipes his hand back over his coiled hair. He doesn't give me an immediate agreement, but the clench of his jaw tells me he's on board.

"We shouldn't leave her by her—"

"Not all of us," I say. "Just you and me. Zian can smack down anyone who comes at him, and Dom'll be here if the worse comes to worst."

Drey's gaze slides over me again. "Are you sure *you're* up to another fight?"

I adjust my weight, flexing my muscles to test them. A faint throbbing lingers inside my skull from how far I strained my powers this afternoon, and a twinge runs through my side where the bullet hit me.

It's all distant compared to the vengeful chill warbling from that forge inside me.

"I've got most of my strength back. And what we're going to do shouldn't take too much of my power."

One corner of Andreas's mouth curls upward, and then I know I have him for sure.

"I distract them, and you knock 'em down?"

A matching smirk crosses my face. "That's the plan."

He turns toward the stairs. "First we have to find them."

"I don't think that'll be a problem."

I pause to yank my sparse belongings out of my pack and stuff in a clear plastic trash bag the boat's owner left crumpled in a corner. Then I climb the stairs after Andreas.

Zian glances over at me from where he's staked out in front of the cabin, but I can tell from the acceptance in his face that Drey has already told him the gist of what we're up to. He dips his head to me.

We leap out onto the rickety dock we tied the small yacht to and scramble up the rocky shoreline to this much more derelict section of the city. Down a dingy street, I spot a car that's rusty and dented enough for me to be sure it has no alarm system.

"We go back to the scene of our 'crime,'" I murmur to Andreas, heading toward the car. "At least some of them will be searching for us around there."

And this late at night, the windows on the city's buildings are nearly all dark, the streets around us empty. It shouldn't be difficult to spot a squad of supposed soldiers marching around on patrol.

I pop the locks on the doors with a tug of my talent and twist the ignition the same way. As Drey drops into the split leather of the passenger seat, the engine rumbles to life.

I have a general sense of where we are relative to the part of the city we fled through earlier—approximately southwest. Easing on the gas, I pull away from the curb.

In the first few minutes, nothing crosses our path except a mangy dog that trots faster at the sight of us. The digital clock on the dash says it's three thirty in the morning.

"We won't want to get too close in the car," Andreas says. "It'll draw attention when the streets are so quiet."

"This is just to get us closer fast enough that it's still dark."

We lapse back into silence. Drey runs his fingers over the mottled armrest.

A flicker of an image passes through my mind: his hand sliding over Riva's dress as they danced together.

My own hands tighten around the steering wheel. For a second, my anger flares hot enough to cut through the chill that's keeping me focused.

But the only one who deserves that anger is me.

"I'm sorry," I say abruptly.

Andreas's head snaps around. "What?"

"You tried to tell me I was fucking up. More than once. And I didn't listen to you. And then, with Riva—I purposefully made what you did sound so much worse..."

Acid gnaws at my stomach as if I've poisoned myself. The part I hate most is that I don't even know how much I really believed I was defending my friends in that moment and how much it was jealousy I was tamping down so hard I couldn't even recognize it.

Andreas says nothing for long enough to leave me queasy. Then he swipes his hand over his face.

"We all messed up. We *are* all messed up. I know that I can't even imagine how hard it's been for you the past four years, without Griffin, believing she sold him and the rest of us out… And I know that I haven't been able to do much to make it any easier."

A splash of shame chases my guilt. "It wasn't your job to make *my* life easier. I never expected—"

"Of course you didn't. I'm just saying I'm not holding any grudges. Were there a few moments in there when I wanted to punch you in the face? Sure. But I don't think that would have fixed things any faster."

His tone has turned lightly wry. He watches me as if to evaluate my reaction.

I swallow thickly. "Maybe not, but I bet it'd have been awfully satisfying. If you get the urge again, feel free to actually punch me."

I tried to match his tone, but Drey has spent enough time in other people's heads that he can be almost as perceptive as my twin was. He must be able to tell I'm serious.

"You already beat yourself up plenty without me adding to it, Jake."

I don't know what to say to that. Then the beam of a flashlight flickers across the street several blocks in the distance, and my foot jams on the brake.

"We'd better stop here."

It's easier, focusing on the mission I intend to carry out. Sinking down into the welcome simmering of icy fury, letting the searing chill carry me out of the car and stealing down the street.

Andreas keeps pace. We dodge the pools of light beneath the sporadic streetlamps, sticking to the thickest of shadows.

From some club or bar in the area, energetic bass is still pounding, distant to our ears. A laugh spills out of a high hotel window that's open to the night breeze. A single car putters by.

Otherwise the night is still and silent. I wouldn't be surprised if the supposed soldiers managed to clear most of the locals out, if any had wanted to still be up.

After seeing what I did to those buildings, maybe it wouldn't have been too hard.

When I spot the gleam of the flashlight again, we're only a couple of blocks away. The figure holding it is beyond our view.

We creep closer with even more care. My ears pick up the scrape of footsteps moving away from us down the cross-street.

Andreas stops me with a hand on my shoulder. "Let me take a look," he says under his breath.

He vanishes from view, as neat a trick as the way the shadowkind can merge into the shadows. I wait in a darkened doorway, grappling with my impatience, as he must venture after our potential targets in his invisible state.

A minute later, he reappears next to me.

"It's them. Some of them. I counted seven, spread out along the street, but one guy talked into a radio, so they're in contact with others. They're patrolling, looking into all the buildings."

Satisfaction sweeps through me. "Good. Then we'll just have to give them some bait."

They think we're in hiding, on the run from them. That we're too scared to face them head on.

The truth is, we just needed a chance to turn the tables and get the upper hand.

I backtrack, seeking out an ideal site for our ambush. After prowling up and down a few streets, I come across a parking lot behind a bar that's closed for the night.

The backs of the surrounding buildings close off the rectangular space, the only entrance and exit a short lane onto the street. The bar itself has a rear second-story patio with a thick stone wall undulating along its border.

Now we just need to lure the bastards here.

I motion to the patio above us. "Get up there and wait for me. I'll bring them around. We want to gather as many of them as possible before I start taking them out. Once they're in, if they look like they're aiming to leave, flood their heads with enough memories to keep them confused."

Andreas nods and reaches for a window ledge to help him scale the lower part of the building.

The training the guardians put us through wasn't a total waste. I hope someday they find out we put it to use cutting down monster-hunters rather than monsters.

I slip out of the parking lot and glance up and down the nearest street. There's no sign of our targets, but I know they aren't far from here.

I train my attention on a statue fixed to the roof of a building on the corner. With a shove of my power, it cracks off its ledge and plummets to the ground.

The cracking thud of the stone form hitting the pavement echoes through the night. I pull back into the mouth of the lane and watch.

It's less than a minute before footsteps pound close enough for me to hear. Several uniformed figures charge into view down the street.

They gather around the fallen statue, glancing from it to the roof with tensed poses and guns in hand. One of them has something that looks like a glittering net slung over his shoulder, whatever the hell that's for.

Definitely not normal soldiers. I have a sneaking suspicion that those shiny bullets they fired at us—and into us—were made out of silver, not lead.

The hunters fan out again to search the street. One of them speaks into his walkie talkie.

Good. Bring more of them this way.

With a nudge of my ability, I send an empty pop can rattling across the sidewalk just a few feet from where I'm standing.

The nearest figures jerk around. I let out a curse I muffle badly and take off down the lane, deliberately letting my shoes smack the asphalt harder than they need to.

Hushed hollers pass between the hunters. They rush after me, the sound of their pursuit mingled with more crackling of radio static as they call for backup.

That's right. Let's get everyone together now.

Every murderous prick who nearly slaughtered the woman I would die for.

I sprint into the parking lot and throw myself toward the patio using the same route Andreas took. He bobs up from behind the surrounding wall to give me a hand up.

We duck down again behind the jutting chunks of stone just as the first men race into the parking lot in pursuit.

I have to keep them engaged while the others pour in after them. Searching rather than shouting warnings to flee.

Peeking over one of the lower sections of wall, I set a window rattling. As soon as the soldiers rush in that direction, I flick a shingle off a roof on the opposite side.

More hunters are storming into the parking lot. Some of them are whirling with obvious wariness in their stance.

We can't afford to wait long enough for them to get suspicious. It's time to end them now.

Like shooting fish in a barrel.

The rage inside me flares through my chest. I lean forward, gripping the edge of the wall, just as the first man steps toward the lane and then stumbles as Andreas's power floods his mind with memories that aren't his.

Before my target has had a chance to let out more than the start of a yelp, I whip him against the corner of the nearest building, head first. His skull bursts open like a smashed jack-o-lantern.

More shouts of alarm rise up, faltering as confusion spreads through their ranks. I grin with my teeth bared and topple them one after the other.

Neck snapped. Back cracked.

Shove that one into his own knife, straight through the heart. Slam this one's face into the pavement until it's a bloody pulp.

My body hums with the energy whipping out of it. Not a single emotion stirs inside me except the burn of resolve.

Die. Die. Die.

No pausing, no resting. Blazing from each to the next the second I've struck them down.

Every last one of the pricks, until Riva can walk safe through these streets again.

But as the skulls shatter and the heads slump, the stabbing sense lances through me that none of this will *ever* be enough.

Twenty-Seven

Riva

The boat rocks, and I jerk awake with a jolt of alarm. My body springs into a defensive crouch, tossing off the covers before I'm even fully aware of where I am.

No shouts or crashes carry from beyond the small bedroom's door. The thin gray light of pre-dawn drifts through the small window, making the plain furniture look outright dingy.

The boat settles, whether from a wave or one of my guys moving around. I sink back down onto my ass and retract my claws.

I've taken one calmer breath when the door swings open and Jacob marches into the room.

He smiles at me immediately, but the friendly expression doesn't quite reach his eyes. His pale irises have darkened like churning storm clouds.

Dark splotches dapple the fabric of his light blue shirt as well—streaking across the sleeves where they're rolled to his elbows, splattering his chest. When he steps to the foot of the bed where the light is a little sharper, the spots glint with a ruddy crimson sheen.

My stomach lurches all over again. "What happened?"

Jacob's smile stretches wide enough to bare all his teeth. He reaches around to yank a bulging plastic bag from his backpack.

"I happened."

He upends the bag, and a deluge of bloody objects tumbles onto the far corner. A meaty smell floods the air.

I stare and abruptly recognize the details—the jutting fingers, the stumps of wrists, a glint of a thick silver ring.

They're all hands.

Hands severed from their bodies and dumped on the end of my bed.

My claws spring back out automatically, my ears tufting with their catlike peaks. My gaze jerks to the door that's clicked closed behind him in anticipation of some even larger threat.

Jacob tosses the bag aside with a plastic warble that brings my attention back to him. "There's nothing to worry about. They're never going to squeeze a trigger at you again. I made sure of it."

His voice is even but fervid. The gleam in his eyes looks almost feverish now.

I stare at him. "You— Those are from—"

"Every last one of them," he says with a slight rasp. "Drey and I tracked them down, and I slaughtered them like they tried to do to us. To you."

He glances down at his trophies. "I'd have brought their heads, but they wouldn't all have fit in the bag. Their hands are what they tried to hurt you with most anyway."

"I…" I don't know what to say.

I should be horrified, right? There's a heap of chopped-off hands lying on my bed.

Some part of me *is* horrified, with a thread of nausea creeping through my gut. But at the same time, a strange lightness is rushing up inside me.

We're safe. Safe from the hunters who tried to murder us.

Because Jacob went out and took care of them before I even had the chance to worry about them again.

He's watching me so intently my skin flares under his gaze. But whatever reaction he was searching for, he must not get it, because something in his expression falters.

The sight sends a twang of regret through me, knowing the lengths he's just gone to on my behalf, but I don't know what he wants. I don't know if I can give it.

"They aren't the only ones who hurt you," he says, his voice gone raw, and jerks a knife out of his pocket. The blood smeared across its heavy blade suggests it's the one that sawed through all those wrists.

Then he brings the knife to his own arm, right below the roll of his sleeve.

Something in my brain stalls. I can't fully process what I'm seeing until he angles the blade to dig it in.

A cry breaks from my throat. I throw myself forward and grab his wrists just as blood starts to spring from his skin.

My hands look tiny against his bulging muscles, but the supernatural might in me gives me the strength to wrench his knife hand away from his forearm.

More blood is flowing from the cut he managed to make before I sprang in. Another pained sound hitches out of me, and I press my palm against it.

"We need Dom."

I suck in a breath to call for our healer, but Jacob shakes his head.

"No. I hurt you. I *poisoned* you with this fucking arm. I don't deserve to keep it."

He means it. Every word propels from his lips with the same fierce resolve I used to hear when he accused me of murdering Griffin.

He barrels onward. "I can't change what happened, but I can show you it's over. I can pay the price. I—"

"Not like this," I break in. "Never like this, Jacob."

I squeeze his arm harder. Only a little blood is streaking out from beneath my hand now—I don't think he'd managed to cut very deep yet—but my heart still aches to see it.

Jacob stares down at me like he can't quite believe I'm refusing him. When the tears burning behind my eyes brim over, he flinches.

With a shudder of his fingers, the knife thumps to the floor. His legs give.

He slumps to the floor, his head tipping forward to lean against the edge of the bed by my knees. But he doesn't pull his arm away from me.

"I hurt you so badly," he mumbles. "I can't take it back. I can't make it better. I don't know how to do this right."

My throat closes up. I keep clutching on to his forearm, but I have no idea what to say.

The boy in front of me seems so lost and alone, but he's already pushed me so far away that I don't know if I could ever reach him.

But I don't want to lose him. Whatever we still have, however much all our history before the past few weeks matters, that one fact resonates through me beyond a shadow of a doubt.

"I don't know either," I say, my voice coming out rough. "But you have to be here, in one piece, to do it."

He inhales with a hiss through his teeth. "What if I'm never going to be in one piece the way I was again?"

I frown. "What do you mean?"

Jacob is silent for a stretch before he speaks again. "I wasn't lying when I said I died that day, even if it wasn't you who killed me. When I saw Griffin fall on that screen, when I knew he was gone… It was my fucking fault. I should have taken lead. I shouldn't have let him—"

He cuts himself off with a strangled sound.

My other hand drifts over as if of its own accord to rest on the rumpled strands of his hair. My tentative touch seems to give him the resolve to go on.

"Everything was wrong, and there wasn't anything I could do. I just wanted to be gone too. There wasn't any point. The only thing… The only thing I felt other than empty was rage at the pricks who shot him down. If I hadn't known I might still get to pay them back, I would have slit my own fucking throat four years ago."

Fresh tears prickle in my eyes. "What about the other guys? You still had them."

Jacob manages a shrug in his slouched position. "I look out for them. I'm not letting them fall if I can help it. Because that's what we do for each other. I don't—there's nothing *in* me—I couldn't manage to be a brother properly so I sure as hell can't handle being a friend."

He lifts his head to gaze up at me. "Until I watched you racing toward that train, and I—I cared, so fucking much, and I was terrified and ashamed and I wanted so many things that I haven't even thought about in years. But I'm not fixed. It's like I just broke more. The emptiness is all filled in with total fucking chaos. I can't even keep my goddamned powers from going haywire."

I feel as if I can see the broken pieces of him behind his distraught eyes. I didn't know that moment made such a difference to him.

But I still have to ask, with a quiver of nerves that rises up despite everything he's said, "So you're not at all angry with *me* anymore? I didn't —I didn't know what would happen that night, but I got distracted; I distracted Griffin. If I hadn't kissed him…"

Jacob is already shaking his head. He meets my gaze again.

"The guardians figured out what we were up to somehow. I don't see how it'd have happened any differently no matter what you did out there. At least he got that little bit of happiness before they murdered him."

I can't sense any trace of rancor in his words. I think he means that too.

But I can't help prodding a little farther. "You believed it was my fault for a long time."

"I—" He exhales harshly. "Maybe it was like Andreas said. Maybe it was easier hating a you that was alive somewhere than believing you were dead and having to mourn you too. I hated and hated until it was all I could do. I didn't know how to turn it off until I hurt you *that* badly that it jolted me out—"

Jacob cuts himself off with a growl that seems directed entirely at himself. He pushes himself onto his feet but stays crouched enough that we're on the same level, and lifts his hand to touch my cheek.

"I'm glad you got to have that moment with Griffin before everything went to hell. I know—I know *you* would rather they'd taken me out than him—I know he was always—"

"Jake," I interrupt with a burst of emotion that cuts off the rest of my words for a moment. My heart feels like it's breaking now.

I rest my free hand over his against my face and repeat the words I know Andreas already told him. But Jacob wasn't in a place where he could hear them then, was he?

Maybe he can now.

"I loved all of you," I say quietly. "Nobody more than anybody else. You were all different but not more or less. I loved *you.* The way you'd spot answers to problems so quickly. The way you could cut through any worries or confusion we got caught up in."

Jacob lets out a sputter of a laugh, but I keep going.

"You could always get us focused and on track, right there with you. It was the best feeling when we'd make it through a training exercise together, and you'd smile at all of us like we'd already defeated the guardians… If I started feeling out of sorts, I could always hang out with you, and you'd have some new challenge we could tackle together…"

His head droops, his hand falling though he's caught my fingers in his. "I don't even know where the track is anymore. I'm the one all out of sorts."

The corner of my mouth ticks upward with a bittersweet smile. "I can't think of anyone else who'd set out on a crusade to kill all the monster-hunters in town before they could find us again."

His gaze jerks back up with a flare of the passionate determination I loved so much too. "Anyone who comes at you has just signed their death sentence. Maybe I can't promise much, Wildcat, but I can guarantee you that."

After this morning's bloody present, there's no way I can doubt his declaration.

"Just don't think you're ever handling them on your own," I retort.

Jacob's mouth twists, but he doesn't argue.

A breeze drifts past the thin curtain. Its cool taint reminds me of the sticky dampness beneath my other hand where it's still pressed to Jacob's forearm.

"Let me bandage your cut? If you're going to insist that Dominic doesn't take care of it right away."

Jacob's expression pulls into an outright grimace. "It'll heal fast enough on its own. He shouldn't have to extend himself any more than he already has." He lays his arm down on the blanket. "Go ahead. Thank you."

He replaces my hand with his as I reach for my backpack to find the first aid gear I stashed there for my own past injury. I can't help thinking that his concern for Dominic sounds a lot like being a damn good friend.

He's cared all along, even if his grief overwhelmed his awareness of it.

I brush an antiseptic wipe over the cut before wrapping a wad of gauze in place with a longer strip of the stuff. As Jacob flexes his arm to check the tightness, I lean back on the bed and wipe my blood-streaked fingers on the sheet.

We really owe a major apology to whoever we stole this boat from. Maybe leaving a nice wad of cash as a thank you will balance the scales?

I'm struggling to decide what to say next when a series of thumps emanate from above, forceful enough to set the boat bobbing in the water.

My pulse stuttering all over again, I jump to my feet.

Zian's voice bellows down from the deck. "Guys! It's those asshole shadowkind."

TWENTY-EIGHT

Riva

Jacob and I don't speak, only dash for the door. One of my hands fumbles in my cargo pants' pockets for a knife; the other flicks its claws free.

I don't know how much good either of those weapons will do me against the monsters and their powers, but I'm not going in unarmed.

Jacob must have the same thought, because the purple spines that hold his poison spring from his forearms. He takes the stairs two at a time, every movement honing to brutal intensity.

I can see in each stride the vulnerability he showed me falling away, his icy confidence snapping back into place as he prepares for battle.

This is what his anger did for him. It gave him armor to face all the shit the guardians threw at him when he had nothing else to hold him together.

I still cringe at the memories of how he aimed his rage at me, but I'm not sure I can say I wish he'd never had it.

Andreas was already hurtling up to the deck ahead of us. At the rasp of footsteps behind, I glance over my shoulder to see Dominic following us.

His tan face has taken on a sickly tone, but he manages to shoot a tight smile at me.

We burst out into the warm morning air on the deck, right on each other's heels. On this small yacht, there's barely room for us to fan out in a semi-circle without bumping into the railing.

Zian stands with muscles bulging threateningly in the middle of the deck, facing the dock. His face is still mostly human, but his wolf-man fangs jut from his mouth, claws twice as thick as mine arcing from his fingertips.

In the crisp early sunlight, five figures watch us from the dock, a few steps away from the bow of our boat.

Cinder has her slim arms folded over her chest, the fingers of one hand drumming the opposite elbow. Kudzu matches Zian's aggressive pose with his ropier muscles flexing.

I don't know the names of the other three, but they stood with Cinder and Kudzu when they kicked us off the ship.

It's almost definitely one of those five who pointed the hunters at us.

There's no sign of anyone potentially friendly to us. How did this bunch track us down?

Why did they track us down? Did they realize their human dupes didn't perform adequately and decided it was time to finish the job?

As that last question passes through my mind, a tremor of caustic energy wakes up at the base of my chest.

These beings wanted us dead. They cast us out, treated us like *we* were the monsters.

My mind feels jumbled from the wrenching conversation with Jacob, but one clear, quivering thread of resolve winds through my body.

I am not letting these fiends hurt any of us again.

In the split-second of that decision, a sixth figure materializes farther up the dock, just across from our yacht's hull. Rollick studies us with a typical air of nonchalance, but there's a fiery smolder in his eyes that I don't like the look of.

"See," Kudzu says in a brusque tone. "I told you they'd all be here where I saw the one guy."

Rollick lets out a dismissive sound. "That's hardly an impressive revelation. I'd have been more surprised if they'd split up."

Cinder hisses through her teeth with an electric sizzle. "They've made a mess of their stolen boat too. Blood and body parts all over the place. They're *beasts*."

I wince inwardly at the reference to Jacob's gift.

His jaw only hardens. "I took care of the real beasts. The ones you sent after us."

One of the other shadowkind scoffs. "You can't blame us if you're such a hazard the local hunters caught on the moment you stepped on shore."

A choked guffaw tumbles out of me. I know we aren't that noticeable.

"We've roamed all across North America before now and never been attacked by anyone other than guardians… oh, and the thugs one of your crew paid off to kill us."

The tremor spreads through my limbs beneath my skin. I want to tear through every one of them—but I don't know if I can.

I don't know how bad the backlash might be if I try and fail. I could make things even worse.

And there's still a chance—Rollick has stood up for us through everything, hasn't he?

The demon is eyeing us with the same edge of skepticism I sensed at first glance. "You did make an awful mess of this city. Pulling down entire buildings, leaving mutilated bodies strewn around parking lots."

Andreas raises his chin, and I remember that Jacob said Drey came with him on his mission tonight. "We did what we had to do to protect ourselves. It'd have been a lot less messy if your people hadn't set us up to be attacked."

"And if they hadn't kicked us off the ship in the first place," Zian growls.

A fierce crackle runs through Cinder's voice. "We were protecting *our* own. You're like rabid dogs—and we all know what humans do with those. Is it so awful for us to take the same tactic?"

Her sneering words fling me back to Ursula Engel's living room, to hearing the woman who created us call us abominations she couldn't wait to see slaughtered. My claws shoot from my knife hand, pricking into my palm.

"We didn't ask to be this way," I snap.

She narrows her eyes at me. "You're not trying very hard to rein yourselves in. You've been arguing with Rollick every step of the way."

"Well, forgive me for not wanting to go around torturing random creatures for my own training." My claws dig right into the flesh of my hand, the pang of pain grounding me just a little against the internal claws scrabbling to break free from my lungs.

The shadowkind woman in front of me isn't an innocent creature. She's made it amply clear that she's my enemy.

But lashing out at her is exactly what they all expect, isn't it? It'd be an excuse to justify slaughtering us all if I can't carry through.

And then where will we be? Stuck here in a country we're not familiar with, where only two of us even speak the language, with resources that'll quickly dwindle and possibly more hunters already on the alert?

"We all make sacrifices," Kudzu mutters. "It's obvious you'd rather hold on to your delicate sensibilities than do what's necessary to keep anyone else safe."

I can't hold back a snort. *My* delicate sensibilities?

Maybe when I was two years old, if then.

Jacob has turned his full attention on Rollick. I can tell from the tension in his stance that he's braced to whip out his telekinetic talent the second it's needed.

"What about you?" he demands. "They tossed us out against your orders, and that's just fine with you?"

Rollick's voice turns slightly brittle. "No, it's not. And they'll face consequences for their actions. But that doesn't mean I can't reevaluate my own decisions in light of new information."

"You're really blaming us for fighting back when those hunters nearly killed us?" I burst out. The quiver of a shriek climbs partway up my throat, nipping at my vocal cords.

"Your methods appear rather overblown compared to the actual threat. I have mentioned at least once or twice how important it is that we keep our abilities under wraps around the regular mortal population."

Cinder nods sharply. "Exactly so that more of those pricks don't decide to take up arms against us."

Dominic speaks up, his voice as even as always but propelled with more force than usual. "We wouldn't have needed to fight at all if *you* hadn't tipped them off. It wasn't because of us. None of us had done more than walk up the street and buy some dinner."

Kudzu grunts. "It makes a lot more sense that you fucked up than that we went running to ally with humans."

"Except one of you already did before," I remind them, my temper flaring hotter. "It wouldn't even be the first time this week."

Rollick swivels on his heel to contemplate his companions. "It is true that there's a precedent for sending murderous mortals after this bunch. If you deliberately provoked them, then—"

"Oh, for fuck's sake," Cinder breaks in, her words warbling with frustration. "Let's just end this. *She's* the biggest problem."

Her slender forefinger jabs at me, and in the same instant, the four shadowkind standing with her spring into action.

Kudzu and one of the beings hurl themselves right over the railing onto the deck of the yacht. Another flings his hand forward, and blazing light sears across my eyes.

I throw myself down on the floor to dodge any other attacks, braced to strike out or roll away. Dark spots stay hazed across my vision.

Jacob lets out a yell, and one of the figures on the deck goes flying all the way across the dock to crash into the rocky shoreline. But Kudzu charges at Jake and heaves him over the side to plummet into the water.

Blinking hard to try to clear my eyes, I lunge at the gangly shadowkind man—but Zian shoves in front of me with a roar. He slashes at Kudzu and reels backward with a bone-cracking punch to his wolfish snout.

Andreas blinks in and out of view, jabbing a knife at Kudzu. But another of the shadowkind has leapt onto the deck and kicks him in the ribs with a spike that juts from the back of her heel.

Kudzu rams Zian over the railing after Jacob. And Cinder steps to the edge of the deck with a current of electricity hissing between her hands.

I leap to the railing, my stomach flipping over. She's going to electrocute them—burn them to oblivion right there in the water.

Because they rushed in to help *me*. They're going to die because they wanted to defend me from the only real villains around here.

The furious anguish of that realization tears up through my chest. The scream explodes from my mouth at full throttle.

I don't even have to think to deflect its effects from my men now. The vicious thing inside me recognizes them from the thrum of our blood, the torture already entwining us through our shared history.

Inflicting more of that torment isn't what it wants. It wants the monsters who tried to tear us down to suffer, every possible drop of agony wrung out of them.

My scream reverberates across the yacht and the deck, slamming into all six of the shadowkind who confronted us. I can taste them yanking and flailing against its grip like bugs on flypaper—and my hunger doesn't know how long I can hold them.

I might not have much time to drink down all the pain this part of me is craving.

My fury narrows down onto Cinder first, my nerves buzzing at the electricity still sizzling in her hands. My intent rips through her from feet to forehead.

Hit her as hard as I can. Batter her, break her.

The shriek still ringing from my throat twists her ankles and shatters her kneecaps. It digs through her innards like a jagged blade.

Split open her ribs. Dislocate both her shoulders. Then blast her menacing skull right in two.

Send her crumpling into the smoky mishmash she's actually made of.

Just as my attention jerks away from her crumpling, mutilated form to latch on to a new target, a slim form bursts out of the shadows at the foot of the dock, racing toward us.

"Leave her alone! You're making her—"

The focus of my scream veers to the newcomer, pummeling him with a hitch of breath and a shock of alarm through my senses.

More, there's more of them than I thought—I have to crush them all before—

"Riva, don't!" a voice I vaguely recognize cries out. "It's Billy! He wanted to help; he was trying to—"

Billy. The name sinks in through the shriek that's echoing through my mind.

The delicate frame that's cracking so easily under the pressure of my voice, the horns poking from the jumbled waves of hair—

Horror hits me like a wave of icy water. I wrench myself backward and trip onto my ass—but the impact of my body against the deck breaks the momentum of my scream.

My voice cuts off with a stutter. And I stare with pulse thrumming and throat aching at the two smoking bodies sprawled across the dock.

The one I meant to destroy—and the one that tried to be my friend.

The cry that tumbles out of me next has no pain in it but my own.

No. Oh, no.

What the fuck have I done?

Twenty-Nine

Dominic

Riva slumps onto the deck, her face drained of all color. The features that had gone rigid as she let out her scream slacken; the white sheen fades from her eyes beneath her plummeting eyelids.

There's chaos all around us—yells of horror and anger, shadowkind looming on the deck in front of me, plumes of dark smoke gushing through the air—but my entire world narrows down to the woman I love. A splinter of her anguish spears through me from the mark on my sternum.

Before I've even processed that I'm moving, I've dashed to her side.

A shudder ripples through her body, and then she keeps shivering despite the warm air, like she's freezing. When I touch her arm, her skin feels clammy.

I yank off my trench coat without a second thought and crouch down next to her to wrap it around her trembling shoulders. The ocean breeze licks over my exposed tentacles, but right now I don't give a shit.

The rest of the world barges into my awareness, as much as I'd like to keep tuning it out.

"You see?" Kudzu is hollering, stomping toward us with his sinewy muscles flexing across his tall frame. "*She's* the fucking monster. We have to destroy her before she—"

My tentacles have already lashed out to defend Riva as well as I can. Andreas steps in too, his face taut but determined, and from the splashing and sputtering that carries from below the boat, I'd imagine Zian and Jacob are doing their best to fight their way back to us.

The second shadowkind being that leapt onto the boat has stepped back to the railing, his eyes bulging with fear. But the other springs forward, joined by the one of their group that'd stayed on the dock before, scrambling after Kudzu with seething hisses and murder in their eyes.

Oh, fuck.

Then Riva raises her head. She doesn't seem to see the monsters bearing down on us—she focuses on the railing as if she can see through the hull to the dock beyond.

"Billy—is he—" Her gaze yanks to me. "Can you heal him, Dom? I tried to stop before it went too far…"

Three raging supernatural fiends are storming toward us intent on ending her life, and she cares more about the life she almost took. She'd send me to protect him rather than have me stay here defending her.

I don't feel like I have a lot of choice, though. I snatch up the knife she dropped and shove between her and Kudzu a second before the massive guy barrels down on her.

"Don't touch her!" I snap, tentacles whipping around me, knife hilt clenched in my hand.

He could probably pummel me into the deck without breaking a sweat, but he'll have to if he wants to get to Riva. He's not setting one fucking finger on her while I can still stand in the way.

The shadowkind man snarls with a hint of a smirk, as if he's *glad* he gets to bash through me first—

And then a voice so deep and dark it sounds like it's echoing up from the depths of hell reverberates through the air.

"Get away from the girl."

The rush of supernatural power that comes with that order washes over me in a prickling wave that sets all the hairs on my body on end.

Kudzu jerks around, his body clenching up like he's been punched.

A monster stands on the dock, glaring at the shadowkind on the ship with eyes like smoldering coals and razor-pointed teeth glinting in his grimace. The inhuman figure has to be well over seven feet tall, muscle-bound beneath his ruddy skin, two long black horns curving upward from the sides of his head.

My mind jars against the image, my thoughts scattering.

Then Kudzu says, in a cringing tone, "But, Rollick—"

"Get. The fuck. Away from her," the monster says in a firm but almost sardonic tone that does remind me of the demon's voice, even if this version is way more booming.

Is that… is that what our benefactor *really* looks like?

I guess he's called a demon for a reason.

There's no missing the brutal energy that radiates off him, even more potent than in his human form. The shadowkind on the deck fall back, one of the smaller beings wincing as if Rollick's demonic presence outright hurts her.

And just like that, it becomes very clear why he's the boss. Even if his associates sometimes turn a little mutinous.

"Billy," Riva says again, louder—a wrenching plea.

"He's alive," Pearl's voice calls up from the dock, unusually squeaky with strain. "He's— It's not good."

The demon that is Rollick meets my eyes and jerks his head toward the dock as if to say, *Well, get on with it.*

I don't want to leave Riva, but knowing that someone is helping Billy in ways she can't obviously means more to her than keeping me here. Rollick's influence seems to be holding his comrades at bay.

My stomach knotting, I dash to the side of the boat.

As I straighten up with my approach, the crumpled bodies on the dock come into view. They're even more unsettling than I expected from my glimpses while Riva's scream cut through our attackers.

I can barely make out the heap of matter that was once Cinder through the streams of smoke gushing off her corpse. It looks as if her flesh is disintegrating into the smoke essence.

There's a knob of something there that might be a knee. A long, lean chunk that's probably her torso, though contorted beyond recognition.

I drag my gaze away to the other, smaller form huddled closer to the shore.

Billy is at least still identifiable as the slender, horned faun. His head appears to be intact, though it's tucked toward his chest with a twisted grimace.

But the rest of him…

The gleam of a rib juts from one side, right through his torn shirt. Both of his legs sprawl bent at unnatural angles.

Wafts of essence trail off his wounds. Pearl is crouched over him, tears shimmering on her rosy cheeks, her pale hands flitting over him as if wanting to piece him back together but not knowing how.

No, that's not good at all.

I shove open the gate and push down the ladder so I can rush down to the dock. The rickety surface bobs under my sudden weight.

Jacob and Zian are just pulling themselves onto the boards farther down, adding to the unsteadiness. Jake swipes his hand back over his drenched hair and stares at the boat as if he's about to launch himself back onto it, his eyes blazing like ice-blue flames.

"If those fuckers touch Riva—"

"They know better," Rollick says in that echoing demonic voice that sends another shiver under my skin.

I dash over to Billy and sink down across from Pearl. My tentacles swing forward, one of them tucking around his waist, and the other trailing through the air.

"I need—I need an energy source," I rasp out.

Rollick snaps his fingers. "Kelp, get the kid some fish. *Now.*"

An eerie warbling sound carries up from below, with a tremor of the dock. Then a gleaming fish as long as my forearm flips out of the water onto the boards next to me.

I don't question it, just smack my other tentacle around its scaled body. The suckers clench on, and life races into me in a tingling torrent.

I compel the energy through my body and out the other tentacle, pouring every shred of the life I'm absorbing into the broken man in front of me.

Billy's shadowkind body doesn't feel the same as the people I've healed. Instead of catching hold of solid bones and organs, the healing power I'm sending into him seems to pool through his entire form. Like it's condensing inside him, making every particle of him stronger and more solid.

Whatever it's doing, my efforts appear to be working at least a little.

The rib vanishes into Billy's body. His legs morph back into a more normal configuration.

The plumes of essence taper off, but thinner ribbons of smoke keep winding upward.

Another fish flops onto the dock, and my tentacle flicks to that one, nudging the desiccated corpse of the first into the water. I yank more life energy through me, but I can't tell if my renewed efforts are actually fixing anything in the muddy sense I have of Billy's internal state.

My voice comes out in a croak. "I don't know what else to do. I don't know if I can do anything else."

Pearl smooths her hand over Billy's tan forehead. To my relief, I spot the halting but visible rise and fall of his chest with a breath.

"I think—I think he needs to be back home to totally heal," the succubus says, and glances at Rollick.

The demon nods. "There's a rift just down the coast. Take him as quickly as you can. You'll be able to find me later."

Pearl gathers her friend up in her arms and murmurs something by his ear. A second later, they both waver out of sight into the shadows along the dock.

My chest feels hollowed out. I look up, my thoughts shooting back to Riva, and find her standing near the railing, watching.

She still looks sickly, and in my first glimpse, another shiver ripples through her frame. But she pulls my trench coat tighter around her and draws her back up straighter as if ready to face judgment.

Seeing her in my clothes sends a strange wobble through my gut that's not at all unpleasant. Somehow I manage to reach the ladder before Jacob or Zian do, hurtling up the rungs so I can sling my arm around her.

Riva leans into me, taking comfort in my embrace. Just like that, I'm complete.

I don't care that my mutations are out for everyone to see. I don't care if I look like a monster to anyone looking on.

I am what I am, and I am hers. If she can love me like this, then I'm damn well going to figure out how to at least like what I've become.

"Are you really going to just let them off after what she did to Cinder and the wimp?" Kudzu demands, scowling down at Rollick but, I notice, not daring to step right up to the railing.

Rollick's attention shifts to the gangly shadowkind with a mild glower. Before my eyes, his body contracts.

The ruddy skin pales to a peachier tone. His frame shrinks to a more realistic six-foot-and-a-few.

The horns vanish, and an elegant suit reforms over the planes of now more subdued muscle.

But the aura of power doesn't diminish. It's as if he twisted a dial up to max, and the force of it keeps humming through the air like the peal of a warning bell.

The demon crosses his arms over his chest. "I never said anything about 'letting them off.' There are gradations between turning a blind eye and slaughtering people."

"She *should* be slaughtered—she tore Cinder apart! They all—"

I can't keep my own anger bottled up any longer. I step away from Riva to face him with my hand still on her shoulder.

"You were going to massacre us! Why the hell should we just roll over and die because it'll make you feel better?"

Kudzu bares his teeth at me, but his attention snaps back to Rollick at the clearing of the demon's throat.

"I will decide what's to be done with them on my own time. But frankly, Cinder got what she asked for."

Kudzu's face hardens. He glances at his companions, some silent communication passing between them.

"Fine," he spits out. "Have fun with your psychotic playthings. We aren't sticking around to help."

He leaps into the shadows, there and then gone, and the other four blink out of view within the next thump of my heart. Then it's just the five of us on the deck, clustered around Riva, staring down at the demon who might have saved us… or might be planning a more complicated doom.

Rollick brushes his hands together as if washing them of bad business and meets our gazes steadily.

"You'd better come with me back to the ship. I have some news about your 'facilities,' but it wouldn't be wise to stick around here any longer what with all the commotion we've already caused."

The harbor area we picked is secluded from the rest of the city by a strip of brush, but the faint grumble of early morning traffic reaches my ears. Has some part of this conversation been seen or overheard?

All the same, I balk. "What news?"

Rollick shoots me a baleful look. "Nothing earth-shattering, but enough to potentially point you in the right direction. Are you coming or not?"

At his question, the others all glance… at me. Even Jacob.

As if the fact that I questioned Rollick, the fact that I told off Kudzu however ineffectively, means my opinion carries the most weight.

"Are you going to hurt her?" I ask. I don't know if he'd tell the truth, but I want to at least evaluate his answer.

Rollick's unperturbed expression doesn't shift. "I have no interest in doing so. As long as she doesn't try to shriek the bones out of my body, I think we'll be fine."

"I won't be doing any shrieking if you don't come at us," Riva says in a raw but firm voice. "So there shouldn't be any problems then."

He did stop the others from continuing their attack. I don't know what changed his mind, or whether it hasn't changed at all and he's wanted more time to evaluate us all along, but accepting his offer feels like a safer bet than taking our chances on our own here in Havana.

"Fine," I say.

"But if any more of your idiot 'associates' try to—" Jacob snarls.

Rollick cuts him off with a flick of his hand. "I believe the trash just took itself out, as some of you mortals like to say." He steps toward our boat. "Come on, then. Since you can't travel by shadow, it'll be easiest if we make use of this convenient craft you've already commandeered."

Andreas moves toward the cabin. "I'll drive."

The rest of us unmoor the boat, always making sure there's someone between Riva and Rollick. Not taking any chances about his good graces just yet.

As Andreas starts the engine and sets us cruising out into the low waves, Riva sinks down on one of the benches. She turns toward the demon.

"Will Billy be all right? He'll heal once he's back… home?"

Rollick is already lounging on the bench across from her. "I can't say how long it'll take, but he'll recover. We *can't* die in the shadow realm. We rarely die even in this one unless we're hit with the right tools—or very thoroughly eviscerated, as you demonstrated with another of my colleagues."

Riva's mouth tightens. She gazes out over the water for a few minutes, the rising sun glancing off her silver and slate-gray hair.

Then her fingers twitch toward the trench coat. She slides it off and offers it to me.

"I'm sorry. I should have given this back earlier."

I drop down next to her and grasp her hand. "It's all right. I'm actually… kind of enjoying not being sweltered."

A soft smile crosses her lips, but it looks fragile, like it could easily be shattered. There's still so much pain shining in her gold-flecked eyes that the sight makes my heart ache.

When we approach the large harbor where the massive yacht is docked, Rollick steps into the cabin to direct Andreas. We pull up beside the vessel to scramble onto the pier and then the larger ship.

Rollick jerks his thumb toward our previous ride, looking at someone I can't see who must be lurking in the shadows. "Take care of the boat and head back to Miami for further instructions."

As he sets a few other members of the crew who waver into sight about casting off immediately, one more figure emerges from the patches of darkness along the deck. Torrent leans back against the cabin wall, taking some of the weight off his supporting tentacles that are much thicker than my own.

My heart leaps. If he's back, then Rollick must have been telling the truth at least about the search for the facilities.

I head over to the shadowkind man with my hand still wrapped around Riva's, the other guys following. Rollick strolls over too, although I assume he's already heard whatever Torrent has to report.

"You found the facilities?" Zian asks with a hopeful expression.

Torrent's mouth slants crookedly. "I've identified three spots I think are likely locations of the type of facility you described. I can't tell you for sure whether any or all of them are actually holding other experimental subjects like you."

"Then we'll have to check them out," Andreas says without hesitation.

"We can make decisions about that when we're back in the right country and I have a better idea what we're working with," Rollick says. "For now, why don't you take a moment to breathe and then you can come back to the discussion—and the others we need to have—fresh?"

Riva's free hand tightens around the strap of her backpack. She doesn't say anything about a potential rescue mission, no eagerness showing on her face.

She tips her head toward me, letting her forehead graze my jaw. "I'm going to my room. I think I need a little time alone."

I press a quick kiss to her temple. "Are you sure?"

"Yeah. Don't worry about me."

She squeezes my hand and then lets it go. As she heads into the ship's interior, the ache that formed before clenches hard around my chest.

But the wound inside her now is one I have no idea how to heal.

Thirty

Riva

The light knock on my door makes my lungs constrict where I'm lying on the bed on top of the covers.

Andreas's softly cajoling voice filters through. "Hey, Tink. I brought you a plate from dinner, whenever you're ready to eat."

"Thank you," I say without stirring.

I know he's hoping I'll come to the door or invite him in, that he'll have a chance to talk to me face to face. But the weight bearing down on my chest holds me in place until I sense him stepping away and heading back down the hall.

When I'm sure he's out of view, I push myself up and trudge over. A large part of me doesn't want to do anything except sink into oblivion, but the rest of me knows that's not really an option.

I need food to keep my strength up. I can't just fall apart.

As much as I feel like I already have.

The scents wafting off the plate Andreas prepared provoke a pang in my stomach, but when I sit cross-legged on the bed with the dish on my lap, I find I can only force down a few bites of the creamy pasta and braised asparagus. After that, my throat closes up.

Grimacing at myself, I set the plate on the bedside table for picking at later and flop down on my back again.

The daylight is dimming beyond the small window. I wonder how far we are from land—where exactly we're headed to.

I haven't talked to Rollick about his plans yet. Every time I think about facing him or any of the other shadowkind, I cringe down to my bones.

Our demon benefactor hasn't pressed the issue, so I've avoided it for now. Maybe if I lie here a little longer, I'll know what I want to say.

I'll know how to sort out the mess inside me into something worth hearing.

I'm not sure how much later it is when another set of footsteps approaches my door. I can tell they don't belong to Andreas or Dominic.

My body tenses, bracing for a summons or impatient questions. What actually happens is the lock clicks over and Jacob barges right into the room.

I jerk upward on the covers with a lurch of my pulse. "What are you doing?"

He kicks the door shut behind him but then simply stands in front of it with his arms crossed over his chest, like he sees no problem with invading my privacy but draws the line at infringing on my personal space.

"You've been hiding away in here all day," he says, with an emotion I can't identify smoldering in his icy eyes. "At this point, it's obvious whatever you're doing on your own isn't helping."

I scowl at him automatically, partly because I can't say he's wrong. "And you figure that *you* can help me?"

His gaze seems to pierce right into me the way his poison spines once did. "I think I'm the only one here who knows what it's like to have to live with the fact that you chose of your own free will to hurt someone who didn't deserve it."

His words sock me right in the gut. I flinch, my head drooping.

My voice comes out raspy. "I stopped as soon as I realized who it was."

"I know. And you realized your mistake a hell of a lot faster than I did. So you can at least give yourself credit for that."

I draw my knees up to my chest and hug them. "I proved the shadowkind who wanted us dead right. I showed that I *can't* really control myself—I'll hurt people I wouldn't even want to. I almost *killed* him."

"I almost killed you," Jacob says quietly. "Maybe not quite as directly, but we both know I'm the one who pushed you to the edge. You might not have forgiven me, but you don't seem to think I deserve to be scrubbed off the face of the planet for it either."

Pain and regret resonate through his words. I swallow thickly before looking up at him.

He's got a fresh bandage wrapped where he tried to cut his forearm off this morning. The one I used would have gotten soaked when our shadowkind attackers tossed him in the ocean.

He sounds calmer than he did when he broke down in front of me, but the anguish he expressed clearly hasn't gone anywhere.

I can understand that urge in a way I didn't totally before. If I could cut into my chest and dig out the parts of me that hold my shrieking power, I'm not sure I wouldn't try.

I grapple for a way to respond to his statement. "We had all those years together before. Billy barely knows me except for what I did today. Anyway, him forgiving me isn't the point."

"You forgiving you is," Jacob agrees. "Do you think you were somehow worse than I was? That you deserve worse than I do?"

I close my eyes. Somehow it hurts even trying to answer that question.

"I don't know. I argued with Rollick about practicing more to make sure I had a better handle on my power. I took that gamble, and Billy paid for it."

Jacob's feet whisper across the carpet. The bed dips as he tentatively sinks down on the edge, still a couple of feet away from me.

"You were scared. You were scared, and you got backed into a corner, and you *mostly* managed to only lash out at the people who were actually a threat."

"I'm not sure mostly is ever good enough."

"Maybe not. But I was there too, Riva. He jumped out of the shadows and bolted up the dock so fast—*I* couldn't even tell whose side he was on in that first second, and I wasn't caught up in my powers."

I peek at him through narrowed eyes. "So, what, you're saying it's okay that I bashed him up?"

Jacob's mouth twists as he holds my gaze. "I'm saying it was an honest mistake. If you'd erred in the other direction and he *had* been joining the attack, we could all be dead."

I can't help snorting at the idea of Billy the faun, the sweetest of all the shadowkind we've met, racing in to slaughter us all, but there isn't much humor in the sound.

"I don't like it," I say after a moment of silence. "The way I feel when I'm sending out that power. Or maybe it's that I like it too much. What if using it even more makes it *harder* for me to back away?"

That's the question that's been simmering inside me all day. The fear that's made me balk rather than march straight to Rollick and say we should get on with my training.

What if I end up hurting even more people than I already have?

Jacob considers for a moment before speaking. "I think you'll be able to tell if that's happening, and then we can figure out other strategies to deal with that problem. You don't like how things are now either. Even when you don't know how to fix something, the only thing you can do is keep trying whatever seems most likely, over and over, until hopefully you get there. Right?"

I think from the shadow that's come over his face that he isn't talking just about me now.

I incline my head. "I guess that makes sense. I just—this isn't anything like how I wanted to be. *Who* I wanted to be."

"The guardians took away a whole lot of our choices. But I'm trying to make the most of the choices I do have. I know you, Riva, just like you know me. You aren't going to let yourself become an actual monster. If you could take on the whole fucking facility to get us out of there, you can handle this."

The confidence in his voice brings an unexpected burn to the back of my eyes. "I wish I knew that for sure so I didn't have to be so scared."

Jacob's expression softens. He leans toward me, his hand reaching out —and then falling to the duvet still several inches from where I'm sitting.

His hesitation hangs in the air between us like a tangible thing. He's afraid too—afraid I wouldn't have accepted even a brief touch of comfort from him.

But he was right to come in and insist on talking to me. It is better not being alone, even when my company is him.

Maybe especially because. He's also right that he understands the guilt that's suffocating me in a way I don't think any of the other guys could, not exactly.

As far as I know, they've never hurt anyone that badly except in self-defense or forced by the guardians.

Sitting with Jacob, talking with him, has opened a crack in the weight that was pressing down on me. And seeping through that crack is not just a hint of relief but a tingle of longing.

He brought me back the severed hands of our enemies. He would have cut off his own arm in retribution if I'd let him.

I hate what he did to me… but I have no doubts anymore that he hates his past cruelty just as much. That he is trying, in every way this damaged man knows how, to save me from any further pain.

To give me something better.

I lift my gaze from Jacob's fallen hand to his uncertain face. It takes another moment before I can push the words from my throat—but they feel right when I do.

"If you want to make up for how brutal you were before, why don't you show me how gentle you can be now?"

Jacob's eyes flicker with a momentary widening. Then he eases across the bed and ever so carefully tucks his hand around mine.

He skims his thumb over the back of my hand, feather light. Just his increased closeness and that simple touch wakes up a sharper quiver of need through the shadows in my blood.

I don't have to act on the sudden awakening. I can take the comfort he wants to offer without it having to turn into anything else.

A faint whiff of pheromones suggests that Jacob is grappling with the same desires, but he restrains himself, sticking to my request for gentleness. His thumb skims back and forth over my skin in several slow strokes.

He turns my hand over against his palm and glides the fingers of his other hand over my wrist. A fresh burst of tingles shoots over my skin.

My skin heats, but I sit still and silent, watching him.

He traces the bones of my forearm up to my elbow and back again with the same care. His lips slant into a bittersweet smile.

"You've always looked so delicate. Quite the trick when you're the strongest one out of all of us."

The corner of my mouth quirks upward. "I think Zian might object to that assessment."

Jacob lets out a soft huff. "I'm counting powers *and* physical strength. Zian can't tear someone apart without even touching them."

Somehow he makes my ability sound admirable rather than horrifying. I suddenly remember the way he talked about the massacre in Ursula Engel's house after we'd first escaped.

He said it was "fucking amazing." Called me a superhero.

I was too scarred and incapable of trusting him then for the knowledge to sink in, but he really did mean it, didn't he?

He doesn't think my power is something wrong with me. He thinks I'm amazing, mistakes and all.

Why else would he be here right now, trying so hard to make me believe the same thing?

Jacob twines my fingers with his and raises his other hand to slide his fingertips across my shoulders.

"Even before," he goes on, "I always thought Griffin's nickname for you was silly. *Moonbeam*. Like you were something fleeting, fragile. You were a wildcat all the way through, fierce and unshakable."

My smile tightens. "I don't know about the unshakable part."

Jacob circles his thumb against the crook of my neck in a soothing massage that makes me want to purr. "Look at all the shit everyone's thrown at you, including me, and you're still standing. I say that counts."

I reply with a noncommittal sound, resisting the urge to press into his touch.

Jacob traces his fingers down my spine and up again, with just enough pressure to be soothing. There isn't a trace of his usual rigidity in the caress.

His voice lowers again. "I did understand it better after a while, though. There was this one day at the facility—a few years before we tried to escape; we must have been around thirteen—when we were doing some training thing outside, and the sunlight caught on you just as you turned around and smiled at the rest of us. And I'd swear you fucking glowed."

"Like a moonbeam?" I joke, with a bit of a wobble.

"More than that. And not only your hair. *All* of you just shone."

His hand pauses against the middle of my back, resting there. "You're a hell of a lot more than a moonbeam, Riva. You're our whole goddamned sun. Wherever you go, you bring that warmth with you. You tether us so we don't spiral out into the abyss. How many times have you pulled each of us back from the edge just in the past few weeks?"

The burn comes back to my eyes, hotter than before. "We all had each other's backs."

"But without you there during those four years, the rest of us got lost."

"Without me and Griffin," I feel the need to say.

Jacob starts rubbing my back with his slow, careful rhythm again. "I don't know that it really would have been better if he'd still been there without you."

He falls silent for a stretch, and I don't know what to say.

The brush of his fingers is siphoning off my ability to speak. More heat kindles under my skin with every stroke, but the ache winding around my heart holds the sting of loss.

My losses. His. All of ours.

Jacob drags in a breath. "That moment in the field was when I realized how much I wanted you. But I also knew I wasn't going to act on that feeling. Griffin loved you too, so much—he might have been the one who could read people's feelings, but he was my *twin*, so I sure as hell could read him—and I could see how you were with him… I never would have thought there was even a chance you'd fall for more than one of us."

My throat constricts. "Jake—"

He shakes his head. "It's okay. That's what I'm trying to say. It was okay then, and it's okay now. You don't ever have to want me the way you want Dominic and Andreas. I never expected to have it anyway. I just hope, so much, that we can get to the point that you believe I'll be standing with you through whatever comes at us. Having that would be enough. I'd be happy—hell, I'd be fucking ecstatic with that."

The emotion swelling in my chest bursts through the crack that'd opened, and I don't know how to do anything but turn toward him and tug his mouth to mine.

Jacob's chest hitches beneath my hand, and then he's kissing me back. There's so much tenderness and heat mingled in the press of his lips that I could melt with it.

Nothing about him is icy now. He cups one hand against my cheek and rests the other on my waist.

The shadowy essence inside me flares, clamoring for more.

My fingers slide into the smooth strands of his hair to grasp them and yank him closer. A groan reverberates from Jacob's lungs.

We fall into each other farther, our kisses deepening, our tongues dancing. Every nerve in my body shivers with anticipation.

When my hand creeps up under the hem of Jacob's shirt to trace the ridges of muscle across his abdomen, he groans again and slides his arm farther around my torso. Then he tips us over, pulling me with him so I'm bowed over his body, straddling him.

His voice comes out in murmurs between the collisions of our mouths. "I'm yours. Whatever you want with me, you can have it. This is your show, Wildcat."

His palm grazes my breast, and a whimper tumbles out of me. I know this feeling, this rush of overwhelming hunger that can only be sated one way, and for a moment, I'm lost in it.

Then I turn my head to give Jacob access to my neck. As his lips sear against my skin, my gaze falls across his forearm raised toward me.

This close, I can't miss the faint pock marks where his toxic spines can emerge.

Something flips over in my gut. The remembered sting and the rippling pain flash from the depths of my mind—and break loose a deluge of other memories.

The frigid blue of his eyes when he hurled his accusations at me. The cutting edge to his voice when he chose the best remarks to flay me open from the inside out.

All the thorns he jabbed in my side, over and over, *hoping* to tear me down.

I gasp for air, and a sob comes out instead. A different sort of crack splits me down the middle with a flood of tears.

Jacob jerks back from the kiss as I sag over him. His hands hitch against my body as if he doesn't know what to do with them.

I can't stop the tears from streaming out. They're streaking down my cheeks and pattering across Jake's shirt, and more seem to breach the walls I've held so firm inside me with every choked breath.

All the anguish and confusion I bottled up, all the pain I tried to bear unflinchingly—it never left. It's been stewing inside me all these weeks, and now it's boiling over.

"Riva," Jacob says raggedly, framing my damp face with tentative hands. "Riva, I'm sorry. I'm so fucking sorry."

I tip my head right against his shoulder, and his arms finally come around me, catching me against him in their solid embrace.

This is Jacob too. This is the Jake I knew, even if parts of him have hardened and turned embittered over the last four years.

He said the boy he used to be died, but he's here. He fought his way up through the rage and misery that consumed him so he could be with me.

But maybe I'm still not capable of forgiving him for how much of that rage and misery he inflicted on me before he pulled free from it, not completely.

With a slight rock of his body, he pushes us so we're sitting upright on the bed. "It will never happen again. I swear it. I'd rather cut off my own *head* than hurt you."

Even through my sobs, I believe him.

I'm smearing tears and snot all over his shirt. "Sorry," I mumble as I struggle to rein all that emotion in again.

Jacob only squeezes me tighter. "*You* have nothing to apologize to me for. Not ever." His lips brush my temple. "You're so strong, Riva, but you don't always have to be. I can be your armor when you need it. I know I can do that much."

He *feels* like a suit of armor braced around me, shielding me from the world while I grapple with my tears. Maybe it doesn't make sense that he could protect me when he's the one who set me on this crying jag in the first place, but most of my uneasiness at the explosion of vulnerability fades away.

The embarrassment lingers. When I finally swipe the last tears from my eyes and inhale without a stutter, I keep my head tucked against his shoulder, not wanting to meet his gaze just yet.

"I love you," Jacob says, his voice rough. "You are my sun, my fucking soul. I'm going to keep showing you how true that is for as long as it takes."

I know I'm not ready to say those three words back to him, even if I could have four years ago.

I know I'm not ready to form the connection that would fuse his essence with mine, even if I teetered on the verge just now.

But that doesn't mean I can't recognize that he's been knitting my heart back together from the moment he stepped into my room.

Here with him, with his words and his embrace, I've found some kind of peace.

"Stay?" I whisper against his chest.

Jacob hugs me with a shuddery exhalation that sounds like relief. "As long as you'll let me, Wildcat."

Thirty-One

Riva

I wake up with Jacob's sharply cool scent filling my lungs and a needy ache pulsing between my thighs.

At some point during the night, without really thinking about it, I kicked off my cargo pants, which make for poor sleepwear with all their lumpy pockets. Unwise move.

Now my bare knee is hooked over Jacob's leg beneath the duvet he pulled over us. At least *he's* still wearing his slacks, thank all that is holy.

The rest of my body decided to press up against his while we slept, my hand resting on his chest. My head lies against his shoulder, cushioned by the arm he's still got tucked around me.

I feel the rise and fall of his breath beneath my hand and try to convince myself to pull away. But it isn't just the shadows in my blood shouting at me to twine myself with him even further.

I've recognized how gorgeous he is even when he was acting like a total jackass. My hormones have gone haywire every time he's been close to me, regardless of how the rest of me felt about it.

And now he isn't being a jackass. He shook me out of my self-berating funk yesterday like I'm not sure anyone else could have.

He held me through the whole night like the armor he promised me he'd be.

The thought of giving him my whole heart is still a little terrifying. But fuck, I don't know how I'm going to concentrate while I'm around him when my defenses against my attraction have crumbled so much.

Is it possible I could satisfy some part of that itch without giving in to the most vulnerable bits?

Is it selfish of me to even want that?

Jacob's breath speeds up a little, and the waft of pheromones that laces the air tells me he's awake… and not exactly unaffected by our current position either.

His hand rises to stroke carefully over my hair. I can feel the tight control he's maintaining over the simple movement, over his entire body where it touches mine.

"Okay, Wildcat?" he murmurs.

"Yeah," I say, but even with that one word, my voice comes out a bit ragged.

Jacob twists a little so he can peer down at my face, managing not to dislodge my hand or my knee. I'm not sure if that's for the best or a precursor to my impending doom.

"What?" His tone firms with a protective edge that only fans the flames nibbling away at my own control.

I swallow hard, my cheeks flushing. Am I really going to say this?

I should peel myself off him *now* and jump in the coldest of cold showers.

But somehow I'm still not moving.

Jacob lifts his other hand to brush his thumb over my cheek. He's definitely taking my instructions to prove himself with gentleness to heart.

When I lift my gaze, the worry shimmering in his eyes nearly cracks me apart. "If something's wrong—"

It suddenly feels ten times more selfish *not* to tell him what's actually on my mind.

Which doesn't make it any easier to spit the truth out. I lower my gaze back to the muscled planes of his chest that show through his button-up shirt and fumble with the words.

"No, I just— I think I want— It doesn't seem right to ask—"

Jacob waits out my babbling patiently, his fingers stilling against my face. When I halt completely, he studies me.

"Ask for what, Riva? You can ask me for *anything*. Hell knows I fucking owe you."

My mouth opens and closes again. My flush spreads down my cheeks. "I—Do you think we could—"

I squeeze my eyes shut and force my thoughts into something vaguely resembling coherency. "Could we… enjoy ourselves a little, without it being anything permanent?"

Jacob goes even more rigid, but a fresh whiff of desire tickles my nose at the same moment.

"Without leaving a mark, you mean," he says, his voice lowering in a way that sends my temperature spiking. "Nothing binding us. Just to get off."

"Yeah," I mumble, and then feel I need to make one thing clear. I meet his gaze again even though my face is flaming. "For now."

I'm not making any promises, but I don't want him to think I expect it to be never. That nothing he's done has meant anything.

A small smile that brings a flutter into my chest crosses Jacob's lips. "I told you last night that I'm yours, didn't I? Whatever you want with me, I'm right here. Take as much as you need."

A tight, hungry sound works from my throat, and then I'm rolling right onto him, straddling him like I did last night.

I splay my hands against his sculpted chest and wet my lips. Leaning over for a kiss feels too risky.

If I'm not going to lose myself in the moment and end up careening past boundaries I'd rather not, I need to keep a little distance.

Jacob trails tentative fingers down my neck, but his eyes have gone stormy with his own desire. "What can I do for you, Wildcat?"

The ache between my legs seems to be pulsing all through my body now. "I—touch me. Make me feel *good*."

A groan he can't quite suppress seeps from his lips.

He drops his hand further to trace the side of my breast through my tank top. I press into the contact, shifting my hips at the same time—and my pussy, covered only by the thin panties, grazes the rock-hard bulge behind the fly of his slacks.

Both of our breaths hitch in unison. As the pleasure of the friction spirals from my core, Jacob cups my breast completely.

He rolls his finger over my nipple and then squeezes it. I whimper at the heady sparks the gesture sets off.

My hips rock. I can't stop myself from grinding against him, seeking more of that delicious friction that's quickening both our pulses.

"Fuck," Jacob mutters shakily. He massages my breast with more forceful strokes that bring a whimper to my lips.

He bucks up to meet me, his erection locking against me even more firmly through our clothes, and my fingers dig into his shirt. I'm afraid to do anything else, to ask for anything else, or I might lose my grip on the reins.

Maybe I should stop this. Maybe it was a stupid idea.

But I'm not sure I know how to stop.

Jacob must see the inner conflict playing out on my face. He hesitates for just a second, and then both his hands slide to my thighs.

"I know what you need. Come here."

Before I can ask what he means, he hefts me up without the slightest sign of effort. My muscles might be supernaturally powered, but I'm still tiny compared to him.

In one smooth movement, he lifts me so I'm kneeling over his face instead of his groin. My hands grasp onto the top of the headboard instinctively.

Then Jacob tugs my panties to the side and swipes his tongue over my throbbing cunt.

The starker rush of pleasure shocks a cry from my lungs. As if that's the confirmation he was waiting for, he pushes up to plant his entire mouth against my folds.

His tongue flicks over my clit and down across my opening. He moves his lips against every sensitive part of me, sending quivers of delight racing through every nerve.

Oh, God. I clutch on to the headboard and sway with his attentions, my body outright quaking with the sensations he's conjuring through it.

It felt incredible when Dominic kissed me there, but something about this position makes the act even more potent. I can set the pace; I can adjust the angle when he moves from what's just the right spot.

Jacob follows my lead without complaint or any sign that I'm smothering him. His hands work up and down my thigh muscles as he devours me from below with every part of his mouth, even the softest graze of his teeth.

He plunges his tongue right inside me and then laps all the way to my clit, and I shudder against him with a moan. My hips can't stop bucking, urging him on.

"That's right," he murmurs with a torturous vibration against my pussy. "Ride me for all you're worth."

He dives back in like I'm the best meal he's ever eaten. The pleasure swells until it's resonating through my whole body.

One of my hands falls to grip the rumpled strands of his pale hair. The other grips the headboard as if for dear life.

He sucks down on my clit, and the rising wave breaks.

It crashes over me, washing away every sensation but the surge of blissful release, whiting out my vision. I sputter another cry, lost in the haze.

Jacob keeps moving his mouth against me until my body starts to sag. Then I ease off him, sated but also a little awkward at how up close and personal we just got.

He's buried his face in the most private part of me, and he hasn't even taken off one piece of clothing.

Of course, that was by my choice more than his.

The shadows twist through my veins, yanking at me, but my baser desires are satisfied enough that I can ignore them as I sink into the mattress.

Jacob licks his lips, the gesture so unexpectedly erotic after what he just did that I practically come all over again. He grins at me, looking nothing but satisfied himself.

I've forgotten how absolutely breathtaking he can be when he's actually happy. I don't know if I've gotten a chance to see it since our escape.

He can't be that happy, can he? His erection is still straining against his slacks.

But he sits up before I can think about offering to repay the favor, his grin unwavering.

"That is exactly how you should always look, Wildcat."

I hesitate. "Do you want—"

He shakes his head before I can finish. "I'm good. That was about you. And it's *really* good to be able to give you something that lights you up for a change."

A different sort of embarrassment heats my cheeks. "I feel like I used you."

He fixes with me a look both heated and determined. "Riva, it's a fucking privilege to be used by you. If that's what you need, I will eat you out every day of the year and take the blue balls as a badge of honor."

Okay, now my cheeks might scald right off. "Um…"

Before I can decide how to respond, reality crashes back into the room with a jaunty rapping on my door.

The heat of our interlude drains out of me. My body tenses, knowing it's Rollick before the demon even speaks.

His voice calls through the door, as lively as his knock. "Rise and shine, little banshee. Breakfast is being served, and then I think it's time we talked. The porcupine can come too."

His summons wipes away the last wisps of the afterglow even as Jacob grunts in mild objection at the sardonic description of him. My heart sinks.

We're on Rollick's ship. We're alive and well because of his mercy.

And after seeing his full demonic form, I'm really not inclined to test his patience or his generosity.

I caught up even *him*, with his millennia of built-up power, in my scream for at least the short while it lasted before I wrenched myself out. That fact is both incredible and unnerving.

I don't think he's going to forget any time soon that I can be a threat to him. One he might want to squash if I start looking like I'm more trouble than I'm worth.

"I'll be there," I reply, sucking in a breath, and gird myself to face the comeuppance I got to put off yesterday.

Thirty-Two

Riva

I'm not really in any state to immediately head to breakfast, regardless of the gurgle of my stomach reminding me that I barely ate anything all yesterday.

I dig through my backpack for a change of clothes and then look up at Jacob. "I'm going to take a quick shower. Er, alone."

The corner of Jacob's mouth ticks upward with a hint of amusement even as his eyes smolder.

"I think I'd better grab one of those myself, with the water set to ice-cold."

He gets off the bed and then reaches to give my shoulder a quick squeeze before he leaves.

"You are all right, aren't you?"

After everything that passed between us last night, that question could refer to a whole lot of things. Maybe all of them.

I pause in the stream of sunlight pouring through the window and really take stock of my internal state.

A whole lot of me still feels tender when prodded. The lump of guilt in my gut hasn't completely dissolved, and I can't say my emotions about the guy I just got awfully close with are free of snarls either.

But beneath the jumbled, painful bits, or maybe around them, my sense of myself holds steady. I was shaken yesterday, but I seem to have found my footing again.

"I will be," I say, and Jacob nods as if that's the best answer he could have expected.

"I'll see you in the dining room, then."

I can't let him just leave like that. He reaches for the door, and his name tumbles from my lips.

"Jake."

He glances back at me, his forehead starting to furrow.

I find I can manage at least half a smile. "Thank you."

For talking me down last night. For shielding me through the night.

For helping me work out other tensions just now…

Jacob's stance relaxes, as much as the guy ever relaxes. "I should be the one thanking you."

He strides out of the room with the athletic poise I can't help admiring now that I'm letting myself feel more than angry at him.

In the ensuite bathroom, I scrub myself all over hastily, taking just a moment to enjoy massaging the fancy shampoo that was part of the bath set Andreas got for me into my hair. The citrus tang wakes up my senses even more.

To face the conversations ahead, I need to be alert and honest and bold. But I have my men with me, in more ways than one.

We're going to get through this too.

I twist my hair into its usual braid even though it's still damp after the toweling and slip out into the hall. Dominic emerges from his room at the exact same moment—which is probably not a coincidence, since he must have known I was on my way out.

It gives me a little thrill I can't totally explain to see him standing assured with his tentacles out in the open. To stop them from dangling at his feet, they fall to his waist and then loop back around to hook over their bases, swaying a little as he steps to meet me.

He'll have to cover up again when we venture out into normal society. But he isn't ashamed for me or any of the shadowkind here to see them anymore.

Even with all the worries still weighing on me, I can't resist pulling him into a hug. Dom hums happily as he hugs me back and presses a kiss to the corner of my jaw.

"You look like you're feeling better, Sugar," he murmurs by my ear.

The new nickname sends a giddier thrill right down the middle of me.

I tip my head against his chest. "I just… needed some time to come to grips with things. Jacob helped."

Another blush tingles in my cheeks, but if Dominic can guess what some of that "help" entailed, I don't think he minds. He strokes his hand over my hair before we ease apart to head to the dining room.

"I'm glad you and him are sorting things out. He was awful, and of course you've been angry, but I know that's not who he really is."

My smile turns crooked. "Maybe we're all still figuring out who we really are now."

Dom pauses for a moment in his contemplative way. "That sounds about right."

The smells of buttery eggs and fried sausages tickle into my nose and set my stomach growling again. My mouth is watering before I even step through the dining room doorway—and then it dries up as I halt in my tracks with a stutter of my pulse.

Pearl has come back. She's perched on the edge of one of the tables, talking with the hulking green-skinned shadowkind who's occasionally emerged as part of Rollick's crew.

As my legs lock, she tosses her glossy blond waves over her shoulder and glances around. When her bright eyes meet mine, the succubus's friendly expression twitches.

I expect her smile to stiffen into a frown, but instead she hops off the table and ambles over to me, if with a little less energy than her typical pace.

"Have you eaten yet? The croissants are extra good today."

My mouth opens and closes and opens again. "I— No. I was just going to get breakfast now."

"Well, come on then. Rollick's stalking around looking like he's building so many plans in his head he'll fall over if he doesn't get the chance to let them out soon."

I follow her tentatively over to the buffet spread. Dominic veers over to the other guys, who've all gathered around one table.

Zian nods to me, and Andreas shoots me a warm grin, but they seem to recognize that they shouldn't interrupt.

I didn't think I was going to see Pearl again. I didn't think she'd want to see me.

I haven't prepared for this conversation, but it's one I know I need to have at least as much as whatever's coming with our host.

Food ends up on my plate somewhat by random rather than any

conscious selection process, because my mind is too busy spinning around what I'm going to say to focus on my options. Pearl grabs herself another croissant and plops into a chair at an otherwise empty table.

I'm not totally sure she wants me to follow, but a day hiding from my screw-ups is long enough.

I carry my plate over and sit down across from her. "I didn't realize you'd come back."

She shrugs in her artfully careless way and takes a bite of her croissant. "I like working with Rollick. And you all have been very interesting."

Interesting isn't the word I'd have thought she'd use. I hesitate, poking my fork into a sausage. "Is Billy healing okay?"

"Oh, yeah, as soon as we got into the shadow realm, everything started binding itself together just fine. It's a pretty dreary place, but it's easier to relax when you're surrounded by the same stuff you're made of."

The reassurance only eases a little of the tension inside me. I force myself to dig into my breakfast, thinking she might bring up any grievances she has, but Pearl chews merrily away, apparently content in my silence.

"I don't know if he's going to want to see me again," I say finally, "so the next time you visit him, if you could tell him how sorry I am. I never meant—I wouldn't have done it if I'd been totally in control."

Pearl snorts. "I didn't think you would have."

I peer at her, still struggling to gauge her reaction. "Aren't *you* upset at me? He's your friend, and I— It could have been you."

The succubus hesitates, turning the last bit of croissant between her fingers. She glances at me.

"You think I don't know how powers can get a grip on you when you haven't had much practice using them?"

I stare at her. "I—I have no idea." I'd kind of gotten the impression that shadowkind came into being simply knowing what they could do and how to wield those talents effectively.

Pearl's gaze slides away from me again. "In one of my early feeds, I had my hand down the guy's pants before I realized that he was terrified under the lust I'd stirred up. He didn't want it at all. We cubi can get glimpses inside people's heads, you know. To make sure they're a good target. The more they're into it, the better it is. But I was *really* hungry, and he was curious at first, and I… just kind of tuned out the bad signs until I'd practically…"

Her mouth tightens, and my chest constricts in sympathy. I can imagine how that kind of realization feels all too vividly.

Pearl shakes herself and manages to brighten as she yanks her gaze back to me. "So I'd be an awful hypocrite if I got mad at you for not having perfect control over your scream-y power."

Even so, I feel the need to make one thing clear. "I'm going to do some training with Rollick, like he's been pushing for. I want to get as much control as I can."

"I'm sure he'll be *very* happy about that. He does like to get his way."

Pearl pops the last piece of croissant into her mouth and lets out a pleased hum. Watching her, it's hard to reconcile the bubbly young woman she looks like so often with the pained regret she expressed just moments ago.

After she swallows, she wags a finger at me. "It's everyone, really. I don't know why, because I've never talked to another cubi who has this—although I guess I haven't met a whole lot of them yet—but after I hook up with a mortal to feed, they always start spilling some deep dark secret they feel awful about. Maybe they can tell I'm not going to blab to anyone they know, so it's a safe way to unload."

I grimace. "That sounds… unpleasant."

"Yeah, it kind of kills the mood. I haven't figured out how to stop it happening. But hearing all those confessions has made it very clear that everybody's done bad things. I figure what matters is whether they care enough to try to do better afterward."

She sounds so genuine that more of the guilt congealed inside me disintegrates. I still want to apologize directly to Billy if he's willing to give me the chance, but maybe I don't have to feel like a total monster.

Or at least not more of one than the actual monsters.

As if summoned by that thought, Rollick saunters into the dining room and sweeps his gaze over all of us with an imperious air. "Are you semi-mortals fueled up yet? We've got decisions to make."

I gulp down the rest of my breakfast at lightning speed and dart over to join my guys. Rollick stays standing, leaning his hands against the back of an empty chair as he considers us.

"I'm sorry about the mess in Havana," I say right off the bat, even though technically the messy parts were mostly Jacob's fault. But he was acting to protect me. "And, um, pissing off most of your crew."

Rollick makes a dismissive sound. "Over the centuries, I've come to terms with the fact that most of my kind are very narrow-minded."

Dominic is studying him, his eyes wary. "When the bunch of you first showed up, you sounded like *you* weren't sure we were more than a liability."

Zian's brawn tenses at the reminder, but Rollick simply chuckles.

"It *was* a mess. I can't say I appreciated needing to clean it up. But it became obvious in the confrontation that my people were at least as much to blame for that as you were."

I can't hold back my incredulous question. "The confrontation… where I killed one of them and nearly did the same to another?"

The demon cocks his head. "You enforced your authority when the people you cared about were threatened and reined yourself in before you went too far overboard. What more proof could I need that you *can* control yourself, if imperfectly? I can work with that. And I think you understand the necessity of said work now too."

I swallow thickly. "I do."

"Why do you want to work with us?" Jacob asks brusquely. "Why don't you figure it'd be easier to destroy us like the others wanted to?"

Well, that's one way to put it all on the table.

Rollick offers a slanted smile. "I have hundreds if not thousands of years more experience than most of my associates can draw on. And some very specific experiences that have suggested that the merging of human and shadowkind can save the world more often than ending it. It seems that the mortal side acts as a decent moderator for those talents… Possibly being so much closer to possible death makes you more inclined to prevent it on the whole."

"You said you'd only met one other hybrid before," Andreas says.

"Yes, well…" The demon's voice softens slightly. "The mortal I happen to love once wielded a power that was more threatening and horrifying to shadowkind than anything the bunch of you have, and she proved it could be used to boost us up rather than bind us. So I have learned not to make assumptions."

He rocks back on his heels, scanning us with renewed analytical curiosity. "And in general, I don't believe in destroying potential resources. I'd very much like to see what you shadowbloods can do given the freedom to make your abilities your own—and that includes your younger counterparts, if we can locate them."

I'm not sure how I feel about being considered a "resource," but his last words capture my attention. "We're going to break them out? You're going to help us do it?"

"I think that course of action is the most likely to diminish your 'guardians' ability to track you, since none of our experiments have borne any fruit so far." Rollick glances toward the dining room windows. "My people in the cities along the southern coast have noticed some activity that suggests they're aware that you've been at sea and are attempting to be prepared for your return."

My stomach knots. "So we'll have to go through them to get to the younger shadowbloods?"

"If what you've said is true, I'd imagine most of their experimental subjects are still back in their facilities. We could start there. The more allies we have on our side, the greater our options."

Zian perks up. "Torrent said he'd found a few facilities—or he thought he had."

Rollick nods. "It would simply be a matter of determining which if any of those your counterparts are being held at and getting them out."

Nothing in that statement sounded particularly simple, but my pulse kicks up a notch in anticipation.

"How are we going to figure out the first part?" Dominic asks. "Are your people going to sneak inside and scope things out?"

Rollick's expression darkens a little. "Unfortunately, that's impossible. Your guardians are obviously familiar with shadowkind ways—and weaknesses. One of the factors that helped Torrent identify the likely locations was the presence of a lot more silver and iron than most of us can easily tolerate. Going straight in would likely be a suicide mission."

My spirits deflate. I guess the shadowkind could watch from afar, but who knows how long it'd taken them to confirm what's going on in those places?

Whatever shadowbloods might be in the facilities, they'll be locked away down in the depths like we were most of the time. Who knows how securely the guardians are holding them now?

At the new building where I found the guys after our first escape attempt, there wasn't even a training field for a small break from captivity…

The answer hits me so squarely I could smack myself for not thinking of it right away.

"*We* can find them," I say. "It's in our blood. We've lived the same lives as them. Maybe we don't know their names or what most of them look like, but I think—if we focus on the parts we do have, the things we all would have gone through—I think our essence will lead us to them."

Those experiences are imbedded deeper in us than anything you could see in a video recording. We *know* the other kids the guardians have held captive, better than anyone else could.

The guys all sit up a little straighter, their eyes flashing at my words. I can tell the idea feels as right to them as it does to me.

Rollick rubs his jaw. "We don't know for sure that your blood play will work with impressions that vague."

I raise my chin. "It's worth a try. It'd be a hell of a lot faster than hoping your spies will spot something from outside the buildings." I hesitate. "But we'd have to make sure the guardians don't track *us* down while we're following the trail."

A small smile crosses Rollick's lips. "That much I can help with."

He leans forward with his hands braced against the top of the chair. "I'm willing to help you with this because it serves my purposes too. But most of the risk won't be mine. As I've already mentioned, we won't be able to go into the buildings with you."

Andreas frowns. "You have some abilities you can use at a distance, don't you?"

"To a small degree. Even with those… The helmets and vests these mortals wear will protect them from most influence we could exert from afar."

So that was what the guardians' strange uniforms had been about. They must have hoped the metals would give them some small bit of protection against our powers too.

But it hadn't worked. We hybrids really are that much more powerful than the full shadowkind.

No wonder Engel was afraid of us. No wonder the shadowkind are too.

I inhale slowly to steady myself. "What does that mean for us, then?"

Rollick's smile has turned grim. "My people would do what we can on the outside—to draw the mortals out and dispose of any who step beyond the stronger protections. We can be prepared to carry the young ones you rescue to safety as soon as they're out. But it'd be up to the five of you to handle everything inside the building, on your own."

A solemn silence descends over the table as we let that declaration sink in.

Just the five of us, unaffected by the guardians' protective measures but with powers we're still struggling to control, no ability to dart away into the shadows if the fight turns against us, no shadow realm we can turn to in order to repair our injuries.

The demon's voice softens. "Do you really want to do this? We can hold off your pursuers from this ship for a long time. If you'd rather, I have no problem with simply continuing to cruise around while continuing our experiments. We may still find another way to cut off their ability to track you."

The thought of sticking to the security of the yacht, of enjoying gourmet food and curling up in my cozy bedroom at night, wraps around me like a warm blanket. It's so tempting.

But the next image that floats through my mind is of my cell in the facility.

The cramped space with its narrow, hard bed.

The plates of bland food delivered through a slot.

The barrage of orders, day in and day out.

All the hurt and destruction we carried out on the guardian's whim.

All the pain they dealt out to us if we resisted.

The younger shadowbloods are living like that right now. If Engel's notes were correct, their powers are weaker than ours.

They have no hope of escape unless we come for them. How could I sit on my ass in luxury while they're being tormented?

And Rollick can't be sure that we really will stay safe on this ship anyway. For now, the guardians are simply preparing for battle along the coast—but they've taken us by surprise before.

None of us—me and my men, our shadowkind allies, or the younger shadowbloods in captivity—will really be safe and free until the guardians can't reach us any longer.

Glancing around the table, I see the same resolve forming in my men's eyes. I feel it humming through my marks from Andreas and Dominic.

I broke in to rescue them all on my own. With the help of Rollick and other shadowkind, with the five of us working together, we have to be able to take on whatever the facility holds.

Or we'll die trying.

I turn back to Rollick with a knot of apprehension forming in my gut but not a single trace of doubt.

"We need to get them out of there. Whatever it takes. As soon as we can find them."

Thirty-Three

Zian

I should probably stop being surprised by how fancy every vehicle Rollick owns is. I mean, do private jets that *aren't* fancy even exist?

The leather seats are wide enough that I don't feel at all squished even when the middle arm is in place, and padded enough that I can sink right into the cushioning. The bathroom is nearly as big and shiny as the one attached to my bedroom on the yacht.

It's too bad I can't enjoy the fanciness more. My pulse is thrumming through my veins at a heightened pace, and it speeds up even more when Rollick swivels his seat into the aisle so he can face all five of us.

"It'll be difficult to come up with a definitive plan before we know what location we're dealing with," he says. "But I've made my calls, and I have people on standby with the supplies to create some excellent disruptions."

Riva straightens up in her seat. "And to get the shadowbloods we break out to someplace safe."

The demon inclines his head. "Of course. I'm not sure how close we'll be able to bring any vehicles while avoiding detection, but we'll carry the young ones on our backs if we need to."

He pauses with a slight grimace. "Unfortunately I won't have as much backup for this mission as I'd prefer… Kudzu and his friends have spread the word through the community. Quite a few of my typical associates balked at getting involved, and I prefer to work with willing help."

"We wouldn't really be able to count on them if you were forcing them into it anyway," Andreas says from where he's sitting in front of me.

"There's that too. But qualms don't apply to my material resources, so we're still well covered there." Rollick's dark eyes glint with amusement.

I haven't been able to tell how much this "mission" is important to him and how much he sees it as a game to pass the time. But I guess it doesn't really matter as long as we pull it off.

He clasps his hands in his lap, squaring his shoulders as if bracing himself. I understand why when he makes his next announcement.

"Also in the interests of avoiding detection… you need to be prepared that if we identify a facility where your counterparts are being held, you won't be able to charge straight at it. That'll give them time to realize you're coming."

I knit my brow. "Won't they have more time if we take longer getting there?"

Rollick's gaze settles on me. "The problem isn't really the time. It's how obvious you make it where you're going. If we don't want them picking up on your route… the five of you will need to split up to make the journey."

A jolt of horror shoots through my body. We haven't been more than a few hundred yards apart from each other in weeks.

The whole point is that we're in this together.

Dominic tenses in his spot behind Riva. "You want us to go off on our own?"

Rollick shakes his head. "Not entirely. I think it should be enough to break off into two groups and then take an indirect route to reach the facility. I have two helicopters already standing by at the airfield we're headed to. We only need to confuse the tracking efforts enough to obscure your intended destination."

Jacob leaps out of his seat, his eyes flashing. "I'm staying with—"

He cuts himself off as he swings around and his gaze sweeps over all four of us. His stance goes rigid, but he dips his head. "No. Never mind. Riva should have Dom and Drey with her. They've proven themselves."

My throat constricts with a pang, both at his clearly pained acceptance—and the knowledge that I'm excluded from that proven circle too.

Before any of the rest of us can jump in, Riva clears her throat. "I don't like the idea of us splitting up at all. But it does make sense. And if we have to, I think either Dominic or Andreas should be in the other group. That way, no matter what happens, we'll be able to find each other."

Her hand brushes over her collarbone where she showed us the marks that've formed on her skin.

The two guys who share those marks tighten their expressions, but neither argues.

The demon is watching our discussion with apparent interest. In the momentary silence, he speaks up.

"That sounds like solid strategy. I'd also suggest that your two physical powerhouses should split up between the groups, so that both have physical might if you need it."

That means me and Riva. There's no chance of me staying by her side, even if I deserved the spot.

But he's right. "That's fine," I mutter reluctantly.

Andreas pushes to his feet like Jacob has so he can more easily look at all of us. "I'll go with Zian, then. The two of us should make a good team if we run into any trouble before we meet up again."

He hesitates and catches Riva's gaze. "As much as I'd like to be right there with you the whole way, I'd rather know you've got Dom nearby in case you're injured."

Riva aims a baleful look at him. "I don't want any of *you* dealing with injuries on your own either."

"I can't be with both groups, as much as *I* would like that," Dominic says in his usual quiet way. "I think we'll all feel better if I'm with you."

I can't help nodding.

Riva lets out a huff. "So I'm outvoted, is what you're saying?"

Jacob has noticeably brightened since it turned out he was getting to stick with Riva after all. "Four to one. No complaining."

She wrinkles her nose at him, but there's more fondness in her gaze than I've seen her direct at him in weeks.

He's reconnected with her too, if not as fully as Drey and Dom have. All at once, my skin itches with the sense that I've found myself separate from our group in a totally different way.

I tried to talk to her the other day on the ship, but I don't know if she really understood what I was getting at. I don't know how to convey half of the things I'm feeling.

And one very big part of it I'd rather not even think about.

I want her to know I'll be here for her as much as I can be, though. That she means just as much to me as she does to the other guys.

How much more time do we have before she's going to be walking away from me, and I might not even get the chance?

As I grapple with my doubts, Rollick chuckles. "It sounds like it's settled, then."

With the discussion over, Riva squirms over toward the window where the sunlight is beaming in. We've all taken a double row for ourselves, sliding the armrest in the middle out of sight so it's like one long seat instead of two.

My chest clenches up as if my ribs are closing in on my lungs. I close my eyes, picturing the move I want to make.

Reassuring myself that I can do this, just this, and it won't be anything like the moments I'm avoiding.

Bit by bit, I gather my self-control. Then I push myself out of my seat and cross the aisle with two careful steps.

"Can I sit with you for the rest of the trip?"

Riva's head snaps around. She blinks at me, obviously startled—and then a small smile crosses her lips.

"Of course. I'd like that."

It feels like a much greater feat than it probably should to lower myself into the seat next to her. Even with my broad frame taking up plenty of space, she's so tiny in comparison that I don't need to worry I'm crowding her as long as I keep to my side.

Riva peers up at me with a little mischief dancing in her bright brown eyes. "Got lonely all by yourself?"

Despite her teasing, I can see the uncertainty in her expression. That's exactly why I needed to do this.

I fumble with my words. "I—I wanted to be close to you for a while, before we have to split up. So you remember that I've got your back too. Even if I'm not right there with you."

The amusement fades from Riva's gaze, softened into something more bittersweet. "I know that, Zee."

"Well, I thought—I thought it'd be good to really show it."

My face has heated to the point that I think it might burn right off my skull, but Riva doesn't laugh at me. She just keeps looking at me with that soft shimmer in her eyes that makes my heart beat twice as fast.

From the tilt of her body, I think she might have reached over and held my hand or something if the situation were different. If I hadn't flinched away every time she's touched me in the past.

I've come this far. I can manage a little more, right?

Slow and calm, totally controlled. Only one precise movement, nothing a friend couldn't offer another friend.

I lift my arm and ever so carefully extend it in offering to wrap around her shoulders. Riva's eyes widen, and then she scoots a little closer to accept the gesture.

I rest my arm across her back, my hand settling loosely to cup the peak of her shoulder. Riva exhales, and her muscles relax against mine.

"Are you sure this is okay?" she asks in a voice as careful as my embrace.

My nerves are jumping around like they've been zapped with a live wire, half panicked, half begging for more. But when I hold still in this position, I can tune them out enough to say, "Yeah. It should always be. We're blood, right?"

"Always," Riva murmurs happily, and leans in to nestle her head against my chest.

I don't have words for the joy that clangs through every inch of my body at her acceptance. I just wish it didn't come with an equal portion of fear.

I have her with me now. What's going to happen in the fight ahead of us?

For the rest of the flight, I barely dare to move. I know that no unwanted flares of emotion will spark inside me as long as I stay just like this.

As we begin the descent, Riva straightens up so she can buckle her seatbelt. The loss of contact wrenches at me.

But once she's secured the belt, she holds out her hand. Not touching mine, just giving me the option.

I hesitate, gathering my resolve, and curl my fingers around hers.

The plane touches down with a bump and a light jostling. My stomach sinks with the knowledge that the hardest part of this mission is still ahead and approaching faster by the second.

We tramp out of the private jet into a field of close-cropped grass surrounded by nothing but trees. There are no buildings in sight, but the two helicopters Rollick mentioned are waiting at the far end of the field.

The demon turns to us. "All right, let's get on with your essence trick. Who's doing the honors?"

"I will," Jacob says without missing a beat.

Riva shakes her head. "I think we all should. We all went through something a little different. If we're all focusing together… we can go by wherever the most essence flows. That should give us the clearest picture."

Her suggestion makes sense to me. I will my wolfish claws from my fingertips.

Riva gives Jake one last pointed glance. "We shouldn't need very *much* from each of us."

He offers a crooked grin in response. "I won't cut too deep this time, Wildcat."

Jacob extends his spines. Andreas and Dominic retrieve the knives they've armed themselves with from their pockets.

Without speaking, we slice thin scratches across our forearms at the same time.

A streak of blood seeps across my skin—and a puff of dark smoke wavers up into the fresh, foresty air. I watch it for a moment and then close my eyes.

Remember the halls and the training rooms. The little bedroom where the guardians shut me away every night.

The blades they sliced into me.

The prod they jolted me with.

All the things, inanimate and living, they made me smash with tests of my strength and will.

Are there other shadowbloods like me trapped in their facilities now? Being tormented in the same ways?

I want to find them. I want to reach out to them so we can pull them out of that nightmare.

So we can all live free together.

Rollick lets out a soft chuckle. "Well, I'd say that's fairly definitive."

My eyes snap open. My breath stops at the sight of the smoke trails streaming out in front of us.

All five wafts of essence have converged into one larger current. A few little trickles veer off in a variety of directions, but by far the most floats away from us to my right, toward the sun that's dipping toward the western horizon.

"One of the locations we had our eye on is a couple hundred miles in exactly that direction," the demon says with the slightest hint of awe. "The other two are nowhere near it. I suppose we know where we're going now."

As we lower our arms, he swipes his hands together in a brisk gesture. "Which means you'd better get going. I've left tablets and phones in the helicopters along with the rest of the equipment we discussed—I'll be sending your pilots flight plans and you all the details I have so far on that specific possible facility. You can look them over on the way there and discuss how you want to proceed. And please keep me in the loop."

"Where are you going to be?" I ask.

He motions to the jet. "I'll take a more direct route, as close as I can get, and make sure our ground support is in place."

Andreas has moved to join me. Riva turns toward the two of us, a flicker of worry crossing her face.

She darts to Drey, and he catches her in his arms. I avert my gaze as they collide with a kiss so potent my skin prickles with my awareness of it.

"We'll see you soon, Tink," he promises, a little hoarsely.

As Riva eases back from him, her gaze slides to me. My body balks, but the images from the facility are still floating in the back of my mind.

What if I never get another chance to do anything at all?

I step forward and tentatively wrap my arms around her. Riva hugs me back with all the strength that's wound through her slim form.

My pulse hiccups, but I find the determination to lower my head and press a kiss to her hair.

My stomach twists itself into a dozen knots. I can feel the other guys watching me, wary and concerned.

On my behalf, or hers?

None of that really matters, though. Not when she releases me and I see the brilliant smile that's lighting up her face, just for me.

"Stay safe, Shrimp," I tell her, as if I'm not worried at all.

Our two groups veer apart as we hustle over to the choppers. I clamber on board, ignoring the nervous tension coiling around my gut as well as I can.

Our pilot materializes out of the shadows into the cockpit. "Your equipment's in the bag there," she says, and starts the motor whirring.

Andreas yanks the door shut and drops into the seat next to me. He glances over, his gray eyes a little darker than usual.

"You've got to tell her, you know."

He doesn't need to spell out what he's talking about. My body goes rigid.

I push through it, reaching for the duffel bag on the floor. "Did you tell her how it was for *you*?"

Drey sinks into the seat with the lurch of the chopper taking off. "Yeah. She didn't blame me for it. She knows none of that shit was our choice."

My hands ball, my claws prickling at my fingertips again.

What he told her isn't half as bad as my own story. It's not even in the same ballpark.

"You could figure something out with her if she knew what you're dealing with," Andreas adds in a gentler tone.

My voice comes out gruff. "We'll see. We've got bigger things to worry about right now."

We're about to break back into one of the facilities. The last place on Earth I'd ever have wanted to go.

And I've got to make sure every one of my friends and the woman I love make it back out again with me.

Thirty-Four

Riva

I pull the black cap tight over my hair and tuck the end of my braid under the springy fabric. Then I slip my cat-and-yarn pendant under my shirt collar, both for safe-keeping and to keep it out of view.

We might not be able to merge right into the shadows, but the stealth gear Rollick got for us cloaks us in darkness from head to toe.

As I hop out of the helicopter after Dominic, Jacob right at my heels, the thick fabric of the mock turtleneck and athletic pants presses against my flexing muscles. The Kevlar in it should protect us from knife slashes and the jab of a tranquilizer dart.

If the guardians decide they'd rather kill us than recapture us, the thin but dense padding across the torso and throat should help protect us from regular bullets. There isn't much that could properly shield our heads, though.

We're working with a balance of security and flexibility so we can dodge the attacks we can't absorb.

Pistols of our own rest against our hips in the dual holsters that hang from our belts. We're prepared in every possible way in case our supernatural abilities aren't enough to get us through the trials ahead.

The military-grade gear should add to my confidence. But as we hustle through the stretch of forest between our landing site and the facility, draped in the shadows of the early night, my pulse wobbles with uncertainty.

No matter how much reconnaissance Rollick's people were able to gather, they've only observed the outside of this place. We have no idea what's waiting for us *inside*, other than it'll probably look uncomfortably like the prisons we've already escaped.

I can't help feeling like a kid playing dress-up, pretending at being the superhero Jacob once claimed I am when I don't actually have any clue how to fight a war.

Go in, take down any guardians who get in our way, get the other shadowbloods out. That's our mission, boiled down to its simplest essence.

Whatever complications arise along the way… we'll just have to deal with them as they come.

A familiar figure wavers out of the gloom up ahead. Rollick tips his head to us silently and makes a few brisk gestures.

After our urgent phone conversations hashing out the initial plan, I follow his meaning well enough.

His people have disabled the few guardians who were patrolling outside the facility's protections. They're waiting to escort the younger shadowbloods to the camouflaged vans parked on the nearest road.

The facility itself is just up ahead.

We nod in acknowledgment, and Rollick vanishes again. My stomach twists tighter.

The shadowkind have a few more tricks up their sleeves, but once we cross the protective barrier that wards them away, we're on our own.

Then again, that's how we started. And for all Rollick's wealth and influence, it's always come down to the five of us when the shit has hit the fan.

If we can't pull off this mission, if we can't even protect the kids who are going through the same things we did, then what was the point of claiming our freedom to begin with?

As the trees start to thin, a glimmering trail catches my eyes through the underbrush up ahead. One of Rollick's allies—one of the few who wasn't too terrified of us to join in the operation—laid down a line of phosphorescence to show us where the boundary of anti-shadowkind protections lies.

They can't cross over that line—at all or without being significantly weakened. Our job is to get the younger shadowbloods past the barrier so the shadowkind can escort them the rest of the way to safety.

All of us know how to slink silently across terrain like this. I don't hear or see our companions approach, but the tingle of my mark tells me Andreas is getting closer.

Jacob, Dominic, and I pause at the edge of the clearing that holds this facility. I glance in the direction where I can sense Andreas is just arriving, twenty feet away.

We can't risk any sound passing between us. I have to assume he wouldn't be here if he and Zian weren't ready.

Then I turn my attention on the structure ahead of us.

From the photographs and descriptions Rollick's people passed on, I had some idea what to expect. Still, seeing the place for real, turned ominous by the darkness, makes my gut drop to my feet.

Here, the guardians took a different tactic from what we're used to. There's no electrified fence, no secure concrete bunker hiding the labyrinth of levels underneath.

They were counting mainly on disguise this time. The nearest proper road is miles away, so no one's likely to stumble on it. All their supplies must be coming on foot or by helicopter to the small clearing at the base of the cliff we're facing.

The cliff that holds the gaping black maw of a cave.

The guardians built this facility into the intimidating natural features of the landscape. The cave opening looms at least ten feet high and nearly the same across, surrounded by mossy crags of stone.

It's pitch black beyond the small strip of moonlight that touches the very edge of the yawning entrance. We have no idea what we're dealing with even before we've gone inside the building itself.

Andreas and Zian steal over to join us. Relief washes through my chest at having our group all together again.

Without speaking, we move farther around the clearing, over to the side. We're going to help clear the way into the facility, but the shadowkind are going to kick off our invasion.

Our allies must be watching. The second we've gotten into place, a resonant *boom* reverberates through the woods, shaking the ground beneath our feet.

As I grab hold of a tree trunk to steady myself, the sound of another blast rattles my eardrums.

Firelight dances through the trees beyond the other side of the clearing. We pull back a little deeper into the forest to ensure its glow doesn't reveal us.

Then we simply watch.

Three guardians in the familiar metal helmets and vests dash from the mouth of the cave. Guns glint in their hands.

One raises a walkie talkie with the other to report to colleagues inside. They march to the edge of the clearing, peering at the flames, but don't venture farther into the forest.

They're being more cautious than when I broke the guys out. Maybe the surviving guardians from that escape told stories about how I diverted them.

This bunch *shouldn't* have any idea that we were heading their way or that we'd even want to invade their workplace. But with every passing moment, the chances increase that the guardians who've been tracking us will figure out where we've converged and spread the word.

Every instant could make a difference.

Thankfully, it doesn't take long for more guardians to come loping out of the cave. A dozen of them set off through the trees to investigate the fire, but five hang back by the cave entrance, scanning the entire clearing.

Yes, they've definitely gotten smarter. But I don't think they've gotten stronger.

We can take five no problem.

I flick my claws from my fingertips.

We don't want to use the guns yet if we can help it. It's better if the guardians who've ventured farther away from the facility don't realize there's trouble back here.

The main force of guardians vanishes into the darkness of the woods. And we launch ourselves forward.

Before we've even reached them, Jacob has already flung two of the figures against the cliffside, denting their helmets and cracking their skulls against the jutting crags. Zian snarls and pummels one into the ground with a heave of his fist.

I throw myself at the figure nearest to me and plunge my claws right into his throat.

The final guard lets out a bark of warning that's cut off with a gurgle. Andreas has blinked out of invisibility behind him, jabbing a knife into his heart.

More shouts echo from the depths of the cave. The hairs on the back of my neck stand on end, but I glance around at the guys and see a resolve in their eyes that solidifies my own determination.

We aren't the monsters here. We're freeing tormented children from the real beasts.

I *can* be a hero, in every way that counts.

And we're working like a team again—a real one with all the trust and understanding that should go with that word. With only a look and imperceptible nods, we spread out to either side of the cave and dash in close to the walls.

The guardians come charging forward down the middle of the space. One has a light fixed to her helmet, the beam bobbing through the darkness.

We spring.

Bodies smash against the walls as Jacob lashes out with his powers.

I sever another throat.

Dominic's tentacles whip from his back to slap around a neck and crush a windpipe.

A guardian next to me stumbles, and Andreas is on him with his knife before I need to whirl around.

"The door!" Zian calls out, his voice low but urgent.

The lit helmet has spun toward the far end of the cave—where we can see a solid wall with a steel door on the verge of slamming shut.

Jacob jerks his hand forward, and the door jolts to a halt just a crack from locking. The muscles in Jake's arm bulge with the strain.

Zian heaves himself forward, and I dart after him just as fast. He catches the edge first, but his thicker fingers can't push inside the crack to yank it farther open.

There's no handle on this side.

I dive in and squeeze my own fingers into the tiny gap. With an ache I feel all the way through my shoulders, I haul at it.

The door shifts toward me, just enough for Zee to get a proper grip too. He yanks it wide—

And another squad of guardians barrels into us.

Electricity crackles with a prod that smacks my arm. My limb spasms, but I hold on to enough control to kick my attacker aside with a force that must crack several ribs.

Jacob hurls himself at the man who jolted me with a growl that could match Zian's wolf. He crushes the guardian's skull against the rocky floor with his bare hands.

Darts whiz toward us, and I fling myself around so my face and head are protected. With another jab of my heel, I snap someone's jaw.

Zian roars. There's a gristly tearing sound and a thump that's probably an arm or maybe a head torn right off.

These people want to destroy us. They've always wanted to destroy us, even if only our free will and our spirits.

They managed to slaughter Griffin, but we won't let them take another one of us.

An arm swings upward with a flash of an unexpected blade. I throw myself between the fallen guardian and Jacob just in time to deflect the slash so it only glances off his cheek.

My claws rake across the woman's throat, and she slumps with a gush of blood. When I glance up, Jacob swipes the thin scarlet streak from his cheek and offers me a smile that reaches all the way up to warm his cool eyes.

Yes, we're a team now—all of us.

The five of us push into the space beyond the steel entrance. Dim light illuminates a short hallway with a door on either side and an elevator at the end.

A helmet glints in the crack where the door on the left is pushed ajar.

Before the guardian there can pull the trigger on his weapon, Jacob's power batters him into the tiled floor. Zian crushes the man's head under his heel as we storm past.

We burst into what's obviously the control room, screens mounted all across three of the walls over a long console of controls.

The guy seated in front of the console whips up a gun, but it flies from his hand to smack against the wall. Jacob and Zian loom over the guardian while the rest of us hang a few steps back, Andreas keeping watch by the door.

"Where are you holding your experimental subjects?" Jake demands. "The ones with powers, like us?"

The man's panicked eyes leap to the screens and back to us. I scan the footage projected from various security cameras around the building.

There's a vast training area that looks more like a cavern than a room. Hallways full of more doors.

No one stirs in any of the images. Have we really eliminated the entire staff of this facility already?

If that's true, then all that stands between us and getting the kids out is this prick.

But we might need him. We don't know what codes or keys it might take to open the cells our fellow shadowbloods are locked inside.

"I—I—" the guardian stutters, and then squares his shoulders, his mouth clamping tight.

Jacob raises his hand, his fingers curling toward his palm, and I have a sudden vision of what he means to do. How he could strangle the life out of this man as easily as clenching a fist.

But we don't need to. The guy is unarmed, defenseless—and I'd like to leave one person here knowing that we're so much more than monsters.

"Wait," I say, quiet but firm.

Jake grimaces but eases to the side as I prowl forward.

What I can see of the guardian's face around the plates of his helmet pales. He swallows audibly, but he still doesn't speak.

I pin him with my stare, every muscle braced for action. "I don't want to—"

I cut myself off, realizing what I was going to say isn't true. And maybe the truth will mean more, even if it's not as pretty.

"No," I correct myself. "I *do* want to hurt you. A whole lot of me would like to make you feel just a fraction of what you and the people you work with put us through."

I flex my claws for emphasis. A shriek tremors in my chest, eager to feed off the pain I've denied it so far in this battle.

The man remains silent, but his jaw ticks with a restrained flinch.

I take another step closer to where I could scrape my claws across his face if I decided to.

"I want you to know that. I want you to know that I'm holding myself back from what I'd like to do right now, because no matter what you people put in me or did to me, I'm not a monster. I can believe there are people out there who'd care if you died, who don't deserve that pain. I can have compassion even for *you*."

"I'm not going to help you," the guardian rasps out.

I shrug, staying tensed. "That's up to you. We've broken out of places like this twice before. We can manage it again without you. We know to leave your eyes and your hands and your face intact in case we need those to unlock the system. The rest of you…"

Leaning in, I hook one claw under his helmet and flip it right off his head. His fear saturates the air, so pungent I wouldn't be surprised if the others can smell it now too.

"I'm giving you the option," I say. "If you want to survive another day to see those people who care about you, who maybe you care about too, you can show us how to find and open the cells. Or we can kill you and then figure it out anyway. The only thing that changes is whether you live. That's your choice."

Jacob inhales roughly behind me but doesn't argue with the bargain I'm attempting to strike.

I don't know if it's going to work. The man's posture has gone even more rigid in his chair.

But then Andreas speaks up from the doorway, even but with a hint of his cajoling tone.

"Chloe would miss you an awful lot, don't you think? And what would she tell Ava? Is this job really worth losing *them*—leaving them alone?"

The man can't suppress his wince this time at the names Drey has pulled from his memories. His face turns an even more sickly shade.

"Do whatever you're going to do to me," he spits out. "But don't—don't touch them. They had nothing to do with this."

He spins his chair toward the console. My teeth grit at the thought that he's only acting because he thinks we were threatening his family—but he's doing something.

I really shouldn't look a gift horse in the mouth, should I? I'm getting what I wanted even if not exactly the way I wanted it.

And he'll know that I meant my promise when he walks out of this building alive.

His hands dart over the controls. He points to one of the screens—a blue-print style rendering of a hall lined with small rooms on either side.

Uncomfortably familiar.

"That's where they are. Three floors down, past the training complex."

"And unlocking the doors?" Dominic asks.

The man wavers for a second and then leans toward a glass pane on the console. A flash of light washes over his face. He jabs a few buttons, and the symbols marking each of the cells blink from red to green.

"There. It's done. Now don't—"

Zian brings his fist down on the man's head with a *thwack* that makes me cringe. But even as he tumbles off his chair, I can see the angle and the impact were only enough to knock him unconscious.

"Tie him," Andreas urges.

I'm already springing over. My claws slice off a few strips of the man's shirt.

I tug one piece of fabric through his mouth as a gag while Jacob and Dominic hurry to secure his wrists and ankles. Then I scan the screens again.

"No more guardians. Everyone else must be outside."

Dead or still dealing with our shadowkind allies.

Jacob smiles grimly. "Let's get those kids out, then."

My heart thudding with a mix of adrenaline and joy, I dart with the others to the opposite door. A stairwell awaits on the other side.

The guardians know better than to put all their faith in an elevator and the electricity that runs it. I'd rather not count on it either.

We hurtle down the stairs as fast as our feet can carry us, Zian's head swerving from side to side as he listens for sounds of pursuit.

On the third floor, we shove out into another hall that leads into the cavernous room I saw on the surveillance. Our footsteps echo eerily through the vast, darkened space.

But there's light up ahead. The gleam of florescent bulbs shines through the window on the door at the far end.

I push myself faster. We have to get the younger shadowbloods out of their rooms and all the way back up to the surface.

We have no idea when reinforcements might be arriving.

The hall beyond the window lies empty. Zian shoulders the door open.

We spill into the hallway, our gazes whipping over the dozens of closed doors we unlocked upstairs.

And half of those doors fling open as a horde of hidden guardians charge out to meet us.

THIRTY-FIVE

Riva

A yelp of warning breaks from my throat, as if the guys won't have seen the threat in the same instant I did. I propel myself backward—

And bang against a set of steel bars that've just dropped from the ceiling to cut off our access to the doorway.

They've locked us in. Was this a trap?

We all duck low instinctively to make ourselves smaller targets. Tranquilizer darts whiz through the air only to be smacked to the side by a wallop of Jacob's telekinesis.

I have only a second to register that the guardians are wearing something odd under their usual helmets before one of them tosses a hissing cannister our way. A plume of blue smoke gushes up into the air around us.

Gas masks—that's what they're wearing. They think they can knock us out this way instead.

Zian sputters and aims a brutal kick at the cannister, sending it spinning past our attackers. The smoke wafts away from us with another push of the invisible force Jacob can conjure, but a hint of dizziness prickles through my mind.

Several of the guardians let out startled shouts, shaking their heads as if trying to clear them. When I glance at Andreas, his eyes have flared red.

He's confusing them with projected memories. But there are so many of them, more tramping out of a door at the other end of the hall.

Dominic yanks out his pistol and fires at our adversaries, but the power Jacob is hurling out to deflect their assault carries bullets from our side too. Dom flinches as the projectile ricochets off the wall.

Shit. We can't shoot at them without opening ourselves up to their own ammunition.

More darts fly. My ears catch the click of another cannister.

If we don't figure out something fast, we're going to suffocate in here.

The thought sends a jolt of panic through my nerves. I sway on my feet, claws out to slash at anyone who dares to come close, knowing it won't be enough.

The vibration in my chest reverberates through my lungs with a swelling scream.

I could end them all—but they know that, they're tossing everything they can our way to stop me first. If I'm doing this, I have to cut them down *now*.

But they're not the only ones with us in this hallway.

Nervous eyes peek from one of the doors that hasn't been thrown fully open. As my power resonates through my bones, I can feel them—the ones like us, the ones with shadows in their blood, shut away in this place for so long.

I can't save us by killing them too. And my scream…

It prickles up my throat, and I clamp down on it. My body balks like it did before when Rollick tried to get me to practice my powers.

But with my next gulp of air, laced with the desperation of all my men around me, my mind latches on to a different memory.

Last night, under Rollick's supervision. Letting out a sliver of a shriek and lancing it through one creature and another.

There are too many guardians. I can't hit them one at a time.

But I shielded my guys before. I *know* them—and I know the kids huddled behind those doors too, in all the ways that matter most, enough that my blood could lead me here.

I won't strike at them. Not the ones like me.

I'm not a killer. I'm a *protector*.

Images flash beyond my eyes of all the moments I've shared with my men over the past week. Not just battles and bloodshed, but tenderness too.

Showing Dominic I adore him even with his strange new features.

Stepping back into Andreas's arms with forgiveness.

Stopping Jacob before he sliced himself open on my behalf and bandaging his wound.

Cuddling up to Zian on the plane just hours ago, proving that whatever he's able to offer me is enough.

I can heal in my own ways. I can defend and champion.

And I will do that now.

I part my lips and let my power out.

The shriek bursts from my throat and blasts down the now-crowded hallway. I aim it past the bodies that pulse blood and shadow together and stab it into every figure before me that's only human.

Human and totally monstrous.

My hunger surges up to saturate my nerves. I wrench through one body and another, devouring their pain, letting the satisfaction of it drown out any tremors of guilt.

All my focus, all my self-control stays on keeping my vicious talent on target.

I'm distantly aware of my men moving around me, not frozen in shock like the first time I let my fury loose.

Zian braces himself in front of me, guarding me from any physical attack, smacking away a dart that careens my way. Jacob heaves one cannister and another back toward their source, his power warbling down the hall as he compels the noxious gas away.

At the back of the crowd, the new figures who barge into the hall stumble into their colleagues in the grips of memories that aren't theirs. In the muddle Andreas is casting over them to distract them for the few instants before my scream catches hold of them too.

And Dominic crouches next to me, one tentacle wound around my bare hand, another clasping the neck of an injured guardian who collapsed on the floor after he attempted to charge us. My healer is flooding me with more and more energy even as I drink down the giddying waves of pain I'm dealing out as well.

We're in this together, and we'll leave together. More of us than came.

Strength thrums through my muscles. The shriek belts on and on as bones snap and tendons tear and—

And then there's no one left. No one who deserves my rage.

My legs wobble with the sudden rush back into normal awareness, but it's all eager adrenaline, not a hint of weakness. When Dominic touches my side to steady me, I've already caught my balance with a flare of urgency.

"We've got to get the kids out. There could be more guardians coming."

There's no way the staff here didn't manage to contact their colleagues elsewhere, right? But we don't know if anyone was close enough to help all that quickly.

It's better not to take the chance.

We hurry down the hall, yanking open the doors that the guardians weren't hiding behind. I find a skinny, dark-complexioned girl who can't be more than twelve and a stout, redheaded boy who looks maybe fifteen.

"Come on," I say, beckoning to them. "We're getting you out of here. No more tests. You'll be free."

As they stir to their feet, apprehension and hope flashing across their faces in tandem, Zian gives a shout of triumph and fishes a controller from one of the mangled guardian's pockets. He hits the button, and the barred gate rises.

Andreas ushers two other kids out through the doorway. "Let's take only a couple each," he shouts over his shoulder. "We need to be able to protect them."

I nod. "And hurry!"

Dominic directs two more kids toward the training area. As I encourage my shell-shocked charges to follow them, motioning toward the door to try to avert their gazes from the bodies on the blood-stained floor, Zian wrenches open the last of the cells and frowns.

"That's all of them down here. Only six?"

I pause in the doorway and glance at the boy, who looks slightly less terrified than the younger girl. "Was it just the six of you in this facility?"

"I—I'm not sure," he says. "We didn't always train with the same people. They came and went."

Well, six is better than none. Six is a start.

Maybe the guardians didn't manage to make all that many more shadowbloods with Engel's adjusted methods after all.

Jacob kicks the last of the still-smoking cannisters into one of the empty cells and yanks the door shut to seal the noxious smoke away. He turns to Zian.

"Go with them! Make sure they get to Rollick okay. I feel like there's something else important down here—come back as soon as you've dropped the kids off and we'll see what else they've been hiding."

I don't love leaving him on his own, but getting the kids to safety matters more. "Don't go too far," I order him.

Andreas and Dominic have already crossed half the cavernous room. I hurry my charges along as quickly as I can, not wanting to slow down the others' escape by calling for them to wait.

They vanish into the stairwell, and we dash after them moments later. The kids finally come out of their stunned state enough to pick up to a run.

I wonder if they've been drugged like the guys say they were after our first escape attempt, their senses dulled.

We'll see them free of that internal prison too.

We scramble out into the short upper hall. Muffled grunts carry from the control room where the man we tied up must have regained consciousness, but I ignore him.

Zian pulls ahead before we race outside and wedges a stone in the door to hold it open. As we approach the mouth of the cave, we both scan our surroundings quickly.

I catch a few shouts off in the distance, and the flames are still crackling as part of Rollick's distraction. But there are no guardians I can see or smell nearby.

A spark of victory lights in my chest. We did it—we saved them.

There's no one left here who can hurt any of us.

Andreas and then Dominic lope past us back toward the facility, their kids already safely passed on. I wave my two charges on toward the gleaming phosphorescent line.

"We have friends here who are going to make sure we all get out of this place without the guardians catching us again. Stick with them, and the rest of us will join you soon."

Pearl and a shadowkind man wave to us from just beyond the boundary, the succubus bouncing eagerly on her feet. I shoot Pearl a quick smile and give the kids a gentle nudge toward them.

"These are the last of them."

Pearl returns my smile brightly. "Are you coming back with us, then?"

My sense of Andreas and Dominic through my marks tugs at me. I think of Jacob still searching below, and shake my head.

"We're going to give the building one last check and then we'll be right with you."

As the shadowkind figures hustle the kids onward through the woods, I wheel around with Zian by my side and dash back into the cave.

That's it. All six of this facility's prisoners are in protective hands now.

But maybe we can hurt the whole organization of guardians even more if we just look a little harder. Find out whether they're holding other young shadowbloods elsewhere.

We could be only just beginning this war.

The upper hall of the hidden facility is empty—I can feel that Andreas and Dominic have headed downstairs. They weren't there to hear that we'd already gotten all of the kids who were being held here, but we need to get back to Jacob anyway.

I dart into the stairwell, and Zian stalls in his tracks behind me with a confused grunt. "What…?"

I start to glance back at him, but Jacob's voice carries up from below. "Riva—hurry! We've got to deal with this fast."

I have no idea what he's found, but my heart lurches with a sudden jolt of panic so sharp it practically shoves me toward him.

"Come on, Zee!" I holler, and take off down the steps.

Jacob has pulled off his black cap. His blond hair gleams in the florescent lights as I dash after him around the twists in the staircase, a couple of levels above him.

He marches past the third-floor landing to the fourth basement level and pushes aside the door there. I run after him, propelled by the still-growing wave of anxiety.

What have the guardians been doing down here?

I barge into the fourth-floor hallway just in time to see Jacob disappearing past a door partway down. His voice carries back to me. "This way! Quick!"

I spring after him and burst past the door. My momentum hurls me forward a few steps before I slow, realizing I've come into a narrow, empty room that appears to have no other exits.

Transparent panes shoot from the walls on either side of me. They smack into place, hemming me in.

With a stutter of my pulse, I slam my fist into one to smash it.

It's definitely not any normal kind of glass. My supernaturally powered blow doesn't open the slightest crack.

My gaze jerks to Jacob, who's standing beyond one of the panes, expecting him to be launching himself at it from his own side. But he's just standing there, watching me.

In the space of a thump of my heart, I notice a few things.

There's no cut marking his cheek where I deflected the jab of the guardian's knife.

His slicked-back hair curls a little longer around his ears than seems quite right.

His clothes, though all black, don't totally match mine. The collar only reaches the base of his throat instead of covering his neck.

And his eyes. The pale blue eyes that've seared into me with anger and lit up with joy look utterly empty in a way I've never seen before, not even at his worst.

The bottom of my stomach drops out.

That's not Jake.

The man who isn't Jacob pushes his mouth into what looks more like an imitation of a smile than the real thing.

"It's been a long time, Moonbeam."

Captured Fate

One

Riva

A painful tightness fills the middle of my throat. Before I've even opened my eyes, the urge to clear it grips me.

But I can't seem to swallow. I can't make a sound.

It's not a lump *in* my throat but something squeezed against my neck from the outside.

My eyes want to spring open. My muscles are braced to jerk into attack mode. But instead my body reacts as if I'm moving through mud.

My eyelids lift sluggishly. My arms and legs squirm against a firmly padded surface.

And jar to a stop when they hit restraints clamped around my wrists and ankles.

I blink with the same blurry sluggishness, fighting to clear my hazy vision. A room comes into focus around me: shadows along the walls but bright light streaming over the center of the space where I'm trapped in this seat.

It's like a dentist's chair. Except I don't think those normally lock you in place.

Of course, I've never been to a proper dentist before, only seen them in TV shows and movies. It could be the reality is much more frightening.

But why the hell would I have been kidnapped by a *dentist*? Some psycho tooth doctor was so desperate to clean my teeth?

My head's been filled with mud too. My thoughts seep along dampened circuits.

There was something, right before—

We were in the facility—we'd gotten a bunch of shadowblood kids out—

Running down the stairs after Jacob, urgency thrumming through my nerves. Dashing down a hall and into a room—

Unbreakable walls thudding into place around me. And Jacob—

Not Jacob.

He called me *Moonbeam*.

My heart lurches, and my limbs yank against the restraints even though I can already tell they're built to withstand my supernatural strength. But as the resurgence of shock and anguish crashes over me, I'm remembering what happened next. The gas that poured down from the ceiling in a thick lavender gush, blotting out the man I was staring at and clouding my mind into nothingness.

That's where the memories stop. I have no idea what happened between that moment and waking up here, now.

Panic trickles through the sludge in my head, sharpening my senses.

Where are my guys? Were they caught too?

What happened to the kids we got out—did Rollick and his people get them to safety?

Where the hell *am* I?

I open my mouth, wanting to call out, but the pressure against my throat chokes off any sound beyond a slurred mumble. A fresh chill winds around me.

I won't be able to scream like this. I can't defend myself with my strength, my claws, or my killing shriek.

Whoever's holding me knows exactly what I can do and figured out a way to chain all of my talents.

I clamp down on the jolt of terror with the instinctive discipline honed by years of training and combat in the ring. Freaking out isn't going to help me.

I have to focus.

When I draw my awareness inside myself to settle my nerves, I pick up on the faint prick of sensation in the two thumbprint-sized blotches that mark my collarbone. The marks that formed when I slept with Andreas and Dominic for the first time.

They're here, wherever here is. Somewhere nearby, anyway.

But I can't tell any more than that they're within maybe a hundred feet of me in different directions, and that they're alive. What state they're in beyond that, I haven't got a clue.

A soft rasp from behind me jerks me out of my thoughts. A shift in the air that tells me a door has opened.

My pulse stutters, and I hold myself still to track the sounds.

Careful footsteps tread across the floor toward me. As I turn my head toward them, an unfamiliar man comes into view.

He walks until he's nearly in front of the chair and stops there, facing me. His blue eyes study me assessingly.

I assess him right back.

He's decently but not epically tall, with a fair bit of muscle under his polo shirt and slacks. Strong but no match for me if it comes down to hand-to-hand combat.

A military-short cropping of carrot-red hair tops his face. His features have a hardness to them that makes me think of military discipline too.

Faint wrinkles mark the corners of his mouth and eyes, and when he shifts his weight from one foot to the other, the light from overhead catches on a few faded strands amid his red hair. I'd guess he's in his late forties.

He isn't wearing the typical metal helmet and vest that the guardians usually do. But I was captured in the depths of a facility. He must be with them, right?

I manage to push a few words from my throat, rough and faint but audible. "Who. The fuck. Are you?"

His thin lips form a reserved smile. "Someone who believes you can be more than what's been offered to you so far, Riva."

What the hell is that supposed to mean? I grimace.

"Someone. Who can't. Talk?"

He lets out a light chuckle that makes me want to punch him in the face. I wasn't making a joke.

Then he motions to my throat. "I'll take the clamp off as soon as I'm sure you aren't going to turn that unexpected power of yours on me. It really wouldn't be in your best interests, and I'm sure you'll realize that for yourself. But I'd rather not take my chances before then, having seen how dire the consequences can be."

Yes, enduring one of my screams should not be on anyone's top ten lists of how to go. My power craves all the pain it can provoke while it's breaking its targets' bodies.

That doesn't mean this prick doesn't deserve every bit of the pain I could deal out.

"Where. Guys?" I force out. My throat is aching just from the little bit of conversation I've been able to carry out.

"Your fellow shadowbloods—the ones you grew up with—are being held in their own rooms. They'll be given the same opportunity. But you do seem to make a lot more trouble when you're all together."

His tone is dry, but I catch the more ominous implications. If we're kept apart, we can't plan a joint escape.

And escaping alone would leave the others in this man's hands, possibly to punish for our rebellion.

If I scream this guy to pieces, I have no idea whether I'd be able to even get out of this room afterward, let alone get to Dominic, Andreas, Jacob, and Zian. Or how many other people might be working in this place who'd make me—or them—pay for my actions.

But the thought brings back the image of the guy who led me into the trap at the last facility I entered—the guy I grew up with but believed was dead.

My throat constricts for more reasons than just the restraint before I croak out, "Griffin?"

"I don't think it's time to get into that subject just yet," the man says evenly. "Let's focus on getting you out of that chair. I don't want to hurt you or the others. I've been trying to get control over the Guardianship for years so that I could take our endeavors in a different direction. This is your second chance. But you have to show you're willing to give *me* a chance."

Every word coming out of his mouth sounds like bullshit to me. I narrow my eyes at him.

"Not. Trusting. Anything. Until. I see. Guys."

By the end of that sentence, my vocal cords are outright throbbing. I'm not sure I'll be able to say much else.

The man's mouth tightens. His gaze flicks away from me, toward the door, as if something has drawn his attention there.

His frown deepens, but he steps to the side as another set of footsteps approaches.

He wasn't the only one who came in. Someone's been listening from just inside the door.

My body tenses all over again, not that it ever really relaxed. And then the last face I ever expected to see appears in front of me.

My heart stops.

My brain wants to think it's Jacob I'm looking at. That's what would make sense given everything I believed.

But just as in that final moment in the facility, I can pick out the differences. The slightly longer fall of his blond hair. The posture that looks a tad looser than Jacob seems to be capable of these days.

The emptiness in the sky-blue eyes that used to shine with every bit of shared joy we could scrounge up in our old prison.

"I've checked on the other guys," says the man who must be Griffin, in a measured voice that holds no hint of emotion whatsoever. "Precautions have been taken when it comes to their powers, but they haven't been harmed. I wouldn't be here talking to you if I thought Clancy meant to do that."

He glances at the older man—Clancy?

My captor raises his chin. "There. You've heard it from one of your own."

Is the guy in front of me 'one of my own' anymore? He doesn't sound like the Griffin I knew.

I watched that Griffin take a bullet that tore right through his back and chest. I watched the blood burst out of him, the mix of crimson liquid and black smoke that earned us the name "shadowbloods."

I saw him crumple like a rag doll as if all the life had already left his body.

My face twitches with a wince, but I manage to cough up one more word, my gaze trained on the impossible figure before me.

"How?"

Clancy answers. "The Guardianship has always had excellent technology at our disposal. The shot only nicked Griffin's heart rather than puncturing it. It took some time, but between our doctors' expertise and the innate shadowblood ability to self-heal, he made a full recovery."

He nods to Griffin. "Why don't you show her the scar?"

Griffin's face remains completely placid, almost dazed, as he reaches for the collar of his button-up shirt. Has he been drugged like the other guys said the guardians did to them after our first escape attempt?

He eases open the top two buttons on his shirt and pulls the fabric down and to the left.

He's healed, but a reminder of the injury remains. A whorl of darker, ridged scar tissue marks the pale skin of his upper chest.

Right where the bullet hit him in my memory of that night.

"She's confused," Griffin says to Clancy in the same empty voice. Whatever they've done to him, apparently he can still read my emotions. "And scared. I think we should let her talk properly so she can ask whatever questions she's got. I don't get any sense that she's preparing to attack."

Clancy pauses and then nods again, this time toward me, though he's still speaking to Griffin. "You can loosen the clamp."

I guess he trusts Griffin to give an accurate assessment. How mixed up is Griffin with the "Guardianship," if that's what this bunch is calling their organization?

If he even really is Griffin. Who knows what else the guardians could be capable of that we don't know?

He steps toward me and fiddles with something by the side of my neck. His presence, so close to me but not quite touching my skin, sends a jitter through my nerves.

The shadows in my blood wake up and tug at me. An itch to reach out to him races through my arm to my hand, not that I can move it even if I wanted to.

Some part of me, below the level of conscious thought, believes it's really him.

But I'm not totally sure I can trust even that impulse. So when the pressure at my throat eases and I can swallow again, I aim my full attention at the man claiming to be Griffin, who's stepping back again with his infuriatingly vacant expression.

My voice comes out hoarse but unimpeded. "Tell me something only Griffin could know."

Griffin pauses, his gaze shifting but becoming distant in a more focused way as if he's giving the matter serious thought. When he brings his attention back to me, his eyes look a little more alert than before.

"A few months before the escape attempt, one of the guardians distracted Jacob during a training exercise, and he started mouthing off at the guy, swearing and stuff. You snapped at him afterward and told him off, but you weren't really angry, even though you were acting like it. You were scared. Probably that it'd mess up the plans we'd been making somehow."

My arm muscles clench with the urge to hug myself. I remember that moment in the training room—the frustration seeping from my mouth while my gut was knotted up with an edge of panic.

"When we left to go back to our rooms," Griffin goes on, "I found a chance to give your hand a quick squeeze when the guardians wouldn't see. I wanted to reassure you."

I remember that too. A pang of loss echoes through my chest even though the man I thought I'd lost is standing right here in front of me.

Only Griffin would know those things. It really is him.

But it couldn't be stranger to hear him talk about reassuring me in a voice that offers no tenderness at all, only flat facts.

Then again, maybe I'm feeling enough for both of us right now.

The pang swells into a wave of grief and guilt, sending a burn of tears into the back of my eyes. "I'm sorry. I didn't know—I thought I saw you *die*. If we'd had any idea you were alive—"

"It's okay," Griffin says, perfectly matter of fact. "There was no way you could have known."

Like he doesn't care. Like he wasn't ripped away from us for those four years just like I was from the other guys.

I don't understand.

What have they done to the boy I knew? The boy I *loved*?

I blink hard, pushing back the tears I can't move my hands to swipe away, and another question surges up from inside.

"Why were you at the facility when we— Why did you help them capture us?"

Griffin dips his head as if he's trying to indicate that he recognizes my turmoil without actually showing any regret himself.

"I've seen some of the things you did after you got out. And to get out. All of you. It became obvious that… it wasn't for the best for you to be out there in the world as you are. You were hurting too many people."

I flinch at his last words as if he's punched me in the stomach. In that moment, it's like the clamp is strangling me again. I can't find my words.

We were hurting too many people?

But even as he says that, images flash behind my eyes.

The mangled bodies in the cage-fighting arena. Most of those people died without ever having actually harmed me.

The buildings toppling into a Havana street with a yank of Jacob's power.

Billy the faun's delicate body turned into a crumpled, disjointed heap.

People *have* gotten hurt who shouldn't have.

"We were only trying to protect ourselves," I protest. "If they'd just let us go free…"

Somehow, Griffin still sounds calm. "Maybe. But even when the guardians weren't after you, there were others who wouldn't leave you alone. And then you'd lash out. It would have happened over and over. What Clancy wants to do is better."

My gaze jerks back to the older man. The military-styled dude offers me another tight smile.

My fingers curl toward my palms. "What exactly do you want?"

He's obviously going to tell me eventually. Might as well get it over with as quickly as possible so I can figure out where we go from here.

What avenues I might have for reaching the other guys. For breaking out of our new prison.

And if Griffin thinks this man is worth listening to, is it possible he's right?

But I don't know how much to trust this altered version of my old love.

Clancy takes a step toward me, putting himself just inches away from my restrained feet. "I should introduce myself properly, Riva. My name is James Clancy, and I've been part of the Guardianship since its inception, alongside my parents. It's only been in the past several months that I've had a chance to take the reins and present a better vision for our shadowbloods."

I resist the urge to make a face. "What vision?"

His posture pulls even straighter. "Chasing after monsters that rarely leave a lasting impact on society is pointless when there are so many bigger issues that human beings face. There are much greater challenges your skills could be put toward resolving. You and your friends have the opportunity to make the entire world a better place."

Two

Riva

To make the entire world a better place.

James Clancy says the words with total confidence, as if he's presenting me with an award or something. As if I should be fucking *honored* that he's chosen me to be trapped in a dentist's chair and half-strangled.

I glower at him. "What are you even talking about? I thought that was already the idea: we protect the world by fighting the 'monsters.'"

Not that the shadowkind—as I've learned those monsters prefer to be called—act beastlier than the guardians do, at least not the ones I met. But I don't see the point in rubbing that fact in just yet.

Clancy shakes his head. A gleam of enthusiasm has come into his eyes. "The three founding families believed hunting monsters should be your purpose. But I've seen a lot over the years. I know you could accomplish so much more than that. You should have the chance to become more than monsters yourselves."

Griffin nods along, and I can't stop a flutter of hope from passing through my chest despite my wariness.

I don't want to like what my new captor is saying. But to be more than what the guardians made us and expected from us—that's a dream I've been chasing from the moment I fled the cage-fighting arena.

On the other hand, this asshole does still have me locked in a chair.

Clancy starts to pace, but it isn't an anxious motion. I don't pick up the slightest hint of nervous pheromones in the air.

He strolls back and forth in front of me like he's gathering momentum, pulling out a phone as he does. "You must have some idea of the larger problems we face from the media you were allowed to consume. There are totally human horrors that run rampant around the globe. Children dragged into slavery. Terrorists killing thousands. Cartels spreading violence and addiction. Extremists carrying out genocide."

He halts and holds out his phone so I can see the screen. His thumb swipes through images that wrench at my gut almost as much as my blood-soaked memories do.

Wide-eyed little kids holding guns. Bombed out buildings. Fields mottled with broken bodies.

So much more devastation than I've ever caused… so far.

I lift my gaze from the screen to Clancy. "And you think we could do something about this?"

His little smile comes back. "I know you could. If you have the skills to battle literal monsters, why couldn't you take down the worst of humanity? You shadowbloods have the ability to turn the tide against the evil forces in this world, to save the innocents they're harming, the lives being destroyed every day… Bring something good to society on a massive scale. Wouldn't you *like* that?"

The truth is, part of me would. If I had the opportunity to prevent even one of those images from becoming real, I'd jump at it.

But I don't trust the man in front of me.

"And I'm going to do all of that while shackled to a chair?" I say pointedly.

The corner of Clancy's mouth twitches. I think he suppressed a larger smile.

Does he find me *amusing*? My teeth set on edge.

The next thing I know, he's walking over to me and pressing buttons on the side of the chair.

The cuffs click open from my neck, wrists, and ankles. A breath of relief rushes into me.

I sit up straighter, rubbing my wrists, fully registering my clothing for the first time. I've lost my mock turtleneck with its Kevlar protection, but given the amount of blood splattered on it during our raid of the facility, it'd probably be rank by now anyway.

I've been left in the wide-strapped black tank top I had on underneath, my pendant necklace tucked beneath the neckline, and a new pair of black sweats. I run my finger along the waistband just enough to confirm that I've got on the same panties as before.

They invaded my privacy, but I can admit it could have been a lot worse.

I glance up at Clancy again. My captor doesn't look frightened of me, and I'm still not picking up any whiffs of anxiety.

He has Griffin monitoring my emotions. Griffin knows I'm not angry enough to go on the attack just yet.

I have the other guys to think about. What happens to them if I let loose my claws and slice open this man's throat?

What if this is the best opportunity we're ever going to get, and reacting with violence would mean consigning us all to a lifetime of total imprisonment and torture instead?

Clancy tilts his head toward the door. "Come with me."

Cautiously, I peel myself out of the chair and follow him.

Griffin trails along behind. As we step out past the steel door into a hallway that I realize looks as if it's roughly carved into stone, I glance back at him.

He offers me a smile of his own, but it's the same stiff kind he gave me right before the gas knocked me out in the facility. Not the way he used to smile, the expression lighting his whole face up.

Did *Clancy* do this to him, or was it the other guardians? Because if the man giving me this grandiose talk was responsible for killing the light in the boy I loved, he's going to end up with his throat severed eventually, one way or another.

As soon as I can figure out how to do it without screwing things up for the rest of my guys.

Panels on the ceiling send an artificial glow over the hallway. More steel doors are imbedded in the rocky walls, labeled with numbers.

I peer at them as we pass. The faint tingle in my marks tells me Dominic and Andreas, at least, are farther behind me.

My claws itch at my fingertips. "Where are my friends? When do I get to see them?"

Clancy casts his voice over his shoulder. "Like I said before, the bunch of you make a lot of trouble when you're all together. I don't think we'll be arranging a full group reunion until you're more settled in. But you'll have the chance to see them one or two at a time once I know where you stand. Assuming you're on board."

"On board with saving the world?" I mutter.

"Something like that."

We turn a corner into a wider hallway with a set of double doors just ahead. Clancy presses his thumb against a panel at waist height while offering his face to another scanner higher up.

The steel slabs whir apart. Daylight and a warm breeze spill through the opening.

My heart lifts of its own accord.

I hadn't realized how dim and cool the rocky interior was until now, as I stepped out onto a stone platform under the bright sun. I stall in my tracks just beyond the entrance, my jaw going slack at the scene before me.

The walls of the building I've just exited are rock because it's carved right into the face of a mountain. A mountain that's part of a range looming in craggy peaks all around a small but lush valley spread out some fifty feet below our vantage point.

Immediately in front of us, water burbles in a crystalline spring. A few acres of cleared land gleam with vibrantly green grass.

Some of that area has been left as a totally open field. Other parts have been set up for training activities: an elaborate jungle gym-slash-obstacle course, shooting or throwing targets, a trampled track.

A couple of running trails veer off into the tropical forest that fills the rest of the valley. I can't make out much through the dense canopy of leaves.

Bird song trills through the air. A flash of red-and-yellow feathers darts through the branches.

A faint perfume drifts on the breeze to my nose, sweet florals with a mossy undertone.

"The Guardianship owns this island," Clancy says, gazing out over the valley with a satisfied expression. "A long time ago, this spot was a crater smashed into the mountains by a meteor. Now it's become a place where life can thrive."

He shoots a pointed look my way. "Even the most desolate things can transform into something spectacular."

I'd wrinkle my nose at the blatant insinuation about my own usefulness, but my attention has been drawn to the figures who are moving amid the training equipment.

My pulse stutters at the thought that I might see my guys among them, but I don't recognize any of the current trainees. They're all young, I determine after studying them for a minute. Mid to late teens.

As that thought passes through my head, one of the guys slips on the climbing ropes. The girl ahead of him jerks around at his yelp and flings out her arm—and an invisible force shoves him back into balance.

My mouth goes dry. "They're shadowbloods. You're training them here now?"

Clancy nods. "I've gathered as many of our subjects as I can at this facility. Those who were away from their facilities—in the interests of tracking your group down—are on their way now. That will be all of them… except the six you led to the monsters."

The six we helped escape from imprisonment, he means.

My mouth tightens, my appreciation of the gorgeous setting fading. I turn toward him, the words to tell him off rising up my throat, and find him already watching me.

"Do you want to know what the creatures who pretended to be your allies did to those children?" he asks in a low voice.

An uneasy prickle ripples over my skin. "What do you mean?"

Clancy takes out his phone. "Some of them can be very persuasive… but we consider them monsters for a reason."

When he points the screen toward me again, my stomach flips over.

It's a photograph of four bodies sprawled on the forest floor under muted daylight. I can't see much of the two farther figures other than that there's blood splashed across them.

The closer two are clearly dead. Eyes staring vacantly, flesh drained to white. Scarlet flecks dapple their cheeks.

I know the girl. She's one of the two I led out of the facility.

Clancy gives me several seconds to take the image in and then slides to another, showing the other two forms. There's the boy I escorted out, equally limp, his arm torn right from its socket.

In my shock, my voice breaks. "But— How did that happen? Who—"

"The beasts you brought them to must have felt it best to eliminate the threat the shadowbloods represented as quickly as possible." Clancy tucks the phone away, his tone now grim. "I'd imagine they only left *you* alive as long as they did in the hopes you'd help them eliminate more of your kind."

My stomach roils. No. That doesn't make sense.

I can't imagine Pearl, the bubbly, curious succubus, planning a slaughter. And Rollick, the demon who was overseeing our mission—he proved over and over that he was on our side.

Could that really have all been an act?

It doesn't need to have been, does it? Other shadowkind working under Rollick tried to kill us in spite of his protection before.

Maybe they were less scared of our younger counterparts—maybe they jumped in and murdered the kids before he realized they were rebelling against his orders.

We gave those kids freedom—for what? A few minutes? And then…

Guilt congeals in my gut. I grapple with the nausea churning inside me.

"That doesn't mean *you* were right," I say roughly. "The things you put us through, everything you forced us to do…"

All the anguish I've witnessed on my guys' faces and heard in their voices as they talked about the four years we were apart, even worse than the time before. The four years when *I* was stuck fighting for my life every week and in shackles every other hour of the day, because the guardians sold me off.

At least the shadowkind didn't torture the kids.

"I haven't had much control over your training," Clancy says. "It took time before I really had a voice, and more time for everyone involved to listen. I don't agree with everything you've endured. But it's toughened you to withstand the worst the villains out there can throw at you."

I scowl at the training equipment below. "And what are we doing here? More toughening up?"

Clancy's voice softens. "I don't think training needs to be torturous. You've already had enough of that. The five of you are more than prepared to go out into the field already. We'd only go through exercises designed to confirm you have specific skills needed for a given mission—and that you're committed to seeing it through. As well as some exercises for increasing your control over your powers."

My gaze jerks to him with a jolt of surprise. The whole reason we turned to the shadowkind to begin with was for help harnessing our supernatural abilities.

"You *know* how to help us control them? Better than we learned before?"

"Your past keepers were mainly concerned with provoking as much ability out of you as possible, not reining it in. My colleagues who've supported my cause and I have developed some strategies that appear to help with focus and moderation."

So I could make sure I only let out my scream when it was deserved? Modulate it to decide how much to hurt, whether to kill?

The guys have been struggling with the wilder side of their abilities too. We've all been longing for this.

Clancy studies me. "It wouldn't take very long before you could start making a difference—a real one, for the people who need it most."

I don't like the lump that's risen in my throat. But the photos he showed me mean I have even more to make up for than I knew before.

If I can believe anything he says.

I cross my arms. "You said there were three founding families. I guess Ursula Engel was part of one of those, and she got pushed out. Did you manage to convince… your parents? And whoever the other founders are to go along with all this?"

Clancy's mouth slants at an uncomfortable angle. "My parents passed away in the last few years, and their other co-founder stepped away during their illnesses with his own concerns. It's become clear he won't be returning. The direction of the Guardianship rests solely in my hands now."

I can't claim his idea sounds like a totally horrible direction, at least not if he's telling the truth. That doesn't mean I'm going to leap to sign up.

"And if we don't commit to your missions?"

He offers a slight shrug. "Then you'll be confined to your room and contribute with the tests we'll run on you, physically and mentally. I'd imagine getting out into the world and taking matters into your own hands will be more satisfying, but the choice is up to you."

Do things his way or go back to being a total prisoner. Such fantastic options.

I hold in my snark, my hand rising instinctively to my necklace. My fingers tug out the cat-and-yarn shape and curl around it.

The feel of it against my skin makes me glance toward the other man standing on the ledge with me—the one who gave this necklace to me years ago.

Griffin hasn't said a word since we came out. He stands there under the warm sunlight, his stance easy but his expression just as blank as it's been since I first saw him.

What would it take to get a real reaction from him?

I raise the pendant so the light flashes off it. "I've held on to your necklace all this time. It helped me get through a lot."

There's no real joy in his smile. "I'm glad it served you that well."

I can't help reaching toward him with my other hand. Maybe it's an echo of the moment he referenced when he offered me that quick squeeze of reassurance.

My fingers brush his, and a spark quivers across my skin and into my veins. My pulse hiccups.

Whatever the guardians have done to him, I'm still just as attuned to him as I am the other guys.

Griffin swivels toward me, moving his hand out of reach with the same motion. He considers me like I'm an interesting piece of art hanging in a gallery rather than one of his closest friends.

Still, I can't hold back the question. "Do you think this is a good idea?"

Griffin inclines his head. "I think we should help. We can, and there aren't many people who could—not as much, not on the same level. I want to know I've done something good with my life. We haven't really had the chance before."

No, we haven't. But it's hard to feel totally convinced when Griffin delivers his answer in that vacant voice.

Clancy motions me back toward the hallway. "Let me show you your actual room here, and you can take some time making your decision. But I hope it won't be a difficult one."

Three

Jacob

I hate this fucking room.

There's nothing in it. Just me and a floor, ceiling, and walls that all look and feel like rock.

A steel door I can't budge with my powers, no matter how hard I pull.

A light fixture sealed behind layers of some translucent material that's so well-secured I can't wrench it out either.

Of course, if I could break it, then it'd be just me and the dark. But at this point I'm too pissed off to care how practical the strategy would be.

I prowl through the small space, my sneakers smacking the flat but rough ground, my hands clenched into fists. My power zings this way and that, snatching at every surface around me for something to catch on to and snap.

The guardians screwed us over somehow. Some stupid trick that I didn't recognize until it was too late.

When we'd gotten the kids out of the facility we invaded, I had the strongest sense that I needed to keep digging, keep searching—that there was something else important there. I remember opening a door with a rush of exhilaration that I'd finally found whatever that was.

Then the door slammed shut behind me, tossing me forward as a hissing sound filled the air. A chemical smell filled my nose.

And before I could do shit about any of it, my mind went black.

Am I still in the same building? The stone surfaces make me think of the cave the other one was built into, but all the rooms and halls there looked like a regular building, not something carved right out of the rock.

When I get my hands—or my powers—on the fuckers who're caging us now…

I march up to the door and pound my fists against it, even though I know it won't budge. Let them know how fucking furious I am.

They're going to have to face me eventually. I can't see them going to the trouble of knocking me out and shutting me in here just to leave me to starve to death.

What have they done to Riva? To the other guys?

I should have been with her—protecting her. If they've gotten her too…

God fucking *damn it.*

I slam my clenched hand into the door once more, hard enough that a lance of pain shoots up my arm. The renewed surge of anger and frustration sends me storming in another circuit of the room.

The guardians have always come down hardest on her. She was the one they took away when we first tried to escape.

They left her on her own to fight for her life at some crime boss's whims. How much worse will they do this time?

"Fuck!" I shout, flinging an invisible force at the wall, which of course doesn't budge.

I'm just coming up on the door again when a panel I didn't notice slides open on the ceiling and a screen whirs down from it.

All I register is a middle-aged man's face on the screen, hard angles topped by short orange hair, and his mouth moving to form words. "Hi there, Jacob. This seems like the safest way to—"

My power whips out of me at the first viable target it's gotten since I woke up on the uncomfortable floor.

The screen shatters. Bits of glass rain down on the floor. Sparks sputter from the electronic frame that held it.

It occurs to me a moment too late that I should have been a little more careful. I should have cracked the glass so I'd have a larger piece to work with as a weapon.

Fuck it. I've got a dozen spines that'll spring from my arms, as sharp as any glass and poisoned on top of that.

I stomp through the glass-littered part of the room for good measure, taking a tiny pleasure in the crunch of the shards under my feet. The panel starts to hum shut again, but I snatch at it too.

With a heave, I bring the camouflaged covering and the metal frame crashing down too.

That's what I think of their attempt at conversation. They want to say something to me, they can come look me in the eyes.

"Where's Riva?" I yell in the vague direction of where the screen once hung. "Where are my friends? Let me out of here, you assho—!"

A current of electricity jolts through my body from the floor and cuts off my last word with a rattling of my jaw. My body spasms.

My legs give, and I fall to my hands and knees. The brief zap has dissipated, but every nerve in my body continues to vibrate with the discharged energy.

I've bitten my tongue. The tang of blood trickles over it.

I grimace and shove myself, wobbling, back onto my feet. I'm going to tear those pricks apart and dance on their fucking—

The roar of anger reverberating through me simmers down like a pot taken off the stove. A strange rush of cool, soothing calm muddies it.

I should be raging. Why the hell am I—

This tantrum is silly. Everything is okay. The others must be okay too.

No, *that's* ridiculous. The guardian bastards grabbed us and—

Another cool wave rolls over me, numbing the searing flames. I suck in a shaky breath.

What is going on in my head?

I'm bewildered and chilled out enough that when the lock in the door clicks, my power doesn't immediately jerk to the ready. I just stand there, staring, somehow sure that I need to wait and get the answer I need when it swings open.

There's a soft hiss of escaping compressed air. The door slides partway into the side of the stone frame rather than swinging inward.

For an instant, I think it's opened to reveal a mirror. That's a reflection of me, gazing back at me with the same pale blue eyes.

But reflections don't walk on their own like this one steps into the room, the door thudding shut behind him. A reflection wouldn't be wearing a green shirt when mine is black.

A reflection wouldn't aim an awkward-looking smile at me while my jaw hangs slack.

"Jake," the other man says in a mild voice that seems to sweep over me on a third swell of calm. "You need to stop fighting. Let's try talking. You can talk to me if you don't want to listen to anyone else yet."

I think I've swallowed my tongue. I can't seem to find it, and a choking sensation constricts my throat.

I cough and sputter and find my voice again as my heart thumps on with an erratic beat.

"Griffin?"

It's hardly more than a hoarse whisper. I'm almost afraid to have made his name audible, as if I'll shatter the illusion by addressing it.

But the man in front of me doesn't fracture. He looks steadily at me, not denying my naming of him.

"I'm sorry it's been so long. Things have been… complicated."

"They—*what*? You—we thought—I saw you—"

A different surge of emotion sweeps away all my words. My gut knots up, and the rest of me lurches forward.

I wrap my arms around my brother and tug him close. Absorbing the warmth of life from his skin, the even rhythm of his pulse thumping in his chest.

He's really here. Right here with me, speaking, breathing.

But not quite the way I remember. The way I know down to my bones that my twin is supposed to be.

Griffin would have laughed, because I'm usually not a hugger, and hugged me back tightly. Griffin would have overflowed with his excitement at the reunion.

The guy I've embraced has lifted his arms to return the hug, but more in a comforting way than with any clear enthusiasm. He stays quiet as I pull away.

I stare at him, trying to connect the figure before me with my expectations and memories. Nothing quite makes sense. My mind feels as if it's been buried under a landslide.

"Where have you *been*?" I blurt out, which maybe isn't the best question to lead with when I should be singing Hallelujah that he's alive at all, but it's the one that careens out first.

Griffin smiles in his new, tight way. "Another facility. It took them a long time to heal me and to make sure that I was prepared for everything I might have to face. And then the guardians said it would be better if I didn't come back and disrupt the habits you all had gotten into. I asked… You know what they were like."

He didn't die. We thought we saw his life leave him in the video they showed us, but his injury wasn't quite so bad that they couldn't patch him up.

He was alive all this time, and they kept rubbing it in our faces that supposedly Riva arranged his murder. That it was her fault he was dead when even the dead part wasn't true.

The realization and my brother's last words spark a renewed flare of frustration. "What they *are* like. Those assholes—"

But Griffin… shakes his head. "New management. Things are changing. We're *here*, and together. It's a fresh start. I'd really like to embark on it with you—with all of you, but especially you, Jake."

I'm gaping at him again, wishing I had Zian's X-ray vision so I could peer inside his skull in case I might find a little gremlin sitting at a set of controls where his brain should be. "A fresh start? What the fuck are you talking about?"

"Someone new has taken over the guardians," Griffin says. "He's got different plans—he's going to let us run missions that actually matter. Take control over our lives. Have a say in our training. You have to give him a chance to explain."

"Whoever he is, he shut me in this prison! He took away the others—Riva—"

Griffin's voice gentles. "They're all here. I just talked to Riva a half hour ago. She's fine. Everyone's fine. You'll be able to see them, talk with them and the younger shadowbloods who are here, go outside—everything. When you've calmed down and we don't have to worry about you hurting anyone by accident. Or on purpose."

Something about that last sentence makes my pulse hitch.

He knows. He knows the people I've already hurt—in both ways.

Griffin never wanted to hurt anyone. He'd feel their pain as well as his own.

He can't understand.

I raise my chin. "I was protecting us. I'd do it again."

"You won't have to," Griffin says. "We're safe here. We don't have to go out and tackle the real villains until we're ready."

I scowl at him. "I'll believe it when I see it."

Griffin sighs. It's a mild sound, but it conveys enough disappointment that I want to cringe away inside my own body, away from the sense that I've let him down.

I let him take lead in the escape—I let him be the one to race out first, where the bullets started flying—

How much of the strangeness I see in him now is my fault too?

I suck in a breath through my teeth. "We can't trust them. We can't trust any of them. Even Engel, the one who *made* us, turned out to hate us."

"Clancy isn't like that." Griffin steps back toward the door. "Show that you're ready to talk and listen, and then we'll get somewhere."

He slips out before I can get another word in, leaving me behind in the cold, empty room.

Four

Riva

The swaying, reed-like strands of plastic sparkle with pink glitter. I eye the narrow opening, tracking their movements in the breeze.

There's a dip in the ground under them. If I roll into it—a little to the side to avoid that root—at just the right moment…

I brace my limbs and then launch myself. As I hit the ground, I tighten my muscles to squish my compact body as small as it'll go.

The pink-and-green strands flash by over my face. Then I'm shoving forward and leaping onto a jutting tree branch to avoid a pool of more glitter—this stuff neon yellow—on the far side.

I crouch there for a moment, breathing hard but with a sense of satisfaction I wasn't totally prepared for. The branch starts to wobble, warning me that it's part of the course's training too.

With a rasp of my feet against the bark, I spring off and slip along a narrow path between the trees. I spot the trip wires seconds before I reach them and hop nimbly over each, just dodging a spinning disc that's careening back and forth along one of them.

It's done. I dart out into the field beyond the jungle with a sigh of relief.

The sun beams down over me, comfortingly warm. My nerves jangle from the high alertness I kept all through the stealth course that's part of this island facility's grounds.

Flopping down on the soft grass, I breathe the warmth and the new stillness in deeply.

I *can* do this. I can lie back and rest, knowing I made it through the course successfully.

Knowing I got to choose to run that course to begin with. Clancy escorted me from my room in the mountain facility this morning after a brief talk, but once we reached the grounds, he told me I could explore and try out anything that interested me.

He *wanted* me to get comfortable here. To see what he's offering and what the life he's talking about could be like.

I'm still having trouble wrapping my head around the idea of a guardian offering me a choice.

I told him I'd give his training style and his missions a try, because it was either that or stay locked up and be prodded like a lab rat. The decision was pretty simple.

But is it possible this option could actually be… good?

I'll feel surer about that when he lets me see my guys again. How much can I really trust him when he doesn't totally trust us?

Of course, he's right not to trust us. If I knew how to reach the guys and had a clear way of getting us and the other shadowbloods out of here, I'd take it in an instant.

But the mountains that surround this crater-turned-valley look ominously steep. I don't know how far we'd have to go beyond their ridges to find the island's shores—or what avenues for further escape we'd find there.

How is Clancy bringing in people and supplies? Helicopter? Boat?

I have no idea which direction we'd even want to go in.

So for now I'll play along, make whatever observations I can, and stay ready.

And if he really can help me get a proper handle on my sadistic talent while I'm here, I might actually leave better than I arrived.

Footsteps rustle across the grass toward me. I sit up in a snap and find two of the younger shadowbloods wandering over.

They hesitate at my sudden motion before continuing toward me. The younger-looking one, who I can't imagine is even in her teens yet, strides forward boldly even as her eyes widen to take me in. A cloth bag swings from one of her hands.

The older one, who I'd guess is in her late teens, comes at more of a stroll, her eyebrows slightly arched beneath the fringe of her dark pixie cut. The wry expression contrasts with her statuesque bearing, tall and solidly built but elegant as well. But what stands out the most is her neon pink T-shirt.

"Did you make it through the whole thing with no glitter at all?" the younger one asks breathlessly, swiping her fawn-brown hair back from her pale face.

I guess they were watching my explorations.

"I think so." I get up and hold out my arms for them to examine me.

They both circle me. The younger girl leans in to tap something on my black tee that I grabbed from the assortment of workout clothes I found in my room and giggles. "Nope, that was just a bit of lint. You really made it! I always get a little dusted."

I look her up and down. "I'd imagine I've been training a while longer than you have. Also, it helps being tiny."

Even the preteen has a couple of inches and maybe ten pounds on my five-foot-one frame. Her companion is at least half a foot taller than me.

"And fast," the older girl says with a smile, and dips her head, the sun shining off her high brown cheeks. "I'm Nadia, and this is Tegan. You're one of the First Gen shadowbloods, right?"

The capitalization of the words comes across in her tone, like it's an official rank. A shiver that's a weird mix of uneasy and proud tickles under my skin.

I shrug. "Yeah. I guess I am. My name's Riva. Have you been here on the island for a while?"

Nadia shakes her head. "I think it's been a week? I'm not great at keeping track."

"Yeah, same." Tegan peers at me again with those big eyes that I'm starting to think are just permanently wide. "Is it true that you and the other Firsts were going around with the *monsters*?"

I blink at her. "You know about the shadowkind?"

The guardians never told me and my guys anything about the "monsters" we were supposed to be training to fight. We only found out what our expected purpose was when we confronted Ursula Engel.

Nadia's eyebrows arch higher. "Shadowkind?"

"That's what they call themselves," I say. "The beings the guardians call monsters. They helped us. Well, some of them did."

My mind darts back to the photos Clancy showed me of the dead kids. The bodies that could have been the two girls in front of me if they'd been held at the facility we broke into.

Tegan claps her hands together. "Of course we know about them! The guardians told us that's why they're working us so hard. So we can go out and stop them. Nadia's even done missions to *kill* them."

The older girl grimaces with a tug at her vibrant tee. "That wasn't anything wonderful. I don't even know what the ones I took out had been doing. I shot them with some special bullets from far away… But it was better than what the guardians would have done if I'd argued about it."

I can imagine—they probably threatened her friends, her fellow shadowbloods, like they did with me and the guys.

Why did the guardians send our younger equivalents out so much sooner than us? What made them change their approach?

The two girls obviously don't realize there's anything strange about it. I swallow that question.

Curiosity itches at me about their talents, but if I ask about theirs, they'll want to know mine… and the thought of trying to explain my brutal scream to sweet Tegan makes my stomach clench up. Instead, I focus on something more immediately important.

"How's it been since you got here? No one's treated you badly?"

"It's great!" Tegan crows. "We get to come outside all the time, and the guardians working with Clancy are way nicer than the ones before. And the food is SO much better."

Nadia nudges her. "You forgot to get out the snack."

"Oh, right!" The younger girl grabs the cloth bag she set down and opens it up. "One of the kitchen staff made brownies for a treat. I was going to see if you wanted one. Or two. However many you'd like."

She smiles at me so shyly but eagerly that I have to smile back. Then my stomach gurgles.

"Sure. Seems like I've worked up an appetite."

She lays the bag down on the grass between us, spreading the opening wide so we have easy access to the several slabs of chewy chocolate stacked inside. I pick one up with instinctive wariness, but it smells and feels like perfect fudgy goodness.

When I take a small bite, it tastes like that too, chocolate heaven melting in my mouth. Normally I'm more of a sour-flavors gal, but I can go for sweets when they're this delicious.

But as I chew, a pang shoots through my chest.

Dominic would love these. Has he gotten to have one?

I can sense that he's somewhere within the mountain facility right now, but nothing about how he's feeling or what he's doing. I guess he can't be in too much distress, because I seem to pick up a trace of particularly strong emotions, but that's not a huge comfort.

It'd be awfully nice if these marks operated like walkie talkies.

As Tegan hums happily over her own brownie, two other teens who look around Nadia's age amble toward us. The guy, whose tan skin and spiky blond hair make him look like he's walked out of a surfer movie, tsks his tongue in mock-offense.

"You didn't think to tell *me* you had the goods?"

Nadia scrambles up in a much more awkward motion than I've seen before, her cheeks reddening as she sweeps up the bag. "Of course you can have one. And you too, Celine."

She nods to the girl who's trailed behind him. From her features, I'd guess she's got a lot of Chinese or Vietnamese in her genetics.

The guardians seem to have liked to experiment with a variety of human ethnic heritages. I suspect Nadia is mostly Native American in background—as much as you can call it a background when we were constructed in a lab rather than out in the real world.

Celine smiles widely with a swish of her long ponytail, the red flecks in her black hair catching the sunlight. "Thanks so much!"

Something about her tone jars me. Like the chipper inflection should remind me of Pearl's bubbly personality, but it doesn't hold as much warmth as I'd expect.

But then, who could blame her if she's a little on edge in this place? It might be nice compared to other facilities, but we are still technically captives.

Nadia is mainly focused on the guy anyway, her gaze lingering on his face as he raises the brownie to his full lips.

I might not be the most socially experienced person ever, but soap operas have more than prepared me to recognize a crush. And that, ladies and gentlemen, is what I'm looking at right now.

Did they train together like I did with my guys? Nadia isn't acting like they have quite the same level of closeness already.

"Nice," he says after swallowing the first bite, and lifts his hand to me in greeting. "And nice to meet you, Firstie. I'm Booker."

"Riva," I reply. *Firstie?* Is that what they're all going to be calling us now?

Celine aims her smile more directly at me. "I'm glad you're all back with us, safe and sound."

Tegan, who's gotten up too, bobs on her feet. "Celine was out with the guardians trying to help you get away from the monsters."

Oh. My lips part, but my words have dried up.

Should I say thank you when I didn't really want to be "helped"?

Celine laughs as if it's no big deal, but her eyelids flicker down for just a second. I think I catch a flash of discomfort, maybe even sadness, before she's smiling fully again.

What did the guardians put her through during their hunt? It's no wonder she'd be struggling, even if she's doing her best to put on a cheerful front.

Before I can figure out how to talk to her, a twinge at my collarbone brings my gaze jerking to the facility entrance. My heart leaps.

Two figures are just walking out onto the ridge in front of the entrance, over the broad stone staircase that winds around to the valley floor. It only takes one glimpse for me to recognize them.

It's probably horrendously rude of me, but I can't stop my feet from bounding forward. I sprint across the field and up the steps as the two men who stepped out hurry down to meet me.

"Drey!" I throw my arms around the leaner guy the second he's within reach, knowing he'll welcome the hug.

Andreas sucks in a hitch of breath and squeezes me hard. He smells like he always has, warm and a little spicy, like cinnamon.

When I force myself to ease back to scan his face, he looks the same too: dark coiled hair, gorgeous brown face, sparkling dark gray eyes. I don't see any injuries on him.

Then he's cupping my jaw and pulling my mouth to his, and there's no part of me that can resist the kiss.

I loop my arm around his neck and kiss him back hard with a giddy quiver through my veins as if the shadows in me are rejoicing at our reunion.

This is something different too. I never would have dared to show this much physical affection in any of the other facilities.

But I don't give a fuck what Clancy thinks. These are my guys, my loves, and I'm not going to pretend they're anything less.

Well, they're my guys to varying extents. As Andreas releases me, keeping one arm slung around my back, I turn toward Zian with a smile that's both joyful and a little cautious.

Zee hasn't generally reacted all that well to even brief touches, let alone a full hug. But he did offer me a very careful embrace right before we set off on our last personal mission.

He's staring at me with so much emotion blazing in his dark brown eyes that it lights up my skin. His brawn flexes all across his broad shoulders.

He reaches out and brushes his fingers tentatively over my shoulder. "They didn't hurt you, Shrimp?"

The question comes out gruff, the silly nickname offset by the concern wound through his voice.

"No. I'm okay. Just… not really sure what to make of all this." My gaze darts between the two of them. "Are you both totally all right? Have you seen Dominic or Jacob?"

Andreas flicks his gaze toward the facility with a trace of the same wariness I feel about our new situation. "We're… as good as we can be. I got to talk to Dominic at breakfast this morning—he wasn't happy that we're being kept apart, but otherwise fine."

Zian knits his brow. "Neither of us has seen Jacob. You haven't either?"

"No. You two are the first." My stomach sinks. "Clancy hasn't been letting us out until we commit to running his missions. Maybe Jacob isn't giving in."

It's way too easy to imagine the rigidly stubborn guy refusing to even pretend to play along if he's angry that we were captured at all. And there's also—

I pause for a second with a constricting of my throat. "You know—Griffin…"

I don't have to say anything more than that. Andreas's face somehow manages to brighten and fall at the same time, and the furrow in Zian's forehead deepens.

"All this time," the bigger guy says in a disbelieving tone, and swipes his hand back over his short black hair.

Drey nods. "That's got to have thrown Jake for a loop. Especially when Griffin is definitely… different, too."

"Yeah." My gut knots at the memory of Griffin's oddly vacant demeanor.

I haven't seen him since the talk with him and Clancy yesterday. I have no idea how he's been spending his days.

How closely do the two of them work together?

"At least this place seems better than many of the alternatives," Andreas says with a hesitantly hopeful note in his voice. He glances across the valley. "I saw a place like this once in some backpacker's memories. He went around scaling mountains, soaking in lagoons, and gorging himself on tropical fruit until he gave himself a stomachache. Even then, he called it paradise. It never occurred to me I'd get to visit somewhere like that in person."

He's fallen into his storyteller's lilt. Andreas has always been our memory-keeper—both of our own past and all kinds of lives that were beyond our reach except through his talent.

His attention comes back to me with a knowing expression. "And it's also a little less restricted. Can't complain about that."

"Nope," I agree. Not when that lack of restriction means more opportunity for escape if we don't like the other opportunities Clancy offers us.

As if drawn by my thoughts, our grand leader himself steps out onto the ridge above us. He sets his hands on his hips and smiles down over his domain and all of us within it.

"All right, folks," he calls out. "You've had some free training time. How about something a little more structured? Capture the Flag—the whole valley's your arena. Three Firsts against the rest of you. That should be fair enough."

An excited murmuring rises up from where the younger shadowbloods—including another two who've joined the bunch I talked to—are gathered below. I glance at my guys and swallow hard.

Clancy is working so hard to make our time here feel like recreation rather than torture. He's given us a home some people would consider paradise.

But he's still one of *them*.

Just how dangerous would it be to trust him?

FIVE

Riva

However skeptical I might be about the intentions of the new man in charge, I have to admit that mealtimes in the mountain facility are a big step up from our past imprisonment.

No more trays of bland food chosen only for nutritional completion shoved through a slot in a door to be eaten in solitude. We get our choice from a spread of dishes set out in shifts, with a random assortment of about ten fellow shadowbloods in the cafeteria for company.

The buffet isn't anywhere near as extensive or gourmet as the meals Rollick provided us with on his yacht, but everything I've sampled so far at least tastes good. And there's something to be said simply for getting to pick.

For this morning's breakfast, I'm debating between omelets stuffed with cheese and fried veggies or bowls of steaming oatmeal laced with berries and brown sugar. I kind of want one of each, but I don't think my stomach will thank me after I've stretched it to twice its regular size.

I end up grabbing a plate with an omelet, add a small scoop of hashbrowns and a bottle of orange juice for good measure, and turn toward the tables.

The rock-carved room holds five rectangular tables that comfortably seat six each, but I've never seen them full. Because we eat in shifts, I have no idea exactly how many shadowbloods are staying here.

Right now, the two of the tables on the left hold three and four of the younger shadowbloods respectively. I spot Nadia and Booker at one, her laughing hard at something he's said and then covering her mouth as if embarrassed.

Today her shirt is neon green. She obviously has a thing for bright clothing.

Everything in my wardrobe is darker shades… Did she ask Clancy for those tees specially?

Did he give her new clothes simply because she asked?

As I'm working through my new debate of whether to be friendly and go sit with them or huddle on my own at one of the empty tables, a familiar blond head passes through the doorway at the right side of the room.

My pulse skips a beat, and my plate wobbles in my hand. For an instant, I'm not sure which of the twins I'm looking at.

Then his gaze collides with mine, and any doubt flies out of my mind. Only Jacob could look at me like a dam's just burst open behind his eyes.

Before I can even part my lips to speak, he's hurtling forward, straight toward me.

He doesn't even veer around the vacant tables between me and him. With a flick of his arm, he sends them flipping over to clear his path.

Both tables clang against the stone wall. Jacob strides by without a split-second of hesitation, his gaze still fixed on me.

Then he stops right in front of me and raises his hand with a gentleness totally at odds with the aggression of his approach.

As he touches my cheek, my fingers tighten around my plate and the neck of the juice bottle as if I'm clutching them for dear life.

My heart pounds against my ribs. I'm too choked up to speak.

To say that Jake and I had a stormy time with our original reunion is like referring to a hurricane as a light breeze. But in the last few days before we ended up here, I came to understand how he acted a lot better than I had before.

To recognize that no one could hate how he first treated me more than he did himself. To see just how far he'd go to ensure nobody ever hurt me again.

And how far he'd go to make me feel *good*, when I'd let him.

The maelstrom of emotion in his sky-blue gaze matches the turmoil his presence has stirred up inside me. He strokes his fingers over my cheek with nothing but tenderness, staring at me as if he can read my experiences of the past few days through my skull.

"Are you okay?" he asks in a low, taut voice, either because he can't tell or he wants me to confirm it.

I manage to get enough of a grip on my internal state to locate a trace of my sense of humor. "I'm fine. I don't know if the tables are."

Jacob doesn't spare the pieces of furniture he upended even the briefest of glances. "Fuck the tables."

I'm not sure Clancy's staff are totally on board with that attitude.

A man and a woman have stepped into the room to eye the results of Jacob's arrival. Like Clancy himself, the guardians working under him don't wear the protections we're used to—but then, we know those are useless against our powers anyway. But they're the only people around who are older than me and my guys, so they're easy to identify.

I tense, expecting them to march over and yank Jacob away from me —Lord only knows how big a catastrophe *that* would turn into—but the woman simply shakes her head in apparent consternation. She and the man heave the tables onto their feet, study the new but small dents along the edges, and nudge the chairs back into place.

Huh. I guess they're choosing their battles.

I have no idea what the younger shadowbloods are making of Jacob's dramatic entrance. I only manage to watch the guardians for a matter of seconds before my attention swings back to him as if drawn by a magnet.

I move as little as I can manage to set my plate and my juice down and then rest my hands against the front of Jake's shirt. "Are *you* okay? You must have— Did Griffin—?"

He nods with a tightening of his mouth, cutting off the question I'd only started. "If you can even call him Griffin anymore," he mutters.

A tremor passes through his body, and he brushes his fingers farther across my face to stroke them over my hair. He hasn't moved one inch closer since I set aside the meal I was holding.

He's waiting for my welcome—or lack thereof. I can feel his tense anticipation like a vibration in the air.

I ease forward and tip my head against his chest.

A breath rushes out of Jacob with a shudder, and his arms encircle me. He hugs me to him tightly but still with a sense of restraint, as if he's afraid he'll hurt me even now.

But if our new prison has proven anything to me so far, it's that Jake has never really been my enemy.

He fucked up, and he shouldn't have treated me the way he did. But the guardians fucked him up first.

They did it on purpose.

And having seen the new Griffin, drained of any noticeable emotion, devoid of warmth, I know just how thoroughly they can break a person.

I may never fully understand exactly how much they wrecked the man I'm holding.

Jacob's voice comes out in a rasp muffled by my hair. "I'm sorry."

I frown and raise my head. "What for?"

I hate how familiar I am with the anguish etched on his chiseled features. "I was supposed to be looking out for you in the other facility—I swore I'd keep you safe—and they still managed to— I got distracted. I wasn't thinking."

"Hey." I touch his cheek the way he cupped mine. "You know that Griffin was *there*, right? He messed with our emotions to get us where the guardians—at least the ones on Clancy's side, I guess—wanted us to be."

Jacob blinks at me, and a muscle ticks in his jaw. Maybe he *hadn't* realized that part.

"Shit. I should have recognized—I should have known—"

"No." I tap the side of his face firmly to emphasize my protest. "We all got caught. It's all of our faults or none of ours. I haven't for one second blamed you. So you're not allowed to blame yourself for this."

Jacob's mouth twists, but he can't seem to find a way to argue with me.

I pull away from him a little reluctantly and pick up my breakfast to bring it to the nearest undented table. Jake snatches the first plate in reach and follows me.

As he sits down across from me, I hover my fork over my omelet. "So, you decided to give Clancy's missions a try? We've been a little worried about you since we hadn't seen you yet."

Dominic joined in my outdoor training session yesterday morning, and I saw Zian and Andreas again at separate meals. Jacob's absence has been weighing on all of us.

Jake shrugs a little stiffly and jabs his fork into the fried egg. "It wasn't really much of a choice, was it? It was the only way they'd let me see you, or the guys. They still made me wait a whole day for that after I said I was in."

Clancy must have been watching him, evaluating whether he could trust Jacob's intentions enough. "They just left you in your room all that time?"

He shakes his head. "I think they take us outside in shifts just like the meals. Clancy and a couple of his underlings brought me out to a training area that's a ways into the forest, along with some of the kids. We didn't see anyone else going to or from."

I haven't been taken to any separate areas of the valley yet, but his explanation doesn't surprise me. Zian said that he and Dominic were escorted to a rock-climbing area yesterday afternoon while I was in the field again.

Jacob takes a bite and considers me over the table as we chew. "We have to get off this island for one of these missions. See how it all works. Then we can make more of a decision."

Exactly what I've been thinking. I offer him a crooked smile in return. "Yeah."

We eat for a few minutes in silence, wary of who might be listening unseen. Then Jacob motions his fork at me.

"You said 'we.' How many of the others have you seen?"

"All of them, now. But only here and there. And never more than three of us together at once." I swallow a lump of cheese-saturated egg, the flavor turning sour as I think about my answer. "Clancy made it clear that he doesn't think it's in his best interests to let all five of us have a chance to collaborate."

Jacob lets out a disdainful huff. "Because we'd run fucking circles around his operation here."

He could be right. But we're not getting to find out, are we?

Even though the omelet is perfectly enjoyable, my stomach has twisted into a knot by the time I've finished eating. I get up to put my dishes away, knowing that in a matter of minutes some of the staff will come by to usher us to our various next destinations.

But I've barely set my plate down in the bin when Clancy himself pokes his red-topped head into the cafeteria.

He walks over to my and Jacob's table at a briskly professional pace. "The two of you appear to be settling in."

Jacob eyes him, looking like he's grappling with his self-control. "I'd like to see the rest of my friends."

"We'll get to that. I'm sure Riva's already told you that they're perfectly fine, as she is." Clancy motions to us. "I was hoping to talk to just the two of you in my office for a moment."

Jake and I exchange a look. Our new captor makes the request sound voluntary, but somehow I don't think he'll be pleased if we refuse.

We'll get more chances to figure out this place and how to leave it the more we dance to his tune.

But I'm not going to let him call all the shots either—at least, as much as he'll let me have a voice.

As we follow him into the hall, I clear my throat. "There were a few things I wanted to ask you about too. Just to understand how we ended up here better."

I don't know whether to be relieved or suspicious that Clancy answers without hesitation. "That's completely fair."

Of course, after we've stepped into an office room that's got the same stone walls as the rest of the mountain facility, it's Jacob who speaks up first. He doesn't even wait until Clancy has moved behind the desk at one end of the room.

"In the other facility, the one we broke into—you set us up to get caught, with my brother's help. How did you know we'd be coming there? Why did you let us get the kids out first?"

I've been wondering a lot along the same lines. I study Clancy's face as he sinks into the simple office chair behind the desk, leaving us standing.

"About your brother's part in things, I think that's something you should discuss with Griffin, as much as he's willing to. As for the rest, I didn't intervene right away because I wasn't sure how the situation would play out. Not everyone working at that facility was completely on board with my approach. I hoped their strategy would work and that I could arrange your transfer to the island regardless."

The knots in my gut pull tighter. "But it didn't work, so we slaughtered a bunch of people who were causing problems for you." How convenient.

And technically, *I* slaughtered most of them.

Clancy doesn't show any reaction to that statement. "I'm not happy about the loss of life. It is what it is. We did have to resort to a certain amount of trickery in the end, but I'd known that if brute force wasn't going to do it, we'd have to be as smart as possible instead."

They'd waited until we'd started to split up and then divided us even further.

"What about the younger shadowbloods—all of them?" I ask. "The ones I've talked to here all already know about the sha—the monsters we're supposed to be fighting. Some of them have already been sent on missions directly against them. That never happened with us."

Clancy folds his hands in his lap as he leans back in his chair. "We've made some modifications to our process from generation to generation. We were able to train in the younger shadowbloods faster because we'd learned from our experiences with you. And after your escape attempt, a significant portion of the Guardianship felt it would be too dangerous for the six of you to leave the facilities under any circumstances."

Modifications in their process. He probably doesn't realize what we learned from Ursula Engel's computer files—that she never gave the rest of the guardians her full formula for creating us.

The kids have weaker powers than we do. *That's* at least as much a part of why the guardians worried less about sending them into the field.

But it also means they'd have been less equipped to actually fight the shadowkind they were up against.

"What are we doing here if you're not actually going to give us anything to do other than train more?" Jacob demands, scowling.

A hint of a smile touches Clancy's lips. "I said a significant portion. I didn't say *I* felt that way. I actually brought you in here so we could discuss your first potential assignment."

Six

Riva

The first moment when I emerge from sleep in my new bed always feels a little empty. It's comfortable enough, with layers of covers I can bundle under against the cave-like chill, but I'm all on my own.

Sometime over the past few weeks, without even realizing it, I got used to waking up next to my guys. Mostly Dominic, but one time him and Andreas both, and once, after a particularly tumultuous evening, Jacob.

We have more freedoms here, but I'm no longer allowed the simple pleasure of a cuddle to greet the day.

I pull myself out from under the covers, wash at the sink in the corner, and dress with quick movements. I'm just slipping on my sneakers when a knock sounds on my door.

I don't cross paths with any of my guys at breakfast, but when I'm ushered out to the facility entrance, Clancy is waiting with Jacob, Dominic, four of the younger shadowbloods, and several other guardians.

Seeing Jake, my heart skips a beat. This must be preparation for the mission we agreed to yesterday.

Clancy confirms my assumption with a nod toward the kids, who look to all be from the oldest of their generations, around seventeen.

"This group will perform some secondary work as part of your assignment off the island. It should be relatively straightforward, but we want to make sure we've covered all the bases before sending you into the field."

Celine is there, flashing me one of her bright smiles as she teases her fingers through her ponytail, but I don't know the others by name yet. As we set off down to the clearing and then along a jungle path, she chatters energetically with a couple of her companions.

Here and there, I think I catch glimpses of that sadness I thought I noticed earlier. I feel like I should apologize to her for the last mission the guardians forced her to take on, even though it wasn't my idea that they should hunt us down across the continent.

Behind them, the three of us "Firsts" walk in silence. I'm too keyed up to make any kind of small talk.

Dominic takes my hand and interlocks my fingers with his. Jacob sticks close to my other side, scanning the wilderness.

Despite the sticky humidity, it isn't really an unpleasant hike. Birds twitter in the trees, and the hazy sunlight dances between the rustling leaves.

It doesn't take long before we stop in a small clearing. Three of the guardians direct the younger shadowbloods off between the trees at the far end for whatever they need to work on. Three others and Clancy stay with us Firsts.

Clancy strolls back and forth in front of us, his hands clasped behind his back. "I know the three of you have already been through extensive training, including some missions outside your facility. And obviously you've added to your real-world skills in the weeks while you were on the run."

Real-world skills that included killing a whole lot of his colleagues. My skin creeps uneasily despite his calm tone, and Dominic squeezes my fingers reassuringly.

His closer tentacle slips around my wrist as if to duplicate the casually affectionate touch with the gentle graze of its suckers. Both times I've seen him since arriving on the island, he's had his strange new appendages uncovered like he'd started to feel comfortable doing on Rollick's yacht.

I catch a couple of the younger shadowbloods glancing his way and nudging each other. My jaw sets on edge, and my grip on his hand tightens in return.

They might be like us, but I'm not going to let *anyone* make him ashamed of the features that are now part of him. Especially not when he's finally found a kind of peace with his situation.

"This operation will require a few very specific skills that will need additional testing and training." Clancy halts and turns to face the three of us. "Riva and Jacob, you'll be taking lead, which will require immense stealth and speed. Dominic, if your healing ability is needed, time will be of the essence there as well. We'd like to see where you're currently at."

He points to a blotch of orange through the trees in the opposite end from where the teens are doing their training. "Start by that marker and run as fast as you can, regardless of the obstacles, to the one you'll see ahead of you." His arm swings to indicate the direction we'll be running.

Then he fixes his gaze on us again. "Please give it your all. I don't want to waste time on additional exercises that aren't really necessary."

I don't want to hang around here training any longer than I need to either. Less than a week, and he's already opened up the possibility of getting off the island.

I have no idea how we can make use of that opportunity, but I want to find out as soon as I can.

This once, we have to leave Andreas and Zian behind. But maybe we'll learn something that could bring us back together, one way or another.

We head toward the marker, Jacob positioning himself between me and the guardians like a shield.

As we turned, we put our backs to the younger shadowbloods with a sway of Dominic's tentacles. A shocked gasp carries after us, followed by nervous giggles and a muffled "What the *hell*?"

Dom's fingers tense momentarily in mine.

"Ignore them," I say under my breath. "They'll get used to it."

They'd better.

Dominic's grip has already relaxed again. "I know. And I do look strange. It's worth the trade-off."

He told me the first night we got together that he'd never want to try to remove the tentacles because then he might not be able to heal me properly if I needed his help in the future.

I raise his hand in mine to press a kiss to his knuckles, and then to the back of his tentacle still tucked around my wrist. Dominic beams at me, and I don't give a shit that the guardian who's following us clears his throat as if to remind us to stay focused.

Jacob shoots a death glare over his shoulder at my critic, so that helps too.

The guardian veers away from us toward the other orange marker that I can now make out through the trees. "Get ready and wait for my signal."

We spread ourselves out in a reasonably straight line in front of the tree that has the first marker, my hand parting from Dominic's reluctantly. I drop into a sprinter's starting stance.

The guardian gives the standard "Ready, set, go!" and I launch myself forward alongside the other guys.

Between the three of us, it's no real contest. I could probably outrun even Zian's similarly super-powered strength here in the forest, where my small size makes it easier for me to slip between the tree trunks and through the underbrush.

My feet thump over the uneven ground in a swift rhythm, finding their balance instinctively. I fly past bushes and low branches and skid to a stop just past the second marker, barely winded.

Jacob charges after me, hurtling forward as fast as his muscular legs can propel him. Dominic follows several paces behind him with his tentacles coiled close to his back.

But even though Dom's always been the least coordinated of us, all our past training has still served him well. He reaches the two of us just seconds behind Jacob.

The guardian gives his timer a third click and studies the results. "Better than you were looking for," he shouts back to Clancy.

"Then we can move on," Clancy says. "Come on back, you three."

When we tramp over to him, he motions Jacob toward another of the guardians. "Lin has some models for you to work your powers on. We want you honing that telekinetic accuracy so you can dispatch enemy combatants with no chance for them to sound a warning."

Clancy turns to me. "I'd like to see if your claws can let you climb up a brick wall without the need for a harness. We've got a setup for that over here."

Then he beckons over the last of the guardians who've stayed with us, who's been lugging a large sack. The man peels it off to reveal a short, dense shrub in a thin plastic pot that's trailing fabric straps.

"You," Clancy says to Dominic, "need a guaranteed energy source if you're going to be healing on the fly. So we're going to see about making an effective harness for you, with the largest plants you can carry that won't interfere with your movements."

Dominic studies the shrub with a slight rise of his eyebrows. "I'm going to be porting bushes around like a baby in a carrier?"

I can't stop a short laugh from slipping out at the image that forms in my mind. "Whatever works, right?"

It's actually a pretty smart idea, even if it'll look funny.

Clancy and the guardian who handled our race lead me over to a section of layered bricks they've set up in another clear patch of forest. I flex my claws out far enough that tufts of fur spring across the shell of my ears too and launch myself at the mottled surface.

After a few tries, I figure out the trick for sinking the tips far enough into the mortar between the rough blocks at the right angle to hold my weight. I can't hold myself in one spot for more than a few seconds, but by quickly jerking my hands upward one by one and scrambling with my feet catching on whatever small notches they can find, I make it to the top of the ten-foot structure in the space of a few breaths.

I push myself off and land on my feet on the ground.

Clancy nods with a satisfied air. "Give that at least ten run-throughs until you're totally comfortable, and then we're going to work on refining your other supernatural talent."

My pulse hiccups at the thought of bringing out my fatal shriek. I glance toward Jacob, his pale hair partly visible through the trees, and think of the task he was sent to do.

By "dispatch," Clancy meant "kill."

"Are you going to tell us who we're going up against and why?" I have to ask.

"We'll get to that."

He turns on his heel and leaves me to it.

I tackle the wall twenty more times just to make sure I'm fully prepared. I might have kept going if the last joints of my fingers didn't feel ready to fall off by that point.

I stop to catch my breath, flexing my hands to stretch out some of the soreness. Clancy returns with a smaller sack I didn't notice the guardians carrying.

He pulls it open to reveal a wire cage containing eight white mice.

I recoil instinctively. "I don't want to kill them."

Clancy gives me an evaluating look. "I don't want you to either. I think your power could be much more useful than that, in ways you might be more comfortable putting it to use. From the video footage I've seen—you can only break one body at a time, but you can hold dozens of them frozen while you work your way through them. Is that right?"

"Yes." I swallow against the sudden dryness in my mouth.

"Then if we can modulate that scream of yours, you should be able to maintain it at lower levels of influence. Simply paralyze your targets without inflicting any damage. Possibly even seek them out without touching them at all, like a sort of sonar."

His even words steady my nerves, but doubts coil in my gut. "I don't know. It… It really *wants* the pain."

Clancy doesn't object to my characterizing my talent as something separate from myself. "It's in you. You can control it. You simply need to learn how."

I drag in a breath. "What did you have in mind?"

Clancy motions for me to sit and sets the cage in front of me. "We'll pull back from your innate impulses by degrees. Can you damage one of the mice without outright killing it?"

I give him a sharp look, and he smiles apologetically. "We have to start somewhere. If you can manage it in one go, we can scale back even more."

Every molecule of my body balks at torturing an innocent animal, but I remember Rollick's admonishments far too well. If I don't learn how to control my power, then it's going to control me when I least want it to.

Like when I nearly tore apart one of the shadowkind who'd been most welcoming to us.

The memory of Billy's twisted, smoking body congeals inside me, stiffening my resolve. "All right. I'll do my best."

Seven

Riva

I kill the first mouse.

I don't mean to. I summon the furious vibration in my lungs, remembering the other guardians chasing us down, the cage-fights in the arena, the attacks of the monster hunters, and part my lips, letting only the thinnest shriek slip out.

But maybe the vicious thing inside me is too hungry after all the days it's lain dormant. Or maybe other parts of me crave the rush of power a little more than I want to admit.

The scream jolts out of me faster than I intended. The mouse twitches and spasms, the flavor of its agony hitting me in a swift smack like a gulp of cold water on a hot day.

The next thing I know, it's lying in a disjointed lump on the cedar chips covering the base of the cage.

I flinch at the sight, but Clancy sets a careful hand on my shoulder.

"It's going to take time. After everything I've heard and observed, I think your problem might be how much you're resisting the urge."

I stare at him, barely holding back a glower. "Isn't the point to resist?"

"Then you're fighting against yourself. You'll only make yourself weaker." Clancy tips his head thoughtfully. "What if you focused on how you *will* get what the power wants? Stretching out the pain so you can absorb more of it—and then you'll have more time to pull back as well. Even holding a creature in place with the sense of something horrible to come is a pretty painful act, if you think about it."

I wet my lips and look at the dead mouse again. I don't know if what he's saying makes sense, but it's true that my past attempts at control haven't gotten me very far.

I've managed to get more specific in *who* I target, but how… not really at all.

Gritting my teeth, I brace myself to try.

The second mouse I don't kill outright, yanking myself out of the scream's trance at the last second. But its mangled twitching showed there'd be no point in keeping it alive if Clancy couldn't scoop it out and pass it to another guardian, telling him to take it to Dominic.

I still feel sick, but knowing I managed to rein myself in a little builds my confidence. With the third mouse, I encourage the demanding need inside me to inflict the pain slowly, drawing out every drop.

One bone snaps. A sliver of flesh rips.

I slam my mouth shut, and the mouse shudders. It's going to need healing too, but it can still walk.

A startled laugh of relief tumbles from my mouth, soothing the vocal cords still quivering from my last shriek.

The next time, I don't break anything at all. I narrow all my attention onto the panic I can sense in the rodents' beady eyes, the twitches of their bodies as my scream grips them, drinking in the thinner stream formed by the torment of that fear—and pull back before the scream can slice any deeper.

I practice again and again, until I've probably given the poor things PTSD. But I haven't done anything worse to them.

Finally, I sag back on my heels and realize that my shirt is damp with sweat.

Clancy's small smile looks almost friendly to me now. "That was good. Very good. You'll have a chance to practice more later. Better not to push yourself too hard all at once."

I find myself accepting his offered hand to help me to my feet. A whisper of elation tickles through me as we return to the main clearing.

He told the truth about at least this much—he's giving me the chance to be something other than a monster.

When I rejoin the others, Dominic still has his harness on. The straps of the shrub-carrier have been constructed well to work around his various appendages, angling under his tentacles and then across the outer part of his shoulders. Another strap around his waist holds the contraption steady, with the pot right in the middle of his back.

"It's not too bad," he tells me with a crooked smile. "I'm going to leave it on for the trek back to the facility just to get more used to it."

Jacob rolls his shoulders, his expression impassive. I can't tell if he's been affected by the mock-killing he's been practicing.

"What now?" he asks Clancy.

Our captor-slash-trainer has brought out a tablet. "We'll go over more of the details of the mission back at the facility this evening. But I want you to start absorbing the key faces now so you're most likely to recognize them later."

He brings up a photograph of a man who looks to be in his sixties, grizzled with slicked back gray hair and lips that are both full and sharply carved in his craggy face. "This is the leader of a child abduction ring that's been operating for decades. His people kidnap vulnerable kids and teens and sell them off into work-slavery or worse."

A shiver of revulsion passes through me. "And there aren't any police or whatever who can stop them?"

Clancy grimaces. "He pays off local law enforcement and operates very carefully so there's as little evidence as possible. I think it's time someone took matters into their own hands."

He flips through several more photographs, pausing on each to give us time to study their faces. "These are his known associates that we've identified. Most of them should be with him in his home on the night we send you in."

"What about the kids?" Dominic asks, frowning.

"They never have more than one or two on their property at a time, and never for very long. And from what we can tell, they don't keep them at the private home. But to take every precaution, we'll pick a time when we're sure they're between transactions."

Clancy lowers the tablet and considers us. "There may be household staff on the premises. We'd prefer you didn't harm them if you can avoid it. I'd imagine you can differentiate between them and your real targets by their behavior and clothing."

One more factor to pay attention to. I won't be able to simply scream at the house and carve up every human being inside it.

This assignment isn't going to be easy. It isn't anything like our past missions, where we had no idea what real purpose the guardians had for sending us out.

But the quiver passing through my veins is as much anticipation as it is nerves. I *would* like the chance to put my deadly skills to use in a way that helps people rather than simply slaughtering those in my way.

And I'm starting to think that might be possible in ways I never imagined before.

How can I say that killing a bunch of child-slavers is a bad thing? These assholes have to know their work is evil, but they're doing it anyway.

If I was willing to shatter Ursula Engel and her men simply for trying to murder us, slaughtering this bunch should be barely a blip on my conscience. Hell, it's balancing the scales, making sure people who deserve it have real *lives* that these pricks would steal from them.

Good fucking riddance.

If we get a better idea of how we could get free again while we're at it, then it's an extra win.

I eye Clancy's tablet as he slips it into his shoulder bag, wondering about the cell reception out here. Would we be able to get our hands on a phone out in the wider world that we could bring back and use?

But who would I contact? I had Rollick's number programmed into my old phone, but I didn't memorize it.

And I'm not sure even our supposedly greatest ally can be trusted to have our backs—or to protect us from his fellow shadowkind—after all.

Well, there's no way to know what we'll have to work with until we get out there.

Clancy claps his hands together. "Riva and Jacob, why don't you two run back to the facility. We've highlighted the trail with more markers at intervals. Consider it a challenge to see how quickly you can get there ahead of the rest of us."

The corners of his eyes crinkle as if with amusement. As if he likes watching us rise to the occasion.

I have no idea what to make of this man.

Jacob jerks his head toward me. "Come on, Wildcat. They can eat our dust."

He springs forward, not waiting for me—but then, he knows I can catch up with him in a matter of seconds. Which I do.

We dash between the trees, noting each orange marker when they flash into view up ahead. I could pull past Jacob and leave him "eating my dust" too, but I only propel myself a few steps ahead of him where I'll have more room to maneuver.

It's more fun when I can hear him right behind me. Like it's a real competition.

And weirdly, for several minutes there, the extended sprint actually does feel almost fun.

The wind whips over my face and braid, the fresh forest air flooding my lungs. Our feet thunder over the ground in a complex joint rhythm that's close to a song.

We're not free. I know we're not.

But for a few moments there, I feel closer to it than I have the whole time we were out of the guardians' clutches but hunted at every turn.

Jacob called me a superhero after I tore down Engel's soldiers with my scream. I managed to believe I was acting like one while we broke those six kids out of the facility days ago, even if that went all wrong.

Could what Clancy's offering us really be our best chance at becoming some kind of heroes for real?

I spot streaks of brighter sunlight in the distance where I think the forest gives way to the main field around the mountainside. I push myself a little faster, our goal in reach—

And stumble at the sight of the guy I thought was behind me emerging from between the trees in front of me instead.

It's not Jacob, though. Jacob slows next to me as my run peters out into a hesitant jog.

The guy who's ambling through the woods, now heading our way after seeing us, is his twin.

I haven't seen Griffin, let alone spoken to him, since my first day in the facility. From Jacob's tensing and the whiff of startled pheromones he gives off, I suspect he hasn't had much chance to reacquaint himself with his brother either.

Griffin offers us a mild smile. "Back from training?" he says in that vaguely friendly way that feels as vacant as his gaze.

I don't know how to talk to him anymore. Is that awful, when I've spent years wishing I had him back?

"Yeah." I come to a stop a few feet away, not sure whether I should keep going, what else he might want to talk about.

Then Jacob barrels between us, his muscles and his voice taut. "You *helped* Clancy get his hands on us, Griffin? What the fuck were you thinking?"

Oh, shit. I forgot that Jacob hadn't realized that part until I told him yesterday morning.

Griffin blinks at his twin, but even his surprise at the outburst is mild. "It seemed like the best thing to do. The right thing to do."

"To see us stuck back in cages? What's the matter with you?"

Griffin's gaze veers around us. "This isn't much of a cage."

I think his calm demeanor is pissing Jacob off even more than he already was. "It doesn't matter how pretty it is—we're still trapped here. Partly because of *you*. You're one of us. Or at least you were."

Griffin studies Jake as if he's a little confused by the entire line of questioning. "I didn't want to see you get into even more trouble or do more things you might regret. I'm sorry that I had to trick you to do it."

"You're sorry?" Jacob rasps. "You betrayed all of us. Me. Riva. You loved her—I know you did—and you helped them drag her back— How could you turn on even *her*?"

A flicker of something passes through Griffin's expression, there and then gone before I can tell if it's anything resembling an emotion. His attention slides to me where I'm standing behind his brother's shoulder, and a pang shoots through my chest.

I loved him too. I don't know if there's anything left of the guy I loved behind those dazed eyes.

"I think I should give you more space," Griffin says, backing up a step. "Seeing me is getting you worked up. I hope we can talk more later."

"You—"

Jacob's hand twitches, and I grab his arm before he can lift it. I don't want him using his powers on his brother—I can't imagine he won't regret *that*.

"Let him go," I say quietly as Griffin strides off toward the clearing. "I don't think he *can* give us any answer we'd be happy with."

Jake's fingers flex and clench at his sides. "There's nothing okay about that."

"I know. It isn't okay at all. But yelling at him isn't going to fix it. Throwing around your power definitely won't."

Jacob lets his breath out in a hiss. His head droops. "Yeah."

Watching him, an ache expands through my chest, eating away all the momentary joy I found. I can remember the two of them together so easily, back when we were all in the facility together.

Any time Griffin faltered in a physical trial, Jacob would be there, ensuring his twin made it through. Every time Jacob's determined incisiveness boiled over into frustration, Griffin would be there, talking him down.

They fit together perfectly, like two halves of a whole, made to complement each other—to balance each other out. I've never seen them argue.

Until now.

We stay there for a few minutes, just standing together as Jake's breaths even out. I figure it's better not to push him to go on to the facility until he's got his anger totally under control.

Just as he finally lifts his head, footsteps crackle behind us. We look over to see Clancy approaching us.

Apparently our captor is a fast walker.

He takes us in with a slight cock of his head that asks a question silently.

"We bumped into Griffin," I say in explanation. "It wasn't a good conversation."

"Ah." Clancy's mouth tightens.

I cross my arms over my chest, just shy of hugging myself. "What did the guardians *do* to him?"

Clancy takes a deep breath, his gaze sliding past us toward the mountainside and then back again. "It's over now. I'd focus on that."

Jacob's voice comes out in a growl. "But—"

The older man cuts him off with a shake of his head and fishes for something in his bag. "I realized there's one thing I wanted to go over with you upfront. While you're out on the assignment, we'll be tracking and monitoring your life signals the entire time. To make sure you haven't gotten diverted, and so we can alert Dominic right away if his powers are needed."

My spine stiffens. "What do you mean?"

He pulls out a couple of metal bands about as thick as my thumb. "You'll each be wearing one of these around an ankle. So you'll never really be alone."

EIGHT

Riva

The lit windows stand out on the face of the mansion like signal flares in the dark night. But we have to avoid those beacons until we're inside.

Jacob topples the last of the three men who were stationed outside the isolated home with a snap of a vertebrae straight through the spinal cord. His power catches the body so it slumps quietly on the ground rather than hitting the lawn with a thump.

That's what he's spent the past two days practicing, while I've been climbing more walls, slipping silently through shadows… and doing my best *not* to kill mice.

Oh, and one of Clancy's guardians did walk me through the fastest ways to kill a person with my claws using a dummy. But when she saw that my cage-fighting days had driven those skills home even deeper than my previous facility training, she decided I was good to go.

I always left my opponents alive if I could, but if it came down to me or them, I needed to know how to end the fight quick.

We stalk swiftly through the darkness to the back of the sprawling two-story mansion. Clancy showed us a rough blueprint of the place—there's a room at the back that the people he's sent to observe never saw the light go on in.

Whatever our targets do in there, they don't do it at night. It's our best chance at entering without alerting anyone.

The second-floor window is closed, and I bet it has a latch on the inside too. But Jacob simply stares at it, and after a moment the sliding pane eases upward with a faint rasp.

I don't even wait for it to be fully raised. I leap at the side of the building, digging my claws in the way I've rehearsed, and fling myself up toward the window.

My ears pick up the tiny scratching of my claws, but I don't think even Jacob will be able to hear the noise below, let alone anyone inside. The second I reach the window, I whip my arm over the ledge to brace myself and lift my other hand to carve open the screen.

I roll inside through the opening I've made, peer through the darkness to confirm that the small room holds nothing but scattered cardboard boxes, and whirl toward the window while unstrapping the coil of rope from my waist.

Jacob's always been able to move small things very precisely and larger things with great force, but he doesn't have enough control with something as heavy as a person to lift them fifteen feet in the air with no chance of them thumping against the wall. So he won't be flying himself or anyone else through windows anytime soon.

Although when Clancy talked us through this part of the plan, I got the impression that Jake was making mental notes to develop that skill too.

I drop the rope, and Jacob catches hold. Bracing his feet against the bricks, he heaves himself up with careful steps until he can scramble in after me.

We glance around the room, our eyes adjusting to the more enclosed darkness. He reaches into a box and lifts up what at first looks like a rag.

No, it's a shirt—a kid's shirt, that could fit a six year old.

My stomach clenches.

Another box I glance into holds an assortment of basic toys—dolls and plastic cars and building blocks. My throat constricts to match my gut.

Clancy said the slavers don't appear to bring the kids to this house, but they clearly stash some supplies to do with their business.

Jacob glances at me with a determined expression, and I nod, squaring my shoulders. I may have led the way into the house, but for most of the mission, he's going first.

He'll "dispatch" every person we see who's part of the slaving ring, and I'll stay ready to leap in if Jake's subtler approach to offing them goes wrong.

Zian's X-ray vision would have been helpful here too, though I guess he might not have even fit through the window. And Clancy is still determined not to let too many of our group work together.

As we steal over to the door, footsteps creak on the floor outside.

Jacob tenses. He cocks his head, judging the sound, and nudges the door open a sliver to get a look outside.

The next thing I know, there's another faint *crack*, and he's yanking a limp corpse into the storage room with his powers.

I catch the body to help break its fall, and we lay it together on the floor. Even slack with death, the face catches on a memory.

It's one of the men from the pictures Clancy showed us. Not the boss, though.

Jacob must recognize him too, because his mouth twists into a grim smile. He catches my gaze again as if to check that I'm still good and returns to the doorway.

The hall outside is empty now. We slip along the thick rug, finding the spots where we can set our weight without provoking creaks of our own, to a room farther down that voices are filtering from.

With my ears pricked, I decipher three different voices. I don't think Jake will be able to drop all of them before the last can sound an alarm.

He's going to need me too.

I touch his arm to catch his attention and hold up three fingers followed by a gesture toward myself. Jacob grimaces, but he nods in reluctant acknowledgment.

He isn't going to gamble both our lives by overestimating his abilities.

To my surprise, instead of leaping straight in, he reaches to me and clasps my hand. Tentatively at first, as if he's afraid I'll yank away—like I probably would have a couple of weeks ago.

But I squeeze his fingers in return with a strange wobble through my pulse.

We're going to do this together. We're *good* together when all the other shit is out of the way.

We position ourselves in front of the door. My muscles coil.

Then Jacob flings it open in one brisk motion.

I don't pause for even an instant to make sure he's handling his part of the problem. I spring straight at the man who's standing the farthest on my side of the room, my claws slashing out to strike his throat.

As I catch his fall while blood gurgles out of him, two more bodies slump at my right. One sways in Jacob's hold, but he manages to push it toward an armchair that muffles the impact.

I scan the faces in the lamplight and swallow a twinge of disappointment. All three were in Clancy's file, but none of these are the man in charge either.

He's the most important one. If we don't get him, he could just start his business all over again once he's hired more people.

Thumps carry up the stairs from outside the room, a voice rising alongside them. The words are in a language I don't know, but they have the cadence of a question.

Jacob and I fall into position silently.

The door still stands partly open. The moment the newcomer is close enough, Jacob grabs him with his power, snaps his neck, and drags him inside with the others.

We shut the door behind us and pause to listen in the hall. No other sounds of human presence reach our ears from the rooms around us, but more remarks travel up from the first floor, along with a tinkling of music.

We have to hurry. Who knows how soon the rest of the inhabitants might start to think it's strange that their companions upstairs have been so quiet?

The banister on the broad staircase only offers partial shelter. I spot a couple more men and a woman—one of the two women included in Clancy's photos—sitting on a leather sofa in a huge living room, laughing at something on the TV.

This time, I don't even need to look at Jacob. He reaches back and rests his hand on my foot, nudging me ahead of him.

He can do his work from here. I need to get closer if I'm going to be speedy enough.

I dart the rest of the way down the stairs and flatten myself against the wall by the living room entrance. When I'm ready, I make a quick gesture to Jacob without shifting my attention from the room's inhabitants.

I trust that he'll act the moment I signal him. And as I hurtle into the room, the first of the men is already crumpling.

The second man starts to yelp, but I cut off the sound with a swift slash, tearing open the woman's throat as well before she can do more than flinch. Blood spurts out over their sagging bodies and splatters my black clothes.

We still haven't found the boss. Is he not even home right now?

Clancy wouldn't have sent us in unless he was sure we'd find our main target, would he?

Jacob descends the stairs. We creep through an empty dining room and out into a wide hall that leads to a kitchen and a few other closed rooms.

The clink of dishes carries from the kitchen. We venture closer, our eyes peeled.

Two figures are moving around between the gleaming stainless-steel appliances and counters. Both the woman and the man are dressed in plain clothes, aprons tied over them, no jewelry or weapons.

And if that wasn't enough to suggest that they don't fit with the house's main residents, they're in the middle of unloading a dishwasher. They must be part of the household staff that Clancy mentioned.

I'm about to move on in the hopes that we can ignore them completely when a man walks into the kitchen from the back door, his confident stride and posher clothes marking him as a target rather than a servant. Shit.

We don't have time to retreat to an easy hiding place. And maybe it'd be stupid to try to continue our assault with the kitchen staff here anyway, when they could potentially wander into the other rooms and stumble on a body at any moment.

At least this way, we control when and how they find out.

Jacob focuses on the man, who's already ambled halfway across the kitchen. As the faint, fatal crack sounds, I hustle into the room.

The kitchen staff spin around, the woman letting out a gasp of surprise at the sight of one of her employers toppling. I press my hands to both of their mouths.

"We don't want to hurt you," I whisper in as low a tone as I can manage. "We just want to stop them from taking more kids. Get out of here, and don't come back."

They both nod, wide-eyed. The man rushes out through the back door first.

The woman treads after him and steps out into the night. But she's only made it a few steps into the lawn before she whirls around and screams out a warning in that language I don't know.

Fucking hell. My claws spring from my fingers again, but I have more vital things to do than get revenge on her for her betrayal.

Heavy footsteps pound toward us—some from the hall and others up from a basement staircase I hadn't even noticed. Someone else is yelling now.

There's an oof and a bang from the hall. Jacob dashes into the kitchen after me.

Two men charge in from the other direction at the same moment, guns in their hands. I swing around, but I'm not close enough to strike either of them in time.

One smacks into the wall with a heave of Jacob's invisible power. He throws himself at me, tackling me to the ground just as the second gun fires.

We roll across the floor behind a storage cart. Nerves jangling, I squirm out from under Jacob just in time to see the gunman barging toward our momentary shelter.

He aims his pistol at Jake, who hasn't quite righted himself yet, and this time I am close enough.

I launch myself at our attacker, my knee slamming into his elbow to send his shot wide, my claws snatching at his throat. With a hiss of breath, I tear the entire front of his neck right off of his body.

At another thud, my head jerks up. A woman who ran into the room, clutching a rifle, is just slumping to the ground, her head seeping blood against the wall from where Jacob cracked it open.

My gaze drops to the man who's just collapsed in front of me.

Slicked-back gray hair. A craggy face with harsh full lips above the gouged-out throat.

My heart leaps.

"It's him," I murmur to Jacob. "We got him. The main boss."

Jacob is staring at me as if he hasn't quite heard me. A shudder runs through his body.

His head jerks around, but no other footsteps reach our ears. That isn't enough of a guarantee that we're done, though.

I open my mouth and let a tiny shriek reverberate out of me, even softer than the ones I've practiced. Just enough to quiver through the walls, seeking out a target to latch on to.

In the middle of my adrenaline high, I don't know if I could have reined it in as well as I did in the controlled environment back on the island. Maybe I'd have ended up tearing into any body it touched.

But I don't have to find out. It flows through the whole house and catches nothing.

I gulp in a relieved breath. "That's it. We got them all."

"Then let's get the fuck out of here," Jacob rasps.

I couldn't agree more.

We race out the back door, scanning the night for assailants drawn by the sounds of the fight. The yard is empty.

The staff fled for safety after all—after the woman screwed us over.

I grit my teeth and run for the surrounding wall. Jacob is right behind me.

He offers me a boost up and I lean over to grab his arm, helping each other in turn. Then we sprint for the van we parked half a mile away in the cover of a short stretch of forest.

The metal band around my ankle shifts with my movements. Clancy will know that we left and that we made it through the attack okay. Dominic will be safe where he's waiting in his own van to find out if he'll need to rush to anyone's rescue.

Safe for now, anyway. I can only hope that the team of younger shadowbloods doesn't need to deal with too many late arrivals.

We leap into the van without breaking stride, Jacob having disengaged the locks from a distance. He starts the engine while I strap myself into the passenger seat.

As we tear off down the road to put even more distance between us and the site of our assignment, a message pops up on the touchscreen mounted on the dashboard between us.

Targets eliminated?

I tap in a hasty answer. *Several including the big one.*

Good work. Get to the rendezvous spot and wait there. Expect the others in approximately 2 hours.

At the command, I can't help looking down at my ankle. Jacob studied his tracking band on the way out here and indicated to me that he couldn't feel any simple way of removing it.

The knowledge passes through my mind that we could make a run for it. We don't have much, but we've gotten by with hardly anything before, and we'd have a two-hour head start.

But even if we can bash the anklets off before Clancy's people find us, even if we could navigate this country without a clue where the plane brought us… we'd be leaving the others behind.

I don't even need to voice the question to know Jacob would reject that idea just as vehemently as my heart is recoiling from it. I'm not even sure we aren't better off in our new circumstances, at least in some ways.

I paid attention during the trip leaving the island, though. I know where the runway the private jet took off from lies relative to the mountain facility, and that there's a harbor in sight within a few miles of it on the island's coast.

We've learned useful things for ourselves on this mission as well as taking out villains who deserved it. If we decide it's time to leave, hope isn't lost, not by a long shot.

Jacob pulls into the open field a short distance from the currently vacant airfield. The second he's turned the engine off, he twists toward me.

His gaze skims over my body. "Are you okay? None of them got to you?"

I adjust my position, cringing inwardly at the feel of the still-damp patches of blood on my shirt. "None of this is mine, as far as I know. We should get out of the bloody clothes, though."

Clancy didn't leave us much in the large space at the back of the van, but we do each have a change of clothes—and a bag where we're supposed to stuff the evidence of our mission for burning. I push into the back and tug at my long-sleeved tee.

Jacob follows me. I expect him to change his own clothes, but when I toss my bloody shirt into the bag and move to reach for the new one, he touches my arm to stop me.

The next sweep of his gaze over my nearly naked torso lights a flicker of heat under my skin despite the cool air. I open my mouth to say something about personal space and privacy, but the turmoil in his eyes when they rise to meet mine stops the sardonic remark in my throat.

"You're really all right?" he says, like he can't quite believe it.

He wasn't checking me out just now. He was confirming I don't have any wounds.

A little of my self-consciousness fades. I hold out my arms so he can see the sides of my torso clearly, everything that isn't covered by my sports bra or the slim chain of my necklace.

"Yeah. Not a scratch. Up until the end, they had no idea what hit them."

Another shudder like the one I saw in the kitchen ripples through Jake's frame. "The asshole with the fucking gun—he almost shot you. I almost didn't get there fast enough."

Oh. That's why he's so keyed up.

I touch his jaw in an attempt at reassurance. "You did. You were my armor, like you promised. And then I got to be yours. That's how it should be, right?"

Jacob lets out a strangled sound and lowers his head so his forehead brushes mine. "Yeah. Yeah. I just never want to see anyone get that close—"

His voice tightens. "I want to tear his head right off his fucking shoulders and dance on it."

"I think he's dead enough already," I say with a hint of dryness. "Are *you* okay?"

He doesn't seem like he's detached from reality the way he has a few times in the past when we'd gotten through a shitload of trouble. Tonight's incident doesn't really compare.

But he's obviously not jumping for joy either.

Jacob sets his hands on my waist, skin to skin, with a bloom of warmth. He swallows audibly. "Nothing you need to knock me out of, Wildcat. But I wish I could keep you out of anything this dangerous completely. What good is fucking armor when there's so many of them?"

His voice drops, getting hoarse. "I love you so much, Riva. If I could make sure no one ever fired another bullet at you to begin with, there's nothing I wouldn't do."

A lump rises in my throat. "I know," I say through it, and I do. I believe him with every fiber of my being.

So nothing could feel more natural than finishing my answer by tugging his lips to meet mine.

Nine

Riva

I've kissed Jacob before. More than once.

There was the time I used a kiss to snap him out of a frenzy he was caught up in, thinking he still needed to protect me from attackers.

And the time we started making out and I bawled all over him.

Not the greatest track record. But then, maybe that's to be expected when our entire reunion has been so messy.

I can feel the tension in him as he kisses me back. Part of it is hunger I know must be flaring in his veins just like it is within mine, our shadows straining toward each other.

And part is him battling that hunger.

His fingers flex where he's raised his hand to cup my cheek. A quiver runs through his body, every muscle taut.

I haven't wanted everything he could give me before. I've asked him to be gentle.

Just like every other moment since the one when he called me away from the train hurtling toward me, he's doing whatever he can to make me happy. Whatever he can to make sure he doesn't damage that happiness again.

But the only ache left inside me is the best sort of pain.

I break the kiss to draw back just a few inches, holding his face between my hands as I do. The words feel like they well up from the very center of me. "I love you too."

Jacob lets out a choked sound and dips his head for another kiss. It's all tenderness and giddy release, but I can still taste the restraint in it.

I need more.

I push him downward, and he moves easily at my prodding. As he sinks down to sit against the inner wall of the van, I straddle his lap like I have before.

Maintaining control. Taking the reins.

But that doesn't mean I'm going to be calling *all* the shots.

I tug at his shirt to pull the blood-dappled fabric off him and slide my hands down his sculpted torso.

Jacob's voice has gone rough. "Riva?"

My tongue darts out to wet my lips. I can taste how much he wants me in the desire that laces the air.

The shadows in my blood thrum with eager anticipation.

I look at him, straight into his blue eyes that smolder like pale flames. "I'm not afraid of you anymore. Let it all out. Show me what you'd do with me if you knew I wanted all of it. Because I do."

The flames flare into a full-out bonfire. Jacob trails his fingers under my chin to pull my mouth back to his.

His hesitation doesn't vanish in an instant. The heat of this kiss could melt me, fierce and demanding, but his hands stay careful as they travel over my body.

I kiss him back hard and splay my fingers over his bare chest, tracing every ridge of muscle, thumbing his nipples, caressing all the way down to the solid planes of his stomach. Taking in every part of him without any hesitation of my own.

With each stroke of my hands, Jacob's touch becomes firmer too. He curls his fingers around the back of my neck as he tilts his head, his tongue delving past my lips, scorching hot.

Then he traces my spine all the way down my back before returning to yank at my bra. I raise my arms so he can peel the stretchy sports bra off me, watching how he lifts it around my necklace so the fabric doesn't catch on the pendant.

The gesture brings his forearm near my face where I can't help tracing the scar just below the elbow with my gaze.

There's nothing I wouldn't do.

An echo of the anguish that hit me when he brought the knife to his arm all those weeks ago rises up through my chest. I grip his wrist and bring my lips to the pink line of the scar.

Jacob holds perfectly still as I chart the evidence of his attempted sacrifice with soft kisses. I hear him swallow.

I lift my head to meet his eyes again. "No matter what you feel like you have to do, don't hurt yourself again. Not even for me. I want you here, every part of you."

Jake brushes a stray strand of hair back behind my ear, his gaze fathomless. "You've got me. Every part. I'm yours, whatever you want to do to me, whatever you want me to do."

I dip my head close to his. My voice comes out in a whisper. "I just want you to love me."

He raises his chin to fulfill that request. As his mouth crashes into mine, he cups my bared breasts.

My curves are just large enough to fill his hands. He swivels his palms against my nipples, cautiously and then with more force at my encouraging whimper.

Every increasingly urgent rotation sends a rush of pleasure through my chest. I can't stop myself from nipping at his lip and drinking in his groan.

The essence inside me is rioting now, clamoring for the connection it's already gotten to solidify with two of my other men. My claws tingle behind my fingertips; my hips rock against Jake's.

He grasps my ass, pressing me tighter against him as I grind. Even through multiple layers of clothing, the friction of my pussy against his stiffening erection makes us both growl.

We've gotten this close before, and I didn't let it go any further. But I'm burning up, and the man beneath me is both fueling the flames and absorbing them with his touch.

I want him. I want Jacob in all his fucked-up, damaged, obsessively devoted glory.

It's because of his damage that he understands the deepest wounds I try to hide.

I don't want to lose him again, not any of the ways it could happen. And when the shadows between us meld and merge, I'll always know where he is.

I'll always be able to find him… and I'll know he can always find me.

My hands drop to his athletic pants, yanking at the waistband. Jake's breath hitches, and he shifts his weight to help me drag them off him.

When I stroke my fingers over his rigid cock through his boxers, he groans—and the first aid kit in the corner of the van goes pinging off one of the walls.

Jacob winces in embarrassment and catches my gaze. "Sorry. I can keep better control."

I'm not sure if that's true, but it won't be his fault. My first times with both Andreas and Dominic, our powers came flaring to the surface of their own accord.

I give him a smile that I suspect looks a little wicked. "Just don't give either of us a concussion, and you can go as wild as you want."

Jacob's gaze turns blazing, and he yanks me back into his embrace.

Our kisses become hungrier, hastier, as he strips my sweatpants off me. The pulsing need between my thighs has me grinding against him again with a gasp at the surge of heady sensation.

Jake echoes the sound, his lips branding my neck, my shoulder. He lifts one breast to clamp his mouth around the peak and flicks his tongue over my nipple until I'm bucking in his arms.

He trails his fingers up and down my bare legs, torturously close to my panties, but he pauses to linger over the metal band around my ankle. He looks up at me with a ragged breath.

"Are you sure—"

Resolve burns in my chest alongside my raging desire. "If they can figure out what we're doing, let them. There's nothing wrong about this."

Those words bring a smile to Jacob's face that's so bright I swear my heart almost leaps right out of my chest.

He pulls me into another kiss, tender as the first ones but with scorching passion simmering underneath. My pussy throbs, and the shadows inside me stretch toward the man I've rediscovered my love for.

My pulse kicks up a notch with renewed urgency. I wrench at Jacob's boxers, and he helps me wriggle out of my panties.

But as I lower myself over his jutting cock, he catches me by my hips before I've quite reached him and exhales in a rush.

"I want you so badly. Once we get started—"

I brush my lips against his. "It'll be fine. It's how it's supposed to be. We're meant for this."

He kisses me hard, and I sink the rest of the way onto him. Jacob jerks upward to meet me, plunging deep enough to send a jolt of bliss all the way to my throat.

I cry out and kiss him fiercely so he knows the sound is all happiness. Our hips roll together, propelling him deeper, in and out, with the giddy swell of heat that rises to fill my whole body.

Another loose object smacks into a wall somewhere behind me. Jacob hisses, his fingers digging into my thigh.

When he adjusts the angle at which we fit together, his cock drives home so perfectly I can't suppress a moan. His grasp urges me on while his other hand traces across my scalp where my hair has loosened from my braid.

I know exactly where he's touching me. His fingers sear against my skin. But moments later, an impression of contact reaches other parts of my body, as if more hands have reached for me.

A careful pressure caresses my breasts. A similar sensation runs down my back and across my belly.

My breath stutters in surprise, and Jacob teases his teeth against the crook of my jaw.

"I want to make this as good for you as it possibly can be," he says in a rasp. "I know where it should feel good, but I can't tell— You've got to show me when I get it right."

He's caressing me with his power as well as his body. I'm too lost in the growing whirlwind of pleasure to fully comprehend what he means by "showing" him until the pressure condenses around one nipple as if in a pinch.

My nerves spark, and I sway faster with the rhythm of his thrusts. A needy sound slips from my lips.

"You like that?" Jacob murmurs in a wash of heat across my neck.

I whimper in answer, and he repeats the gesture, tweaking both of my nipples with his telekinetic talent simultaneously. The rush of bliss makes me buck faster.

My voice comes out in a mumble. "So good. More."

Jake chuckles, raw and jerky. "You feel so fucking good too, Wildcat. Never going to let you down again. Never going to stop making you feel fantastic."

The invisible touch massages my ass and strokes my hair, toys with my nipples and wraps around my torso. I spur on his attentions with gasps and moans as he discovers every spot that sets me on fire.

Then the pressure dips right down to the place where we're joined to strum my clit.

Pleasure crackles through me in a rampant blaze. A louder moan of approval careens from my lungs.

Jacob growls and plunges up into me harder, faster.

I want to bury myself in him and swallow him up, all at the same time.

He thrusts up inside me just as his power seems to set off every point of pleasure in the rest of my body, and I hurtle into my release. My nerves sizzle with the smoky essence reaching to twine with his.

The wave of bliss hazes my vision. My claws spring from my fingertips.

Jacob grates out a curse with a twitch of his arms to angle the poison spines that've just shot from his skin away from me.

He slams home once more with a groan that reverberates through the van. The sound tosses me even higher.

I cling to him, riding the wave, shivering with the intensity of the moment. Feeling his heart thump in time with mine, our breaths mingling at the same panting pace.

We are one. Forever.

The tingling races all through my body, but I know it'll condense on my upper chest. This time, when I start to sag over him and glance down between us, I'm not at all startled to see the mark like a thumbprint-sized bruise that's formed at the top of his sternum.

A matching spot has bloomed on my left clavicle, next to the one that formed when I first hooked up with Andreas.

Jacob's chest is still heaving, but he touches the mark with absolute gentleness, his expression full of awe.

"I marked you. Like Drey and Dom did."

"Of course you did. We're blood. Our shadows *want* to meld together." I beam at him. "And now we'll always know how to make our way back to each other, no matter what comes between us."

He lets out a shaky chuckle. "I wasn't totally sure, after everything…"

"You're mine," I inform him, in case he wasn't already aware of that. As if he hasn't been telling *me* that over and over for the last few weeks. A pang of emotion cuts off my voice for a second before I can add, "And I'm yours."

Still inside me, Jake hugs me to him, tipping his head against my shoulder. "For as long as you want to be, Riva."

A quiver passes through his frame, but it feels different from the tremors that shook him before. More energized, less tense.

He tilts my head to claim another kiss. Then his attention falls to my chest again, but not to the marks on my pale skin.

Jacob curls his fingers cautiously around the cat-and-yarn charm dangling from my neck. The one his twin gave me all those years ago.

He lifts his gaze to meet mine. "We're going to fix this too. There has to be a way, and I'll find it."

He got one of the shadowkind to fix the charm itself already, but I know that's not what he's talking about. He means Griffin himself.

The memories of the times he's talked about his feelings for me and his recognition of his brother's send a tightness around my heart. Jacob thought he couldn't have me at all because he didn't want to get between me and Griffin.

I touch the side of his face, grazing my thumb over his cheek. "I know if there is one, you will. But I don't need him *more* than I need you, Jake. I don't love him more. I wanted *you*."

The corner of Jacob's mouth twitches into a hint of a smile. He hugs me again, and I nestle into his embrace for the short time we have before we need to return our minds to the end of our mission.

Before we need to head back into our new cage, gilded as it is.

TEN

Dominic

I stretch out my legs in the back of the van, then tuck them into a cross-legged pose, and pretend I don't notice our local contact shooting uneasy glances my way. He's sitting sideways in the driver's seat so he can alternate between looking out through the windows and over toward me.

I know I'm not much to look *at* right now. Clancy outfitted me with a track jacket even lighter weight than the trench coats I used to use to hide my tentacles.

It only falls to my hips, so I have to keep my unusual appendages coiled a couple of times over. But he must have had the jacket custom made, because the inner lining holds loops of soft fabric to help support them.

I hadn't realized that spreading out the weight across my body would make them feel like less of a burden.

In any case, all the stranger can see is that my back is oddly shaped. I've been holding the tentacles still—holding my whole self pretty much still as we wait to see if I'll be called in to save any of my fellow shadowbloods.

He rubs his hand across his chapped lips and shoots me another glance. "Do you want something to drink? I have water bottles up here."

His accented voice should give me a clue about where Clancy has sent us, but all I can tell for sure is his native tongue isn't Spanish or anything in that family of languages. Maybe German? Or some variation of Eastern European?

Hell, it could be Swedish or Turkish and I'm not sure I'd know the difference. I don't even know if he's a long-time local to this place or a more recent transplant from abroad.

"That's okay." I pat the knapsack resting on the thinly carpeted floor next to me. "I've got a canteen."

He grunts in acceptance and goes back to gazing through the windows, though there isn't much to see out there in the night. With the van's overhead light on at its dimmest setting, the world beyond the windshield looks totally black to me.

I understand why Clancy arranged for his man as my sort-of guide. The de facto leader of the guardians needed to be in touch with people on the ground to find out exactly what we'd be dealing with.

If there's a problem, this guy will know the roads and the rules of them better than any of the guardians would. He'll get me straight to my friends if they need help.

He'll recognize the signs of trouble faster.

But I can't help wishing, for the first time in my life, that I had a guardian for company instead. Someone who already knew about my strangeness and wasn't fazed by it.

What have they told this guy? What is he going to think if I do have to rush in and whip out my tentacles to pour healing power into one of the other shadowbloods?

God forbid.

I shift my weight, my pulse picking up a faster beat. Will Riva and Jacob already be inside the house?

How long will it take them to carry out their first part of the mission —the most dangerous part?

Has the man sitting with me and whatever colleagues he's had helping Clancy given us all the information we needed to keep them safe?

I brush my fingertips over the thin leaves of the shrub that's poised on the floor next to me, its harness ready to fling onto my back in a matter of seconds. The tingle of energy I can sense within them settles my nerves just a little.

I gave the plant a bit of water from my canteen right after we hunkered down here, about a mile from the house—not close enough to draw attention but not too far to cross the distance quickly if I have to rush in. Its crisp herbal scent tickles my nose.

Please, don't let me have to kill it. For all our sakes.

I'd rather not have to destroy any more life. Even a plant's.

The screen on the van's dashboard stays empty. No news so far.

I close my eyes, inhaling the smell of the shrub. My mind strays back to my new room at the island facility.

After our first training session for his assignment, I asked Clancy if I could have some potted plants in my bedroom. I told him it'd help me feel more at home, since that seems to be what he wants.

I didn't really think he'd go along with it anyway, but by the evening, he'd come to escort me to a different room that must be near the face of the mountainside. My old one had no windows, but this one came with a skylight where one wall slanted into the ceiling.

Three potted shrubs of different types and an assortment of flowers waited for me, right where the sunlight would hit them best. A whole garden.

Just remembering it sends a little thrill through me. This isn't the life I expected to be living, and I'm not done sorting out how I feel about Clancy and his plans… but is it possible this new facility *could* be a real kind of home, eventually?

It already feels more mine than any other place I've stayed, both at past facilities and when we were on the run.

My guide is peering at me again. He lifts his chin toward the shrub.

"Your special power—you can make injuries better? But you need the plant?"

I brush my fingers over the leaves again. "If it's a big injury, I need to draw the energy to heal it from something else. Plants are… easiest."

They make me feel the least guilty about the life I've stolen. But I don't want this guy thinking about what else I might suck the energy out of.

He hums to himself and adjusts his weight in the seat. I guess he's probably getting a little restless too, stuck in this van with a particularly strange stranger.

He's curious, though. Maybe I should be trying to make more of the opportunity.

Do more than sit here like a lump hoping I won't need to do anything else.

When we were first driving out to this spot from the airfield, I tried nudging him for clues about where we are, but he shut those down quickly. Clancy must have instructed him not to tell us anything identifying.

"It's safer for all of us," was how he put it to us shadowbloods.

But even having more of an idea about how Clancy is reaching out to people beyond his Guardianship could be useful to know.

"The man who set up this mission with you," I venture. "He told you about our powers?"

My guide shrugs. "Some. Not a lot. Enough to be sure that you should accomplish what you're here to do."

"It doesn't bother you? Or did you already know that people like me and my friends exist?"

"Many unexpected things exist in the world. Better to work with those you can when it benefits you, not dismiss them or run away."

He chuckles lightly, but his gaze flicks toward my back for just a second with the same wariness I've noticed before.

He's happy to *use* our services, but that doesn't mean he trusts us.

His mouth tightens with a momentary frown, and he twists a little farther in the seat to face me. "Your friends—they won't touch anything they find in the house, will they? They only destroy the people."

"That's what we were told to do." I can't say whether Clancy might have given Riva and Jacob other instructions at the last minute. "Is there something important inside?"

He waves his hand dismissively. "Don't worry about it. That's for us. That was the deal."

An uneasy prickle runs down my spine at his words. Who is "us"? What "deal"?

I thought he was helping our mission because he wanted to see the child-slavery ring taken down too—for the good of his community. What would that have to do with anything the perpetrators are keeping in the house?

I try to tell myself that he could simply be thinking of records about the kids and where they've been sold or something understandable like that, but I can't quite shake the sense that he didn't mean it that way. Why would he avoid talking about it if that's all he meant?

"Our boss does take his deals seriously," I say carefully, watching the man's expression.

He lets out a guffaw. "He should, with what he's getting out of it."

The prickle jabs deeper under my skin.

I try to keep my voice even, but I'm not sure I totally succeed. "What exactly is he getting out of the deal this time?"

This time, the man's gaze darts toward my face rather than my back, with a flicker of panic as if he's realized he's said something he shouldn't have. Then he turns to face the windshield.

"That's between us and him. Not your concern, right?"

I'm sure as hell concerned now. "Are you saying that you *paid* him to take on these guys?"

That isn't necessarily so bad, right? They could be a group of outraged citizens who raised the funds to hire someone to deal with a problem they couldn't tackle themselves.

But the way he's acting is setting off my internal alarms. And Clancy never mentioned anything about getting compensation—or about being called by the locals.

He made it sound like he'd found the slavers and decided they needed to be taken out all on his own.

"Did he come to you first or did you come to him?" I ask.

The man shakes his head. "We're done talking about this."

"I just want to understand what's going on. I'm part of this too."

"You work for your boss. I work for mine. We all get what we want. That's all you need to know."

No, it's not, not when everything he adds to the puzzle makes the pieces look more ominous. He has a boss—helping with this mission is *work* for him?

I wish Andreas was here to peer right inside this guy's head and find out what's going on. But he's not.

It's just me.

"Please," I say. "I came all the way out here. It's my mission too—why shouldn't I know all of it?"

My guide keeps his mouth clamped shut. He appears to have decided he's not going to talk at all.

The old me might have given up. This me has faced off with literal monsters and murderous gunmen.

This me has watched the woman he loves torn apart and then melded her back to life.

If there's something going on here beyond what we know, I have to find out what that is. All of our lives could depend on it.

I'm not going to be the weak one. I can't let this slide.

I push to my feet, ducking my head under the low ceiling of the van.

"How were you and your 'boss' involved in setting up this mission? I need you to tell me."

"You can ask your own boss if you want to know more."

I step toward the guy and take in his flinch with a wince of my own. But underneath my revulsion at his reaction, I know I can use it.

He's scared of me. And fear can be an incredible motivator.

"I don't need you," I say. "I can drive this van myself. I could tell my boss that you freaked out about my abilities and tried to hurt me. It was self-defense."

The man's head jerks toward me. "What are you talking about?"

I hate using my physical differences this way, like a threat, but it's the only thing I'm sure will work. I shrug off my jacket and let my tentacles rise on either side of my shoulders.

I aim a firm gaze straight into the man's twitching eyes. "I can use anything living to draw energy from. I can drain a whole human being in a couple of minutes. I know, because I've needed to before."

The man cringes in his seat against the door of the van. He snatches at the handle, but I whip out one tentacle and snag it around his nearer wrist.

"You're not going anywhere. Just tell me the terms of the deal, and we can go back to just sitting here like we never talked at all."

"Get that thing *off* me!" The man jerks at his arm, but my suckers and the sinewy muscles within the tentacle clamp tight.

"I can start siphoning off your life right now," I warn him, but he keeps struggling.

I need to prove it. I need to make him feel what he could be losing.

My mouth goes dry. I managed to take just part of a fish's life once, back when Rollick and his people were helping us get control of our abilities on his yacht. That last set of exercises I attempted with him, I was just starting to get the hang of refusing the deeper hunger.

But that was only once, in a perfectly controlled situation.

On the other hand, a fish has a lot less life than a human being.

I can do this. I *have* to do this, or what did I even start threatening this man for?

I clench my teeth and give a tug through my tentacle. My will catches hold of the streams of life energy that thrum through the man's body alongside his pulse.

The first spurt of it rushes through me with a giddying warmth, like drinking the richest hot chocolate in the world. I want more—I want to drown myself in it—

My mind flails, and for a second I almost do lose myself.

Then I yank up a memory of Riva. Riva smiling at me. Riva stroking the tentacles and telling me I'm not a monster.

With her, I'm not. Right now, I don't need to be either.

I cut off the flow of energy that was flooding me. The man's shoulders slump, a shudder passing through his body.

But he's alive. He's breathing properly, if rapidly. His skin hasn't lost his color.

I didn't take too much.

Only enough for him to know what it feels like. For him to get a sense of how far I could go.

My stomach lists queasily, but at the same time his now-watery eyes dart to mine.

"I'm sorry. I wasn't supposed to say. It's very simple. We give him the money, he clears out the house and leaves it for us."

I knit my brow, not letting up my hold on the man's wrist. "What do you want the house for? What's in there that's so special?"

My guide gestures vaguely with his free hand. "Not so much the house. Records, equipment, connections. They had a good business going. We move in and take over. Everyone wins."

I stare at him. "You're going to take over their business?"

The man starts squirming against my hold again. "Not *me*. My boss wants to expand. That's all it is. Just business."

Acid burns the base of my throat. For a second, I think I might actually vomit.

It's not business to the kids who've been getting snatched and sold.

We aren't really protecting them. If I'm understanding this guy right, there'll be a brief respite, and then a new syndicate is going to take over where the group we're slaughtering left off.

And they paid Clancy for the opportunity. They paid him to send us in and do their dirty work.

How much does he even know about what they're planning?

What else that he's told us has been a total fucking lie?

Eleven

Riva

I expected to feel relieved the moment we all clambered back onto the private plane that's going to take us back to the island. One look at Dominic's face turns any joy inside me to dust.

He isn't like Jacob—he doesn't carry his discontent like a storm cloud wrapped around him. I don't think anyone who doesn't know him well would even notice.

But I see the way the corners of his mouth stay tight when he aims his smile of welcome at me. I notice the slight hunching of his shoulders, like he's reverting back to his old uncertain self.

Back in the old facility, he always withdrew into himself like that right before he had to say something hard. The memory rises up, as if Andreas is telling it to me, of the complex strategy game the guardians had us play maybe a year before we tried to escape, with the promise that we'd get a full day to train and relax outside if we beat it.

Dom looked like he does right now in the moment before he told us in a rough voice that he'd just realized we'd made a fatal mistake several steps back… one there was no longer any way of recovering from. Any chance of claiming the reward we'd all longed for was gone.

Those were the kind of stakes we usually dealt with back then. These days, it could be so much worse.

My gaze jerks to the other figures on the plane. Did one of the younger shadowbloods get hurt? That could have been awful to see—what if he couldn't even save them?

That can't be true, though, because all four of them are tucked into their seats in a cluster, chattering quietly but with an easygoing air.

"Everything went okay on your end?" I call over to them, leaning my arm on the back of a seat.

Celine laughs and brushes her hand over her shoulder with a swish of her black and red-flecked ponytail. "No one even came. We just sat there the whole time."

One of the boys shoots a grin at me. "You two must have done a good job. Made it easy for the rest of us."

Celine laughs a little louder, and I find myself thinking of her missions before, hunting us down.

I don't know whether she was ever close to the actual fighting. Maybe I'm assuming she must be bothered about it underneath when those were easy for her too.

"It's always good to have backup," I say, because I don't want them to think we didn't appreciate them being there.

If anyone else working with the slavers had shown up while we were inside, they could have thrown the whole operation off. And having the teens monitoring the road for any late arrivals after the fact allowed Jacob and me our break, with all the unexpected enjoyment it brought.

"You shouldn't have to take all the responsibility on your shoulders," Clancy told us before, when we were going over the plan. "One of your greatest strengths is how well you rely on each other."

The private jet's seats are arranged in clusters of four along one side of the plane, two pairs facing each other with a tiny table in between. Narrow sofas and a refreshments cabinet stand along the opposite wall.

The teens have claimed one cluster for themselves. Jacob drops into a seat next to the window, across from Dominic.

I have the urge to follow him. To hold on to the new closeness we've formed between us.

But Dominic's expression tugs at me more.

I sink down beside him and slip my hand around his. "Everything went okay for you too, then?"

His smile doesn't reach his hazel eyes. "Pretty boring, but I'd rather that than needing to rush in to heal any of you."

He hooks his arm right around mine and leans in close, and I instinctively tilt toward him. His lips brush my cheek and then veer toward my ear as if he's making an intimate gesture.

"Pretend I'm saying nice things to you," he murmurs, so soft I'm not sure even Zian's sharp hearing could have picked up the words if he were in the seat across from me. "I don't know how closely they're monitoring us on the plane."

I squeeze his hand in agreement and push my lips into a small smile, willing down the nervous twist of my gut.

Dominic keeps talking, low and steady but quickly as if he's afraid he might get cut off. "Clancy didn't come up with this mission out of the goodness of his heart. Some other gang paid him to eliminate those guys. And they're planning on taking over the business. They were just looking to off the competition."

With every sentence, my muscles tense more. It takes all my willpower not to clench my jaw in a horrified grimace.

So I don't have to hold the increasingly stiff smile any longer, I turn as if to nuzzle his head in response. My voice comes out in a thin whisper. "Are you sure?"

He nods without hesitation.

I close my eyes. The images from our mission waver behind the lids—bodies crumpling, blood splashing.

They still deserved it. We stopped them from doing horrible things.

But what if someone even worse steps in to fill the void?

How could Clancy be making decisions about what wrongs to set right based on getting *paid*?

When I look up again, Jacob is watching the two of us, but without a trace of jealousy. From the furrow on his brow, he's picked up on the fact that our PDA is a cover for a more serious conversation.

I could tell him the same way that Dominic just told me—but I'm not sure Jake could hide his reaction well enough. I'm having enough trouble myself.

If the snack packets start bouncing off the ceiling, the guardians who've come along to escort us home will know something's up.

We can't keep quiet about this for long. I'm not going on another mission without understanding what the new leader of the guardians is really up to.

But I'd rather not hash it out with his underlings while we're thousands of feet in the air.

It'll be better if we can confront him without him knowing that we're on to him. Observe his unguarded response before he recovers from the surprise.

We can fill Jacob in at the same time.

I give Dom's cheek an actual kiss and whisper, "We'll see what Clancy has to say about it when we get back."

He nods again and slings his arm right around me to give me a brief but emphatic hug. The love we share seems to pulse through the mark on my collarbone.

After several minutes, I switch seats to cuddle up with Jacob, but all I tell him is, "There's something Clancy hasn't been telling us. We'll bring it up with him when we see him."

Jake manages to restrain a full frown, but his muscles tense even at that vague news. He glances at Dominic, who offers a small, crooked grin, and sighs.

Then he loops his arm around my shoulders as if he's determined to be some kind of armor for me even here. Even without knowing what he might be protecting me against.

I run through the possible scenarios dozens of times in my head during the flight until I fall into a doze. At the jolt of the wheels hitting the mountain-top runway, I wake up with a jerk.

As we straighten up in our seats, everyone looking a bit groggy, the door swings open.

Another guardian appears in the glow of the jet's interior lights. "Clancy wants a briefing from each of you, in your own teams. Jacob and Riva first."

My pulse stutters. I assumed we'd all go together—that I'd have the backup of five other shadowbloods when we confronted him.

That Dominic would be able to say exactly what he found out.

There isn't time to hash out an alternate plan. The guardian is motioning to us impatiently.

I peel myself out of my seat and hurry over with Jacob right behind me.

It'll be okay. The two of us can handle the conversation ahead.

It's better for us to address it than to leave Dominic to take Clancy to task on his own.

Outside the plane, a warm breeze washes over us, carrying the hum of nighttime insect life. Dawn is just starting to tint the horizon.

We head down the path carved into the mountainside from the plateau that serves as a landing strip, our shoes rasping against the rough stone. Our escort leads us straight to Clancy's office.

In spite of the early hour, the head of the Guardianship looks perfectly alert standing behind his desk to greet us. Did he sleep while we flew, or has he been up all night?

As he motions us into the room, my gaze catches on the other figure waiting with him, and my heart hitches in my chest.

Griffin is sitting in a chair in the far corner, watching us with his unnervingly blank expression.

What's he doing here? The only explanation I can think of is that Clancy wants him to read our emotions, to make sure we're telling the truth.

I guess it's a good thing I decided I was going to call out our captor now, because I'm sure Griffin would have picked up on the fact that I was hiding something major if I held off.

We come to a stop in front of the desk, but Jacob's attention has fixed on his brother. His jaw works.

Griffin simply tips his head in greeting as if this is a totally normal situation. Jake wrenches his gaze back to Clancy without acknowledging the gesture.

Even with all the other concerns gnawing at me, grief ripples through my gut. Have the guardians managed to destroy their brotherly connection forever?

I make myself focus on the man behind the desk.

Clancy is studying us with an intensity that feels more penetrating than I remember from our past conversations. As if he already knows there's something we'll have to say beyond the basics of the mission.

My skin creeps in uneasy anticipation.

"It seems the assignment went well," Clancy says with typical briskness. "But I'd like to hear the full account from your own mouths. It appeared that you had a bit of a hiccup toward the end of your time in the house."

My mouth twists. He must have been able to tell something went wrong from our physiological signals broadcast from our ankle bands.

"We didn't have any trouble with most of the mission," I start. "We took down the first several people we found in the house before they even realized what was happening."

I give him my account of our progress into and through the house, trading the story back and forth with Jacob, from our first kills to the kitchen staff's warning to our ultimate victory.

With every word, the nausea gripping my stomach expands. At the time, it *did* feel like a victory.

Dominic's revelation has drained all the justice out of that triumph, turning it hollow.

Why did I ever trust this man even a little? The guardians have never done anything except manipulate us and betray us.

I should never have believed he was any different, no matter what he said or did.

But I still need to hear what he'll say for himself. I need to know just how aware he was of the shit he dragged us into.

Clancy takes our account in with occasional nods and sounds of encouragement. When we've finished, he contemplates us with a satisfied expression. "It sounds as though you fulfilled your tasks as well as I could have hoped. There can always be unexpected obstacles along the way—it's impossible to avoid them entirely."

"There was something else unexpected that came up," I say, girding myself for the conversation ahead.

Clancy arches his eyebrows slightly, almost as if he's amused. I don't think he can have any idea what I'm about to say. "Is that so?"

I cross my arms in front of me. "Yes. Why didn't you tell us that someone was paying you to send us in there? It wasn't a humanitarian mission."

Our captor's gaze flickers with a momentary tensing of his jaw. Oh, he had no clue at all that I was going to bring that subject up.

A faint whiff of stress pheromones reaches my nose, but he recovers quickly. "An organization on this scale requires funding. Our operations can be both humanitarian and paid for."

Griffin is looking at Clancy instead of us now, with a furrow on his brow. He didn't know about this part either, apparently.

I raise my chin. "Sure, that's possible. But not when the people paying you off only want you to get rid of the criminals so they can take over the same slaving business for themselves."

"What?" Jacob snaps. He narrows his eyes at Clancy. "You hired us out to *help* some child-abducting assholes?"

Clancy's whole expression has tightened now. "I didn't inquire about the plans of the group that hired us. They wanted to take out a target I was happy to see gone. If you heard something that led you to believe our sponsors had malicious intentions, you were probably mistaken."

I snort. "Probably? You don't even know. It didn't occur to you to ask why these people were willing to spend who knows how much money for a mass assassination?"

Dominic wouldn't have told me with so much certainty if he hadn't found out enough to be totally convinced. And the fact that Clancy admits he didn't really know one way or the other only makes me surer that Dom was right.

"It doesn't matter," Clancy says firmly. "You did a good thing today—you removed people who were doing horrible things from the world. We can't control who might step in to fill a vacuum that's been created, but if someone else picks up where they left off, they can be dealt with too."

Jacob scowls. "As long as someone coughs up enough money to make it worth your while?"

Clancy gazes steadily back at him. "There's a lot of injustice in the world. I see no reason we shouldn't address it while also avoiding bankruptcy."

He makes the whole thing sound so reasonable, but every inch of my skin is crawling at his matter-of-fact tone.

Destroying awful things could be awful in turn if it's done for the wrong purpose.

Can't he see that? He must.

He just doesn't give a fuck as long as his bank account gets larger.

I catch Jacob's eye. We don't need to speak for me to recognize that we're on exactly the same page.

Being paid mercenaries is a totally different thing from acting as superheroes. We don't want this.

But as long as we're here under Clancy's control, we're either carrying out his missions or he's going to lock us up as lab rats.

Which means we're going to have to get out of here, no question about it. All of us—the younger shadowbloods too.

And I have no idea how the hell we're going to pull that off.

Clancy steps around the desk toward us. I brace myself for another attempt at justifying himself, but instead he cocks his head, his gaze skimming over our bodies.

"That's not the only interesting thing that happened after you completed your part of the assignment, is it?"

My heart skips a beat. After Dominic's report, I totally forgot to wonder how much the guardians might have realized about my and Jacob's intimate activities.

"I don't think anything happened that would be interesting to *you*," I shoot back.

Jacob steps closer to me in solidarity. "You're just trying to change the subject from your shitty attitude."

Clancy tsks his tongue. "Or maybe you're trying to divert *me*. I did hear some very intriguing things while I was monitoring the missions."

He reaches out, a gesture I wasn't prepared for, and tugs down the collar of Jacob's clean tee. Just far enough to reveal the dark spot that's formed at the top of his sternum.

Jake is shoving him away a second later, but Clancy mostly dodges the blow with a backward step, anticipating it. He rocks on his feet, brushes himself off, and glances at me.

"I'm guessing you have a third of those now. A mark. We made note of them when you arrived, but I didn't realize they were connected to your powers."

My pulse thumps faster. "What are you talking about?" I blurt out, praying that there's some chance he doesn't really understand.

Griffin stands up. "You're upsetting them," he says, his voice as calm as ever but the furrow on his forehead deepening.

Clancy ignores him. "I suppose I didn't mention that your tracking bands also transmit audio. I heard everything you said after your little interlude. Sex creates a connection between you? An extra awareness of each other? That's fascinating. We didn't anticipate anything like—"

"Shut the fuck up!" Jacob snarls, and throws himself at the other man with a clench of his fist that I think is directing a smack of telekinetic force ahead of him.

But Clancy is ready for that assault too. His arm whips out, and Jacob's body spasms with the crackle of a taser.

A cry bursts from my throat as Jake stumbles to his knees. "Stop!"

My claws spring out, but Clancy holds up his hand. "Let me remind you that you aren't gambling only with your own well-being but his and your other friends' as well."

I stop, the vibration of a scream burning in my lungs, my fingers curling.

I want to slash his throat out like I did to the thugs in the mansion we just invaded. I want to shriek pain through his joints until they break.

But I don't know what will happen to us—all of us—if I give in to that impulse. I don't know how much worse things could get.

Taking in my stillness, Clancy rolls his shoulders, the taser still held between us. The door clicks as several more guardians enter the room to surround us.

"I think this conversation is over," he says. "You've simply opened a new avenue of inquiry—a process I'll need to study more closely to fully understand."

TWELVE

Riva

Nadia bobs on the balls of her feet in the grass, her latest neon T-shirt flashing under the sunlight in the yard. "I can't wait until I can get out there on a mission. They only let the non-Firsts who've already done a *lot* of fieldwork join in for that one."

I look up at her from where I've been stretching out my legs on the grass. The morning's exercise hasn't done anything to loosen the knot in my gut that's lingered since my talk with Clancy yesterday.

"You wouldn't want to go until you're definitely ready anyway," I say, not knowing what else to tell her.

You shouldn't want to go at all. Clancy's just using us. And I don't know how much worse it could get.

What would be the consequences of laying out the things I've discovered? Before I left Clancy's office, he warned Jacob and me to keep what we'd learned to ourselves… or we wouldn't get the chance to work with the other shadowbloods at all.

He's got his guardians watching us, I'm sure. How much could I even tell Nadia or the rest of them before I got dragged away?

I need to keep training, keep watching, and figure out a way to actually get us out of here. None of the rest matters as long as Clancy's calling the shots.

Nadia lets out a huff and swipes the short strands of her thick black hair back from her face. "I guess not. But even if it is nicer here than it was in the old facility, I want to see more of what's out there."

My chest constricts, knowing that longing for freedom so well. "Yeah. You'll get there."

On my terms rather than Clancy's, if I can manage it.

The carnage from the photos he showed me of the last kids we tried to rescue flashes through my mind, and the knots in my gut pull tighter. My terms have to be safer this time.

Booker saunters over from where he just finished a round of strength training. "When they send you on one of those missions, you'll have to trade in the neon for stealth-wear. Are you sure you can handle that?"

Nadia rolls her eyes at his teasing, but a hint of a blush appears on her brown cheeks at the same time. "Maybe, maybe not. My whole job is lighting things up."

Her words tickle my curiosity. "That's your shadowblood power?"

She nods and picks up the jump rope she brought out for an aerobics workout. "I'm a human glowworm. Lucky me."

She flips the rope over her head and starts up a brisk rhythm, moving her feet back and forth rather than simply keeping them in place. A shimmer appears beneath her skin.

Within a matter of seconds, the glow has risen to the surface, shining off her as if she's a signal beacon.

Booker laughs and claps his hands in approval. "We'll never get lost in the dark with you around, anyway."

As I get up, planning on taking another run through the stealth course—since stealth is definitely going to be key in working around Clancy's security systems—Booker glances at me. "The mission went okay, didn't it? You're all right?"

I hesitate, startled. The questions are perfectly straightforward, but his concern sounds genuine.

What's the best way to answer? I roll the words around in my mouth. "Things got more complicated than we expected. I'm still figuring out how I feel about that. Why? Did you hear something from Celine's group?"

Did the younger shadowbloods who came along pick up on something being off even though we never said as much in front of them?

But Booker shakes his head with a flash of sunlight off his pale hair. "Nah. Just your vibe." He waves vaguely around my body. "I see auras, basically. Like a haze that gives an idea of where a person's at, physically and mentally. Yours looks kind of uneasy."

Oh, shit. I had no idea he could pick up on my internal state while I've been doing my best to put a good face forward.

"I'm still not totally used to the whole setup here," I say in the best explanation I can give. "This island isn't where I was planning on ending up."

He lets out another chuckle. "Yeah, I guess that's the same for all of us."

Nadia pauses in her rope-jumping. Booker bumps his knuckles against her shoulder in a playful but affectionate gesture. "I'm going to go tackle the ropes. See you around, Glowworm."

She watches him go, the rope swaying in her hands. I recognize the longing in her expression, all the way down to my bones.

"Were you in the same facility before?"

Nadia jerks her gaze back to me with an embarrassed purse of her lips. "Some of the time, anyway. When we were kids. There was a point when they started only letting girls train with other girls—and the guys with the guys. Until now."

A chill washes over me. That might be kind of my fault too.

When my guys and I tried to escape the first time, one of the guardians who caught me said something about it being a mistake to include a "female" in the mix. Maybe they figured the emotional connections forming between us had given us extra motivation to want to get out.

Apparently once they came to that conclusion, they applied their new principles to the younger shadowbloods.

"I'm sorry," I can't help saying.

Nadia shrugs. "Maybe it was better like that. It's not like anything could have happened in the kind of place we were before. I mean…" She trails off awkwardly, tensing as if she expects me to mock her for her romantic aspirations.

I don't really know how to do this whole role-model thing. I'm only four years older than her, barely more experienced.

But I want to be something like that for her and all the other shadowbloods. If the guys and I are blood, then we're connected to the rest of them too, if not quite as closely.

There's no one else in the whole world who could really understand what we've been through.

I offer her the best smile I can. "I know. I've been there. We'll get a real life eventually, where everything's… a little easier."

God, I hope I can fulfill that promise. Especially after the way she smiles back at me after my encouragement.

Another swell of cold wraps around my stomach. What if I end up leading them to their deaths instead?

Before I can shake off the thought and head over to the course like I intended, a couple of guardians jog down the mountainside steps. Their slacks shift with their brisk movements, and for the first time I notice a glimpse of a monitoring band around the man's ankle, just like the ones Clancy had us all wear on the mission.

The ones he made a point of taking off us when we returned. But the guardians wear them?

Understanding hits me like a slap to the face.

Clancy's monitoring the guardians—so that he knows immediately if any of us tries to hurt them. If I went on a rampage out here and slaughtered these two, no doubt an alarm would go off somewhere and the whole place would be locked down before I could get any farther.

Knowing the guardians are okay is more useful to him than tracking our exact movements when we're confined to the valley anyway.

They let us shadowbloods go without those anklets to give us the illusion of freedom. The guardians don't need the illusion, because they *know* they're actually free.

All more of his manipulative lies.

As the two guardians stride toward me, I force my hands to unclench. It's clear from their gazes that I'm their intended target.

I move forward instinctively to meet them before they get closer to Nadia, even though I'm not really sure what I'd be shielding her from.

She and the other younger ones haven't had to see half of what the rest of us have. Haven't had to *do* what we've been forced to in order to survive.

And I'd rather keep it that way if I possibly can.

"We've got a different task for you, inside," one of the guardians says with a jerk of her thumb toward the facility.

I frown. "Right now? I thought I had the whole morning out here."

The other guardian rests his hands on his hips—by his electrified baton. "Change of plans. Clancy's orders."

A prickle of apprehension runs down my back, but I nod and go with them. Let's find out what the man in charge wants from me today.

The guardians lead me to a different part of the facility than the areas I've become familiar with. In a small room with a vaguely medical vibe, they have me take off my running shoes.

Then they wrap a band around each of my arms, just below the sleeve of my T-shirt. The outer material feels like fleece, but something more solid presses against my skin from within.

As they click into place, tiny bumps jut out against my skin with a faint prick that fades away almost instantly.

I study the gray fabric warily. "What are these for?"

"Monitoring equipment," the woman says. "They give a closer look at your internal state, but you'll forget they're even there."

I find that hard to believe. And something about her phrasing sets off a sharper alarm bell in my head.

The man opens a door at the other side of the room and ushers me into a slightly larger space. The door thumps shut the second I've stepped over the threshold.

Zian turns at the sound where he's standing at the far end of the room, his expression uncertain. Other than him, the room holds only a shag rug, a polka dot loveseat, and a double bed with two pillows and a duvet, all lit by a soft glow from the panel set in the ceiling.

My entire body is jittering with discomfort now. Something about this whole scenario feels way too wrong.

I glance at Zian, noting the matching bands against the peachy-brown skin of his bulging biceps. "Do you have any idea what this is about?"

He shakes his head, his mouth tight. "They didn't tell me anything. I don't get it."

I'm starting to wonder if anyone else from our original group will be sent in to join us when Clancy's voice warbles from a speaker set somewhere in the walls.

"It looks like we're all set up now. Why don't you two get comfortable? You can take things at your own pace, although of course the faster you move things along, the sooner you can go back to your typical day."

I peer at the stone wall in the general direction the voice seems to be coming from. "Move what along? What are we supposed to be doing?"

There's a slight hesitation. I can imagine Clancy clearing his throat as if preparing for a not-entirely-comfortable announcement.

"You've already formed this marked bond of yours with Jacob,

Dominic, and Andreas. If we're going to study the mechanics of the process, that leaves Zian."

My gut plummets. Zian goes rigid, every muscle tensing as a shudder ripples through his body.

I glare at the wall, but my voice wavers. "You're ordering us to have *sex*? While you watch? Are you out of your fucking mind?"

The last two words crackle with a mix of anger and desperation. He wouldn't really go *that* far…

No, I can't say that for sure. I have no idea how twisted our new captor's mind might actually be.

Some small part of me is still hoping he'll chuckle and say I've got it all wrong. No dice.

"We won't be watching. There are no cameras in the room. The changes in your bodies and your shadowblood energies will be monitored through the bands you're wearing—that's the data we're interested in."

A process I'll need to study more closely. He practically told me he was going to do this when he dismissed me and Jake yesterday.

The fact that he isn't going to be sitting there directing us in his own personal porno doesn't really make the situation any better. Even if I believe him that we're not being secretly recorded.

Zian retreats from me until his back hits the far wall. He slides along the wall to the corner and wedges himself there, his massive frame outright quaking now.

Watching his obvious agitation, my heart wrenches even more than it had already.

"We won't do anything you don't want to do," I tell him in as soothing a voice as I can manage. "We don't have to listen to them."

I can't tell if Zee even hears me. His gaze has gone vague with horror, panicked pheromones flooding the air from his corner.

Clancy pipes up again as if I give a shit what else he has to say on the subject. "Allowing us to study the process will mean we can help *you* understand what the connection means too. What benefits there might be to it that you haven't discovered on your own, or any potential pitfalls."

My hands ball at my sides. "Don't tell us you're trying to force us into hooking up for our own good. Forget it. This whole thing is sick."

"I'm not going to force anything. The two of you care about each other—you're attracted to each other. Griffin has sensed as much in just the last few days. I'd imagine this would have happened before too long regardless. We're simply—"

"Fuck you!" I snap, and whirl around as if I can figure out where he and whoever's with him might be relative to this room. "Are you in on this right now, Griffin? You really think what this asshole's doing is okay?"

I don't get any answer. Zian rocks in little jolts between the two walls, a faint growl seeping from his throat.

"Take as long as you need," Clancy says, so fucking calm I want to tear his face off his skull. "You'll remain confined to this room until you decide to take that step. But be aware that your three friends will also remain in solitary confinement for the same length of time. It's up to you how long the process takes."

There's a crackle, and I have the sense he's shut off the mic.

I fling myself at the door, but even my superhuman strength can't yank it open. As much as I strain at it, I can't break the lock.

"No, no, no," Zian is muttering in his corner. He rakes his hands through his short hair, and I wince at the sight of the little red scratches he's drawn in their wake—from the claws that've poked from his fingertips.

My stomach is churning so wildly it's a wonder I haven't already spewed my breakfast on this nice rug. "We can wait him out, Zee. He can't make us do this."

I take a couple of steps toward him, groping for some way to reassure him more, and his head jerks up with a snarl. Fur has sprung up along the sides of his neck; the beginning of his wolf-man snout contorts his face.

"Get away from me!" he yells in a guttural voice that barely sounds like the Zian I know.

I freeze and then back up. If he needs space, I'll give it to him, even if it kills me to see his distress.

The last thing I want to do is add to it.

With a click, Clancy's voice drifts into the room again. "There's no need to get so worked up about the situation. You'll both enjoy yourselves. If you—"

I don't find out what fantastic tips he has for us now, because Zian's roar cuts off our captor's voice. He barrels out of his corner with a ferocity that makes me flinch.

His full wolf-man face has taken over, fangs protruding from a wrinkled muzzle. His body looks at least half a foot taller and broader than his usual size.

He hurls himself at the bed and gouges his claws right through the duvet into the mattress. Chunks of fabric and foam careen through the air.

I scramble backward and leap onto the loveseat, my pulse racing. I've never seen Zian quite this wild before—and I'm the only person in the room.

I don't want to think he'd hurt me, but if he's so upset that he isn't even aware of what he's doing…

His arms swing, smashing the bed's plain wooden frame. Splinters fly across the floor.

When he spins around toward me with a feral howl, my heart nearly stops. His eyes blaze with fury and anguish.

He lunges forward—and the door bursts open. Several guardians hurtle into the room, two zapping him with batons, another stabbing him with a syringe as his body spasms.

"Don't hurt him!" I shout through my constricted throat. Tears burn behind my eyes.

It isn't his fault. They pushed him until he snapped.

As Zian slumps on the floor, Clancy himself appears in the doorway. He meets my gaze with just a little regret in his expression.

"I'm sorry this attempt went so badly," he says. "Let's get you out of here. We can try again with a new approach another day."

"Are you *insane*?" I sputter.

Before I can say anything else, the prick of a needle radiates from my shoulder. I hadn't heard the guardian turning toward me.

I teeter over, the rest of my caustic words dying in my mouth.

Thirteen

Riva

I scale the mountainside with swift, efficient movements, ignoring the growing burn in my arms. Whenever the terrain ahead of me is predictable enough that I can risk it, I take swift glances around at my surroundings.

I specifically picked this training exercise today so that I could get a better sense of the island's landscape. Maybe even catch a glimpse of something that'd indicate a potential escape route.

We can't fly away using Clancy's private jet, since none of us knows how to pilot a plane. But if I could spot an obvious route through the mountains to a harbor or any sign of human civilization beyond the facility…

The latter option feels more and more impossible. It would make sense for Clancy to buy an entire island for his purposes rather than take the chance that we'd be discovered.

But surely they have *some* method of transportation other than the air route. He doesn't seem like the type to put all his eggs in one basket.

Hell, I'd be willing to attempt a swim to the mainland if it turns out there's some in sight.

Anything to not get dragged into more of his sick schemes.

When I reach the top of the climbing path and perch on the shallow ledge there, the view doesn't offer much. There's no easy way to scale the last fifty or so feet to the very top of the cliff, which is smooth and sheer probably by design, so I can't look over the other side of this peak.

All I see sprawled out in front of me is the dense jungle that once looked so appealing. Now it seems to glower ominously at me.

I worry at my lip in the few minutes I can reasonably rest before I should start the climb down to avoid raising suspicion. Maybe we do need to focus on getting a plane—hijacking it, forcing one of the guardian pilots to take us off the island.

Although if the jets they have access to are all the same size as the one that took us on our mission, I'm not sure we could safely fit all of the shadowbloods on it. There are at least a few dozen of us here, and I don't know if I've met all of the facility's inhabitants yet.

Not only are the training periods staggered and unpredictable, there could be just as many prisoners who aren't allowed out at all because they haven't agreed to Clancy's terms. Or he's decided they're even more volatile than the rest of us.

And I have no idea which of the guardians is trained as a pilot, or how we'd threaten them into complying if I can figure that out.

A wave of hopelessness washes over me. I close my eyes against it and then propel myself onward.

I start the scramble back down, relying mostly on my clawed fingers and my feet in their flexible athletic shoes, keeping the safety rope loose. When I figure out a plan, I want to be ready for whatever it'll require.

Voices carry through the trees during the last short stretch before my feet hit the ground. Celine, Booker, and a few of the other older teen shadowbloods emerge along the path through the jungle to the climbing site.

The five of them keep chattering away as they stretch their arms and legs in a quick warm-up. The smiles flashing between them and relaxed tone to their conversation make my stomach knot.

I'm not sure how easily it'll even be to convince the other shadowbloods that we *should* escape. They haven't seen the darker side of this place—and Celine knows firsthand just how ruthlessly the guardians will hunt us down to reclaim their supposed "property."

Funny that Clancy spoke about the child slavers with so much disdain when he and his colleagues have treated us like slaves since we were old enough to walk.

The guardians here make a show of giving us our space, but I can pick out a couple of figures hanging back among the trees along the fringes of the climbing site. I can't talk safely here.

But I might be able to get a general sense of how content our younger counterparts actually are.

After I've stripped off the climbing harness, I amble over to where the teens are stretching. "It's a good day for a climb," I say, just to start the conversation. "Not too sweltering for once."

One of the girls laughs. "I'm just glad to be getting out in the sunlight every day. It can swelter us all it wants."

Okay, no sign of mutiny there. I drift a little closer to Celine. "Too bad the guardians didn't give you more of a break to enjoy your new life here before sending you off on missions again, huh?"

I try to keep my tone light, as if I'm making a joke out of it rather than criticizing our keepers. Celine lets out a quick giggle with an energetic shake of her head.

"I like getting out there. Knowing I'm being useful. Maybe the next mission, I'll get to do more than sit in a van!"

She sounds upbeat enough, but a trace of apprehension tickles my nose with its heightened sense of smell. There's something about the subject she isn't totally happy about.

I prop myself against the side of the cliff while the first couple of climbers gear up. "You ever think about what you'd want to be doing if we weren't part of this whole Guardianship thing? Like what job you'd do or where you'd want to live?"

Booker snaps his fingers. "Hell, yes. I don't know about jobs, but New York City is where it's at. At least out of the places I've been. Could be there's someplace I'd like more outside of the US."

As he cocks his head with a contemplative air that clashes with his surfer-dude appearance, Celine shrugs. "I don't know. With the missions, we could end up seeing all kinds of places anyway."

"As much of them as you see from the inside of the van," I say.

She giggles again. "Well, yeah. I'm sure we'll have more action on other missions. And once we've proven ourselves more. Maybe Clancy will even let us take vacations or whatever!"

So she would like a chance to have more freedom, whether she's fully recognized how stuck we still are or not. That's a start.

And Booker seems to have dreamed about other things, despite his easy-going attitude.

"I like to think about that stuff sometimes," he says, his grin going a bit crooked, "but mostly it makes more sense to focus on what we've got right now. Especially when this is a heck of a lot better than we ever had it before."

I force a smile in return. "That's true." Though I'm not so sure I'd agree about the "a lot."

Celine wanders away to watch her friends on their climb, but Booker lingers near me, his stance turning unusually hesitant. Has he guessed why I was asking these questions?

He glances at the ground and then back at me, and asks in a lowered voice, "You and Nadia have gotten kind of friendly, yeah?"

Huh. Where's he going with that?

I dip my head. "Sure, I'd like to think so. Not that we've had the chance to get to know each other all that well yet."

"I just wondered—and maybe this is a weird thing to ask, so you totally don't have to say—has she mentioned anything I did that bothered her?"

I blink at him, feeling totally out of my depth. He thinks Nadia is *upset* with him?

At my startled silence, Booker barrels onward. "It's just, her aura gets kind of… strange when I'm around, like agitated or something, even though she always acts nice. If I did offend her or something, I'd want to apologize. I mean, I really like her."

He stops abruptly, a flush coloring his cheeks.

I've never had anything like a normal family, but in that moment, swept up in a rush of amused affection, I have the urge to ruffle his hair like I'm the worldly big sister in a sitcom. Except it'd be a bit of a reach when he's nearly a foot taller than me.

I can't stop a real smile from tugging at my lips. I'm not going to betray Nadia's secrets, but it seems fair to say, "I think she'd really like to hear that. She's definitely not upset with you."

Booker studies me as if trying to read more into my words and lets out a chuckle with a rush of breath. "That's—that's good to hear. Sorry if it was a strange thing to bring up—"

"No," I say quickly, meaning it. "I don't mind at all. I know most of us have only just met, but we're all kind of family, right? We should help each other when we can. At least, I want to."

"Yeah." He flashes me a more confident grin. "Thanks." Then he lopes over to join the others at the base of the climbing route.

I watch them for a moment with an uneasy twist of fondness and apprehension in my gut.

Maybe he and Nadia will find something special together like I have with my guys.

Maybe Clancy will force the issue if he realizes they're into each other, to see if they'll form the same kind of connection we have.

My teeth set on edge. I can't let that happen.

I don't know the best way to get us out of here or how to protect us once we're gone, but I know we can't stay here any longer than we can help.

I have a while yet before I'm due back at the facility for my lunch period, so I set off for my other planned training activity: firearms. I might prefer close combat where I can use my supernatural strength and claws, but when it comes to dealing with people as well-equipped as the guardians, weapons could definitely come in handy.

And I want to take into consideration all the weapons we could have access to.

The shooting range is set up in a cavernous room at the top of a carved flight of steps leading from the valley floor. A broad waterfall covers the entrance, the warbling of the water drowning out any sound that resonates out of the mountain.

When I duck past the waterfall, a guardian is standing several feet down the hall on the other side, keeping an eye on things. No doubt I was watched along the path I took to get here as well.

I could kill any of them if I wanted to—but that wouldn't do us any good. Clancy knows I'm not going to go rogue without my guys. And the second I attack any of his people, their ankle bands will let him know.

We're still shackled; he's just given us a longer chain.

As I step into the shooting range, my spirits lift a bit. Andreas is standing down by the end, next to a younger guy I don't know and little Tegan.

There is something deeply wrong about watching a twelve-year-old raise a pistol and blast away a target with cool focus.

Andreas brightens at the sight of me, and my pulse stutters with the sudden thought of all the things he doesn't know. I haven't seen him since getting back from my mission.

There's no sign in his expression that any of my other guys have filled him in on the pieces he's missing.

I grab a pair of earmuffs and examine the array of weapons on offer, presided over by another guardian. They're basic handguns and rifles, including a couple with sniper scopes.

I haven't done much work with long-distance shooting. I pick up one of those and move to a lane that's deeper, with a more intricate target at the far end.

Something about the process of positioning the gun and focusing on the stick figures I'm supposed to pick out in the target drawing is unnervingly reassuring in its familiarity. I sink into the same focused state Tegan must have found.

Squeeze the trigger. One, two, three, four times.

I miss one of the targets by half an inch, but the bullets tear straight through the others. The finished sheet whirs away, and another takes its place.

I've blasted my way through five of them when I notice Andreas heading over to the equipment area. As he takes off his earmuffs, I lower my rifle.

I have to talk to him. That's more important than just about anything.

We can't come up with any plan at all until we're on the same page.

Andreas waits for me and catches my hand as we head down the hall, away from the thunder of the range. He probably figures we'll hang out in the valley for a bit, but I stop him right by the waterfall.

Its noise can cover our voices too.

I bob up, looping my arms around his neck when he bends to meet me. For all my determination, in that first moment I can't help simply hugging his leanly muscular frame to me.

"Hey," Andreas murmurs by my ear, embracing me just as eagerly. "I missed you too."

I let out a rough laugh and squeeze him tighter, shutting my eyes against a sudden burn of tears. Cool flecks dapple our skin from the waterfall next to us, but I tune out the sensation.

I tuck my head against his shoulder so I can speak right by his ear like he did with me. "Things are even more messed up than we realized. Dominic found out that Clancy's picking missions based on what he gets paid to do. And he doesn't really care who's paying him or why they want the job done."

Drey kisses my cheek, but his mouth has drawn into a grimace. "He managed to tell me about some of that when I saw him yesterday. Not what the guy pitched to us, is it?"

"No." I let out a shaky breath. "But it's gotten even worse than that.

He found out about our marks. Because Jake and I—after the mission, we…"

I trail off, abruptly uncertain of my words, but Andreas gives a low chuckle. "You don't have to feel bad about that. You told me right from the start how you felt about all of us. I'm glad Jake's done enough for you to trust him again."

I swallow thickly, simultaneously warmed by his response and sickened by the rest I have to tell him. "That's not the problem. Clancy didn't know any of us had formed that kind of connection before. He wants to study how it happens—*what* actually happens. So he stuck me and Zian in a room together and tried to make us put on a demonstration."

Drey's whole body goes rigid against mine. He pulls back just far enough for me to see the fury flashing in his dark gray eyes. "What the fuck? I'll kill the asshole myself."

He's managed to keep his voice low enough even in his anger that the guardian down the hall doesn't react, but my heart skips a beat anyway. I pull him back to me to hide his expression.

"Nothing happened. Well, Zian really freaked out. Have you seen him since yesterday morning? They tranqed him."

Andreas pauses, his muscles flexing with the tension coursing through his body. "He was there at breakfast this morning. Quieter than usual, but then, we don't usually feel comfortable talking all that much anyway."

A little of my own worry releases. "Okay. Good. I just—I think Clancy's going to try again. Not the same way, but… He really wants to figure out why our powers are bonding like that."

Drey lets out a sound that's close to one of Zian's wolf-man growls and hugs me like he thinks if he can hold me tight enough, Clancy won't be able to reach me. Right now, I think if our captor stepped into view, Drey might actually murder the guy, consequences be damned.

"We can't stay here," I say. "But I haven't been able to figure out any way we could make a run for it without getting caught before we're even out of the valley."

Andreas's breath hisses through his teeth. "I've been searching the guardians' memories here and there when I get the chance, looking for anything that might be useful in case we wanted to break out. Nothing useful has come up so far, but I'll start pushing harder. There's got to be a chance."

He nuzzles my hair and squeezes me in another hug. "We made it so far before, Tink. We can do it again. I'm *not* letting him turn you into some kind of sex experiment. If you need to fight back in the moment, fight. Don't worry about the rest of us."

Pressed against his solid chest, I choke up with a swell of emotion. Because it just might come to that.

And deciding between my personal autonomy and my guys' well-being is the last choice I'd want to make.

FOURTEEN

Zian

When the pair of guardians who seem to have been assigned to me come to collect me after dinner, I assume they're going to lead me back to my room. That's where I've been locked up for most of yesterday and today other than meals, since my freak-out with Riva.

Instead, they direct me toward the entrance to the facility. I walk along hesitantly, my nerves on edge.

What is Clancy going to do with me now?

Fractured memories of my panicked rage yesterday morning flit through the back of my mind, but I do my best not to look at them too closely. I focus on what's ahead instead.

We step out onto the wide ridge into the warm evening air. The sun hasn't quite set, the sky cast with a golden haze.

A few shadowbloods are training in the field below, but I don't recognize any of them. I haven't gotten many of the younger ones' names so far.

I'm always a little afraid that if I approach them, they'll see me as a threatening presence rather than a friendly one.

"This way," one of the guardians says. They both walk with me down the steps and along one of the jungle paths.

The sound of burbling water reaches my supernaturally keen ears well before I see the source. When we come to the edge of a glade between the trees, I stall in my tracks.

It should be a pretty scene. A waterfall, much thinner than the one that hides the shooting range, tumbles several feet down the cliffside into a clear pond ringed by polished rocks, obviously set up for swimming. Ferns and bushes with vibrant flowers frame most of the pool.

And Riva is sitting on the grassy patch near the bank, her knees drawn up to her chest, alone.

"Clancy thought the two of you should have a chance to talk after what happened yesterday," the guardian next to me says. "You'll be given your privacy. As long as you stay in this clearing, you won't be disturbed. When you're ready, you can walk back to the facility—or we'll come to escort you if you get off track."

Without waiting for my response, she and the other guardian vanish into the thickening shadows of the path. I stay where I halted, looking at Riva.

Clancy wants us to *talk*? He's giving us our privacy?

They say that, but Riva's got the bands around her upper arms like they put on us yesterday. Maybe the guardians never took them off.

They've left mine on, a faint weight against my biceps.

The fabric is a little scuffed on mine because I tried to tear them away after I woke up in my room. The metal bits underneath wouldn't give.

They're obviously still monitoring us. And I'd bet they want us to do a lot more than talk. This is just a different tactic.

Riva gazes back at me from where she's sitting. Her mouth forms a tight smile.

She tips her head toward a couple of baskets sitting on the ground next to her. "They left us swimsuits in case we wanted to get in the water and some snacks if we get hungry. I think this is Clancy's insane idea of a date."

Her tone is dry. I'd snort in amusement if I didn't feel so sick.

"Something like that," I mutter.

Riva studies me for a few moments longer, her pretty face turning so serious it sends a different sort of ache through my gut.

Her voice softens. "Are you okay after yesterday? They came at you so hard when you got upset—I've been worried about you the whole time."

The ache digs deeper at her phrasing, as if what the guardians did to subdue me was more violent than my destruction of the room. There was a point when my entire world dissolved into a frantic fury to smash every piece of Clancy's plan.

I duck my head. "I was fine after the tranquilizer wore off. Other than feeling pretty awful about the whole thing. I'm sorry if I scared you."

Riva makes a dismissive sound. "It wasn't your fault. It was a psychotic plan—of course you were upset."

She was upset too, but she didn't fly into an uncontrollable rage. I bite my lip and then force out the words.

"I can't do it. Even like this, without being so trapped. Even if he keeps pushing it on us over and over. I just—I *can't*."

When I dare to look at Riva again, her eyes have widened. "Don't even think about that," she says firmly. "Even if you could make yourself go through with it, *I* wouldn't want to. Not like this. If anything… If anything's ever going to happen between us, it'll be because we both want to for ourselves, not to satisfy some sick tyrant."

Her gaze flicks toward the jungle around us, her chin lifting at a defiant angle, as if challenging Clancy in case he's watching.

A bit of the tension that's twisted up inside me loosens. I finally convince my feet to move again.

As I walk over, Riva pushes one of the baskets forward so that it can sit between us. A little shield, confirming that we aren't even going to touch.

The sight relaxes me even more. I sink down on the grass next to her and peer at the crystalline water of the pool in the fading sunlight.

"It is a nice spot."

"Yeah. Under different circumstances, I'd appreciate the gesture." Riva laughs roughly and then digs into the basket. "I guess we might as well make the most of it."

Under the cloth covering, we find raspberry and custard tarts, a container of popcorn, miniature sandwiches, and a couple of bottles of what turns out to be lemonade.

Riva sips hers and wrinkles her nose at it. "Not sour enough."

I find I'm capable of smiling at her. "You'll have to ask them to import some lemons so you can make your own, Shrimp."

"That's not likely to happen. I don't think Clancy is very happy with me right now in general."

I pause, my stomach clenching all over again. "I saw Dom at lunch. We talked a little."

I don't know how much I should say out loud in case Clancy's monitoring us. But Riva can obviously guess that Dominic told me about their mission—and what they found out about Clancy's approach to global activism—from my brief remark.

She sighs and takes a bite of one of the tarts. "It was too good to be true right from the start, wasn't it? We'll figure something out."

She's already working on a plan—I know her well enough to tell. She got us out of a facility before.

But that one wasn't on an isolated island. And it was only the four of us she needed to break out.

"At least we have the chance to train and improve our skills while we're here," I say. "I've been working on the exercises Rollick suggested for controlling my shifts. Obviously they didn't help yesterday, but in less tense situations, I think I'm making progress. He wasn't wrong about some things even if… things have turned out badly here too."

I wince inwardly as images come back to me of the pictures Clancy showed me when he was first pitching his new plan for us shadowbloods. Things went very badly before—there's no denying that fact.

Riva considers my expression. "You heard about what the shadowkind did to the kids we got free."

"I saw the photos he has."

She gives a soft hum but doesn't say anything else, her gaze going momentarily distant. I wish I could read her mind.

This whole situation would be so much easier if we all could communicate through thoughts alone. Although I'm not sure I'd want Riva seeing everything that's in my head.

She slips off her running shoes and socks before scooting onto one of the smooth stones around the pool. With a tug of her pantlegs to her knees, she dips her feet into the water.

"Not bad." She swishes her feet back and forth. "Not as warm as I'd usually like, but I guess it'd be a little much to expect a hot tub."

The rippling water tempts me. We spent all that time on the yacht sailing around the ocean, and I never really got the chance to swim.

I hesitate and then ease over to the pool's edge too. The water laps around my feet and calves, as warm as the tropical air around us.

I shoot Riva a sideways glance. "I don't know what you're complaining about. This is perfect."

She laughs more openly this time, the bright, buoyant sound that sends a giddy shiver right down the middle of me. "No one's stopping you from diving in."

I suppose that's true. I look down at myself and then at the other basket with the swimming clothes. But I don't really want to get changed with Riva right here, even though I know she'd avert her eyes for my privacy.

I don't want to deal with the feelings that'd rise up in me, getting undressed with her so close by.

But it's not as if I'm particularly attached to the tee and sweats I'm wearing. Without letting myself second-guess the impulse, I push off right into the water in my regular clothes.

Riva laughs again, the perfect soundtrack to the delight of the warm water closing around my large frame. I kick off from one end of the pool to the other, but it's only about fifteen feet across, so not much of a workout.

Oh, well. It isn't the swimming I like most anyway.

I stretch out on my back, flexing my muscles in the right places to keep me afloat. My body bobs in the peaceful water.

For a moment, I feel as if I weigh nothing at all.

I close my eyes, absorbing the sensation of floating free. My body drifts toward the spray of the waterfall, and I scull briefly to nudge myself away.

There's a soft splash and a shift in the water's gentle currents. I glance up to see Riva has joined me, leaving on her tee and sweats like I did.

Her silvery braid trails behind her head in the water. She grins at me and paddles around the pool.

I can't help following her movements, unwilling to return to the meditative state of my float.

Her slim arms dart through the water with both strength and grace. The water darkens her eyelashes, bringing out her bright brown eyes.

It's only about a minute before she paddles back over to the bank where she was sitting before. She scrambles out and gives herself a quick rubdown with one of the towels from the basket before hunkering down at the edge of the water again. "That's enough of that."

Her damp top clings to her curves. My gaze traces them before I jerk it away, with heat flaring through my veins.

In my pants, my dick rises.

There's a part of me that wants to swim right over to her, yank her back into the water, and press my body against every bit of hers. Kiss her until our lips are on fire.

But I know that if I tried, I'd be recoiling in another jarring smack of panic before I did much more than graze my fingers over her leg. I'm not sure I could touch her at all right now, no matter how carefully, without setting off the instinctive jolt of horror that Clancy provoked so badly with his experiment.

Riva cocks her head, catching me staring. I turn, glad that the flush staining my cheeks won't show in the twilight.

How the hell is she ever going to understand why I keep pushing her away?

Andreas's voice travels up from my memories. *You've got to tell her, you know.*

Every particle of my being balks at the idea, still. But maybe he was right, because she's already gotten the wrong idea.

She pulls her legs up in front of her to hug her knees. "It's okay, you know. I'd *never* want you to do anything more than you'd want to. I love you, Zee, as you are, without you needing to do anything else. What we already have is enough for me. That's not going to change."

My throat closes up at the raw affection in her words. For a second, I'm afraid to speak, but I know I have to say at least one thing.

The statement seems to yank at my heart as I push my voice from my mouth. "I love you too."

The smile that springs to her lips could kill me.

She does need to know the rest. She *deserves* to know.

I don't want to be treading water while I'm doing it. I clamber out of the pool a safe distance from Riva and wrap the other towel around my bulky shoulders.

When I sit down with the picnic basket between us like before, my thoughts jumble together. I don't know where to start.

No, maybe that's not really true. My dick is still half-hard—it's taking conscious effort not to let my eyes trail over her body again.

I fix my attention on the water instead. "The worst thing is that I do want more. A lot more. Even now. I just don't think I'll ever be able to act on wanting it."

Riva gives me a moment and then ventures into my silence. "I heard from the other guys about what the guardians did after I left—how they brought in that woman… and something went really badly."

Should I be glad there's one part I don't need to explain? All I feel is the weight of the story pressing down on me.

"She took Andreas first," I say. "He said he told you about that. I could see afterward how sick he felt about the whole thing, and then she came to me. She was leaning into me and touching me to encourage me to come to the other room, and I—"

I stop, gathering myself, my gaze still glued to the water.

Riva's voice comes out painfully gentle. "It's okay. You don't have to talk about it if—"

I shake my head. "No. I do. You need to know…"

I inhale sharply and force myself to go on. "I've never wanted anyone other than you, Riva. And my head was a mess right then because she wasn't you, and that wasn't right, but the guardians had told us all that shit about you turning on us, so I didn't know how to feel about you anymore. And I was just so angry about everything."

"Anyone would have been."

"Maybe, but anyone else wouldn't have—" I close my eyes with a wince. "She started tugging on my arm for me to join her, and something in me just snapped. The wolf-man came roaring to the surface all raging. I just wanted her to *stop*, I wanted her to be gone, to leave me and my friends alone…"

My voice trails off into the stillness around the pool. I inhale raggedly, my stomach churning as I put the memory that's haunted me for nearly four years into words.

"I was hardly aware of what I was doing. But then the guardians zapped me back to reality, and she was there on the floor… in pieces… all the blood…"

I press my hand against my face. "It wasn't her fault. They'd hired her, they'd told her what to do. She might not even have had any more of a choice than we did."

My whole body is tensed against Riva's reaction. But when her voice reaches me, it's quiet and steady.

"That's right. It was the guardians' fault. They should never have put you in that position."

"I shouldn't have lashed out that harshly. I shouldn't have lost control." My breath rushes out of me. "And now, when I'm in any situation that feels like that scenario even a little, all the feelings come back. The disgust and the anger and the horror about what I did. And I'm terrified. If I can't control the feelings, then how do I know I can keep control of myself?"

It could be Riva lying in a puddle of blood, chest gouged open and limbs strewn by my vicious hands. Not because she did anything wrong. Because I'm just too fucking messed up to protect her from myself.

And here she is, still trying to help me after everything I've told her. "That makes sense. Of course you'd want to be careful."

I manage to raise my head to finally meet her eyes. "It isn't fair to you. It's the *worst* with you, because even a totally innocent touch can set me off, because… because I do want you, so it always affects me more. But nothing's gotten better as we've spent more time together. I might be like this forever."

Riva's eyes glint with a shimmer that might be tears. For me?

"If you are, then that's how you are," she says. "But you haven't had that much time to see how we could work through it, right? We'll just have to take it as it goes and see what happens. When we're in a place where we can actually do that without any… pressure hanging over us."

A burn forms behind my own eyes. I want so badly to hug her right now.

Instead, I reach, ever so tentatively, to rest my hand on the basket between us.

Riva watches and carefully sets her hand just a few inches from mine. An offering, take it or leave it.

I swallow hard and evaluate the emotions whirling inside me. Then I let myself slide my hand that last short distance to curl my fingers around hers.

Riva responds with a gentle squeeze that sends a pang through my heart. Her smile is tight, but I know the pain in it is empathy for me, not her own distress.

"This is enough," she says, like she told me before. "It will always be enough."

I thought I already loved her as much as a person could, but somehow in that moment, the feeling grips me twice as hard.

How can I care about her so fucking much and still not be sure I won't destroy her?

Darkness settles over the glade. The warmth starts to fade from the air, chilling my damp clothes and probably Riva's too.

We grab another tart each and then pack up the baskets. Before we can set off for the facility, lights glow along the path.

Clancy arrives with another two guardians in tow. One moves to collect the boxes, while the other goes to Riva.

She offers Riva a poncho to warm her up—and removes the bands from her arms without a word.

As the guardian motions for Riva to walk along the path, Clancy reaches for my own arms. I hold myself tensed as he detaches the bands.

"I'm sorry," he says in a low voice for only my ears. "I was aware of the incident at your old facility, but I failed to realize how deep the trauma ran. I shouldn't have put any pressure on you at all. Nothing like this will happen again."

I blink at him, but all he adds is a brisk nod. Then, without any sign of expecting forgiveness, he ushers me ahead of him down the path.

I follow the light that glimmers off Riva's hair, tension still humming through my body. Should I even believe his apology?

It's hard to imagine we've won any kind of victory here. All we can do is wait and see what Clancy and his guardians will try next… until we're free of them.

Fifteen

Andreas

It's another bright day, which means I can wear the sunglasses I requested without looking at all strange. I adjust the frames on my nose and lean back on my hands where I'm taking a brief break from training in the yard.

The dark lenses let me train my eyes on each of the guardians monitoring our progress or moving to and from the facility without them noticing the reddish gleam that gives away my talent. For the past few days, I've been riffling through as many memories as I can reach, at every possible opportunity.

One of them has to have seen or experienced something that could help us get off this island.

It's hard to narrow down my search. The only way I've found I can focus my ability to pry inside people's heads is by targeting a specific person.

I started by digging up memories involving me or my friends, but those didn't get me very far. Glimpses of moments like the attaching of bands around Riva's arms and walking her into a bedroom to meet Zian only left me twisted up with fury and a sense of helplessness.

Clancy didn't get to see through his plan. Riva's okay. But just thinking about what he tried to force them into makes me want to batter him with my fists and feet until he looks worse than the victims of Riva's screams.

Who knows what messed-up plan he's going to come up with next? We have to escape.

I have to find a way how.

If I'd been paying more attention, we might not have gotten stuck here at all. If I'd taken a moment to scan Griffin's mind when the guy I thought was Jacob beckoned me and Dominic down that hall in the facility…

All it would have taken was a brief peek, and I'd have known it wasn't Jacob. That it was a trick.

I could have stopped us before we ended up trapped in that room, before he had a chance to go back to trick the others as well. I could have warned everyone.

And maybe we'd have gotten away.

I'm the only one with a talent that would have let me realize the problem before it was too late, and I fucking failed all of us.

Guilt gnaws at my gut as I adjust my position on the grass. I'm not going to miss a crucial detail like that again.

For my current quest, I've switched to homing in on memories involving the man in charge. Clancy gives the orders to the other guardians—he introduced most of his staff to this place.

He knows its inner workings better than anyone, so the things he told his underlings could hold the key.

The man I'm currently studying surreptitiously from behind my shades isn't offering anything all that useful, to my disappointment. I sink into a memory of Clancy telling him to escort a group of younger shadowbloods to the climbing course, leap from that to a moment seeing Clancy at the other side of the cafeteria, and from there to a conversation Clancy was a part of involving some sports team in the regular world.

I grimace and push myself off the coarse grass, knowing I can't rest for long without the guardians hassling me about keeping up my training. As if I'll be a willing volunteer for any of their missions now that I know their motivations are more about financial gain than making the world a better place.

We have to play along for now, or we'll end up shut away in our rooms, no chance to discover a way out at all.

I make my way through the trees to the rope course, knowing it'll allow me a vantage point where I can check out the guardians monitoring the area without them seeing what I'm up to all that well. It can't hurt to keep both my muscles and my agility in tiptop shape too.

After I've clambered up one of the ladders and set out across the hanging boards between my starting platform and the next, one of the younger shadowbloods emerges below me. Even from above in the mottled jungle light, I recognize him immediately from his skin tone, so dark it's almost literally black.

I've made a point of chatting with all the shadowbloods I've crossed paths with during training and meals. I *want* to find out what their lives have been like—and who knows when one of them might have something useful to contribute.

So I know that the kid down below is named Ajax, and that he's part of what appears to be the middle "generation" of younger shadowbloods: the ones who are currently fourteen or fifteen years old. The few times I've seen him around, he's been pretty quiet.

Now, he glances up at me, runs his hand over the stubble of hair on his scalp, and moves to the ladder on a tree ahead of me. He times it so that he reaches the platform just moments before I swing off the last board to join him.

"Hey," he says in a low voice the guardians on the jungle floor won't hear, with a careful but intent look at me.

He's positioned himself like this on purpose—because he wanted to talk to me?

I walk slowly around the platform as if considering my options for my next trek. "Hey. Everything good?"

"About as good as it can be, huh." Ajax rests his hand against the tree trunk. "You know, with my power—I've got a little bit of telepathy. Can't pick up much, but I catch bits and pieces of thoughts. Stuff people are thinking the most loudly."

A chill washes over my skin. I keep my voice quiet and even. "Oh, really? You must 'hear' a lot of interesting things."

"Nah, mostly it's boring—or I can't even make sense of it. But yours have gotten me curious." He pauses with a swift glance toward the guardians below. The only one in view isn't even facing us at the moment.

Ajax drops his voice even lower. "You really think we could leave?"

I grip one of the ropes, my mouth going dry. Can I trust this kid?

For all I know, he could turn tail and inform Clancy of anything I tell him.

I measure out my words. "Anything's possible. Why—are you thinking you'd want to?"

The boy gives a barely perceptible shrug. "I know a lot of 'em like it here. But there's someone who matters a lot to me that I hardly ever get to see. Back in the old facility, we were together every day."

My mouth tightens in a grimace. I can understand his frustration too well. "That sucks."

"Yeah. And it's not much fun being stuck around the guardians with the way they think about us anyway."

Ajax lifts his head, and I let myself meet his dark brown gaze. "I just wanted to say… If you find a way, I want in."

He doesn't sound like a schemer trying to manipulate me into a confession. He sounds like a nervous but hopeful kid.

I study him for a moment, slipping through his skull into his memories.

I see him sitting on his own in a corner, wincing at the insult that tumbles out of a guardian's mind into his head. I see him waving goodbye to a group of other kids, his other hand clenched, as he's escorted out of a facility's training room.

Emotions don't come through with my talent, not directly, but I can sense how unhappy he was in those memories from the feel of his body.

I pull back out and re-focus on him here in the present. "I'm just… considering my options. But if you pick up on any thoughts that might help with that goal, even a little, you should let me or one of the other Firsts know ASAP." I hesitate. "Well, any of the firsts other than Griffin."

Ajax makes a face. "He's always with Clancy anyway. What's his deal?"

I wish I had a better answer. "I don't know. He wasn't like that before."

I don't want to linger any longer in conversation in case the guardians take notice. Ajax turns toward a net-like configuration of ropes, and I set off along another path of hanging boards.

An ache has formed in the pit of my stomach. It isn't just Riva and my friends counting on me.

I've just given that kid a reason to hope. I need to have something more for him the next time we talk.

I've scaled most of the course when one of the guardians calls up that it's time for lunch. Ajax has already left, and I don't see him again on my way to the mountain facility.

They switch up our shifts and never let us know when we'll see each other again specifically to make it harder for us to plan anything. They pretend it's freedom, but really it's just another kind of cage.

As I'm climbing the steps to the mountainside entrance, Clancy himself appears. He gives me a brisk nod and gazes out over the training grounds for a moment before returning inside.

I have to take off the sunglasses once I step into the facility to avoid raising suspicions, but I can't resist fixing my gaze on him while I follow him down the hall. Imagine all the useful information that's tucked inside *his* memories.

But I only glimpse a fancy dinner someplace that's got to be nowhere near the island, with crystal chandeliers and people in tuxedos and evening gowns, and then a fragment of a childhood elementary-school test. Before I can dig any farther, a guardian steps out of the cafeteria ahead of me.

I jerk my gaze away, hoping she didn't notice me using my talent. When she doesn't say anything, only motions me inside, I exhale softly in relief.

Even if the quest feels pointless, I have to keep trying. Giving up *definitely* won't get us anywhere.

As subtly as I can manage, I flit through the memories of the guardian standing near the buffet table while I grab a hamburger, fries, and salad for my lunch. Clancy yelled at him one time for showing up late to his post, but I don't see how that could factor into our plans.

Keep trying, keep trying, keep trying.

My lack of progress makes it hard to appreciate seeing Zian walk into the room. How much of a friend am I if I can't get us closer to freedom?

Freedom he needs even more than I do.

He shoots me a small smile and makes a gesture to indicate he'll sit with me. My gaze slides past him to the guardian who escorted him in.

I've seen that guy talking to Clancy pretty often. Maybe he's a closer associate than the others.

But he stands there by the doorway watching all of us. If my eyes flare red for more than a few seconds, he's bound to notice.

Fuck. I don't want to let the chance go.

"Zee," I murmur when the bigger guy sits down across from me. "Could you go keep the guardian who came in with you busy for a bit? Ask him about your schedule for the rest of the day or something like that —just keep his attention away from me?"

Zian's forehead furrows. "I can give it a shot. I don't know how long I can keep him talking for."

"Whatever you can manage is fine."

He sets off without question or complaint. Trusting that I'd only ask him to do this if it was important.

Zian approaches the guardian from the side, and the man turns to better face him. His frown doesn't indicate much patience for the interruption.

I train my gaze on him and leap in.

Clancy, Clancy, Clancy. Grabbing breakfast together, a briefing on training progress, daily orders.

I'm aware of Zian shuffling his feet at the edge of my awareness, but I force myself to keep digging. He's doing his best, and I have to too.

Then I stumble into a memory of what looks like a facility control room, though with the stone walls specific to the island. Clancy is gesturing to a set of controls.

An emergency system? asks the guardian whose head I'm in.

Clancy nods. *Earthquakes in this region are infrequent and rarely severe, but we need to be prepared. If a tremor strikes that sets off the sensors, the rooms will automatically unlock. We'll need to get all of the shadowbloods out into the valley as quickly as possible. As few assets lost as possible.*

My host stares at the pane Clancy pointed at with its zigzag symbol, so I stare at it with him. Sensors that'll make our rooms unlock?

Of course, we'd need an earthquake to make that happen.

But Jacob once toppled two three-story buildings with his power. Maybe…

Zian passes between me and the guardian on his return, cutting off my connection—and ensuring the man doesn't see the fading flash of red in my gaze. He drops back into his seat and gives me a curious look.

"Get anywhere?"

"You know, I just might have." A hint of a smile touches my lips. "I could use a little more help—from your X-ray vision this time. Look through the walls around here and check if you see this symbol anywhere."

I squirt ketchup next to my fries and scrape the tines of my salad fork through the scarlet liquid. Sketching out the emblem from the guardian's memory, that just might be the key we so desperately need.

Sixteen

Riva

I'm getting a little tired of the guardians' surprises. Especially the ones where I can't even tell whether the unexpected event is good or bad, like being ushered into a random room in the facility to find Griffin standing there waiting for me.

I stop in the doorway, my pulse stuttering.

Is this guy my friend or my enemy now?

Does *he* even know?

"Hey, Moonbeam," Griffin says, with the vacant smile that makes me want to claw the sound of the childhood nickname out of my ears.

I'm afraid hearing him say it like that will write over my memories of all the times he spoke it with real affection. Of when he was still himself.

I don't answer, tearing my gaze from him to take in the rest of the room.

It's a hotchpotch of furnishings: a sofa against one wall, a utilitarian table along another, and a couple of round, ringed targets hanging at the far end. Like whoever set it up couldn't decide whether it was for lounging in or training.

The table holds a row of gleaming knives. My fingers twitch at my side.

Griffin is watching me. "You always liked practicing with throwing knives. And I thought you might feel more comfortable if you had weapons available while we talk."

My attention jerks back to him. "Are you planning on saying something that'll make me want to stab you?"

He lifts his shoulders in a gentle shrug. "I hope not. But I know the last week here has been a lot more stressful for you than any of us would have wanted. You have every reason not to feel totally safe."

I walk over to the table and skim my fingers along the edge while I eye the blades on offer. "What did you want to talk to me about?"

"Clancy knows he fucked up. I've told him how badly he did. He'd like to find a workable solution, but he thought you might prefer to talk things through with me first. Since you know me better."

I don't know the guy talking in that unnervingly even voice at all.

But I *would* rather talk to Griffin than that asshole Clancy. If only because there are questions that've been gnawing at me that no one except Griffin can answer.

I select one of the knives—a particularly slim one that looks sharp enough to slice through flesh like butter. "Are you just his puppet, then? You speak for him and not yourself?"

Griffin shakes his head. "I make my own decisions. But I still think what he's trying to do here could be for the best for all of us. It's a work in progress."

A work in progress that traumatized Zian more than he already had been, that forced me and Jacob to murder one gang on behalf of another that might be even worse…

My jaw tightens. I curl my fingers around the hilt of the knife and turn toward Griffin.

"Then you're on his side. And I've got a lot of reasons to be pissed off with him. Aren't you afraid I'll stab you no matter what you say?"

I could kill him for real. He knows I could. One slash deep enough through his throat, and he'd be too far gone before the guardians could rush Dominic in here.

With my supernatural speed, I could land the blow before Griffin even has time to try to deflect me.

But he simply gazes calmly back at me, without the slightest sign of being disturbed by my suggestion.

"You're not that angry," he says. "You don't want to hurt me."

I grit my teeth. I might not be feeling particularly murderous, but the fact that he can read my emotions irritates the hell out of me.

Especially when he doesn't appear to be remotely affected by them.

What the hell would it take to jolt a little emotion of out *him*?

I adjust the knife in my hand, willing myself into a state of calm focus that won't betray my intentions. Then I lunge at Griffin.

I slam him back into the stone wall he was standing by, hard enough to bruise but not to break any bones, and whip the knife up to brace it at the base of his throat.

Griffin's expression twitches with the impact, but it settles back into its usual placid state a second later. I can't say the reaction was anything more than physical.

He gazes down at me with those uncomfortably blank sky-blue eyes.

If anything, he looks *curious*. Not rattled, not annoyed.

"Maybe I don't need to be angry to think we'd be better off if you really were dead," I snap, but I know even as the words come out that they aren't going to land right. Because just saying them sends a twist of guilt and horror through my gut that no doubt he can pick up on.

He is right that I don't want to hurt him, no matter what he's become.

Griffin cocks his head, not seeming to care that the blade nicks his skin with the movement before I tug it back a fraction. "You're upset with me, but not like that. What are you doing this for?"

I grimace at him. "You're acting like nothing matters. I'm trying to figure out if anything *does* matter to you."

He lifts his hand to set it over mine—the one that's pressed flat against his chest just beneath his shoulder. The second his fingers brush over my skin, a tingle races through my veins.

All the shadows in my blood wake up and quiver with anticipation. And something flickers in Griffin's eyes, the closest thing to an emotional response I've seen in him so far.

Huh. Does touching me affect him like it does me?

I guess that would make sense. The other guys all feel the same magnetic pull between us, the urge to connect physically and let our shadows meld together.

Whatever the guardians did to Griffin, maybe they couldn't stamp out that one aspect of his nature.

His gaze stays a little more intense, a little more *present*, as he tucks his hand around mine.

"You matter to me, Riva. The guys matter to me. All the shadowbloods here do."

The physical contact and our closeness are distracting me more than I like. I shove away from him, yanking my hand from his and lowering the knife.

"You have a funny way of showing it. We finally got out like we'd always wanted to—we'd have come for you too if we'd known you were alive—and you helped the guardians drag us back into their prison."

I regret stepping back when I see the vagueness creep back over Griffin's expression. Like he really was more here with me for a moment and now it's gone.

"I told you why I helped them," he says. "You were doing a lot of damage out in the world. Destroying things, killing people."

"People who were attacking us!"

Griffin is silent for a moment, studying me. When he speaks again, his voice has gone quieter.

"I didn't help right away, you know. Some of the guardians came to me and told me what had happened, showed me pictures from the place where they said you'd been doing cage fights, said you were the one who murdered all those people. I didn't believe them."

My throat closes up. It takes a moment before I can speak. "That wasn't— I didn't *mean* to kill the whole audience. I didn't even know it was going to happen."

"But that's a problem, isn't it?" Griffin's tone has turned coaxing, as if I'm a wild animal he's working at taming. "Most of those people were just there to watch. They weren't the ones controlling you. Did they all deserve to die?"

My whole body tenses with the surge of anguish. "I had no idea I even had that power then. I'm learning how to control it."

"It wasn't just that," Griffin says. "It isn't just you." He pauses. "I didn't believe it until they showed me video footage from Ursula Engel's cabin. She had surveillance cameras, you know? So I could see the way you twisted and broke the bodies, just like at the arena."

"That's when you started tracking us for them," I say with a lurch of my gut as the understanding hits me.

After Engel's house—that was when the guardians started finding us so much faster. We couldn't stay anywhere for more than a day without them showing up.

Griffin inclines his head. "For a little while. But then, in Miami… Their strategy wasn't working. They couldn't take you in, and one of the shadowbloods died while they were trying, and I thought maybe I'd been wrong. That it was safer letting you go."

I swallow thickly. "But then you changed your mind again?"

"They showed me what Jacob did in Havana. All those people *he* broke—and then cut off their hands..." Griffin knits his brow as if the thought confuses him. "He was getting worse, being out in the world. More violent. And then Clancy came to me and told me how he was going to change things, so the Guardianship wouldn't work like it had before. So you wouldn't be trapped the same way. So you could use your powers to make things better."

"And you believed him."

"He didn't lie. Here we are."

I flip the knife in my hand and fling it at one of the targets. It smacks straight into the central ring, but I get no satisfaction out of the sight.

"Here we are," I say. "Working as hired goons for whatever criminals feel like paying him to take on their dirtiest work. How is murdering people for money better than murdering them to protect ourselves, Griffin?"

Griffin walks over to the table by the knives, but he only looks at them. He never liked weapons practice much even in our old lives.

"I didn't know about Clancy getting paid. But he does need money to keep things running—to keep supporting us. If he chooses the jobs that do the most good for the world at the same time, it doesn't have to be a problem."

I snatch up a smaller knife and whip it after the first. It strikes the target a couple of inches from the center.

"And how can you be sure he is choosing those jobs and not whichever get him the most money?"

"He's said he'll be more careful from now on about vetting who hires us."

I snort. "Funny. Somehow I don't automatically believe everything he says."

Griffin replies with the air of patience that annoys the shit out of me. "I've known him since before he managed to bring us here. He worked hard to give us this opportunity. And he *is* better than the guardians who were in charge before."

"Better doesn't mean good."

"But if there isn't any option that's good in every way, you have to go with the closest one."

I take another knife but simply toss it from one hand to the other, eyeing Griffin. "And what about how he treated me and Zian? How is that anything close to good?"

Griffin's voice firms. "That wasn't okay. At all. I didn't realize he was going to try something like that. But he knows it was an awful mistake. He hasn't pushed you two together again, has he?"

It's true that I've only seen Zian twice in the past four days, and those were during regular training sessions, no one forcing us to even work together.

"It was still sick that he tried to force us at all," I have to say.

Griffin's gaze drifts away from me, somehow going even more distant than before. "I think… the guardians aren't used to seeing us as people instead of test subjects. Even the ones who are trying to do the right thing. That might take time."

I swallow a growl of frustration. I'm obviously not going to get Griffin to reject Clancy's approach right now.

If we get a chance to make a break for it, using the emergency system Andreas told me about in a secretive murmur during dinner two evenings ago, would we even be able to take Griffin with us? Would he be willing to go or try to stop us?

But if we leave him behind… he'll point the guardians right to us like he did before, won't he?

I change subjects to get at the most vital information he could still give me. I'm not sure if he'd answer if I ask directly, but that doesn't mean I can't prod my way there.

"We're talking about the people who made you bleed all over the country tracing our movements too. I'm surprised they didn't drain you dry over all those days you must have been following us."

Griffin offers a faint smile as if he thinks he's reassuring me. "It wasn't like that. My powers have evolved and grown too."

I raise an eyebrow at him. "Our emotions led you to us?"

"In a way. We've determined that if I focus on someone I know reasonably well, I can pinpoint their location on a visual display like a map. I just… feel where they're feeling things, you could see it as."

He can pinpoint us on a fucking map? A chill races over my skin.

We'd never get far enough away from the guardians while Griffin's willing to serve as a tracking device. Even crossing the ocean only worked because he was momentarily refusing.

But I have no idea how to get through to him.

No, maybe that's not totally true. I know the one thing that's provoked anything close to a real reaction in him the entire time we've been in the room together.

Setting down the knife, I turn to fully face him. I reach out and take one of his hands in my smaller ones.

The simple skin-to-skin contact sets my nerves alight. They spark brighter when I stroke my fingertips over his knuckles, the shadows inside me flaring with the impulse to step closer.

And a hint of the same longing wavers in Griffin's suddenly uncertain gaze.

"You know me that well," I say softly, holding on to him. "You've always known me the best out of anyone. Can't you see that I'm not some kind of monster who needs to be locked in a cage? We were figuring it out—we were getting a grip on our powers. None of us would have hurt *anyone* if we'd been left alone to live our lives."

His mouth tightens. "I don't know that for sure. And if you lose control again—if Jacob goes on a rampage— I can't just let that happen."

I squeeze his hand, and his fingers wrap around mine in return. A pang resonates through my chest. "It wouldn't be your fault. Nothing we did was your fault."

Griffin laughs, a strangely rough sound after the eerie calm I've gotten so used to. His voice drops until it's barely a whisper. "You have no idea how much is my fault."

What is he talking about?

Anguish shines in his eyes, there and then gone so quickly I can't tell whether I only imagined it. I let myself step closer, lifting one hand, meaning to touch his face—

But Griffin pulls back, dragging his hand from my grasp.

Whatever tenuous connection I forged vanishes. He blinks, his expression evening out.

Before I can try again, the door behind him opens. A guardian pokes her head into the room.

"Griffin, Riva—since your talk is going well, Clancy wants me to move you on to dinner."

Your talk is going well. The words roll over me, and something clicks in my head.

Horrified certainty spikes through my veins. I jerk my gaze back to Griffin. "For fuck's sake. You know what this is, don't you?"

Griffin knits his brow. "What *what* is?"

I can't read his mind even as much as he can read mine, but I think he genuinely didn't realize.

I step farther away from him and cross my arms over my chest defensively. "You said Clancy learned from his mistakes? He's only gotten sneakier about them. This is a fucking *date*. He wanted us to get friendly again—why now, after he couldn't force me to hook up with Zian? Why would he care other than because you're the only other guy from our original six I haven't already been with?"

Griffin stares at me. Before he can respond, whether he'd deny it or argue in Clancy's defense, I decide I can't stand to hear any more from him.

I march over to the guardian at the door. "I'd like dinner, but I'm not having it with Griffin. Let me go to the cafeteria. *Now.* And tell Clancy he can fuck off to the goddamn moon, if he isn't already listening to hear me say it himself."

Seventeen

Griffin

The twining melodies of violin and piano swell through my room. They wind around me as I lean back in my armchair.

The music stirs emotion in some people. I've seen videos of audiences weeping while listening to this song.

But nothing rises up inside my chest. My heart beats on at the same steady pace.

I used to put on music like this to test myself. To confirm just how deep the guardians' training ran.

This is one of the rare moments when I can't help thinking I might prefer it if I noticed it getting to me just a little. If I knew the things that affect other people could still affect me, if only slightly.

A normal person would be irritated, even angry, that Clancy was taking so long to come talk to me. I told the guardian who tried to bring me and Riva to dinner that I wanted to see him immediately, in the firmest tone I'm capable of.

But it's been… hours? Definitely at least one of those.

My sense of time has gotten foggy with the fading of my emotions, as if feeling things about what was happening helped define those events concretely in my head.

By any measure, it's been a lot more time than *immediately.* My thoughts won't settle until I can address him directly.

And yet with each passing minute, my heart thumps on in the same steady rhythm. My gut stays relaxed.

The tension in my mind doesn't seep beyond my skull.

Maybe he's gone to talk to Riva first, which might be fair, and that's what's keeping him.

At the thought of Riva, one of my hands brushes over the other unbidden. The graze of my fingertips over my knuckles doesn't summon even a ghost of the sensation I'm unconsciously seeking, but it does provoke a flicker of memory.

Her hands, tucking around my own. Her fingers stroking my skin.

The tiny but heated quivers that shot through my nerves and had my pulse momentarily hitching.

The memory in turn provokes a faint twinge of aversion. No, that shouldn't happen. No, that's nothing I want.

The source of that reaction is buried so deep now that it doesn't contain any emotion of its own, only a dull impression of recoiling within my head.

What am I recoiling from, though? It was Riva— It was *good.*

The urge to walk straight to wherever she is and feel it again nibbles at the edges of my mind.

No.

Even feeling things because of her can be a problem. Those kinds of feelings could be the *worst* problem.

Couldn't they?

I rub my forehead as if the gesture will sort out my uncertainties.

All I know for sure is that Clancy created a problem much bigger than any turmoil inside me. How could he have thought it made sense to send me to Riva as if I could take Zian's place in his disturbing plan?

Unless Riva was wrong, and that wasn't what he intended after all.

If it wasn't, if he has nothing to justify, why hasn't he already come to tell me that?

Jacob would be furious. I've felt my brother's anger, sharper and harsher than it ever was when I knew him before.

I've felt it aimed at me. How am I going to make *him* understand that I was trying to keep him safe in my own way?

I thought, once we could see each other again…

At a plaintive meow, I lift my head. Lua is stalking over to me, her tail standing straight and her ears perked in anticipation.

My cat might not be able to talk, but I can instantly tell what she wants, although I can't read animal emotions at all. Even without the inner insight, she's so much simpler than any of the human beings I encounter.

As she rubs her cheek against my leg, I reach down and give her a gentle scratch down the length of her spine. With an encouraging meow, Lua jumps right onto my lap.

She stretches out in her favorite spot, squeezed into the narrow space between my thigh and the arm of the chair, and offers up her white-furred belly for more pets. A smile crosses my lips as I oblige.

It isn't the same as feeling something, but I get a general satisfaction out of knowing I can cater to her needs. Make *her* happy.

That the emptiness of my body doesn't stop me from showing I care in the ways I can.

When I told Clancy I was bringing Lua with me from the facility I'd been kept at before, he started to ask if that was really necessary. The look I gave him stopped him halfway through the question.

I'm not totally sure why the guardians who worked on me after the escape attempt brought her to me as a kitten, but she's mine now. She counts on me.

And maybe I need her a little bit as well.

At the knock on my door, Lua twitches in surprise and then goes right back to purring avidly. I scoop her up and get to my feet, reaching to switch off the music.

"Come in."

I know it's Clancy already, well before he opens the door. Every person in this place has a different feel to them, and I'm more familiar with his overall air than most.

He steps inside and stays by the door, his arms folded loosely in front of him. The fact that I have no emotions roiling in my own chest makes me twice as aware of his own, as detached as I am from the visceral sensations of them.

He's apprehensive but mostly calm and determined. Prepared for this to be an uncomfortable talk but assuming everything will be smoothed over without much difficulty.

I hope he's right.

"I take it your visit with Riva didn't go all that well?" he says. "Is that what you wanted to talk to me about?"

I study him, watching the outward signs of his mood even as I monitor him from the inside out. "It was going fine until she got the idea that you were hoping us re-establishing our friendship would lead to something more. Was that the larger plan? That she might warm up to me enough that she'd want to have sex with me, since she isn't going to with Zian?"

My straightforward question sends a flicker of discomfort through the older man. As if his intentions would be any better or worse depending on how I phrase it.

He adjusts his weight. "I can see I pushed too hard with the two of them. I wasn't going to force anything. But if we'd reached that outcome, getting more data on the connections she's been able to form within your group would have been a welcome side benefit."

"And would you have encouraged me to talk with her at all if it wasn't for that possible 'side benefit'?"

Clancy simply avoids answering that question. "Griffin, you know the work we're trying to do here—how difficult it'll be. I'm looking out for all of you, searching for every possible advantage."

A pang of self-righteous defiance resonates through his emotions. He's on the defensive—because I'm getting at the truth, and he doesn't want to admit there could have been anything wrong about his plans.

My fingers continue their rhythmic stroking of Lua's fur where she's sprawled in my arms, but my thoughts jitter as the new information shuffles into my understanding of the situation.

He was using me like he tried to use Zian. He didn't even *tell* me he was trying to use me.

I wouldn't have thought he'd go that far. Just hours ago, I was telling Riva he'd realized his mistake.

Clancy sighs. "If you talk to her again, you could help her warm up to you with your powers, couldn't you? I know you couldn't intervene very well with Zian, but her hesitation is much less… aggressive."

I frown at him. "I tried to calm Zian down when he went into that rage because I was afraid he'd hurt someone, not to make it easier for them to hook up. To push Riva to feel happier around me…"

That would be just like forcing myself on her, wouldn't it? Worse than doing it physically, because she wouldn't be able to see the attack and ward it off.

A flinch ripples through me, my thoughts narrowing down to a surge of denial. "I don't understand why you'd ask me that. It'd be a horrible thing to do to her."

So horrible a twinge of nausea ripples through my gut, as if just for an instant I'm actually feeling that horror.

Clancy shakes his head. "Sorry, it was a reflexive thought. Obviously as soon as you left, your influence would fade, and that could have adverse effects that would counteract any progress we made."

Adverse effects? How about the fact that she's one of my oldest friends, and there is no universe where coercing her into any kind of intimacy, even only renewed friendship, would be seen as anything but morally appalling?

The flicker of emotion has vanished, but my abhorrence at the idea hasn't wavered. I need to be completely clear about this.

I draw my posture straighter. "Even if it wouldn't fade, I would never do that to her. She's my *friend*. I'm here to stop people from being exploited, not to do it myself."

"Of course, of course," Clancy says, holding up his hands. "I won't mention it again."

He's uneasy, but I can tell from the way he's eyeing me that it's only about my response. He doesn't feel any concern or guilt at all about the tactic he just suggested.

What if Riva was right about that too? What if I've failed to recognize just how detached this man is from *us*?

Does he still see us as so subhuman that he can't be trusted to have even our basest best interests at heart?

The other accusations Riva threw to me flood through my head. I find myself saying, "You know, she'd be happier naturally—they'd all be happier—if the Guardianship gave them even more freedom. Chances to go out into the wider world for their own reasons, to do what they want, not just for missions."

Clancy exhales in a huff. "You of all people should realize how dangerous that could be. We can't risk it until we're absolutely sure they wouldn't give in to their more violent impulses."

I fix my gaze on him even more intently than before. "Well, what about me? What if I wanted to have some time for myself? I've never hurt anyone. My powers can't do any permanent damage."

"You're a key part of getting our operations into gear, Griffin," Clancy says without missing a beat. "I hope you wouldn't try to bow out on us when we need you to make sure we achieve everything we're aiming for."

He's dodging the question again. He could have said I could take a brief trip, or that he'd be willing to arrange something in the future, but instead he's saying no while doing his best to make it sound as if he's only being reasonable.

James Clancy is a very controlled man. I've never sensed his emotional state going wild the way Zian or Jacob can.

But the impressions I pick up from him still tell a story. And right now, I taste not just the fear I can assume is about what might happen to the world if shadowbloods were allowed to roam freely through it, but also an anxious twinge of anticipated loss.

He doesn't want to let go of us. And not because he cares about *us* all that deeply, it's clear.

Because we're the key to his grand master plan, and he can't carry it out properly without us. We're tools he's counting on putting to use.

He hasn't shown any concern about what I might be going through that I'd want to ask that question. Any sign that *my* happiness matters at all to him beyond carrying out his goals.

Has he ever? Or was I so caught up in the idea of fixing everything that's gone wrong, making a better future for us all in alignment with his vision, that I never paid enough attention before?

"I want to do what's best for all of us," I say, an answer that's both true and that I know he'll accept.

Clancy gives me a tight smile. "I'm glad to hear that. Don't worry about this whole situation anymore. Or about Riva. She just needs time to fully grasp the bigger picture."

He leaves without checking if there's anything else I hoped to ask him. The door clicks shut behind him.

Clicks shut and locks, because I'm never allowed to go looking for *him*.

For a few minutes, I stand in the same place, running my fingers over Lua's back and under her chin, gazing at the door without really seeing it.

This facility and the missions carried out from it were built off Clancy's vision… but they wouldn't have happened without me. Without me, I doubt any of the guardians stood a chance of catching up with my former friends, let alone capturing them.

At the time I was sure I'd made the right decision. That it really was best for them and me as well as him.

I have no gut feeling to guide me, no innate sense of whether these are the results I should have expected, but fuck, do I wish I did.

What if I've actually screwed up our lives all over again?

Eighteen

Riva

The low, thin voice reaches my ears as I secure the last pieces of my climbing gear.

"Riva? That's your name, right?"

I glance around at the same time as Dominic does where he was gearing up a few feet away from me—more carefully to work around his tentacles.

A slim boy in his early teens has approached us, so quietly I didn't notice him coming. The bright afternoon sun gleams off the rounded planes of his dark face and the stubble of even darker hair over his scalp.

His intent gaze is fixed on me. I recognize him from seeing him here and there around the facility, but we've never spoken before.

I tip my head in acknowledgment. "Yeah, I'm Riva. Are you going to climb too? There's room for three on the course."

He steps closer with a flick of his eyes toward one of the guardians stationed at the edge of the jungle around the climbing site. His voice lowers so it's barely a murmur.

"Andreas told me I should let the Firsts know if I picked up anything that might give us a way out. I caught something from a guardian at breakfast—the supply helicopter is coming right after the last dinner shift tonight."

Understanding clicks in my head: this is the kid Drey mentioned to me, the one who can read thoughts, just a little. Ajax—that was the name he said.

I push a smile onto my face, keeping it as relaxed as possible for the sake of the watching guardians. "Thank you for the heads up. We might check out the course after we're done here."

Ajax's mouth twitches upward with a faint smile of his own, accepting the cover story I've offered. "I figured you'd want to hear about it," he says, and turns to go.

I meet Dominic's gaze and find it even more pensive than usual. He pauses and then nods to the cliffside in front of us. "We'd better get climbing."

We can't really talk while we're scaling the rocky surface. I push myself faster than usual both in anticipation of the conversation to come and to let the burn of the exertion focus my thoughts.

Of course, that means I reach the ledge partway up the cliff well before Dominic does. I brace my feet on it and lean my weight against the cliffside as I give him time to catch up, rolling my shoulders.

The guardians won't think there's anything strange about us taking a brief break here. That's the whole reason they included the ledge, even if on my own I'd clamber right past it.

Dominic scrambles up to join me with a huff of ragged breath and a weary smile. "I think you've gotten even faster since the old days."

I give him a crooked grin in return. "I've had a lot more motivating me."

He balances himself carefully on the ledge and lets one of his tentacles slip over to wrap around my wrist, the monstrous equivalent of holding my hand. "What do you think about the news?"

I bite my lip, gazing down at the jungle where I can only barely make out the forms of the watching guardians now. There's no way they can hear us up here.

The wind gusts over me as I consider my answer, whipping my braid across my neck. "I don't know. I guess a cargo helicopter must have a decent amount of room in it—but enough for all of us?"

Dominic strokes the tip of his tentacle over my palm in a soothing gesture. "You know we might not be able to get *everyone* out all at once. I don't even know how many shadowbloods are living here."

Neither do I, but every part of me balks at his suggestion. I push my thoughts toward other considerations. "We'd still have to figure out a way to *get* to the chopper and take it over without being caught along the way."

"Yeah." Dominic's mouth twists. "I guess we don't know for sure if Jake even can set off the emergency system. And we'll only get one chance to try that trick."

"He's got to make it feel like a whole earthquake. A *big* earthquake."

That seems like a lot, even for Jacob. I've seen him pull down two three-story buildings in one go, but nothing on the scale of shaking up an entire mountain.

Dominic chuckles roughly. "You know he'll try, even if he practically kills himself doing it. The number of times he ran himself to the point of injury in the last few years at the old facility, pushing himself past his limits like he thought he was proving something…"

A melancholy cast comes over his face. I wonder how many times Dom needed to patch Jacob up after he overexerted himself.

A tickle of inspiration ripples through me. We should probably start climbing again, but I have to put the idea out there.

"Dom… You told me that you can take energy out of things even when you're not using it to heal, right? That it makes you feel stronger, exhilarated, like my scream does for me?"

Dominic's shoulders tense, and I reach to grasp his actual hand in the hopes of conveying that I didn't mean any judgment in the question.

"Yeah," he says quietly. "Why?"

"I was just thinking… if you can pass energy on to someone else to heal them, maybe you could pass it on to boost them when they're already fine too."

Dominic blinks at me, and understanding dawns on his face with a strange mix of hope and horror. "If I can get to Jacob at the right moment, maybe I can pump up his powers."

"It could be worth trying. If you're okay with it."

He gives both my fingers and my wrist one last affectionate squeeze and turns toward the cliffside again. "If it would get us out of here, I'd try just about anything."

I take the second half of the climb slower, making sure I don't get too far ahead of Dominic. I still reach the upper ledge a couple of minutes ahead of him.

Stretching out my arms, I peer over the craggy landscape in the direction of the facility. The landing strip where our private plane took us to and from our mission lies above it. That's probably where the cargo chopper lands too.

Supplies must be delivered pretty regularly. It's not like this is the only chance we'll get.

I'm just not sure how much better prepared we could be. Or how much worse our circumstances might become the longer we delay.

When Dominic reaches me, he takes one look at my face and slings his arm around me. I hug him back, tucking my head against the crook of his neck and breathing in his familiar tangy scent, sharper now with the sweat he's worked up during the climb.

"We'll figure it out," he murmurs to me. "One way or another. One time or another."

I wish I could feel as sure as he sounds.

He cups my cheek and brings my mouth to his. My skin lights up from head to toe as our breaths mingle.

I haven't gotten to kiss any of my guys more than briefly since I hooked up with Jacob in the van. The soft but determined press of Dominic's lips against mine leaves all my nerves tingling—and aching for more.

He draws back only far enough to rest his forehead against mine. His voice comes out with an unusually husky note.

"I've missed getting to be this close with you."

My throat chokes up. "Me too."

"One more thing to look forward to when we get out of this, Sugar."

The new nickname heats me up even more. I can't resist claiming one more lingering kiss before we head down the mountainside again.

We chuck off our gear for the trio of preteen shadowbloods who've come for a climb and set off toward the facility. My thoughts spin in my head.

Dominic doesn't push for further answers. He knows that a problem like this needs to be contemplated carefully.

We come out into the clearing beneath the facility in time to see a procession scaling the winding path higher above the entrance.

I stop in my tracks, squinting at the figures who are just cresting the peak of this part of the mountain range. My heart thumps harder, but I don't make out the forms of any of my guys—or any other shadowbloods I recognize.

I do catch the ruddy gleam of the short-cropped hair on the man at the back of the line. I'd know that color and the confident gait anywhere.

Clancy is directing a bunch of the shadowbloods off somewhere.

"Another assignment?" Dominic murmurs next to me.

"Must be." My stomach knots with the question of what mess he's bringing them into this time.

Dom hesitates before he speaks again. "It means some of the kids won't be here… but he won't be either. And last time he brought at least a few other guardians with him. You were gone until the next day, weren't you?"

The knot clenches tighter. "Yeah."

I know what he's saying. The mission gives us an additional opening.

The facility's leader will be away, out of easy reach to give orders, when the supplies arrive. There'll be fewer guardians in general to tackle a rebellion.

How many opportunities are we going to get like *that*?

One of the guardians still here strides over to us with a curt air. "Riva, you're having lunch now. Dominic, you have another hour of training time."

Splitting us up as they always like to do. They wouldn't want us to have too long at once to feel comfortable in each other's company.

Except when they're trying to force me to fuck one of the guys, that is.

I grab Dominic's hand for a quick squeeze before the guardian gets insistent. He surprises me by tugging me right to him in an embrace.

The jolt of pleasure at his kiss mingles with my apprehension. We've avoided most overt PDAs in front of our captors.

But the gesture isn't really about stealing a momentary make-out session. Dom's lips brush my cheek next, and the faintest whisper travels to my ears.

"It's your call. Say the word, and we'll be with you."

He steps back at the guardian's clearing of her throat. I shoot him a nervous smile and hustle up the stone steps to the facility.

The knot in my stomach feels like a boulder now. Why is it up to me?

But I already know the answer to that. I'm the one who instigated our last escape and our attempt at breaking the younger shadowbloods out of a different facility.

I'm the one who has the most need to escape from here, the one Clancy has imposed on the most.

My men don't want to drag me into a plan I don't agree with. They trust me to judge when the balance of opportunity to risk skews right.

Too bad I'm not sure how much I trust myself. That last escape we carried out is what got us captured.

It led to those gory photographs Clancy showed me.

We definitely won't be able to bring everyone with us, not when a bunch of the shadowbloods are on this mission. Hell, for all I know Clancy did bring one of my guys with him and I just didn't spot him. I can tell Andreas and Jacob are still in the area, but I don't have that kind of awareness of Zian.

I slip into the cafeteria in a daze and am hit with a wave of relief seeing Zee by the food table. He notices me at the same moment and gives me a smile so bright and yet shy that it wrenches at my heart.

I hurry over to fill my plate next to him, careful not to stand close enough to touch. He tilts a little toward me as he snatches an enchilada off a platter with a pair of tongs.

"I saw Jake last night. Told him where I've spotted the markings Drey showed me for the emergency system."

My pulse stutters with this new piece of information added to the puzzle of "What the hell am I going to do?" All the factors are starting to line up, pointing toward a conclusion I can't ignore.

It isn't really a sudden decision. We've been prepping for a moment like this for days.

"Good," I murmur in response, taking an enchilada of my own.

As I drop some salad onto my plate, Zian backs up abruptly to make room for a younger shadowblood who's darting to the dessert tray. In his haste, Zee's elbow brushes my forearm.

He jerks his arm close to his chest like he's been burned, the now-familiar panic crossing his face for an instant before his jaw tightens.

I swallow thickly as I give him a slight nod to indicate that I'm okay. That I'm not offended by his reaction.

And anger sparks in my chest.

The flames of my fury smolder while I add a cookie to my meal, while I walk behind Zian over to one of the tables, while I sit across from him and take in the longing I can now recognize in his gaze when he looks at me briefly before digging into his lunch. The burn spreads all through my abdomen.

He's gotten worse—he's still worse than he was before, even though Clancy finished his sick games almost a week ago. The guy in front of me, the guy I *love*, has taken even more damage in the short time we've been here than he'd already endured before.

How long can we let them keep manipulating us, using us? How much farther will they go?

Who will they hurt next? How many of the younger shadows have they already screwed up without my even knowing it?

The anger sears into a swell of resolve. We can't stay here any longer.

Every day, every hour, each of us dies a little more.

And it isn't just me. I might be lighting the signal fire, but we made this plan together.

We all have a choice. Me and my guys and the other shadowbloods who can join us or not. We won't force them.

I tap my fork lightly against my plate, and Zian looks up.

"Tonight," I mouth, not even a whisper.

The way his face lights up tells me this is right.

As I gulp down my lunch without tasting it, I focus on the marks dappled across my collarbone. On my sense of Jacob and his taut, brutal energy.

He's outside right now, but not far. In the clearing just outside the facility, I think.

I construct an excuse in my head. When I stand up from the table, I make a show of patting my hip pockets.

Then I jog over to the door, where one of the guardians is monitoring, as always. "I think I dropped one of my earbuds outside while I was training. Can I quickly check the clearing?"

The man eyes me, but I really do have a portable radio and a set of wireless buds that Clancy supplied me with back in my room. I've been on good behavior my whole time here.

They have no reason to think I'd be up to anything nefarious—and they'll be watching me the whole time anyway.

"I want you back inside in five minutes," he says brusquely.

"Thanks!"

I dart out the entrance and down to the clearing. Jacob is poised near the trees with a couple of weights from a rack the guardians have set out, but the second I appear, his attention snaps to me.

To avoid being obvious about my real intentions, I stalk over to the edge of the jungle by the path that leads to the climbing area. I don't need to do more than be here—Jake joins me a moment later.

"What's up?"

I keep my tone casual. "Dropped something. Help me look?"

I crouch down as if peering through the underbrush. Jacob squats next to me, his shoulder brushing mine.

"Tonight," I say under my breath. "Right after last dinner. Dom might help you."

Jacob reins in any reaction he might have to the news other than the glitter of his cool blue eyes. "You got it, Wildcat."

We veer in separate directions, and then I let out a huff as if in frustration. "I'll have to look by the climbing range next time I'm out."

As I lope back to the facility, my heart thuds in my chest. We're really doing this—if we can get coordinated in time.

My hand rises to my cat-and-yarn necklace, flicking over the silver surface without quite swiveling the joints. And a different thought jabs through me like an icy spear.

If we're going to get out of here and stay free from Clancy's grasp, we're going to have to deal with Griffin.

Nineteen

Riva

We don't have watches or clocks, but I know my dinner is one of the middle shifts. A few shadowbloods are heading out of the cafeteria when the guardian escorts me over, and more are just arriving when I'm ushered out.

Back in my bedroom, the door thuds shut behind me with the hiss of the lock engaging. My pulse skitters through my veins as I sink down on the side of the bed.

It's not even a bad room. It's three times as big as the cells we were confined in at the old facility, with a soft-toned overhead fixture that mimics daylight and a cupboard to store the possessions I've actually been allowed to hold on to.

A few changes of clothes, picked by me out of the selection Clancy offered us—all practical and flexible, but that's how I like them. The radio he gave me, programmed to only offer stations with no hosts talking about the outside world, just music.

A couple of novels from the small fiction library we're allowed to borrow from, that I tried to read to pass the time but lost interest in. An assortment of weights, bands, and other exercise equipment so I can work on my strength and flexibility between outside training sessions.

How is it possible that our new captors have treated us both better and worse than any before?

Maybe that's why it's most important that we get out of this place. The better parts lulled me into enough complacency that the worse parts took me by surprise.

No matter how people like Clancy dress up the situation, no matter what grand ideals they announce, in the end, we're still prisoners as long as the guardians have us.

I should never have let myself feel like somehow that could be an okay life. Like it wasn't reasonable for me to want to make my own choices beyond someone else's tight restrictions.

I turn on the radio and switch it to a station playing a soft but steady beat and lowkey melodies. Nothing that makes me want to dance. Just enough to focus my mind without distracting me.

It occurs to me that it might be smart to have some extra clothes along. Even the radio could be useful in some way.

But I don't have anything to carry them with. And even though I can't see any, I'm sure the guardians have cameras monitoring the room.

Just like the first time, we have to act normal, or we could betray our plans before we get to act on them.

And I won't think about how badly that first escape attempt ended.

The flickers of memory bring my mind back to Griffin. A new ache forms in my stomach.

I wish I could talk to the other guys properly—make a real strategy, confirm that we're all on the same page. We'll have to scramble to organize ourselves once the doors open.

At least four of us can find each other through our marks.

But we have to bring Griffin with us too. It's either that or kill him, and no matter how he's helped Clancy or what he's agreed to, every cell in my body recoils from the thought.

I can't imagine the others will feel any different.

As long as he's with the guardians, he can pinpoint our location almost instantly. The only way to make sure he isn't with them is to keep him with us.

I'm just not sure how we're going to accomplish that when I doubt he's going to come willingly.

As that uneasy thought passes through my head, the floor beneath my feet vibrates with a faint tremor. My breath catches in my throat.

That's got to be Jacob. He's starting to shake the whole fucking mountain.

When I concentrate on my marks, I can sense that he and Dominic are together, somewhere near the facility entrance. Twinges of strain resonate from both of them.

They must be pouring a ton of effort into the attempt if a hint of it is seeping through our connection. Will their powers be enough to trigger the emergency system?

Or has all my worrying been pointless?

As I get up to turn off the music, the tremor expands. The quivering sensation spreads through my bones from the floor.

My heart pounds faster alongside it. What if the guardians realize what's happening?

For a few seconds, the vibration plateaus, not getting any stronger or weaker. Then the stone floor lurches so hard I have to smack my hand against the wall to catch my balance.

An unnerving creaking sound resonates through the air, followed by a distant peal of an alarm—and the whir of my bedroom door sliding open.

Adrenaline jolts me into action. I dash into the hall, my attention split between possible threats in the hall outside and my awareness of my three guys through our marks.

Dom and Jake are rushing deeper into the facility, toward me. Andreas is… farther down the hall in the opposite direction, around at least one bend, but hurrying toward me too.

A few confused faces appear around the doorways nearby—younger shadowbloods trying to figure out what's going on. Before I've taken more than a step toward them, two guardians hurtle into view.

They're carrying their electrified batons and a tranq gun, but I don't give them a chance to use either. With only a slight pang of guilt, I shriek at the one who's slightly closer—a short, sharp scream designed to tear right through the most vital parts of him as quickly as possible.

He crumples, and the other guardian slams into the wall headfirst. Not because of me. As she slumps to the ground amid pooling blood, Jacob charges up from behind her with Dominic at his heels.

"Come on!" I shout to the younger shadowbloods, darting down the hall and beckoning them. "Everyone out—out to the facility entrance. We're taking off!"

Nadia and Tegan venture from nearby rooms, their eyes wide but chins up. Other kids duck back into their rooms as if more afraid of escaping than staying.

Why wouldn't they be? They have no idea what we'll face out there.

Most of them don't even really know me.

Andreas dashes around a corner farther down with Zian beside him. Relief flickers through me, but it isn't enough just to have my guys.

"Let's go!" I call out. "You don't have to live with guardians controlling everything you do, forced to go on missions and train and the rest. We can find something better."

My guys peer into the open rooms, motioning to the kids who are hesitating. Booker and Ajax must have joined Andreas and Zian as they rushed this way, because I spot them in the increasingly crowded hall.

Another guardian sprints into view, only to be tossed aside by a shove of Jacob's power. Jake comes up beside me, his hair sweat-damp along his forehead and his jaw tight.

"We've got to get moving quickly while they're still confused."

"We need Griffin," I say.

The darkening of Jacob's eyes shows that he understands why without me saying anything more. He pauses for an instant and then strides onward. "I can find him."

As Jake's twin awareness leads him around the bend in the opposite direction from where Andreas came, the other guys fall into step with us. We point every shadowblood kid we pass toward the entrance, hoping they'll listen, and hustle onward.

"We have to be ready," Jacob says. "I don't think Griffin can push emotions on more than one or two of us at the same time. You see it happening to someone, jump in there and interrupt him."

Zian frowns. "I don't want to hurt him."

A shudder runs down my spine. "None of us do. But we'll all be hurt if he can track us down for the guardians again. Knocking him out would be better for everyone in the long run."

Two guardians appear in the hallway up ahead. Zian barrels forward to crash into one; I cut the other down with another truncated shriek.

Then Griffin emerges from a room just beyond their broken bodies.

He looks at the corpses and then at us, and like so often now, I can't read the slightest emotion in his gaze. But he can obviously tell what's going on.

"You're breaking out," he says in that new, vacant voice of his.

Jacob grabs his brother's arm. "And you're coming with us. Get moving."

I tense, waiting for Griffin to put up some kind of fight. But after a second's hesitation, resolve tightens his expression. "All right. I just need to get Lua. I can't leave her here."

Lua?

My momentary confusion is broken by a meow from just inside the doorway. Griffin shoots Jacob a look of appeal, and his twin nods.

Griffin's fast about it. He ducks into the room and emerges within a matter of seconds, a backpack slung over one shoulder and a cat's white-furred face poking from the unzipped top.

As we hurry toward the entrance, I check the other guys. I don't see any sign of him warping their emotions.

Would he have grabbed his pet if he was only planning to turn the tables on us at the right moment? Or is it just to convince us to trust him?

I turn and narrow my eyes at him. "No argument? You're happy to join us?"

Griffin blinks at me. "I don't know if happy is the right word, but it's become clear that none of us are better off staying here."

It has? Since when?

As much as I'd like to badger him with questions, this isn't the time for it.

A particularly young-looking kid with spiky white hair flits past us toward the entrance, his body seeming to stutter as he blinks out of view and reappears a few feet farther ahead in an instant. I catch sight of Celine braced in the doorway to her room, her expression taut with worry.

I wave to her as we pass. "Come with us. There's room for everyone who'll come."

At least, I hope there is.

She wavers a second longer and then sprints ahead of us. Her dark hair swings as she veers into a room near the entrance, but she's returned by the time we've caught up.

I guess, like Griffin, she had something here she didn't want to leave behind, although I can't see any sign of what that was.

A dozen or so younger shadowbloods are gathered on the dusk-draped ledge outside the entrance. *Is that all?* a voice in the back of my head murmurs, but I don't let myself dwell on my disappointment.

We have to get the kids who were willing to flee out of here ASAP. That's what matters most.

Especially because feet are thundering in the halls behind us. The guardians must be regrouping, preparing to recapture us.

There's no time to go back and try to convince the others to join our escape if we want to escape at all.

"Up the path!" I shout over the racing of my pulse, jabbing my hand toward the narrow, shadowy track that weaves back and forth up the mountain over our heads.

Jacob and Andreas push to the front of the crowd, dragging Griffin with them.

"Follow us," Jake calls out, and the kids start to stream after them into the thickening dusk.

Good. Whoever reaches the plateau first will need to deal with the helicopter's pilot, and my guys are more equipped to do that than the kids. I should have thought that part through more carefully.

But when did we have time to put our heads together and really plan?

I hustle along at the back of the group, ushering the kids ahead of me with Dominic and Zian on either side. When the spiky-haired boy I noticed earlier stumbles, Zee grabs his elbow to steady him.

We're not moving fast enough. As we swerve around the first bend, some of the kids already slowing as the unexpected climb saps their energy, a squad of guardians hurtles up the path toward us.

I spin around and let out a shriek, but one of our pursuers fires a weapon at the same time. A projectile whizzes through the evening and smacks me right in the throat.

My voice fizzles out with a squeak. I try to force another sound out and only rasp.

Shit.

As a chilly wave of panic washes over me, Zian throws himself at the guardians—only to hurl himself backward, barely dodging the bolt of electricity that shoots from one of their batons.

"Go, go, go!" Dominic hollers to the kids ahead of us, urging them onward, but my stomach has started to sink.

More shots blare through the night. Zian smacks a dart to the side with a swing of his hand.

Another plunges into the back of a kid just beyond him. The boy crumples, and I stumble as I avoid stepping on his slack form.

We can't afford to stop and try to carry him, or the guardians will be on us.

One of them must hit a control, because the next thing I know, a section of path in the middle of our frantic procession crumbles away. Three of the younger shadowbloods tumble down the mountainside to a thick net that's waiting to confine them below.

"Jump!" I manage to force out in a thin voice. Zee and I catch Dominic between us and spring at the same moment.

It's at least a five-foot gap, but we clear it. Unfortunately, the guardians were prepared for that possibility too.

One of them jabs the side of the mountain, and a new ledge of rock protrudes to fill the gap so they can continue their pursuit. Another arc of electricity whips through the air, close enough that my fingers jitter.

I cough and try to propel a shriek from my mouth, but my throat is throbbing from the impact. The strangled noise that pops out of me does nothing at all.

Just in front of us now, Tegan sways on her feet, her fawn-brown hair sticking to the sweat that's broken out on her neck. Her breaths are so ragged I can hear them over the pounding footsteps around us.

I'm considering swinging her small form onto my back—or gesturing for Zian to do it—when she spins around. Her eyes have stretched even wider, but her mouth is set in a line of total determination.

"I can stop them!" she says. "I can give you enough time."

She squeezes between us before I can say a word. When I jerk around, she's already facing off against the guardians—with her mouth open as she exhales in a rush.

I never asked what her power was. Now I get to see it up close.

A current of dark smoke like the shadows that bleed from our veins gushes over her lips. The cloud sweeps over the guardians, setting off shouts of alarm that make me think it's doing more than obscuring their vision.

"Tegan!" I rasp, taking a step back toward her, but Zian tugs me in the opposite direction.

"We have to let her. We might not make it otherwise."

I know he's right. But the sense of abandoning her yanks at my heart with every step I take away from her toward the top of the cliff.

As we veer around another bend and race the last distance to the top of the mountainside, Dominic's breath breaks into panting. I'm not sure how much longer he can keep up this pace.

But we've arrived. We burst onto the air strip in the midst of the cluster of younger shadowbloods who've made it this far—who are staring at Jacob where his hand is pressed against the helicopter's windshield, lit by the glow of its running lights.

It's a huge chopper with a propeller on the tail as well as one over the long main cabin. The pilot gapes at us from inside, both in shock and because Jake's power has a grip on his throat.

"Open the fucking doors!" Jacob snarls.

Griffin steps up beside him, his presence weirdly calm amid all the turmoil. "Force isn't working. Let me try."

Jake narrows his eyes at his twin. "You—"

Andreas cuts him off with a grasp of his shoulder.

Griffin doesn't appear to be paying much attention to the other guys anyway. He peers through the window at the pilot, and my skin prickles with the sense of exuded power.

The pilot's expression shifts, loosening other than the worried slant of his mouth. "What do you need? How can I help?"

Griffin only offers the slightest of triumphant smiles. "Open the doors and let us on."

The hatch halfway down the body of the chopper opens up. I wave the remaining shadowbloods on board, my mouth gone dry.

Will Griffin really be able to manipulate this guy into doing everything we need? Should we even believe Griffin is looking out for us?

But then, how else are we going to get a flight out of here? Jacob and Zian can't beat the guy into submission and then expect him to coherently direct an aircraft.

If it seems like something's wrong during the flight… we'll just have to deal with it then.

We squeeze into the dim, metallic-smelling space alongside several plastic crates and cardboard boxes that must be the supplies the guardians were expecting. Griffin comes around to the cockpit, leaning against the back of the pilot's seat.

Jacob stations himself right beside his brother, poised for potential trouble.

"Take us into the air," Griffin says in a voice that's almost hypnotic in its smoothness. "We need to leave this spot."

He may as well have hypnotized the pilot from how quickly the man moves to follow his suggestion.

As the helicopter lurches into the air with a whir of the blades, Griffin glances back at me. His backpack wobbles as his cat squirms inside it, her head ducked down in the chaos.

"Where do we want him to go?"

God, that is the question, isn't it? I can't see anything but darkness beyond the windshield right now.

I freeze up, both because I'm not sure what the right answer is and because I don't know if I could say it loud enough for Griffin to hear me anyway.

Dominic catches my hand and answers for me. "The nearest major city on the mainland. As quickly as we can get there."

Griffin nods at the pilot. "You heard him."

The helicopter swings around with a bob of the floor beneath our feet. I snatch at the corner of a box for balance and glance around at our fellow escapees.

A few of the kids I know have made it—Nadia and Booker, Celine, Ajax. The spiky-haired kid is here. And then a few others I haven't specifically noticed before.

They're all huddled together in the cramped space. Booker is gripping Nadia's hand like Dominic has mine, but she looks too frightened to appreciate the gesture of affection. Ajax has wrapped his arm right around another boy who looks about the same age, with dark hair, brown skin, and features that make me suspect the human part of his genetic heritage is Middle Eastern.

"What do we do now?" Celine asks from where she's sitting against a stack of crates, her normally perky voice gone a bit shaky.

I swallow and find I can speak a little more loudly, though it's not much better than a croak. "I guess we get to the city and get our bearings, and then make more decisions."

I can reach out to Rollick without telling him where we are. Find out exactly what went down after our break-in at the other facility.

Zian stiffens abruptly. "Tracking devices."

I stare at him for a split-second before my gut lurches.

Right. When we made our first escape, he'd figured out that we all had trackers embedded in our teeth.

We got rid of them by yanking the molars out of our jaws—or having Zian do it, for those who didn't have the same brutal strength. The thought of asking all these kids to do the same makes me queasy.

But if we don't take care of them quickly, the guardians will be able to figure out exactly where we've gone even without Griffin's help.

Celine has gone rigid too. "What?"

Andreas comes up beside me, resting his hand on my back. "We all had tracking devices in our teeth. We dealt with ours before, but you probably still have them. We'll need to do something about that."

"Something like what?" Booker asks in a wary tone, adjusting his grip on Nadia's hand.

Dominic answers in a gentle tone. "Zian pulled the tooth out for each of us. It isn't fun, but I can heal you all up as soon as it's done."

Celine shivers, and the boy Ajax is embracing cringes in his arms. Ajax looks down at his friend—boyfriend?—and then his gaze jerks up to meet mine.

"Devon might be able to do it another way. The devices are made out of metal, right? He can create heat… Not a lot if it's a big space, but if he concentrated it on something really small, he should be able to melt circuits."

He glances down at the other guy with a fond but concerned expression that clearly indicates *boyfriend*. "Don't you think so? If you want to try."

Devon lets out a halting sigh and offers a crooked smile. "I guess it'd be better than having my teeth yanked out. How do we know which tooth it is?"

Zian's shoulders come down at hearing there's an alternative to him disfiguring all these teens and preteens we're trying to save. He moves over to the young couple. "I can find it. Let's start with the two of you to see how it goes."

For the next fifteen minutes or so, Zian's eyes flash as he uses his X-ray vision to locate each tracker and then confirm that it's sufficiently melted by Devon's power. The knots in my stomach gradually unravel.

Maybe we're actually going to be okay. Maybe the worst part is over.

It doesn't matter that the radio crackles with questions about where the pilot is going. Jacob silences the device with a bash of his power.

It doesn't matter that I'm not totally sure about what we're going to do once we've landed. We'll figure it out once we're there.

This time, the guardians don't have Griffin as an ace up their sleeve. They tracked us down once without his help, but only after we'd stayed in the same place for a whole week.

Then Zian steps away from Celine, who submitted herself to the heat treatment last, and she points a finger at Griffin. "What about him? He's got a tracker too, doesn't he? He never ran away before."

We all glance over at the twins. Jacob shoots his brother a grim look. "She's right. Let's destroy whatever you're carrying too."

As Zian and Devon move to flank Griffin, who raises no protest, Booker raises his eyebrows. "Are we sure we should have this guy along at all? He was helping Clancy."

"If we left him behind, then he'd have been able to help track us down," I say in my roughened voice.

Griffin turns toward Booker. "I'd rather be here with all of you. Clancy misled me about his plans too. I apologize for anything I've been a part of that's harmed you."

"You don't *sound* sorry," one of the other kids mutters.

"I—I'm working on that."

Griffin opens his mouth wide for Zian and Devon to do their work. Watching them, Booker abruptly pushes to his feet.

I don't know if he isn't satisfied with Griffin's answer—I don't think *I* am.

Whatever his intentions, the movement must distract Griffin. Because just as Devon turns away, the pilot yanks on the controls.

"What the fuck are you doing?" Jacob demands, his gaze snapping around.

The kid who muttered about Griffin being sorry jumps up. "He pretended to be on our side, and now he's letting the guardians catch us again!"

The pilot whips a phone I didn't know he had to his ear. "Yes," he gasps out in the frantic tone of a man who knows his time is limited, "They've got me—"

I don't really know who's to blame for what happens next. Jacob whirls all the way toward the pilot and sends the phone flying from his hand. At the same moment, the spiky-haired boy launches himself toward the cockpit with a cry of, "I'll stop him!"

He blinks a few steps forward like I saw him do in the hallway and slams into the pilot's seat as he appears, his arm whacking the guy across the back of the head in a blow that doesn't look totally intentional.

As the boy yelps, the pilot careens forward. His head bashes into the controls.

The helicopter heaves. Those of us standing bang into the walls and boxes.

Griffin's even voice cuts through the chaos of gasps and exclamations. "You can still do this. Get the helicopter steady."

The pilot has straightened up a little, but he lets out a pained moan. Blood is trickling down his forehead and from his nose.

"I can't—I can't see—it's broken."

"Just try. Try your best. There, you're doing so well."

It doesn't feel like anything's going well. The next lurch tosses me right onto my knees.

"Hold on to something!" I call out hoarsely to the kids.

A plummeting sensation melds with the forward momentum. The darkened sky beyond the windows tilts.

We're falling—faster, faster, rushing onward at the same time. All at once, branches crackle against the windows.

Then there's a boom of impact, and we slam to a sudden halt.

TWENTY

Riva

My head smacks into the box I'm crouched against. For a few seconds, my thoughts spin as pain splinters through them.

Something creaks. Gasps and a few sobs fill the air around me, along with a panicked feline yowl.

I shake myself out of my daze with a hitch of my pulse and peer through the darkness. "Is—is everyone okay?"

I can't tell if my voice is still strained from the thing the guardians shot at my throat or if it's all the shock of our crash now. In the dim moonlight that seeps through the windows, I vaguely make out the younger shadowbloods amid the tumbled boxes and crates.

A bag of rice has fallen out and split open, pale grains spilling across the floor. Celine has her hand pressed to her beige forehead, a trickle of blood streaking down from beneath her palm.

"Dominic!" I cry out automatically, and feel his hand on my shoulder.

He squints at me in the dimness and touches the side of my head where I smacked it. The tender spot makes me wince, but there's no coolness of blood.

"I'm all right. The kids…"

"I'm on it," he murmurs, and moves deeper into the helicopter's cargo area with a slight sway to his steps that makes me wonder if *he's* completely all right.

"Riva!"

It's Jacob's voice, taut and ragged.

I spin toward the cockpit, the direction where I last saw him. "I'm here. I bumped my head, but not too badly."

Zian staggers to his feet near me. Andreas catches my arm, his fingers curling around my elbow.

Jacob, silhouetted by the faint light through the shattered windshield, takes an urgent step toward me and then glances back at Griffin. His jaw tightens.

He still doesn't trust his brother enough to feel comfortable leaving him to his own devices. I'm not sure I do either.

I push myself toward them instead. "The pilot—"

The words snag in my throat. With just a couple of paces, I've come close enough to see the full consequences of the crash.

The front of the helicopter rammed right into a thick tree trunk—right at the pilot's seat. The metal and glass there have crumpled inward.

You can't tell that the man's nose was bleeding before because now his entire body is bashed beyond recognition.

My stomach flips over.

Griffin is staring at the pilot from just behind him, blood smearing the back of his hand from a thin cut—maybe from the breaking glass. Hugging his backpack and the quivering cat inside it to his chest, he blinks and glances over at the rest of us.

"I didn't mean for— I was hoping we could still land properly."

"It's okay," Andreas says in the warm voice that comes so naturally to him. "The crash could have been a lot worse."

Jacob scowls. "At least this way we know he won't be reaching out to the guardians."

With a twitch of his fingers, he summons the phone he wrenched from the pilot's hand just minutes ago. As his power tugs it through the air to us, his scowl deepens.

Cracks form a spiderweb on the screen. He pushes the wake button just in case, but no light flickers on the fractured surface.

Zian looks around. "Where are we?"

All that's visible through the windows are the shadowy shapes of more trees. I can't make out any sign of civilization, not the slightest gleam of artificial light in the distance.

"No way of telling from the navigation screen," Jacob says. "But we were heading toward a city like Dominic told him to. I could see a big patch of lights in the distance."

Andreas nods. "North… northwest. It was just to the right of where the sun was setting."

A flicker of hope rises in my chest. "How far away?"

Jacob shakes his head. "I don't know. It wasn't *close*."

"We won't be able to tell which direction is northwest until the sun's back up," Zian says.

Griffin's voice comes out calm but more tentative than usual. "I know where it is."

All our gazes jerk to him.

Jacob's eyes narrow. "How?"

His twin gazes back at him steadily. "There are a lot of people there. A lot of emotions. I can only pick up on a general impression, and faintly, but there mustn't be much of anyone else around, because it's mostly coming from that way."

He points at an angle from the windshield, into the jungle outside.

Zian lets out a rough guffaw. "Griffin can be our compass."

From Jacob's expression, he isn't happy about the idea. But we can't be beggars and choosers.

"He did help with the escape," I remind Jake. "And we've got to get moving in some direction as soon as possible. We'd only just disabled the last tracking device when we started to crash. The guardians might be able to find us here if we stay with the chopper all night."

Jacob sighs in frustration, but he doesn't argue. He just shoots his brother another steely look.

I scramble back to the cargo area where Dominic is tending to the younger shadowbloods' injuries. Devon and the spiky-haired kid who hit the pilot were tossed back by the impact, squatting on opposite sides of the bay now.

Devon winces and then relaxes as Dom grips his ankle with a healing hand. The spiky-haired kid, who can't be more than twelve, watches with darting eyes.

His gaze catches on me, and his shoulders curl in on himself. "I'm sorry. I didn't mean to run right into him. I didn't mean to hop at all. It just *happens* when I'm worried."

I'm not anyone to criticize people for having erratic control over their powers.

I crouch down across from him. "Hopping—is that what you call it when you flash forward like you're not even there for a second?"

He nods. "The guardians said it's teleporting. But they were always mad I couldn't go farther."

Of course they would have been. Skipping a few steps isn't going to make that much difference on a mission.

"We're here now," I tell him. "And we're going to keep going. What's your name?"

He swipes his hand across his eyes like he's rubbing away tears before they fully formed. "George."

When I turn around, Dominic has finished healing Devon, and Ajax has come over to help his boyfriend to his feet. Booker and Nadia are standing close together, his hand at her back, her face tight with worry.

Booker rakes his fingers through his pale hair, his expression too serious now to conjure the surfer dude impression he gave me when we first met. "What now? Can the guardians find us here?"

"I don't know," I admit. "So we're moving out. But…"

My gaze travels over the jumbled assortment of supplies, and I manage a small smile. "At least we shouldn't have to worry about going hungry. Let's quickly dig through all of this and grab whatever's easiest to carry and doesn't need cooking."

A girl whose name I haven't caught points toward the back of the helicopter. "There are some things that look kind of like backpacks that would help for carrying stuff. I think they might be emergency parachutes, but we could tear the parachute part out."

Celine, the scratch on her forehead sealed, lets out a tinkling laugh that doesn't hold much real humor. "If we can even see what we're doing in here."

Nadia perks up, the tension falling away from her face for the first time since we ran to the helicopter. "Finally, it's my time to shine! Literally."

As she grins, her brown skin lights up the way she showed me before.

In the daylight of the clearing, it was hard to tell just how potent her inner light is. Now, the warm glow washes over the entire interior of the storage bay as if the overhead lights have turned on.

"Wow," Booker says with admiration that's obviously genuine. "You're really something, Glowworm."

As we all get to work digging through the boxes and crates, Dominic turns pensive. "Can you adjust how strong the light is? To make sure you don't wear yourself out—and so it'll be harder for anyone to spot us from above?"

"Oh, sure." Nadia pauses, and her glow fades as if she's pushed down a dimmer switch to halfway. "Is that good?"

Andreas shoves open the hatch and takes in the jungle beyond. "I think that'll be safe enough. The tree cover is pretty thick, at least right around here."

In the end, the six of us "Firsts" end up carrying most of the supplies in the limited number of makeshift backpacks. I stuff mine full of crackers, cheese, apples, carrots, and a couple of jugs of juice.

We might be relying on that to stay hydrated, since it doesn't appear that the supplies included water, and we have no way of making sure any streams or ponds we pass are safe to drink from.

Each of the younger shadowbloods gathers a small assortment of their own, tying swaths of parachute fabric around their backs and shoulders however feels most comfortable as makeshift carry-sacks. When we're all loaded up, I glance over our motley group again, holding tightly to the spark of hope that lit when Jacob said he'd seen a city.

"Is everyone ready to go?"

There are nods and murmurs all around. They don't exactly sound enthusiastic, but then, I don't think any of us would take this trek if we had the choice.

We just know it's better than the alternative.

Nadia leads the way with her innate light, Booker sticking close to her side and Zian tramping along at her flank in case we encounter any threats. The rest of us Firsts spread out through the procession, monitoring the kids for signs of faltering.

I end up at the rear of the line, making sure no one falls behind. Andreas eases back next to me as we tramp over the uneven ground, weaving between the trees and scrambling over jutting roots.

"We won't be able to keep this up all night," he murmurs. "None of us has slept since yesterday."

The stress of the escape has worn at my nerves enough that exhaustion is already nibbling at the edges of my awareness. "I know. But we should get as much distance from the crash site as we can."

"Yeah, let's see how they do. I think we can get away with a fairly short rest and then keep going as soon as it's daylight. We can have a longer break the next night, if it takes that long. It'll be better not to let

Nadia drain herself too badly—and we'll be harder to find when we won't stand out against the darkness anyway."

I dodge a waxy-leafed bush and rub my arms. A fly buzzes around me and starts to land on my elbow before I swat it away.

The jungle air is humid, nearly as warm at night as it was on the island, but my fears send a chill through the sweat on my skin.

I told these kids we'd get them to someplace better than the facility. I have to make sure that this time I keep my promise.

As we push on through the brush, the minutes blur into hours. Stars glint overhead in the small gaps in the canopy of leaves.

From time to time, Andreas lifts his voice with his storyteller's cadence. Because of course he has stories to go with even this trek.

"One time, I came across a woman who'd done a hike all the way from one end of the States to the other," he says. "All on her own. It took weeks, and most of that time some part of her was aching, and she'd get hungry for food she couldn't have carried on the trail. But when she got back, if anyone asked, she'd tell them the worst part was the loneliness. She said she'd do it over again if she had the right company."

He glances around at us with a weary but honest smile. "We don't have anywhere near that far to go, and we've got each other. I think we've got this."

His assurance helps steady me, so I hope it does the same for the younger shadowbloods as well.

But even my supernaturally strong legs are feeling the burn by the time the ground starts to slant upward in an increasingly steep slope. I notice George and Devon wobbling as they trudge onward.

Have we come far enough that it's safe to stop? How can I possibly know?

The sound of trickling water is what decides the issue. Zian turns his head toward it, no doubt hearing it much more clearly than I can.

"I think there's a waterfall," he says. "Running water is safer than still, right?"

Dominic nods. "Let's take a look at it and see if we want to risk it. Either way, this might be a good time to set up some kind of camp. We'll tackle the hill better after we've gotten some rest."

I don't miss the sighs of relief that carry through our younger charges. Yes, it was definitely time to stop.

We veer toward the sound of the water and halt our march when Nadia's light glints off a current about a foot wide burbling down a sheerer section of the hill. As she heads over with Dominic and Andreas to inspect the water, the rest of us hunker down among the trees.

"Have a snack if you're hungry, and then I guess curl up wherever you can make yourself decently comfortable," I tell the kids. At least it's warm and reasonably dry for the moment.

I don't want to think about what we'll do if it starts raining.

Our three water analysts return with uncertain expressions. "It looks pretty clean, but there are flecks of dirt in it," Andreas says. "I took a gulp, and if I'm still okay by tomorrow, we can all have a drink." He nudges Dominic. "Otherwise I'm relying on Dom to cure me."

I don't love him using himself as a test subject, but I guess we don't have a lot of choice. "Juice for tonight, then, anyone who's thirsty."

Celine stretches out a hand. "I could use some of that right now!"

As she drinks, Griffin hunkers down near me, watching her with an intentness I don't understand. I wait for him to make a comment to explain his attention, but he doesn't say anything, even after Celine passes the jug on to Ajax.

After a moment, he reaches into his old backpack and guides out the white cat and a tin of cat food he must have snatched up when he grabbed her. He peels back the lid, and Lua sniffs it tentatively before taking some cautious bites.

I've been drinking regularly along the trek, so my throat isn't too parched, but my skin feels uncomfortably grimy. I push to my feet with a quick glance around at my guys. "I'm going to wash up a little before I try and sleep."

It only takes a minute to walk the last short distance to the waterfall and its winding stream. The hillside there is rockier but still has clumps of soil clinging in pockets.

I can see why the guys hesitated to trust the water washing over those rocks for ingestion. But to splash it on my face shouldn't be a big deal.

I dampen not just my face but my neck as well, then swipe under my armpits for good measure. As I give my hands a final rinse, the brush rustles behind me.

When I glance over my shoulder, I find Griffin emerging onto the rocky bank next to me. Not who I would have expected.

My stomach shifts with a hitch of uneasiness. It feels wrong to be this wary around the one guy I once trusted more than anyone in the world… but completely necessary at the same time.

"Hey," I say in a low voice, adjusting my weight to stand. "The stream's all yours."

Griffin catches my wrist before I can rise more than a few inches, his grip firm but careful. "I didn't come for the water. I wanted to talk to you."

I settle back into my crouch, studying his face in the dimness. As usual, I can't read his intentions in it—but for once he does actually look concerned, if only vaguely. "What about?"

Griffin glances at the ground and then back at me, leaving his fingers curled gently around my wrist. "I'm sorry. For getting you caught, in the facility, before—I need to apologize to everyone for that—but especially for trying to tell you that you should still work with Clancy. For not realizing what he was doing when he had us meet up."

The words are right, but I don't hear any anguish in them.

I frown. "Are you saying that because you really mean it or because you know I'd want you to be sorry?"

"I mean it. I just—" He sucks in a breath, and his mouth tightens. His thumb glides over the underside of my wrist, sending a tingle shooting up my arm.

"I don't feel very much," he says, low and even. "I pick up on what others do, but inside *myself*… I haven't felt anything in years. The guardians decided I was too affected by the emotions I absorbed, it was a liability, and they decided to fix that problem. And for a while, I thought I was better off that way too."

My throat constricts. "Feeling nothing could never be better. What did they do?"

Griffin shakes his head. "It doesn't matter. The point is… I do feel something, when we're touching. I don't know why, but the contact seems to wake up something they didn't totally suppress."

He traces the fragile bones of my wrist again, setting off a more heated tingle. A flush courses over my skin.

"You pulled away from me, before," I point out, remembering our conversation in the training room.

Griffin's fingers go still. "I—I wasn't sure if it was a good thing. It's been a long time. I've gotten used to having my head clear."

He pauses. "But I don't know if it ever really was clear. I was missing something all along. I'm starting to think I can't actually make the right decisions if I don't have any emotional reactions to guide me along with pure information."

I swallow thickly. "I think everyone needs both."

"I have to find a good balance. I can't let—I still need to be careful." He knits his brow. Then he strokes his hand right up my arm from wrist to elbow, provoking a full-out flare of heat.

When Griffin meets my eyes again, I catch a flicker of longing there. A clearer emotion than anything I've seen in him since we reunited.

"I'm not going to ask for anything from you," he says. "You're upset with me and confused, and that makes sense. But every time we touch, I feel a little closer to where I need to be. So… if *you* want to—to hold my hand, or sit close to me, or anything like that, I hope you will."

Sudden tears prick at the back of my eyes. I *am* upset and confused, but I can also hear the boy I loved so much in his halting admission.

Griffin has been just as much a victim of the guardians' schemes as the rest of us. Maybe more so, if they somehow managed to sear every feeling out of the guy who was once the most compassionate person I've ever encountered.

Part of me balks, but not enough to override the urge to lean toward him right now—to wrap my arms around his slender but toned shoulders and hug him hard.

Griffin lets out a shaky breath and hugs me back, his bare forearm resting against my neck, his hand skimming the band of skin where my tee has ridden up at my waist. Keeping that bodily contact in place.

"I'm sorry," he whispers again, and this time I feel it as well as hear it.

I rest my head against his, absorbing the rhythm of his breath and the warmth of his body. "The people who really should be sorry never will be. So we just have to make sure they can't hurt any of us ever again."

"Yeah." His breath tickles against my ear. His arms squeeze me a little tighter. "Ever since the other day with the throwing knives… I've been dreaming about the night we broke out. The moment when you kissed me."

I wince inwardly. "When they shot you. That must be an awful memory."

"No. It's not. I wish everything after had gone differently, but the pain I went through is nothing compared to the joy before. Right then—that's the best I've ever felt in my life. And for years, I never even thought about it. They took it away from me."

My threatening tears rush back with a vengeance. I'm too choked up to speak.

My hand rises of its own accord to Griffin's jaw. Nothing could feel more right than tilting my head so I can brush my lips against his.

The kiss stays butterfly-soft. Griffin barely seems to breathe, but a tremor runs through his body as he kisses me back so tenderly I want to melt right into his arms.

But I don't know if I trust him quite that completely just yet.

And before I can decide either way, he eases back and turns his head. I follow his gaze.

Jacob is standing between the trees just a few steps from the waterfall. Watching us with eyes so stormy I can make out the turmoil in them despite the darkness.

Griffin releases me from his embrace as we get up. He offers his brother a lopsided smile.

"I'm not trying to get between you—any of you—and Riva. If she had to choose right now, she wouldn't pick me anyway."

He's probably right about that, but the comments Jake's made in the past—about knowing he had to stand back so his brother could be happy with me, about believing that I'd rather he'd died instead of Griffin—form a lump in my gut.

"Jake," I start, not sure exactly what I'm going to say. We found a peace with each other in the past few weeks, but it suddenly feels so tenuous.

Jacob breaks in before I can get any farther. "It's fine. I only came to make sure you're okay. I'm going to take one of the first watches. Everyone who's going to sleep should stick together."

I nod. "We'll head right back."

Griffin strides ahead of me through the trees on our way back to the campsite, not touching me at all, but Jacob's gaze trails after us with a prickling sensation down my spine.

Twenty-One

Jacob

I thought the island we were stuck on was fucking hot, but somehow the jungle we've crashed into is even worse.

The interlacing branches overhead, heavy with leaves, block out most of the direct sunlight, but humidity saturates the air underneath. Trudging along feels more like wading than walking.

Bugs buzz past, some of them stopping to nip at us. I guess the island breezes kept the worst of them away back by the facility.

Our group skirts a patch of huge ferns, the edges of the fronds tickling over my arm. I swipe at the sweat collecting on the back of my neck and scan our surroundings.

I used to like the occasional opportunities the guardians gave us to explore the forest beyond the facility where we grew up. Gazing up at the leaves and breathing in the wild scents loosened something inside me, like a trace of freedom.

I'm not sure I'm ever going to feel the same way about the jungle. Between our training on the island and this trek, I can't help associating the dense vegetation and heavy warmth with restrictions and perils rather than peace.

We've been walking since sun-up, other than a short snack break partway through the morning and a slightly longer break for lunch a couple of hours ago. The younger kids appear to be drooping with the sticky heat, but the older teens are carrying themselves pretty well, I have to admit.

Well, they've been through the same brutal training as the rest of us. At seventeen, they're practically adults, not kids at all.

We were around that age the first time we made a run for it.

The thought brings my gaze veering back to my friends.

Andreas is loping along as quickly as the dense underbrush allows, no sign of sickness from the jungle water he drank last night. We filled up two emptied juice jugs at the waterfall before we moved on from our campsite.

He's got a cord he picked up somewhere wrapped around one hand. On the easier stretches of terrain, he's fallen into a rhythm of twisting it into knots and loosening them again, like he used to do sometimes back at the old facility. Maybe it helps him focus.

Zian pushes ahead at the front of the group, snapping branches and crumpling shrubs to allow easier passage for all of us behind. And probably terrifying any wildlife that might notice us into giving us a wide berth.

Well, other than the damned bugs.

Dominic has stuck to the middle of the group, his head swiveling periodically as he conducts a similar scan to mine. Any time one of the younger shadowbloods so much as stubs their toe, he's there, siphoning life out of a twig or a wildflower to set them right again.

His short ponytail clings damply to his neck. I hope he's keeping *his* health in mind just as much as everyone else's.

Riva prefers to stick to the rear of the group where she can monitor the whole bunch more easily, so I've hung back too. It means I'm close by if the brush happens to trip her up, although she's scrambling through it perfectly fine so far even with her tiny frame.

And it means I can keep an eye on my brother wherever he happens to drift through the group.

Griffin does drift quite a bit. One hour he'll be at the left of the pack, the next at the right. Sometimes he presses forward until he's just behind Zian and other times he slows until he falls into stride with Riva.

When that's happened, she's reached out and taken his hand. Nothing spoken, not much more than a brief glance exchanged, but something in his expression softens just a tad when her fingers curl around his.

It makes him look almost like he really is my brother again.

Can I trust that impression? Is he actually coming around, snapping out of the demented stupor the guardians inflicted on him?

Or is he simply making the best moves he can to win us over so that he can then betray us when he has an ideal opportunity?

I can't read the answers in his face or his behavior. And the knowledge that he can sense my uneasiness without even trying gnaws at me.

We always thought that Griffin was the weakest out of us, at least when it came to combat skills. But knowing how your enemies are feeling, being able to twist those emotions to your will if you want to…

I'd rather deal with another guy like me, with telekinetic talents and poison spikes, than face off with my brother.

At least I haven't seen any sign that he's manipulating us. Riva might have kissed him last night, whatever he said to her that encouraged the gesture of affection, and she's offering moments of companionship now, but her gaze stays wary when she looks at him.

She isn't convinced he's really come back to us either. And if he was going to mess with anyone's emotions to his benefit, presumably it'd be mine or hers.

The kids in front of us clamber over a fallen tree that rises to my thighs, and I extend my hand automatically to heft Riva with me over it. She accepts the help with a soft smile that rearranges my insides and gives my hand a squeeze before she lets go on the other side.

Even when we're not touching, it feels like we are through the mark now burned into my flesh at the top of my collarbone. I can sense exactly where she is in an instant.

I'll never really lose her again.

But somehow I can't convince myself that even that closeness is enough. Can't shake the vague impression that there must be something more I should offer that I haven't worked out yet.

It turns out that not every wild creature around has been warded off by Zian's might. We're just ducking around the low branches of a vine-draped tree when one of those "vines" lifts its head with a threatening hiss.

The huge snake's head swings toward Riva. With a jolt of panic, I hurl out a surge of power that smacks it backward but doesn't dislodge it from its perch.

Before I can launch a more aggressive defense, Riva sets her hand on my shoulder and parts her lips. The sound that seeps from them echoes the snake's hiss with a hint of one of her deadly shrieks.

A flinch ripples through the snake's body. It recoils and slithers away higher into the tree.

Riva shoots me another smile. "I appreciate the protection, but I wanted to see if that would work. I'd rather not kill the animals if we don't have to."

She looks so pleased with herself—with the control she's gaining over her powers, with the kindness she was able to offer that beast I'd have smashed to pieces—that my heart just about bursts.

I rein in the urge to grab her and pour all my adoration into a kiss of my own. We've both got to stay alert.

But the longing lingers as we tramp onward.

The jumpy kid with the spiky white hair does one of his teleporting hops and nearly trips onto his face. Riva dashes forward in an instant and catches him before he hits the ground.

She walks on next to him, getting into a murmured conversation. I'm torn between wanting to catch up so I'm close at hand if *she* needs help again—not that she ever needs that much—and knowing she'd rather at least one of us was at the back of the pack to keep track of all the kids.

Then Griffin drifts backward again, falling into step beside me. The weird pang that hits me every time my twin is nearby radiates through my chest.

It feels wrong to still be grieving him when he's right *here*. But he's not exactly. Not one piece of my body has come to grips with that fact.

"You don't miss the comforts of the facility?" I hear myself saying before I've considered the question. It's not a bad one, though. If I could assume he'd answer honestly.

Griffin shakes his head without hesitation. "It wasn't really that comfortable when you got down to it, was it? I just… I was looking at things too narrowly."

I guess that's one way of saying he royally screwed us over.

As if he's read that thought as well as my emotions, he glances over at me. "I am sorry, you know. I made mistakes—I misjudged the situation. I hope… I hope that none of us will have to hurt people the way you had to before, but I can see why you didn't feel you had much choice."

I gaze back at him, letting my gaze harden. "Anyone we hurt, it was to make sure they couldn't kill us. Or turn us back into slaves."

"I know. I know you did the best you could."

He pauses, a crease forming in his forehead as if he isn't sure of what he's going to say next. He exhales softly.

His voice comes out quieter. "I'm sorry I wasn't there, too. It always seemed… wrong, being apart from the rest of you. Especially *you*. I tried to tell the guardians, to convince them. We supported each other in a way they didn't seem to understand. And I didn't know what you were thinking with me being gone, how that would affect you, but it bothered me, so it couldn't be good."

Another pause. His head bows. "I'm not sure it would really have made things much better if they had let me come back the way I am now, though."

"It would have been better," I burst out. "I wouldn't have been thinking you were *murdered* because of a plan I helped come up with. They couldn't have messed with us making us believe that was mostly Riva's fault."

I aim a scowl at my twin. "You realize that's the main reason they kept us apart, right? It was an easy way to lie to us, to fuck us up even more than they already had."

"I didn't know what they'd told you," Griffin says. "If I had, I'd like to think I'd have fought harder to get back to you. Maybe I wouldn't have trusted Clancy at all, even though he acted like he wanted nothing to do with the group who'd been handling me since the escape."

I can't conceive of what our lives would have been like if Griffin had turned up, in his currently vacant state or not, before Riva crashed back into our lives. If we'd known from the start that the guardians had lied to us about his fate—and therefore probably hers too.

It kills me even trying to picture it in comparison to what actually went down.

"All we can do is go forward from here." Griffin glances over at me tentatively. "You're going to be angry at me for a long time, just like the others, and I don't resent that. But I'm doing *my* best to figure out how to head in a better direction. And if you feel like you could lean on me for anything, in any way… I want to be there like I wasn't all those years. As well as I can."

I can't tell how earnest he is when his tone holds only the faintest trace of emotion, but the words make my throat tighten anyway.

Lean on him? I always saw myself as the one he leaned on. When the training pushed us hard, when the guardians wouldn't let up.

But I know that's not really accurate. Something about his knowing but compassionate gaze, the ease to his words, could settle the rest of us down no matter what upset us, even when we were little. He kept us centered.

Where has that guy gone?

Before I have to decide how to respond, my brother's gaze slides forward, to where Riva is just giving the teleporting kid a reassuring pat on the back.

"She loves you so much, you know," he says. "Every time she looks at you, it's there, shining like an entire full moon, not just a moonbeam. She wants you to be happy. Whatever you're worried about when it comes to her, I don't think you have to be anymore."

He picks up his pace, leaving me grappling with a tangle of my own emotions.

It isn't as if Riva hasn't told me how she feels. I'm not sure I've totally believed it, though.

After everything I put her through…

I might not completely believe in Griffin, but hearing him say it so confidently smooths out a few rough edges inside me that I hadn't even noticed scraping at my heart.

So maybe he hasn't totally lost his centering gift after all.

When Riva returns to her position at the back, she gives me a curious look. "Are you and Griffin okay?"

I rub my mouth as I debate my answer. "I don't know. But it's possible we could get there."

Our afternoon break stretches a little longer than the morning one. Some of the younger shadowbloods massage their calves and stretch their arms in attempts to relieve the strain.

New hope comes in the form of a strip of thinner underbrush we stumble on maybe an hour after our stop.

Zian steps out into the clearer stretch cautiously, his shoulders flexing as he glances up and down it. The rest of us follow.

I toe the grass-choked ground and make out faint ridges in the packed soil. Bits of gravel rasp against the sole of my sneaker.

"It was a road," Dominic says, coming to the same conclusion I have a little faster. "Just a small one, like a private lane or something, and obviously not used in a while."

Andreas peers along it into the distance. "That's got to mean there are people around *somewhere* not too far away."

He turns to Griffin, whose eyes go even more vague as he must tap into his empathic sense. My twin's mouth slants crookedly.

"Other than our group, I'm not picking up on anyone really close. I'm still aware of the big population northwest of here. But that doesn't mean there isn't anyone closer. At longer distances, I can only pick up on a whole lot of emotion condensed in the same place, unless it's someone I already know."

Riva cocks her head, her eyes glinting with sudden inspiration. "Can you tell where Clancy is?"

Griffin takes another moment to focus inwardly. "Nowhere near us. Someplace south. I'd need a map to pinpoint him."

"Nowhere near sounds good enough to me." I motion toward the section of overgrown road that heads in approximately the same direction we were already headed. "We might as well walk along this route while it's taking us where we need to go, right? We'll move faster with fewer obstacles."

"I'll watch and listen for any sign that we're getting close to the locals," Zian says, his face settling into a mask of concentration.

I'm not surprised that none of the younger shadowbloods argue. Some of them even get more of a spring in their step as we set off along the easier terrain.

I start to doubt my suggestion when the road takes on an upward slope. But unless we wanted to spend an extra day or two walking all the way around the looming hill ahead of us, I guess we'd be stuck scaling it either way.

The sun has sunk below the level of the canopy when Zee lets out a low shout to alert us and stops in his tracks.

"There's a building up there," he says, squinting through the trees. "I can see part of a roof."

We all gather around him. A couple of the kids shift nervously on their feet.

"Any sign of people?" Riva asks.

Zian shakes his head. "I can't make out a whole lot from here, though."

Griffin gazes off in the direction Zee indicated. "I think I'd be able to sense if anyone was over there. I'm not picking up any emotional impressions strong enough to be coming from a building that close."

Andreas steps to the front of our pack. "I'll take a quick look around incognito."

He tips his head jauntily and vanishes from view in a blink.

The lanky, blond-haired guy near me—Booker, I think his name is—

sucks in a breath of surprise. A startled murmur passes through the younger shadowbloods.

I forgot that most of them aren't familiar with our powers. I don't think I'll be showing off my spines anytime soon.

Zian moves a little farther ahead to keep scanning the area while we wait. Riva pulls a jug of water out of her pack and passes it around, checking on the kids with Dominic flanking her, ready to treat any injury.

Seeing her dote on them sends another quiver through my chest, not as heated as the impact of her smiles but with a soft glow of warmth I'm not used to.

She's been so worried about her powers, about being someone destructive. A monster. Does she even realize how easily she's taken on this nurturing role?

She's a badass, brilliant superhero of a woman, but I bet she'd be a fantastic mother someday too, if that's something she wants.

Whether I'd be much of a dad…

That idea leaves me unsteady enough that I yank my mind back to the present.

Andreas reappears in the lengthening shadows with a grin. "It looks like it was some kind of eco hotel. Solar panels on the roof, a cistern that's set up for catching rainwater. It's been abandoned for a while, and the jungle's crept in on it, but there's still some power going and the plumbing works. And it's got actual beds."

My instinct is to balk at the idea of staying anywhere it looks like people would want to stay, but the relief that crosses several of the kids' faces keeps my mouth shut.

Dominic is already thinking cautiously for all of us anyway. "How noticeable do you think it'd be from above?" he asks.

Andreas motions to us. "You can all come take a look, but there's tree cover over a lot of the roof now. The building was only a couple of stories tall anyway. I don't think we'd want to have the lights on once it really gets dark, but otherwise I doubt it'd stand out."

We tramp on up the road for a few more minutes before the hotel comes clearly into view.

The trees have grown right up against the tan walls, in some places jutting through windows or broken sections of thatched roof. They block what was once probably a pretty view over the hillside. But they also camouflage the place to a degree that satisfies the worst of my worries.

We slip inside onto the dirt-strewn hardwood floor of what was once the lobby. The boards sigh under our feet.

A vine has crept over the reception desk and around a couple of sagging armchairs. A little monkey chitters at us and darts out through a broken window.

The air flow through the space has kept it from getting musty, though. The faint perfume of jungle flowers laces the breeze that washes through the hallways.

Andreas leads us to the kitchen, which is deep enough inside the building that it's remained mostly unaffected by the jungle's imposition. At his twist of a fixture, clear water burbles from a tap.

"The stoves have power," he says, pointing to a couple of rows of burners. "And there's a little food left in the pantry that might be edible—rice, dried beans, and lentils that I don't think would really go bad."

The tall girl who lit our way through the night lets out a low chuckle. "I could go for a real dinner."

Riva takes in the space with a contemplative air and gives a short nod. "I think we should spend the night here. Get some real rest before we keep going with the journey. But we'll need people keeping watch at all times just in case."

Zian moves closer to her, his expression turning abruptly fierce. "The guardians aren't getting their hands on us again."

Riva beams at him, so much affection shining in her eyes that my chest clenches up—even more so at the hesitant but bright smile Zee offers in return. At the momentary lifting of his hand as if he's thinking of offering her a brief touch, only to jerk his arm back to his side at the last second.

I don't need Griffin's talent to know how much he wants her… or how hard it is for him to grapple with that longing. My stomach twists in pained sympathy, and I find myself remembering Griffin's comments to me in the jungle.

He tried to make it easier for me to embrace everything Riva's been willing to offer me. To help the two of us understand each other.

If she wants to see me happy, I want the same for her at least as much. For all of my friends, including Zian, who has so much trouble reaching for that happiness himself.

But just telling him how much Riva cares about him wouldn't be enough. I'm pretty sure he already knows. That isn't the problem.

I keep part of my attention on Zian as I move to help the others sort through the kitchen equipment, the gears in my head spinning.

Maybe I don't have to only be the guy who races into a fight and bashes any possible threat. It's not like those impulses have been helping my friends or the woman I love a whole lot recently anyway.

Maybe I could be as generous as it seemed Griffin meant to be—fill the hole where Zian has faltered.

I just need to figure out how. For both him and her.

Twenty-Two

Riva

Our mishmash of rice, lentils, and the few spices we scrounged up isn't fit for a five-star restaurant, but after twenty-four hours of crackers, hard cheese, and bruised fruit, I have to hold myself back from licking the plate when I'm done.

We've hunkered down in the vast kitchen, one of the cleanest rooms in the abandoned hotel. The terrace on the other side of the hall looks like it served as the main dining area, but it's been consumed by jungle: tree branches jutting through the broken railings and vines strangling the chair-and-table sets.

The daylight has almost completely faded. As I glance around at my fellow shadowbloods, I catch a couple yawning.

I raise my voice to carry to the entire group. "We should get some rest while it's dark. It wouldn't be safe to turn on any lights at night anyway. And as soon as the sun comes up, we'll want to get moving again."

Mumbles of agreement reach me. Dominic stands up with the more confident air that's starting to come naturally to him.

"There are lots of bedrooms farther down the halls," he says to the group. "Pick one that's reasonably neat, and stay at least in pairs so you have someone to turn to if there's a problem. I think we should avoid the second floor since the roof obviously isn't in great repair."

"And give yourselves a good wash if you want," I add. "Running the water shouldn't give us away, and we don't know when we'll have another chance."

After another day of trekking, the dirt and dried sweat on my own skin itches at me.

A few of the younger kids drift out of the room, Ajax and Devon hand in hand. Celine gets to her feet with a swish of her ponytail and manages a smile that only looks a little tired.

"You Firsts should get a break. You've been running yourselves ragged looking after the rest of us—you organized the whole plan to get us out. We can take the first watch."

She motions to herself, Booker, and Nadia—the oldest of the kids who escaped with us. Nadia nods without hesitation, but my stomach dips uneasily.

"I think at least one of us—" I start.

Griffin interrupts so smoothly it barely feels rude, looking up from where he's stroking Lua's fur. "I can watch over the younger shadowbloods for the first shift. I don't think I'm ready to sleep yet anyway."

I hesitate again, appreciating the offer but not sure it's quite what I needed. If Griffin has actually been lying about his intentions, this would be a perfect opportunity to work against us.

My instincts tell me he's been honest. But what if they're wrong?

I thought we could trust Rollick to keep the other kids safe, and look how that turned out.

Andreas steps close to me and lowers his head by my ear. "I've had Ajax monitoring Griffin's thoughts as well as he can. He told me he's only picked up things that confirm his story. Ideas about how to help, worries about how his past actions might have hurt us."

I exhale slowly, releasing a little of the tension that's gripped me since we first got the opportunity to flee the island. I don't think Griffin is skilled enough to conceal every suspicious thought, if he'd even realize that Ajax would be searching his mind.

I can believe that my instincts were right this time with that outside confirmation.

"Okay." I offer Griffin a slightly guilty smile because of my initial uncertainty and aim a brighter one at Celine. "Thank you. A couple of us will take over in a few hours. You should spread out so you can keep an eye out all around the hotel."

Booker gives me a playful salute. “We’re on it, Captain. Don’t worry—we’ve been training our whole lives for this.”

The wryness of his tone makes Andreas’s lips twitch. “Hopefully we’ll find something better to do with our lives once we’re out of the jungle.”

Celine cocks her head, her tone still light. “Are you thinking we’ll go to the monsters to see if they’ll help us like you did before?”

I hesitate, my regrets about my past decisions still stark in my mind. “I—I don’t know yet. We can’t turn to *anyone* without being really careful about it.”

She nods and casts her gaze away. I hope my uncertainty won’t add to whatever worries she must already be grappling with.

Most of the kids have already shuffled out of the kitchen. The five of us Firsts meander down the hall after them.

I’m not totally sure what we’re searching for. We pass the first several rooms that’ve already been claimed by the younger shadowbloods and then start peeking through doorways at random.

I skip past a bedroom with a large water stain in the ceiling and another where some jungle creature appears to have crashed through the window and made a nest out of the bed. Then Zian lets out an awed sound from farther down the hall.

The rest of us hustle over to join him.

He’s stepped inside a massive suite that must have been reserved for honeymooners and high-profile guests. In the dim moonlight that seeps past the vast windows, the four-poster bed in the center of the far wall is bigger than any I’ve ever seen, the duvet barely wrinkled.

One window is cracked, a vine winding its way partway to the floor, but only a thin smattering of dirt and dust has coated the floor. The mirror mounted on the ornate vanity still gleams.

But Zian’s attention has been captured by the tub.

A huge jacuzzi bathtub stands across from the bed, half embedded in the wooden floor. Its white walls are dappled with dirt, but Zee gazes at it like it’s the most glorious thing he’s ever seen.

I can’t stop a fond grin from crossing my lips. He’s always been drawn to the water on the rare chances we had to appreciate it.

The image of him floating in the jungle pond near the island facility drifts up from my memory. He looked so peaceful, so content, just for those few minutes.

I walk over and prod the controls on the side of the tub. “I bet we could rinse it out and then fill it up. You can have first dibs, Zee.”

At a twist of a knob, water gushes from several of the jets. It carries the dirt in swirls down the drain. With a few swipes of my hand over the smooth surface, I bring back a faint gleam of white.

When I look up, Zian is watching me, not the water. Watching me with an expression that brings back other memories from that night by the pond.

Desire glimmers in his eyes, and uncertainty twists his mouth. The signs of his inner turmoil bring a lump to my throat.

"We'll give you your privacy, of course," I say, and lean down to push in the stopper so the tub will fill. "There are lots of other rooms where we—"

Jacob clears his throat, stopping me in mid-sentence. "I have a better idea."

We all glance over at him, and he gives the rest of us an unusually soft smile. "The tub's big enough for us all to share, don't you think? What have we got to hide at this point?"

He holds my gaze for a moment with a warily hopeful air and then shifts his attention to Zian with a flicker of concern. Jake must know as well as I do that Zee has the most reason to balk at the idea.

Zian shifts his weight, peering at the water and then the group of us. His eyes linger on me, the mix of longing and uneasiness only starker now.

I pause. "We wouldn't have to get totally undressed. I'll stay at the opposite end of the tub."

Andreas taps his knuckles against Zee's arm. "We'll all be in there, just hanging out. No pressure, no expectations."

Zian wavers for a few seconds longer and then squares his shoulders. "Yeah. Why shouldn't we?"

A gentle smile curves Dominic's lips too. "Why don't you get in first so you can enjoy a good float before the rest of us join in? We should scrounge up some towels anyway."

We leave Zian by the jacuzzi to prowl through the rest of the room. Dominic checks the actual bathroom and emerges with a stack of fluffy beige towels that he shakes a little dust off of.

Andreas and I give the bed the same treatment, stripping off the duvet and fluffing it out. The sheets underneath look almost pristine.

I'm tempted to sprawl on them right now, except *I'd* get them all dirty.

Jacob returns from his own search through the bathroom with a crow of victory. "Biodegradable bath oils. Now we're living in real luxury."

He carries the glossy green bottles over to the tub, where Zian has stripped down to his boxers and gotten in. His brawny body just barely fits without bumping against the sides, drifting on the rising water.

It's nearly reached the overflow drain now. Zee reaches to tweak one of the controls, and a hint of steam puffs into the air from the jets.

He dunks his head to slick his short hair back and grins at Jake, looking much more relaxed now that he's actually in the water. "Well, pour that stuff in then. We should have the full experience."

As Jacob drizzles the oil in the tub, a thin froth of bubbles forms on the surface of the water. Andreas shucks off his facility-issue tee and athletic pants and slides into the jacuzzi kitty-corner from Zian.

I guess we're all getting in now. All four of these guys have seen me at least partly undressed, and the room is dark enough that I'll be mostly cloaked in shadows anyway, but all at once my skin tightens with self-consciousness.

They don't pressure me either, though. Dominic tugs off his shirt with a little extra effort to work around his tentacles, not even glancing my way. Jake sheds his pants like it's no big deal at all.

With the attention off me, I relax enough to peel off my own tee and pants, leaving my necklace on like usual. The air is so warm that I'm not at all chilled even in my sports bra and panties.

They're like a bikini. Like I'm just going for a dip in a pool.

No big deal at all.

As I promised Zian, I slip into the water at the far end from where he's settled. We form a ring around the edges of the tub, my calf brushing Andreas's next to me, one of Dominic's tentacles coiling around my elbow beneath the bubbles.

Zee's set the temperature nice and warm. I let out a sigh and sink a little deeper until the bubbles tickle my chin.

"Maybe a soak will make tomorrow's hike a little easier," Jacob says, stretching one arm and then the other in front of him.

Zian leans back against the smooth wall. "Are there any other roads around this place that aren't so overgrown? If they left any vehicles behind…"

Drey shakes his head. "I did a circuit of the whole hotel when I was first checking it out. There is another road, a little wider than the one we came along but just as choked. And I didn't see any cars around anyway."

Dominic hums to himself. "We could head that way tomorrow and see where it takes us."

"It's a totally different direction from where we were heading before," Andreas says. "I don't think it'll take us to the city."

I tip my head back, letting the water seep through my braid and up my scalp while I consider the possibilities. "Griffin hasn't sensed any large populations any closer than the city we knew about. And a little town might not have the resources we'd need to make a real escape."

However exactly that's going to work once we see what we have to work with.

Drey gives my braid a teasing tug. "You've led us well so far, Tink. I trust your judgment."

The brush of his fingertips against my neck sets off a heat much more potent than the water's steam. As my face flushes, he traces his fingers across my cheek.

All at once, pheromones of desire lace the air from all around me. A shiver of need travels through my body, the shadows in my blood quaking with it.

I've been forced apart from my guys, from the most concrete manifestation of our connection, for too long. And I can tell they feel it too.

But one of them isn't ready to act on that longing.

Zian must sense the shift in the air, because he straightens up with a slosh of the water. Even in the dimness, I can tell his peachy-brown skin has taken on a ruddier cast that I don't think is just because of the bath.

"I can give *you* guys some privacy," he says in a rough voice, turning to heft himself out.

Jacob stops him with a hand on his arm. His blue eyes blaze with sudden intensity.

"What if you could be a part of it too? Without risking any of the things you're scared of?"

Zian's gaze jerks to him, his eyes widening. "What are you talking about?"

Jake pauses as if he's still figuring that out himself. He glances at me with a look so scorching my nerves tingle.

Then he turns back to Zee. "Use us. We can be your hands, your mouth. Tell us what you'd want to do to her, and we'll do it for you. Like you're acting through us. That would work without setting anything off in you, wouldn't it?"

A fresh wave of heat courses through me at the idea.

Zian draws in a breath, his pupils dilating with unfulfilled hunger. "That would— I mean—"

His gaze sears into mine. "Would you even be okay with that?"

Every nerve in my body is trembling with anticipation. I've collided with Dominic and Andreas at the same time before, but only the once. And never more than the two of them.

The possibilities flooding my head light me up from the inside out. "Yes. If you'd like it too."

Zian's next inhalation comes shakily. The other guys remain silent, Andreas's hand gone still by my cheek, all of us giving Zee the space he needs to come to his decision.

He wets his lips, the smolder in his dark eyes deepening. Then he nods to Drey.

"Kiss her. Kiss her until she's squirming for more."

A sly grin curves Andreas's mouth, and he tips my chin up so my lips can meet his.

It doesn't take much for him to summon a needy whimper out of me. His mouth claims mine with weeks of bottled passion neither of us has had the chance to really let out.

I clutch at his coiled hair and kiss him back hard. My lips part instantly at the flick of his tongue, welcoming him in.

Through the eager thundering of my pulse, Zian's voice reaches my ears, gone ragged. "Dominic, you know how to make her squirm too, don't you? Touch her—everywhere she likes it."

Dominic chuckles softly and presses a kiss to the peak of my shoulder. Both his tentacles glide around me, one across my back and the other over my belly, the suckers stroking my skin in a multitude of puckered kisses.

His hand glides over my chest at the same time. When he swipes one thumb over the tip of my breast, my breath stutters into Drey's mouth.

As I arch into Dom's touch, Andreas makes an urgent sound low in his throat and deepens our kiss. Our tongues tangle together, bliss racing through me from the melding of our mouths all the way down my body over the terrain Dominic is caressing.

Dom massages my breast with swivels of his thumb over the peak until my nipple is straining stiff against the fabric of my bra. A growl escapes me with the growing ache between my thighs.

I pull my mouth from Andreas's and catch Zian's gaze for just an instant. Hoping he can feel through the heated glance how happy I'd be if he really were joining in too.

Then I can't help seeking out Dominic's lips, pulling him tighter against me.

Jacob hasn't moved toward me yet, but his words travel over the water in a low purr that sets the shadows in my veins shivering twice as giddily. "Look at how much she's enjoying it, Zee. You've got three mouths to work with. Six hands. A couple of tentacles as a bonus."

He stops, and his voice dips even farther. "Why don't we get her out of the water so you can see just how well she's responding?"

"Yeah," Zian says roughly. "Bring—bring her to the bed."

I don't put up an ounce of protest when Dominic and Andreas lift me between them. They set me on the edge of the tub, clamber out themselves, and then Jake is there behind me, scooping me up in his arms.

"My turn," he says, blue fire dancing in his eyes.

I cup his jaw, remembering the uneasiness I saw in him when he caught me kissing Griffin and all the ways he's still been trying to make up to me what I've already forgiven.

"I need you just as much," I say quietly.

His arms tighten around me. He strides toward the bed, his head bowing to catch my mouth with his at the same time.

I could burn up in the feral demand of Jacob's kiss. The electric shock of his hunger races all the way to the tips of my fingers and toes.

He lowers me onto the sheets we cleared and drags his lips away, staying by my shoulder. The dampness of my body seeps into the silky fabric.

Dominic and Andreas follow us, Dominic sitting at my other side and Andreas sinking down next to my knee. In the faint moonlight drifting through the windows, their eyes shine with intensity.

The water warbles as Zian heaves himself out too. He walks right past the stack of towels to stand by the foot of the bed, heedless of the rivulets trickling over his sculpted brawn.

I want to lick the droplets right off his burnished flesh. I rein in the urge but lift my gaze to his face.

"What would you do with me now?"

His hands flex at his sides as if he's imagining his fingers trailing over me for real. He watches Dominic trace the band of my bra.

"Take it off of her, Dom," he says hoarsely. "I want to really see her. You and Jake—touch her, kiss her there."

I push upward a little so Dominic and Jacob can pull the sports bra up over my head together. I've barely leaned back into the sheets before Jake has lowered his head to suck my nipple into his mouth.

As I gasp, Dom takes a more gradual approach. He rolls the other peak between his thumb and forefinger and then slides one tentacle across it.

Each sucker that grazes my pebbled nipple gives it a firm squeeze. In a matter of seconds, I'm moaning at the flashes of delight.

Having Zian's gaze on me feels like another caress in itself. Will it help him, seeing that he can call the shots and direct my pleasure without any disaster crashing down on us?

I hope he's enjoying the moment at least half as much as I am.

My thighs have started rubbing together of their own accord in an instinctive attempt to relieve the ache between them. Andreas strokes his fingers up and down my leg.

"I think she needs more, Zee."

A sound like a strangled groan escapes Zian. "Take the rest of her clothes off. And then—get her off, whatever will feel best for her—hands, mouth…"

As he trails off with another strained noise, Drey yanks my panties down. He teases his fingers over my clit and my drenched folds beneath.

My head pushes back into the pillow as a soft cry of longing breaks from my lips. The familiar burn of desire courses all through my body, my nerves and my shadows forming a chorus clamoring for *More, more, more.*

Andreas massages my pussy until I'm rocking with his strokes, one hand twined in Jacob's hair and the other clutching Dominic's arm. When Drey delves two fingers right into my slit, a blissful shudder runs up my spine.

He plunges them in and out of my slickness a few times before holding the digits, gleaming with my arousal, back toward Zian in his taut pose. His own voice has gone ragged. "You can taste her."

Zian freezes, but only for an instant. He hurtles the last couple of steps to the foot of the bed and bends in to accept Drey's offering.

The sight of his tongue swiping over Andreas's fingers, lapping me off the other guy, has my breath hitching to the point of panting. Zian gazes down at me with so much conflicted emotion in his expression my nerves crackle with it.

"Keep tasting her," he says. "Right at the source. Until she comes."

Andreas doesn't miss a beat following that directive. He leans down and melds his mouth to my sex.

Oh, fuck. The rush of sensation floods me alongside the pleasure Jacob and Dominic are already summoning from my body.

Dom chooses the same moment to latch his mouth around my breast. I'm being devoured from three angles, lips and tongues and careful scrapes of teeth playing a symphony of bliss all across my body.

Andreas laps his tongue right inside me, and my hips buck up to meet him. As he works over every sensitive place I need it most, my gasp blends into a whimper and then into a louder moan.

Jacob raises his head and caresses my cheek. "Better not to get too noisy, Wildcat. Wouldn't want the kids to realize what we're getting up to. Clamp down when you need to."

He slides his fingers past my lips, between my teeth, muffling my next cry.

I don't mean to take him up on his suggestion. But he pinches my nipple with increasing friction, and Dominic's tentacles strum even more pleasure from my skin while he worships my other breast.

And then Drey is sucking so hard on my clit it's like he's dragged a tidal wave of ecstasy smashing through a dam I didn't know I'd built inside me.

My throat vibrates with a muffled moan, and my jaw clenches on Jacob's hand. The tang of blood that laces my tongue somehow heightens the rush of my release.

I jerk against Andreas's mouth and then sag with the gentler swell of the afterglow. Jacob withdraws his hand without hiding the streak of scarlet from the imprints of my teeth.

My gut lurches with guilt. "Dom, you need to heal—"

"It's fine," Jacob interrupts, in a tone so thick with satisfaction I can't doubt his claim. He grins down at me, as ferally devoted as the night when he poured the severed hands of my enemies at the foot of my bed. "I hope it leaves a scar—another way you've marked me."

Zian exhales with a groan. One of his hands is braced against the bedpost now, the other balled against the bulge in the front of his boxers.

"She needs someone inside her," he rasps. "Properly. Until she comes all over again."

I have no idea how the guys decide, and maybe they don't know either. Like one being, they shift around me, with Dominic settling between my splayed legs.

He looks up at me as if in question, as if he doesn't realize my heart swells with affection at the matching desire in his gaze. I reach up to tangle my fingers in the auburn strands that've come loose from his damp ponytail and beam at him.

"Please."

As he tugs off his boxers, Jacob captures my mouth with a kiss. Andreas applies his talented lips to my breast.

I'm completely encompassed in their joint embrace, their arms around me, Dominic's tentacles stroking along the sides of my torso.

Jake releases my lips just as Dom slides into me. My moan catches in my throat at the feeling of total fullness.

My knees lift to encompass his hips automatically, welcoming him deeper. He bows over me, the two other guys drawing back to make room but still keeping up their combined caresses.

"Love you," Dominic murmurs, with a hitch of breath as he drives farther into me that sets off a gasp of my own. "So much."

Joy radiates through my chest even though I've heard the words from him more than once before. "I love you too." I cast my gaze around to the other guys around us. "All of you. Always."

Andreas nips my earlobe, his words a warm wash of breath. "You're everything I'll ever want."

"Going to keep doing everything I can to deserve it, Wildcat," Jacob mutters, his fingers squeezing briefly around mine before he cups my breast again.

Zian's voice carries to me from the end of the bed, little more than a rasp. "Riva…"

He's gripping himself through his boxers now, his hunger etched across his handsome face. As Dominic surges into me again, propelling me toward another heady release, I manage to hold Zee's gaze.

"Come with me?"

He sputters a curse, every muscle tensing. Then he delves into his boxers to pump his erection skin to skin.

The slap of his palm against his cock merges with the rhythm of Dominic's thrusts inside me, the warble of all our broken breaths, the whirlwind of pleasure racing through me. He might not be touching me himself, but right then, it feels as if he's just as close to the others, just as much a part of this.

The thought sets off a brighter spark inside me. Its glow expands alongside the rising wave of bliss, on and on until the shadows are dancing in my veins and my body is trembling.

I press up to meet Dominic, urging him into me harder, faster. Tip my head to invite Drey's kiss. Tease my fingers down Jacob's chest.

And then shatter apart in time with Zian's final groan.

As I quake between the other three guys, our director slumps toward the mattress, spilling himself. His shoulders heave.

Then he drops his head a little farther and presses the most careful of kisses to the ball of my foot where I've just lowered it.

Right here with me. Where they're all meant to be.

But the peal of joy comes with a twist in my gut.

I have to figure out how to make sure they stay with me this time—that none of the villains beyond these walls ever come between us again.

Twenty-Three

Zian

It sure would have been nice if the hotel had come with some kind of vehicle. I guess that would have been too much to ask.

Instead, we're tramping along through the dense jungle vegetation again, slapping away bugs and stubbing our toes on stones hidden in the underbrush.

I push forward in the lead, because with my size and strength it's easier for me to smash through the worst of the obstacles than it would be for any of the others. But that also means I don't have the greatest sense of what's going on behind me.

Even my supernaturally keen ears are focused more on any hint of danger from farther away than the murmured conversations and weary sighs of our group of shadowbloods.

So I have no idea that George's teleportation talent is on the fritz until he jolts into view a step ahead of me and promptly trips over a tree root his foot slammed right into. He sprawls forward with a whoomph of breath and then a growled swear word that twelve-year-olds probably shouldn't know.

I reach out to help him up. "You okay?"

He swipes his hand through his odd white hair and grimaces at me.

"Yeah, fine. I didn't mean to do that. It just starts happening when I want to be moving faster than I am, whether that's actually a good idea or not."

His whole face is shiny with sweat, his hair's usual spikes drooping with dampness. His shirt clings to his skinny frame in patches.

I give him a quick onceover and decide I can pitch in a little more without it affecting my endurance all that much. "Here, why don't you take a breather on me?"

I heft him up onto my shoulders in a piggyback ride, balancing him over the bulge of my pack. He's so scrawny I barely feel the extra weight.

"You don't have to do this," he says as I tramp onward. "I can manage."

I shrug—carefully so I don't dislodge him. "I can too. Just keep your head low so I don't accidentally brain you on any of the lower branches."

George ends up resting his forearms gently on the top of my head, letting out a soft sigh that suggests he appreciates the rest more than he's letting on. He might be the youngest kid here—it's not surprising he's tiring out the fastest.

His voice reaches me in a low mutter I don't think he wants anyone else to hear. "Just for a few minutes. I'll keep up, really."

Something about his tone tugs at my gut. I wish I could see his face now to judge his expression, not that I'm the best at reading emotions even then.

"It's no big deal for me," I assure him. "I could keep going like this for hours."

His head droops closer to mine. "You shouldn't have to. It's my fault we're here at all."

As I snap a few vines that crisscross our path, I frown. "Why would you say that?"

"We wouldn't have crashed if I hadn't hit the pilot so hard—because I made that stupid hop when I wasn't even trying to. I'm always screwing up like that, but that time—that time I screwed things up for everyone."

Oh. The thread of emotion I caught in his voice before must have tugged at me because it's so uncomfortably familiar from my own life.

But with the recognition comes an unexpected sense of certainty. The words leave my lips without any hesitation.

"I think all of us have had issues getting control over our powers. The guardians never really taught us how to use them properly."

Clancy's done a little work with us, but only to serve his missions. I don't know if he's even bothered with this kid.

George lets out a soft huff. "Yeah, well, no one else made the helicopter crash."

I consider his statement. "No, but a bunch of us could have. And some of us would be more likely to screw up in different ways that could be just as bad. As long as… as long as we're *trying* to help rather than hurt people, I think we'll end up doing more good than bad in the end. The balance will be more right than wrong."

The kid is silent for several seconds. "Are you sure? I do try."

"As sure as I can be about anything," I say, and realize as I'm saying it how true that is.

Is this the first time I've thought of my own mistakes and not immediately started beating myself up over them?

I'm not happy about my fuck-ups. I wish I could take back the pain I've dealt out that wasn't deserved.

But I didn't ask for this power or the feral defensiveness that's intertwined with it. I can put more good into the world than pain myself, can't I?

I'm doing a little of that now by giving this kid a hand. And maybe not just by taking some weight off him in the literal sense.

A smile crosses my face, and my own steps feel even lighter. For a little while.

The direction we've been heading in, based on Jacob's observations from the cockpit before the crash and Griffin's emotional compass, is taking us toward a range of tall hills. Maybe even small mountains, from the looks of the green-draped peaks I'm getting glimpses of through the leaves.

The breaths of my companions become rougher as we veer upward again. How high are we going to have to climb this time?

We can't count on stumbling on another abandoned hotel for shelter.

I skirt a clump of jutting boulders with the others trailing behind me and knock a path through a grove of sprouting saplings. George sways on my shoulders.

My calves are starting to prickle with exertion now. I'm going to have to put him down soon after all.

I glance up at the sun, just past its peak in the sky and searing even through the thin haze of clouds, and then back at the others. "Are we sure we definitely want to keep going this way? I haven't gotten us off-course?"

Dominic peers up at the sun too. "I think this is still northwest."

Griffin nods with that unnervingly vague expression of his. "It feels like we're going the right way to me, if we want to reach the biggest city around."

I guess we just keep trudging for as long as it takes, then.

I turn back to face the jungle, debating whether I can handle carrying George a while longer or should preserve my strength by setting him back on his feet now, and realize one of the other kids has sidled up next to me. The mousy-haired girl looks to be about fourteen, but she's been so quiet throughout the trek that I haven't caught her name.

"I, um," she mumbles, her head dipping shyly. "I think I might be able to tell where we could walk more easily."

I'm not going to say no to that offer. I smile down at her in an attempt to offset my imposing size, in case that's part of what's making her nervous. "How's that?"

Her hands twist together in front of her. "Well, I—my abilities have to do with the earth. Like, dirt and stuff. And I've been noticing I can kind of *feel* the ground around us. Where it's steeper or… not so steep. Where there are more roots in it or less."

"Less roots would mean less plants to push through," Booker pipes up. "Sounds good to me."

Jacob's voice reaches me with an impatient note. "We don't want to get too far off track. An easy path could still take longer if we wander off the wrong way."

Before my eyes, the girl deflates. The sight gnaws at me just like George's admission of guilt did.

She's trying to do something good for us too. Jake's just a natural skeptic.

"Do you think you could tell how far we'd need to go to get to the better routes?" I ask her. "Make sure it's not too long a diversion?"

She peeks up at me, biting her lip. "Yeah. I can't feel things very far away anyway. There's a spot that's pretty close that we could try."

"We might as well give it a shot," Andreas says in his easygoing way. "Especially with how much more walking we've got ahead of us."

A murmur of general agreement passes through the group. I give the girl's shoulder the gentlest pat I can manage.

"Why don't you take the lead for a bit? Sounds like you know where you're going better than I do."

The swift grin she flashes at me makes the gamble worthwhile all on its own. She darts a little ahead of me, picking her way across the terrain so deftly my confidence in this plan has grown before I'm even walking again.

I check behind me to make sure everyone's on board. My gaze collides with Riva's, and she shoots me a wider smile that makes my pulse wobble in the best possible way.

She's been championing these kids from the moment she found out they existed. But she doesn't have to be alone in it.

She doesn't have to be alone any way at all. A flicker of heat washes through my veins at the memories from last night—her taste on my lips, her face flushed with bliss.

I played a part in giving her that pleasure, and I didn't have to push myself too close to my limits to do it. Even if that's the best I can ever offer her, it's more than I thought I could.

The shy girl guides us onto a narrow but trampled path that I'd bet animals use to traverse the jungle more quickly. My strides lengthen as we set off along it, the strain easing back.

"This is great," I tell her, and she smiles a little longer than before.

"I feel like it's going to take us on a lower path between the higher hills," she says. "So we won't have to go right up any of them."

Nadia lets out a whoop of approval. "I'm all for that. No pain, no gain is definitely not my philosophy."

At our faster pace, we find ourselves surrounded by the looming peaks within a couple of hours. The ground keeps veering upward with plenty of hillside still to cover, but my spirits are high.

Of course, the others still need their breaks even with an easier hike. Andreas calls for a pit stop when we come up on a couple of fallen trees that can act as benches, and he and Riva pass around the drinks and snacks while Dominic checks everyone for possible injuries.

Griffin scoops his cat out of his pack and scratches her shoulders while she cuddles on his lap. As I watch him, wondering what's going on in that head of his now, he focuses on the perky girl from the older kids.

"I think we know everyone's talent now except yours, Celine," he says calmly. "What powers do you have? It'd be good to know in case they might come in handy."

She lets out a giggle with an awkward dip of her head. "I'm not sure how likely that is out here. The guardians say my abilities have something to do with magnetism… I can manipulate certain metals a little, and sometimes I pick up on things like radio waves, cell phone signals… Haven't heard any of that on this trip."

She motions to the wilderness around us with a wry grin.

Nadia gives her a teasing nudge. "We'll have to put you to work once we make it to the city."

"It could definitely be useful there." Jacob stretches his arms over his head and then considers the mousy girl with the earth affinity. "Any chance you can tell us how much farther we've got to go before we're heading down again instead of up?"

Her shoulders come up a bit at his demanding tone. "I—I can't really feel that far ahead. It's farther ahead than I can tell, anyway, but I think that only means it's not, like, ten minutes away."

Andreas cocks his head, studying the peaks on either side of us. "From the looks of things, I doubt it's more than a few hours farther. We're not going to make it all the way down the other side before it gets totally dark, but it'd be good if we can push on until we reach the highest point. We might be able to see the city from there. It'll give us something to inspire good dreams before we set off again."

Riva stretches her arms out in front of her with a gleam in her eyes. "That would be amazing—to know our goal is in sight."

Once we've reached civilization, we can find out where we are. Start making more plans. See if we can gather more allies.

My heart thumps faster in anticipation, even though those events are at least a day in the future. Then my attention snags on Riva's next movement.

She sat down a couple of feet away from Griffin, and she's just slipped her hand around his.

As he looks at her with a quiet smile, my hackles rise automatically.

He's been helping us with the escape. He hasn't given me any reason to distrust him since we fled the facility.

But he hasn't really explained himself either. Justified all the ways he worked against us with Clancy and whatever other guardians.

He helped Clancy form his plan to shove me and Riva together. Shared some of my most private feelings—and hers.

A growl forms at the base of my throat.

I don't care if Riva's decided she can trust him. He should *prove* it—to all of us. Or at least to my three friends who are tied to her as completely as anyone can be with the marks I might never be able to take on my own skin.

Maybe it's not his fault. The guardians could have put him through all kinds of hell that we don't know about.

We still need to hear it.

I confessed all my past shit to her. It was a good thing I did.

He should want to for all of our sakes, including his.

I stand up abruptly, my wolf-man features itching at my face. I'm not going to threaten him into it, even if part of me would like to.

When the others glance up at me, I jerk my head toward the area to the left of our path. "I can hear a stream somewhere off that way. Why don't those of us carrying the jugs go see if it's worth refilling them."

That's just us Firsts. We've shouldered the heaviest packs. And we've each got at least one empty jug by this point.

We wouldn't really all need to go, but Dominic gives me a thoughtful nod as he gets to his feet as if he understands I must have some other motivation. Jacob's eyes flash with sharpened alertness, and Andreas's easy grin fades.

Riva looks around at the kids with a slight frown. "You're all okay on your own for a few minutes?"

"Hey, we're not toddlers," Nadia says, her tone light enough to show she isn't offended. She swipes the fringe of her dark pixie cut away from her damp forehead. "And I don't think any of us would argue with having a plentiful supply of water."

Griffin has stayed seated on the log. He ruffles his cat's fur. "I'll be here with them."

I fix him with a firm stare. "You should fill up too if it looks like a good source. Come on."

Griffin gazes back at me, and I know he can pick up on how I'm feeling. The threads of aggression, the determination behind my demand.

Riva makes a small noise as if she's about to speak, but then Griffin gets up. He lets the cat leap out of his arms and go to the empty can he filled with water for it.

"That's no problem. I want to do my fair share."

I have to lead the way, of course, since I'm the one who can supposedly hear the running water. But when I check to confirm that the others are all with me, Riva has twined her fingers with Griffin's again.

My fingers flex, my claws prickling with the urge to spring free. I keep walking in as straight a line as I can manage until the chatter of the younger shadowbloods has completely faded into the rustling of the leaves and buzzing of the jungle insects.

If my wolfish ears can't hear them, they definitely won't hear us.

I turn to face the others, folding my arms over my chest. "There isn't any stream—at least, not that I've heard. I just thought we should talk. The six of us, alone."

Riva knits her brow. "About what?"

I can protect her and my friends with more than my brutal strength. I can protect her from the secrets we need to be sure won't come back to haunt us.

I lift my chin toward Griffin. "I think it's time you told us exactly what happened to you in the past four years—and why we should believe anything you tell us now."

TWENTY-FOUR

Riva

Zian's words come out with the edge of a snarl. I instinctively step even closer to Griffin, my fingers tightening around his.

I don't know how much of a chance he's gotten to talk to the others—to apologize, to explain… Does Zian have any idea at all of the reasons Griffin decided to side with the guardians over us?

But then, *I* still can't totally wrap my head around his reasoning either, can I? I've been willing to do what I can to see the hints of the boy I knew rise to the surface through the robotic being he's become, but I wouldn't put my life in his hands.

Not now. Not yet.

A beam of sunlight streaks between the leaves overhead to glare off Griffin's blond hair. He's still standing calmly beside me amid the jungle vegetation, but a whiff of nervous pheromones reaches my nose.

What is he afraid of?

Should I be worried that he's unnerved or happy that he's capable of being scared at all?

He keeps his attention on Zian, though all five of us are watching him now. "I've tried to explain it. Clancy acted like he wanted to take the Guardianship in a new direction, one that sounded like it'd be good for us. You all thought that might be possible too, when you first got to the island."

He isn't wrong, but Jacob's lips pull into a grimace. "I wouldn't have dragged my friends back into captivity after they'd gotten free, no matter what I thought was 'possible.'"

"It made sense at the time. I—I didn't know what to think about everything he was showing me, about what you were doing, the people you'd hurt. *How* you'd hurt them. And my sense of who you all were was muddled. I hadn't seen you in so long."

"But you *knew* us," Zian insists. "Riva hadn't seen us in four years, and she did everything she could to help us even after we'd been assholes to her."

Griffin swallows audibly. "It's not the same. I don't know how to describe how it's been. Like everything was flat but also blurry at the same time…"

As he trails off, the shade of sadness in his expression wrenches at my heart. He obviously doesn't want to talk about how he ended up in his current state, but I'm not sure there's any other way of unraveling the tension between us.

I stroke my thumb over his knuckles in an attempt at reassuring him. "What did the guardians do to you that erased all your emotions, Griffin? How did it even happen?"

His mouth twists, and he grips my hand harder. There's pain in the answer to my question, and I've never really wanted to hurt him.

But maybe because he can tell that, he doesn't refuse me.

His gaze trails off toward the wilderness as if it's easier for him to bring back those memories when he isn't looking at any of us. "They called it 'desensitization.' The basic idea seemed to be to make feeling things worse than not feeling them."

Dominic brushes aside a fern frond that grazes his arm with the heavy breeze, his hazel eyes shadowed. "How did they do that?" he asks quietly.

Griffin's stance stiffens a little more with each word. "They started small. Showing me video clips that would provoke a little generic emotion in most people: a kid having a happy birthday party, a tense car chase, stuff like that. And they had me hooked up to a machine with different sensors. When they could tell that I was having an emotional response—from my heartrate and my breathing and I don't know what else—they'd overwhelm it."

Jacob's posture has turned equally rigid, as if he's matching his twin's discomfort. "Overwhelm it with *what*?"

Griffin's mouth twitches. "Physical pain. Electric shocks or chemicals that set off different types of aches or burns."

Andreas's eyes widen. "Fuck."

Griffin blinks hard, a tremor running through his body. I set my free hand on his arm a little above our clasped hands, doing my best to steady him.

"It was a long process," he says in a thin voice. "They'd show a clip, catch a reaction, lance the emotions like a boil. Then they'd play the same clip again. Over and over until my body just… didn't register whatever had made me feel something before. Like a connection was snapped. And then they'd move on to the next clip."

Jacob's fingers flex at his sides. A branch cracks overhead, whipping against the trunk of a neighboring tree.

"Those fucking pricks," he spits out. More rage burns in his blue eyes than I've seen in weeks.

My own anger at the guardians sears through my gut, but what chokes me up is a thicker anguish. "That must have taken a long time."

"Yes." Griffin swallows again, his eyes gone even hazier than usual, as if he's retreating inside his head. "They had to—to work up through every possibility to the most intense, and destroy those automatic reactions too. I didn't have much concept of time. During it or after. It was more than a year, at least."

More than a year of constant agony for every emotion that stirred inside him. Tears prick at the back of my eyes.

"I still don't understand why they wanted to do that in the first place," I say roughly.

"So my own emotions wouldn't confuse what I was reading in other people. So I wouldn't be affected by the things I read."

Jacob scowls. "And your feelings are just gone? You can't bring them back?"

Griffin raises his shoulders in an awkward shrug. "I'm not sure I even know how to try. By the end, the whole concept of what it was like to feel things wasn't something I could grasp." He pauses. "And by then, I—I kind of thought maybe they were right. Maybe it was better like that."

"What?" Zian sputters. "How could them torturing you be good?"

I feel Griffin bracing himself in the shift of his stance. Another whiff of anxiety reaches my nose.

His jaw works, and then he glances around at each of us with obvious effort. "It's because I couldn't control my emotions that they caught us. The first time. I gave away that we were going to try to escape."

Andreas's forehead furrows. "What do you mean?"

A rasp creeps into Griffin's voice. "They showed me the surveillance video when they told me. The afternoon before we were going to break out—right before we went back to our cells. I must have been thinking about getting free, and just for a moment I smiled at all of you. So bright they couldn't miss it."

I shake my head. "One moment couldn't have given everything away."

Griffin hangs his head. "They said they already suspected we were planning something. I guess it would have been hard to completely hide the conversations we were having, no matter how careful we were being. But they didn't think we were ready to make a move until they saw that. I guess I normally looked sad when it was time for us to leave."

His free hand clenches, and then he raises his chin. "I'm sorry. I'm so fucking sorry. I can't even—I can't even *feel* how sorry I know I am, but I ruined everything, and none of this would ever have gone so wrong if my emotions hadn't been so noticeable, and—"

My chest hitches with a sob I can't totally suppress, and I yank Griffin into a full embrace. He bows his head next to mine, his jaw coming to rest against my cheek.

"They were probably lying," I insist, my voice shaking with vehemence. "They couldn't have been that sure just because you *smiled.* And even if it was that, it wasn't your fault. You couldn't help being happy."

"They made it so I wouldn't be any more. I couldn't be happy or sad or angry or anything."

"And that isn't better. That isn't *you.* If we couldn't have escaped without you being broken, then it wasn't the right time to escape. You weren't the problem."

Andreas clears his throat, sounding pretty choked up himself. "In case it isn't clear, we all agree on that point. I'd never have blamed you, Griffin."

Zian's foot scuffs against the uneven ground. "I'm sorry for coming down so hard on you. I didn't realize—"

"It's okay." Griffin pulls a few inches back from me, his hands coming to rest on my forearms. "I wasn't sure how much I should talk about it—if you're going to accept what I did, it should be because I've made up for it *now*, not because you feel bad about what happened to me before."

Jacob's eyes still blaze with fury, but I don't think that rage is directed at his brother anymore. "Can we fix it?" He glances at Dom. "Can you heal whatever they fucked up inside him?"

Dominic extends a cautious tentacle to rest on Griffin's elbow and pauses. "I can't pick up on any physical damage. It's not like a typical injury."

I turn my hands to grip Griffin's arms like he's holding mine. "You said that you're starting to feel things again."

He nods, gazing down at me. "The more I'm close to you, the more things are reemerging. It's—it's a little unsettling after all this time, and I'm still figuring out how to sort through all the sensations, but I think it's better than staying numb."

It makes sense that it took the draw between our shadowy essences to get through to him. I've never experienced anything like the urgent clamor in my blood except when I'm physically close with these five men.

The guardians could never have provoked that one feeling in him to torment it out of him.

Imagining the torture they inflicted on him makes my stomach plummet. "The feelings that are coming back—are they triggering the pain the guardians put you through?"

It's got to all be tangled up in a big mess inside him.

Griffin manages to give me a smile that's only slightly strained. "That's part of what I'm sorting through. But I have to deal with it before it can get better. You've been helping a lot. Don't feel bad about it. I want everything you're willing to offer."

He sounds so sure that I only hesitate for a second before giving in to the urge that sweeps through me at his words. Bobbing up on my toes, I press my mouth to his.

As he kisses me back, one of his hands rises to the back of my neck. The stroke of his fingers over my skin stirs up all kinds of hungry emotions inside me, not that this is a good time for indulging in them.

When we ease apart, I don't see a trace of disapproval in any of the other guys' expressions.

Jacob wavers on his feet and then steps toward his brother. As Griffin turns to meet him, Jake yanks him into a hug of his own.

"I should have been there," he mutters. "I'd have done everything I could to stop them."

Griffin hugs him back hard. "I know you would have. I can feel how angry you are on my behalf. I haven't blamed you for being angry with me at first, Jake. I deserved it."

"They fucking deserved it."

"They're gone now. I don't even know if they're still working with the Guardianship. Clancy told me what they'd done was barbaric." Griffin frowns as he draws away from his brother. "But he might have just said that to encourage me to trust him."

"It doesn't matter," I say. "We have plenty of other reasons *not* to trust him now. And we're not going to have anything to do with him again except to get the other shadowbloods free."

Zian reaches out to squeeze Griffin's shoulder. "Thank you for telling us everything, even if I kind of bullied you into it. I guess we should be getting back… and explain why we don't have any more water."

Andreas waves his hand dismissively. "We'll just say it looked too muddy to risk it. Simple enough."

I might have liked to have topped up our supply of hydration, but my spirits have lifted as we tramp back to the path anyway. The simmering tension between all of my guys has melted away, the vibe between us feeling almost as companionable as back when we were teens.

We rejoin the younger shadowbloods just in time to see Celine slipping through the trees toward the group from the other side.

Griffin aims a pointed look at her that I don't totally understand. "Where did you go on your own?"

She laughs with a tug at her clothes. "Needed a trip to the 'ladies room.'"

Griffin still seems pensive, but then his gaze travels across the group, and his eyebrows draw together. "Where's Lua? My cat?"

Booker, Nadia, and Devon look over from where they were standing in a cluster farther down the path, matching guilt on all their faces.

"I'm sorry," Nadia says, her shoulders slumping. "She was hanging out with us getting pets all around, and then all of a sudden she freaked out. Fur puffed out, hissing at us. She raced off this way."

"It was only a couple of minutes ago," Booker adds. "Maybe she saw or smelled something weird that freaked her out a bit, and she'll come back when she realizes there's no problem."

Zian's head jerks around in response to something I didn't pick up on. "Unless there is a problem. Everyone, stay where you are."

We all freeze, our voices fading into the humid air. My heart thuds so loud I can barely make out the twitter of the birds overhead.

Then I catch a hint of movement between the trees. A striped, muscular body prowling through the jungle several feet from the path.

We've got a feline companion, but it's not Griffin's little housecat. No wonder Lua panicked.

I glance at the guys, not sure what to say. How do you deal with a tiger on the hunt?

I don't want to risk pissing it off and making it more inclined to attack.

"Let's get moving, slowly and calmly," Dominic says. "Stick close together, and—"

"What's there?" The girl who found our path interrupts him with a nervous shiver, her gaze scanning the jungle. Then she lets out a squeak and scrambles farther down the path.

As if her fear has lit a fuse in the youngest shadowbloods, Ajax, Devon, George, and a couple others dash after her, George blinking in and out of view every few steps. But clearly that's the wrong move.

Paws thump over the ground. The tiger barrels through the jungle toward the fleeing kids.

"No!" I cry out, throwing myself after them.

The giant cat lunges onto the cleared path right at their heels, and a shriek jolts up my throat before I can even think about it.

The tiger's body seizes up. My power radiates up from my lungs, latching on to every nerve and bone in its immense body.

I've shattered a shadowkind monster before. A mortal jungle creature is nothing.

The energy vibrates through my body as the scream peals louder. This beast was going to hurt the kids—the kids I swore I'd protect.

I can't let it get another chance.

The tiger's legs crumple with a groan of agony.

Its tail kinks. Its back twists. Its jaw snaps open and sideways.

The crack of its skull resonates through my veins with a rush of power. In that instant, I feel as if I've just woken up fresh for the day, not a single step taken yet.

The furry creature slumps in the middle of the path, limp and deformed.

The young shadowbloods huddle together, staring at the tiger and then at me. My stomach knotting, I glance behind me to find similar shock etched on the faces of the older teens.

They had some idea what I can do, but they've never seen my power on full display before.

They've never seen the sadistic edge it takes… or how much satisfaction I take from the torment, even if I wish I didn't.

None of them have abilities anything like this. They couldn't have been prepared.

Jacob sets his hand on my back and lifts his voice. "You got it just in time, Riva. That thing would have mowed all of them down if you hadn't hit it so fast."

His steely gaze dares anyone to complain about my methods.

"Let's grab our things and get moving," Andreas adds, brisk but warm. "We've had enough of a break."

And we don't want the kids spending any more time gaping at the tiger's mutilated body than they have to.

Ajax squares his shoulders and meets my eyes. "Thank you, Riva."

The girl who ran first nods shakily, though she's clutching George's arm. "Thank you."

But as we skirt the tiger's broken body, a gloom seems to have fallen over our group that not even the brilliance of the late-afternoon sun can beam away.

Twenty-Five

Riva

Our pathfinder—whose name she's finally told us is Lindsay—lifts her head abruptly in the thickening darkness.

"I can feel it. The land slopes down again right up ahead. Like it keeps going that way, not a little dip."

She's gotten our hopes up over what was just a dip a couple of times already in the past hour. This time she sounds a lot more confident than before, though.

At the skeptical looks a couple of the younger shadowbloods shoot her through the dusk, she raises her chin. "It's clearer than last time. And we *should* be getting almost to the highest spot by now, right?"

Nadia smothers a yawn. "I sure hope so."

Zian and Lindsay tramp on at the head of the pack. Andreas eases back along the line to where Jacob and I are bringing up the rear like usual.

Drey glances over the motley procession before turning to us with a low voice. "I think if we haven't reached the top yet this time, we should make camp anyway. Everyone's getting pretty tired."

My mouth twists. "Yeah."

We took another short break about an hour ago after Lindsay had to divert us from one animal track that veered off along the side of the hills to a clearer passage continuing upward. At that point, I think Dominic killed half a dozen twigs healing blisters.

My shoulders are aching under the straps of my pack. The pain is faint compared to the sharper sensation digging into my chest that has nothing to do with the exertion of the hike.

We've finished off all the juice, and we're getting low on water. The sky clotted with more clouds for part of the afternoon, but they burned off before any rain fell.

At this point, I'd rather we got rained on so we could collect some of it even if we all end up drenched.

And of course there's also the memory of the kids' shocked stares after my scream wrenched through the tiger, hovering at the back of my mind.

Jacob frowns. "The kids will have an easier time resting if they know the goal's in sight."

I swallow down the worry it's probably better I don't voice—that our goal might not be in sight at all. That we could reach the crest of this section of hills and see nothing but more jungle.

And then what?

"If we push them to total exhaustion," Andreas murmurs, "it's only going to—"

Zian's excited shout cuts him off, an eager squeal from Lindsay mingling with it.

"You've got to see this," he calls back to us.

We all hustle forward, breathless remarks passing between the younger shadowbloods. My pulse kicks up a notch, partly spurred by the whiffs of anticipation lacing the air from the group.

Zian and Lindsay have stopped up ahead, eased off into the thicker vegetation to make room for the rest of us to come up alongside them. The gasps and exclamations of our younger companions as they reach that spot wash away most of the gloom that'd fallen over me.

The three of us arrive at their heels, and for a second I lose my breath.

The landscape below us is draped in the same black as the shadowed jungle around us—except for a broad patch of gleaming lights piercing the night. In the darkness, I can't tell how far away from the hills it is, but it's definitely *there*: a big, vibrant city.

We'll be able to get food and water, one way or another. We'll have access to vehicles and phones.

The worst part of the trek is nearly behind us.

The kids let out soft whoops, grabbing each other in a jumble of hugs in their relief. Andreas shoots me a grin.

"Guess I didn't need to worry after all. Let's figure out a good place to hunker down for the night and who'll take first watch."

"I'll go first," I offer automatically. "I'm too keyed up to sleep right away anyway."

Jacob nods. "Then I'm with you. We'll get one of the older teens too —that should be enough eyes."

Settling into camp is a chaotic business. We hand out a little more food from our stash and try to make sure each of the kids has a decently comfortable patch of ground to curl up on.

We brought some sheets from the hotel, but anything heavier like an actual blanket would have been too much cargo. They bundle part of those up as thin pillows and drape the rest over their bodies.

The jungle terrain hardly makes for a cozy bed. I know that from our first night.

But everyone makes the most of it without complaint, maybe with dreams of finding actual beds again by the end of tomorrow.

I pick out a perch on a stump overlooking the other side of the hill and the city below. Jacob is still prowling around the perimeter of our camp, checking for immediate threats, but I suspect he'll stick close to me once he's done.

At the rustle of brush, I turn my head, but it's Nadia venturing toward me, her statuesque frame giving off a faint glow to help light her way.

"Hey," I say, abruptly hesitant. Nadia is probably the closest to a new friend I've made among the younger shadowbloods, but I have no idea what she thinks of me now. "Did you want to take first watch?"

She rubs her mouth. "Yeah. I'll keep an eye on things at the other end of the camp once everyone's settled. I just wanted to look at the city a little more first."

I can't hold back a smile. "Sure. I get that. If you want to take this post, I can cover the other side and—"

Nadia cuts me off with a shake of her head. "Nah. I'll get too distracted if I have that view in front of me the whole time. But… thank you."

She sounds a little uncertain too. I shut my mouth and simply gaze off over the darkened landscape with her, trying to chart the path we'll take even though that's impossible when I can barely make out the trees.

After a minute or two, Nadia inhales audibly. "The other Firsts… Do you all have abilities like what you did to the tiger? I mean, that strong?"

Oh. Yeah, it does make sense for that question to be on her mind. She'll never have seen any of her facility-mates pull off something like that.

"We've all got different powers," I say carefully. "But they're all pretty strong. That's the only reason we were able to escape—before and now. Jacob had to basically set off an entire earthquake to get us out, you know."

"Wow." She gazes at the city lights for a few beats longer and then looks at me. "None of the rest of us can pull off anything like that. At least, I've never met any shadowblood my age or younger who could even get close to that kind of impact."

She hasn't asked a question outright, but it's implicit in her words. I roll my answer around in my head, debating how much to tell her.

But she deserves the truth as much as we did, doesn't she?

I swallow down my doubts. "When we escaped the first time, we tracked down one of the founders of the Guardianship—a woman who worked with Clancy's parents. She's the one who figured out the process for merging humans with… with what they think of as monsters. She told us that when we—the Firsts—were very young and she saw how we were developing, she decided she'd made a mistake. She wanted us dead."

Nadia's eyebrows shoot up. "But they kept making more of us."

"It seems like the other founders and whoever else had control by then didn't agree with her. They shut her out more and more."

I tilt my head, thinking of the laptop we stole from her home in the Canadian wilderness, the one that's either still in Rollick's hands with the rest of our old supplies or tossed in the trash if he didn't bother to hold on to our packs.

"We found some records from her work," I go on. "We couldn't understand much of it, but as far as we could tell, when the other guardians pushed her for her process, she left out some parts. She might have been hoping it wouldn't work at all. It looks like what actually happened was the later shadowbloods they created had a lot less of the 'monstrous' stuff working for them."

Nadia hums to herself. Then, to my surprise, she lets out a dry bark of a laugh. "Well, that sucks."

It's my turn to have my eyebrows shoot up. "You'd rather you had more power?"

"Sure." She runs her hands through her thick black hair, rumpling the short strands. "Right now I can just glow a bit. If I could set off a whole solar bomb or something… We'd have a lot easier time keeping out of the guardians' hands, wouldn't we?"

Somehow it hadn't occurred to me that she might feel that way.

"It isn't always a good feeling," I have to point out. "I don't really like seeing what I've done, even if it helps us."

"But you wouldn't get rid of the power if you had the choice, would you?"

I open my mouth and close it again.

There was a time when I'd hoped the real monsters, the shadowkind, might be able to tell us how to carve our monstrous parts out of us. That was before I knew about all the younger shadowbloods who needed our help to escape.

Before I realized just how far-reaching the Guardianship's influence extended.

"No," I admit. "Not right now. Not as long as we might still need it."

Ajax's measured voice travels from behind us, making me startle. "I wish I could read a lot more of people's minds. Even if I'd probably see stuff that's disturbing."

I turn to face him where he's standing a few steps back on the path, chiding myself for getting so caught up in the conversation that I didn't hear him coming. Although he'll have trained in all the same non-supernatural skills like stealth that the rest of us have, so maybe it's not totally my fault.

I guess I haven't horrified the younger shadowbloods after all, at least not all of them.

"You might get stronger," I say, shifting my gaze between him and Nadia. "The six of us all had our powers expand over time, especially once we were technically adults. I didn't know I could scream like that until a few months ago."

Nadia perks up visibly. She rubs her hands together with a smirk that looks a little devious. "Maybe we'll figure out ways to develop the talents more when we get to decide how we train for ourselves."

I suppose that's possible, although I'd imagine the guardians have prodded as much ability out of the younger shadowbloods as they possibly could already. It seems kinder to keep that thought to myself for now.

"You never know."

Ajax yawns and drifts away. After giving the city one last longing glance, Nadia does the same.

As their footsteps rasp off through the jungle, Jacob rejoins me. He rests his hand on the back of my head, the gesture still tentative after everything we've been through until I lean into his touch.

"They'll be okay," he says. "We'll all be okay. Because you're making sure of it."

I don't know how to answer. Do I even think that's true?

But looking out over the glow of the city we've pushed ourselves so hard to find, it's a little easier to believe it than before.

I wake up on my uneven bed of soil and fallen leaves to a sorrowful *meow* that carries through the underbrush.

As I push myself upright, Griffin is already shoving through the nearby bushes. "Lua?"

The cat meows again, and a moment later he's turning with his pet tucked in his arms. Her white fur is mottled with bits of debris, but she nestles against his chest with a purr I can hear from five feet away.

Griffin smiles down at her, his expression so tender with affection that my pulse skips a beat. He really is coming back to us bit by bit, just like Lua found her way back to him.

Our fellow shadowbloods are stirring throughout our hasty camp. Dominic approaches Griffin, his tentacles unfurling from their coils against his back.

"Do you want me to check her over? In case she got any scratches or sprains that aren't totally obvious?"

Griffin hesitates, whether because he doesn't want to loosen his hug yet or because he knows what the healing costs Dom, I'm not sure. Maybe some of both.

Then he takes a step toward Dominic. "Yes, that would be a good idea."

I get to my feet, gathering my meager belongings, and raise my voice to carry through the jungle around me. "Let's have a quick breakfast and then move out. We're almost there!"

Energetic murmurs rise up after my reminder. I weave through the trees back onto our narrow path and peer down the opposite hillside again.

The city doesn't stand out as much amid the jungle greenery by daylight. But it's still undeniably there, a grayish blotch that feels even more within reach now that I can distinguish actual buildings.

And maybe a highway cutting through the trees running parallel to the hills? If we can reach that, the hike will be even easier.

I turn back toward the camp with a lighter heart—and freeze at a rhythmic whirring that reaches my ears in the same moment.

Farther down the path, Zian has already stiffened. His head swivels as he knits his brow.

"That sounds like—"

A big military-style helicopter veers into view around one of the higher peaks nearby. From the expanding cacophony of sound, it isn't alone.

"Shadowbloods," a voice blares from a loudspeaker. "Stay where you are and prepare to be collected."

"What the fuck?" Booker says, staring up at the swiftly advancing chopper.

Griffin whirls around, Lua still clutched in his arms. His gaze latches on to… Celine.

His voice comes out cool with certainty but a little shaky. "You. You signaled them somehow. You're *happy* that they're here."

My stomach lurches. Griffin's been keeping an eye on Celine, questioning her here and there from the start, hasn't he?

Was he picking up on something in her emotions that made him suspicious? I guess not enough that he felt confident mentioning it to the rest of us until now.

Celine stares back at him, her hands clenched at her sides, her usual sunny smile vanished with the flattening of her mouth.

"How is this better than what we had before?" she bursts out with a wild gesture toward the jungle around us. She jabs a finger toward me. "She—she wants to take us back to the fucking *monsters* like she did before. I've seen what those things can do."

More nausea bubbles up inside me. "I wouldn't—it was just a possibility. We'd have been careful about it."

Celine narrows her eyes at me. "You can't be *careful* with those things. I saw what they did to one of my friends when we tried to help the guardians bring you back in Miami. I saw the pictures of what they did to the shadowbloods you thought you were 'rescuing' afterward. They're psychotic beasts."

Oh, no. The image flashes through my mind of the girl slumped in a pool of blood at the parking garage where we were attacked with Rollick.

I didn't want that to happen. When we asked Rollick and his people to help us push back the guardians, I asked them not to hurt any of the kids.

But they did anyway. I can't even promise her that it was unavoidable or a mistake, because I honestly don't know.

I don't even know which of the shadowkind killed her.

Nadia gapes at the other girl. "Are you kidding me, Celine? We came all this way—"

Celine glares at her. "We've been attacked by a tiger, almost ran out of water—we're sleeping in the dirt—to get to what? Maybe I don't love the facility, but we're a hell of a lot safer there."

She jogs forward toward the crest of our section of hill, raising her arms as if to beckon the helicopters, a second of which has swung into view.

"Celine!" I cry out, not even sure what I want to do, and spring at her.

A *boom* resonates through the air from the closer chopper. An invisible force smacks into me in mid-leap and hurls me into a tree trunk.

TWENTY-SIX

Dominic

As the thunderous sound splits the air, I throw myself into the shelter of two broad tree trunks. That might be the only reason I escape being knocked right off my feet.

As it is, I sway and clutch at the nearest branch to keep my balance. Shrieks and grunts carry through the air from all around me.

The mark on my sternum prickles with echoed pain. Riva's fallen somewhere out there—fallen hard.

My heart lurches. I push myself around the trees, searching for her slim form in the chaos.

My gaze catches on Jacob first. He's sprawled on his ass in the middle of the path, his hands raised, his face tight with fury.

He's aiming his telekinetic power at the helicopter. But the same instant that becomes obvious to me, the chopper sweeps by overhead—and drops something from a hatch in its belly.

A strange, glinting net plummets over the path, large enough to slam into Jake and a few of the younger shadowbloods who'd tumbled around him. An electric hiss ripples through its metallic strands, and their bodies jerk with spasms.

Fuck. He won't be able to toss the helicopters away while he's being electrocuted.

Where's Riva? I can't tell if she's even okay.

But if she can aim a scream at the guardians—

I scramble forward through the jungle and glimpse her farther up the path near the crest of our section of hill. She must have fallen to her hands and knees, but she's shoving herself upright with a wobble.

Zian has reached her already. He grasps her elbow to steady her—and the helicopter whips by again with another glittering release.

Riva and Zian try to spring out of the way, but they don't quite clear the edge of the net. The electric current jolts through their bodies with a searing pain that jabs into me.

The helicopter circles around. Clancy's voice booms from the loudspeaker. "Stay where you are, and we will collect you. There's no need to make this a fight."

My jaw clenches. He's already turned it into a fight himself.

But how the hell are we going to hit back when the shadowbloods with the strongest talents are tangled up in electrified cords?

I shove through the underbrush toward Riva, careful not to expose myself on the path where another net could catch me. She's struggling, trying to claw her way free.

But the moment she jerks one shoulder out from under the twined ropes, another electric shock sizzles through her limbs. Her cry hollows out my gut.

She slumps next to Zian, whose head is lolling with a dazed expression.

I have to help her—I have to help everyone. But what can I do that won't get me shocked and stunned too?

I swivel around, hastily taking stock of who's stayed free of the nets.

Up by the crest, Griffin has pulled back into the shelter of the trees on one side of the path. Celine stands across from him, only about ten feet from where I'm poised, her face lifted toward the two helicopters as they hover in search of a landing spot.

She's obviously not going to be any help. She's the reason the assholes found us.

Ajax and Devon crouch deeper in the jungle beyond Griffin, but neither of them have talents that could destroy or deflect a helicopter. Glancing farther down the path, I spot Andreas several feet behind me with his arms out as if to shield George, who's ended up next to him.

Drey is staring up at the choppers. Then his gaze drops to meet mine, his face taut with strain.

"I can't see any of them to mess with their heads. I can't project memories unless I'm looking at my target."

Maybe it doesn't matter. If the helicopters can't land anywhere nearby, we'll have a chance to make a run for it.

The thought has just passed through my mind when another earth-shaking *boom* reverberates from one of the choppers. With an unsettling creaking sound, several trees topple over farther along the crest of the hill, past Griffin's position.

With another thunderous impact, the same thing happens beyond Celine. She teeters on her feet but spins toward the sound with a smile that looks like relief.

The helicopters descend in unison toward the makeshift landing pads they've apparently created for themselves. My pulse drums frantically in my veins.

The second they're on the ground, who knows what else the guardians will throw at us.

We're running out of time. I have to do *something*.

I've got to use the talents *I* have, however I can.

I haven't formed more of a plan than that before I'm sprinting forward, charging toward Celine.

She brought them here. She's loyal to Clancy.

If I'm going to take back some kind of leverage for us, who better than her?

My tentacles fling forward over my shoulders in anticipation—but before I'm close enough to touch her, Celine flinches.

In the same instant, a rush of thrilling energy smacks into me.

My steps stumble. Did I just suck away some of her life without even touching her?

If my powers work from a distance now… I don't even know how to grapple with the mix of awe and revulsion that rises up at the possibility.

There isn't time to mull it over now. I flick a tentacle in the helicopter's direction but feel nothing at all.

It only worked across a distance of a couple of feet. Still not all that useful in a fight… except as I intended to use it anyway.

But taking a hostage only works if the threat is obvious.

As Celine sways on her feet, I hurtle the last few steps toward Celine and slam my tentacles around her.

One grips her by the throat. The other pins her arms to her sides.

I yank her toward me, staying in view of the closer helicopter that's just touched down but partly sheltered by the trees. I'm not risking the chances that they have some way to fling one of those nets at me even from the ground.

Celine gasps and struggles in my hold. I tighten the tentacle around her neck enough to make it hard for her to speak, holding back the urge to drink in more of the energy my suckers can sense thrumming through her frame.

"Stay still, and we all get out of this," I say in a low voice that's more ragged than I'd like. Even going this far has made me queasy.

She might have betrayed us, but she's really still a kid. I can't totally blame her for being scared after everything she's experienced.

But I can't think of any other way to get us out of this standoff—or at least buy us enough time that one of the others can figure something out.

The roaring whir of the helicopter blades cuts out. I pitch my voice to carry as far as possible.

"Don't come any closer! I'll kill her if you try to take us."

Celine starts to squirm again, and I drop my voice so only she can hear. "They don't want any of us dead. If you decide to go back to them after the rest of us have gotten away, I won't stop you."

The guardians have always avoided any kind of attack that could kill us in the past. We're valuable property, after all.

With so few of us shadowbloods, they wouldn't want to lose any of us completely. Especially not one who's both proven her loyalty to them and shown that her skills have a clear use in the field.

Celine doesn't appear to believe me, though, because she keeps twisting against my hold, forcing me to tense my extra appendages even tighter.

Clancy's voice resonates from his loudspeaker. "I don't think you want to do this, Dominic."

I can only make out the front half of the helicopter from my current position, its windows tinted too dark for me to decipher any figures inside. Even if Andreas joined me, he won't be able to help.

"I don't want you to take us back to the island," I holler back. "You try to grab any of my friends, and you can say goodbye to the rest of your shadowbloods."

He doesn't know what I'm capable of, not really. Sometimes *I'm* not even sure what I might do.

Celine lets out a choking sound. A shudder I do my best to suppress ripples through me.

The guardians have to back off—they have to—

Clancy breaks through my frantic thoughts. "If that's the price you want to pay, it's up to you. It's the six of you who matter the most."

The creak of a hinge and the thump of multiple sets of feet travel through the air. My heart stutters.

He doesn't care. Are the younger shadowbloods really expendable to him?

Celine whimpers in my grasp, a hopeless expression coming over her face. That's obviously how she's taken his words.

She thinks I'm actually going to murder her now.

My gambit wasn't enough. He's calling my bluff—and I'm not sure killing her would do us any good even if I wasn't bluffing.

A tiny whisper in the back of my head asks if maybe I should find out. I've never sapped all the life out of another human being purely for my own satisfaction before.

And this girl has already betrayed us once. Should I give her the chance to do it again?

I recoil from the impulse, yanking back my tentacles as a cold sweat breaks on my back.

No. *No*. I'm not a fucking murderer, no matter what else the guardians made me into.

At the same moment, Griffin steps forward, across the path, where he'll be in view of both helicopters. There's an unnerving intensity in his gaze.

He must have set down his cat sometime before. His arms are empty, one hand pressed close to his side as if he's concealing something against the fabric of his pants.

"Let's stop all the resisting now," he says, cool and even but loud enough for everyone including Clancy to hear him. "You should have known you were never getting away from the guardians. I led you to them before, and now I've led them to you."

I stare at him in bewilderment. But he said—he said it was Celine who signaled them somehow. She *admitted* it.

He was upset with her. She ran to greet them.

And now he's saying—

Celine whirls toward him. "You traitor! You ruined everything."

Fury vibrates through her hoarse voice, and understanding hits me in an icy smack.

Griffin's using his power on her—he's making her angry at him. He's tricking the guardians so they'll trust him and not her?

Or was he using his ability to manipulate her before, when she confessed, and he's been working on a way to get us back to the facility all along?

After everything Griffin's told us and how well I once knew him, my kneejerk reaction is to reject that thought. But I have no idea what his full plan is either way.

I never would have thought he'd have turned on us in the first place.

The only thing I'm sure of is that the guardians are the biggest threat we're facing. I take a step back into the trees, watching for their approach and bracing myself to fend them off if need be, as well as I can.

Celine marches part of the way toward Griffin and stalls there, wavering. "You're such a fucking asshole!"

"I've done what I needed to do to get by," Griffin replies, so calmly it's hard to imagine he could be generating all the rage she's showing at the same time. "Now it's time to go home."

"I don't want to go anywhere with *you*."

Clancy's voice carries through the jungle, unaltered by the loudspeaker this time. He's close.

"Let's keep our tempers cool and think this situation through rationally. We can all go back to the facility. No one will be punished."

Griffin nods as if agreeing with him. "It's for the best for everyone."

Celine lets out a sound that's close to a growl. She snatches a rock off the ground, large enough that she can't totally close her fingers around it.

"All you think about is yourself. You let us go through all this shit, and now you're laughing at us."

My pulse kicks up another notch. Should I try to use my power?

I twist my tentacles, testing the atmosphere around me, but no one's close enough for me to latch on to their energy now. Maybe Griffin will lure Clancy close enough that I can take him down?

But if that's what Griffin intended, it isn't how things go down.

"It was silly of you to think you could ever have things your way," Griffin tells Celine.

She barks out a wordless rasp of fury and launches herself at him with the stone raised.

As she comes, Griffin jerks up his lowered hand. A blade flashes in the sunlight.

He's got a small knife, maybe taken from the hotel kitchen. He's prepared to stab her with it—in what will look like self-defense.

It isn't really, though, it occurs to me with sickening clarity. He's basically reeled her straight toward that blade like a fish hooked on a line.

Is this some kind of revenge for her betrayal? Or—

"Griffin!"

A body hurtles up the path, singe marks darkening pale skin and hair, arms heaving forward.

Jacob managed to break free from the net to race to his twin's protection.

The wallop of his power slams into Celine before Griffin's knife can. Her body whips backward, her neck wrenching to the side with a crack of her spine that rings through the air.

"Jake," Griffin says in a pained tone, his eyes wide with shock.

Jacob stumbles onto his knees. "I couldn't let her…"

Then a stream of electricity crashes into my back, and my brain short-circuits to blackness.

Twenty-Seven

Riva

As the guardians usher us back into the island facility, I steal as many glances at Griffin as I can. My gut has been tangled in queasy knots since I woke up with my wrists cuffed and the clamp around my neck that squashes my throat, braced with my fellow shadowbloods in the back of a helicopter.

Griffin wasn't locked up like that then, and he strides along beside Clancy and the guardians now as if he's one of them. He holds his head high, his gaze steady.

My memories of the guardians' assault on us are blurry, bits and pieces scrambled by the electric jolts of the net that caught me. I saw Griffin claiming that he called Clancy to our spot—I saw Celine fly into a rage and lunge at him.

I believed her when she confessed before. I don't know how he could have provoked those specific details out of her about the girl she saw die and her fear of the "monsters" I might turn to for help.

Is it possible he somehow found the right emotional button to push on to make her admit to a betrayal she hadn't committed? Or was it only in the end he was manipulating her, so he could take credit for that betrayal?

Even if it's the latter, even if he was honest with us every moment before then… why did he do it?

He had a knife ready. I think he'd have killed her, with the excuse of self-defense, if Jacob hadn't thrown himself in there first.

None of it makes sense. All I know is that in the next few frantic seconds, I squirmed in the net, which zapped me hard enough that my vision whited out.

And then there was a prick on the back of my neck, and everything went dark until the helicopter.

The guardians obviously overwhelmed the shadowbloods who escaped the nets. All of us from our group of escapees are cuffed alongside me in our procession—except for Celine, of course.

I don't know what Clancy ordered the others to do with her body. He wouldn't have left it as evidence.

Even though chances are high that she's the one who ruined our chance at freedom, a twinge of guilt runs through my stomach, remembering her frantic expression and her neck snapping with the force of Jacob's power.

She didn't want to be there with us. If I hadn't pushed for all the kids we encountered to come with us, if I'd realized how hesitant she was sooner…

It's too late for that now. One more death that's at least partly on my conscience.

Ahead of me in the line, Jacob sways and shakes his head as if trying to clear it. I think they drugged him like the guys told me the guardians used to after our first escape attempt, to dampen their powers.

They've wrapped a heavy blindfold around Andreas's face so he can't aim projected memories at anyone. He's relying on Dominic to keep him on the right track, a tentacle tucked around his hand like a lead.

I can't see Zian, who's behind me now, but from his glazed eyes on the chopper, I'd bet they drugged him too. There aren't many ways to contain his combination of brawn and monstrous strength.

The cuffs are pretty solid on their own, though. The guardians have had lots of time to experiment with what can hold us shadowbloods back. I can't feel the effects of any drug, but I can tell from my furtive tests that I wouldn't be able to snap the chain.

Clancy stops partway down the front hall, just past the door to the cafeteria, and the rest of the procession halts with him. An older man stands there, looking over the line of us captives with a dour expression that fits perfectly with his sagging features and posture.

Despite the sense of deflation he gives off, his voice comes out crisp and firm. "This is all of them, then?"

Clancy holds his posture with easy certainty, as if he isn't the slightest bit ruffled by the events of the past couple of days. "We lost one of the second generation. Not an especially valuable talent."

The older man grunts, his frown deepening. "We'll talk about it later. You'd better get them shut away before they flee on you again."

"If they do, we'll simply round them up like we did this time," Clancy says without showing a hint of concern.

I grit my teeth at his dismissiveness. He *wouldn't* have rounded us up if Celine—or Griffin—hadn't signaled him.

But what are the chances we'll get another opportunity as good as the one we just lost? He'll have figured out that we triggered the emergency system—and he'll have adjusted it to prevent the same gambit.

Every helicopter delivery will be heavily guarded from now on, no doubt.

We had our chance, by far the best chance we were ever going to get, and it's been wrenched from our grasp.

The guardians march us on down the hallway, pausing here and there to direct one kid or another into their rooms. I think we've passed mine, although it's a little hard to tell when the rocky walls look so similar throughout the facility.

My nerves prickle with uneasiness when the last of the younger shadowbloods, a drooping Lindsay, disappears behind her thudding door.

It's just the six of us "Firsts" now. Does Clancy have something else in mind for us?

Most of the guardians have drifted off during our walk. Only four remain with Clancy, two up ahead with him and Griffin and two others bringing up the rear.

They all grip the gun-like weapons that can shoot streams of electricity like something out of that ghost-capturing movie we all watched years ago. Although the sizzling bolts zap our bodies rather than our spirits.

The end result is the same—trapped and under their control.

I never expected to relate to the ghosts.

Clancy escorts us into a slightly larger room with a row of five chairs spaced wide apart along the middle of the space. As the guardians lead each of us to a chair, they position themselves between us.

Our collaborating is always what Clancy's been most worried about. He's not taking any chances.

Will he let us even be in the same room together again after this?

My worries form a pulsing ache in my stomach. I swallow against the collar and wince at the choking sensation.

Clancy strides to the front of the room where a large screen about five feet across hangs on the wall. He picks up a control from a small metal side table and paces past the screen.

Griffin hangs back by the side table, watching. His face remains as blank as it was during our first reunion here.

I can't tell if he's still feeling anything at all.

Even if his ploy with Celine was meant to help us, could the chaos of the fight have screwed up the progress he's made? Sent him back into his closed-off state, every flicker of emotion automatically dismissed?

Clancy clicks a button, and the screen lights up, though it's only a flat, pale gray at the moment. He swivels to face the five of us.

"You have not abided by the terms of our agreement. I've offered you the opportunity to do something incredibly constructive with your powers while learning how to use them in the best possible ways, and you threw that generosity in my face."

The choke-collar suppresses my derisive laugh.

Generosity? He was using us to fill his bank account.

No awareness of his hypocrisy shows in Clancy's expression. He taps the controller lightly against his thigh, considering all of us like a professor contemplating the expulsion of a bunch of disruptive students.

"You must see now how impossible striking out on your own is," he goes on, with a condescending edge that raises my hackles even more. "You were never meant to have normal lives. You *aren't* normal. But if we work together, you can have something better than anyone else in the Guardianship would be willing to offer you."

Does he expect a response?

Jacob and Zian stare at him dully. Andreas can't see him at all.

Dominic sits in the chair next to me, a shiver running through his tentacles and his mouth set in a flat line. His gaze darts around the room, but I'm not sure what he's looking for.

And with my voice cut off, I can't answer even if I wanted to.

Clancy squares his shoulders with an imperious air. "I'm hoping that you've learned your lesson, and we can move forward as I planned. But I can't allow more diversions. I have a mission that some of you will be sent on, one you should want to see fulfilled as much as I do. You can accept that challenge with full cooperation, or I'll assign you to continued testing until we find an effective way of harnessing your powers and ensuring your compliance."

That doesn't sound ominous at all. I contain a shiver of my own.

Jacob manages to cock his head with a trace of alertness. But there's still a faint slur in his voice from the drugs. "What mission?"

Clancy brings up an image on the screen—a video, panning through a dusty village of ramshackle huts and a few cars that look at least three decades out of date. The only detail giving away the modern time period is the high-tech army tank standing off to the side in the first shot.

The scene is mostly brown and gray except for the blotches of deepening red that scatter the ground… and the bodies slumped there. The camera takes in a few dozen corpses, fresh enough that blood still seeps from some of their wounds.

Men. Women. Children. All of them dressed in simple tees or blouses, ratty jeans or canvas slacks.

Despite my resistance to anything Clancy wants to show us, my chest clenches up in horror.

Clancy motions toward the video. "The national government of the country where this slaughter took place has been dealing with a large group of hostile insurgents for several years. The group's current MO is to hold an entire rural village hostage, killing the civilians one by one until the government complies with their demands. When the military has attempted to intervene, the insurgents use the villagers as shields and have mostly escaped unscathed… while leaving no survivors behind."

He rests his cool gaze on us. "Government officials heard of my services and reached out to me. They expect based on past behavior patterns that the terrorists will strike again within a week. To ensure the villagers' safety and push back against the insurgents to discourage or even prevent future attacks, they need a team with skills beyond their own."

And that's where he wants us to come in.

The worst part is that the sight of the decimated village tugs at my heart. I *would* want to protect people like that if my powers could shield them.

But how can we trust anything Clancy says now? Who knows what other ulterior motives he could have?

Those officials are probably offering him a huge fee, for one thing.

Does it really matter, though? Would I rather go back to being prodded and tested, knowing I let a bunch of innocent people die that I could have saved, just to spite him?

That's exactly the dilemma Clancy wants us to face.

He crosses his arms over his chest, his blue eyes turning penetrating. "You'll need to agree to take on this mission without knowing which of you will actually be sent out. And understanding that if you agree and you sabotage the assignment, your friends *will* suffer for it. There are lengths I'd have preferred not to go to, but if that's what's necessary for you to respect the responsibility you're being given, so be it."

My skin turns clammy beneath my shirt.

Of course, he's made it clear that if we *don't* agree, we'll all be tormented regardless.

We've gotten out of every tight spot we've found ourselves in before now… but my scrambling mind can't identify a single shimmer of hope.

Clancy nods to the guardians around us. "I'm sending you back to your rooms to recover and think on it. Any harm that you inflict on my people will be inflicted on yours twice over, so be careful how you use your powers. You have twenty-four hours to make a decision. Choose wisely."

With a rasp of his heel, he turns his back on us.

TWENTY-EIGHT

Andreas

At the sight of Riva sitting at the far end of the cafeteria, my heart just about leaps out of my chest.

I haven't crossed paths with any of my fellow Firsts since Clancy gave us his little presentation two days ago, even though yesterday I agreed to go along with his mission.

The others must have too. I can't imagine any of them consigning themselves to total isolation and torture instead.

At least this way we might have some wiggle room to decide our fate.

But I was starting to think he wasn't going to let us mingle with each other at all anymore. Not on the island, anyway.

As I walk over, holding myself back from sprinting to her side in case that would provoke the guardians, Riva glances up from her plate and sees me. The brightening of her face washes away the stress of the past two days.

At the same time, my stomach dips. I glance around the room, noting the two guardians in their usual posts near the door.

Nothing about the cafeteria looks different. I can't believe that Clancy is offering us this opportunity to talk out of the goodness of his heart, though.

The fact that he's letting it happen means it could benefit him in some way. He's got to be monitoring us even more closely than he was before.

We'll have to watch every word so carefully. Not let a single hint of mutiny show.

A wobble of doubt runs through my pulse, and there's an instant when I almost avoid Riva's table altogether, as desperately as I want to bask in her presence. What if I'm misjudging the situation even with my sense of caution?

Wouldn't it look more suspicious if I *don't* even talk to her? Any problems we had in the past were nothing to do with things I said.

I shoot her a smile and a nod, passing by, and quickly spoon chili onto my plate from a tureen. The hearty, spicy scent does nothing to settle my nerves as I sit down across from her.

"It's good to see you."

Riva smiles back at me, but the corners of her mouth stay tight. "Same. You've been okay?"

She's taking the same careful approach I meant to. Good.

"Yeah." I dig my fork in among the beans and bits of ground beef. "I haven't seen anyone except the younger shadowbloods until now."

"Me neither." She takes a bite from her mostly cleaned plate and scans the room warily. "I guess Clancy decided *everyone* here was better off if we still had some contact."

"Everyone" as in him too. Yep, she's definitely come to the same conclusions about his motivations as I have.

"Wouldn't want morale to dip too low," I say with forced wryness.

Riva's head droops. She tears a chunk off her roll but then just holds the piece rather than bringing it to her mouth.

Then she drags in a breath. "I guess we're stuck with this place. Might as well make the best of it."

The strain in her voice and the quiver of anguish that touches my chest through my mark fill in the blanks in her words. She's afraid of how true those statements might be.

A similar hopelessness swells inside me. I've been thinking it over since the moment I regained consciousness on the helicopter, heading back here—how could we pull off another escape?

No brilliant plans have occurred to me. Or even mediocre plans, for that matter.

Every spark of an idea that lights in my mind sputters out before I follow it more than a couple of steps from its instigation.

Clancy has too much power. He'll have safeguarded all the weaknesses of the facility that we've discovered.

And the very fact of being on an island with little means to leave it limits our options to barely any.

"We'll make the best of it," I agree, attempting to push a little energy into the words. A nudge of encouragement that if there is an opportunity to turn this situation around, we'll find it.

Riva aims another smile at me, smaller but softer, so I think I've succeeded. She pops the bit of roll into her mouth and chews thoughtfully. "Have you found out anything more from Clancy about his mission or whatever else he's working on?"

Her wording and her tone give me the sense that she doesn't mean finding out only by conventional means. She thinks I might have learned something interesting from his memories.

But I haven't dared to sneak a peek inside the facility leader's head since we've gotten back. I've only seen him briefly anyway, when he came to collect my answer yesterday.

I shake my head. "No. He hasn't come around to talk to me."

She hums to herself, her gaze going momentarily distant. "I wondered a little about the older man from the Guardianship who talked to him when we got back. It sounded like he might have some say in the missions or other things." She pauses. "I guess you didn't even see him to recognize him—they had your eyes covered at that point."

"I didn't." But she's caught my interest. I did hear a fragment of conversation between Clancy and a gravelly voice I didn't recognize.

Is there still someone else who has authority over Clancy himself? Could there be a weakness we could exploit not in the facility's construction but in the hierarchy of the guardians?

"I'm not sure I could describe him all that well," Riva goes on in a casual tone. "I've never been as good at bringing memories to life as you are."

She flicks her gaze toward me, a meaningful look, and understanding snaps into place. If I wanted to search the other guardians' memories for this man, I could get a solid impression of him by looking inside *her* mind first.

My spirits lift, but the rest of me balks with a twinge of uneasiness. I obviously don't do a good enough job suppressing my discomfort, because Riva's brow knits with concern. "What's the matter?"

"I..." I grapple with the words and decide that it doesn't matter if I express this regret. The past has already happened—Clancy can't expect me to feel *happy* about how our escape fell apart.

Swallowing thickly, I meet Riva's gaze. "It's been bothering me that I didn't figure out what was going on with Griffin in time. I *should* have been able to pick up on these things—I'm supposed to be good at reading people in all kinds of ways—but I totally missed something so important…"

The previous time we were caught, I missed recognizing that Griffin was there at all, pretending to be Jacob. This time, I missed what he'd picked up on: that Celine wasn't actually happy about gaining her freedom.

That she was looking for opportunities to signal the guardians and screw the rest of us over.

I'd been searching *his* memories when I got the chance, checking for any sign that his efforts to help us weren't genuine. My guilt about my previous lapse made me extra conscientious… but in the wrong way.

I know that his act in the end, when they caught us, really was an act. Claiming he'd called them in was the first lie he told through the whole trek.

But I was so focused on confirming his loyalty, it didn't even occur to me to worry about the younger shadowbloods. I got misdirected all over again, and now I can only blame myself.

If I'd checked the kids earlier, if I'd noticed the signs of Celine's discomfort, maybe we could have stopped her before she alerted Clancy. Maybe we'd have made it to the city, however things would have played out from there.

Riva doesn't challenge my implying that Griffin was the one who betrayed us—for all I know, she thinks it's actually possible. "It was a chaotic situation, and we were dealing with a lot. We all had the chance to notice that something was off, and none of us did. You can't take the responsibility."

That's not what I'm really stewing over, though. I'm afraid that if I try to get us out of this mess again, I'll miss yet another crucial detail.

But as Riva gazes back at me with the taint of sorrow in her bright brown eyes, a renewed sense of resolve grips my chest.

It's better to try than to give up, right? We definitely aren't getting anywhere if we all throw up our hands and roll over.

I want to turn the sadness in Riva's expression into hope.

I reach out to take her hand, leaning closer as if with a lover's intent.

But really it's to make it harder for any outside party to spot the ruddy gleam I know comes into my eyes as I slip into her memories.

She doesn't have all that many of Clancy, considering we've only been here for a matter of weeks and his appearances have been sporadic. I flit through the images that I know don't match our arrival yesterday, wincing inwardly at a glimpse of a bedroom where Zian crouches with obvious agitation in a corner.

There. We're walking down the main hall in a line, Clancy in the lead, me with the blindfold I've only worn one other time—when I first woke up in the facility.

I linger in the recollection, focusing as Riva did on the grim white-haired man Clancy pauses to talk to. Etching his doughy features in my own memory.

To look for him again, I don't have to know his name. I only need a clear sense of his presence.

When I'm sure I've absorbed every detail, I pull back out of Riva's skull, squeezing her fingers as I do. She returns the gesture, studying me.

"We still have each other," I say. "That's what's most important."

And we'll keep working with each other to get away from Clancy. Let her hear that underlying message, the one I don't dare say out loud.

Clancy makes no further appearances throughout the rest of that day and the next. When I'm ushered into my stone-walled bedroom in the evening, my stomach churns with impatient tension.

He expected to be sending us on his new mission within a week. We're almost halfway through.

How can I get a glimpse inside his mind without him realizing that I'm up to something? If he catches me at it, I have no idea how he'll punish me… or the others, knowing their torment will hurt me more.

I sprawl on my bed and stew on the problem, running through possibility after possibility for both bringing him to me and ensuring he's otherwise occupied enough that I can get a good fix on his memories. Maybe I'm not giving up, but I still have to make sure I consider every angle if I'm going to do this right.

It must be at least a couple of hours before an inspiration strikes that I don't immediately dismiss. I turn the idea over, poking and prodding at it.

It's by far the best I've thought of, but that doesn't mean it's *good.*

Fuck, I wish I could talk to Dominic for his thoughtful insight, or even Jacob with his incisive logic.

Even if I could see them, I wouldn't be able to talk about this, though. So it comes down to me.

I take a few slow, deep breaths, summoning the image of Riva's face in my mind. Reminding myself of why it's so important that I get this done.

Then I wrap my arm around my abdomen and double over on the bed.

A fake groan spills from my mouth. I twist and shudder as if in the grip of a wave of nausea.

The play-acting isn't enough. I need a blast of reality to really sell the performance.

I've told my friends dozens of stories from the minds I've dipped into over the years, across our early missions. Always picking the amusing or intriguing.

But there've been darker memories I've uncovered, that I never wanted to think about myself, let alone inflict on anyone else. Moments of the violence and horror humans are just as capable of as monsters.

They linger on in the back of my head where I've buried them as deep as I can. I dredge up one of the worst now and hug my belly tighter.

Gore. Gurgled cries. Slashes of a knife. A spray of blood, and organs jumbling—

I lurch right over the side of the bed to vomit onto the floor. The acid sears my throat as I gag and sputter.

The guardians have been watching me, because of course they have. I've barely had time to let out another groan when the door to my room hisses open.

Two guardians lift me onto a rolling hospital-style cot, murmuring urgently to each other as they do. I keep my eyes closed and jerk one way and another as if in the throes of internal agony.

They hurry me to a room that holds brighter lights and a woman who speaks in puzzled tones as she takes my temperature and a blood sample. I figured they'd have a doctor on staff somewhere in this place.

But shadowbloods don't generally get sick. Our enhanced bodies come with hyperactive healing skills. I can't remember ever having more than a brief sniffle growing up.

Clancy will have to come—out of concern for his "resources" if nothing else—won't he?

I lie there through a couple more spells of gagging and mumbled answers to the doctor's questions. My heart gradually sinks.

I could have miscalculated. Maybe I haven't accomplished anything beyond giving myself a stomachache.

Then brisk footsteps rap outside. The leader of the facility strides into the room—and he's brought a bonus I hadn't even let myself hope for.

Through my lowered eyelashes, I see Dominic trailing behind Clancy, my friend's mouth tight with worry.

"See if you can sense any internal injuries," Clancy orders him.

Dominic comes up beside me and rests his tentacles gently on the bare skin of my wrist and neck. I crack my eyes open just enough to make out Clancy behind him—turned mostly away from me in hushed conference with the doctor.

He's let down his guard. He doesn't suspect anything from me. Perfect.

I give Dominic's hand a light tap, the tiniest of nudges to the left so he'll completely block the doctor's view of my face if she happens to glance our way. That's all it takes.

The connection we each share with Riva might be marked on our skin, but the five of us—no, the *six* of us—all know each other down to our bones. Deeper than I think Clancy can even conceive of.

Dom's eyebrows rise just a smidge. He shifts over without a word.

Keeping my eyelids low, I stare at the back of Clancy's head—and tumble into it.

I hold the image of the man Riva saw at the front of my thoughts and prod the whirl of Clancy's past impressions with it. One after another, memories float to the surface of him speaking to that older man: in a video chat, in person, on the phone.

In every conversation, tension runs through Clancy's body. He keeps his voice smooth, but I can feel the urge in his throat to become terser.

He calls the other man Richmond. And Richmond has a lot of ideas about how Clancy should be running things, often referring to "the board" of the Guardianship that it sounds like he speaks for.

I push harder, faster, for a snippet of anything relevant to our current situation. And then I slide into a vision of Clancy's cave-like office here, Richmond wearing the same clothes Riva saw three days ago.

"Even with all your precautions, thirteen of them made it right off the island," Richmond is saying in a patronizing tone. "Including the six that are by far the most valuable."

Clancy stands stiffly behind his desk. "I retrieved all of them before there was any trouble."

Richmond snorts. "Any trouble other than two deaths and a whole lot of manpower expended. Look, the board has given you the leeway to try your approach, but a misstep like this calls the whole endeavor into question. There's been talk of superseding your right to direct the Guardianship. You know you'd never have taken it at all if Balthazar hadn't vanished on us."

Balthazar? My focus momentarily wavers, but then I remember the conversation Riva related to the rest of us, asking Clancy about the three founding families of the Guardianship.

He told her that one of the three founders had pulled back from the guardians. I have to guess that's who Richmond means.

At the implied threat, Clancy's spine goes even more rigid. Richmond is purposefully not mentioning his own opinion, but I can taste in his tone that he's been a vocal participant in the "talking" he mentioned.

"I've just landed a major contract," Clancy says quickly. "Now that I have a better idea of how the shadowbloods operate, I'll be able to keep them in line—and show just how much I can accomplish with them. You have to give me the chance to prove it."

Richmond rubs his fleshy chin. "I'll discuss the matter with the others. You can be sure we'll be watching closely. If you—"

A tug of my arm brings me back to the present. Dominic is leaning over me, his gaze intent.

"Thank you," he says over his shoulder.

Clancy is approaching, carrying a glass of water. Through my cluttered awareness, I piece together what must have happened: Clancy was going to come over earlier, but Dominic diverted him for long enough to snap me out of my power's daze.

Dom pats my shoulder. "Can you sit up?"

I push myself upright with a sway to sell my performance and sip the water. Clancy inspects me with his penetrating gaze.

"The best we can determine, something you ate must have disagreed with you that's now out of your system," he says in a clipped tone. "There's no sign of illness or internal damage. You can sleep here for the night while we get your room cleaned."

I nod my thanks and lie back down as he escorts Dominic out of the room. My thoughts keep buzzing, louder than the hum of the overhead lights.

Clancy is in danger of losing his grand dream. He's got a lot riding on this upcoming mission.

I don't know what we can do with that yet, but it gives us a foothold. If he's desperate, then we have leverage.

But who the hell can I tell that to without giving any budding scheme we could form away? I can't plan a coup and pull it off all by myself.

I roll onto my side on the thin cot mattress, closing my eyes again. The answer comes to me like a ghost rising from the grave.

Griffin. Griffin is at the middle of this mess, tangled between Clancy's objectives and ours.

He's just proven his loyalty to the guardians—in Clancy's eyes, anyway.

I don't know what the others think, but I've looked inside our former friend's head. I've followed the reasoning in his words and the cadence of his voice.

He understands us just as well as we do each other. He's with us.

And now he's the only one I can turn to.

Twenty-Nine

Riva

I hear Nadia before I see her—her dry laugh carrying from between the trees by the row of obstacle courses. I recognize it, but there's a dull edge to it that wasn't there before.

It's harder to spot her than I expect. I find her standing with one of the other older teen shadowbloods and Ajax near the climbing course, dressed in black sweats and a dark gray tee that blend with the shadows between the trees.

Before I've even spoken to her, my heart sinks.

The three of them glance over at me as I emerge into the clearing by the first of the rope ladders. I nod to them all, my gaze holding Nadia's.

"Hey. No neon today?"

She rubs her toned arms self-consciously. "I guess I just haven't been feeling all that bright lately."

Her mouth tilts into a half-smile, but I can't find even a hint of good humor in it. If my heart was heavy before, now it feels like it's morphed into a lump of lead.

Ajax runs his hand over the sheen of stubble on his dark scalp, but he can't seem to think of anything to say at all. Only the third kid, the one who wasn't part of our escape, shows any energy.

He claps his hands together. "Come on! Are we going to climb or what?"

The form of a guardian stirs farther away along the edge of the clearing, with a clearing of her throat. "This is time for training, not talking."

I hold back a bitter snort. When have they ever given us much time to talk—to do anything other than train and bodily necessities like eat?

The guy who clapped his hands grasps the ladder, and Nadia and Ajax shuffle into line behind him automatically. The droop of Nadia's shoulders and sluggishness of Ajax's movements send a jabbing sensation through my gut.

I touch Nadia's arm. "Your brightness got us through a lot. Remember that." And Ajax's shoulder. "You heard things the rest of us couldn't."

I don't know how well my attempt at raising their spirits lands. Nadia only dips her head, and the smile Ajax shoots at me is fleeting. The energy in the clearing remains downcast.

What else can I say?

A weird sense of homesickness winds through me, missing the brief days we had our freedom. Not because I loved tramping through the jungle with not much more than crackers to eat, but because we did all help each other.

It's not just the six Firsts who can accomplish a lot together. All of us shadowbloods make an amazing team.

When we have the chance.

As I watch Nadia and then Ajax scale the ladder with obvious reluctance, my heart seems to plummet all the way to the ground.

As difficult as our trek on the mainland was, it was better than this. We deserve to be free.

We aren't the tools Clancy sees us as or the experimental property we are to most of the other guardians. We're *people*—we shouldn't be owned by anyone.

We sure as hell don't owe the Guardianship anything after the hell we've already been through at their hands.

Who would Nadia and Ajax and all the others be if they could simply… *be*? Have the space and peace to explore what a regular human life could look like, on their terms?

I want to give them that, so fucking badly. But I don't have a clue how.

I'm just reaching for the ladder myself—not that I really want to go through the course, but I've got to do something to look like a participant and not a rebel—when the underbrush rustles behind me. "Riva?"

My pulse hiccups before I even glance back. It's Griffin's voice, soft and even.

As I turn around, he comes to a stop at the end of the path.

It's hard to imagine that I confused him with his twin just weeks ago. All I can see now are the ways they differ—the shagginess of Griffin's slightly longer blond hair in contrast with Jacob's smoothness, the gentler lines of his face.

The distance in his eyes, as if the whole sky really is contained in their blue irises.

I clamp down on the urge to hug myself. "What's up?"

His mouth forms a small smile. "I was hoping we could spend a little time together. We haven't seen each other since… everything. There are some things I'd like to explain."

Searching his gaze, I grapple with my response. I'm pretty sure he did what he did to protect the rest of us, not because he was the real traitor among us. But not one hundred percent sure.

And either way, I'm *supposed* to believe he betrayed us. What reaction would the guardians expect to see to keep up that ruse?

I raise one shoulder in a partial shrug. "I'm not interested in hearing your explanations."

He holds out his hand. "Please. For old time's sake?"

Have I resisted enough to sell my wariness? I'm also supposed to be trying to cooperate with the new status quo, to avoid me or the other guys getting punished.

I settle for ignoring his hand, as much as I'd like to take it, but stepping toward him. "Fine. What did you have in mind?"

Griffin's expression twitches as he lowers his hand, a trace of discomfort crossing it that I wouldn't have expected to see even a week ago. The feelings that've woken up inside him haven't vanished, then.

He motions for me to follow him and doesn't speak again until we're partway along the narrow path. "You seemed to enjoy tossing the knives during our last meeting. Clancy agreed to give us private use of the shooting range."

I press my hand to my mouth to contain a sputter of laughter. "And you're not worried you'll end up with a bullet in you?"

Griffin's tone lightens—just slightly, but any break from his new typical monotone is a relief to hear. "You managed not to stab me last time, so I think my chances are good."

We cross the stone bridge over the thin but deep river that courses away from the waterfall and climb the damp stone steps to the hidden entrance. The cool spray flecks my skin, sharp against the tropical heat.

Just inside the entrance to the shooting range, with the water rushing down inches away, Griffin stops me with a careful grasp of my wrist. He leans in so I can hear him over the warble of the falls.

"We aren't being directly monitored here. Clancy went along with a lot of concessions… because he thinks I'm trying to get him the data he wants."

He pushes up one sleeve to reveal a band like the ones the guardians made Zian and me wear—in the hopes of monitoring the forming of our marked connection.

My stomach clenches. "I—"

"It's okay," Griffin murmurs. He takes my hand, interlacing our fingers, and lets out a sigh that speaks of days of bottled tension releasing. "I wouldn't want to 'help' him like that anyway. It just buys us a little privacy. He said it only records physiological data, not voices, but I thought we should be extra careful."

Hence talking by the waterfall. I nod.

Griffin's head dips closer, the side of his face grazing mine. "I'm sorry. This isn't—I didn't want us to end up back here. I don't know…"

He trails off, but the anguish in his words is unmistakable. Any lingering doubts I felt disintegrate.

I ease closer to him, slipping my arm around his back in a loose embrace. The crisply airy scent that clings to him fills my lungs and tingles through the shadows in my blood.

"Why didn't you tell us you were worried about Celine?"

Griffin exhales raggedly. "I couldn't tell if there was really something to be worried about or if I was misreading her. It wasn't anything obvious. Just here and there, especially when we were in the helicopter, I got flickers of emotion from her that felt upset, or defiant, in ways that didn't match everyone else. I didn't want to accuse her of anything when I had no idea what was actually going on with her."

"You were sure in the end, though."

"Yeah." He swallows audibly. "She was so relieved—*happy*—when she heard the choppers coming for us. And a little triumphant. It was obvious then that she'd done something… I think she'd brought a device that would send out a location, but one that couldn't be set up properly if she was trying to carry it on her. I was watching her pretty carefully before Zian pulled us away."

I have a vague memory of Celine darting out of sight in the middle of our rush out of the facility. She could have grabbed something then.

But I also remember what she said to me when she acknowledged her betrayal. "It might not have been you stopping her before. It's possible she wasn't totally sure if she should use it or not… until after I admitted that we might turn to the shadowkind for help."

"Either way…" I feel Griffin's wince in the movement of his features next to mine. "I didn't want her dead. It was just—in the moment, when they'd arrived and they'd already incapacitated most of you, and Dominic's strategy didn't work—all I could think was that the guardians were going to take us back either way. And the only way I'd be able to fix things was if Clancy believed I was still on his side."

"And he wouldn't have believed that if Celine was alive to tell him she'd signaled them," I fill in.

"But maybe I was wrong. Maybe there was some way we could have still escaped. It was hard to see clearly with my feelings and my ideas all jumbled together—I'm not used to sorting through them anymore. I thought I saw our best chance, so I took it, because I thought I had to, but I can't say that was right."

A tremor runs through his lanky frame. "I'm going to get better. I'll get used to balancing both again. Andreas managed to arrange to see me yesterday—he's found out a few things—I have some ideas for using this mission to turn things back in our favor."

Hope flutters up through my chest. "What?"

"I'll have to see what I can pull off. Clancy might believe I'm standing with him, but that doesn't mean he listens to me all that much." Griffin pauses. "I don't think we can end this while *he's* still alive, though."

I absorb that statement with only the faintest twinge of uneasiness.

The current head of the guardians is willing to torture us to bend us to his will. Why should we give a shit about his well-being?

"Whatever you figure out, let me know as much as you can," I tell him, my nerves thrumming with the possibility of a new plan within reach.

"I'll do my best. He seems to still trust me, but he's being even more cautious with the rest of you." Griffin brushes a tentative kiss to my forehead that lights up my nerves in a totally different way and then eases back. "We should probably do a little shooting so he doesn't wonder why we'd have skipped that part completely."

I cock my head. "A chance for me to let out my aggression before you start your supposed seduction."

Griffin chuckles, but his cheeks flush at the same time. "Something like that."

Farther into the cave, I pick a pistol off the rack somewhat at random, set a pair of earmuffs in place, and let out a few rounds at one of the targets. Griffin takes a more measured approach, selecting his gun with care and then firing each shot with a moment of contemplation in between.

Even so, my bullseyes end up tattered while his shots dapple the two inner rings more haphazardly.

His mouth twists as he studies the result. "Blasting things apart was never something I took to naturally."

"We all have our own talents," I say, with a fond smile to show I think that's a good thing.

He reloads his gun and then gazes down at it. "Do you want to keep going?"

I consider my new target and wrinkle my nose. "I think I've worked through all my urge to shoot things. You're definitely safe now."

Griffin laughs. "Then maybe we could talk a little more? If there's anything else you'd want to ask me to feel better about how things went down, you can go ahead."

I recognize his phrasing as being for the benefit of any guardians listening in. "Yeah. I'm ready to hear you out."

We set aside our guns and earmuffs before meandering back to the waterfall. Griffin turns to me, setting one hand on my waist with his thumb stroking up over the bare skin beneath my tee.

"I— Can I just hold you for a bit?" he murmurs. "I never feel as much like myself as when we're touching."

Affection swells inside me so abruptly I lose my breath. "Yeah, of course."

He lowers his head next to mine again until we're cheek to cheek, sliding his arm around me so his whole forearm rests against my lower back where my tee has ridden up. His other hand traces along my arm to align them side by side, his fingers loosely cupping my elbow.

His warmth wraps around me, and every inch of my skin tingles with his closeness.

A breath shudders out of him as if he's found some peace in me that he's been missing for ages. He hugs me a little tighter.

"I missed you so much. All that time before… I didn't even know how much I did because I couldn't *feel* it—but it was all there underneath, and now all that pent-up loss is hitting me."

Tears well behind my eyes. "I missed you too. Every single day."

"I want to be everything I should have been before. I want to give you what you really needed. I don't know—I don't know if I'll ever be totally back to normal, but I'm going to try."

I choke up at the rawness of his voice. "I know you are. You've already done a lot. We've all made mistakes."

We've all had to do things we'd rather not have done in the fight for our freedom. I can't blame Griffin for the life he meant to take without condemning the rest of us dozens of times over.

Griffin's fingertips trace a gentle circle on my back. "My moonbeam, lighting the way for me."

Suddenly the tears that welled up before are flooding my eyes. I blink hard and turn my head to seek out Griffin's mouth.

Our lips collide with a rush of heated breath. He kisses me tenderly at first and then harder, as if he's pouring himself into the embrace.

As if he's offering himself up to me in every way he can, showing me I've got all of him.

Desire flares low in my belly. I wrap my arms around him, and he nudges us backward with a stifled groan.

My shoulders press against the rock wall of the hall. The need blazing through me sears away the brief chill of the damp surface.

I force myself to pull back a few inches, to gaze up into Griffin's face. He stares down at me with a wildness in his expression that I've never seen before, here or in the past.

The storm of adoration and hunger in his brilliant eyes unravels me. I'm bringing him back to his old self with every touch, every embrace.

Every brush of skin against skin.

I want more. I want to see every bit of the boy I lost surfacing through the frightening emptiness of the guardians' torture.

My hand rises to his cheek. My voice comes out in a whisper. "How much would you like to feel right now?"

Griffin wets his lips, the intensity in his gaze only deepening. "Everything I can."

I reach for the hem of his shirt and tug. Griffin lifts his arms to help me peel it off him, peering at me avidly.

When I reach for my own tee, his chest hitches. "Riva…"

"We won't give him what he's looking for," I say, tipping my head toward one of the bands that circle his upper arms. "There's so much else we can do."

For a second, Griffin's expression shifts with a trace of what might be fear. I hesitate, knowing the awakening of his emotions has come with a heap of pain.

Then he sets his hands over mine, and we strip off my shirt together.

Griffin lets out a low sound from deep in his throat and bows his head to kiss my shoulder. I slip one arm around his leanly muscled back and tangle my fingers in his rumpled hair.

Everywhere our chests touch, bliss sparks. The dark essence twined through my body roars louder than the waterfall.

This man is meant for me, and I am meant for him. Just as much as the others.

Maybe it makes sense that I lost him first and found him last.

I yank Griffin's mouth back to mine. He trails his fingers along my spine and around my waist.

They pause at the band of my sports bra. I nip his lower lip between my teeth, reveling in his stuttered breath, and yank that off too so I'm completely bare from the waist up.

Griffin traces the soft ridges of my abdomen up to the curves of my breasts. He curls his fingers around the slopes carefully.

I've never seen anything as miraculous as the interplay of tender devotion and scorching lust etched across his features.

"I don't—I don't know exactly what I'm doing," he admits haltingly. "I've never—I imagined, before, but that's all. But I can feel what makes you feel good."

It hadn't occurred to me that he'd have even less idea about sex than the other guys. Of course the guardians wouldn't have exposed him to provocative videos and encouraged that kind of release while they were attempting to erase every emotion from him.

They didn't have to worry about giving him an outlet for his urges because they were stealing his entire capacity for desire.

"Your approach seems to be working just fine," I reassure him. "We've all been figuring it out as we go."

Something inside us calls to each other—directs our desire toward completion. I can already tell that the hardest part won't be enjoying this interlude but avoiding giving in to the hunger to fully consummate our connection.

Griffin kisses me again, teasing our mouths against each other until he finds just the right angle to press harder. When I whimper against his lips, he starts caressing my breasts.

He tests every bit of that terrain with his palms, his fingers, his thumbs. Stroking softer and harder, back and forth and in quickening circles.

When he catches one nipple between two of his fingers with a swift squeeze, the moan that tumbles from my lips is echoed by his matching groan. He repeats the gesture, kissing me harder as if drinking down the pleasure he's conjuring in my body.

My hips rock toward him of their own accord. Griffin drops one hand to trace the curve of my hip.

His voice comes out in a ragged murmur. "You need more. But we can't—"

He cuts himself off as if coming to a decision on his own—and hefts me against him braced between his body and the passage wall. The rough stone digs into my back, probably leaving a dimpled impression, but I can't find it in me to care when I'm melded this tightly with the man I've loved for so long.

As my legs splay around him, our groins locking together through our clothes, a different sort of need grips me.

I kiss him again and hold my face close to his. "I love you."

The second the words come out, I feel abruptly sheepish. "But you already know that, don't you? You always knew."

Griffin nuzzles the side of my face, his breath washing over me in its own caress. "This is the first time I've gotten to hear you say it out loud. I—I love you too. I don't think I even know how much yet. The feeling just keeps growing."

I close my eyes against a renewed rush of tears, bittersweet. The joy of being back with him; the pain of knowing how trapped we still are.

The darkness inside spurs me on, desperate for the merging I'm going to refuse it. I grind against the erection straining at Griffin's pants, and he muffles a groan in my hair.

We can't have that ultimate fusion yet. I'm not sure either of us is quite ready for it anyway, regardless of what ideas our bodies might have.

But we can still claim a different kind of satisfaction.

My fingertips skate across Griffin's back. He works over one breast with an increasingly confident hand as he keeps me balanced with the other.

We buck against each other through frantic kisses. The friction against my pussy floods me with waves of giddy heat.

And Griffin can sense every swell of delight. He adjusts his angle by increments, finding just the spot to send me spiraling higher.

Oh, God, to actually *fuck* this man—

I bury that thought under the rising whirlwind of bliss. We rut and groan and devour each other, my heart drumming out a desperate rhythm.

My essence screams out for him—and my release crashes over me. I quake in Griffin's embrace, biting his lip hard enough to draw blood.

Griffin lets out a growl low in his throat, his hips still bucking. Then his shoulders stiffen.

A final groan reverberates from his lungs. He clutches me to him, mumbling a litany of devotion by my ear.

"Riva. Love you. Love you. Moonbeam."

We stay clasped together for a few minutes, simply breathing in tandem. I don't want to let him go.

But Griffin draws back with an embarrassed glance at the wet splotch that's formed on his pants. "Well, that's… a bit of a mess."

His uncertainty only intensifies the love humming through my chest. I smile up at him. "Good thing we have this handy river to wash off in, huh?"

His gaze catches mine. He leans in again to bring our foreheads together.

"It is good. It's all good. Everything you give me."

My throat tightens, but there's a glow of hope in my chest that wasn't there before.

THIRTY

Griffin

I didn't remember how much feeling my body was capable of containing. Or maybe it never held so much emotion before, when our existence was so strictly regimented, when I'd never shared anything more with Riva than smiles and the occasional hug.

Now my adoration radiates through every pore, like I'm shining with it right down to my soul.

It's incredible and also overwhelming. I don't want to let go of her, even just to walk down the path to the river.

The slide of my arms around her bare back sends fresh shivers of sensation through my body. Slivers of pain lance through the joy here and there, punishing me for the indulgence, but the eager thunder of my pulse drowns those out enough that I can ignore them.

I can't keep all this happiness in.

"I love you," I murmur, kissing her forehead, her cheek. "I love you. I love you."

Can I say it enough times to make up for the years when I wasn't there to say it at all? For all the time I've been aware of her and then around her in the last few months when I couldn't even feel it?

My mind slips back to images from our shared past—to a younger Riva tucking herself next to me on the sofa in the facility's lounge area, trusting me not to betray the eagerness only I could sense to the others. To the spirited arguments with Jacob that neither of them took too seriously back then. To the strength that flowed through her body when she pushed herself through a challenge.

But with each of those memories, sharper shocks of pain jolt through my nerves. My stomach starts to cramp.

I have to clamp my jaw against the other memories that try to rise up, that the guardians seared into my brain in tandem with every image they could find that provoked the slightest emotional reaction in me.

But every memory since we came to the island is safe. I can revel in the hunger that winds through my veins at the touch of her, not satisfied even after the intimacy we just shared.

I can think of the compassion in her gaze and the tenderness of her kiss after I first told her what her touch was doing for me. Of the flash in her eyes when she told off Clancy for profiting off us.

I don't think there's any part of her I don't love.

A matching emotion shines from her into me. She was right that I don't need her to say it for me to know her heart, but my pulse still skips when the words pass from her lips again.

"I love you too, Griffin. I know… I know now that all six of us are back together—really *together*—we can figure this out eventually."

I capture her lips, losing myself in their softness and heat—but not totally. Her last comment echoes through my mind.

Eventually isn't good enough. I screwed this up—it's because of me that she and the others ended up under Clancy's thumb to begin with.

I will make this right. I was willing to end Celine's life to make sure I was in a position to save us, as sick as *that* memory makes me feel.

I would give up my own life if it comes to that. There's no sacrifice that wouldn't be worth it.

Better to die knowing I gave them everything I could than to live with the awareness that I was nothing more than their downfall.

The unsettling thoughts finally loosen my need to hold on to her. What we're doing here isn't going to save anyone.

I take a step back, ignoring the protests of my desire pleading for more. "I guess we'd better get on with washing up."

Riva smiles bright enough to almost compensate for the loss of her embrace and tugs her bra and tee back on. I collect my shirt from the ground and pull it over my head reluctantly.

But I haven't lost her yet. She curls her fingers around mine to walk with me down the mountainside.

The guardians keeping watch have stayed far enough back in the jungle that I'm not sure Riva will see them. I can sense their presence, their mix of boredom and apprehension—and the jolts of alertness when they spot us coming into view.

I head straight for the riverbank at the base of the waterfall and slip over the coarse grass along the water's edge to plunge in waist deep.

Riva dips her feet in with a wince, though nothing on the island is really cold. It's more lukewarm.

I wade around, adjusting my pants so the current will carry away the outcome of our interlude and trying not to think about exactly what I'm doing. But Riva's gaze follows me, and my face gradually flushes hotter until I think it might burn right off.

I sensed her with the other guys that night in the abandoned hotel. I didn't set out to pry, but with the invisible bonds we've already formed, it's hard not to pick up on how they're feeling when they're nearby.

I know how much pleasure they gave her and how much enthusiasm they brought to the task. *They* all know that side of her so much better than I do, even when I can read her from the inside out.

How can I catch up when I'm not even totally sure how to feel anymore?

But I also know that she doesn't care. There's nothing in her now as she watches me except the warm glow of affection and a little worry that I can tell is for my own well-being, not hers.

And when I walk over to where she's sitting on the bank, my clothes clinging to my frame and my hair slicked back, a flare of desire sears through her too.

She doesn't let it show other than the brief flick of her tongue over her lips. The tiny movement acts like a magnet, drawing me in.

Without speaking, I step right up to her, set my hand on her cheek, and kiss her.

Riva trails her hands down my chest, the heat of them seeping through the damp fabric of my shirt. I wish it was off again—I wish I'd never put it back on.

Maybe Riva's thoughts are traveling along similar lines. When our mouths part, she leans close so only I can hear her whisper. "There are a lot of places I haven't gotten to touch you yet."

I swear my dick rises to half-mast in an instant, as if volunteering for duty.

I lower my head to nibble her jaw where I know I can set off a spark of bliss before answering. "I've missed out too."

"Hmm. But I bet the guardians are monitoring us out here."

"Yes." I drink in her heat and the flavor of her desire, and an impulse grips me that I can't shake. "But we could work around that."

She cocks her head, but before she can voice her question, I scoop her off the bank. As Riva lets out a gasp of startled laughter, I push through the current to the waterfall—and propel us right under it.

The torrent washes right over us and then we're mostly beyond it. I press Riva up against the wet rock beneath, heedless of the current streaming down my back.

I was already soaked anyway. And back here, no one can see what we're doing.

No one can hear the breathier gasp that escapes her when I trace my fingers right down the center of her to the apex of her thighs.

When I stroke over the spot that before I only bucked against artlessly, Riva's fingers clench in my shirt. If I had any doubts about whether I'm moving too quickly, she dispels them with the yank of my mouth to hers.

I don't know how much more time the guardians will give us. So I'm going to make sure I leave her with the best possible memories of our reunion.

I delve my hand under the waistband of her track pants and her panties. At the feel of her slick folds, I groan against her mouth.

She already came for me once, but I can make this one better. I can make it as close as possible to the total joining we're both craving but resisting.

I tease my fingertips over her sex until I've charted every spot that provokes the greatest rushes of pleasure and exactly what kind of pressure works best on each. The exact bodily sensations don't pass into me, but I can trace their intensity echoing through the flashes of satisfaction, exhilaration, and impatience whirling through Riva.

As my confidence grows, I delve two of my fingers right inside her wet heat. The physical evidence of her enjoyment sets off a thrill in me that's almost as intense as her quake of need.

"Griffin," she mumbles, burying her face in the crook of my shoulder. Begging for what I'm only too happy to give her.

I match her pose, kissing and nipping the sensitive spots on her neck while I pump my fingers in and out of her. The rhythmic swivels of the heel of my hand send even more desire flooding through both of us.

Riva whimpers, swaying into my hold. I can't even feel the waterfall behind me anymore.

Everything is her and us and the intoxicating symphony of our coming together.

My hand grazes a spot inside her that makes her cry out. I stroke it again and again, fanning the flames until she's shaking.

And then it happens, even more delicious than the first time. Ecstasy crackles through her, electrifying both of us.

She quivers and sags against me, wrung out. My erection throbs, but I want the moment to stay only about her.

I want her to know through every particle of her being how much I'm here for her, in every possible way.

"I love you," she says again, barely audible through the roar of the waterfall. Then she looks up and catches my gaze, as if she's read something inside me that I didn't realize would be obvious. "If we make it out of here again, you're coming with us. It's only worth it if it's all of us."

A lump rises in my throat. "Okay."

The urgency that brought me down to the river sweeps through me again. I carry Riva back to the bank and clamber out next to her.

The guardians adjust their positions among the trees, but don't move to stop us as we head down the path.

No one steps out to intercept us until we reach the clearing outside the facility. A woman raises her hand toward Riva.

"You're still in a training period. You'll go in for dinner in an hour."

Riva catches my gaze, and I nod, a gesture that feels totally inadequate. I carry her quiet answering smile with me all the way up to the facility and down the stone halls.

I need to find out what I can about Clancy's plans so far and see if I can direct him down a path that would benefit us. I can tell him that I found out something useful from Riva—that'll get his attention and kick off the conversation.

My clothes are still damp in the warm air, but it'll sell my story better if I go straight to him rather than stopping to change. Convince him it's important.

When I reach his office, a sense of keyed-up tension flows right through the door to me alongside with the hasty ruffling of papers. Something's already happened.

"Clancy?" I say with a knock.

"Come in."

His voice is curt. I step into the office to find him jabbing at the keys on his laptop while he stands over his desk, his face rigid.

I need to exercise plenty of self-control even seeing him in his regular moods these days. Keeping a tight rein on the flares of resentment and anger his presence provokes.

He lied to me, hid things from me. Tricked me into dragging the people I care most about in the world into this mess. Stole our chance at freedom from us.

He didn't even let me keep Lua. She ran off into the jungle, unnerved by the fighting, and Clancy forced me to march onto the helicopter before I could call her back.

He said he was sorry, but he didn't feel it. Not about anything.

I wasn't prepared for this level of agitation from him, though. My chest tightens. "What's going on?"

Clancy doesn't even look at me. "I got the call five minutes ago. The insurgents have invaded another village. My clients want us there ASAP." He grimaces at his laptop screen. "There are more of the fighters than usual—it's a bigger village. For us to overwhelm them without too many casualties…"

Inspiration hits me with Riva's steady voice carrying from the back of my mind. *It's only worth it if it's all of us.*

I approach the desk. "You were planning on going in with just a few of the Firsts, right?"

The red-haired man shoots me a narrow look. "I can't risk bringing all of them. Especially not after the stunt they just pulled. You know that."

I shrug. "I know they've realized how hopeless trying to escape is. And the six of us do have the strongest abilities by far. It'd go much smoother with all of us helping, along with however many of the younger shadowbloods you think could pitch in effectively."

I was trying to keep my tone cool and practical, as if I'm being totally logical about my suggestion, but a tremor of skepticism—maybe even suspicion—weaves through Clancy's whirl of emotions.

"Or they could screw me over," he snaps, and turns back to his computer.

I grope for a way to make the tactic easier for him to swallow. "They wouldn't all need to be in the field. You could keep Dominic back wherever you'll be monitoring the mission from—and maybe Andreas too? Just use his invisibility to scope out the scene before you send the others in. They'll be on hand if necessary, but having them right there, where you could put pressure on them if the others act out—that'd make for plenty of motivation to comply."

Clancy looks up at me again. "Did Riva ask you to push for this?"

Shit. How have I already started to lose the foothold I managed to gain with him.

"No," I say quickly. "We didn't talk about the possible mission at all. I only thought—"

I hesitate, feeling his wariness expand through the rest of his presence. My stomach lurches.

He isn't going to simply listen to me. The only chance I have of swaying him… is if I *really* sway him.

I haven't dared to use my powers on Clancy yet. I've been too afraid he might notice.

And now, after drawing my friends into his traps in the mainland facility, after compelling Celine to her violent death, even thinking about warping anyone's emotions fills my gut with nausea.

With every moment I waver, I'm losing ground with him. I was willing to *die* to see the others free—I have to do this.

I put on a calm expression and extend the slightest tendril of concentrated emotion toward the man in front of me. A thread of hope laced with faith.

You see a way through in the things I'm saying. You know I wouldn't lead you astray.

My stomach keeps churning, but I manage to keep my voice even. "I understand why you're worried about keeping the Firsts together. But I think you're letting your fears cloud your better judgment. They wouldn't even be *together* or in contact with each other. Just somewhat nearby. And you could have at least two of them ready to be punished the second any of the others steps out of line, more easily than if you left some back here."

Clancy pauses. He *is* afraid, but it's a desperate sort of fear, like Andreas guessed from his memories.

He needs a victory. He wants to see a clear way to get it.

His suspicious vibe has faded but not vanished. I inhale slowly and apply a fraction more pressure to my imposing emotions.

"You could bring along a bunch of the kids too. Not just ones who can help, but the less useful ones who were part of the escape. The Firsts feel particularly protective of them. You'll have the perfect means to ensure they follow your orders to the letter."

Riva wants to get as many of the younger shadowbloods out as she can too, after all.

Clancy's shoulders relax just a smidge. He rubs his chin, the conflicting tensions in him starting to unwind.

"You might have a point there, Griffin. There's something to be said for a more immediate pressure point. And plenty of motivation."

"Exactly." I aim another smile at him and pray to whatever gods might exist that I've just opened a new doorway to freedom—not to our destruction.

Thirty-One

Riva

The wind flicks grit in our faces. A tang of smoke and iron prickles my nose, leaving me with the impression that I've bitten my tongue.

I peer down the low slope through our cover of gaunt shrubs, studying the village of clay-brick buildings. In the thin dawn light, the shadows stretch long.

My pulse thumps at a frenetic rhythm.

The insurgents gave the government of whatever country or state we've arrived in a deadline of twelve hours to meet their demands before they started a full-scale slaughter of the inhabitants. It took Clancy eleven hours to finalize his plans, transport us out here, and have Andreas conduct an initial survey of the situation while invisible.

We've got only one more to save the people huddled and hunched with fear in the broad courtyard at the edge of the village.

As many of them as we can still save. The terrorists have already murdered a few—whether because those civilians resisted or simply to make a point about how serious they are, I don't know.

The bodies of two men and a woman lie sprawled at the outskirts of the courtyard, dark stains marking the packed dirt beneath their corpses.

I swallow thickly, which rather than clearing the uncomfortable flavor from my mouth only intensifies it.

I don't want to be here. I don't want to be carrying out Clancy's mission for him or earning him money and acclaim.

But there've got to be at least a hundred innocent people down there in their tight huddle, many of them kids or elders, without much hope of defending themselves. I also don't want all of them to die if I can help it.

That's the worst part of our new circumstances, isn't it? If Clancy honestly wanted to help people out of the goodness of his heart, including us shadowbloods, I might have been okay continuing the life he set up for us.

If I could really be a superhero, sweeping in to save the day with powers that would suddenly seem more awe-inspiring than monstrous, would I turn down the opportunity so I could claim my own freedom instead?

I don't think I would. Not if it was a real choice with its own kind of freedom woven in.

And Clancy knows that. It's why he made his initial pitch to us the way he did, and why I didn't resist from the start.

He manipulated our emotions as deftly as Griffin can, in his own way. Even now, he's arranging the scales so that any attempt we make to have lives of our own will result in someone else's death.

I am not a monster. Even though I'll never trust Clancy to put what's right over his own self-interests, even though I have no intention of returning to the island after today if I can help it, I'm still going to do all I can to ensure every captive below survives the day.

What happens after is on Clancy's conscience, not mine. He set the stage; we're just working with the scripts he gave us.

I've noted fourteen of the insurgents in their positions around the village, mostly where Andreas reported seeing them. Nine are stationed in a loose circle around the cluster of hostages, strolling a little this way and that, rifles held at the ready. Five others roam more widely around the village, keeping watch for new arrivals.

I don't need Griffin's sensitivity to read the wariness in their postures. They're perfectly aware that the officials they're bargaining with would rather kill them than give in to their demands.

They just aren't prepared for the resources those officials were able to bring to bear this time.

They aren't remotely ready to deal with us.

"I can see all eight of the men Andreas said were in the taller buildings around the courtyard," Zian says from beside me, where he's hunkered down behind the scrubs too. "A couple of them are in different rooms from what he reported, but that's all. If there's anyone else farther into the village, they're too far away for me to make out."

Jacob lets out a rough sound by my other shoulder. "Drey searched the whole village. He'd have noticed if there were more. I'd only be worried if you couldn't find everyone he saw."

He lifts his head to eye the terrain down the slope leading toward the nearest buildings and the courtyard. "We should start with the pricks in the buildings. I can take them out at a distance as long as I know where they are—and without the others realizing anything's wrong."

I smile grimly. "The more of them we can eliminate before they go on the defensive, the better."

My scream is going to be the ultimate key to our victory, but as soon as that shriek careens from my lungs, we might as well have bellowed out a war cry. And I'm not sure if I can target the figures I can't even see while keeping my hunger for pain under tight enough control that I won't catch any of the civilians in its net.

A small herd of sheep stirs in a pen just beyond the courtyard. One of them pushes at the weathered boards of the fence with an emphatic bleat loud enough to reach our ears.

The nearest insurgent spins and squeezes his trigger.

The blare of the shot reverberates through the air. As I flinch, the sheep thuds over on its side.

Behind me, Griffin draws in a shaky breath. Whiffs of nervous pheromones tickle my nose from his direction.

He's never been right in a battle like this before. Never had to see the violence firsthand.

He speaks steadily enough, though. "I'll keep the attackers as calm as possible. If you think a different emotional effect would help more, just say the word."

Jacob looks over at Griffin and nods. There's still a bit of tension in his stance when he interacts with his brother, but even when we were speaking apart from Griffin, he hasn't expressed the slightest doubt about his twin's loyalties now.

With the understanding they reforged that day in the jungle, he probably recognized Griffin's gambit with Celine more clearly than any of us.

We're back to how we were—or as close as we can get to the old days while there's damage not fully healed and Andreas and Dominic are back in Clancy's mobile military base, torture instruments poised to make them pay for any missteps on our end. We're all *here* as the family we were meant to be.

More than just the six of us.

I glance down the opposite side of the low hill to where the four younger shadowbloods Clancy sent along with us are crouched. He picked out the few he thought would be the most useful for the mission.

Lindsay can use her earthen talents to jolt the ground beneath our enemies' feet, setting them off balance.

The older teen who's joined us, a guy named Sully, can conjure distracting illusions. I have the feeling the five of us Firsts encountered his ability before, during our time out in the wider world, attempting to avoid re-capture.

George can hop not just over short distances but through walls, in case Zian notices something we need to grab quickly within one of the buildings.

And if worse comes to worst, Tegan can hit any attacker nearby with the toxic smoke she can expel from her lungs.

But having them with us means more people we need to watch out for, more people to protect. I can't help suspecting that Clancy included them at least as much to ensure we'd take every care to pull off this mission well as because he thought they'd contribute with their powers.

He's keeping track of us through the monitoring bands around our ankles that we know from past experience are picking up our voices too. We have to be careful about what we say.

I catch the gazes of the three guys around me. "We're going to save everyone today."

Griffin dips his head. Determination hardens his features so that just for a moment, he looks even more like Jake's mirror image. "*Everyone.*"

His swift gesture encompasses the four of us and the younger shadowbloods behind us.

One corner of Jacob's mouth curls up in a harsh smile. "And take *all* of the villains down."

Zian bares his teeth. "Like they deserve."

We're all in agreement that after we destroy the terrorists, we're turning our abilities on the guardians who've terrorized *us*. Unfortunately, we won't be able to figure out exactly how to do that until we see what we've got to work with after this part of the mission is over.

I wet my lips, my pulse picking up to an even faster tempo. "Okay. So we split up now? Jake, you could go with Zian to pick off the men in the buildings—and bring George with you in case you need him to hop inside. I'll stay farther back with Griffin, Lindsay, and Sully where we can keep an eye on the bigger picture."

I hesitate at the thought of Tegan. Her talent won't do any good unless she's close to her targets… but she's only twelve.

I don't care how useful her power could be in a pinch. Clancy is sick for sending any of the youngest shadowbloods out here, but especially her, when she only could be useful if she's right within reach of a murderous attacker.

"She'll come with us," Jacob says firmly. "Zee and I can make sure nothing happens to her."

Somehow it's a relief to have one decision taken out of my hands.

We scuttle down to the younger shadowbloods and convey the plan in murmurs. Sully's expression firms with the resolve of someone who's been in the line of fire before, but the younger kids look understandably jittery.

"Stick close to us, and don't do anything unless Griffin or I say so," I murmur. "If everything goes the way we're hoping, you might not need to get involved at all."

Lindsay clenches her hands. "I want to help if I can." But she doesn't look any less terrified.

I squeeze her shoulder. "I know. Come on—we don't have much time left."

We creep back to the crest of the hill, diverging into our two groups when we reach the top. My heart stutters as I watch Jacob and Zian pull away from us, even though I can sense exactly where Jacob is whether I can see him or not.

We can do this. We can protect these people, as much as this mission is really designed to protect them, lull Clancy into a brief complacency, and then strike at him too.

The scattered scrubs and gnarled trees give us enough shelter that we can steal halfway down the slope without being seen as long as we stay close to the ground. We move in spurts, Griffin gesturing when none of the men are looking in our direction and he can sense a lapse in their wariness, holding up his hand to stop us when they start to turn our way.

He's scanning the emotions of everyone in our vicinity—including the insurgents staked out in the two-story buildings that give them a higher vantage point over the village and its surrounding terrain. After a few minutes, he pauses and lifts his hand toward me with his forefinger raised.

Jacob has taken out one. Seven more to go.

It'll be slow going for Jake. He has to know exactly where his targets are, and he can't risk them noticing something's wrong before he gets a grip on them.

He'll be relying on seeing them through windows, but at least they should be staying near those while they keep watch.

As we crouch in our new positions, close enough to the sheep pen that the pungent odor of manure laces the air, Griffin raises his hand again and again.

Two down. Three. Four.

I study the men stationed around the villagers. None of their faces betray any heightened concern.

One of the insurgents patrolling farther out strides past us, just twenty feet from our crouched position. Next to me, Lindsay quivers.

I think I can direct my scream at both the men around the hostages and the five who are patrolling the outskirts at the same time without my control slipping. They're far enough away from the main cluster of figures that it shouldn't be too hard to distinguish them.

But if Jacob and Zian can deal with some of them first as well, that'd be better.

Griffin indicates five gone, and then six. After he lowers his hands, he picks up a stick and draws a Z and a line in the dirt.

We don't dare speak here, but I understand. Zee managed to tackle one of the men on patrol.

Two more are left in the buildings near the courtyard, four on the outskirts, nine surrounding the villagers. We're closer and closer to our goal, and so far, no alarm has been raised.

A murmur carries from the group of hostages. Some of the figures near the edge of the huddle are stirring.

The voices that reach my ears hold the edge of a hushed argument. I tense, spotting a woman clutching at the arm of the man next to her.

Is one of the villagers thinking of rebelling? Can't he see the insurgents will simply shoot him?

But the locals don't know that we're already in the process of freeing them. He might assume they'll end up dead either way.

Two of the terrorists march over. One of them barks something in a language I don't know at the source of the disruption.

The villagers go still, but it's too late. And what the insurgents do is even worse than I expected.

The one who spoke reaches into the huddle and yanks a kid out by the elbow—a little boy who can't be more than five or six years old. He squeals and babbles in terror as the woman who must be his mother grasps after him.

The insurgent hefts up the kid, dangling, and points his rifle right at the boy's face.

My gut lurches, and my lips spring open before I've even thought about it. But Lindsay is even faster.

The dirt beneath the gunman's feet juts upward in a sudden bump. He stumbles, losing his balance, and the kid slips from his grasp.

Griffin's face has gone taut with concentration, no doubt trying to rein in the violence. But the other men scramble to snatch up the kid, and one grabs another child from the far side of the huddle.

Her cry wrenches at me. I might not understand their words, but their harsh voices tell me they're determined to punish the villagers for even considering resisting.

God only knows what'll happen if they start firing. Maybe they'd cow the rest of the villagers—or maybe they'd provoke a larger rebellion that will end with them slaughtering so many more.

The boy wails as he's jerked around toward the second man's rifle, and I can't hold back any longer. All the anguish of watching the villagers' pain bursts from my lips in a monstrous shriek.

The sound peals out of me and hurtles across the landscape to smack into my targets. The hunger inside me twitches and yawns, eager to be sated after weeks of denial, but I narrow the jabs of my power to lance only into the nine gunmen poised around the hostages.

I can't feel the more distant patrollers right now—and I'm afraid to loosen my grip even enough to seek them out. This has to be enough.

Please, let my fellow shadowbloods manage to handle the rest.

My power radiates through all nine men, freezing them in its clutches, but I can only tear apart one at a time. I pitch the shriek louder, harder.

My latent senses know exactly how to break and rend each victim for maximum pain. My scream rips through one body and another, shattering bones, splitting sinews and organs.

The agony ripples back into me, flooding me with an exhilarating strength.

For a long time, the pleasure that came with the pain I deal out has horrified me. But in this moment, knowing how many lives are at stake, I give myself over to it.

I need the strength. I need every bit of might I can get to ensure the larger massacre never happens.

These men would have murdered little kids. They were willing to kill every person in this village to get their demands met.

They don't deserve the life I'm tearing out of them.

My fingers dig into the dry earth, claws jutting out. Body after body crumples in their ring around the hostages.

I'm distantly aware of cries and shouts, but I can't even decipher where they're coming from while my focus is trained on my targets. I have to trust that my friends and colleagues are holding their own.

Then there's only one left. The man that first hauled the little boy out of the crowd, the one who stumbled at Lindsay's shove.

I propel a sharper scream from my lungs, snapping his feet, then severing the tendons at the backs of his knees. Raking destruction up through his body swiftly but methodically.

Drinking down the last swell of agony before his life blinks out.

Then I sway forward, my own body caught in the rush of power. The sound fades from my throat.

Griffin touches my back, helping to ground me. His voice spills out in a rush of relief. "We got all of them. Jake and Zee and the others caught the sentries before they could hurt anyone—Sully helped divert them with his illusions. We—"

"Someone's coming!" Zian's frantic holler splits through the air from farther away. "I can hear it."

The words have barely left his lips when I hear it too—the roar of what sounds like a dozen engines. I leap to my feet, thinking that if we can just hurry the villagers to safety in time, it won't matter.

But I don't know where we could take them that *is* safe. And as I straighten up, a barrage of brown armored trucks careen into view over the top of a nearby ridge.

Did the insurgents here realize something was wrong in time to summon reinforcements, or were these men already on their way? Are they even with the original terrorists, or are they some new hostile group?

It doesn't matter. A hail of machine-gun fire blares across the landscape, and all I can do is yank Lindsay down with me as we flatten ourselves to the ground.

Our battle isn't over. It looks like it's barely even begun.

THIRTY-TWO

Riva

I hug the earth through another thunder of bullets, grit prickling into my mouth.

Tires are grating against the hard-packed dirt as the trucks grind to a halt. Voices holler unfamiliar words.

And a sliver of pain jabs me right through one of my marks.

Jacob's mark.

The chill of fear prickles through me. He's a few hundred feet away, farther down by the buildings and the courtyard—closer to the incoming attackers.

Griffin puts words to my fear where he's sprawled behind me. "Jake's hit. Zian too. They're still conscious. Jake's more pissed off than worried, but Zee's panicking a bit."

Shit. My own worry constricts my insides from my throat down to my gut.

I dare to lift my head to get a look at what's going on. I only manage to make out a couple dozen figures with massive guns marching toward the courtyard before a few of them aim their weapons at the hillside again.

Bullets batter the soil and the twisted shrubs. Chunks of twig and leaf spray around us—and Lindsay lets out a pained gasp.

I twist toward her as she cringes closer to me. Blood streaks across the side of her arm where one of the bullets hit her.

It doesn't look serious, but guilt knots my stomach anyway.

"Stay quiet," I murmur to her urgently. "It'll be okay as long as we don't draw more attention."

Those definitely aren't any government soldiers come to thank us for our service. They were dressed similarly in earthen tones but nothing like an official uniform.

And I can already hear them yelling at the villagers with hostility rather than relief.

As Griffin shuffles closer to Lindsay with a bandage he's pulled from his pocket, I peer through the brush again. I have to get to Jacob and Zian —make sure they're okay, do what we can to pick up the pieces of our mission.

Frustration and fear tangle in my chest to form a prickling vibration. I'll scream all these assholes who've barged in to ruin our victory to pieces.

But when I judge it safe to lift my head so I can stare down into the courtyard, my spirits deflate.

The new arrivals have obviously figured out that something very bad happened to the insurgents who were here first. They're herding the hostages into the largest of the two-story buildings around the courtyard, shouting and shoving—many of them already inside.

Even with my practice under Clancy's supervision, I doubt I can keep track of who I'm tearing into with my scream when I can't even see who I'm aiming it at. I'd end up ripping through a bunch of the innocent villagers too.

Shit, shit, *shit.*

But if these men are with the first bunch, how long will they wait before *they* start killing more of the hostages in retribution for our attack? We don't have time to figure out a new plan.

Behind those walls, they could be slaughtering hostages to hold up as examples right now.

I feel like I'm going to vomit. I still need to reach Jacob and Zian, help them if they need it.

What is Clancy going to do if we have to pull out to get them to Dominic for healing?

Too many thoughts are whirling in my head. Just move—figure it out one step at a time.

I drag in a rough breath and glance at Griffin. "I'm going to the others. Keep making the insurgents as calm as you can manage."

"Riva—"

I don't wait to hear what he's going to say. The seconds are slipping past me—I might already have wavered too long.

The last of the gunmen is disappearing into the building. I heave myself forward, scuttling along the slope staying as low to the ground as I can, following the line of spindly shrubs for the cover they provide.

Jacob hasn't moved much from where I sensed him before. Hopefully Zian and the younger two are still with him.

I have to run the last short distance from the patches of vegetation to the fence around the sheep pen, and then another short dash to nearest structure by the courtyard. Thankfully, I've already passed out of view of the building the terrorists ushered their captives into.

As I sprint to the mud-brick wall, the boom of a single gunshot splits the air from the other direction.

My wince radiates through my body. The scream swells in my lungs, but I don't have a proper target.

I dash around the corner of the structure—and make out a shed I can sense Jacob is behind up ahead. My footfalls echo the pounding of my heart.

I dart around the shed and freeze with a sharper lurch of my gut.

Jacob is leaning against the side of the shed, looking pissed off just like Griffin said. Blood has pooled beneath his thigh and is seeping through the hasty bandage already wrapped around the wound.

He might not even be able to walk like that.

And Zian looks even worse off. He must have caught a bullet in the side—the hem of his shirt and the left hip of his pants are dark with blood.

Tegan huddles close to him, helping him press a couple of balled bandages to the wound in an effort to stop the bleeding. She looks all right.

But George lies in the dust just around the corner of the shed, back of his skull blasted right open, the rest of his white-blond hair drenched red.

Zian somehow looks twice as upset when he takes in my expression. "I'm going to be all right," he insists with a hint of a growl. "But he—I couldn't get to him in time…"

Lindsay lifts her head, her wide eyes flicking from him to me and back again. "I think the bleeding is slowing."

Jacob hefts himself farther upright. "That's what matters. Just tore up a little muscle on this hulk."

He taps Zian lightly with his elbow, but his face is tight with concentration. His jaw works when he glances at George's body.

His expression hardens even more at another crackling gunshot. He catches my eyes. "They're killing the hostages?"

I nod, my mouth dry. "Must be. I don't know…"

I don't know what we do now. I don't have the slightest clue how to salvage this mission.

For all we know, if we go back in failure and Clancy loses control over the guardianship… the remaining guardians will decide that Engel was right and murder us after all. Or send us off to be lab rats the way Clancy's always threatened.

But how the hell are we going to take down all those gunmen when only one of us who's much good at killing anyone has all her flesh intact?

Jacob is still watching me. "You tell us what you need, Wildcat. We'll do whatever we can."

None of us can touch the insurgents without getting inside the building. And I can't see Jacob or Zian launching themselves into a full-out brawl with their injuries.

Which leaves just me.

But how the hell could I manage to take down all of our enemies in an enclosed space without them shooting me first? Without slaughtering all the innocents with them at the same time?

Even if I got in there and brought every supernatural talent I have to bear as quickly as possible…

The quivers of the exhilaration of my last scream still thrum through my veins, but that's not enough to take on an entire squad of terrorists unscathed.

Not on its own. I need more.

A restless bleat reaches my ears. My head jerks toward the sheep pen.

The bottom of my stomach drops out with the idea that's just occurred to me.

I can't deny the solution that's right in front of me, no matter how horrific I find it. If I have to become more of a monster to save us all, so be it.

I won't be able to save *anyone* if the mission completely falls apart.

"I need to see what I'm working with out there," I say.

Jacob pushes to his feet without another word, gripping the side of the shed for balance so he isn't putting too much weight on his wounded leg. Zian sways after him.

A protest tumbles from my lips. "You should—"

Zee shakes his head. "We're in this together. Like always."

Tegan looks terrified and fierce at the same time. "I'm coming too."

The truth is, no matter how powerful I get, I'm not sure I can pull this off alone. So I grasp Jake's arm to help him, and we shuffle as quickly as the guys can manage through a narrow gap between two of the buildings to where we can peek into the courtyard.

The sheep are pacing in their pen back the way I came from. The building with the hostages stands almost directly opposite it.

There's a pane-less window on the second floor, large enough that I'm sure my small frame could fit through it without a squeeze.

Two more shots ring out just in the brief moment I'm taking it in. My jaw clenches so abruptly I bite my lip.

I don't know how easy it'd be able to climb that material, not the same construction as the bricks I tackled before. It might give our enemies enough time to hear me coming and shoot me on sight.

There is another way I could get up there, though.

I jerk my gaze across the bodies of our first targets still strewn around the courtyard. One several feet away has a smaller rifle that looks easier to handle.

I touch Jacob's arm for his attention. "I need you to pull that gun over here. Once I have it, I'm going to circle around until I'm close to the building they're in. When I run for it, can you throw me through the biggest window on the second floor?"

Jake blinks at me, his stance tensing. "With that much effort, you know I don't have the best control. I could hurt—"

"You won't," I interrupt, my tone firm. "Just fling me up there, and I can handle the rest. Once I'm ready."

Zian frowns. "What are you going to do?"

I can't bear to answer him.

Jacob extends his power to the gun and drags it over to us. I pick it up, backtrack between the buildings, and dart along a dusty street until I can slip through a passage that takes me within ten feet of the front of my goal.

There, braced between two of the neighboring buildings, I fix my gaze on the sheep and open my mouth.

The shriek seeps out, constrained so it's low but still piercing. I'm hoping the terrorists won't notice it.

The hunger inside me squirms eagerly. I aim all its reverberating power at the undeserving livestock across the courtyard.

My scream rips through one animal and another even more easily than it cut down the men before. I shatter their windpipes first to cut off any bleats or groans that might have alerted my next targets.

But only to silence them, not to kill them just yet. I need them to live through plenty more agony if their sacrifice is going to mean anything.

Wrench. Snap. Puncture. Crack. Flesh rent and bones smashed.

Pain floods my chest with each four-legged corpse toppling to the ground—and transforms into a nauseating flare of strength. The sense of power flows through my limbs and tingles all the way up to my scalp.

More and more and more. I'll need every bit if I'm going to have any hope at all.

I can only imagine the guys staring at the carnage from their vantage point. I hate to think what Tegan is making of the slaughter I'm carrying out.

Blood is starting to creep across the ground beneath the pen's fence. But there are still a few more sheep standing.

I propel the shriek from my lungs, drinking in every drop of anguish. My body vibrates with the unnerving thrill of it, as if I've been lit up with an electric current.

Please, let this be enough. Please, let them not have died for nothing.

The last sheep crumples. I tuck the rifle under my arm and race toward the building before one fragment of the power I've dragged into myself can dissipate.

My feet fly across the packed ground faster than I've ever felt, even with my usual supernatural speed. The wind warbles in my ears.

I stare up at the window I'm hurtling toward—and Jake is there for me. An invisible force whips me off my feet, straight toward the opening.

Between my speed and his shaky control, my shoulder might have glanced off the edge of the frame, but I twist sideways the second I see the danger. Then I'm careening into a crowded room over the heads of dozens of sitting hostages.

All my instincts spark to life with the hum of bottled power within my body. My hands whip out, and a shriek sears from my lungs.

It isn't even hard to figure out who my targets are now that I can see them—they're the only figures standing. I ricochet across the room, each spring of my feet adding to my momentum, and carve a path through them.

Bullets from the rifle I grabbed burst open several skulls. The claws of my free hand slash through one throat and another.

And my scream echoes off the walls, gutting the rest of the insurgents from the inside out.

Several of the hostages yelp or add their own shrieks to the mix, but thankfully they only duck lower. One of the terrorists charges at me, raising his gun, and I lance my scream straight through his innards so he crashes to the ground with a spurt of blood over his lips.

I'm flying, nothing but strength, speed, and fury—but this is only the upper floor. The instant I see the last of the terrorists around me collapse, I throw myself toward the stairwell.

The pain I drank in from the latest targets of my shriek replaces the energy I expended in my attack. I blaze down the stairs and slice through four more militants with my shriek and my gun before anyone below has a chance to think about reacting.

Then the rifle's trigger gives a hollow click. I toss it aside, rebound off a wall to tear one man's head right off his body, carve open another with the force of my scream—

And the front door bursts open.

Zian barrels into the building with a feral roar, his face contorted with its full wolf-man visage. The transformation must have rallied his own strength, because he slams one gunman into the wall and gouges open another's chest in the space of a blink.

Most of the hostages are crying out now, their terror pricking at me. I can't imagine Zian likes hearing how our rescue is being received either, but he rampages on, focusing on the insurgents who were gathered around the doorway.

The second he's tossed the last aside, I let my scream fade just long enough to call out. "Get out of here! Hide in your homes until it's safe!"

I gesture with my arms at the same time, knowing it's likely none of them can understand my words. Zian stumbles back out into the courtyard.

The hostages hesitate until I crash into the last remaining terrorist with another vicious shriek. Then they scramble toward the doorway with a babble of panic.

The rush of pain-powered strength ebbs in my limbs. My breath stutters with a jitter of my nerves.

I won't be able to bring this heightened state all the way back to Clancy—but I have to use it in every way possible while I can.

Bending down, I smash my fist across the monitoring band clinging to my ankle.

I have just enough pain-driven might left to crack the metal and then to yank the band the rest of the way off me. I stomp on it to a sizzle of sparks.

We can tell Clancy it was destroyed in the fight. Technically that's even true.

When we meet him again, I don't want him to have a single clue what's going on inside me.

Thirty-Three

Riva

I leap through the doorway to rejoin the others. The hostages have scattered across the village, ducking into the other buildings. Doors thud decisively.

Not a single additional gunshot rings out. No armed men appear around the boundaries of the courtyard.

I wait for several beats of my heart, my ears pricked, but no further catastrophe descends on us.

We did it. It wasn't tidy, but we did it.

Zian has slumped down on the ground, his face returned to normal and shining with sweat but a broad grin baring his teeth. Jacob is hobbling over to him with Tegan helping balance him.

"We have to get out of here," I say, knowing my voice will carry through their own ankle bands—that it'll tell Clancy that I survived even if my own monitor didn't. "Regroup with the guardians—Dominic will be able to heal you too."

I pause with a fresh punch of nausea. There'll be no healing George.

I'm just opening my mouth to speak again when a faint rustle reaches my ears. Jacob has whipped his arm upward before I can even turn around.

The purple poisoned spikes jut from the side of his forearm—and spring free. They zing through the air like a set of darts and spear the insurgent who was still alive enough to drag himself to the doorway across the chest.

The man sprawls, his eyes glazing. The gun he was raising toward me slips from his limp hand.

Jacob stares at his arm. "I— They've never done that before."

I swallow thickly, thinking of the power that pealed through me just moments ago, more than I've ever felt in my life. "Our abilities are still evolving, apparently."

Jacob's mouth sets in a slanted line as if he isn't sure whether to be happy about that development. Then he motions me toward him.

"You're right. We've got to get going. I'm pretty sure whoever hired Clancy would rather we cleared out before they show up. Where's my brother?"

As we tramp across the courtyard, Jake, Zian, and I all pause briefly to confiscate a weapon. We don't speak about it, not when our voices would be transmitted straight to the guardians, but the solemn glances we exchange say enough.

We still have another fight ahead of us.

Griffin, Sully, and Lindsay emerge from the brush along the slope to meet us as we hurry over. Griffin makes a beeline for his twin and lifts Jacob's arm to support him.

"I can manage," Jake mutters, but I think I see him relax a little at the same time.

Sully glances at the sheep pen with its blood-stained earth and mangled corpses. He doesn't need to say anything.

My shoulders tense. "I did what I had to do."

His jaw works, but he nods.

Jacob lets out a rough dismissive sound. "Better us than them."

Lindsay is scanning the courtyard behind us, her face tight with worry. "Where's George?"

Zian winces. "He—when the new trucks first showed up, spraying bullets everywhere—we didn't get to shelter in time."

I hate the shadow of anguish that crosses her face. She's silent for a moment and then asks, "What about the hostages? Are they okay?"

My mind trips back to the scene in the building I just unleashed my powers on. A few of the bodies that remained after the hostages fled were villagers, but most of the corpses were the terrorists I destroyed.

"Almost all of them," I say, turning that fact over in my mind. The insurgents decided not to punish too many of the villagers even though everything had gone wrong.

Griffin directs us toward the van we arrived in, concealed about a mile away. "They were greedy. I could feel it, the whole time—the bunch of them were angry when they saw what had happened, but mostly they were still hopeful, hungry… wanting whatever it was they demanded as ransom."

"They didn't want to lose too many of their bargaining chips," I fill in with a shudder.

Zian lets out a rasp of a chuckle. "If they'd given up after our first round, *they* would have lived too. Guess they got a little too greedy."

"Maybe it works out better for Clancy this way. He'll get everything he's owed."

I keep my tone even, but I know the guys pick up on the extra meaning in my last words. We all know what he's earned from us.

Griffin nods. "Andreas and Dominic will be worrying about us, but they were ready for whatever might happen. When they see us and what state we're in, they'll jump in to help."

They're waiting for us to take the lead in our rebellion, he means, and then they'll pitch in however they can. That makes sense.

We're the ones who've had the chance to arm ourselves. We'll have the most room to maneuver when we make it back to the temporary base Clancy set up to monitor the mission.

As the cluster of trees that hide our vehicle come into view up ahead, my mind starts spinning through the possibilities. But even once we've clambered in and buckled up, I'm still not sure.

With their injuries, Zian and Jacob won't be able to maneuver quickly. Griffin isn't much of a fighter, no matter how he was trained.

I'm going to be the key, again. That's just the way it is.

Clancy and his guardian colleagues have Drey, Dom, and a few of the younger shadowbloods with them as their own kind of hostages. I don't think they'd hesitate to go as far as killing the younger ones if they realize we're defying them.

It's only the six of us Firsts they really think are valuable, after all. Clancy proved that when he all but dared Dominic to kill Celine.

And they won't be kind even to Dom and Drey if they catch wind of our rebellion too soon. Our friends won't be able to help us if they're drowning in agony.

I need to tackle him first. Without him giving the orders, it'll be so much easier to deal with the others.

Where would he make a fatal misstep that could get him killed? What is he afraid to lose, enough that he might act without thinking?

The answer soars up from the depths of my mind like a signal flare: It's us.

That's all there is to it, isn't there? He's spent his entire career working to get us under his control, and now we're essential to taking on the savior-hero role he's obviously been dreaming of.

There has to be a way I can use that fear.

I reach into my shirt to pull out my cat-and-yarn necklace, allowing myself to carefully click it open and snap it back together. The simple, familiar rhythm melds with the rumble of the van's engine.

The start of a plan forms piece by piece. I can't see how it'll end, because so much depends on exactly how Clancy reacts. But the longer I sit with it, the surer I feel.

"When we get back to the base," I say quietly, "wait for me. Then do what you need to."

Jacob squeezes my hand from the seat next to me, and Zian lets out a grunt of acknowledgment from behind. Behind the wheel, Griffin doesn't give any visible sign at all, but a flicker of emotion passes through me, all warm acceptance.

A wordless message that says all it needs to.

Clancy's base squats on the side of the dirt road, a military-style truck attached to a long trailer with most of his monitoring equipment, both of them painted in camouflage colors. As we crest one last hill before it comes into view, his even voice crackles from our radio.

"Park twenty feet away and walk the rest of the distance. Enter through the back of the trailer."

We're not using the guns we grabbed, then. They're all too big to conceal under our clothes.

Griffin cruises to the indicated spot and parks. We clamber out and head toward the trailer.

I hang back, letting the others go ahead. Dragging my feet across the ground as if I can't quite lift my feet.

Clancy knows I'm not dead, that my monitoring band must have simply been broken. He'll have no idea what else might have happened to me.

He's probably already been on edge, hoping that my ability to speak coherently means there isn't an outright emergency.

Well, he's going to get an emergency now.

As our procession comes up on the attached truck, I purposefully stagger. My knees buckle under me.

I fall, catching myself with my palms in the dirt and swaying. A groan breaks from my lips.

"Riva!"

I don't think Jacob even needs to fake his panic. He lurches back to me as fast as his wounded leg allows, his face paling.

Zian follows with a defensive snarl, his gaze skimming the landscape as if searching for new foes.

I slump over on my side, letting my head loll. And through the slits left by my nearly closed eyelids, I see Clancy burst from the truck.

I hadn't known if he'd simply send Dominic racing over or come himself. Maybe I should be gratified that he cares enough, even if it's for totally selfish reasons, to stick his neck out.

Although it might not even be his motivation alone. Griffin heard my instructions too—he's smart enough to have realized an extra shove of panic would work in our favor.

Even so, a sudden pang of loss ripples through me. This man has been a monster to us, but he's also the only guardian who's ever attempted to give us anything remotely close to a real life.

We're giving up on that dream the moment I go through with my plan. We'll be nothing but fugitives again—nothing but monsters ourselves.

To them. I know, with a resolve that steadies me through the pang, that we can be so much more for ourselves than even our new keeper ever imagined.

Another guardian hustles out behind Clancy. As they race over, I shudder and go limp again.

"Come on, get her legs—we'll carry her into the back for Dominic," Clancy says to his underling, his voice taut with concern. He bends over to grasp my shoulders.

My claws slide from my fingertips. It's now or never.

For the little bit of good he tried to do amid the bad, he deserves at least to have his death witnessed.

Opening my eyes, I whip my arm upward to rake my hand across Clancy's throat.

His blood splatters down over my face and hair. There's just an instant before his body crumples when he stares down at me, shock and denial and the briefest flash of emerging rage contorting his features.

You asked for this, I think. *You wanted us too badly to let us go.*

As Clancy's dying body hits the ground, the other guardian starts to yelp—but the sound is lost in the crack of Jacob's talent wrenching her neck around. Before she's even fallen, I'm sprinting for the trailer.

I throw open the doors to total chaos. Andreas and Dominic must have taken their cue and run with it.

Three of the guardians are circling each other and yelling in what sounds like bewilderment. Dominic has a stranglehold on another with one tentacle.

Another sprawls at Andreas's feet, still twitching from the jolt Drey must have given the man with the baton he's snatched.

I lunge forward, determined to end this now. To end everyone who'd have continued our torture.

I'm not sure the guardians even know what hit them. I sever one's throat and plunge my claws into another's chest, and then Zian is there behind me, bashing a skull into the trailer's floor.

Dominic's jaw clenches, and the man he's clutching purples as the tentacle around his neck squeezes and sucks the life out of him simultaneously. Andreas yanks a knife from one of the other guardian's belts and jabs it into the back of the man he toppled.

We stop, all of us panting. My nerves jangle through my body as if waiting for another shoe to drop. "That's—that's all of them?"

"That's all," Dom says, quiet and grim as he releases his victim.

I exhale with a sound like a sob. My knees wobble for real this time as all the pent-up stress and effort catches up with me.

We don't know what country we're in or where we're going next. But right now, we're more free than we've ever been before.

THIRTY-FOUR

Riva

We might be free, but we're not exactly done.

Dominic hustles over to Zian, having spotted the evidence of his wound on his clothes. As he ushers him outside to find a shrub or tree to draw healing power from, I turn toward the three younger shadowbloods crouched in the back of the trailer.

Devon is there, and Booker, and a fourteen-year-old girl named Harriet who was caught up in our escape but mostly kept stoically quiet. Clancy decided to separate the two couples who were part of our earlier escape, leaving Ajax and Nadia behind, maybe to give him more leverage over their significant others as well as us Firsts.

They peer at the carnage left in our wake in silence and then at me. Clancy's blood still saturates my hair and smears my skin.

I swipe at my face with my sleeve, but it's a little too late to make a cleaner entrance. Booker's jaw works.

We didn't have any way of looping them in on our plans. This is a much gorier revolt than the first one they joined.

"We'll go back to get the others," I promise. "Right away. Without Clancy giving orders, the whole organization falls apart, at least while the guardians are scrambling to figure out what to do next. We'll head back to the plane, and a few of us will make the pilot take us back to the island to get the rest of the shadowbloods while the rest figure out a safe place for us to regroup. Okay?"

Devon rubs his hand across his mouth with a little shudder. "Are you going to kill all the guardians on the island too?"

"Not if they don't get in our way," Jacob mutters. "It'll be up to them."

He slips from the back of the trailer at Dominic's beckoning and limps over to our healer. Griffin comes up beside me and squats down to put himself eye to eye with the younger shadowbloods.

"It makes sense that you're unsettled," he says. "You're probably not all that sure about me either. We all wish we could have let you in on what we were planning sooner, but there wasn't any way that wouldn't have tipped off the guardians too."

Andreas dips his head, his voice low and rough. "There was no way they were letting us go while they were still alive. I think if you look back on everything you've seen of the guardians, you know that."

Booker hesitates. "They were ready to hurt us, maybe even kill the three of us, to keep you in line."

"Yeah." I grimace. "You should never be in that position again—not you three or Nadia or Ajax—or any of the others. We look out for each other. We're blood, and they can't take that away from us, no matter what they do."

Harriet's head droops. "I don't want to go back to the island. Or any other facility. I never liked any of it."

"You won't have to," Griffin assures her. "Will you come with us? I think we'd better leave the trailer behind."

Andreas glances around the interior at the slumped bodies, the splattered blood, and the tools the guardians meant to use to torment their "leverage" if we disobeyed. "Yeah. It'll only slow us down."

The younger shadowbloods cautiously creep forward. As Griffin ushers them out of the trailer, I turn to Andreas. "What did you do to the guardians to get them so confused?"

His mouth twists at a pained angle. "I wiped one guy's memories completely so he had no idea who he was or what he was doing here. Then I wiped another from all the others' minds so they didn't understand where he'd come from. And after that, I threw a bunch of projected images into the mix to throw them off even more."

A thread of strain winds through his voice, and I don't think it's just because of the energy using his ability to that extent took out of him. He's no more comfortable with the most monstrous side of his abilities than I am with mine.

I squeeze his arm. "We all did what we had to do. Now we can really take charge of our lives."

"Yeah." He leans in to give me a quick but heated kiss and brushes his forehead against mine. "I'm right here with you every step of the way, Tink."

We gather the guardians' phones and weapons for possible later use and clamber out of the trailer to find Zian already unhitching it from the truck.

"We're going to need both of them to carry all of us," he says, nodding to the van we arrived in.

Tegan watches the proceedings with her arms wrapped around her chest, hugging herself. "Even after we get everyone off the island, aren't the other guardians going to keep chasing us?"

"I can handle that," Andreas tells her. "At least partly. Once we have the other kids out of there, I'm going to erase Clancy from everyone's minds. If none of the guardians can remember him, they won't remember his project or where he organized it or any of that. There'll be records, but it'll take them a while to piece things together—time we can use to cover our tracks completely."

I peer into the front of Clancy's truck, where Jacob has taken the driver's seat. "Does this one have a working radio? If there are any local stations, we can figure out where exactly we are on the drive to the plane."

He frowns at the controls. "Looks like it. Let's get out of here, and we can check in with each other before we get to the runway to decide the final details."

"Sounds good to me." I like the idea of putting some distance between us and Clancy's worksite, if only because I have no idea how aware his clients are of the details of his operations—or when they might arrive to confirm his success.

Dominic comes up beside me, resting a gentle tentacle on my waist. "You're completely okay, Riva?"

I smile at him, letting myself lean into his offered embrace just for a moment. "Getting there. I'm looking forward to my next shower, though."

He gives a rough chuckle and presses a kiss to my cheek, heedless of what I recently wiped off my skin. "Here's hoping we can give you that soon."

We climb into the vehicles—Jacob, Dom, me, and the kids from our mission in the truck while Griffin, Zian, and Andreas head to the van with the guardians' hostages. Jacob guns the engine and spins the wheel to take us back onto the road.

"Good-bye and good riddance," he says without a backward glance.

The van roars ahead of us, and Jake speeds after it. I take a long breath, feeling my nerves just beginning to settle down, and shift in my seat to check on the others behind me.

Just as I turn, an explosion booms and sears through the air beyond the rearview window.

It's the trailer—it's just blasted apart in a surge of flames. The impact jolts the ground beneath the tires, and Jacob swears.

"I didn't think we were going to—" he starts.

Dominic is shaking his head, his body tensed. "That wasn't us. That—"

Another force wallops into the side of the truck, wrenching away his voice.

Our vehicle skids and tumbles into a roll.

The doors fly right off their hinges. We crash into the dry earth on the side of the road, my head smacking the steel frame.

Jacob lolls, dangling from his seatbelt, mumbling. Dominic has been flung out onto the roadside just beyond my reach.

Not that I seem to know *how* to reach anymore. My head is aching and spinning at the same time.

I can't collect my voice; I can't remember how to move. Pain washes through my limbs in waves.

Footsteps thud across the cracked dirt. I have a blurred impression of two figures standing over me—a broad-shouldered man and a wiry woman.

"You did a good job, my shadowbloods," the man says in a roughly amused baritone. "You did half of *my* job for me."

My mouth opens and closes as I grasp for words. For a shriek. For anything.

The man turns to the woman. "Toni, we need them to know right from the start that I'm no one to fool with. That one first—the one with the tentacles."

He points, and the woman raises a gun I hadn't noticed clutched in her hand. "Of course, Mr. Balthazar."

"No!" I choke out, barely a whisper. I manage to jerk my arm forward—

And something slams into my head from behind, knocking all the thoughts out of my head.

Right before the darkness closes in, the last thing I hear is the blare of a gunshot.

About the Author

Eva Chase lives in Canada with her family. She loves stories both swoony and supernatural, and strong women and the men who appreciate them. Along with the Shadowblood Souls series, she is the author of the Heart of a Monster series, the Gang of Ghouls series, the Bound to the Fae series, the Flirting with Monsters series, the Cursed Studies trilogy, the Royals of Villain Academy series, the Moriarty's Men series, the Looking Glass Curse trilogy, the Their Dark Valkyrie series, the Witch's Consorts series, the Dragon Shifter's Mates series, the Demons of Fame series, and the Legends Reborn trilogy.

Connect with Eva online:
www.evachase.com
eva@evachase.com

www.ingramcontent.com/pod-product-compliance
Lightning Source LLC
Chambersburg PA
CBHW020345310726
48979CB00015B/2515/J

* 9 7 8 1 9 9 8 5 8 2 5 9 4 *